# Best for Winter

# Best for Winter

A SELECTION FROM TWENTY-FIVE YEARS OF

## Winter's Tales

EDITED BY

## A. D. Maclean

ST. MARTIN'S PRESS
NEW YORK

The stories are copyright respectively:

Copyright © 1979 by A. D. Maclean
All rights reserved. For information, write:
St. Martin's Press, Inc. 175 Fifth Ave., New York, N.Y. 10010
Manufactured in the United States of America

**Library of Congress Cataloging in Publication Data**

Main entry under title:

Best for winter.

1.   Short stories, English.   2.   English
fiction—20th century.   I.   Maclean, Alan Duart.
PZ1.B446599   1980     [PR1309.S5]     823'.01
ISBN 0-312-07708-4                         79-22851

# Contents

# Editor's Note

THE first *Winter's Tales* was published in 1955, and the twenty-fifth volume will appear later this year. When I joined Macmillan in 1954 they were considering the possibility of reviving *Macmillan's Magazine*, which had flourished for forty-eight years between 1859 and 1907. For various practical reasons the idea was abandoned, and we decided instead to start an annual anthology, which would at least provide a vehicle for long stories that neither the weeklies nor the current literary magazines had room for. It seemed a shame at the time that we could not relaunch the magazine, but it would certainly have needed a heavy subsidy and might well, like so many others, have become a casualty quite early in its second incarnation. The infinitely more modest venture of *Winter's Tales* has, however, kept going under its own steam for twenty-five years, and this selection from nearly 250 stories is a mild celebration of that fact.

*Winter's Tales* has two thriving siblings. *Winter's Crimes* is now in its eleventh year and was invented by George Hardinge when he came to Macmillan in 1967 to start a range of suspense novels that has few rivals today. *Young Winter's Tales* has been published each year (except for 1977) for nine years and was preceded by three volumes of *Allsorts* edited by Ann Thwaite, and before that by *Winter's Tales for Children*. M. R. Hodgkin and D. J. Denney have been responsible for all the *Young Winter's Tales*. Our Australian colleagues published two volumes of *Summer's Tales*, and Gill and Macmillan published *Winter's Tales from Ireland* in 1970 and 1972.

*Winter's Tales* was intended primarily for long stories written in English on this side of the Atlantic, and, although we have not kept absolutely rigidly to that, I have not included any North American stories in *Best for Winter*. I have also equally regretfully excluded translations, which rules out *Winter's Tales 7*, which was devoted to translations of modern Russian stories and edited by C. P. Snow and Pamela Hansford Johnson. It was an excellent and interesting collection.

The process of selection proved to be both exciting and agonising, and it would certainly be possible to produce at least four volumes of the same length and of equal quality and range. I won't attempt a justification for my choice of stories; they speak for themselves. But there is one story which needs a word of introduction and explanation.

The late Zeno's 'Suspense of Judgement' is the only true story to have been published in *Winter's Tales*, and I include it now. He first told it to me when we were sitting idly chatting in his cell in Wormwood Scrubs (he was serving a life sentence) and he mentioned that he was an atheist. When I said that I thought most people were agnostics rather than atheists, he said rather sharply, 'Well, I once had half-an-hour to think about it.' He wrote the story, won one of the first Arthur Koestler Awards for it, and went on to write some fine books, including *Life* and *The Cauldron*.

The first three volumes of *Winter's Tales* contained pen-and-ink drawings, each story being illustrated by a different artist. As costs rose and sales settled down we had to drop the illustrations, and I don't altogether regret it. It was inevitably rather a hit or miss plan, and it was never the intention to make *Winter's Tales* into what is loathsomely called a 'gift book'. It was meant to be a plain vehicle for the long story, and that is what it has been and will, I hope, continue to be.

I am not making extravagant claims for *Best for Winter*, but it is at least representative of what *Winter's Tales* has been about in the last quarter of a century, and I think that those who believe in the form of the long or short story, and want writers to cherish and practise it, can take heart from it.

I am grateful to all the writers who have contributed stories over the years, and also to my colleagues and former colleagues, Peter Collenette (*W.T. 23*), Kevin Crossley-Holland (*W.T. 14*), Caroline Hobhouse (*W.T. 17* and *25*), James Wright (*W.T. 22*) and C. P. Snow and Pamela Hansford Johnson (*W.T. 7*) for sharing the editorial load.

A.D.M.

# Best for Winter

V. S. PRITCHETT

# The Satisfactory

'WHEN one says that what one is still inclined to call civilisation is passing through a crisis,' Mr Plymbell used to say during the last war and after it when food was hard to get, and standing in his very expensive antique shop, raising a white and more than Roman nose and watching the words go off one by one on the air and circle the foreign customer, 'one is tempted to ask oneself whether or not a few possibly idle phrases that one let fall to one's old friend Lady Hackthorpe at a moment of national distress in 1940 are not, in fact, still pertinent. One recalls observing, rightly or wrongly, at that time that one was probably witnessing not the surrender of an heroic ally but the defeat of sauces. *Béarnaise, hollandaise, madère* – one saw them overrun. One can conceive of the future historian's inquiring whether the wars of the last ten years, and indeed what one calls "the peace", have not been essentially an attack on gastronomy, on the stomach and palate of the human race. One could offer the modest example of one's daily luncheon. . . .'

Mr Plymbell can talk like *The Times* for ever. Not all the campaigns of our generation have been fought on the battlefield. His lunch in those bad days was a study.

At two minutes before half-past twelve every day, Plymbell was first in the queue in the foyer outside the locked glass doors of Polli's Restaurant, a few yards from his shop. On one side of the glass Plymbell floated – handsome, Roman, silver-haired, as white-skinned and consequent as a turbot of fifty; on the other side of the glass, in the next aquarium, stood Polli with the key in his hand waiting for the clock to strike the half-hour – a man liverish and suspended in misanthropy like a tench in the weed of a canal. Plymbell stared clean through Polli to the sixty empty tables beyond; Polli stared clean through the middle of Plymbell into the miasma of the restaurant keeper's life. Two fish gazed with the indifference of creatures who had accepted the fact that neither of them was edible. What they wanted, what the whole of England was crying for, was not fish but red meat, and to get meat at Polli's one had to be there at half-past twelve, on the dot.

First customer in was Plymbell. He had his table, in the middle of this chipped Edwardian place, with his back to one of those white pillars that gave it the appearance of a shop-soiled wedding-cake mounted on a red carpet, and he faced the serving-hatch. Putting up a monocle to his more annoyed eye, he watched the chef standing over his pans, and while he watched he tapped the table with lightly frantic fingers. Polli's waiters were old men, and the one who served Plymbell had the dejected smirk of a convict.

I

Plymbell used hardly to glance at the farcical menu and never looked at the waiter when he coldly gave his order. 'Two soups,' said Plymbell. 'Two roast beefs . . . Cheese and biscuits,' he added. 'Bring me mine now and you can bring the second order in a quarter of an hour, when my secretary arrives.'

It was a daily scene. Plymbell's waiter came forward with his dishes like one hurrying a funeral in a hot country, feebly averting his nose from the mess he was carrying on his dish. He scraped his serving spoons and, at the end, eyed his customer with criminal scorn. Plymbell's jaws moved over this stuff with a slow social agony. In fifteen minutes he had eaten his last biscuit, and was wetting his finger to pick up the small heap of crumbs he had worked to one side of his plate. Plymbell looked at his watch.

Exactly at this moment Plymbell's assistant used to come in. Shabby, thin, with wrinkled cotton stockings and dressed in black, a woman of forty-five, Miss Tell scraped on poor shoes to the table. She carried newspapers in a bundle under an arm and a basket in her hand. He would look carefully away from her as she alighted like some dingy fly at the other side of the table. It was astonishing to see a man so well dressed lunching with a woman so bowed and faded. But presently she used to do a conjuring trick. Opening her bundle, Miss Tell put a newspaper down on the roll of bread on her side plate and then picked it up again. The roll of bread had gone. She had slipped it into her lap. A minute passed while she wriggled to and fro like a laying hen, and then she would drop the roll into the basket by the leg of her chair.

Plymbell would be looking away from her while she did this and, his lips hardly moving, he would speak one word.

'What?' was the word.

She replied also with one word – the word naturally varied – cringing toward him, looking with fear, trying to get him to look at her.

'Sausages,' she might whisper.

'How many?' Plymbell would ask. He still did not look at her.

'Half-pound,' she said. On some fortunate days: 'A pound.'

Plymbell studied the domed skylight in the ceiling of the restaurant. The glass was still out in those days; the boards put there during the war when a bomb blew out the glass had not been replaced. Meanwhile the waiter brought a plate of soup to Miss Tell. She would stare at the soup without interest. When the waiter went, she lifted the plate across the table and put it in Plymbell's place, and then lowered her head in case other customers had seen. Plymbell had not seen, because he had been gazing at the ceiling, but, as if absent-mindedly, he picked up a spoon and began to drink Miss Tell's soup, and when he had finished, put the plate back on her side of the table, and the waiter took it away.

Plymbell had been lunching at Polli's for years. He used to lunch there before the war with Lady Hackthorpe. She was a handsome woman – well-cut clothes, well-cut diamonds, brilliantly-cut eyes and sharply-cut losses. Plymbell bought and sold for her, decorated her house.

Miss Tell used to go home to her parents in the evenings and say, 'I don't understand it. I make out her bill every month and he says, "Miss Tell, give me Lady Hackthorpe's bill," and tears it up.'

Miss Tell lived by what she did not understand. It was an appetite.

After 1940, no more Lady Hackthorpe. A bomb cut down half of her house and left a Hepplewhite bed full of broken glass and ceiling plaster on the first floor, and a servant's washstand on the floor above. Lady Hackthorpe went to Ireland.

Plymbell got the bed and a lot of other things out of the house into his shop. Here again, there was something Miss Tell did not understand. She was supposed to 'keep the books straight'. Were Lady Hackthorpe's things being 'stored' or were they being 'returned to stock'?

'I mean,' Miss Tell said, 'if anyone was killed when a thing is left open it's unsatisfactory.'

Plymbell listened and did not answer. He was thinking of other things. The war on the stomach and the palate had begun. Not only had Lady Hackthorpe gone. Plymbell's business was a function of Lady Hackthorpe's luncheons and dinners, and other people's, too. He was left with his mouth open in astonishment and hunger.

'Trade has stopped now,' Miss Tell said one night when she ducked into the air-raid shelter with her parents. 'Poor Mr Plymbell never goes out.'

'Why doesn't he close the business, Kitty?' Miss Tell's mother said.

'And leave all that valuable stock?' said Mr Tell. 'Where's your brain?'

'I never could fathom business,' said Mrs Tell.

'It's the time to pick up things,' said Mr Tell.

'That's a way to talk when we may all be dead in a minute,' said Mrs Tell.

Mr Tell said something about prices being bound to go up, but a huge explosion occurred and he stopped.

'And this Lady Hackthorpe – is she *friendly* with this Plymbell?' said old Mrs Tell when the explosion settled in as part of the furniture of their lives.

'*Mr* Plymbell,' Miss Tell corrected her mother. Miss Tell had a poor, fog-coloured London skin and blushed in a patch across her forehead. 'I don't *query* his private life.'

'He's a man,' sighed Mrs Tell. 'To hear you talk he might be the Fairy Prince or Lord Muck himself. Listen to those guns. You've been there fifteen years.'

'It takes two to be friendly,' said Miss Tell, who sometimes spoke like a poem. 'When one goes away it may be left open one way or another, I mean, and that –' Miss Tell searched for a new word but returned to the old one, the only one that ever, for her, met the human case, 'And that,' she said, 'is unsatisfactory.'

'You're neurotic,' her mother said. 'You never have any news.'

And then Miss Tell had a terrible thought. 'Mum!' she cried, dropping the poetic accent she brought back from the West End every night, 'where's Tiger? We've left him in the house.'

Her mother became swollen with shame.

'You left him,' accused Miss Tell. 'You left him in the kitchen.' She got up. 'No one's got any heart. I'm going to get him.'

'You stay here, my girl,' said Mr Tell.

'Come back, Kitty,' said Mrs Tell.

But Miss Tell (followed across the garden, as it seemed to her, by an aeroplane) went to the house. In her panic Mrs Tell had left not only the cat, she had left her handbag and her ration books on the kitchen table. Miss Tell picked up the bag, and then kneeled under the table looking for Tiger. 'Tiger, dear! Tiger!' she called. He was not there. It was at this instant that the aeroplane outside seemed to have followed her into the house. When Miss Tell was dug out alive and unhurt, black with dust, six hours later, Mr and Mrs Tell were dead in the garden.

When Plymbell talks of that time now, he says there were moments when one was inclined to ask oneself whether the computed odds of something like eight hundred and ninety-seven thousand to one in favour of one's nightly survival were not, perhaps, an evasion of a private estimate one had arrived at without any special statistical apparatus – that it was fifty-fifty, and even providential. It was a point, he said, one recollected making to one's assistant at the time, when she came back.

Miss Tell came back to Plymbell's at lunch-time one day a fortnight after she had been dug out. She was singular: she had been saved by looking for her cat. Mr Plymbell was not at the shop, or in his rooms above it. In the vainglory of her escape she went round to Polli's. Plymbell was more than half-way through his meal when he saw her come in. She was wearing no hat on her dusty black hair, and under her black coat, which so often had ends of cotton on it, she was wearing navy-blue trousers. Plymbell winced: it was the human aspect of war that was so lowering; he saw at once that Miss Tell had become a personality. Watching the wag of her narrow shoulders as she walked, he saw she had caught the general immodesty of the 'bombed out'.

Without being invited, she sat down at his table and put herself sideways, at her ease, crossing her legs to show her trousers. Her face had filled out into two little puffs of vanity on either side of her mouth, as if she were eating or were containing a yawn. The two rings of age on her neck looked like a cheap necklace. Lipstick was for the first time on her lips. It looked like blood.

'One inquired in vain,' said Plymbell with condescension. 'I am glad to see you back.'

'I thought I might as well pop round,' said Miss Tell.

Mr Plymbell was alarmed; her note was breezy. 'Aren't you coming back?'

'I haven't found Tiger,' said Miss Tell.

'Tiger?'

Miss Tell told him her story.

Plymbell saw that he must try and put himself for a moment in his employee's situation and think of her grief. 'One recalls the thought that passed through one's mind when one's own mother died,' he said.

'They had had their life,' said Miss Tell.

A connoisseur by trade, Plymbell was disappointed by the banality of Miss Tell's remark. What was grief? It was a hunger. Not merely personal, emotional and spiritual; it was physical. Plymbell had been forty-two when his mother died, and he, her only child, had always lived with her. Her skill with money, her jackdaw eye had made the business. The morning she died in hospital he had felt that a cave had been opened inside his body under the ribs, a cave getting larger and colder and emptier. He went out and ate one of the largest meals of his life.

While Miss Tell, a little fleshed already in her tragedy, was still talking, the waiter came to the table with Plymbell's allowance of cheese and biscuits.

Plymbell remembered his grief. 'Bring me another portion for my secretary,' he said.

'Oh no, not for me,' said Miss Tell. She was too dazed by the importance of loss to eat. 'I couldn't.'

But Polli's waiter had a tired, dead head. He came back with biscuits for Miss Tell.

Miss Tell looked about the restaurant until the waiter left and then coquettishly she passed her plate to Plymbell. 'For you,' she said. 'I couldn't.'

Plymbell thought Miss Tell ill-bred to suggest that he would eat what she did not want. He affected not to notice and gazed over her head, but his white hand had already taken the plate, and in a moment, still looking disparagingly beyond her, in order not to catch her eye, Mr Plymbell bit into one of Miss Tell's biscuits. Miss Tell was smiling slyly.

After he had eaten her food, Mr Plymbell looked at Miss Tell with a warmer interest. She had come to work for him in his mother's time, more than fifteen years before. Her hair was still black, her skin was now grey and yellow with a lilac streak on the jaw, there were sharp stains like poor coffee under her eyes. These were brown with a circle of gold in the pupils, and they seemed to burn as if there were a fever in their shadows. Her black coat, her trousers, her cotton blouse were cheap, and even her body seemed to be thin with cheapness. Her speech was awkward, for part of her throat was trying to speak in a refined accent and the effect was half arrogant, half disheartened. Now, as he swallowed the last piece of biscuit, she seemed to him to change. Her eyes were brilliant. She had become quietly a human being.

What is a human being? The chef whom he could see through the hatch was one; Polli, who was looking at the menu by the cash desk, was another; his mother, who had made remarkable *ravioli*; people like Lady Hackthorpe, who had given such wonderful dinner-parties before the war; that circle which the war had scattered and where he had moved from one lunch to the next in a life that rippled to the sound of changing plates that tasted of sauces now never made. These people had been human beings. One knew a human being when the juices flowed over one's teeth. A human being was a creature who fed one. Plymbell moved his jaws. Miss Tell's sly smile went. He looked as though he was going to eat *her*.

'You had better take the top room at the shop,' he said. 'Take the top room if you have nowhere to live.'

'But I haven't found Tiger,' Miss Tell said. 'He must be starving.'

'You won't be alone,' said Plymbell. 'I sleep at the shop.'

Miss Tell considered him. Plymbell could see she was weighing him against Tiger in her mind. He had offered her the room because she had fed him.

'You have had your lunch, I presume,' said Plymbell as they walked back to the shop.

'No – I mean yes. Yes, no,' said Miss Tell secretively, and again here was the blush like a birthmark on her forehead.

'Where do you go?' said Plymbell, making a shameful inquiry.

'Oh,' said Miss Tell defensively, as if it were a question of chastity. 'Anywhere. I manage. I vary.' And when she said she varied, Miss Tell looked with a virginal importance first one way and then the other.

'That place starves one,' said Plymbell indignantly. 'One comes out of there some days and one is weak with hunger.'

Miss Tell's flush went. She was taken by one of those rages that shake the voices and the bones of unmarried women, as if they were going to shake the nation by the scruff of its neck. 'It's wrong, Mr Plymbell. The government ought to give men more rations. A man needs food. Myself, it never worries me. I never eat. Poor mother used to say, "Eat, girl, eat." ' A tear came to Miss Tell's right eye, enlarged it and made it liquid, burning, beautiful. 'It was funny, I didn't seem to fancy anything. I just picked things over and left them.'

'I never heard of anyone who found the rations too much,' said Mr Plymbell with horror.

'I hardly touch mine since I was bombed out,' said Miss Tell, and she straightened her thin, once humble body, raised her small bosom, which was ribbed like a wicker basket, gave her hair a touch or two, and looked with delicate resolution at Plymbell. 'I sometimes think of giving my ration books away,' she said in an offhand way.

Plymbell gaped at the human being in front of him. 'Give them away!' he exclaimed. '*Them?* Have you got more than one?'

'I've got father's and mother's, too.'

'But one had gathered that the law required one to surrender the official documents of the deceased,' said Plymbell, narrowing his eyes suggestively. His heart had livened, his mouth was watering.

Miss Tell moved her erring shoulders, her eyes became larger, her lips drooped. 'It's wicked of me,' she said.

Plymbell took her thin elbow in his hand and contained his anxiety. 'I should be very careful about those ration books. I shouldn't mention it. There was a case in the paper the other day.'

They had reached the door of the shop. 'How is Lady Hackthorpe?' Miss Tell asked. 'Is she still away?'

Miss Tell had gone too far; she was being familiar. Plymbell put up his monocle and did not reply.

A time of torture began for Plymbell when Miss Tell moved in. He invited her to the cellar on the bad nights, but Miss Tell had become light-headed with fatalism and would not move from her bed on the top floor. In decency Plymbell had to remain in his bed and take shelter no more. Above him slept the rarest of human beings, a creature who had three ration books, a woman who was technically three people. He feared for her at every explosion. His mouth watered when he saw her: the woman with three books who did not eat and who thought only of how hungry Tiger must be. If he could have turned himself into a cat!

At one point Plymbell decided that Miss Tell was like Lady Hackthorpe with her furniture; Miss Tell wanted money. He went to the dark corner behind a screen between his own office and the shop, where sometimes she sewed. When he stood by the screen he was nearly on top of her. 'If,' he said in a high, breaking voice that was strange even to himself, 'if you are ever thinking of *selling* your books . . .'

He had made a mistake. Miss Tell was mending and the needle was pointing at him as she stood up. 'I couldn't do that,' she said. 'It is forbidden by the law.' And she looked at him strictly.

Plymbell gaped before her hypocrisy. Miss Tell's eyes became larger, deeper and liquid in the dusk of the corner where she worked. Her chin moved up in a number of amused, resentful movements; her lips moved. Good God, thought Plymbell, is she eating? Her thin arms were slack, her body was inert. She continued to move her dry lips. She leaned her head sideways and raised one eye. Plymbell could not believe what he saw. Miss Tell was plainly telling him: 'Yes, I *have* got something in my mouth. It is the desire to be kissed.'

Or was he wrong? Plymbell was not a kissing man. His white, demanding face was indeed white with passion, and his lips were shaped for sensuality, but the passion of the gourmet, the libidinousness of the palate gave him his pallor. He had felt desire, in his way, for Lady Hackthorpe, but it had been consummated in *bisques*, in *crêpes*, in *flambées*, in *langouste* done in many manners, in *ailloli*, in *bouillabaisse* and vintage wines. That passion had been starved, and he was perturbed by Miss Tell's signal. One asks oneself (he reflected, going to his office and considering reproachfully his mother's photograph, which stood on his desk) – one asks oneself whether or not a familiar adage about Nature's abhorrence of a vacuum has not a certain relevance, and indeed whether one would not be justified in coining a vulgar phrase to the effect that when one shuts the front door on Nature, she comes in at the back. Miss Tell was certainly the back; one might call her the scullery of the emotions.

Plymbell lowered his pale eyelids in a flutter of infidelity, unable honestly to face his mother's stare. Her elderly aquiline nose, her close-curled silver hair tipped with a touch of fashionable idiocy off the forehead, her too-jewelled, hawking, grabbing, slapdash face derided him for the languor of the male symptom, and at the same time, with the ratty double-facedness of her sex, spoke sharply about flirtations with employees. Plymbell's eyes lied to her image. All the same, he tried to calm himself by taking a piece of violet notepaper and dashing off a letter to Lady Hackthorpe. Avocado pear, he wrote, whitebait (did she think?) *bœuf bourguignon*, or what about *dindonneau* in those Italian pastes? It was a letter of lust. He addressed the envelope, and, telling Miss Tell to post it, Plymbell pulled down the points of his slack waist-coat and felt saved.

So saved that when Miss Tell came back and stood close to his desk, narrow and flat in her horrible trousers, and with her head turned to the window, showing him her profile, Plymbell felt she was satirically flirting with his hunger. Indignantly he got up and, before he knew what he was doing, he put his hand under her shoulder blade and kissed her on the lips.

A small frown came between Miss Tell's eyebrows. Her lips were tight and set. She did not move. 'Was that a bill you sent to Lady Hackthorpe?' she asked.

'No,' said Plymbell. 'A personal letter.'

Miss Tell left his office.

Mr Plymbell wiped his mouth on his handkerchief. He was shocked by himself; even more by the set lips, the closed teeth, the hard chin of Miss Tell; most of all by her impertinence. He had committed a folly for nothing and he had been insulted.


The following morning Plymbell went out on his weekly search for food, but he was too presumptuous for the game. In the coarse world of provisions and the black market, the monocle was too fine. Plymbell lacked the touch; in a long day all he managed to get was four fancy cakes. Miss Tell came out of her dark corner and looked impersonally at him. He was worn out.

'No offal,' he said in an appalled, hoarse voice. 'No offal in the whole of London.'

'Ooh,' said Miss Tell, quick as a sparrow. 'I got some. Look.' And she showed him her disgusting, bloodstained triumph on its piece of newspaper.

Never had Miss Tell seemed so common, so flagrant, so lacking in sensibility, but, also, never had she seemed so desirable. And then, as before, she became limp and neutral and she raised her chin. There were the unmistakable crumb-licking movements of her lips. Plymbell saw her look sideways at him as she turned. Was she inviting him to wipe out the error of the previous day? With one eye on the meat, Plymbell made a step toward her, and in a moment Miss Tell was on him, kissing him, open-mouthed and with frenzy, her finger-nails in his arms, and pressing herself to him to the bone.

'Sweetbreads,' she said. 'For you. I never eat them. Let me cook them for you.'

An hour later she was knocking at the door of his room, and carrying a loaded tray. It was laid, he was glad to notice, for one person only. Plymbell said, 'One had forgotten what sweetbreads were.'

'It was nothing. I have enjoyed your confidence for fifteen years,' said Miss Tell in her poetic style. And the enlarged eyes looked at him with an intimate hunger.

That night, as usual, Plymbell changed into a brilliant dressing-gown, and, standing before the mirror, he did his hair, massaging with the fingers, brushing first with the hard ivory brush and then with the soft one. As he looked into the glass, Miss Tell's inquiring face kept floating into it, displacing his own.

'Enjoyed my confidence!' said Plymbell.

In her bedroom Miss Tell turned out the light, drew back the curtains, and looked into the London black and at the inane triangles of the searchlights. She stood there listening. 'Tiger, Tiger,' she murmured. 'Where are you? Why did you go away from me? I miss you in my bed. Are you hungry? I had a lovely dinner ready for you – sweetbreads. I had to give it to him because you didn't come.'

In answer, the hungry siren went like the wail of some monstrous, disembodied Tiger, like all the dead cats of London restless beyond the grave.

Miss Tell drew the curtains and lay down on her bed. 'Tiger,' she said crossly, 'if you don't come tomorrow, I shall give everything to him. He needs it. Not that he deserves it. Filling up the shop with that woman's furniture, storing it free of charge, writing her letters, ruining himself for her. I hate her. I always have. I don't understand him and her, how she gets away with it, owing money all round. She's got a hold——'

The guns broke out. They were declaring war upon Lady Hackthorpe.

Tiger did not come back, and rabbit was dished up for Plymbell. He kissed Miss Tell a third time. It gave him the agreeable sensation that he was doing something for the war. After the fourth kiss, Plymbell became worried. Miss Tell had mentioned stuffed veal. She had spoken of mushrooms. He had thoughtlessly exceeded in his embrace. He had felt for the first time in his life – voluptuousness; he had discovered how close to eating kissing is, and as he allowed his arm to rest on Miss Tell's lower-class waist, he had had the inadvertent impression of picking up a cutlet in his fingers. Plymbell felt he had done enough for the vanity of Miss Tell. He was in the middle of this alarmed condition when Miss Tell came into his office and turned his alarm to consternation.

'I've come to give my notice,' she said.

Plymbell was appalled. 'What is wrong, Miss Tell?' he said.

'Nothing's wrong,' said Miss Tell. 'I feel I am not needed.'

'Have I offended you?' said Plymbell suspiciously. 'Is it money?'

Miss Tell looked sharply. She was insulted. 'No,' she said. 'Money is of no interest to me. I've got nothing to do. Trade's stopped.'

Plymbell made a speech about trade.

'I think I must have got—' Miss Tell searched for a word and lost her poetic touch – 'browned off,' she said, and blushed. 'I'll get a job in a canteen. I like cooking.'

Plymbell in a panic saw not one woman but three women leaving him. 'But you are cooking for me,' he said.

Miss Tell shrugged.

'Oh yes, you are. Miss Tell – be my housekeeper.'

Good God, thought Plymbell afterwards, so that was all she wanted. I needn't have kissed her at all.

How slowly one learns about human nature, he thought. Here was a woman with one simple desire; to serve him – to slave for him, to stand in queues, to cook, to run his business, do everything. And who did not eat.

'I shall certainly not kiss her again,' he said.

At this period of his life, with roofs leaving their buildings and servants leaving their places all round him, Plymbell often reflected guardedly upon his situation. There was, he had often hinted, an art in managing servants. He appeared, he noted, to have this art. But would he keep it? What was it? Words of his mother's came back to him: 'Miss Tell left a better job and higher wages to come to me. This job is more flattering to her self-importance.' 'Never consider them, never promise; they will despise you. The only way to keep servants is to treat them like hell. Look at Lady Hackthorpe's couple. They'd die for her. They probably will.'

Two thousand years of civilization lay in those remarks.

'And never be familiar.' Guiltily, he could imagine Lady Hackthorpe putting in her word. As the year passed, as his nourishment improved, the imaginary Lady Hackthorpe rather harped on the point.

There was no doubt about it, Plymbell admitted, he *had* been familiar. But only four times, he protested. And what is a kiss, in an office? At this he could almost hear Lady Hackthorpe laughing, in an insinuating way, that she hardly imagined there could be any question of his going any further.

Plymbell, now full of food, blew up into a temper with the accusing voices. He pitched into Miss Tell. He worked out a plan of timely dissatisfaction. His first attack upon her was made in the shop in the presence of one of the rare customers of those days.

'Why no extra liver this week, Miss Tell? My friend here has got some,' he said.

Miss Tell started, then blushed on the forehead. It was, he saw, a blush of pleasure. Public humiliation seemed to delight Miss Tell. He made it harder. 'Why no eggs?' he shouted down the stairs, and on another day, as if he had a whip in his hand, 'Anyone can get olive oil.' Miss Tell smiled and looked a little sideways at him.

Seeing he had not hurt her in public, Plymbell then made a false move. He called her to his room above the shop and decided to 'blow her up' privately.

'I can't *live* on fish,' he began. But whereas, delighted to be noticed, she listened to his public complaints in the shop, she did not listen in his room. By his second sentence, she had turned her back and wandered to the sofa. From there she went to his writing-table, trailing a finger on it. She was certainly not listening. In the middle of his speech and as his astounded, colourless eyes followed her, she stopped and pointed through the double doors where his bedroom was and she pointed to the Hepplewhite bed.

'Is that Lady Hackthorpe's, too? she said.

'Yes,' said Plymbell.

'Why do you have it up here?' she said rudely.

'Because I like it,' said Plymbell, snubbing her.

'I think four-posters are unhealthy,' said Miss Tell, and circled with meandering impertinence to the window and looked out onto the street. 'That old man,' she said, admitting the vulgar world into the room, 'is always going by.'

Miss Tell shrugged at the window and considered the bed again across the space of two rooms. Then, impersonally, she made a speech. 'I never married,' she said. 'I have been friendly but not married. One great friend went away. There was no agreement, nothing said, he didn't write and I didn't write. In those cases I sympathise with the wife, but I wondered when he didn't communicate. I didn't know whether it was over or not over, and when you don't know, it isn't satisfactory. I don't say it was anything, but I would have liked to know whether it was or not. I never mention it to anyone.'

'Oh,' said Plymbell.

'It upset Dad,' said Miss Tell, and of that she was proud.

'I don't follow,' said Plymbell. He wanted to open the window and let Miss Tell's private life out.

'It's hard to describe something unsatisfactory,' said Miss Tell. And then, 'Dad was conventional.'

Mr Plymbell shuddered.

'Are you interested?' asked Miss Tell.

'Please, please go on,' said Plymbell.

'I have been "the other woman" three times,' said Miss Tell primly.

Plymbell put up his monocle, but as far as he could judge, all Miss Tell had done was make a public statement. He could think of no reply. His mind drifted. Suddenly he heard the voice of Miss Tell again, trembling, passionate, raging as it had been once before, at Polli's, attacking him.

'She uses you,' Miss Tell was saying. 'She puts all her rubbish into your shop, she fills up your flat. She won't let you sell it. She hasn't paid you. Storage is the dearest thing in London. You could make a profit, you would turn over your stock. Now is the time to buy, Dad said. . . .'

Plymbell picked up his paper.

'Lady Hackthorpe,' explained Miss Tell, and he saw her face, small-mouthed and sick and shaking with jealousy.

'Lady Hackthorpe has gone to America,' Plymbell said, in his snubbing voice.

Miss Tell's rage had spent itself. 'If you were not so horrible to me, I would tell you an idea,' she said.

'Horrible? My dear Miss Tell,' said Mr Plymbell, leaning back as far as he could in his chair.

'It doesn't matter,' said Miss Tell, and she walked away. 'When is Lady Hackthorpe coming back?' she said.

'After the war, I suppose,' said Plymbell.

'Oh,' said Miss Tell, without belief.

'What is your idea?'

'Oh no. It was about lunch. At Polli's. It is nothing,' said Miss Tell.

'Lunch,' said Plymbell with a start, dropping his eyeglass. 'What about lunch?' And his mouth stayed open.

Miss Tell turned about and approached him. 'No, it's unsatisfactory,' said Miss Tell. She gave a small laugh and then made the crumb movements with her chin.

'Come here,' commanded Plymbell. 'What idea about lunch?'

Miss Tell did not move, and so he got up, in a panic now. A suspicion came to him that Polli's had been bombed, that someone – perhaps Miss Tell herself – was going to take his lunch away from him. Miss Tell did not move. Mr Plymbell did not move. Feeling weak, Mr Plymbell decided to sit down again. Miss Tell came and sat on the arm of his chair.

'Nothing,' she said, looking into his eyes for a long time and then turning away. 'You have been horrible to me for ten months and thirteen days. You know you have.' Her back was to him.

Slices of pork, he saw, mutton, beef. He went through a nightmare that he arrived at Polli's late, all the customers were inside, and the glass doors were locked. The head waiter was standing there refusing to open. Miss Tell's unnourished back made him think of this. He did no more than put his hand on her shoulder, as slight as a chicken bone, and as he did so, he seemed to hear a sharp warning snap from Lady Hackthorpe. 'Gus,' Lady Hackthorpe seemed to say, 'what are you doing? Are you mad? Don't you know why Miss Tell had to leave her last place?' But Lady Hackthorpe's words were smothered. A mere touch – without intention on Plymbell's part – had impelled Miss Tell to slide backward onto his lap.

'How have I been horrid to you?' said Plymbell, forgetting to put inverted commas round the word 'horrid'.

'You know,' said Miss Tell.

'What was this idea of yours?' he said quietly, and he kissed her neck. 'No, no,' she said, and moved her head to the other side of his neck. There was suddenly a sound that checked them both. Her shoe fell off. And then an extraordinary thing happened to Plymbell. The sight of Miss Tell's foot without its shoe did it. At fifty, he felt the first indubitable symptom. A scream went off inside his head – Lady Hackthorpe nagging him about some man she had known who had gone to bed with his housekeeper. 'Ruin,' Lady Hackthorpe was saying.

'About lunch – it was a good idea,' Miss Tell said tenderly into his collar.

But it was not until three in the morning that Miss Tell told Plymbell what the idea was.

And so, every week-day, there was the modest example of Mr Plymbell's daily luncheon. The waiter used to take the empty soup plate away from Miss Tell and presently came forward with the meat and vegetables. He scraped them off his serving dish onto her plate. She would keep her head lowered for a while, and then, with a glance to see if other customers were looking, she would lift the plate over to Mr Plymbell's place. He, of course, did not notice. Then, absently, he settled down to eat her food. While he did this, he muttered, 'What did you get?' She nodded at her stuffed basket and answered. Mr Plymbell ate two lunches. While this went on, Miss Tell looked at him. She was in a strong position now. Hunger is the basis of life and, for her, a great change had taken place. The satisfactory had occurred.

But now, of course, French cookery has come back.

# KINGSLEY AMIS

# My Enemy's Enemy

'Yes, I know all about that, Tom,' the Adjutant said through a mouthful of stew. 'But technical qualifications aren't everything. There's other sides to a Signal officer's job, you know, especially while we're still pretty well static. The communications are running themselves and we don't want to start getting complacent. My personal view is, and has been from the word go, that your friend Dally's a standing bloody reproach to this unit, never mind how much he knows about the six-channel and the other boxes of tricks. That's a lineman-mechanic's job, anyway, not an officer's. And I can tell you for a fact I mean to do something about it, do you see?' He laid down his knife, though not his fork, and took three or four swallows of wine.

'Well, your boy Cleaver doesn't impress me all that much, Bill,' Thurston, who hated the Adjutant, said to him. 'The only time we've tried him on duty he flapped.'

'Just inexperience, Tom,' the Adjutant said. 'He'd soon snap out of that if we gave him command of the section. Sergeant Beech would carry him until he found his feet.'

'Mm, I'd like to see that, I must say. The line duty officer getting his sergeant out of bed to hold his hand while he changes a valve.'

'Now look here, old boy.' The Adjutant levered a piece of meat out from between two teeth and ate it. 'You know as well as I do that young Cleaver's got the best technical qualifications of anyone in the whole unit. It's not his fault he's been stuck on office work ever since he came to us. There's a fellow that'd smarten up that bunch of goons and long-haired bloody mathematical wizards they call a line-maintenance section. As it is, the N.C.O.s don't chase the blokes and Dally isn't interested in chasing the N.C.O.s. Isn't interested in anything but his bloody circuit diagrams and test-frames and what-have-you.'

To cover his irritation, Thurston summoned the Mess corporal, who stood by the wall in a posture that compromised between that of an attendant waiter and the regulation stand-at-ease position. The Adjutant had schooled him in Mess procedure, though not in Mess etiquette. 'Gin and lime, please, Gordon. . . . Just as well in a way he is interested in line apparatus, isn't it, Bill? We'd have looked pretty silly without him during the move out of Normandy and across France. He worked as hard as any two of the rest of us. And as well.'

'He got his bouquet from the Colonel, didn't he? I don't grudge him that, I admit he did good work then. Not as good as some of his chaps, probably, but still, he served his turn. Yes, that's exactly it, Tom, he's served his——'

'According to Major Rylands he was the lynchpin of the whole issue,'

Thurston said, lighting a cigarette with fingers that were starting to tremble. 'And I'm prepared to take his word for it. The war isn't over yet, you know. Christ knows what may happen in the spring. If Dally isn't around to hold the line-maintenance end up for Rylands, the whole unit might end up in a mess with the Staff jumping on its back. Cleaver might be all right, I agree. We just can't afford to take the risk.'

This was an unusually long speech for anyone below the rank of major to make in the Adjutant's presence. Temporarily gagged by a mouthful of stew, that officer was eating as fast as he could and shaking his forefinger to indicate that he would as soon as possible propose some decisive amendment to what he had just been told. With his other hand he scratched the crown of his glossy black head, looking momentarily like a tic-tac man working through his lunch-break. He said indistinctly: 'You're on to the crux of the whole thing, old boy. Rylands is the root of all the trouble. Bad example at the top, do you see?' Swallowing, he went on: 'If the second-in-command goes round looking like a latrines detail and calling the blokes by their Christian names, what can you expect? You can't get away from it, familiarity breeds contempt. Trouble with him is he thinks he's still working in the Post Office.'

A hot foam of anger seemed to fizz up in Thurston's chest. 'Major Rylands is the only field officer in this entire unit who knows his job. It is due to him and Dally, plus Sergeant Beech and the lineman-mechs., that our line communications have worked so smoothly during this campaign. To them and to no one else. If they can go on doing that, they can walk about with bare arses for all I care.'

The Adjutant frowned at Thurston. After running his tongue round his upper teeth, he said: 'You seem to forget, Tom, that I'm responsible for the discipline of officers in this unit.' He paused to let the other reflect on the personal implications of this, then nodded to where Corporal Gordon was approaching with Thurston's drink.

As he signed the chit, Thurston was thinking that Gordon had probably been listening to the conversation from the passage. If so, he would probably discuss it with Hill, the Colonel's batman, who would probably report it to his master. It was often said, especially by Lieutenant Dalessio, the 'Dally' now under discussion, that the Colonel's chief contact with his unit was through the rumours and allegations Hill and, to a less extent, the Adjutant took to him. A tweak of disquiet made Thurston drink deeply and resolve to say no more for a bit.

The Adjutant was brushing crumbs off his battle-dress, which was of the greenish hue current in the Canadian Army. This little affectation, like the gamboge gloves and the bamboo walking-stick, perhaps suited a man who had helped to advertise men's clothes in civilian life. He went on to say in his rapid quacking monotone: 'I'd advise you, Tom, not to stick your neck out too far in supporting a man who's going to be out of this unit on his ear before very long.'

'Rylands, you mean?'

'No no no. Unfortunately not. But Dally's going.'

'That's gen, is it?'

'Not yet, but it will be.'

'I don't follow you.'

The Adjutant looked up in Gordon's direction, then leaned forward across the table to Thurston. 'It only needs one more thing,' he said quietly, 'to turn the scale. The C.O.'s been watching Dally for some time, on my suggestion. I know the old man pretty well, as you know, after being in his company for three years at North Midland Command. He's waiting to make up his mind, do you see? If Dally puts up a black in the near future – a real black – that'll be enough for the C.O. Cleaver'll get his chance at last.'

'Suppose Dally doesn't put up a black?'

'He will.'

'He hasn't yet, you know. The terminal equipment's all on the top line, and Dally knows it inside out.'

'I'm not talking about that kind of a black. I'm talking about the administrative and disciplinary side. Those vehicles of his are in a shocking condition. I thought of working a snap 406 inspection on one of them, but that wouldn't look too good. Too much like discrimination. But there'll be something. Just give me time.'

Thurston thought of saying that those vehicles, though covered with months-old mud and otherwise offensive to the inspecting eye, were in good running order, thanks to the efficiency of the section's transport corporal. Instead, he let his mind wander back to one of the many stories of the Colonel's spell as a company commander in England. Three weeks running he had presented his weekly prize of £1 for the smartest vehicle to the driver of an obsolete wireless-truck immobilised for lack of spare parts. The company sergeant-major had won a bet about it.

'We'll have some fun then, Tom, old boy,' the Adjutant was saying in as festive a tone as his voice allowed. He was unaware that Thurston disliked him. His own feelings towards Thurston were a mixture of respect and patronage: respect for Thurston's Oxford degree and accent, job at a minor public school, and competence as a non-technical officer; patronage for his practice of reading literary magazines and for his vaguely scholarly manner and appearance. The affinity between Thurston's unmilitary look and the more frankly ragamuffin demeanour of Dalessio could hardly explain, the Adjutant wonderingly felt, the otherwise unaccountable tendency of the one to defend the other. It was true that they'd known each other at the officer's training unit at Catterick, but what could that have to do with it? The Adjutant was unaccustomed to having his opinions contested and he now voiced the slight bafflement that had been growing on him for the last few minutes. 'It rather beats me,' he said, 'why you're taking this line about friend Dally. You're not at all thick with him. In fact he seems to needle you whenever he speaks to you. My impression is, old boy, for what it's worth, you've got no bloody use for him at all. And yet you stick up for him. Why?'

Thurston amazed him by saying coldly: 'I don't see why the fact that a man's an Italian should be held against him when he does his job as well as anyone in the sodding Army.'

'Just a minute, Tom,' the Adjutant said, taking a cigarette from his silver case, given him by his mistress in Brussels. 'That's being a bit unfair, you know. You ever heard me say a word about Dalessio being an Eyeteye? Never. You were the one who brought it up. It makes no difference to me if a fellow's father's been interned, provided——'

'Uncle.'

'All right, uncle, then. As I say, that's no affair of mine. Presumably he's okay from that point of view or he'd never have got here. And that's all there is to it as far as I'm concerned. I'm not holding it against him, not for a moment. I don't quite know where you picked up that impression, old boy.'

Thurston shook his head, blushing slightly. 'Sorry, Bill,' he said. 'I must have got it mixed. It used to get on my wick at Catterick, the way some of the blokes took it out of him about his pal Musso and so on. I suppose it must be through that somehow, in a way, I keep feeling people have got it in for him on that score. Sorry.' He was not sorry. He knew quite certainly that his charge was well-founded, and that the other's silence about Dalessio's descent was a matter of circumspection only. If anyone in the Mess admired Mussolini, Thurston suspected, it was the Adjutant, although he kept quiet about that as well. It was tempting to dig at his prejudices on these and other questions, but Thurston did his best never to succumb to that temptation. The Adjutant's displeasure was always strongly urged and sometimes, rumour said, followed up by retaliatory persecution. Enough, dangerously much, had already been said in Dalessio's defence.

The Adjutant's manner had grown genial again and, with a muttered apology, he now offered Thurston a cigarette. 'What about another of those?' he asked, pointing his head at Thurston's glass.

'Thank you, I will, but I must be off in a minute. We're opening that teleprinter to the Poles at twenty-hundred and I want to see it's working.'

Two more officers now entered the Mess dining-room. They were Captain Bentham, a forty-year-old Regular soldier who had been a company sergeant-major in India at the outbreak of war, and Captain Rowney, who besides being in charge of the unit's administration was also the Mess's catering officer. Rowney nodded to Thurston and grinned at the Adjutant, whose Canadian battle-dress he had been responsible for securing. He himself was wearing a sheepskin jacket, made on the Belgian black market. 'Hello, William,' he said. 'Won the war yet?' Although he was a great chum of the Adjutant's, some of his remarks to him, Thurston had noticed, carried a curious vein of satire. Bentham sat stolidly down a couple of places along the table, running his hands over his thin grey hair.

'Tom and I have been doing a little plotting,' the Adjutant said. 'We've decided a certain officer's career with this unit needs terminating.'

Bentham glanced up casually and caught Thurston's eye. This, coming on top of the Adjutant's misrepresentation of the recent discussion, made Thurston feel slightly uncomfortable. That was ludicrous, because he had long ago written Bentham off as of no particular account, as the most uninteresting type of Regular Army ex-ranker, good only at cable-laying, supervising cable-laying and looking after the men who did the actual cable-laying. Despite this, Thurston found himself saying: 'It wasn't quite like that,' but at that moment Rowney asked the Adjutant a question, and the protest, mild as it was, went unheard.

'Your friend Dally, of course,' the Adjutant answered Rowney.

'Why, what's he been up to?' Bentham asked in his slow Yorkshire voice. 'Having his hair cut?'

There was a general laugh, then a token silence while Gordon laid plates of stew in front of the new arrivals. His inquiry whether the Adjutant wanted any rice pudding was met with a facetious and impracticable instruction for the disposal of that foodstuff by an often-quoted route. 'Can't you do better than that, Jack?' the Adjutant asked Rowney. 'Third night we've had Chinese wedding-cake this week.'

'Sorry, William. My Belgian friend's had a little misunderstanding with the civvy police. I'm still looking round for another pal with the right views on how the officers of a liberating army should be fed. Just possess your soul in patience.'

'What's this about Dally?' Bentham persisted. 'If there's a move to give him a wash and a change of clothes, count me in.'

Thurston got up before the topic could be reopened. 'By the way, Jack,' he said to Rowney, 'young Malone asked me to remind you that he still hasn't had those cigarettes for the blokes he's lent to Special Wireless.'

Rowney sighed. 'Tell him it's not my pigeon, will you, Thomas? I've been into it all with him. They're under Special Wireless for everything now.'

'Not NAAFI rations. He told me you'd agreed to supply them.'

'Up until last week. They're off my hands now.'

'Oh no, they're not,' Thurston said nastily. 'According to Malone, they still haven't had last week's.'

'Well, tell him——'

'Look, Jack, you tell him. It's nothing to do with me, is it?'

Rowney stared at him. 'All right, Thomas,' he said, abruptly diving his fork into his stew. 'I'll tell him.'

Dodging the hanging lampshade, which at its lowest point was no more than five feet from the floor, Thurston hurried out, his greatcoat over his arm.

'What's eating our intellectual friend?' Rowney asked.

The Adjutant rubbed his blue chin. 'Don't know quite. He was behaving rather oddly before you blokes came in. He's getting too sort of wrapped up in himself. Needs shaking up.' He was just deciding, having previously decided against it, to inflict some small but salutary injustice on Thurston through the medium of unit orders. He might compel the various sections to start handing in their stores records for check, beginning with Thurston's section and stopping after it. Nice, but perhaps a bit too drastic. What about pinching his jeep for some tiresome extra duty? That might be just the thing.

'If you ask me,' Bentham was saying, 'he's too bloody stuck-up by half. Wants a lesson of some kind, he does.'

'You're going too far there, Ben,' the Adjutant said decisively. He disliked having Bentham in the Officers' Mess, declaring its tone to be thereby lowered, and often said he thought the old boy would be much happier back in the Sergeants' Mess with people of his own type. 'Tom Thurston's about the only chap round here you can carry on a reasonable intelligent discussion with.'

Bentham, unabashed, broke off a piece of bread and ran it round his plate in a way that Thurston and the Adjutant were, unknown to each other, united in finding unpleasant. 'What's all this about a plot about Dally?' he asked.

'You got that, Reg?' Dalessio asked. 'If you get any more interference on this circuit, put it back on plain speech straight away. Then they can see how they like that. I don't believe for a bloody moment the line's been relaid for a single bastard yard. Still, it's being ceased in a week or two, and it never was of the slightest importance, so there's no real worry. Now, what about the gallant Poles?' He spoke with a strong Glamorganshire accent diversified by an occasional Italian vowel.

'They're still on here,' Reg, the lineman-mechanic, said, gesturing towards the test teleprinter. 'Want to see 'em?'

'Yes, please. It's nearly time to switch 'em through to the teleprinter room. We'll get that done before I go.'

Reg bent to the keyboard of the machine and typed:

HOW U GETTING ON THERE READING ME OK KKKK

There was a humming pause while Reg scratched his armpit and said: 'Gone for a piss, I expect. . . . Ah, here he is.' In typical but inextinguishably eerie fashion the teleprinter took on a life of its own, performed a carriage-return, moved the glossy white paper up a couple of lines, and typed:

4 CHRISTS SAKE QUIT BOTHERING ME NOT 2000 HRS YET KKK

Dalessio, grinning to himself, shoved Reg out of the way and typed:

CHIEF SIGNAL OFFICER BRITISH LIBERATION ARMY ERE WATCH YR LANGUAGE MY MAN KKKK

Without hesitation the distant operator typed:

U GO AND S C R E W YRSELF JACK SORRY I MEAN SIR

At this Dalessio went into roars of laughter, digging his knuckle into one deep eye-socket and throwing back his large dark head. It was exactly the kind of joke he liked best. He rotated a little in the narrow aisle between the banks of apparatus and test-panels, still laughing, while Reg watched him with a slight smile. At last Dalessio recovered and shouldered his way down to the phone at the other end of the vehicle.

'Give me the teleprinter room, please. What? Who? All right, I'll speak to him. . . . Terminal Equipment, Dalessio here. Yes. Oh, really? It hasn't?' His voice changed completely, became that of a slightly unbalanced uncle commiserating with a disappointed child: 'Now isn't that just too bad? Well, I do think that's hard lines. Just when you were all excited about it, too, eh?' Over his shoulder he squealed to Reg, in soprano parody of Thurston's educated tones: 'Captain Thurston is tewwibly gwieved that he hasn't got his pwinter to the Poles yet. He's afwaid we've got some howwid scheme on over heah to depwive him of it. . . . All right, Thurston, I'll come over. Yes, now.'

Reg smiled again and put a cigarette in his mouth, striking the match, from long habit, on the metal 'No Smoking' notice tacked up over the ventilator.

'Give me one of those, Reg, I want to cool my nerves before I go into the beauty-parlour across the way. Thanks. Now listen: switch the Poles through to the teleprinter room at one minute to eight exactly, so that there's working communication at eight but not before. Do Thurston good to bite his nails for a few minutes. Put it through on number . . .' – his glance and fore-finger went momentarily to a test-frame across the aisle – 'number six. That's just been rewired. Ring up Teleprinters and tell 'em, will you? See you before I go off.'

It was dark and cold outside and Dalessio shivered on his way over to the signal office. He tripped up on the cable which ran shin-high between a line of blue-and-white posts outside the entrance, and applied an unclean expression to the Adjutant, who had had this amenity provided in an attempt to dignify the working area. Inside the crowded, brilliantly lighted office, he was half-asphyxiated by the smoke from the stove and half-deafened by the thumping of date-stamps, the ringing of telephones, the enraged bark of one sergeant and the loud, tremulous singing of the other. A red-headed man was rushing about bawling 'Emergency Ops for Z Corps' in the accents of County Cork. Nobody took any notice of him: they had all dealt with far too many Emergency Ops messages in the last eight months.

Thurston was in his office, a small room partitioned off from the main one. The unit was occupying what had once been a Belgian military school and later an S.S. training establishment. This building had obviously formed part of the original barrack area, and Thurston often wondered what whim of the Adjutant's had located the offices and stores down here and the men's living-quarters in former offices and stores. The cubicle where Thurston spent so much of his time had no doubt been the abode of the cadet, and then *Unter-offizier*, in charge of barrack-room. He was fond of imagining the heavily built Walloons and high-cheeked Prussians who had slept in here, and had insisted on preserving as a historical document the chalked *Wir kommen zurück* on the plank wall. Like his predecessors, he fancied, he felt cut off from all the life going on just outside the partition, somehow isolated. 'Alone, withouten any company,' he used to quote to himself. He would laugh then, sometimes, and go on to think of the unique lavatory at the far end of the building, where the defecator was required to plant his feet on two metal plates, grasp two handles, and curve his body into the shape of a bow over a kind of trough.

He was not laughing now. His phone conversation with Dalessio had convinced him, even more thoroughly than phone conversations with Dalessio commonly did, that the other despised him for his lack of technical knowledge and took advantage of it to irritate and humiliate him. He tried to reread a letter from one of the two married women in England with whom, besides his wife, he was corresponding, but the thought of seeing Dalessio still troubled him.

Actually seeing Dalessio troubled him even more. Not for the first time it occurred to him that Dalessio's long, matted hair, grease-spotted, cylindrical trouser-legs and ill-fitting battle-dress blouse were designed as an offensive burlesque of his own neat but irremediably civilian appearance. He was smoking, too, and Thurston himself was punctilious in observing inside his office the rule that prohibited smoking on duty until ten at night, but it was no use telling him to put it out. Dalessio, he felt, never obeyed orders unless it suited him. 'Hallo, Thurston,' he said amiably. 'Not still having a baby about the Poles, I hope?'

'I don't think I ever was, was I? I just wanted to make sure what the position was.'

'Oh, you wanted to make sure of that, did you? All right, then. It's quite simple. Physically, the circuit remains unchanged, of course. But, as you know, we have ways of providing extra circuits by means of electrical apparatus, notably by utilising the electron-radiating properties of the thermionic valve, or vacuum-tube. If a signal is applied to the grid . . .'

Thurston's phone rang and he picked it up gratefully. 'Signal-master?' said the voice of Brigadier the Lord Fawcett, the largest and sharpest thorn in the side of the entire Signals unit. 'I want a special despatch-rider to go to Brussels for me. Will you send him round to my office for briefing in ten minutes?'

Thurston considered. Apart from its being over a hundred miles to Brussels, he suspected that the story told by previous special D.R.s who had been given this job was probably quite true: the purpose of the trip was to take in the Brigadier's soiled laundry and bring back the clean stuff, plus any wines, spirits and cigars that the Brigadier's Brussels agent, an R.A.S.C. colonel at the headquarters of the reserve Army Corps, might have got together for him. But he could hardly ask the Lord Fawcett to confirm this. Why was it that his army career seemed littered with such problems? 'The regular D.R. run goes out at oh-five-hundred, sir,' he said in a conciliatory tone. 'Would that do instead, perhaps?'

'No, it certainly would not do instead. You have a man available, I take it?'

'Oh yes, sir.' This was true. It was also true that the departure of this man with the dirty washing would necessitate another, who might have been driving all day, being got out of the section billet and condemned, at best to a night on the signal-office floor, more likely to a run half across Belgium in the small hours with a genuine message of some kind. 'Yes, we have a man.'

'Well, I'm afraid in that case I don't see your difficulty. Get him round to me right away, will you?'

'Very good, sir.' There was never anything one could do.

'Who was that?' Dalessio asked when Thurston had rung off.

'Brigadier Fawcett,' Thurston said unguardedly. But Dally probably didn't know about the laundry rumour. He had little to do with the despatch-rider sections.

'Oh, the washerwoman's friend. I heard a bit about that from Beech. Not on the old game again, is he? Sounded as if he wanted a special D.R. to me.'

'Yes, he did.' Thurston raised his voice. 'Prosser!'

'Sir!' came from outside the partition.

'Ask Sergeant Baker to come and see me, will you?'

'Sir.'

Dalessio's large pale face became serious. He pulled at his moustache. Eventually he said: 'You're letting him have one, are you?' If asked his opinion of Thurston, he would have described him as a plausible bastard. His acquiescence in such matters as this, Dalessio would have added, was bloody typical.

'I can't do anything else.'

'I would. There's nothing to it. Get God's Adjutant on the blower and complain. He's an ignorant bloody oaf, we know, but I bet he'd take this up.'

Thurston had tried this, only to be informed at length that the job of Signals was to give service to the Staff. Before he could tell Dalessio about it, Baker, the D.R. sergeant, arrived to be acquainted with the Lord Fawcett's desires. Thurston thought he detected a glance of protest and commiseration pass between the other two men. When Baker had gone, he turned on Dalessio almost savagely and said: 'Now look, Dally, leaving aside the properties of the thermionic bleeding valve, would you kindly put me in the picture about this teleprinter to the Poles? Is it working or isn't it? Quite a bit of stuff has piled up for them and I've been holding it in the hope the line'll be through on time.'

'No harm in hoping,' Dalessio said. 'I hope it'll be working all right, too.' He dropped his fag-end on the swept floor and trod on it.

'Is it working or is it not?' Thurston asked very loudly. His eyes wandered up and down the other's fat body, remembering how it had looked in a pair of shorts, doing physical training at the officers' training unit. It had proved incapable of the simplest tasks laid upon it, crumpling feebly in the forward-roll exercise, hanging like a crucified sack from the wall-bars, climbing by slow and ugly degrees over the vaulting-horse. Perhaps its owner had simply not felt like exerting it. That would have been bloody typical.

Before Dalessio could answer, a knock came at the plywood door Thurston had had made for his cubicle. In response to the latter's bellow, the red-headed man came in. 'Sergeant Fleming sent to tell you, sir,' he said, 'we're just after getting them Polish fellows on the printer. You'll be wanting me to start sending off the messages we have for them, will you, sir?'

Both Thurston and Dalessio looked up at the travelling-clock that stood on a high shelf in the corner. It said eight o'clock.

'That's just about all, gentlemen,' the Colonel said. 'Except for one last point. Now that our difficulties from the point of view of communication have been removed, and the whole show's going quite smoothly, there are other aspects of our work which need attention. This unit has certain traditions I want kept up. One of them, of course, is an absolutely hundred-per-cent degree of efficiency in all matters affecting the disposal of Signals traffic, from the time the In-Clerk signs for a message from the Staff to the time we get . . .'

He means the Out-Clerk, Thurston thought to himself. The little room where the officers, warrant-officers and senior N.C.O.s of the unit held their conferences was unheated, and the Colonel was wearing his knee-length sheepskin coat, another piece of merchandise supplied through the good offices of Jack Rowney in Exchange, perhaps, for a few gallons of petrol or a couple of hundred cigarettes; Malone's men's cigarettes, probably. The coat, added to the C.O.'s platinum-blond hair and moustache, increased his resemblance to a polar bear. Thurston was in a good mood, having just received the letter which finally buttoned up arrangements for his forthcoming leave: four days with Denise in Oxford, and then a nice little run up to Town for five days with Margot. Just the job. He began composing a nature note on the polar bear: 'This animal, although of poor intelligence, possesses considerable cunning of a low order. It displays the utmost ferocity when menaced in any way. It shows fantastic patience in pursuit of its prey, and a vindictiveness which . . .'

The Colonel was talking now about another tradition of his unit, its almost unparalleled soldier-like quality, its demonstration of the verity that a Signals formation *of any kind* was not a collection of down-at-heel scientists and long-haired mathematical wizards. Thurston reflected it was not for nothing that the Adjutant so frequently described himself as the Colonel's staff officer. Yes, there he was, Arctic fox or, if they had them, Arctic jackal, smiling in proprietary fashion at his chief's oratory. What a bunch they all were. Most of the higher-ranking ones had been lower-ranking officers in the Territorial Army during the 'thirties, the Colonel, for instance, a captain, the Adjutant a second lieutenant. The war had given them responsibility and quick promotion, and their continued enjoyment of such privileges rested not on their own abilities, but on those of people who had arrived in the unit by a different route: Post Office engineers whipped in with a commission, older Regular soldiers promoted from the ranks, officers who had been the conscripts of 1940 and 1941. Yes, what a bunch. Thurston remembered the parting words of a former sergeant of his who had been posted home a few months previously: 'Now I'm going I suppose I can say what I shouldn't. You never had a dog's bloody chance in this lot unless you'd been at North Midland Command with the Adj. and the C.O. And we all know it's the same in that Mess of yours. If you'd been in the T.A. like them you were a blue-eyed boy, otherwise you'd had it from the start. It's all right, sir, everybody knows it. No need to deny it.'

The exception to the rule, presumably, was Cleaver, now making what was no doubt a shorthand transcript of the Colonel's harangue. Thurston hated him as the Adjutant's blue-eyed boy and also for his silky fair hair, his Hitler Youth appearance and his thunderous laugh. His glance moved to Bentham, also busily writing. Bentham, too, fitted into the picture, as much as the Adjutant would let him, which was odd when compared with the attitude of other Regulars in the Mess. But Bentham had less individuality than they.

'So what I propose,' the Colonel said, 'is this. Beginning next week the Adjutant and I will be making a series of snap inspections of section barrack rooms. Now I don't expect anything in the nature of spit-and-polish, of course. Just ordinary soldierly cleanliness and tidiness is all I want.'

In other words, just ordinary spit-and-polish, Thurston thought, making a note for his sergeant on his pad just below the polar-bear *vignette*. He glanced up and saw Dalessio licking the flap of an envelope; it was his invariable practice to write letters during the Colonel's addresses, when once the serious business of line-communications had been got through. Had he heard what had just been said? It was unlikely.

The conference broke up soon afterwards and in the Mess ante-room, where a few officers had gathered for a drink before the evening meal, Thurston was confronted by an exuberant Adjutant who at once bought him a drink. 'Well, Tom,' he said, 'I reckon that fixes things up nice and neat.'

'I don't follow you, Bill.'

'Step number one in cooking your friend Dally's goose. Step number two will be on Monday, oh-nine-thirty hours, when I take the Colonel round the line-maintenance billet. You know what we'll find there, don't you?'

Thurston stared blankly at the Adjutant, whose eyes were sparkling like those of a child who has been promised a treat. 'I still don't get you, Bill.'

'Use your loaf, Tommy. Dally's blokes' boudoir, can't you imagine what it'll be like? There'll be dirt enough in there to raise a crop of potatoes, fag-ends and night buckets all over the shop and the rest of it. The Colonel will eat Dally for his lunch when he sees it.'

'Dally's got three days to get it cleaned up, though.'

'He would have if he paid attention to what his Commanding Officer says. But I know bloody well he was writing a letter when that warning was given. Serves the bastard right, do you see? He'll be off to the mysterious East before you can turn round.'

'How much does the Colonel know about this?'

'What I've told him.'

'You don't really think it'll work, do you?'

'I know the old man. You don't, if you'll excuse my saying so.'

'It's a lousy trick and you know it, Bill,' Thurston said violently. 'I think it's completely bloody.'

'Not at all. An officer who's bolshie enough to disobey a C.O.'s order deserves all he gets,' the Adjutant said, looking sententious. 'Coming in?'

Still fuming, Thurston allowed himself to be led into the dining-room. The massive green-tiled stove was working well and the room was warm and cheerful. The house had belonged to the commandant of the Belgian military school. Its solid furniture and tenebrous landscape pictures had survived German occupation, though there was a large burn in the carpet that had been imputed, perhaps rightly, to the festivities of the *Schutz Staffel*. Jack Rowney, by importing photographs of popular entertainers, half-naked young women and the Commander-in-Chief, had done his best to document the Colonel's thesis that the Officers' Mess was also their home. The Adjutant, in excellent spirits, his hand on Thurston's shoulder, sent Corporal Gordon running for a bottle of Burgundy. Then, before they sat down, he looked very closely at Thurston.

'Oh, and by the way, old boy,' he said, a note of menace intensifying the quack in his voice, 'you wouldn't think of tipping your friend Dally the wink about this little treat we've got lined up for him, would you? If you do, I'll have your guts for garters.' Laughing heartily, he dug Thurston in the ribs and added: 'Your leave's due at the end of the month, isn't it? Better watch out you don't make yourself indispensable here. We might not be able to let you go, do you see?'

Early on Monday morning Thurston was walking up from the signal office towards the area where the men's barrack rooms were. He was going to find his batman and arrange to be driven some twenty miles to the department of the Advocate-General's branch which handled divorce. The divorce in question was not his own, which would have to wait until after the war, but that of his section cook, whose wife had developed an immoderate fondness for R.A.F. and U.S.A.A.F. personnel.

Thurston was thinking less about the cook's wife than about the fateful inspection, scheduled to take place any minute now. He realised he had timed things badly, but his trip had only just become possible and he hoped to be out of the area before the Colonel and the Adjutant finished their task. He was keen to do this because the sight of a triumphant Adjutant would be more than he could stand, especially since his conscience was very uneasy about the whole affair.

There were all sorts of reasons why he should have tipped Dalessio off about the inspection. The worst of it was, as he had realised in bed last night, when it was too late to do anything about it, that his irritation with Dalessio over the matter of the Polish teleprinter had been a prime cause of his keeping quiet about it. He remembered actually thinking more than once that a thorough shaking-up would do Dalessio no harm, and that perhaps the son of an Italian café proprietor in Cascade, Glamorganshire, had certain disqualifications for the role of British regimental officer. He twisted up his face when he thought of this and started wondering just why it was that the Adjutant was persecuting Dalessio. Perhaps the latter's original offence had been his habit of doing bird-warbles while the Adjutant and Rowney listened to broadcast performances of *The Warsaw Concerto*, the intermezzo from *Cavalleria Rusticana* and other sub-classics dear to their hearts. Cheeping, trilling and twittering, occasionally gargling like a seagull, Dalessio had been told to shut up or get out and had done neither.

Thurston's way took him past the door of the notorious line-maintenance billet. There seemed to be nobody about. Then he was startled by the sudden manifestation of two soldiers carrying brooms and a bucket. One of them had once been in his section and had been transferred early that year to one of the cable sections, he had forgotten which one. 'Good-morning, Maclean,' he said.

The man addressed came sketchily to attention. 'Morning, sir.'

'Getting on all right in No. 1 Company?'

'Yes, thank you, sir, I like it fine.'

'Good. What are you fellows up to so early in the morning?'

They looked at each other and the other man said: 'Cleaning up, sir. Fatigue party, sir.'

'I see; right, carry on.'

Thurston soon found his batman, who agreed with some reluctance to the proposed trip and said he would see if he could get the jeep down to the signal office in ten minutes. The jeep was a bone of contention between Thurston and his batman, and the batman always won, in the sense that never in his life had he permitted Thurston to drive the jeep in his absence. He was within his rights, but Thurston often wished, as now, that he could be allowed a treat occasionally. He wished it more strongly when a jeep with no exhaust and with seven men in it came bouncing down the track from the No. 1 Company billet area. They were laughing and two of them were pretending to fight. The driver was a lance-corporal.

Suddenly the laughing and fighting stopped and the men assumed an unnatural sobriety. The reason for this was provided by the immediate emergence into view of the Colonel and the Adjutant, moving across Thurston's front.

They saw him at once; he hastily saluted and the Adjutant, as usual, returned the salute. His gaze met Thurston's under lowered brows and his lips were gathered in the fiercest scowl they were capable of.

Thurston waited till they were out of sight and hurried to the door of the line-maintenance billet. The place was deserted. Except in illustrations to Army manuals and the like, he had never seen such perfection of order and cleanliness. It was obviously the result of hours of devoted labour.

He leant against the door-post and began to laugh.

'I gather the plot against our pal Dally misfired somewhat,' Bentham said in the Mess dining-room later that day.

Thurston looked up rather wearily. His jeep had broken down on the way back from the divorce expert and his return had been delayed for some hours. He had made part of the journey on the back of a motor-bike. Further, he had just read a unit order requiring him to make the jeep available at the Orderly Room the next morning. It wasn't his turn yet. The Adjutant had struck again.

'You know, I'm quite pleased,' Bentham went on, lighting a cigarette and moving towards the stove where Thurston stood.

'Oh, so am I.'

'You are? Now that's rather interesting. Surprising, even. I should have thought you'd be downcast.'

Something in his tone made Thurston glance at him sharply and put down the unit order. Bentham was standing with his feet apart in an intent attitude. 'Why should you think that, Ben?'

'I'll tell you. Glad of the opportunity. First of all I'll tell you why it misfired, if you don't already know. Because I tipped Dally off. Lent him some of my blokes and all, to get the place spick and span.'

Thurston nodded, thinking of the two men he had seen outside the billet that morning. 'I see.'

'You do, do you? Good. Now I'll tell you why I did it. First of all, the Army's not the place for this kind of plotting and scheming. The job's too important. Secondly, I did it because I don't like seeing an able man taken down by a bunch of ignorant jumped-up so-called bloody gentlemen from the Territorial Army. Not that I hold any brief for Dalessio outside his technical abilities. As you know, I'm a Regular soldier and I disapprove most strongly of anything damn slovenly. It's part of my nature now and I don't mind either. But one glance at the Adj.'s face when he was telling me the form for this morning and I knew where my duty lay. I hope I always do. I do my best to play it his way as a rule for the sake of peace and quiet. But this business was different. Wasn't it?'

Thurston had lowered his gaze. 'Yes, Ben.'

'It came as a bit of shock to me, you know, to find that Dalessio needed tipping off.'

'How do you mean?'

'I mean that I'd have expected someone else to have told him already. I only heard about this last night. I was the only one here later on and I suppose the Adj. felt he had to tell someone. I should have thought by that time someone else would have let the cat out of the bag to Dally. You, for instance. You were in on this from the start, weren't you?'

Thurston said nothing.

'I've no doubt you have your reasons, your excuses for not letting on. In spite of the fact that I've always understood you were the great one for pouring scorn on the Adj. and Rowney and Cleaver and the rest of that crowd. Yes, you could talk about them till you were black in the face, but when it came to doing something, talking where it would do some good, you kept your mouth shut. And, if I remember rightly, you were the one who used to stick up for Dally when the others were laying into him behind his back. You know what I think? I don't think you care tuppence. You don't care beyond talking, any road. I think you're really quite sold on the Adj.'s crowd, never mind what you say about them. Chew that over. And chew this over and all: I think you're a bastard, just like the rest of 'em. Tell that to your friend the Adjutant, Captain bloody Thurston.'

Thurston stood there for some time after Bentham had gone, tearing up the unit order and throwing the pieces into the stove.

MURIEL SPARK

# The Portobello Road

ONE day in my young youth at high summer, lolling with my lovely companions
upon a haystack, I found a needle. Already and privately for some years I had
been guessing that I was set apart from the common run, but this of the needle
attested the fact to my whole public, George, Kathleen and Skinny. I sucked my
thumb, for when I had thrust my idle hand deep into the hay, the thumb was
where the needle had stuck.

When everyone had recovered George said, 'She put in her thumb and pulled
out a plum.' Then away we were into our merciless hacking-hecking laughter
again.

The needle had gone fairly deep into the thumby cushion and a small red river
flowed and spread from this tiny puncture. So that nothing of our joy should lag,
George put in quickly,

'Mind your bloody thumb on my shirt.'

Then hac-hec-hoo, we shrieked into the hot Borderland afternoon. Really I
should not care to be so young of heart again. That is my thought every time I
turn over my old papers and come across the photograph. Skinny, Kathleen and
myself are in the photo atop the haystack. Skinny had just finished analysing the
inwards of my find.

'It couldn't have been done by brains. You haven't much brains but you're a
lucky wee thing.'

Everyone agreed that the needle betokened extraordinary luck. As it was
becoming a serious conversation George said,

'I'll take a photo.'

I wrapped my hanky round my thumb and got myself organised. George
pointed up from his camera and shouted,

'Look, there's a mouse!'

Kathleen screamed and I screamed although I think we knew there was no
mouse. But this gave us an extra session of squalling hee-hoo's. Finally we three
composed ourselves for George's picture. We look lovely and it was a great day at
the time, but I would not care for it all over again. From that day I was known as
Needle.

One Saturday in recent years I was mooching down the Portobello Road from
the Ladbroke Grove end, threading among the crowds of marketers on the
narrow pavement, when I saw a woman. She had a haggard careworn wealthy
look, thin but for the breasts forced up high like a pigeon's. I had not seen her for
nearly five years. How changed she was! But I recognised Kathleen my friend,

her features had already begun to sink and protrude in the way that mouths and noses do in people destined always to be old for their years. When I had last seen her, nearly five years ago, Kathleen, barely thirty, had said,

'I've lost all my looks, it's in the family. All the women are handsome as girls but we go off early, we go brown and nosey.'

I stood silently among the people, watching. As you will see, I wasn't in a position to speak to Kathleen. I saw her shoving in her avid manner from stall to stall. She was always fond of antique jewellery and of bargains. I wondered that I had not seen her before in the Portobello Road on my Saturday morning ambles. Her long stiff-crooked fingers pounced to select a jade ring from amongst the jumble of brooches and pendants, onyx, moonstone and gold, set out on the stall.

'What d'you think of this?' she said.

I saw then who was with her. I had been half-conscious of the huge man following several paces behind her, and now I noticed him.

'It looks all right,' he said. 'How much is it?'

'How much is it?' Kathleen asked the vendor.

I took a good look at this man accompanying Kathleen. It was her husband. The beard was unfamiliar, but I recognised beneath it his enormous mouth, the bright sensuous lips, the large brown eyes for ever brimming with pathos.

It was not for me to speak to Kathleen, but I had a sudden inspiration which caused me to say quietly,

'Hallo, George.'

The giant of a man turned round to face the direction of my voice. There were so many people – but at length he saw me.

'Hallo, George,' I said again.

Kathleen had started to haggle with the stall-owner, in her old way, over the price of the jade ring. George continued to stare at me, his big mouth slightly parted so that I could see a wide slit of red lips and white teeth between the fair grassy growths of beard and moustache.

'My God!' he said.

'What's the matter?' said Kathleen.

'Hallo, George!' I said again, quite loud this time, and cheerfully.

'Look!' said George. 'Look who's there, over beside the fruit stall.'

Kathleen looked but didn't see.

'Who is it?' she said impatiently.

'It's Needle,' he said. 'She said, "Hallo, George".'

'*Needle*,' said Kathleen. 'Who do you mean? You don't mean our old friend *Needle* who——'

'Yes. There she is. My God!'

He looked very ill, although when I had said 'Hallo, George' I had spoken friendly enough.

'I don't see anyone faintly resembling poor Needle,' said Kathleen, looking at him. She was worried.

George pointed straight at me. 'Look *there*. I tell you that is Needle.'

'You're ill, George. Heavens, you must be seeing things. Come on home. Needle isn't there. You know as well as I do, Needle is dead.'

I must explain that I departed this life nearly five years ago. But I did not altogether depart this world. There were those odd things still to be done which one's executors can never do properly. Papers to be looked over, even after the executors have torn them up. Lots of business except, of course, on Sundays and Holidays of Obligation, plenty to take an interest in for the time being. I take my recreation on Saturday mornings. If it is a wet Saturday I wander up and down the substantial lanes of Woolworths as I did when I was young and visible. There is a pleasurable spread of objects on the counters which I now perceive and exploit with a certain detachment, since it suits with my condition of life. Creams, toothpastes, combs and hankies, cotton gloves, flimsy flowering scarves, writing-paper and crayons, ice-cream cones and orangeade, screwdrivers, boxes of tacks, tins of paint, of glue, of marmalade; I always liked them, but far more now that I have no need of any. When Saturdays are fine I go instead to the Portobello Road where formerly I would jaunt with Kathleen in our grown-up days. The barrow-loads do not change much, of apples and rayon vests in common blues and low-taste mauve, of silver plate, trays and teapots long since changed hands from the bygone citizens to dealers, from shops to the new flats and breakable homes, then over to the barrow-stalls and the dealers again: Georgian spoons, rings, earrings of turquoise and opal set in the butterfly pattern or true-lovers' knot, patch-boxes with miniature paintings of ladies on ivory, snuff-boxes of silver with Scotch pebbles inset.

Sometimes as occasion arises on a Saturday morning, my friend Kathleen, who is a Catholic, has a Mass said for my soul, and then I am in attendance as it were at the church. But most Saturdays I take my delight among the solemn crowds with their aimless purposes, their eternal life not far away, who push past the counters and stalls, who handle, buy, steal, touch, desire and ogle the merchandise. I hear the tinkling tills, I hear the jangle of loose change and tongues and children wanting to hold and have.

That is how I came to be in the Portobello Road that Saturday morning when I saw George and Kathleen. I could not have spoken had I not been inspired to it. And most extraordinary, on that morning as I spoke, a degree of visibility set in. I suppose from poor George's point of view it was like seeing a ghost when he saw me standing by the fruit barrow repeating, 'Hallo, George!'

We were bound for the South. When our education, what we could get of it from the North, was thought to be finished, one by one we were sent or sent for to London. John Skinner, whom we called Skinny, went to study more archae-ology, George to join his uncle's tobacco firm, Kathleen to stay with her rich connections and to potter intermittently in the Mayfair hat shop which one of them owned. A little later I also went to London to see life, for it was my ambition to write about life, which first I had to see.

'We four must stick together,' George said very often in that yearning way of his. He was always desperately afraid of neglect. We four looked likely to shift off in different directions and George did not trust the other three of us not to forget all about him. More and more as the time came for him to depart for his uncle's tobacco farm in Africa he said,

'We four must keep in touch.'

And before he left he told each of us anxiously,

'I'll write regularly, once a month. We must keep together for the sake of the old times.' He had three prints taken from the negative of that photo on the haystack, wrote on the back of them, 'George took this the day that Needle found the needle' and gave us a copy each. I think we all wished he could become a bit more callous.

During my lifetime I was a drifter, nothing organised. It was difficult for my friends to follow the logic of my life. By the normal reckonings I should have come to starvation and ruin, which I never did. Of course, I did not live to write about life as I wanted to do. Possibly that is why I am inspired to do so now in these peculiar circumstances.

I taught in a private school in Kensington for almost three months, very small children. I didn't know what to do with them, but I was kept fairly busy escorting incontinent little boys to the lavatory and telling the little girls to use their handkerchiefs. After that I lived a winter holiday in London on my small capital, and when that had run out I found a diamond bracelet in the cinema for which I received a reward of fifty pounds. When it was used up I got a job with a publicity man, writing speeches for absorbed industrialists, in which the Dictionary of Quotations came in very useful. So it went on. I got engaged to Skinny, but shortly after that I was left a small legacy, enough to keep me for six months. This somehow decided me that I didn't love Skinny so I gave him back the ring.

But it was through Skinny that I went to Africa. He was engaged with a party of researchers to investigate King Solomon's mines, that series of ancient workings ranging from the ancient port of Ophir, now called Beira, across Portuguese East Africa and Southern Rhodesia, to the mighty jungle-city of Zimbabwe whose temple walls still stand by the approach to an ancient and sacred mountain, where the rubble of that civilisation scatters itself over the surrounding Rhodesian waste. I accompanied the party as a sort of Secretary. Skinny vouched for me, he paid my fare, he sympathised by his action with my inconsequential life, although when he spoke of it he disapproved. A life like mine annoys most people; they go to their jobs every day, attend to things, give orders, pummel typewriters and get two or three weeks off every year, and it vexes them to see someone else not bothering to do these things and yet getting away with it, not starving, being lucky as they call it. Skinny, when I had broken off our engagement, lectured me about this, but still he took me to Africa knowing I should probably leave his unit within a few months.

We were there a few weeks before we began inquiring for George, who was farming about four hundred miles away to the north. We had not told him of our plans.

'If we tell George to expect us in his part of the world he'll come rushing to pester us the first week. After all, we're going on business,' Skinny had said.

Before we left, Kathleen told us, 'Give George my love and tell him not to send frantic cables every time I don't answer his letters right away. Tell him I'm busy in the hat shop and being presented. You would think he hadn't another friend in the world the way he carries on.'

We had settled first at Fort Victoria, our nearest place of access to the Zimbabwe ruins. There we made inquiries about George. It was clear he hadn't many friends. The older settlers were the most tolerant about the half-caste woman he was living with, as we learned, but they were furious about his methods of raising tobacco, which we learned were most unprofessional and in some mysterious way disloyal to the whites. We could never discover how it was that George's style of tobacco farming gave the blacks opinions about themselves, but that's what the older settlers claimed. The newer immigrants thought he was unsociable and, of course, his living with that nig made visiting impossible.

I must say I was myself a bit off-put by this news about the brown woman. I was brought up in a university town where there were Indian, African and Asiatic students abounding in a variety of tints and hues. I was brought up to avoid them for reasons connected with local reputation and God's ordinances. You cannot easily go against what you were brought up to do unless you are a rebel by nature.

Anyhow, we visited George eventually, taking advantage of the offer of transport from some people bound north in search of game. He had heard of our arrival in Rhodesia and though he was glad, almost relieved, to see us, he pursued a policy of sullenness for the first hour.

'We wanted to give you a surprise, George.'

'How were we to know that you'd get to hear of our arrival, George? News here must travel faster than light, George.'

'We did hope to give you a surprise, George.'

At last he said, 'Well, I must say it's good to see you. All we need now is Kathleen. We four simply must stick together. You find when you're in a place like this, there's nothing like old friends.'

He showed us his drying sheds. He showed us a paddock where he was experimenting with a horse and a zebra mare, attempting to mate them. They were frolicking happily, but not together. They passed each other in their private play, time and again, but without acknowledgement and without resentment.

'It's been done before,' George said. 'It makes a fine strong beast, more intelligent than a mule and sturdier than a horse. But I'm not having any success with this pair, they won't look at each other.'

After a while he said, 'Come in for a drink and meet Matilda.'

She was dark brown, with a subservient hollow chest and round shoulders, a gawky woman, very snappy with the houseboys. We said pleasant things as we drank on the stoep before dinner, but we found George difficult. For some reason he began to rail at me for breaking off my engagement to Skinny, saying what a dirty trick it was after all those good times in the old days. I diverted attention to Matilda. I supposed, I said, she knew this part of the country well?

'No,' said she, 'I been a-shellitered my life. I not put out to working. Me nothing to go from place to place is allowed like dirty girls does.' In her speech she gave every syllable equal stress.

George explained, 'Her father was a white magistrate in Natal. She had a sheltered upbringing, different from the other coloureds, you realise.'

'Man, me no black-eyed Susan,' said Matilda, 'no, no.'

On the whole, George treated her as a servant. She was about four months advanced in pregnancy, but he made her get up and fetch for him, many times. Soap: that was one of the things Matilda had to fetch. George made his own bath soap, showed it proudly, gave us the receipt, which I did not trouble to remember; I was fond of nice soaps during my lifetime and George's smelt of brilliantine and looked likely to soil one's skin.

'D'yo brahn?' Matilda asked me.

George said, 'She is asking if you go brown in the sun.'

'No, I go freckled.'

'I got sister-in-law go freckles.'

She never spoke another word to Skinny nor to me, and we never saw her again.

Some months later I said to Skinny,

'I'm fed up with being a camp-follower.'

He was not surprised that I was leaving his unit, but he hated my way of expressing it. He gave me a Presbyterian look.

'Don't talk like that. Are you going back to England or staying?'

'Staying, for a while.'

'Well, don't wander too far off.'

I was able to live on the fee I got for writing a gossip column in a local weekly, which wasn't my idea of writing about life. I made friends, more than I could cope with, after I left Skinny's exclusive little band of archaeologists. I had the attractions of being newly out from England and of wanting to see life. Of the countless young men and go-ahead families who purred me along the Rhodesian roads, hundred after hundred miles, I only kept up with one family when I returned to my native land. I think that was because they were the most representative, they stood for all the rest: people in those parts are very typical of each other, as one group of standing stones in that wilderness is like the next.

I met George once more in a hotel in Bulawayo. We drank highballs and spoke of war. Skinny's party were just then deciding whether to remain in the country or return home. They had reached an exciting part of their research, and whenever I got a chance to visit Zimbabwe he would take me for a moonlight walk in the ruined temple and try to make me see phantom Phoenicians flitting ahead of us, or along the walls. I had half a mind to marry Skinny; perhaps, I thought, when his studies were finished. The impending war was in our bones: so I remarked to George as we sat drinking highballs on the hotel stoep in the hard bright sunny July winter of that year.

George was inquisitive about my relations with Skinny. He tried to pump me for about half an hour and when at last I said, 'You are becoming aggressive, George,' he stopped. He became quite pathetic. He said, 'War or no war I'm clearing out of this.'

'It's the heat does it,' I said.

'I'm clearing out in any case. I've lost a fortune in tobacco. My uncle is making a fuss. It's the other bloody planters – once you get the wrong side of them you're finished in this wide land.'

'What about Matilda?' I asked.

He said, 'She'll be all right. She's got hundreds of relatives.'

I had already heard about the baby girl. Coal black, by repute, with George's features. And another on the way, they said.

'What about the child?'

He didn't say anything to that. He ordered more highballs and when they arrived he swizzled his for a long time with a stick. 'Why didn't you ask me to your twenty-first?' he said then.

'I didn't have anything special, no party, George. We had a quiet drink among ourselves, George, just Skinny and the old professors and two of the wives and me, George.'

'You didn't ask me to your twenty-first,' he said. 'Kathleen writes to me regularly.'

This wasn't true. Kathleen sent me letters fairly often in which she said, 'Don't tell George I wrote to you as he will be expecting word from me and I can't be bothered actually.'

'But you,' said George, 'don't seem to have any sense of old friendships, you and Skinny.'

'Oh, George!' I said.

'Remember the times we had?' George said. 'We used to have times.' His large brown eyes began to water.

'I'll have to be getting along,' I said.

'Please don't go. Don't leave me just yet. I've something to tell you.'

'Something nice?' I laid on an eager smile. All responses to George had to be overdone.

'You don't know how lucky you are,' George said.

'How?' I said. Sometimes I got tired of being called lucky by everybody. There were times when, privately practising my writings about life, I knew the bitter side of my fortune. When I failed again and again to reproduce life in some satisfactory and perfect form, I was the more imprisoned, for all my carefree living, within my craving for this satisfaction. Sometimes, in my impotence and need I secreted a venom which infected all my life for days on end and which spurted out indiscriminately on Skinny or on anyone who crossed my path.

'You aren't bound by anyone,' George said. 'You come and go as you please. Something always turns up for you. You're free, and you don't know your luck.'

'You're a damn sight more free than I am,' I said sharply. 'You've got your rich uncle.'

'He's losing interest in me,' George said. 'He's had enough.'

'Oh, well, you're young yet. What was it you wanted to tell me?'

'A secret,' George said. 'Remember we used to have those secrets?'

'Oh yes, we did.'

'Did you ever tell any of mine?'

'Oh no, George.' In reality, I couldn't remember any particular secret out of the dozens we must have exchanged from our schooldays onwards.

'Well, this is a secret, mind. Promise not to tell.'

'Promise.'

'I'm married.'

'Married, George! Oh, who to?'

'Matilda.'

'How dreadful!' I spoke before I could think, but he agreed with me.

'Yes, it's awful, but what could I do?'

'You might have asked my advice,' I said pompously.

'I'm two years older than you are. I don't ask advice from you, Needle, little beast.'

'Don't ask for sympathy then.'

'A nice friend you are,' he said, 'I must say, after all these years.'

'Poor George!' I said.

'There are three white men to one white woman in this country,' said George. 'An isolated planter doesn't see a white woman and if he sees one she doesn't see him. What could I do? I needed the woman.'

I was nearly sick. One, because of my Scottish upbringing. Two, because of my horror of corny phrases like 'I needed the woman', which George repeated twice again.

'And Matilda got tough,' said George, 'after you and Skinny came to visit us. She had some friends at the Mission, and she packed up and went to them.'

'You should have let her go,' I said.

'I went after her,' George said. 'She insisted on being married, so I married her.'

'That's not a proper secret, then,' I said. 'The news of a mixed marriage soon gets about.'

'I took care of that,' George said. 'Crazy as I was, I took her to the Congo and married her there. She promised to keep quiet about it.'

'Well, you can't clear off and leave her now, surely,' I said.

'I'm going to get out of this place. I can't stand the woman and I can't stand the country. I didn't realise what it would be like. Two years of the country and three months of my wife have been enough.'

'Will you get a divorce?'

'No, Matilda's Catholic. She won't divorce.'

George was fairly getting through the highballs, and I wasn't far behind him. His brown eyes floated shiny and liquid as he told me how he had written to tell his uncle of his plight. 'Except, of course, I didn't say we were married, that would have been too much for him. He's a prejudiced hardened old Colonial. I only said I'd had a child by a coloured woman and was expecting another, and he perfectly understood. He came at once by plane a few weeks ago. He's made a settlement on her, providing she keeps her mouth shut about her association with me.'

'Will she do that?'

'Oh, yes, or she won't get the money.'

'But as your wife she has a claim on you, in any case.'

'If she claimed as my wife she'd get far less. Matilda knows what she's doing, greedy bitch she is. She'll keep her mouth shut.'

'Only, you won't be able to marry again, will you, George?'

'Not unless she dies,' he said. 'And she's as strong as a trek ox.'

'Well, I'm sorry, George,' I said.

'Good of you to say so,' he said. 'But I can see by your chin that you disapprove of me. My old uncle understood better.'

'Oh, George, I quite understand. You were lonely, I suppose.'

'You didn't even ask me to your twenty-first. If you and Skinny had been nicer to me, I would never have lost my head and married the woman, never.'

'You didn't ask me to your wedding,' I said.

'You're a catty bissom, Needle, not like what you were in the old times when you used to tell us your wee stories.'

'I'll have to be getting along,' I said.

'Mind you keep the secret,' George said.

'Can't I tell Skinny? He would be very sorry for you, George.'

'You mustn't tell anyone. Keep it a secret. Promise.'

'Promise,' I said. I understood that he wished to enforce some sort of bond between us with this secret, and I thought, 'Oh, well, I suppose he's lonely. Keeping his secret won't do any harm.'

I returned to England with Skinny's party just before the war.

I did not see George again till just before my death, five years ago.

\*

After the war Skinny returned to his studies. He had two more exams, over a period of eighteen months, and I thought I might marry him when the exams were over.

'You might do worse than Skinny,' Kathleen used to say to me on our Saturday morning excursions to the antique shops and the junk stalls.

She too was getting on in years. The remainder of our families in Scotland were hinting that it was time we settled down with husbands. Kathleen was a little younger than me, but looked much older. She knew her chances were diminishing but at that time I did not think she cared very much. As for myself, the main attraction of marrying Skinny was his prospective expeditions in Mesopotamia. My desire to marry him had to be stimulated by the continual reading of books about Babylon and Assyria; perhaps Skinny felt this, because he supplied the books and even started instructing me in the art of deciphering cuneiform tables.

Kathleen was more interested in marriage than I thought. Like me, she had racketed around a good deal during the war; she had actually been engaged to an officer in the U.S. Navy, who was killed. Now she kept an antique shop near Lambeth, was doing very nicely, lived in a Chelsea square, but for all that she must have wanted to be married and have children. She would stop and look into all the prams which the mothers had left outside shops or area gates.

'The poet Swinburne used to do that,' I told her once.

'Really? Did he want children of his own?'

'I shouldn't think so. He simply liked babies.'

Before Skinny's final exam he fell ill and was sent to a sanatorium in Switzerland.

'You're fortunate after all not to be married to him,' Kathleen said. 'You might have caught T.B.'

I was fortunate, I was lucky . . . so everyone kept telling me on different occasions. Although it annoyed me to hear, I knew they were right, but in a way that was different from what they meant. It took very small effort to make a living: book reviews, odd jobs for Kathleen, a few months with the publicity man again, still getting up speeches about literature, art and life for industrial tycoons. I was waiting to write about life and it seemed to me that the good fortune lay in this, whenever it should be. And until then I was assured of my charmed life, the necessities of existence always coming my way, and I with far more leisure than anyone else. I thought of my type of luck after I became a Catholic and was being confirmed. The Bishop touches the candidate on the cheek, a symbolic reminder of the sufferings a Christian is supposed to undertake. I thought, how lucky, what a feathery symbol to stand for the hellish violence of its true meaning.

I visited Skinny twice in the two years that he was in the sanatorium. He was almost cured, and expected to be home within a few months. I told Kathleen after my last visit,

'Maybe I'll marry Skinny when he's well again.'

'Make it definite, Needle, and not so much of the maybe. You don't know when you're well off,' she said.

That was five years ago, in the last year of my life. Kathleen and I had become very close friends. We met several times each week, and after our Saturday morning excursions in the Portobello Road very often I would accompany Kathleen to her aunt's house in Kent for a long week-end.

One day in the June of that year I met Kathleen specially for lunch because she had phoned me to say she had news.

'Guess who came into the shop this afternoon,' she said.

'Who?'

'George.'

We had half-imagined George was dead. We had received no letters in the past ten years. Early in the war we had heard rumours of his keeping a night club in Durban, but nothing after that. We could have made inquiries if we had felt moved to do so.

At one time, when we discussed him, Kathleen had said,

'I ought to get in touch with poor George. But then I think he would write back. He would demand a regular correspondence again.'

'We four must stick together,' I mimicked.

'I can visualise his reproachful limpid orbs,' Kathleen said.

Skinny said, 'He's probably gone native. With his coffee concubine and a dozen mahogany kids.'

'Perhaps he's dead,' Kathleen said.

I did not speak of George's marriage, nor any of his confidences in the hotel at Bulawayo. As the years passed we ceased to mention him except in passing, as someone more or less dead so far as we were concerned.

Kathleen was excited about George's turning up. She had forgotten her impatience with him in former days; she said,

'It was so wonderful to see old George. He seems to need a friend, feels neglected, out of touch with things.'

'He needs mothering, I suppose.'

Kathleen didn't notice the malice. She declared, 'That's exactly the case with George. It always has been, I can see it now.'

She seemed ready to come to any rapid new and happy conclusion about George. In the course of the morning he had told her of his war-time night club in Durban, his game-shooting expeditions since. It was clear he had not mentioned Matilda. He had put on weight, Kathleen told me, but he could carry it.

I was curious to see this version of George, but I was leaving for Scotland next day and did not see him till September of that year, just before my death.

While I was in Scotland I gathered from Kathleen's letters that she was seeing George very frequently, finding enjoyable company in him, looking after him.

'You'll be surprised to see how he has developed.' Apparently he would hang round Kathleen in her shop most days; 'it makes him feel useful', she maternally expressed it. He had an old relative in Kent whom he visited at week-ends; this old lady lived a few miles from Kathleen's aunt, which made it easy for them to travel down together on Saturdays, and go for long country walks.

'You'll see such a difference in George,' Kathleen said on my return to London in September. I was to meet him that night, a Saturday. Kathleen's aunt was abroad, the maid on holiday, and I was to keep Kathleen company in the empty house.

George had left London for Kent a few days earlier. 'He's actually helping with the harvest down there!' Kathleen told me lovingly.

Kathleen and I had planned to travel down together, but on that Saturday she was unexpectedly delayed in London on some business. It was arranged that I should go ahead of her in the early afternoon to see to the provisions for our party; Kathleen had invited George to dinner at her aunt's house that night.

'I should be with you by seven,' she said. 'Sure you won't mind the empty house? I hate arriving at empty houses, myself.'

I said no, I liked an empty house.

So I did, when I got there. I had never found the house more likeable. A large Georgian vicarage in about eight acres, most of the rooms shut and sheeted, there being only one servant. I discovered that I wouldn't need to go shopping, Kathleen's aunt had left many and delicate supplies with notes attached to them: 'Eat this up please do see also fridge' and 'A treat for three hungry people see also 2 bttles beaune for yr party on back kn table'. It was like a treasure hunt as I followed clue after clue through the cool, silent domestic quarters. A house in which there are no people – but with all the signs of tenancy – can be a most tranquil good place. People take up space in a house out of proportion to their size. On my previous visits I had seen the rooms overflowing, as it seemed, with Kathleen, her aunt, and the little fat maid-servant; they were always on the move. As I wandered through that part of the house which was in use, opening windows to let in the pale-yellow air of September, I was not conscious that I, Needle, was taking up any space at all, I might have been a ghost.

The only thing to be fetched was the milk. I waited till after four when the milking should be done, then set off for the farm which lay across two fields at the back of the orchard. There, when the byreman was handing me the bottle, I saw George.

'Hallo, George,' I said.

'Needle! What are you doing here?' he said.

'Fetching milk,' I said.

'So am I. Well, it's good to see you, I must say.'

As we paid the farm hand, George said, 'I'll walk back with you part of the way. But I mustn't stop, my old cousin's without any milk for her tea. How's Kathleen?'

'She was kept in London. She's coming on later, about seven, she expects.'

We had reached the end of the first field. George's way led to the left and on to the main road.

'We'll see you tonight, then?' I said.

'Yes, and talk about old times.'

'Grand,' I said.

But George got over the stile with me.

'Look here,' he said. 'I'd like to talk to you, Needle.'

'We'll talk tonight, George. Better not keep your cousin waiting for the milk.' I found myself speaking to him almost as if he were a child.

'No, I want to talk to you alone. This is a good opportunity.'

We began to cross the second field. I had been hoping to have the house to myself for a couple more hours and I was rather petulant.

'See,' he said suddenly, 'that haystack?'

'Yes,' I said absently.

'Let's sit there and talk. I'd like to see you up on a haystack again. I still keep that photo. Remember that time when——'

'I found the needle,' I said very quickly, to get it over.

But I was glad to rest. The stack had been broken up, but we managed to find a nest in it. I buried my bottle of milk in the hay for coolness. George placed his carefully at the foot of the stack.

'My old cousin is terribly vague, poor soul. A bit hazy in her head. She hasn't the least sense of time. If I tell her I've only been gone ten minutes she'll believe it.'

I giggled, and looked at him. His face had grown much larger, his lips full, wide and with a ripe colour that is strange in a man. His brown eyes were abounding as before with some inarticulate plea.

'So you're going to marry Skinny after all these years?'

'I really don't know, George.'

'You played him up properly.'

'It isn't for you to judge. I have my own reasons for what I do.'

'Don't get sharp,' he said, 'I was only funning.' To prove it, he lifted a tuft of hay and brushed my face with it.

'D'you know,' he said next, 'I didn't think you and Skinny treated me very decently in Rhodesia.'

'Well, we were busy, George. And we were younger then, we had a lot to do and see. After all, we could see you any other time, George.'

'A touch of selfishness,' he said.

'I'll have to be getting along, George.' I made to get down from the stack. He pulled me back. 'Wait, I've got something to tell you.'

'O.K., George, tell me.'

'First promise not to tell Kathleen. She wants it kept a secret so that she can tell you herself.'

'All right. Promise.'

'I'm going to marry Kathleen.'

'But you're already married.'

Sometimes I heard news of Matilda from the one Rhodesian family with whom I still kept up. They referred to her as 'George's Dark Lady' and, of course, they did not know he was married to her. She had apparently made a good thing out of George, they said, for she minced around all tarted up, never did a stroke of work and was always unsettling the respectable coloured girls in their neighbourhood. According to accounts, she was a living example of the folly of behaving as George did.

'I married Matilda in the Congo,' George was saying.

'It would still be bigamy,' I said.

He was furious when I used that word bigamy. He lifted a handful of hay as if he would throw it in my face, but controlling himself meanwhile he fanned it at me playfully.

'I'm not sure that the Congo marriage was valid,' he continued. 'Anyway, as far as I'm concerned, it isn't.'

'You can't do a thing like that,' I said.

'I need Kathleen. She's been decent to me. I think we were always meant for each other, me and Kathleen.'

'I'll have to be going,' I said.

But he put his knee over my ankles, so that I couldn't move. I sat still and gazed into space.

He tickled my face with a wisp of hay.

'Smile up, Needle,' he said, 'let's talk like old times.'

'Well?'

'No one knows about my marriage to Matilda except you and me.'

'And Matilda,' I said.

'She'll hold her tongue so long as she gets her payments. My uncle left an annuity for the purpose, his lawyers see to it.'

'Let me go, George.'

'You promised to keep it a secret,' he said, 'you promised.'

'Yes, I promised.'

'And now that you're going to marry Skinny, we'll be properly coupled off as we should have been years ago. We should have been – but youth! – our youth got in the way, didn't it?'

'Life got in the way,' I said.

'But everything's going to be all right now. You'll keep my secret, won't you? You promised.' He had released my feet. I edged a little further from him.

I said, 'If Kathleen intends to marry you, I shall tell her that you're already married.'

'You wouldn't do a dirty trick like that, Needle? You're going to be happy with Skinny, you wouldn't stand in the way of my——'

'I must, Kathleen's my best friend,' I said swiftly.

He looked as if he would murder me and he did, he stuffed hay into my mouth until it could hold no more, kneeling on my body to keep it prone, holding both my wrists tight in his huge left hand. I saw the red full lines of his mouth and the white slit of his teeth last thing on earth. Not another soul passed by as he pressed my body into the stack, as he made a deep nest for me, tearing up the hay to make a groove the length of my corpse, and finally pulling the warm dry stuff in a mound over this concealment, so natural-looking in a broken haystack. Then George climbed down, took up his bottle of milk and went his way. I suppose that was why he looked so unwell when I stood, nearly five years later, by the barrow in the Portobello Road and said in easy tones, 'Hallo, George!'

The Haystack Murder was one of the notorious crimes of that year.

My friends said, 'A girl who had everything to live for.'

After a search that lasted twenty hours, when my body was found, the evening papers said, ' "Needle" is found: in haystack!'

Kathleen, speaking from that Catholic point of view which takes some getting used to, said, 'She was at Confession only the day before she died – wasn't she lucky?'

The poor byre-hand who sold us the milk was grilled for hour after hour by the local police, and later by Scotland Yard. So was George. He admitted walking as far as the haystack with me, but he denied lingering there.

'You hadn't seen your friend for ten years?' the Inspector asked him.

'That's right,' said George.

'And you didn't stop to have a chat?'

'No. We'd arranged to meet later at dinner. My cousin was waiting for the milk, I couldn't stop.'

The old soul, his cousin, swore that he hadn't been gone more than ten minutes in all, and she believed it to the day of her death a few months later. There was the microscopic evidence of hay on George's jacket, of course, but the same evidence was on every man's jacket in the district that fine harvest year. Unfortunately, the byreman's hands were even brawnier and mightier than George's. The marks on my wrists had been done by such hands, so the laboratory charts indicated when my post mortem was all completed. But the wristmarks weren't enough to pin down the crime to either man. If I hadn't been wearing my long-sleeved cardigan, it was said, the bruises might have matched up properly with someone's fingers.

Kathleen, to prove that George had absolutely no motive, told the police that she was engaged to him. George thought this a little foolish. They checked up on his life in Africa, right back to his living with Matilda. But the marriage didn't come out – who would think of looking up registers in the Congo? Not that this would have proved any motive for murder. All the same, George was relieved when the inquiries were over without the marriage to Matilda being disclosed.

He was able to have his nervous breakdown at the same time as Kathleen had hers, and they recovered together and got married, long after the police had shifted their inquiries to an Air Force camp five miles from Kathleen's aunt's home. Only a lot of excitement and drinks came of those investigations. The Haystack Murder was one of the unsolved crimes that year.

Shortly afterwards the byre-hand emigrated to Canada to start afresh, with the help of Skinny who felt sorry for him.

After seeing George taken away home by Kathleen that Saturday in the Portobello Road, I thought that perhaps I might be seeing more of him in similar circumstances. The next Saturday I looked out for him, and at last there he was, without Kathleen, half-worried, half-hopeful.

I dashed his hopes, I said, 'Hallo, George!'

He looked in my direction, rooted in the midst of the flowing market-mongers in that convivial street. I thought to myself, 'He looks as if he had a mouthful of hay.' It was the new bristly maize-coloured beard and moustache surrounding his great mouth suggested the thought, gay and lyrical as life.

'Hallo, George!' I said again.

I might have been inspired to say more on that agreeable morning, but he didn't wait. He was away down a side-street and along another street and down one more, zigzag, as far and as devious as he could take himself from the Portobello Road.

Nevertheless he was back again next week. Poor Kathleen had brought him in her car. She left it at the top of the street, and got out with him, holding him tight by the arm. It grieved me to see Kathleen ignoring the spread of scintillations on the stalls. I had myself seen a charming Battersea box quite to her taste, also a pair of enamelled silver earrings. But she took no notice of these wares, clinging close to George, and, poor Kathleen – I hate to say how she looked.

And George was haggard. His eyes seemed to have got smaller as if he had been recently in pain. He advanced up the road with Kathleen on his arm, letting himself lurch from side to side with his wife bobbing beside him, as the crowds asserted their rights of way.

'Oh, George!' I said. 'You don't look at all well, George.'

'Look!' said George. 'Over there by the hardware barrow. That's Needle.'

Kathleen was crying. 'Come back home, dear,' she said.

'Oh, you don't look well, George!' I said.

They took him to a nursing home. He was fairly quiet, except on Saturday mornings when they had a hard time of it to keep him indoors and away from the Portobello Road.

But a couple of months later he did escape. It was a Monday.

They searched for him in the Portobello Road, but actually he had gone off to Kent to the village near the scene of the Haystack Murder. There he went to the police and gave himself up, but they could tell from the way he was talking that there was something wrong with the man.

'I saw Needle in the Portobello Road three Saturdays running,' he explained, 'and they put me in a private ward, but I got away while the nurses were seeing to the new patient. You remember the murder of Needle, well, I did it. Now you know the truth, and that will keep bloody Needle's mouth shut.'

Dozens of poor mad fellows confess to every murder. The police obtained an ambulance to take him back to the nursing home. He wasn't there long. Kathleen gave up her shop and devoted herself to looking after him at home. But she found that the Saturday mornings were a strain. He insisted on going to see me in the Portobello Road and would come back to insist that he'd murdered Needle. Once he tried to tell her something about Matilda, but Kathleen was so kind and solicitous, I don't think he had the courage to remember what he had to say.

Skinny had always been rather reserved with George since the murder. But he was kind to Kathleen. It was he who persuaded them to emigrate to Canada so that George should be well out of reach of the Portobello Road.

George has recovered somewhat in Canada but, of course, he will never be the old George again, as Kathleen writes to Skinny. 'That Haystack tragedy did for George,' she writes. 'I feel sorrier for George sometimes than I am for poor Needle. But I do often have Masses said for Needle's soul.'

I doubt if George will ever see me again in the Portobello Road. He broods much over the crumpled snapshot he took of us on the haystack. Kathleen does not like the photograph, I don't wonder. For my part, I consider it quite a jolly snap, but I don't think we were any of us so lovely as we look in it, gazing blatantly over the ripe cornfields, Skinny with his humorous expression, I secure in my difference from the rest, Kathleen with her head prettily perched on her hand, each reflecting fearlessly in the face of George's camera the glory of the world, as if it would never pass.

# IRIS MURDOCH

# *Something Special*

—————————————————

'WHY wouldn't you take him now?' said Mrs Geary. She was setting the evening papers to rights on the counter.

Yvonne sat astride a chair in the middle of the shop. She had it tilting precariously and was rubbing her small head animal fashion on the wood of the back, while her long legs were braced to prevent herself from toppling over. In answer to the question she said nothing.

'She's cross again,' said her uncle, who was standing at the door of the inner room.

'Who's she? She's the cat!' said Yvonne. She began to rock the chair violently to and fro.

'Don't be breaking down that chair,' said her mother. 'It's the last we have of the decent ones till the cane man is back. Why wouldn't you take him is what I asked.'

Close outside the shop the tram for Dublin came rattling by, darkening the scene for a moment and making little objects on the higher shelves jump and tinkle. It was a hot evening and the doors stood wide open to the dust of the street.

'Oh leave off, leave off!' said Yvonne. 'I don't *want* him, I don't *want* to marry. He's nothing special.'

'Nothing special is it?' said her uncle. 'He's a nice young man in a steady job and he wants to wed you and you no longer so young. Or would you be living all your life on your ma?'

'If you won't wed him you shouldn't be leading him up the garden,' said her mother, 'and leave breaking that chair.'

'Can't I be ordinary friends with a boy,' said Yvonne, 'without the pair of you being at me? I'm twenty-four and I know what I'm about.'

'You're twenty-four indeed,' said her mother, 'and there's Betty Nolan and Maureen Burke are married these three years and they in a lower form than you at school.'

'I'm not the like of those two,' said Yvonne.

'True for you!' said her mother.

'It's the women's magazines,' said her uncle, 'and the little novels she's for ever reading that are putting ideas in her head until she won't marry except it's the Sheik of Araby.'

'It's little enough she finds to do with her time,' said her mother, 'so that she's always in there in the little dark room, flat on her tum with her nose inside a novel till it's a wonder her two eyes aren't worn away in her head.'

'Can't I live my life as I please,' said Yvonne, 'since it's the only thing I have?

It's that I can't see him as something special and I won't marry him if I can't.'

'He's one of the Chosen People,' said her uncle. 'Isn't that special enough?'

'Don't start on that thing again,' said her mother. 'Sam's a nice young fellow, and not like the run of the Jew-boys at all. He'd bring the children up Church of Ireland.'

'At that,' said her uncle, 'it's better than the other lot with the little priest after them the whole time and bobbing their hats at the chapel doors so you can't even have a peaceful ride on the tram. I've nothing against the Jews.'

'Our Lord was a Jew,' said Yvonne.

'Don't be saying bold things like that!' said her mother.

'Our Lord was the Son of God,' said her uncle, 'and that's neither Jew nor Greek.'

'Is it this evening the Christmas card man is coming?' said Yvonne.

'It is,' said her mother, 'though why they want to be bothering us with Christmas cards in the middle of summer I'm at a loss to know.'

'I'll wait by and see him,' said Yvonne. 'You always pick the dull ones.'

'I pick the ones that sell,' said her mother, 'and don't you be after hanging around acting the maggot when Sam comes, there's little enough room in there.'

'If you were married at least you'd be out of this,' said her uncle, 'and it isn't your ma you'd be sharing a bed with then, and you always complaining about the poky hole this place is.'

'It is a poky hole,' said Yvonne, 'but then I'd be in another poky hole some other place.'

'I'm tired telling you,' said her mother, 'you could get one of those new little houses off the Drumcondra Road. The man in Macmullan's shop knows the man that keeps the list.'

'I don't want a new little house,' said Yvonne. 'I tell you I don't see him right and that's that!'

'If you wait till you marry for love,' said her uncle, 'you'll wait ten years and then make a foolish match. You're not Greta Garbo and you're lucky there's a young fellow after you at all. Sensible people marry because they want to be in the married state and not because of feelings they have in their breasts.'

'She's still stuck on the English lad,' said her mother, 'the tall fellow, Tony Thingummy was his name.'

'I am not!' said Yvonne. 'Good riddance to bad rubbish!'

'I could not abide his voice,' said her uncle. 'He had his mouth all prissed up when he talked, like a man was acting in a play.'

'Isn't it the like of the bloody English to win the Sweep again this year?' said her mother.

'He brought me flowers,' said Yvonne.

'Flowers is it!' said her uncle. 'And singing little songs to you you said once!'

'He was a jaunty boy,' said her mother, 'and a fine slim thing with some pretty ways to him, but he's gone now. And you wait till you see what Sam'll bring you one of these days.'

'Ah, you're potty with that diamond ring story,' said her uncle. 'You'll turn the child's head on her. That fellow's as poor as we are.'

'There's nobody is as poor as we are,' said Yvonne.

'He's a hired man,' said her uncle. 'I don't deny he may get to have his own tailoring shop one day and be his own master. I can see that in him, that he's not a Jew for nothing. But he's no fancy worker now and he's poorly off.'

'Those ones are never poor,' said her mother. 'They just pretend to be so their own people won't be taking their bits of money off them.'

'It's near his time to come,' said Yvonne. 'Don't be talking about him when he comes in, it's not manners.'

'Listen who's mentioning manners!' said her uncle.

'You recall the time,' said her mother, 'we met him at poor Mr Stacey's sale and we went to Sullavan's bar after and he paid for two rounds?'

'He was for catching Yvonne's eye,' said her uncle, 'with flashing his wad round. I'll lay he had to walk home.'

'You're a fine one,' said her mother, 'and you telling me to encourage the child!'

'Did I ever say she should marry him for his money?' said her uncle.

'Well, you'll see,' said her mother. 'It's the custom of those ones. When they want to be engaged to a girl they suddenly bring the diamond ring out and the girl says yes.'

'If they do it's on hire from the pop shop,' said her uncle, 'and it's back in the window directly.'

'What's Julia Batey's ring then?' said her mother, 'and what's her name, young Polly's sister, who married Jews the pair of them, and it happened that way with both. One evening quite suddenly "I want to show you something" says he, and there was the ring and they were engaged from then. I tell you it's a custom.'

'Well, I hope you're right I'm sure,' said her uncle. 'It might be just the thing that would make up the grand young lady's mind. A diamond ring now, that would be something special, wouldn't it?'

'A diamond ring,' said Yvonne, 'would be a change at least.'

'Perhaps he'll have it with him this very night!' said her mother.

'I *don't* think!' said Yvonne.

'Where are you off to anyway?' said her mother.

'I haven't the faintest,' said Yvonne. 'Into town, I suppose.'

'You might go down the pier,' said her uncle, 'and see the mail boat out. That would be better for you than sitting in those stuffy bars or walking along the Liffey breathing the foul airs of the river, and coming home smelling of Guinness.'

'Besides, you know Sam likes the sea,' said her mother. 'He's been all day long dying of suffocation in that steamy room with the clothes press.'

'It's more fun in town,' said Yvonne. 'They've the decorations up for Ireland At Home. And I've been all day long dying of boredom in Kingstown.'

'It's well for you,' said her uncle, 'that it's Sam that pays!'

'And I don't like your going into those low places,' said her mother. 'That's not Sam's idea, I know, it's you. Sam's not a one for sitting dreaming in a bar. That's another thing I like about him.'

'Kimball's have got a new saloon lounge,' said Yvonne, 'like a real drawing-room done up with flowers and those crystal lights. Maybe we'll go there.'

'You'll pay extra!' said her uncle.

'Let Sam worry about that!' said her mother. 'It's a relief they have those saloon lounges in the pubs nowadays where you can get away from the smell of porter and a lady can sit there without being taken for something else.'

'Here's the Christmas card man!' said Yvonne, and jumped up from her chair.

'Why, Mr Lynch,' said Mrs Geary, 'it's a pleasure to see you again, who'd think a whole year had gone by, it seems like yesterday you were here before.'

'Good evening, Mrs Geary,' said Mr Lynch, 'it's a blessing to see you looking so well, and Miss Geary and Mr O'Brien still with you. Change and decay in all around we see. I'm told poor Mrs Taylor at the place in Monkstown has passed on since now a year ago.'

'Yes, the poor old faggot,' said Mrs Geary, 'but after seventy years you can't complain, can you? The good Lord's lending it to you after that.'

'Our time is always on loan, Mrs Geary,' said Mr Lynch, 'and who knows when the great Creditor will call? We are as grass which today flourisheth and tomorrow it is cast into the oven.'

'We'll go through,' said Mrs Geary, 'and Mr O'Brien will mind the shop.'

Yvonne and her mother went into the inner room, followed by Mr Lynch. The inner room was very dark, lit only on the far side by a window of frosted glass that gave onto the kitchen. It had a bedroom smell of ancient fabrics and perspiration and dust. Mrs Geary turned on the light. The mountainous double bed with its great white quilt and brass knobs and rails, wherein she and her daughter slept, took up half of the room. A shiny horsehair sofa took up most of the other half, leaving space for a small velvet-topped table and three black chairs which stood in a row in front of the towering mantelshelf where photographs and brass animals rose in tiers to the ceiling. Mr Lynch opened his suitcase and began to spread out the Christmas cards on the faded red velvet.

'The robin and the snow go well,' said Mrs Geary, 'and the stage-coach is popular and the church lit up at night.'

'The traditional themes of Christmas-tide,' said Mr Lynch, 'have a universal appeal.'

'Oh look,' said Yvonne, 'that's the nicest one I've *ever* seen! Now that's really special.' She held it aloft. A frame of glossy golden cardboard enclosed a little square of white silk on which some roses were embroidered.

'That's a novelty,' said Mr Lynch, 'and comes a bit more expensive.'

'It's not like a true Christmas card, the fancy thing,' said Mrs Geary. 'I always think a nice picture and a nice verse is what you want. The sentiment is all.'

'Here's Sam,' said Mr O'Brien from the shop.

Sam came and stood in the doorway from the shop, frowning in the electric light. He was a short man, 'portly' Mr O'Brien called him, and he could hardly count as handsome. He had a pale moon-face and fugitive hands, but his eyes were dark, and his dark bushy head of hair was like the brave plume of a bird. He had his best suit on, which was a midnight blue with a grey stripe, and his tie was of light yellow silk.

'Come on in, Sam,' said Mrs Geary. 'Yvonne's been ready this long time. Mr Lynch, this is Mr Goldman.'

'How do you do?' they said.

'You're mighty smart tonight, Sam,' said Mrs Geary. 'Going to have a special evening?'

'We're choosing the Christmas cards,' said Yvonne. 'Have you got any with the ox and the ass on, Mr Lynch?'

'Here,' said Mr Lynch, 'we have the ox and the ass, and here we see our Lord lying in the manger, and His Mother by, and here the three Magi with their costly gifts, and here the angels coming to the poor shepherds by night, and here the star of glory that led them on. When Jesus was born in Bethlehem of Judaea in the days of Herod the King——'

'I still like this one best,' said Yvonne. 'Look, Sam, isn't that pretty?' She held up the card with the golden frame.

'You two be off now,' said Mrs Geary, 'and leave troubling Sam with these Christian things.'

'I don't mind,' said Sam. 'I always observe Christmas just as you do, Mrs Geary. I take it as a sort of emblem.'

'That's right,' said Mr Lynch. 'What after all divides us one from another? In My Father's house are many mansions. If it were not so I would have told you.'

'I'll just get my coat,' said Yvonne.

'Don't keep her out late, Sam,' said Mrs Geary. 'Good-bye now, and mind you have a really nice evening.'

'Abyssinia,' said Yvonne.

They left the cool musty air of the shop and emerged into the big warm perfumed summer dusk. Yvonne threw her head back, and pranced along in her high-heeled shoes, wearing the look of petulant intensity which she always affected for the benefit of Sam. She would not take his arm, and they went a little aimlessly down the street.

'Where shall we go?' said Sam.

'I don't mind,' she said.

'We might walk a bit by the sea,' said Sam, 'and sit on the rocks beyond the Baths.'

'It's too windy down there and I can't go on the rocks in these shoes.'

'Well, let's go into town.'

At that moment from the seaward side came a sonorous booming sound, very deep and sad. It came again, was sustained in a melancholy roar, and died slowly away.

'Ah, the mail boat!' said Sam. 'Let's just see it out, it's ages since I saw it out.'

They walked briskly as far as the Mariners' Church and turned along the front into the racing breeze. In the evening light the scene before them glowed like a coloured postcard. The mail boat had its lights on already, making pale, shifting reflections in the water which was still glossy with daylight. As they came nearer the boat began to move very slowly, and drew away from the big brown wooden quay revealing upon it the rows and rows of people left behind agitating their white handkerchiefs in the darkening air. The scene was utterly silent. A curly plume of black smoke gathered upon the metallic water, hid the ship for a moment, and then lifted to show it gliding away between the two lighthouses, whose beams were kindled at that very time, and into the open sea. Beyond it a large pale moon was rising over Howth Head.

'The moon hath raised her lamp above,' said Sam.

'I've seen the mail boat out a hundred times,' said Yvonne, 'and one day I'll be on it.'

'Would you like to go to England then?' said Sam.

Yvonne gave him a look of exaggerated scorn. 'Doesn't every Irish person with a soul in them want to go to England?' she said.

They walked more slowly back now, past the golden windows of Ross's Hotel to take the Dublin tram. By the time they had climbed the hill the ship was half-way toward the horizon, its trail of smoke taken up into the gathering night, and by the time they got off the tram at Nelson's Pillar the daylight was gone entirely.

'Now where would you like to go?' said Sam.

'Don't be eternally asking me that question!' she said. 'Just go somewhere yourself and I'll probably follow!'

Sam took her arm, which she let him hold this time, and walked her back toward O'Connell Bridge and along onto the quays. The Liffey flowed past them, oily and glistening, as black as Guinness, bound for Dublin Bay. It had not far to go now. Along the parapet at intervals, and hanging suspended from the iron tracery of the street lamps, were metal baskets full of flowers, while a banner hanging on the bridge announced in English and in Irish that Ireland was At Home to visitors. There was a mingled smell of garbage and pollen.

Sam turned her toward the river, and was for lingering there in a sentimental way, his arm creeping about her waist. The moon was risen now over the top of the houses. But Yvonne said firmly, 'You'll get your death with the smell of the drains here. Let's go to Kimball's place and try the new saloon lounge.'

They turned up the side street that led to Kimball's. It was a dirty, dark little street, but a blaze of light and a good deal of hubbub at the far end of it declared the whereabouts of that hostelry. The ordinary bar, which had formerly been the only one, was in the basement, while on the street level was Kimball's grocery store, and above this the saloon lounge before mentioned. From the well of the stairs below came an odour of men and drink and the tinkling of a piano and an uproar of male voices.

Sam and Yvonne turned aside and mounted a brightly lit carpeted stairway, which smelt strongly of new paint, and emerged into the lounge. The door shut itself quietly behind them. Here everything was still. Yvonne walked across the heavy carpet and sat down on a fat chintz sofa and arranged her dress. In the gilded mirror behind the bar she could see the reflection of Sam's face as he ordered a gin and lime for her and a draught Guinness for himself. For an instant she concentrated the glow of her imagination upon him; but could only notice that he leaned forward in an apologetic way to the barman, and how absurdly his small feet turned out as he stood there. He gave the order in a low voice, as if he were asking for something not quite nice at the chemist's. A few couples sat scattered about the room, huddled under the shaded lights, murmuring to each other.

When Sam came back with the drinks Yvonne said loudly, 'You'd think you were in a church here, not in a public-house!'

'Sssh!' said Sam. One or two people stared. Sam sat down close beside her on the sofa, trying to make himself drink. He edged nearer still, but curling into himself like a hedgehog so as to be as near as possible without giving offence. He put down his glass on the table and began laboriously in his mind the long search for words, for the simple words that would lead on to the more important ones. His pale stumpy hand caressed Yvonne's bony brown hand. Hers lay there listlessly in a way that was familiar to him. He squeezed it a little and tried to draw her back towards him, deeper into the sofa. So they sat there a while in silence, Sam searching and holding, and Yvonne stiff. The upholstered stillness around them was not good for their talk. The barman chinked a glass and everyone in the room jumped.

'This place gives me heart disease', said Yvonne. 'It's like a lot of dead people giving a party. Let's go and see what it's like downstairs. I've never been downstairs here.'

'It's not nice,' said Sam. 'Ladies don't go downstairs. Why not let's go back to Henry Street? There's the little coffee bar you liked once.'

'That was a silly place!' said Yvonne. 'I'm going downstairs anyway. You can do as you like.' She said this in a loud voice, and then got up and walked firmly toward the door. Sam, red with embarrassment, jumped up too, took a hasty pull at his drink, and followed her out. They descended into the street and took the iron staircase that led to the basement. The noise and the smell were stronger than before.

Yvonne hesitated half-way down. 'You'd better lead,' she said. Sam stumbled past her and pushed at the blackened door of the bar. He had never been down those stairs either.

They came out into a very big low-roofed room with white tiled walls and blazing unshaded lights. The floor was slimy with spilt drink and beery sawdust and the atmosphere was thick. The pounding repetitive beat of a piano, its melody absorbed into the continuous din of voices, was felt rather than heard. A great many men who were adhering to a circular bar in the centre, turned to stare at Yvonne as she entered. It looked at first as if no women were present, but as the haze shifted here and there it was possible to discern one or two lurking in the darkened alcoves.

'There *are* women here!' called Yvonne triumphantly.

'Not nice ones,' said Sam. 'What's your drink?' He hated being looked at.

'Whisky,' said Yvonne. She refused to sit down, but stood there swaying slightly and holding onto one of the ironwork pillars that circled the bar. The men near by studied her with insolent appreciation and made remarks. She coloured a little, but stared straight in front of her, bright-eyed.

It was not easy for poor Sam to get at the bar. The clients who were standing in his way were in no hurry to move, though they looked at him amiably enough. The bar-tender, an infernal version of his upstairs colleague, pointedly served two later-comers first, and then with ironic politeness handed Sam the drinks.

'Isn't this better than up there?' Yvonne shouted, seizing her glass from him as he got back to her side.

'That's the stuff'll put the red neck on you!' observed a man with a penetrating voice, who was standing close to Yvonne.

'Your mother something or other,' Sam shouted back, propelling Yvonne fussily into a space in the middle of the floor, where he stood holding tightly onto her arm.

She stopped trying to hear his voice and gave herself up to the pleasure of being part of such a noisy crowded drunken scene. By the time she had sipped the half of her whisky she was perceptibly enjoying herself very much indeed. Upon the confused flood of noise and movement she was now afloat.

After a short while there was something quite particular to watch: a little scene which seemed to be developing on the near side of the bar. Someone was waving his arms and shouting in an angry voice. Whereon the publican in even higher tones was heard to cry, 'Just raise your hand again, mister, and you're out in the street! Patsy, put that gentleman out in the street!'

People crowded quickly forward from the alcoves to see the fun. The piano stopped abruptly and the sound of voices became suddenly jagged and harsh. A woman with a red carnation in her hair and an overwhelming perfume came and stood beside Yvonne, her bare arm touching the girl's sleeve. Yvonne could see at once that she was not a nice sort of woman at all, and she removed herself from the contact. The woman gave her a provoking stare.

'Time for us to make tracks,' said Sam to Yvonne.

'Ah shut up!' she said, looking past him with glowing eyes to where the drama was unfolding.

A tall thin young fellow, the prey designate of Patsy, was swaying to and fro, still flourishing his fist, and trying to make a statement, intended no doubt as insult or vindication, but whose complexity was such that he began it several times over without succeeding in making himself clear. His antagonist, a thick man with a Cork accent, who accompanied these attempts with a continual sneering noise, suddenly gave him a violent jab in the stomach. The young man oscillated, and lurched back amid laughter, with a look of extreme surprise. To keep his balance he twisted dexterously about on his heel and found himself face to face with Yvonne.

'Ah!' said the young man. He stood there poised, frozen in the gesture of turning, with one hand outstretched ballet-wise, and slowly allowed a look of imbecile delight to transfigure his features. Another laugh went up.

'Ah!' said the young man. 'I thought the flowers were all falling, but here is a rose in the bud!' He seemed to have found his tongue.

The woman with the red carnation clapped Yvonne on the shoulder. 'Come along the little pet,' she cried, 'and give the kind gentleman a good answer!'

The thin young man turned upon her. 'You leave the young lady alone,' he shouted, 'she isn't your like!' And with that he darted out his hand and plucked the red carnation from the women's hair and thrust it with another lurch into the bosom of Yvonne's frock. There was a roar of applause.

Yvonne sprang away. The woman turned quick as a flash and slapped the young man in the face. But quicker still the woman's escort, a brown man with an arm like an ape, had snatched the flower back from where it hung at Yvonne's breast and given her a push which sent her flying back against the wall. There was a momentary delighted silence. People by now had climbed on chairs to get a better view, and tiers of grinning unshaven faces peered down through the haze. Yvonne was crimson. For a moment she leaned there rigid, as if pinned to the tiles. Then Sam had taken her by the hand and was leading her quickly out of the bar.

Before the heavy doors were shut again they heard the yell which followed them up into the street. 'It's safer upstairs, mister!' screamed a woman's voice.

When Yvonne got out onto the pavement she wrenched her hand away from Sam and began to run. She ran like a hare down the dark and ill-smelling street toward the open lamplight of the quays, and here Sam caught her up, leaning against the parapet of the river and drooping her head down and panting.

'Oh my dear darling, didn't—' Sam began to say; but he was interrupted. Out of the hazy darkness beyond the street lamps a third figure had emerged. It was the thin young man, also at a run. He gripped Sam by the arm.

'No offence, mister,' said the young man, 'no offence! It was a tribute, a sincere tribute, from one of Ireland's poets – a true poet, mister—' He stood there, still holding onto Sam with one hand, and staring wide-eyed at Yvonne, while the other hand fumbled in his coat pocket.

'That's all right,' said Sam. 'It wasn't your fault surely. We've just got to go now.' He began gently but vigorouly to detach the clutching fingers from his arm.

The young man held on tight. 'If I could only find me bloody poem,' he said, 'a sincere tribute, a humble and sincere tribute, to one of the wonders of Nature, a beautiful woman is one of the wonders of Nature, a flower——'

'Yes, yes, all right,' said Sam. 'We don't mind, we've just got to go now to get our tram.'

'——fitting homage,' said the young man. 'Sweets to the sweet!' He let go abruptly of Sam and struck a graceful attitude. The post proving too difficult to maintain, he heeled over slowly against the edge of the quay and came into violent contact with one of the metal flower baskets.

'Did I mention flowers?' he cried. 'And here they are! Flowers for her, for a gift, for a tribute——' He plunged his fingers into the basket and brought out a handful of geraniums together with a great quantity of earth, all of which fell to the ground in a heap, partly engulfing Yvonne's shoes.

'Come on!' said Sam. But Yvonne had already turned and was walking away very fast, swinging her arms, and shaking her feet as she walked in order to get some of the earth out. Sam followed quickly after her, and the young man followed after Sam, still talking.

'What is her name?' he was crying in an aggrieved tone. 'What is her name, who makes rose petals rain from heaven, and with oh such eyes and lips, this was something that I spoke about in a poem——' And as they walked on, the three of them, in Indian file and with quickening pace in the direction of O'Connell Street, the young man plucked the flowers from the baskets and drew their stems through his fingers to gather tight handfuls of petals which he cast high over Sam's head so that they should rain down upon Yvonne.

'Now then, young fellow,' said the policeman, who suddenly materialised as the little procession neared O'Connell Bridge. 'Let me remind you it's public money is spent on those flowers you are defiling in a way renders you liable for prosecution.'

'Nature intended——' the young man began.

'That may well be,' said the policeman, 'and I intend to have you up for wilful and malicious damages.' The two figures converged. Sam and Yvonne drew away.

As they were passing Hannah's bookshop Sam caught up with her. Her face was stony. He began to ask her was she all right.

At first she would say nothing, but turned savagely away over the bridge in the direction of Westmoreland Street. Then she cried in a weary voice, 'Oh be silent, I've enough of this, just come to the tram.'

Sam raised his hands and then spread them out, opening the palms. For a while he trotted behind her in silence, his plume of black hair bobbing over his eyes. 'Yvonne,' he said then, 'don't go away yet. Let me just make you forget those things. You'll never pardon me if you go away with those things between us.'

Yvonne slowed her step and looked round at him sullenly. 'It isn't that anything matters,' she said, 'or that I'm surprised at all. It's that I thought it might be – a specially nice evening. More fool me and that's all!'

Sam's hands clasped themselves in front of him and then spread wide once more. He made her stop now and face him. They were well up the street. 'It can be still,' he said urgently, 'a special evening. Don't spoil it now by being cross. Wait a bit. It's not the last tram yet.'

Yvonne hesitated, and let Sam pull her limp arm through his. 'But where can we put ourselves at this hour?'

'Never you mind!' said Sam with a sudden confidence. 'You come along with me, and if you're a good girl there's something special I've got to show you.'

'Something – to show me?' said Yvonne. She let him lead her along in the direction of Grafton Street. As they turned the corner Sam boldly locked his fingers through hers and kneaded her thin hand in the palm of his own. She welcomed him with a very little pressure. So they walked the length of the street linked in a precarious and conscious hold. The dark mass of Stephen's Green was appearing now in front of them and they crossed the road towards it. A few people were gathered still in the golden glow outside the Shelbourne, but on the farther side of the square there was no one. Sam began to draw her along, slinking close beside the railings.

'I'm destroyed walking in these shoes,' said Yvonne. 'Where is the place you are going to?'

'Here it is,' said Sam. He stopped and pointed suddenly to a gap in the railings. 'There's a rail out and we can go through inside the garden.'

'It's not allowed,' said Yvonne, 'it's shut to the public now.'

'We're not the public, you and me,' said Sam. He put his feet boldly through the hole and ducked to the other side. Then with authority he pulled the girl in after him.

She gave a little cry, finding herself in a tangle of damp undergrowth. 'It's horrid in here, my stockings are tearing!'

'Give me your hands back,' said Sam. He took both her hands and half-lifted her out onto a dark lawn of grass. She took a few steps across its moist spongy surface and then felt the hard grit of the path underneath her feet. They emerged into bright moonlight beside the water. The big moon looked up at them from the lake, clear-cut and almost full, intensely bright.

'Oh dear!' said Yvonne, silenced for a moment by the ghostly radiance. They stood hand in hand looking into the black mirror of the lake, their long moon-shadows stretched out behind them.

Yvonne began to peer nervously about her. 'Sam,' she said in a whisper, 'I don't like this being here, someone'll find us, please let us go back———'

'I won't hurt you,' said Sam, whispering too in a caressing exultant tender whisper, 'I'll look after you, I'll always look after you. I just wanted to show you something nice.'

'Well—?' said Yvonne. She followed him a few steps as he moved, and looked up into his face.

'Here it is,' said Sam.

'Where?'

'Here, look—' He reached his hand towards a dark shape.

Yvonne recoiled from him violently. What seemed a monster was there in the darkness. Then she made out that there was a fallen tree lying right across the path beside the lake, its topmost branches just touching the water.

'What is it?' she said with revulsion.

'A fallen tree,' said Sam. 'I don't know what kind.'

Yvonne looked at him. She saw his two eyes gleam almost cat-like in the darkness in the light of the reflected moon, but they were not looking at her.

'But you were going to show me something.'

'Yes, this, the poor tree.'

Yvonne was dumb for a moment. Then she came choking into speech. 'This was it then you stopped me from the tram for and made me walk a mile for and tear my stockings, just a dirty rotten maggoty old tree!' Her voice rose higher and she hit out wildly with her hand, whipping a flurry of foliage across Sam's round moonlit face.

'But no,' said Sam, quite calmly now beside her, 'only see it, Yvonne, be quiet for a minute and see it. It's so beautiful, though indeed it's a sad thing for a tree to lie like this, all fresh with its green leaves on the ground, like a flower that's been picked. I know it's a sad thing. But come to me now and we'll be a pair of birds up in the branches.' He took her against her will and drew her to him among the rustling leaves which lay in a tall fan across the path. He kissed the girl very gently on the cheek.

Yvonne got free of his grasp and stumbled back, beating away the leafy twigs from her neck. 'Was this all?' she said with violence. 'Was this all that you wanted me to see? It's nothing, and I hate it. I hate your beastly tree and its dirt and the worms and beetles falling down inside my dress.' She began to cry.

Sam came out of the leaves and stood ruefully beside her, trying to get hold of her hand. 'I only wanted to please you,' he said. 'It's a sad thing to show you, I know, and not very exciting, but I thought it was beautiful, and———'

'I *hate* it,' said Yvonne, and began to run away from him across the grass, blubbering as she ran. She was before him at the hole in the railings, and he had to run after her as she hurried along the pavement, trailing a sort of bramble behind her from her skirt.

Now Sam's confidence was all gone. 'Yvonne,' he called, 'don't be holding it against me, Yvonne. I didn't mean———'

'Oh shut up!' said Yvonne.

'Don't be holding it against me.'

'Oh stop whingeing!' she said.

The tram for Dun Laoghaire came lurching into sight as Sam still followed after Yvonne, pawing at her arm and asking her to forgive him. Yvonne got onto the tram and without looking back at him climbed the stairs quickly to the top. Sam stood still on the pavement and was left behind, his two hands raised in the air in a gesture of dereliction.

Once upon the tram Yvonne shed no more tears. When she got back to Upper George's Street she fumbled in her bag for the latch-key, which she had not had for long, and let herself into the shop. It was very still in the shop. The familiar smell of wood and old paper made itself quietly known. Behind her the last cars and trams were rumbling by, and in the dark space in front of her was to be heard the heavy breathing of her mother, already sleeping in the inner room. But in the shop it was very silent and all the objects upon the shelves were alert and quiet like little listening animals. Yvonne stood quite still there for ten minutes, for nearly fifteen minutes. She had never stood still for so long in her whole life. Then she went through into the inner room on tiptoe and began to undress in the dark.

Her mother had taken up the deep centre of the bed as usual. When Yvonne put her knee upon the edge in order to get in, the whole structure groaned and rocked. Her mother woke up.

'It's you, is it?' said Yvonne's mother. 'I didn't hear you come in. Well, how did the evening go off? What did you do with yourselves?'

'Oh, nothing special,' said Yvonne. She thrust her long legs down under the clothes and reclined stiffly upon the high cold edge of the bed.

'You always say that,' said her mother, 'but you must have done something.'

'Nothing, I say,' said Yvonne.

'What did Sam have to show you?'

'Nothing, nothing,' she said.

'Don't keep repeating that word at me,' said her mother. 'Say something else, or has the cat got your tongue?'

'Did you get the Christmas cards with the roses on?' said Yvonne.

'I did not,' said her mother, 'at tenpence the piece! Have you anything to say at all about your evening, or shall we go to sleep now?'

'Yes,' said Yvonne, 'I'm going to marry Sam.'

'Glory be to God!' said her mother. 'So he got you convinced.'

'He did not convince me,' said Yvonne, 'but I'm going to marry him now, I've decided.'

'You've decided, have you?' said her mother. 'Well, I'm glad of it. And why, may I ask, did your Majesty decide it just tonight?'

'For nothing,' said Yvonne, 'for nothing, for nothing.' She snuggled her head under the sheet and began to slide her hips down toward the centre of the bed.

'You make me tired!' said her mother. 'Can you not tell me why at all?'

'No,' said Yvonne. 'It's a sad thing,' she added, 'oh, it's a sad thing!' She was silent then and would say no more.

All was quiet at last in the inner room and in the shop. There would be no more trams passing now until the following day. Yvonne Geary buried her face deep in the pillow, so deep that her mother should not be able to hear that she was just starting to cry. The long night was ahead.

# Death of a Duchess

THE Marquise de Caudebec-en-Caux was very sorry she had ever known his grandmother.

It was windy on the corner, and he had no right to keep her there. She told herself that if she had inherited the spirit of her ancestors it would be perfectly easy to cut through the flow of compliments, bid him good-bye and walk smartly away: but obviously she had not inherited that spirit. Behind the ramparts of chinchilla and Parma violets her eyes blazed: she felt them blazing. He ought to be frightened of her, the babble should die on his lips, he should fade, speechless, rebuked, away into the blur of passers-by. He did not grow speechless, he did not fade. His lemur's face glowed with reverent cordiality and he went on talking. He had so admired, so intensely admired, the Duchesse de Moriat's enchanting little book of *Pensées*. Even Pascal had written nothing so fine. The Duchess's reflections were feminine, yes, essentially feminine: but were they not the essence of Woman, the bead of honey in the multifoliate clover of Woman? He would like to send her some token of his appreciation – not flowers, not, for instance, purple four-leaved clovers from his garden, that would be presumptuous: but a little note? Three lines, no more, so as not to weary her with reading, not to deprive her divine energy of just that grain which might burst into some new and exquisite thought?

'Monsieur Noir—' Madame de Caudebec began firmly.

To have the happiness of seeing her, of hearing her voice, that would, he was sure, never be for him. It was enough for him to address her friend the Marquise, to behold the charming ear just visible below the little fur hat, knowing that into this very ear the voice of the Duchess had poured.

'It is indeed difficult to *see* her,' said Madame de Caudebec, 'since she receives only three persons, perhaps four. She is almost a recluse. she hardly ever goes out. She seldom appears even at *my* "Days".'

She felt someone just behind her elbow, turned away with relief. 'Adalbert! How charming to meet you, and in such weather! The very sight of you warms me up, and I am quite frozen with standing here.'

This should have sent M. Noir away, but it did not. He stood there, waiting to be introduced.

She introduced him reluctantly. 'Adalbert, permit me to present to you M. Hector Noir. M. Noir, my cousin, the Comte de Vimy-Latour.'

Adalbert, like a fool (she reflected), smiled amiably in response. He had no *instinct*. There were times when one would almost think (if one did not know otherwise) that Adalbert was not a gentleman.

She was forced to chat to him, however, for a moment or so longer, while M. Noir continued, brightly, respectfully, to stand by. At last she said, 'My dear cousin, my feet are so cold that I simply can't feel them. If you could find me a cab I should be so grateful.'

It was M. Noir who leaped into the gutter to find it, who helped her in, who picked up her fallen umbrella. She was driving off, much relieved, when it occurred to her to look back; he was walking away at the side of the fool Adalbert, prattling happily.

However, she forgot about him. Her drawing-room was warm and bright, charmingly decorated with forced and leafless lilac. She lay on the couch before the dancing fire, enjoying tea and toast and a Russian cigarette.

She was just thinking of dressing for dinner when the little Duchesse de Moriat called, full of friendliness and her first literary triumph. Madame de Caudebec was not surprised to see her, since the Duchess (despite what had been said to M. Noir) was indefatigable both as hostess and guest.

'My darling Éliane!' the Duchess cried, 'how lovely to see you. I haven't set eyes on you for two whole days. If I'm in the way you must send me packing; I shan't in the least mind.'

'My dearest Marie-Ulysse,' replied the Marquise, 'you know I can never have too much of you. I saw a magnificent piece about your book in the *Revue* this morning.'

'Weren't they kind? I don't know why everyone is being so kind to me. I'm sure I am the merest amateur.'

'How can you say that, when even the greatest writers are praising you?'

'Perhaps it's because I ask them to my parties,' said the Duchess thoughtfully. She had a touch of the realist in her.

'Now, you must know that's not true! You've never invited M. Anatole France, and yet Adalbert, whom I ran into in the street today, says he hears that M. France is praising it to everyone.'

'Oh, Adalbert! Yes, my dear, I've just been talking to him myself, just outside your lodge, in fact. He wanted to introduce me to such a funny little fellow with big black eyes whom he said was an admirer of mine, but I said I simply had to run. After all, Adalbert does lack discrimination sometimes, and I can't possibly know everyone in Paris!'

'You are perfectly right about Adalbert,' said Madame de Caudebec, 'and you must not let yourself meet that young man. I used to know his grandmother when they lived in the country. She was a very decent sort of woman and did all kinds of good works and the whole family's as rich as Croesus, but they're absolute nobodies and little Hector Noir is a social climber of the very first order. He presses himself on one so, and he speaks so extravagantly! He tries to write himself, I believe.'

'Oh, my dear, *no*! Why, I believe that was the name at the foot of an absurd article Ulysse read out to me this morning' (Ulysse was the Duke: people coupled

Marie's name with his to distinguish her from her cousin, Marie-Antioche), 'all about music, which he doesn't in the least understand, he must be tone-deaf – we simply shouted with laughter!'

'That's the one,' said Madame de Caudebec, 'that is he.'

'Well, I shall take great care not to know him,' said the Duchess, 'not because he's common – you know how little these things matter to me – but because he's obviously a bore. Not that *I* mind bores, I can even bear them talking me to death, but Ulysse would be furious. I should never hear the last of it.'

She did not stay long with Madame de Caudebec as she was giving a small dinner-party for various literary persons who had been kind to her book. Most of them were writing noblemen of the younger generation (the Duchess, though she was only thirty, considered herself of an older and better one, and thought of her own literary effort as a kind of amusing freak permitted only to one established enough to afford an occasional step-down), but present also was M. Demasse, the famous novelist, who had accorded her the honour of his printed admiration.

Now M. Demasse, regarding the nobility of the intellect as vastly superior to that of the Gotha and knowing himself a prime favourite with the Princesse Mathilde, was perfectly at ease and ate an enormous meal while talking all the time. He could speak with his mouth full without the slightest blurring of his words or diminution of his resonance; the Duchess found herself wishing Ulysse could do the same.

He talked to the company of Balzac, of General Mercier, of the German Peasant Wars; he addressed it upon the struggles and patrons of his youth, the triumphs and protégés of his middle life. 'What I had from the generous when I was in need,' he said, 'I try to return in full measure to the needy, now that I myself am in a position to be generous. We old fellows must encourage the young fliers; we must boost them up the ladder a little way, just a little way. For we must die; and must have successors. It is up to us to train our successors in the way we would have them go, so that they are sufficiently of our school to take upon themselves the task of saving us from oblivion.'

The Duchess saw a marquis covertly yawning, and thought this was not one of her best evenings.

'For instance, Madame,' said M. Demasse, 'I have a young protégé, a pretentious little cit to be sure, but with something to him, something of the Pierian spring. For his sake, believing in him (absurd though he is), I would put my head into the lion's mouth. I would even ask you and the Duke a favour.'

The Duchess knew what was coming, and felt a tightening of the spine. She weighed in the balance the ruination of her drawing-room and the withdrawal of the favour of so great a man as M. Demasse.

'Ortolans,' he said thoughtfully, 'ortolans! Madame, this is a feast of Lucullus that you are giving us. I have a passion for ortolans. Yes. – Oh, yes, a favour.'

'Why, we'll do anything within the power of human beings, won't we, Ulysse?'

the Duchess said. 'We shall be enchanted.' But the scales had already fallen on the drawing-room side.

'My protégé, a certain young M. Hector Noir, has a passion for your book, Madame, and has entreated me to entreat *you* to receive him, just once, so that he may pay homage to the writer and to the work. If you would permit me to present him——'

'Why, we'd adore it!' cried the Duchess. 'Ulysse and I adore youth, we'd do anything to help it on its way. But, don't you know, though I said we'd do anything within the power of human beings, this simply isn't within human power! Ulysse and I are leaving for Algeria next week, and won't be back for months!'

'Algeria? Right in the middle of the season?' M. Demasse looked stupefied. So did Ulysse.

'The season's a pure convention,' said the Duchess firmly, 'and quite outworn. Nobody cares about it any more. And, do you know, Ulysse and I have never visited Algeria before – what do you think of that, eh? People like us knowing nothing about our own empire? It ain't patriotic to be so ignorant. So we have decided to put patriotism above the season, and pack our bags.'

The Duke, when his guests had gone, made it clear that he was furious. With the fun at its height, with his costumes ordered for two great fancy-dress balls, he was to pack up and exile himself to Africa! He would do almost anything out of respect for his wife's drawing-room, but this was too much.

'Nothing,' the Duchess insisted, 'nothing is too much, in a good cause. And of course we shall have to go, now that I have announced it publicly.'

So they went to Algeria, where they were very bored, and stayed there until the spring. Meanwhile, of course, the stock of the Duchess rose even higher. Could anyone but Marie-Ulysse have the boldness to leave Paris at the most glittering time of the year, cancel all her engagements with the utmost sangfroid, and write home enthusiastically about the peace of the desert? Certainly not. Hostesses whose big crushes had been ruined by her absence this year were all the more eager to invite her to next year's. Her letters were passed from hand to hand at the dinner-tables, and the more delicious witticisms repeated from end to end of the Faubourg.

Meanwhile, M. Noir had not yet met anybody but Madame de Caudebec and Adalbert.

But there was one thing with which the Duchess had never reckoned, and that was the force of sheer, simple-minded persistence. Her kinsmen, the Guermantes, could have withstood it; but they were made of sterner stuff than Marie-Ulysse. Their sterner stuff was, in fact, the chief ingredient of their genius, and true genius was just what Madame de Moriat happened to lack.

M. Demasse had been disappointed to find that the Duchess was not in a position immediately to receive his protégé, but he understood the splendour of her patriotic gesture and was perfectly content to wait until she came home. For, of course, she had to come home: she could not stay in Africa for ever.

When she was settled again in Paris, therefore, one of the first of her callers was M. Demasse. He was not particularly importunate: he saw no need to be. He merely asked whether he might now bring young M. Noir to the next of her 'Days'.

Doubtless any Guermantes would have seen a way out, even of this: but so far as Marie-Ulysse knew, they had never been accustomed to direct requests. She tried feebly to temporise.

'But he'll hate it! If he's young and a true artist, he'll be bored to death among the crowned heads of Europe! He won't know anyone at all, and I'm sure he won't want to. I should never forgive myself if I let you expose him to boredom for my sake.'

'He would love to see the crowned heads,' M. Demasse said simply.

On her next 'Day', Madame de Moriat contrived to be ill, and on the next also: but she could not keep it up. Ill-health seriously reduces one's *mana*, which is the reason why men in public life frequently conceal the worm at the breast until it suddenly strikes them down, to the amazement of all their associates. Marie-Ulysse knew that people were beginning already to speak of the 'poor. little Duchess', and that certain of her rivals were confiding to appreciative ears the confidence that poor Marie was failing not only physically but mentally, that she wasn't half the fun she used to be, that in fact she was beginning to sound quite stupid.

So in the third week she gave the most brilliant 'Day' of all, and waited with despair in her heart to receive M. Noir. (She had taken care to make her reappearance at a time when the Marquise de Caudebec was in the country attending the funeral of a relation. She could not bear the thought of Éliane's raised eyebrows.)

Of course she was crowded out, by people eager to see with their own eyes whether Marie-Ulysse was 'failing' or not. She was quite glad about this, firstly, because a large gathering always stimulated her, and secondly, because she hoped M. Noir would be lost in the turmoil.

Never had her eyes been so bright, a hundred candlepower apiece. Never had her strawberry tarts been more perfect. Never had the other women looked so much like cows.

She was at the top of her form, holding forth upon Victor Hugo to a foreign Royalty and two dukes, when she saw, out of the corner of her eye, that M. Demasse was entering the room, big, happy, smiling behind his lovely tinselled beard. She thought for one joyful moment that he had come alone; then saw, standing in his shadow, a little, lemur-faced young man, dark as a Persian, who had not even troubled to remove his shabby black greatcoat but stood shivering inside it like a timid recruit in a sentry-box.

'Madame la Duchesse,' said M. Demasse, 'will you permit me the honour of presenting——'

'How d'ye do,' said Marie-Ulysse to M. Noir, tartly.

The young man bowed so low that she saw the length of his spine.

'Madame——' he began.

'A future in front of him,' said M. Demasse, 'certainly a future. Indeed, as a fanatical admirer of yourself I should expect him to have exceptional sensibility; but in addition to that——'

'If I might tell Madame,' said M. Noir, 'if I could begin to tell her how, for me, the rain of her marvellous vision playing over the light of thought has made an incomparable rainbow——'

'I expect M. Noir would like to see the Bouchers,' said the Duchess. 'I don't suppose he's ever seen such fine ones before. Why don't you take him into the library, M. Demasse?'

But M. Demasse had turned to speak to another lady, and M. Noir was at Marie-Ulysse's elbow, breathing respectfully something she could not catch.

'What?' she said.

'That lady, Madame, am I right in thinking that lady is the Queen of Greece?'

She gave him her long, motionless smile. She said nothing. The Royalty, she observed with relief, was now in conversation with the Duke. She went on smiling at M. Noir, who shrank.

She might have got rid of him had it not been for Adalbert who, entering the room at the moment, strutted straight up to the young man and tenderly pinched his ear.

'You again? What are you doing here, may I ask? You know my cousin the Duchess, eh? I hope you've been making yourself agreeable.'

'I have been hoping to make Madame understand how her book has become, for me, a field of clover filling the whole world with its adorable perfume.'

'Very nice of you,' Marie-Ulysse said, tartness undiminished. 'Well, Adalbert, it's good to see you looking so well.'

'And to see you looking so exquisitely cool in this preposterous crush, which is clever of you, considering that you must still be warmed by the African sun. 'Pon my soul, Marie, you do the most amazing things!'

'Adalbert,' said the Duchess in a low voice, 'M. Noir is anxious to see the Bouchers. Will you kindly take him to the library, and ask them to bring him some refreshment there?'

The Comte de Vimy-Latour had no option but to obey, and indeed, was pleased to do so, since he had taken a fancy to the young man.

'Don't keep him too long, though,' M. Demasse bellowed suddenly, seeing that his protégé was being removed from the drawing-room. 'I want him to tell Madame about the book he's going to write himself one of these days. Her advice would be invaluable to him!'

'Keep him away just as long as you like, Adalbert,' the Duchess breathed between her teeth.

She had just caught sight of old General Champenac, to whom she very much wished to talk, since there was a question of getting her nephew released from his military service.

When the Count and M. Noir had disappeared from view, she sighed with relief and bore the General off into a corner. 'Now, my dear Léofric, you mustn't put me off any longer. Lucien may be called up any day now, and he has only just recovered from bronchitis. His chest is truly dreadful, he wouldn't do the army the slightest credit. I rely on you to pull the strings. After all, it's really for your country that you're doing it, not for me; it wouldn't redound to our credit here or abroad if it became known that the French army was full of bronchitic privates.'

The General did not seem very happy. Madame knew as well as he did, he said, how difficult things were getting, how they were tightening up the army regulations. It wasn't at all like the old days. Strange as it might seem to her, he really had no influence at all, not on these levels. 'Ask me to get him made captain, or even major, and I dare say it could be done: but to get him out of it altogether – my dear Duchess, it's more than a Field-Marshal could do!'

'Can you tell me what's the use of being a General if you can't make improvements?' Marie-Ulysse demanded. 'For it would be an improvement,' she continued, 'to ensure that the army did not enlist men with a tendency to bronchitis. – Now really, Léofric, as an old friend——'

'I would fall on my sword for you, Duchess,' the General protested, 'but there are some things quite outside my province. These affairs are decided by civil servants, not by soldiers. If you had any influence in those quarters——'

'Well, now, I know what you want,' said Adalbert, appearing at the side of Marie-Ulysse. He had come to fetch with his own hands, for M. Noir, a glass of orangeade and a strawberry tart. 'I know who would be able to help. Our young friend, now studying your Bouchers in the library – which, by the way, is rather chilly, so I have had to lend him my muffler – happens to be the nephew of the Permanent Secretary at the Ministry of War. If it's Lucien you're worrying about, you ought to talk to M. Noir.'

'Ought I?' asked the Duchess fearfully. It was a bad moment for her. On the one hand, she was desperately anxious that Lucien should not be taken into the army, since that, at the present juncture, would almost certainly spoil his chance of a match with Mademoiselle de la Tour du Pont de l'Arche; and if he didn't make her marry him next spring Madame de Pougny would certainly step in with her own son, and fifty million francs would go up in smoke: on the other hand, the idea of asking a favour of the common little man in greatcoat and muffler filled her with horror.

'Why, certainly you ought,' said Adalbert, 'I'll bring him back, shall I?'

She shuddered. 'You'll do nothing of the sort. Please take him out of my house——'

'What, don't you like him?'

'—as quickly as you can, and bring him to dine here tomorrow night. Tell him we shall be quite alone, without any of these society bores, and we can talk about Art.'

'And I can see him home afterwards,' said Adalbert, blushing slightly. 'His chest's weak too. Like Lucien's.'

The thought that God could have been so tasteless as to make the least similarity between these two chests made her shudder again. 'I am quite sure it isn't like Lucien's,' she said coldly.

But the next evening at dinner, with no one but her husband and Adalbert to observe the company she kept, Marie-Ulysse discovered to her surprise that the company of M. Noir was not altogether displeasing. Divested of the greatcoat (which the Duke had firmly and personally taken away from him) he didn't look so bad at all, though his dinner-suit was rather rusty and the gardenia in his button-hole somewhat too big and too pungent. As he talked to her of her own beauty and genius, the words coiling exquisitely from his small red lips, his black eyes huge and sombre, he seemed like some minuscule magician; she felt that he might be possessed of strange powers. Certainly it had heartened her to discover that he possessed the extraordinary power to get Lucien released from his military service.

'My uncle, Madame,' he had said, 'would do anything in the world to release from the least suffering or anxiety a lady for whom he has, though at a great distance, so profound, so marvelling a respect.' Even though he had added, 'But I think it might make things easier if the Duchess were herself to explain to my uncle the nature of her nephew's malady,' and she knew that this meant admitting the uncle, also, to her house, she felt that the game (if she could call it a game, which she felt disinclined to do) was well worth the candle. And she need admit the uncle no more than once.

The uncle came once, and proved to be quite presentable in an agreeably stiff and anonymous fashion. At least he caused not the slightest comment; not a soul asked afterwards who he was.

But Madame de Moriat found herself inviting M. Noir to her house quite often. After all, she had (like anyone else) a heart; everyone knew that Marie-Ulysse was freakish enough to take in a lame duck now and then, if it pleased her fancy, and when that lame duck proved to be quite an amusing talker and (strangely enough) socially acceptable to Adalbert, who had driven a parvenu duke from her drawing-room before now, comment died away and little M. Noir received invitations to the drawing-rooms of other quite impeccable ladies of the Faubourg.

In fact, she grew quite fond of him. He became her little black magician, her little troubadour, her *cavaliere servente*. She suspected that he had indeed some literary talent (though not, of course, in the same street as her own), and when he finally completed his book of small sketches and stories, she was gracious enough to accept the dedication.

The success of the Duchess's own *Pensées* had been so great (no drawing-room was without a copy, bound in watered silk of windflower mauve and lettered in silver) that, with her customary good sense, she decided not to spoil it by writing anything else. Also, she was too busy. Lucien had married Mademoiselle de la Tour du Pont de l'Arche, and Marie-Ulysse had her work cut out to keep this new drawing-room to concert pitch, for there was no doubt that the young woman was a dullard who didn't know her way about and would let the Moriats down in ten minutes were the Duchess to remove her benevolent supervision. And then there was the business of Adalbert, who had become involved in some peculiar scandal she could not altogether comprehend, and who had to be restored, by a series of visits of denial and derision, to his proper status. Also there was Ulysse, who had for once formed what promised to be a serious attachment, and who had to be lured back to decent conjugal observance.

Madame de Moriat discovered, to her surprise, that M. Noir's advice, once it could be disentangled from the compliments, was well worth having. He was not only an amusing little creature but a useful one; with those enormous black eyes of his he seemed to see, not only through people, but all the way round them at one and the same time. If that were not enough ('My little paragon!' she once called him, when introducing him to the Queen of Sweden), he was quite knowledgeable about the stock exchange, and when the Marquise de Caudebec lost her husband, was able to suggest a highly profitable investment of her inheritance.

Really, the Marquise herself had become quite jealous of the Duchess's *cicisbeo*. Had it not been she, after all, who had brought them together? She was extremely annoyed when M. Noir did not put in an appearance at her own 'Days', and even caught herself wondering whether she could spread just enough false rumours about him to bring about his gradual exclusion from the 'Days' of her friends.

She had no chance, however, to convert this scheme from dream to reality, for she suddenly found an extremely wealthy Scottish husband and went off to live with him in an historic and freezing castle in Banffshire.

Éliane, once Marquise de Caudebec-en-Caux, now Countess of Banff, grew old on Scottish soil, and did it very well. She learned to dance an eightsome reel and to eat porridge standing up. She acquired a British outline, stockier than her French one, and a strange red British furze appeared on her cheeks. She visited Paris less and less; it had lost its appeal for her. Her old friends seemed to her like dream nobility, now that she was part of a real one. She often made the most delicious fun of them to Scottish lords who, unhappily, did not understand her. Scottish lords had little appreciation of irony.

But she kept in touch with France through the newspapers; she did not entirely let culture die, and devoted as she was to the habits and customs of her own new life, found Robert Burns and the Sage of Abbotsford insufficient nourishment (or perhaps too heavy a permanent diet) for a lady reared on Molière, Racine, Pascal, Anatole France, Barrès, Bourget. She observed that M. Noir had written a very long book, said by some to have merit. She realised that he must now be middle-aged. What a time he had taken to do a real day's work! She thought she must sent for the book and read it, but when she found that it consisted of fifteen volumes, closed her eyes and the pages, and put it on a top shelf of the library above the Earl's hand-tooled edition of the Waverley novels.

This was Éliane's last attempt at serious reading; henceforth she confined herself to *Le Temps* and *The Times*.

And now it had become a very long time since she had corresponded with any of her friends of the Faubourg. During the war they had been unable to write to her, and this inability had finally broken the habit. She knew that M. Noir had died in Switzerland many years ago. She knew that Adalbert had run away to America just before the German occupation, and that Marie-Ulysse (now a widow) had retired to her estates in Haute-Savoie. How old must they both be now? Ulysse was dead, had been dead these fifteen years, now she came to think of it. Marie-Ulysse could be no *jeune fille*.

But then, one day upon opening *The Times*, Éliane saw that her friend, also, was dead. There was an announcement on page 6: the obituary would be found on page 8.

She looked for it, and as she read it her eyebrows rose into her fringe of hair which, like the rest of her, had acquired with the years a russet, Scotch appearance.

### MADAME DE MORIAT

Our Paris correspondent reports the death recently of Marie de St.-Jean-de-Maurienne, Duchesse de Moriat, at the age of 83. She was a friend of Noir, who dedicated his first book to her, and was herself the author of *Des Pensées mauves*, published in 1900.

'What an obituary!' Éliane exclaimed aloud to the Earl, who had just set down his plate of porridge, opened the window, picked up his gun (which was always kept loaded in readiness for the unexpected sport) and was now taking careful aim at a rabbit.

'A friend of Noir! Of that little *poseur*! They say it as though it were a passport to fame! To couple the name of Marie-Ulysse, who was so . . . so . . .'

The Earl pulled the trigger and missed. He sighed. He closed the window. He had not heard a word.

'Eighty-three,' said Éliane. She looked again at the obituary notice. 'A friend of Noir. Marie-Ulysse, a friend of *his* . . .'

Then she realised that, after all, she might be out of touch. One tended to model one's friends in the Musée Grévin of memory, measuring their features, painting their cheeks, knotting the golden hairs into their heads, as they were in the high afternoon of their days, so that they remained eternally as one had known them best. For ever Marie-Ulysse stood in her radiant pride, her arm stuck out to greet and at the same time to repel, her periwinkle eyes young, sardonic and assured: for ever Hector Noir bowed deeply before her, showing the whole length of his spine even to the wrinkle at the waistline caused by buttoning the greatcoat too tightly across too many woollen under-garments; her suitor, her slave, her quaint little magician whose compliments were as soft, as seductive as Turkish Delight.

But that was half a century ago. Ah well, Eliane said to herself, Times change. And we have to keep up with the times, as best we can.

The Earl banged up the window and took a pot shot. This time the rabbit fell.

JEAN RHYS

# Outside the Machine

THE big clinic near Versailles was run on strictly English lines, so every morning the patients in the women's general ward were woken up at six. They had tea and bread and butter. Then they lay and waited while the nurses brought tin basins and soap. When they had washed they lay and waited again.

There were fifteen beds in the tall, narrow room. The walls were painted grey. The windows were long but high up, so that you could see only the topmost branches of the trees in the grounds outside. Through the glass the sky had no colour.

At half past ten the matron, attended by a sister, came in to inspect the ward, walking as though she were royalty opening a public building. She stopped every now and again, glanced at a patient's temperature-chart here, said a few words there. The young woman in the last bed but one on the left-hand side was a new-comer. 'Best, Inez,' the chart said.

'You came last evening, didn't you?'

'Yes.'

'Quite comfortable?'

'Oh yes, quite.'

'Can't you do without all those things while you are here?' the matron asked, meaning the rouge, powder, lipstick and hand-mirror on the bed-table.

'It's so that I shouldn't look too awful, because then I always feel much worse.'

But the matron shook her head and walked on without smiling, and Inez drew the sheets up to her chin, feeling bewildered and weak. *I'm cold, I'm tired.*

'Has anyone ever told you that you're very much like Raquel Meller?' the old lady in the next bed said. She was sitting up, wrapped in a black shawl embroidered with pink and yellow flowers.

'Am I? Oh, am I really?'

'Yes, very much like.'

'Do you think so?' Inez said.

The tune of *La Violetera*, Raquel Meller's song, started up in her head. She felt happier – then quite happy and rather gay. 'Why should I be so damned sad?' she thought. 'It's ridiculous. The day after I come out of this place something lucky might happen.'

And it was not so bad lying there and having everything done for you. It was only when you moved that you got frightened because you couldn't imagine ever moving again without hurting yourself.

She looked at the row of beds opposite and sighed. 'It's rum here, isn't it?'

'Oh, you'll feel different tomorrow,' the old lady said. She spoke English hesitatingly – not with an accent, but as if her tongue were used to another language.

The two talked a good deal that day, off and on.

'. . . And how was I to know,' Inez complained, 'that, on top of everything else, my inside would go *kaput* like this? And of course it must happen at the wrong time.'

'Now, shut up,' she told herself, 'shut up. Don't say, "Just when I haven't any money." Don't give yourself away. What a fool you are!' But she could not stop the flood of words.

At intervals the old lady clicked her tongue compassionately or said 'Poor child.' She had a broad, placid face. Her hair was black – surely dyed, Inez thought. She wore two rings with coloured stones on the third finger of her left hand and one – a thick gold ring carved into an indistinguishable pattern – on the little finger. There was something wrong with her knee, it appeared, and she had tried several other hospitals.

'French hospitals are more easy-going, but I was very lucky to get into this place; it has quite a reputation. There's nothing like English nursing. And, considering what you get, you pay hardly anything. An English matron, a resident English doctor, several of the nurses are English. I believe the private rooms are *most* luxurious, but of course they are very expensive.'

Her name was Tavernier. She had left England as a young girl and had never been back. She had been married twice. Her first husband was a bad man, her second husband was a good man. Just like that. Her second husband was a good man who had left her a little money.

When she talked about the first husband you could tell that she still hated him, after all those years. When she talked about the good one tears came into her eyes. She said that they were perfectly happy, completely happy, never an unkind word, and tears came into her eyes.

'Poor old mutt,' Inez thought, 'she really has persuaded herself to believe that.'

Madame Tavernier said in a low voice, 'Do you know what he said in the last letter he wrote to me? "You are everything to me." Yes, that's what he said in the last letter I had.'

'Poor old mutt,' Inez thought again.

Madame Tavernier wiped her eyes. Her face looked calm and gentle, as if she were repeating to herself, 'Nobody can say this isn't true, because I've got the letter and I can show it.'

The fat, fair woman in the bed opposite was also chatting with her neighbour. They were both blonde, very clean and aggressively respectable. For some reason they fitted in so well with their surroundings that they made everyone else seem dubious, out of place. The fat one discussed the weather, and her neighbour's answers were like an echo. 'Hot . . . Oh yes, very hot. . . . Hotter than yesterday. . . . Yes, much hotter. . . . I wish the weather would break. . . . Yes, I wish it would, but no chance of that. . . . No, I suppose not. . . . Oh, I rather fancy so. . . .'

Under cover of this meaningless conversation the fair woman's stare at Inez was sharp, sly and inquisitive. 'An English person? English, what sort of English? To which of the seven divisions, sixty-nine sub-divisions, and thousand-and-three sub-sub-divisions do you belong? (*But only one sauce, damn you!*) My world is a stable, decent world. If you withhold information, or if you confuse me by jumping from one category to another, I can be extremely disagreeable, and I am not without subtlety and inventive powers when I want to be disagreeable. Don't underrate me. I have set the machine in motion and crushed many like you. Many like you.'

Madame Tavernier shifted uneasily in her bed, as if she sensed this clash of personalities – stares meeting in mid-air, sparks flying.

'Those two ladies just opposite are English,' she whispered.

'Oh, are they?'

'And so is the one in the bed on the other side of you.'

'The sleepy one they make such a fuss about?'

'She's a dancer – a "girl", you know. One of the Yetta Kauffman girls. She's had an operation for appendicitis.'

'Oh, has she?'

'The one with the screen round her bed,' Madame Tavernier chattered on, 'is very ill. She's not expected to—— And the one . . .'

Inez interrupted after a while. 'They seem to have stuck all the English down this end, don't they? I wish they had mixed us up a bit more.'

'They never do,' Madame Tavernier answered. 'I've often noticed it.'

'It's a mistake,' said Inez. 'English people are usually pleasanter to foreigners than they are to each other.'

After a silence Madame Tavernier inquired politely, 'Have you travelled a lot?'

'Oh, a bit.'

'And do you like it here?'

'Yes, I like Paris much the best.'

'I suppose you feel at home,' Madame Tavernier said. Her voice was ironical. 'Like many people. There's something for every taste.'

'No, I don't feel particularly at home. That's not why I like it.'

She turned away and shut her eyes. She knew the pain was going to start again. And, sure enough, it did. They gave her an injection and she went to sleep.

Next morning she woke feeling dazed. She lay and watched two nurses charging about, very brisk and busy and silent. They did not even say 'Come along,' or 'Now, now,' or 'Drink that up.'

They moved about surely and quickly. They did everything in an impersonal way. They were like parts of a machine, she thought, that was working smoothly. The women in the beds bobbed up and down and in and out. They too were parts of a machine. They had a strength, a certainty, because all their lives they had belonged to the machine and worked smoothly, in and out, just as they were told. Even if the machine got out of control, even if it went mad, they would still work in and out, just as they were told, whirling smoothly, faster and faster, to destruction.

She lay very still, so that nobody should know she was afraid. Because she was outside the machine they might come along any time with a pair of huge iron tongs and pick her up and put her on the rubbish heap, and there she would lie and rot. 'Useless, this one,' they would say; and throw her away before she could explain, 'It isn't like you think it is, not at all. It isn't like they say it is. Wait a bit. You must listen; it's very important.'

But in the evening she felt better.

The girl in the bed on the right, who was sitting up, said she wanted to write to a friend at the theatre.

'In French,' she said. 'Can anybody write the letter for me, because I don't know French?'

'I'll write it for you,' Madame Tavernier offered.

' "Dear Lili . . ." L-i-l-i. "Dear Lili . . ." Well, say: "I'm getting all right again. Come and see me on Monday or Thursday. Any time from two to four. And when you come will you bring me some note-paper and stamps? I hope it won't be long before I get out of this place. I'll tell you about that on Monday. Don't forget the stamps. Tell the others that they can come to see me, and tell them how to get here. Your affectionate friend, and so on, Pat . . ." Give it to me and I'll sign it. Thanks."

The girl's voice had two sounds in it. One was clear and light, the other heavy and ruthless.

'You seem to be having a rotten time, you in the next bed,' she said.

'I feel better now.'

'Have you been in Paris long?'

'I live here.'

'Ah, then you'll be having your pals along to cheer you up.'

'I don't think so. I don't expect anybody.'

The girl stared. She was not much over twenty and her clear blue eyes slanted upwards. She looked as if, standing up, she would be short with sturdy dancer's legs. Stocky, like a little pony.

*Oh God, let her go on talking about herself and not looking at me, or sizing me up, or anything like that.*

'This French girl, this friend of mine, she's a perfect scream,' Pat said. 'But she's an awfully obliging girl. If I say, "Turn up with stamps," she will turn up with stamps. That's why I'm writing to her and not to one of our lot. Our lot might turn up or they might not. You know. But she's a perfect scream, really. . . . As a matter of fact, she's not bad-looking, but the way she walks is too funny. She's a *femme nue*, and they've taught her to walk like that. It's all right without shoes, but with shoes it's – well . . . You'll see when she comes here. They only get paid half what we do, too. Anyway, she's an awfully obliging kid; she's a sweet kid, poor devil.'

A nurse brought in supper.

'The girls are nice and the actors are nice,' Pat went on. 'But the stage hands hate us. Isn't it funny? You see, one of them tried to kiss one of our lot and she smacked his face. He looked sort of surprised, she said. And then do you know what he did? He hit her back! Well, and do you know what we did? We said to the stage manager, "If that man doesn't get the sack, we won't go on." They tried one show without us and then they gave in. The principals whose numbers were spoilt made a hell of a row. The French girls can't do our stuff because they can't keep together. They're all right alone – very good sometimes, but they don't understand team work. . . . And now, my God, the stage hands don't half hate us. We have to go in twos to the lavatory. And yet, the girls and the actors are awfully nice; it's only the stage hands who hate us.'

The fat woman opposite – her name was Mrs Wilson – listened to all this, at first suspiciously, then approvingly. Yes, this is permissible; it has its uses. Pretty English chorus-girl – north country – with a happy, independent disposition and bright, teasing eyes. Placed! All correct.

Pat finished eating and then went off to sleep again very suddenly, like a child.

'A saucy girl, isn't she?' Madame Tavernier said. Her eyes were half-shut, the corners of her mouth turned downwards.

Through the windows the light turned from dim yellow to mauve, from mauve to grey, from grey to black. Then it was dark, except for the unshaded bulbs tinted red all along the ward. Inez put her arm round her head and turned her face to the pillow.

'Good-night,' the old lady said. And after a long while she said, 'Don't cry, don't cry.'

Inez whispered, 'They kill you so slowly. . . .'

The ward was a long, grey river; the beds were ships in a mist.

The next day was Sunday. Even through those window-panes the sky looked blue, and the sun made patterns on the highly polished floor. The patients had breakfast half an hour later – seven instead of half past six.

'Only milk for you today,' the nurse said. Inez was going to ask why; then she remembered that her operation was fixed for Monday. *Don't think of it yet. There's still quite a long time to go.*

After the midday meal the matron told them that an English clergyman was going to visit the ward and hold a short service if nobody minded. Nobody did mind, and after a while the parson came in through an unsuspected door, looking as if he felt very cold, as if he had never been warm in his life. He had grey hair and a shy, shut-in face.

He stood at the end of the ward and the patients turned their heads to look at him. The screen round the bed on the other side had been taken away and the yellow-faced, shrunken woman who lay there turned her head like the others and looked.

The clergyman said a prayer and most of the patients said 'Amen.' ('Amen,' they said. 'We are listening,' they said. . . . . 'I am poor, bewildered, unhappy, comfort me, I am dying, console me, of course I don't let on that I know I'm dying, but I know, I know. Don't talk about life as it is because it has nothing to do with me now. Say something, go on, say something, because I'm so darned sick of women's voices. Christ, how I hate women. Say something funny that I can laugh at, but anything you say will be funny, you old geezer you. Never mind, say something. . . .' 'We are listening,' they said, 'we are listening. . . .') But the parson was determined to stick to life as it is, for his address was a warning against those vices which would antagonise their fellows and make things worse for them. Self-pity, for instance. Where does that lead you? Ah, where? . . . Cynicism. So cheap. . . . Rebellion. . . . So useless. . . . 'Let us remember,' he ended, 'that God is a just God and that man, made in His image, is also just. On the whole. And so, dear sisters, let us try to live useful, righteous and God-fearing lives in that state to which it has pleased Him to call us. Amen.'

He said another prayer and then went round shaking hands. 'How do you do, how do you do, how do you do?' All along the two lines. Then he went out again.

After he had gone there was silence in the ward for a few seconds, then somebody sighed.

Madame Tavernier remarked, 'Poor little man, he was so nervous.'

'Well, it didn't last long, anyway,' Pat said. 'On and off like the Demon King.' She began to sing:

> 'Oh, he doesn't look much like a lover,
> But you can't tell a book by its cover.'

Then she sang *The Sheik of Araby*. She tied a towel round her head for a turban and began again: '"Over the desert wild and free . . ." Sing up, girls, chorus. "I'm the Sheik of Arabee . . ."'

Everybody looked at Pat and laughed; the dying woman's small yellow face was convulsed with laughter.

'There's lots of time before tomorrow,' Inez thought. 'I needn't bother about it yet.'

'"I'm the Sheik of Arabee . . ."' Somebody was singing it in French – '"*Je cherche Antinéa*."' It was a curious translation – significant when you came to think of it.

Pat shouted, 'Listen to this. Anybody recognise it? Old but good. "Who's that knocking at my door? said the fair young ladye . . ."'

The tall English sister came in. She had a narrow face, small deep-set eyes of an unusual reddish-brown colour and a large mouth. Her pale lips lay calmly one on the other, as if she were very good-tempered, or perhaps very self-controlled. She smiled blandly and said, 'Now then, Pat, you must stop this,' arranged the screen round the bed on the other side and pulled down the blind of the window at the back.

It was really very hot and after she had gone out again most of the women lay in a stupor, but Pat went on talking: the sound of her own voice seemed to excite her. She became emphatic, as if someone was arguing with her.

She talked about love and the difference between glamour and dirt. The real difference was £ s. d., she said. If there was some money about there could be some glamour; otherwise, say what you liked, it was simply dirty – as well as foolish.

'Plenty of survival-value there,' Inez thought. She lay with her eyes closed, trying to see trees and smooth water. But the pictures she made slipped through her mind too quickly, so that they became distorted and malignant.

That night everybody in the ward was wakeful. Somebody moaned. The nurse rushed about with a bed-pan, grumbling under her breath.

II

At nine o'clock on Monday morning the tall English sister was saying, 'You'll be quite all right. I'm going to give you a morphine injection now.'

After this, Inez was still frightened, but in a much duller way.

'I hope you'll be there,' she said drowsily. But there was another nurse in the operating room. She was wearing a mask and she looked horrible, Inez thought – like a torturer.

Floating in the air, which was easy and natural after the morphine – *Of course, I've always been able to do this. Why did I ever forget? How stupid of me!* – she watched herself walking across the floor with tears streaming down her cheeks, supported by the terrifying stranger.

'Now, don't be silly,' the nurse said irritably.

Inez sat down on the edge of the couch, not floating now, not divided. One, and heavy as lead.

'You don't know why I'm crying,' she thought.

She tried to look at the sky, but there was a mist before her eyes and she could not see it. She felt hands pressing hard on her shoulders.

'No, no, no, leave her alone,' somebody said in French.

The English doctor was not there – only this man, who was also wearing a mask.

'They're so stupid,' Inez said, in a high, complaining voice. 'It's terrible. Oh, what's going to happen, what's going to happen?'

'Don't be afraid,' the doctor said. His brown eyes looked kind. '*N'ayez pas peur, n'ayez pas peur.*' 'All right,' Inez said, and lay down.

The English doctor's voice said. 'Now breathe deeply. Count slowly. One – two – three – four – five – six . . .'

III

'Do you feel better today?' the old lady asked.

'Yes, much better.'

The blind at the back of her bed was down. It tapped a bit. She was sleepy; she felt as if she could sleep for weeks.

'Hullo,' said Pat, 'come to life again?'

'I'm much better now.'

'You've been awfully bad,' Pat said. 'You were awfully ill on Monday, weren't you?'

'Yes, I suppose I was.'

The screen which had been up round her bed for three days had shut her away even from her hand-mirror; and now she took it up and looked at herself as if she were looking at a stranger. She had lain seeing nothing but a succession of pictures of the past, always sinister, always too highly coloured, always distorted. She had heard nothing but the incoherent, interminable conversations in her head.

'I look different,' she thought.

'I look awful,' she thought, staring anxiously at her thin, grey face and the hollows under her eyes. This was very important; her principal asset was threatened.

'I must rest,' she thought. 'Rest, not worry.'

She passed her powder-puff over her face and put some rouge on.

Pat was watching her. 'D'you know what I've noticed? People who look ghastly oughtn't to put make-up on. You only look worse if you aren't all right underneath – much older. My pal Lili came along on Monday. You should have seen how pretty she looked. I will say for these Paris girls they do know how to make up. . . .'

Yap, yap, yap . . .

'Even if they aren't anything much – and often they aren't, mind you – they know how to make themselves look all right. I mean, you see prettier girls in London, but in my opinion . . .'

The screen round the bed on the opposite side had been taken away. The bed was empty. Inez looked at it and said nothing. Madame Tavernier, who saw her looking at it, also said nothing, but for a moment her eyes were frightened.

IV

The next day, the ward sister brought in some English novels.

'You'll find these very soothing,' she said, and there was a twinkle in her eye. A splendid nurse, that one; she knew her job. What they call a born nurse.

A born nurse, as they say. Or you could be a born cook, or a born clown or a born fool, a born this, a born that . . .

'What's the joke now?' Pat asked suspiciously.

'Oh, nothing. I was thinking how hard it is to believe in free will.'

'I suppose you know what you're talking about,' Pat answered coldly. She had become hostile for some reason. Not that it mattered.

'Everything will be all right; I needn't worry,' Inez assured herself. 'There's still heaps of time.'

And soon she believed it. Lying there, being looked after and waking obediently at dawn, she began to feel like a child, as if the future would surely be pleasant, though it was hardly conceivable. It was as if she had always lain there and had known everyone else in the ward all her life – Madame Tavernier, her shawl, her rings, her crochet and her travel books, Pat and her repertoire of songs, the two fair, fat women who always looked so sanctimonious when they washed.

The room was long and the beds widely spaced, but now she knew something of the others too. There was a mysterious girl with long plaits and a sullen face who sometimes helped the nurse to make the beds in the morning – mysterious, because there did not seem to be anything the matter with her. She ought to have been pretty, but she always kept her head down, and if by chance you met her eyes, she would blink and glance away. And there was the one who wore luxury pyjamas, the one who knitted, the other constant reader – watching her was sometimes a frightening game – the one who had a great many visitors, the ugly one, rather like a monkey, who, all day, sewed something that looked like a pink crêpe de Chine chemise.

But her dreams were uneasy, and if a book fell or a door banged her heart would jump – a painful echo. And she found herself disliking some of the novels the sister brought. One day when she was reading her face reddened with anger. *Why, it's not a bit like that. My Lord, what liars these people are! And nobody to stand up and tell them so. Yah, Judas! Thinks it's the truth! You're telling me!*

She glanced sideways. Pat, who was staring at her, laughed, raised her eyebrows and tapped her forehead. Inez laughed back, also tapped her forehead and a moment afterwards was reading again, peacefully.

The days were like that, but when night came she burrowed into the middle of the earth to sleep. 'Never wake up, never wake up,' her wise heart told her. But the morning always came, the tin basins, the smell of soap, the long, sunlit, monotonous day.

At last she was well enough to walk into the bathroom by herself. Going there was all right, but coming back her legs gave way and she had to put her hand on the wall of the passage for support. There was a weight round the middle of her body which was dragging her to earth.

She got back into bed again. Darkness, quiet, safety – all the same, it was time to face up to things, to arrange them neatly. 'One, I feel much worse than I expected; two, I must ask the matron tomorrow if I can stay for another week – they won't want me to pay in advance; three, as soon as I know that I'm all right for another week, I must start writing round and trying to raise some money. A thousand francs when I get out! What's a thousand francs when you feel like this?'

That night she lay awake for a long time, making plans. But next morning, when the matron came round, she became nervous of a refusal. 'I'll ask her tomorrow for certain.' However, the whole of the next day passed and she did not say a word.

She ate and slept and read soothing English novels about the respectable and the respected, and she did not say a word nor write a letter. Any excuse was good enough: 'She doesn't look in a good temper today. . . . Oh, the doctor's with her; I don't think he likes me much. (Well, I don't like you much either, old cock; your eyes are too close together.) . . . Today's Friday, not my lucky day. . . . I'll write when my head is clearer.'

A long brown passage smelling of turpentine led from the ward to the washroom. There were rows of basins along either whitewashed wall, three water-closets and two bathrooms at the far end.

Inez went to one of the wash-basins. She was carrying a sponge-bag. She took out of it soap, a tooth-brush, tooth-paste and peroxide.

Somebody opened the door stealthily, hesitated for a moment, then walked past and stood over one of the basins at the far end. It was the sullen girl, the one with the long plaits. She was wearing a blue kimono.

'She does look fed up,' Inez thought.

The girl leant over the basin with both hands on its edge. Was she going to be sick? Then she gave a long, shivering sigh and opened her sponge-bag.

Inez turned away without speaking and began to clean her teeth.

The door opened again and a nurse came in and glanced round the washroom. It was curious to see the expression on her plump, pink face change in a few moments from indifference to inquisitiveness, to astonishment, to shocked anger.

Then she ran across the room, shouting 'Stop that. Come along, Mrs Murphy. Give it up.'

Inez watched them struggling. Something metallic fell to the floor. Mrs Murphy was twisting like a snake.

'Come on, help me, can't you? Hold her arms,' the nurse said breathlessly.

'Oh, leave me alone, leave alone,' Mrs Murphy wailed. 'Do for God's sake leave me alone. What do you know about it anyway?'

'Go and call the sister. She's in the ward.'

'She's speaking to me,' Inez thought.

'Oh, leave me alone, leave me alone. Oh, please, please, please, please, please,' Mrs Murphy sobbed.

'What's she done?' Inez said. 'Why don't you leave her alone?'

As she spoke, two other nurses rushed in at the door and flung themselves on Mrs Murphy, who began to scream loudly, with her mouth open and her head back.

Inez held on to the basins, one by one, and got to the door. Then she held on to the door-post, then to the wall of the passage. She reached her bed and lay down shaking.

'What's up? What's the matter?' Pat asked excitedly.

'I don't know.'

'Was it Murphy? You're all right, aren't you? We were wondering if it was Murphy, or . . .'

'"Or you," she means,' Inez thought. '"Or you."'

All that evening Pat and the fair woman, Mrs Wilson, who had become very friendly, talked excitedly. It seemed that they knew all about Mrs Murphy. They knew that she had tried the same thing on before. Suddenly, by magic, they seemed to know all about her. And what a thing to do, to try to kill yourself! If it had been a man, now, you might have been a bit sorry. You might have said, 'Perhaps the poor devil has had a rotten time.' But a woman!

'A married woman with two sweet little kiddies.'

'The fool,' said Pat. 'My God, what would you do with a fool like that?'

Mrs Wilson, who had been in the clinic for some time explained that there was a medicine-cupboard just outside the ward.

'It must have been open,' she said. 'In *which* case, somebody will get into a row. Perhaps Murphy got hold of the key. That's where she might get the morphine tablets.'

But Pat was of the opinion – she said she knew it for a fact, a nurse had told her – that Mrs Murphy had had the hypodermic syringe and the tablets hidden for weeks, ever since she had been in the clinic.

'She's one of these idiotic neurasthenics, neurotics or whatever you call them. She says she's frightened of life, I ask you. That's why she's here. Under observation. And it only shows you how cunning they are, that she managed to hide the things.'

'I'm so awfully sorry for her husband,' said Mrs Wilson. 'And her children. So sorry. The poor kiddies, the poor sweet little kiddies. . . . Oughtn't a woman like that to be hung?'

Even after the lights had been put out they still talked.

'What's she got to be neurasthenic and neurotic about, anyway?' Pat demanded. 'If she has a perfectly good husband and kiddies, what's she got to be neurasthenic and neurotic about?'

Stone and iron, their voices were. One was stone and one was iron.

Inez interrupted the duet in a tremulous voice. 'Oh, she's neurasthenic, and they've sent her to a place like this to be cured? That was a swell idea. What a place for a cure for neurasthenia! Who thought that up? The perfectly good, kind husband, I suppose.'

Pat said, 'For God's sake! You get on my nerves. Stop always trying to be different from everybody else.'

'Who's everybody else?'

Nobody answered her.

'What a herd of swine they are!' she thought, but no heat of rage came to warm or comfort her. Sized her up, Pat had. *Why should you care about a girl like that? She's as stupid as a foot. But not when it comes to sizing people up, not when it comes to knowing who is done for. I'm cold, I'm tired, I'm tired, I'm cold.*

The next morning Mrs Murphy appeared in time to help make the beds. As usual she walked with her head down and her eyes down and her shoulders stooped. She went very slowly along the opposite side of the ward, and everybody stared at her with hard, inquisitive eyes.

'What are you muttering about, Inez?' Pat said, sharply.

Mrs Murphy and the nurse reached the end of the row opposite. Then they began the other row. Slowly they were coming nearer.

'Shut up, it's nothing to do with you,' Inez told herself, but her cold hands were clenched under the sheet.

The nurse said, 'Pat, you're well enough to give a hand, aren't you? I won't be a moment.'

'Idiot,' Inez thought. 'She oughtn't to have gone away. They never know what's happening. But yes, they know. The machine works smoothly, that's all.'

In silence, Pat and Mrs Murphy started pulling and stretching and patting the sheets and pillows.

'Hullo, Pat,' Mrs Murphy said at last in a low voice.

Pat closed her lips with a righteously disgusted expression.

They turned the sheet under at the bottom. They smoothed it down at the top. They began to shake the pillows.

Mrs Murphy's face broke up and she started to cry. 'Oh God,' she said, 'they won't let me get out. They won't.'

Pat said, 'Don't snivel over my pillow. People like you make me sick,' and Mrs Wilson laughed, like a horse neighing.

The voice and the laughter were so much alike that they might have belonged to the same person. *Greasy and cold, silly and raw, coarse and thin; everything unutterably horrible.*

'Well, here's bad luck to you,' Inez burst out, 'you pair of bitches. Behaving like that to a sad woman! What do you know about her? . . . You hold your head up and curse them back, Mrs Murphy. It'll do you a lot of good.'

Mrs Murphy rushed out of the room sobbing.

'Who was speaking to you?' Pat said.

Inez heard words coming round and full and satisfying out of her mouth – exactly what she thought about them, exactly what they were, exactly what she hoped would happen to them.

'Disgusting,' said Mrs Wilson. 'I *told* you so,' she added triumphantly. 'I knew it, I knew the sort she was from the first.'

At this moment the door opened and the doctor came in, accompanied not as usual by the matron but by the tall ward sister.

Once more, for a gesture, Inez shouted, 'This and that to the lot of you!' 'Not the nurse,' she whispered to the pillow, 'I don't mean her.'

Mrs Wilson announced in a loud, clear voice, 'I think that people who use filthy language oughtn't to be allowed to associate with decent people. I think it's a shame that some women are allowed to associate with ladies at all – a shame. It oughtn't to be allowed.'

The doctor blinked, but the sister's long, narrow face was expressionless. The two went round the beds glancing at the temperature-charts here, saying a few words there. 'Best, Inez . . .'

The doctor asked, 'Does this hurt you?'

'No.'

'When I press here does it hurt you?'

'No.'

They were very tall, thin and far away. They turned their heads a little and she could not hear what they said. And when she began, 'I wanted to . . .' she saw that they could not hear her either, and stopped.

v

'You can dress in the washroom after lunch,' the sister said next morning.

'Oh, yes?'

There was nothing to be surprised about. So much time had been paid for and now the time was up and she would have to go. There was nothing to be surprised about.

Inez said, 'Would it be possible to stay two or three days longer? I wanted to make some arrangements. It would be more convenient. I was idiotic not to speak about it before.'

The sister's raised eyebrows were very thin – like two thin new moons.

She said, 'I'm sorry, I'm afraid it's not possible. Why didn't you ask before? I told the doctor yesterday that I didn't think you were very strong yet. But we are expecting four patients this evening and several others tomorrow afternoon. Unfortunately, we are going to be very full up and he thinks you are well enough to go. You must rest when you get back home. Move as little as possible.'

'Yes, of course,' Inez said; but she thought, 'No, this time I won't be able to pull it off, this time I'm done. "*We wondered if it was Murphy – or you.*" *Well, it's both of us.*'

Then her body relaxed and she lay and did not think of anything, for there is peace in despair in exactly the same way as there is despair in peace. Everything in her body relaxed. She did not make any more plans, she just lay there.

They had their midday dinner – roast beef, potatoes and beans, and then a milk pudding. Just like England. Inez ate and enjoyed it, and then lay back with her arm over her eyes. She knew that Pat was watching her but she lay still, peaceful, and thought of nothing.

'Here are your things,' the nurse said. 'Will you get dressed now?'

'All right.'

'I'm afraid you're not feeling up to much. Well, you'll have some tea before you go, won't you? And you must go straight to bed as soon as you get back.'

'Get back where?' Inez thought. 'Why should you always take it for granted that everybody has somewhere to get back to?'

'Oh yes,' she said, 'I will.'

And all the time she dressed she saw the street, the buses and taxis charging at her, the people jostling her. She heard their voices, saw their eyes. . . . When you fall you don't ever get up; they take care of that.

She leant against the wall thinking of Mrs Murphy's voice when she said, 'Please, please, please, please, please . . .'

After a while, she wiped the tears off her face. She did not put any powder on, and when she got into the ward she could only see the bed she was going to lie on and wait till they came with the tongs to throw her out.

'Will you come over here for a moment?'

There was a chair at the head of each bed. She sat down and looked at the fan-shaped wrinkles under Madame Tavernier's small, dark, melancholy eyes, the swollen blue veins on her hands and the pattern of the gold ring – two roses, the petals touching each other. She read a sentence of the open book lying on the bed: '*De là-haut le paysage qu'on découvre est d'une beauté indescriptible . . .*'

Madame Tavernier said, 'That's a charming dress, and you look very nice – very nice indeed.'

'My God!' Inez said. 'That's funny.'

Madame Tavernier whispered, 'S-sh, listen! Turn the chair round. I want to talk to you.'

Inez turned the chair so that her back was towards the rest of the room.

Madame Tavernier took a handkerchief from under her pillow – a white, old-fashioned handkerchief, not small, of very fine linen trimmed with lace. She put it into Inez' hands. 'Here,' she said. 'S-sh . . . Here!'

Inez took the handkerchief. It smelt of vanilla. She felt the notes inside it.

'Take care. Don't let the others see. Don't let them notice you crying. . . .' She whispered, 'You mustn't mind these people; they don't know anything about life. You mustn't mind them. So many people don't know anything about life . . . so many of them . . . and sometimes I wonder if it isn't getting worse instead of better.' She sighed. 'You hadn't any money, had you?'

Inez shook her head.

'I thought you hadn't. There's enough there for a week or perhaps two. If you are careful.'

'Yes, yes,' Inez said. 'Now I'll be quite all right.'

She stopped crying. She felt tired, rested and rather degraded. She had never taken money from a woman before. She did not like women, she had always told herself, or trust them.

Madame Tavernier went on talking. That is quite a lot of money if you use it carefully, she meant. But that was not what she said.

'Thank you,' Inez said. 'Oh, thank you.'

'You'd like some tea before you go, wouldn't you?' the nurse said.

Inez drank the tea, went into the washroom and made up her face. She went back to the old lady's bed.

'Will you give me a kiss?' Madame Tavernier said.

Her powdered skin was soft and flabby as used elastic; it smelt, like her handkerchief, of vanilla. When Inez said, 'I'll never forget your kindness, it's made such a difference to me,' she closed her eyes in a way that meant, 'All right, all right, all right.'

'I'll have a taxi to the station,' Inez decided.

But in the taxi she could only wonder what Madame Tavernier would say if she were suddenly asked what it is like to be old (perhaps she would answer, 'Sometimes it's peaceful'), remember the gold ring carved into two roses, and above all wish she were back in her bed in the ward with the sheets drawn over her head. Because you can't die and come to life again for a few thousand francs. It takes more than that. It takes more, perhaps, than anybody is ever willing to give.

FRANK TUOHY

# A Survivor in Salvador

I

THE airport was far away from Salvador, out in the scrub-country.

While the engines whirred down into silence, a steward came round, puffing at the roof and windows with a spray against mosquitoes. Then the door was opened and some rusty steps, which looked like apparatus from a public swimming-pool, were trundled up. The passengers descended, one by one, into a bath of soft heat, with the new silence drumming in their ears.

The swept area of dust was bounded by a line of jungle. There was nothing else: no sign of the city of Salvador, with all its bell-towers and palm-trees, that they had passed over a few minutes ago; and only a rumour, somewhere near at hand, of the tropical sea.

Christophe – Prince Krzystof Wawelski – was the tallest and oddest-looking of the passengers, and his colourless hair and gaunt features made him look older, and somehow more important, than he actually was. He was fifty-three; an amateur painter, if he was anything. He could speak nothing of the language. He walked out of the airport into a world of pure sensation that required an effort of his dazed attention, a conscious recall of the danger he was in. The sun waved a sheet of fire at his screwed-up features, and while he was blinded his precious valise was snatched from him. There was nothing he could do: porters and taxi-drivers had decided his fate. With five other passengers, and his valise lost among their baggage tied to the car's roof, he was dispatched on the journey to Salvador.

The other passengers were all men. In lustrous suits of chestnut or dove-grey, they were shiny from their oiled hair to their polished shoes. Approaching the fabled city they began to get excited, like school children on their way to a treat. Christophe guessed that they were boasting of their successes with women. He was sure of this when one of them, a young man with a squeaky voice, ostentatiously pulled off his wedding ring and put it in an inside pocket of his coat. The others roared with laughter.

Christophe sat cramped, a head taller than any of them, his face twitching a little with heat and tiredness. His life was far simpler than theirs, for at the moment he was merely trying to survive. In his way of going about this, he was perhaps like many exiled Poles. A sort of arrogance let him stoop to almost anything, as if he believed that his contempt for his associates kept him from losing honour. What you noticed about him was this arrogance, and then also the look of kindness, almost of love, which lay in the eyes blinking on the worn territory of his face. To be an aristocrat, even a minor one, and an artist, although a bad one, cannot leave you untouched in one way or another, and Christophe was helped by both these things.

Today he was wearing his last suit. His shirts, his hair-net and some elaborate toilet gear were in the valise on the roof, and there also was the small package that he believed to represent his future.

Christophe had been living for the last eight months – living on promises, on his title, on his bridge game – among the Polish colony of Porto Alegre, in southern Brazil. Something was always going to turn up, and speaking Polish or German he was able to get around easily. When he was finally broke, and in debt, a friend told him about Blom. Blom, who was imprecisely described as a 'business man', invited him to lunch.

The house was in a suburb of Porto Alegre, with small villas, oleander-shaded gardens and garages for Fords and Chevrolets. Standing at noon in the red-tiled porch, Christophe already bristled with native distrusts and phobias – of Jews, of the middle classes and of work. It was only the immediate prospect of a good meal that kept him there. After that, he thought, he might be able to force himself to listen to Blom's proposals.

A black servant-girl let him in. He saw walls lined with books and there was a strong smell of the chemical used to kill tropical book-grubs. While he waited, he read some of the titles near him: *Zen Buddhism*, the American edition of the works of C. G. Jung, the *Kama Sutra*. Hearing footsteps, he swivelled round. He was still so suspicious that when he saw them he thought for a moment they were midgets. He hadn't imagined Blom having children.

They were a boy and a girl of about ten and twelve. '*Vati kommt gleich.*'

'*Vati! Vati!*'

'*Ruhig, Liebchen!*'

Blom shook hands softly, then he ran his fingers over his daughter's shoulders and her long black hair. 'This is Gerda,' he said, 'and my son Dov. My dear Prince, these young rascals do not speak English and so perhaps we shall do so. Little pitchers have big ears. May I offer you some vodka?'

Mrs Blom, a comfortable-looking woman, joined them, bringing a plate of pickled herring. To Christophe she spoke Polish with a ghetto accent that made him wince.

'I can understand nothing,' her husband said, with great satisfaction. 'You see, I am lucky enough to stem from that famous old city of Frankfurt-am-Main.' Everything he said was bitten down with deprecating irony, a way in which Englishmen are believed to talk, but seldom do. But his accent, which he had modelled on that of Leslie Howard many years before, was far better than Christophe's.

They ate heavily, braised meat, thick with gravy, rice and sweet purple cabbage, and the little servant girl waited on them. Christophe watched her, his hot eyes inventing her body: she was barefoot, and possibly even naked under the plain shift hanging from her shoulders.

As they filled themselves with the warm heavy food, the atmosphere became easy. From time to time the children looked at Christophe, looked away, and broke into wild pubescent giggles, which the little black girl joined in, staggering round the table with the heavy dish of rice. Christophe laughed back, and with the warmth of the room, and first vodka and now tumblers of Chilean wine, he found that he was enjoying himself. Long afterwards, he would remember the giggling middle-class Jewish children and the Negro maidservant as innocents living before the Fall, his Fall.

Perhaps he was off his guard, then, when he was alone with his host. Without any warning – Christophe believed himself a little shocked by this – Blom began to talk business.

'Our friend Mister . . . I am afraid I am very bad at names . . . has told me you are anxious to try your luck up north. I believe there are many possibilities there. I was wondering if you would do me a small service? It is merely to deliver a little package or parcel.'

Christophe nodded. The room became quiet and still while Blom unlocked a safe in the wall. The children's laughter was miles away beyond the bookshelves.

'In return I should be willing to pay the cost of the plane fare. And my correspondent, Mister Lemberg, will pay five thousand *cruzeiros* on delivery. Is that satisfactory? They tell me that life is far cheaper up there.'

Christophe lifted the package and dropped it, as if measuring its weight. It was about the size of a tin of coffee. 'It is valuable?'

'I think it worth about three thousand dollars.' He giggled. 'Of course, it would be most dangerous for anyone to try and sell it. For you, a new-comer without the necessary contacts, it would be impossible. That is my guarantee. Also, Mr Lemberg will know you are coming.'

They went towards the door. 'For a painter, the city of Salvador should be most picturesque,' Blom said. 'Tell me, do you prefer oils or water-colour?'

For Christophe, who had been educated for idleness, all ways for making money involved a racket, and up to now his life had confirmed him in this belief. He was an exile three times over: firstly, from Poland and then, an officer in Sikorski's army, from France in 1940. After the war he and his brother, who was married to an English girl, started a restaurant in Bayswater. There was black-market trouble and Christophe, the unmarried one, had done six months in jail. On leaving Wormwood Scrubs he was deported and obliged to sign a paper saying he would never enter England again. Typically, when recounting this experience, he blamed it automatically and almost without malice on the Jews. Anywhere else he would have needed a lot of forgiving; in Brazil, however, people didn't really understand what he meant.

Tonight, in Salvador, Christophe waited in the taxi until all the other passengers had been left at their different hotels. Then he gave the driver Lemberg's address. It turned out to be quite close, in one of the few modern apartment buildings in this section of the city.

There was a single lift, by which he ascended jerkily to the seventh floor. Standing there, feeling the package sliding up and down inside his valise, Christophe was overcome with an exhausting sensation of relief. He even yawned several times.

He pressed the door-bell. There was a scuffling sound behind the dark wood, and a woman's voice speaking German, frightened and scornful at the same time.

The door opened a little.

'Mister Lemberg? I am sent by Mister Blom.'

At this, a small excited man shot out at him.

'*Nein! Nein!* You must go away!' A hand pawed at Christophe's middle, pushing him towards the concrete stairs at the side of the lift. 'Please, Mister. Down here, hurry, please. Police coming.'

Christophe descended a few steps. The door slammed shut and the woman's voice started up again, more desperate than ever.

He stood in the shadow, two flights lower down. Then he saw the tacky wire ropes begin to tremble in the lift shaft beside him, and the cage climbed slowly upwards, with three Civil Guards inside it.

Christophe ran out of the building, crossed the road and stood among the crowd on the opposite pavement. A black police van was parked near the kerb, but no one took any notice of him. After a few moments, Lemberg came out between two of the Civil Guards. Behind him, weeping, was a plump woman who looked rather like Mrs Blom.

Standing among the crowd in the upper city of Salvador, Christophe knew that he was effectively stopped in his tracks. South America was the end of the line for him. Now they could not deport him anywhere except behind the Iron Curtain. Again he swung the valise to and fro and felt the package sliding about at the bottom of it. It was his greatest danger, and his only wealth: about this, he was going to prove that Blom was wrong.

The city of São Salvador da Bahia de Todos os Santos is one of those raddled beauties whose poverty has kept them intact from change. Night was falling as Christophe stood there outside Lemberg's apartment block in the upper city, and the bells from several churches clanged discordantly. Around him, streets ran downhill into the darkness. They were filled with women walking to and fro. The beauties of mixed blood, who give the city one of its reputations, were like flames lit at intervals. Tonight Christophe avoided them. Choosing a less crowded street between two churches, he looked for somewhere to sleep and to leave his possessions. Wherever he went the inhabitants watched him, without hostility or interest, the tall foreigner with colourless hair, whose white face was constructed out of a different set of feelings from theirs.

A fanlight had 'Hotel Nova Iorque' written on it. Inside an effeminate-looking boy led him up to a room with a single iron bedstead and a row of hooks on the wall. It was what Christophe wanted, and he paid the boy's mother enough for three days: this used up nearly all his money. Now he was gambling on the package, which he took from the valise and put into his pocket. He was not afraid of Blom: the distance, the half-continent that separated them, made it almost impossible to believe in Blom.

Downstairs, he asked the way to the port. The boy accompanied him to the top of the street and pointed across the square with all the churches.

'*Elevador*,' he said. He watched Christophe with humorous, almost patronising curiosity.

By the lift, Christophe descended through layers of heat to the lower city. At the bottom there was a tree-shaded square, inhabited by shoeshines and peanut-sellers. Old black women with charcoal stoves were selling coconut sweets and mealy-cakes fried up in palm-oil. There were bars, and cheap restaurants, but nothing of the type he was looking for.

Christophe walked through the streets of the commercial quarter until he came to the docks. Here there were neon signs: 'Scandinavia', 'Texas', 'Good Beer Serve By Women'. He looked into two or three bars, but they were empty, except for women knitting. Evidently, he was too early, or there were few ships in harbour.

Finally, in the 'Scandinavia', he got into conversation with two young Englishmen, merchant seamen. They were sitting quietly together near the wall, with glasses of beer in front of them.

'Know this place? Just think we do. Must be our fourth time here, isn't it, Ted?'

'That's right.'

They were both large, and seemed very white, with small blue emblems tattooed on their forearms. Christophe pulled out the chair opposite them and sat down. He told them that he had arrived today and knew nobody. He was going to put himself into their hands gently, as one tests a deck-chair.

'You want to watch out,' the first sailor said. In spite of his massive appearance his voice was refined and finicky, like a tenor's in a cathedral choir. You could imagine him sewing on buttons. 'We know all about that, don't we, Ted?'

His friend nodded; he was perhaps stunned with drink.

'What is it you know?' Christophe leaned forward, dropping his voice.

'You don't want to get too friendly, see what I mean?' He indicated the cluster of women who were watching them.

Christophe's interest faded. For him, knowledge of the women came first in one's attack on a place. 'What about the other bars?'

'No good,' the sailor said, 'Never been in any of them. Might pick up something nasty.'

'But in the upper city, perhaps?'

'Where's that?'

'I mean, up the elevator.' It was obvious that they did not know what he was talking about. 'You always stay in this bar?'

'As long as we're in port. We only take the beer, mind. With these other things, you never know what you're getting. That's right, isn't it, Ted?'

The other hardly moved.

'Ted's got one of his upsets again. He had one of these *cuba libres*, rum and that. Never know what they put into them.'

Christophe was up against that transparent protective shell which Europeans think they touch on meeting an Englishman. He prepared to go.

The sailor patted his mouth delicately. 'Not that the beer's any too fancy. It repeats.'

Christophe walked out into the street and followed the tramlines along the dock. He spoke to two Norwegians, one of whom, with mad blue eyes, trembled all over, like an aeroplane about to take off; they had jumped ship and were as lost as he was. He had a long conversation, completely at cross-purposes, with a mulatto from British Guiana. Then, as he walked on, he realised that he was moving away from the area of bars. The warehouses beside him smelt of foul straw, and on the other side the ships lay quiet under the starlight. Only an American liner was fully illuminated. Christophe could see passengers in white dinner-jackets walking on the promenade deck, watching the loading which was going on under arc-lights. A booming sound came from the machine, like an escalator, which trundled raceme after raceme of green bananas, creaking and stiff with unripeness, into the hold of the white ship. On the dock, groups of uniformed officials were standing round. While Christophe watched them, guessing that among them, though unapproachable, was the corruption he was looking for, there came a sudden downpour of rain. The loading machine stopped. The stevedores, whose bare limbs gleamed under the arc-lights, ran to put up their umbrellas. A tarpaulin was dragged over the open hold of the ship.

On the dock, umbrellas sprang up everywhere: all the officials had them. Christophe stood in the shelter of a warehouse roof. His feet were in soft leafy rubbish and the rain beat on the *pavé* in front of him. He shivered, for the fruitless conversations of this evening had affected him more deeply than he thought. One of Christophe's brothers had been murdered, shot in the neck, at the Katyn massacre; his mother had died during the 1944 Warsaw rising. They were remembered with pride. But what pride was there in survival in a foreign city, without money or friends or trust?

He put his hand into his pocket and gripped the hard package. He was beginning to be frightened of it now, and to hate it for the demands it was going to make on his endurance and his courage.

When the rain stopped, he retraced his steps towards the lighted bars. By now, there were a lot of people about and among the soldiers and seamen who crowded the pavements he saw some more of the Civil Guard – he had learned to recognise their holstered belts and white truncheons. Who were they looking for? His fears gave him the answer. After Lemberg's arrest they had discovered something, a letter perhaps, that led directly to himself. They had only to throw a cordon across the street and he'd be done for.

It was in a moment of panic hurry that he stumbled against the American.

The American, who wore a fringe of ginger hair and was dressed in a suit of dark-blue silk, held on. He was slightly drunk and obviously lonely, and though he looked far too innocent to be of any use to Christophe, his presence while the police were about was almost as good as an American passport.

Back in the 'Scandinavia' bar, the American beamed at Christophe across a pair of gin and tonics.

'Where you from?'

With a bow, Christophe presented his card, which at first created the impression he expected. But in the midst of his tipsiness the American carried, rather proudly, a few grains of suspicion.

'But if you're a prince, what you doing here?'

'I am a portrait painter, but I have yet no commissions here.'

'Ah, that's too bad.' The decent, unreal face frowned. 'You're Polish. I met up with a Polish lady last evening. Well, no, perhaps I shouldn't have said that, you see, she keeps a house. Wonderful character, though, wonderful personality. . . .'

The American stopped drinking. He was rotating his glass in his hand, watching the wheel of lemon circling slowly round. For a moment, the other was frightened that drunkenness was going to claim his new friend.

'Please go on, I am very interested.'

'Maybe she could help you, might want her picture painted or something. These madams here must make out pretty well.'

'If you will give me the address I will go there.'

'Ah, no.' A calculating look came into the American's eyes. 'You hold on and I'll come with you. Let's have another of these and stick together.'

He probably thinks I can get him a woman more cheaply, Christophe thought. But he accepted this rôle as he had accepted all the others. He did not want to drink any more for fear he might get careless and lose the hard grip on himself which, at this time, was the only thing he could be certain of. The American, however, insisted, and he couldn't desert the American without learning the address. A woman like that would know everything he wanted.

The moment of calculation had passed, and now the American was watching him with increasing affection. The warmth of a lover of humanity had come back into the American's eyes; he was eating life, as though here it had a savour which his native nourishment had lacked.

Then, suddenly and everywhere, shantung suits, pink plump skin, rimless spectacles: the bar was crowded with his fellow tourists.

'My friend Prince—' 'Hey, listen, Prince—' 'Another of those—'

A quarter of an hour later, among them, almost drowned out by voices, Christophe recovered his friend. He leaned down. 'Please, the address. You give me the Polish lady's address.'

'Ah, wait a minute, can't you? They'll wait for you, won't they?'

'What address, Rud, what address?'

The first American flushed under his ginger hair. 'It's nothing at all. Some idea this guy's got. Who is he, anyway?' Now his eyes had changed again, and were scared and cruel. 'You know, I don't credit he's a prince at all. You meet all sorts of people.'

Christophe clenched his fist in his pocket. His knuckles touched the package, and he controlled himself.

'Some kind of a ponce,' a voice said.

Christophe glanced round him, but none of them were looking at him any more. Then he walked away between the tables towards the door.

A man opened it for him. '*Bonsoir, monsieur.*'

Turning to him, Christophe recognised a life-worn, European face. The ground was under his feet again, a tussock in the middle of the bog.

'*La maison d'une Polonaise,*' he asked, '*vous la connaissez?*'

'*Mais certainement.* Madame Daisy, Rua Gloria 47.'

Christophe knew, the moment she entered the little room with the plush sofas, that he had found what he was looking for.

'*Senhor,* I am afraid all my girls are busy. If you would care to wait . . .'

He spoke to her in Polish and presented his card. He asked only to be allowed to talk with Madame for a few moments.

'You may talk as you wish. None of my girls understands.'

Round-shouldered, almost hunched, Madame Daisy sat opposite him, holding his gaze. Though the tropical night was as hot as ever after the rain, she was bundled up in a cocoa-coloured knitted shawl. Her face was powdered thickly but the mouth was unpainted and so thin that the lips seemed to hook together, like the catch of a child's purse: if this was what the American considered a wonderful personality, he deserved to be deluded wherever he went.

Yet, in spite of Madame Daisy's baleful appearance, Christophe felt at home with her. She too was from the Old World, she would understand these little problems of survival. He offered her an American cigarette and spoke to her of Poland. He had not much imagination and, when he told her his recent history, he kept as close to the truth as he could: he had disembarked with an immigrant's *visa,* and he had something valuable to sell.

At this point, Madame Daisy shifted a little in her seat and pulled her shawl together. But she still held his eye. She had been humiliated by his class in the old days, and now she was not displeased to have him begging for favours.

'If you tell me what it is, I think I can help you. But not jewels' – she wagged her finger – 'Here you don't have a good market.'

Christophe expressed his profound gratitude. He had known at once, he said, that he had found the right person, and an *ambiance* in which he was at home. If she would help him, he said, he would like to throw a party, with champagne, for all her girls.

'Then you waste your money. They are poor silly girls, these ones, and don't appreciate a party.' The sofa creaked and she stood up. 'Well, what is it you have?'

Christophe put the back of his wrist up to his nostrils and sniffed.

'Good. I write you an address. This man will help you and you can trust him.'

She went to a table and scrawled a few words on a piece of paper, which she folded up and pressed into his hand.

'Not thanks, please. I shall hear very soon what this man will give you, and I shall ask for my share. I do not give information for nothing.'

Christophe was not angry at this. Instead he felt the rather masochistic pleasure you get when people revert to type and behave exactly as you expect them to. Whatever happened, he would now be able to sell his package, and even a small part of its value would set him up quite adequately: of an artist's talents, he had at least that of living poor. He left the house and walked some distance to the nearest street lamp, before he opened the paper she had given him and tried to read it.

His first impression was of the handwriting they had taught at free schools in Poland: he had not seen it for many years. Then he began to make out the words. There was no name, but the street and the number were of Lemberg's apartment.

He tore the paper into small fragments and threw them in the gutter.


II


Christophe lay on his bed, feeling the day burn hotter and hotter through the room. Sweat streaked off him in runnels into the mattress and his smell brought in flies, which tried to settle on the corners of his mouth. From outside, he heard the noise of wooden sandals and handcarts on the cobbles. He moved, and felt his hunger. When he sat up, he remembered why he was afraid.

In his mind, the previous day became an area of appalling innocence, an Eden in which he had committed almost every sort of blunder. (Lemberg's clients had been expecting him to receive a consignment. . . . Blom, in Porto Alegre, had heard of the arrest and knew who had the package. . . . Madame Daisy had published the fact that she had been offered it.) From the window, dressed in his underpants, Christophe looked out on the eighteenth-century city. Even in the bright sunlight, he was scared. The shouts in the unknown language from the stalls below had a note of menace, and he felt no pleasure at all in the satisfying thump of knives going into the rose-scarlet flesh of pawpaws and water-melons.

He went back to bed. When the morning was half gone, the boy he had spoken to the night before came in and swept the floor, then leaned on his broom and chatted amiably and incomprehensibly. Christophe watched him, his interest momentarily aroused. Compact and self-reliant, the boy had been able to come to terms with himself more quickly in a society in which there was absolutely no question of being respectable. You could trust him with life, Christophe thought, in a way you could never have trusted the English sailors or the American.

While the boy went on talking, Christophe stared up at the bumps and patches on the white-washed ceiling, forming them into maps of all the countries in the world where he could never go any more until he died. 'No!' he shouted, suddenly. He was talking to himself, exploding out of pressure within, the ingrowing smoulder of his life.

The boy looked up, without surprise.

Christophe pointed to his watch. He made the boy understand that he wanted to sell it. The boy nodded at once and beckoned to him to come out. Christophe pulled on his clothes; he took the package from under the pillow and replaced it in his pocket. When he felt it there, heavy against his side, he knew he was back in his situation once more.

The boy led him across the square to a jeweller's shop. But he refused vehemently when the other asked him to come in.

'No, no.' The jeweller would think he had stolen the watch. Christophe accepted his knowledge, and went in alone.

A silence settled round him and staring people made way for him up to the counter. The jeweller, a dark, furious little man, snatched the watch away and a few seconds later pushed across some money. Christophe counted it. It was not nearly enough and he began to object, but the man ignored him, talking to someone else. You got money out of the poor by surliness and anger, when they were too far gone to resist. Christophe bowed his head and folded the thin wad of notes into his wallet. Everyone was still watching him. It was like the moment when madness strikes, but he seized hold of himself and went out into the street into the glare of sunlight and trams.

At the hotel, his friend was standing in the doorway talking to a young woman.

'This is Antonieta,' the boy said.

They shook hands and Antonieta smiled, showing small bluish-white teeth.

Christophe looked at her again. Her skin was the colour of dark caramel, but she had European features. A ribbon was fastened with a brooch round her neck. She was wearing a black skirt and a white blouse and though these clothes were tight fitting over the breasts and thighs, there was a primness, almost a schoolgirlishness, about her which immediately interested him.

'He told me you were a foreigner,' she said. '*Allemand?*'

'*Polonais.*'

The girl spoke French well. Christophe was amazed, for it was as though there was a gap in the wall in front of him: he could go through it, and live.

'This is a good girl,' the boy said, poking at her and whistling vulgarly. Antonieta pretended to hit him, and there was a scuffle which ended with her arm affectionately round the boy's neck. The ease of their contact surprised Christophe: there was a quality like innocence about them both, though of course you could not call it that. But it made him remember Blom's children, in Porto Alegre.

Christophe invited the girl to come and drink with him.

'Willingly.'

She led him to a bar near by. Though she must have learned from the boy that the Pole had no money, she was obviously glad of his company. He suspected, too, that speaking French gave her a certain status among the other women who came to the bar. Unlike them, however, Antonieta sat stiffly upright, her knees and feet together, her skirt pulled down. She looked charming and entirely presentable. There even seemed a sort of wit, a strong, perhaps unconscious, private joke, about the way she dressed and held herself.

She had learned French, she said, from a Belgian who had been representative of a shipping line. She never told Christophe his name: he remained always '*le Belge*'.

'My mother was the cook in his house. At the beginning I was only a child, but he was always watching me and joking with me. It started when I was thirteen and I lived with him five years. He was not always good to me – he suffered from *amoebas*, poor man, and had very bad humours – but he taught me many things. He was often sick, and I nursed him, changing the sheets, everything. In the end he had to return to Belgium, he was so sick. He left quite a lot of money for me, as a *dot*, but I did not get married and the lover of my mother, Seu Silvio, spent it all gambling.'

'Why didn't you get married? You are very pretty.'

'There was no one special. It is difficult, like this.' She scratched gently on the back of her left hand as if testing whether the darkness would come away under the nail. 'Besides, I cannot have children. When I was fourteen the Belgian gave me one but I was very ill and nearly died.' She smiled at him. 'Now I do not mind any more. I am twenty-one and still new. I have kept my figure.'

Compared with Antonieta, the people Christophe had met in Salvador, the English sailors, the tourist, Madame Daisy herself, became intangible, part of a nightmare that was over. He spent the rest of the afternoon talking to her and told her something of his past. He soon realised, however, that anything that happened outside this city had no reality for her. Yet their conversation was easy, for there was no need for them to pretend to one another. She pleased him more and more, and if he did not yet desire her, it was because the package still obsessed him. With his hand in his pocket he held it to him, his unadmitted vice. He knew that, sooner or later, he would confess its existence to Antonieta. Already he trusted her enough.

About five o'clock the boy came to fetch her. 'The Portuguese is waiting for you at the hotel.'

Antonieta was quite frank about her departure. 'He is rather old, this Portuguese, but he is good to me. He is a grocer and quite rich. You never know, perhaps he would like his portrait painted. I will ask him.'

On her way out, she stopped and looked down at Christophe: there was something else she had to declare. 'But the moment I find someone I love, I stop at once' – she banged the edge of her hand like a cutting blade on the table – 'like that. It is my character, you understand?'

This little blaze-up made her eyes glisten, her features grow taut, and yet it was still a comic passion, which seemed to mock at itself.

When he met her the following day, however, she was in deep melancholy, her face clouded by an African sullenness.

'*J'ai des ennuis avec la police.* But not what you think. I will tell you one day, perhaps.'

Christophe was annoyed at her troubles, because today he had meant to ask her help. In spite of her youth and humble station, she knew things about the city which, without her, he would take years to learn. Whereas he still saw only the narrow streets where coloured people shouted incomprehensible things, the churches like gold-encrusted grottoes and the gardens dark with aged and magnificent mango-trees and palms, Antonieta knew the city as a pattern created out of her struggle to live, a series of shelves down the rock with people scrambling on them, fighting for existence.

'Christophe, I have had enough of it, this life. If I had a room, I could work making clothes for people. But at my mother's there is always Seu Silvio; he doesn't do any work. Perhaps I will go back to Albertinho, it was he who taught me to sew when *le Belge* went away and Seu Silvio took my money. Did you know Albertinho was a friend of mine?'

'Who is this Albertinho?'

She was astonished. 'But he is famous! They know about him even in Rio, and there was an American woman who put him into a book.'

The hotel boy, who had joined them, said something which was obviously derogatory. Antonieta turned on him and they quarrelled violently, like two children. Then she said to Christophe: 'This one, also, walks in the street with paint on his face. He cannot speak against Albertinho.'

The boy smiled and was quiet, preening himself.

'Albertinho was good to me when no one else was,' Antonieta went on. 'He taught me to sew in many ways. Also, I was a *filha do santo* in his *terreiro*. He receives the *orixá* of Yansan. Yansan has been very good to me.'

Christophe realised that she was talking *candomblé*, which is voodoo, but the words meant nothing to him.

'You believe this?' he asked.

'Naturally. Everybody here believes in the old ones. Apart from that,

Albertinho is my friend. He knows everyone. If you are ever in trouble, if you need help, I just say that you are my friend and Albertinho will help us. He has great influence, here in Salvador. The politicians go to church but also they go to Albertinho for advice.'

The boy began talking to Antonieta again. For a time Christophe watched them with the detachment you can feel from those much younger than yourself, but then his own troubles surged up in front of him again. When the boy went away, Christophe did not come out of his silence.

'You are not there!' She was suddenly jealous, fearing she had lost his interest. 'You don't like me?' She smirked. 'I am wondering, perhaps you are not a man at all?'

He looked up at her, his face lined with hatred and strain.

It had been one of her professional gambits and she quickly repented of it. Across the table she placed her dark hand on his. 'Our fingers look like piano keys,' he thought.

He pulled his hand away roughly. 'Come with me.'

'To the hotel?'

He did not answer, but led her out of the bar. They climbed the narrow street and crossed the three squares to the elevator. They were in the middle of the upper city, at the edge of the cliff. Below lay the roofs of the lower city, the fish-market, the little port crowded with sail-boats, the streets, mean and squalid with sunlight, where Christophe had wandered two nights ago. Far off in the heat haze, arrivals from an exterior civilisation, stood the great aluminium drums of an oil refinery.

'*Chérie, je veux que vous m'aidiez.*'

'What is it?'

He told her.

He spoke very low, between flattened lips, although there was nothing but air surrounding them, and the nearest people were at the entrance to the elevator, thirty yards away. She listened to him with her whole soul, and at the end she wept a little.

'Why are you crying?'

'Three thousand dollars! It is impossible to think of so much money.'

'*Enfin*, you see I am in trouble.'

'You are in great trouble. Of course you cannot make love when you are like this.'

Although her taunt had forced him to tell her, it was the best thing he could have done. Now, moving closer to her, he felt himself for the first time alive in the body. But it was like the lust you feel when you are very tired, in a strange town, after a long train journey.

'I thought of throwing the package away.'

'You must be mad.'

'Well, what shall I do?'

'We will go and see Albertinho tomorrow. He will know.'

Christophe nodded; for the moment he was prepared to leave the matter in her hands. A true Slav, he believed that you could never dominate a situation or inhabit a country, unless you first had a woman in it taped. A new-found coloniser, he held her arm with a preliminary knowledge of possession.

Later, he told her about his adventures, about Blom, Lemberg and Madame Daisy. When he spoke of Lemberg, Antonieta said: 'I have seen his name in a newspaper, a day or two ago.'

They got a pile of newspapers from the boy at the hotel.

'Here it is.' She translated for him. The Public Prosecutor, in a statement to journalists, demanded Lemberg's deportation.

'It will be the same for me,' Christophe said. 'In my case, to the Russians.'

Her eyes shone at him in admiration for his importance. He smiled – how grateful he was that such things were completely strange territory to her!

Her fingers touched him experimentally. He put his arm round her and they helped each other up the stairs to his room.

Behind them, the boy crowed in triumph.

They rode to the end of the tramline and got down, under a white sky. The tram rounded the circular track, rang a bell and clanked away, as if happy that its expedition to the interior was over.

There were no houses, only a bar thatched with palm-leaves, where some men were drinking *aguardiente*. Everyone stared at Christophe, who was the only white man in sight, and at Antonieta walking quietly beside him, picking her way on pin-heeled shoes.

'Where are we going?'

'To his house. The *terreiro* is a long way away.'

He now saw that there were several entrances into the mass of vegetation that surrounded them. Electric light poles followed paths that bare feet had trodden, winding between clumps of thorn and castor-oil plant. Antonieta led the way, and small houses began to appear, half-hidden behind the foliage of banana trees. Walls of bamboo sticks shut in little patches of maize, but in front of each house there was always a bare patch, running with waste water and coated with the thin foul mud that is made by the feet of chickens.

When they came to Albertinho's house, dogs started barking. On the veranda, a girl working a sewing-machine gave a cry. Other women came running out. They all shouted to Antonieta and then, when they saw Christophe, fell silent.

'You stay here. I will go alone. It is a house of women, *filhas do santo*.'

She climbed the steps to the veranda. In a little while she was embracing them all, first a mud-coloured old woman with a tightly kerchiefed head, then half a dozen of the girls. A man came out and joined them. He stayed in the shadow and Christophe could not see his face. But he felt a curious lowering of spirit, derived from his own belief in mediums and fortune-tellers, and a memory, from his childhood in Poland, of the servants' stories of witches and ghosts.

Antonieta disappeared into the house.

The women on the verandah had stopped giggling and chattering and were watching Christophe. It seemed to him that there was a peculiar meaninglessness and lack of interest about their gaze: they were like a row of chickens when you turn a torch on them at night. Christophe paced up and down the bare patch of earth. The house and the land round it were in the shadow of a hill. The afternoon stood at a distance on either side, and here everything was in twilight. Bamboo clumps, pathways, the roof-ridge, where two buzzards were sitting, the while porcelain insulators on the wires, seemed to acquire a sort of luminosity: you got very conscious of the edges of things.

The door on to the verandah opened. Antonieta reappeared with Albertinho, who accompanied her down the steps.

He was wearing a shirt of shiny crimson sateen and white trousers, heavy rings and a bracelet. Albertinho was the 'horse of Yansan' and when in trance his body was ridden by the goddess of winds and storms, and he wore her long skirts and purple beads and received her sacrifice of goats. Apart from the tinge of African blood, he had a face, soft and creamy, from the Place Pigalle or Shaftesbury Avenue.

The meeting was not a success. The Pole was depressed by the atmosphere and impatient at having been kept waiting under the hen-like eyes of the women. The mulatto seemed coy and sulky, fearful of contempt or criticism. Antonieta separated them as quickly as possible.

'What happened?' Christophe asked, when they were out of earshot.

'He knows a man. This man came to him for a cure, but his wife will not let him come again. He is *granfino*, you see, this man, from an old white family, very rich. And because his wife despises *candomblé*, Albertinho cannot help him.'

Christophe recognised the usual excuses of the unsuccessful witch-doctor. 'How would a man like that come to believe in this?'

'Probably from his black nurse. Albertinho says he is now ill and without this stuff he is going mad. He will pay anything for it, if you can get it to him without his wife knowing.'

They were back at the tram terminus. Antonieta took off her shoes and wiped them carefully on the grass.

'You found out his address?'

'Yes, when we get back to the city I'll show you where it is. You must go there tonight and speak to his manservant. I will meet you afterwards at the hotel.'

But when Christophe came late that night to the Hotel Nova Iorque, he did not find Antonieta. By then, he was in despair.

It had all seemed too simple: Albertinho had given the address and Antonieta had told him how to reach the house. But by now, the city itself was working against him. The house, which was established with a sort of brutal dominance at the top of the city, was a standing insult to all who were defeated and came begging. The poor of Salvador are not allowed to forget other people's success.

All along the *avenida* Christophe felt the house waiting for him. Porters were on sentry duty at the gates, and police dogs were ready to growl at any passer-by who smelt furtive. Christophe had to hand his card to a Negro in khaki livery, like a member of a private army.

Christophe had asked to see the owner of the house and at the front door the major-domo received the request and acted without hesitation. He was shown into a high room furnished in the North American taste: low tables with playing-cards fossilised under glass in them; some enormous gilt madonnas, such as you still might find in the ruined churches of the interior of the state; on the walls, French pictures, Kisling, Van Dongen, Léger.

Christophe was standing between two doors: the rooms led from one to another in the traditional form of the Portuguese town house. And now he could hear someone approaching along the string of rooms. A woman's footsteps. 'The Senhora is coming now.' Christophe's heart sank. He knew already that it was not going to be any good.

'Madame.'

She was a mere child, of sixteen or seventeen. She was holding his card in her hand. '*Vous êtes vraiment un prince?*' she asked, in shrill convent French. 'How can I help you?'

She was wearing a shirt and tapered pants. Her eyes, which were slightly protruding, kept looking up and down him. But she was charming – she reminded him of a little frog, one of those pretty, throbbing tree-frogs that have almost the delicacy of insects.

'Forgive me, madame. There has been a mistake. It was with monsieur your husband——'

'My husband is ill again. Please speak to me.' She sounded almost as though she were pleading for his company and conversation.

'It is a matter of private business.'

'Please tell me.' She moved towards him, blinking her eyes: she had lived alone and had become uncertain of her effect on other people. As well as guessing her loneliness, Christophe noticed that she was not greatly concerned about her husband. Perhaps, when it had been arranged for her to marry, she had been told 'he will be ill' and had accepted it as a permanent factor in her life.

She settled on the arm of a chair, frowning and swinging her foot, and went on: 'I know all about it, you see. My husband has had this trouble a long time, and first there was the German who came here, and later my husband went to a *pai do santo* – you know what that is, the voodoo? – but the priest told me that I mustn't let him go there any more. Then this doctor came from Rio, with the new treatment, and no one may speak to him, not even me. He has nurses, everything.'

Christophe said nothing, and suddenly she asked him: 'You come from this German?'

It must have been Lemberg. 'No, Madame.'

'You don't?' She frowned again, nervous that she had made a mistake. He saw that she was trembling violently: she was desperately frightened, not of himself, but of everything her life had brought her.

'I have changed my mind about this. I would do anything to make him happy again.'

Christophe was a Pole, a refugee from East Europe. He had to survive. He was a makeweight in the balance of the world: that part of the human race which had never suffered enough, the rich and the untouched, was prey for his exploitation. But not, he decided, this girl. If she had been older, he might have sold his package and survived. But they were not the right people for the situation, he, penniless in his last suit, and she only a child, a little girl with a fat bottom, who couldn't have been married more than a few months. The butler was there the whole time, because her husband could not allow her a minute alone with a strange man.

'No, madame. The situation is different from what I had expected.'

'You won't help me?' She was suddenly angry. 'I could call the Police, you know. That German was arrested – I saw his picture in the paper!'

Christophe bowed, and drew himself to his full height. It was still an imposing front, and below him on the chair she quailed a little. 'I wish your husband every success in his cure.'

The major-domo accompanied him as far as the gate. The moment Christophe was outside the dogs were released again, and their breath roared out, like a gas burner, a few inches behind his calves.

By now the thick darkness had settled down, buzzing with crickets and gassy with rotting vegetation. There were fireflies in the gardens along the street. From the echoing distances of the city, faint shouts came from those who were still involved with the world.

When Christophe came in sight of the sea, he knew he was approaching the centre of the upper city. Then the shouting turned into the sirens of police cars: the sound was muffled, blocked off by houses, and returned again, swooping up the funnels of the narrow streets.

He was cold with shock, the package bouncing against his thigh. The little frog-girl had betrayed him, of course. What else could she do alone there but try to hurt? What other mark could she make on anyone's existence? But he took the blow all over him, shivering and coughing. After this, there came a minute or two when he could think quite calmly. He walked up the steps of a church. He would stay here, and later, at the hotel, he would find Antonieta, and she would have somewhere to hide the package until the opportunity to sell it arose again.

When he sat down in the church his mind was quite empty. The emotions aroused by danger soon faded away. He was getting old, and there were pains and sorenesses in various parts of his body. The night before he had not slept enough after making love, and as he sat in the half-darkness of the church he felt his body groaning and settling down like furniture in a house at the end of a hot day.

While he waited, the church gradually manifested itself around him, the gold carving against the shell-white stone. There was a smell of tallow and incense and dirt. Many years had passed since he had sat long in a church, and it all meant very little to him. When he had been cornered, as he was now, he had always looked for a woman and always found one. It was the thing he did, the way he took out of circumstances.

The streets had grown silent outside and Christophe was bored. A bell struck nine overhead. It must have been the eve of some Saint's day, because candles were being lit and whispering and shuffling drew nearer and nearer to him. He tried to shut out the sounds. But when they were close behind him he turned round. He almost cried out: it was a violent shock, of awe and dread.

The whole church was filled with people, row on row of dark and white faces in the candlelight. It was as though they had pursued him as far as the shrine. But they meant no harm to anyone. It was his recurrent experience in Salvador: he had looked for evil, had needed it, but each time he had met innocence.

He felt his skin contract, his eyes prickle with tears. For the first time he himself was part of the patient despair of the city, and now there seemed to be no point in trying to escape from it, in being the one man in search of a better fate. The hopes that had been wrecked for Poland and himself had never even been born here. Antonieta too would become one of these work-worn crones, scrabbling and muttering after God. And if he failed, wasn't it honourable to fail in such circumstances? For Christophe, twenty years separated from his country and his class, there was certainly no honour in anything else.

He left the church reconciled to his idea of his fate, which was that God will beat us down until we beg for His mercy. Civil Guards, like the angels of punishment, were still standing on street corners, but they were not stopping anyone.

'Where is Antonieta?'

The boy, who had been asleep in his chair behind the hotel door, awoke with scared eyes; he looked very small in the half-darkness.

'She is not here. She is not coming tonight.'

Suspicion hung between them, and the boy twisted guiltily in his chair. Christophe took his key and went upstairs.

He threw the package on the bed, hating it. Then, with his head in his hands, he knelt and prayed. Afterwards he moved aimlessly about the room for a few minutes, breathing deeply, like a swimmer who has taken longer than he believed possible to reach dry land.

On the window-sill Antonieta had left a bottle of cane-spirit mixed with sugar and the juice of green lemons. She had prepared this for him with great pride. Now he poured a little into a tumbler and drank it: it was like some mixture that you use to trap insects. He took another gulp and felt better. He finished the bottle.

The next moment, he was awake in the hot sunlight with the flies buzzing over him. The sun was high in the air, small and concentrated, as though a magnifying glass was directing its heat on the house. The boy had forgotten to wake him.

Christophe found him downstairs. 'Antonieta?' he asked.

But it still wasn't any good. The boy looked away, sulking. His eyes were puffy, his face a drab colour and he had been plucking his eyebrows. 'She will come back,' he said.

'When?'

'I don't know.'

The boy disappeared into a room behind, where his mother was lying, and closed the door. Christophe heard whispering.

The boy came out, rubbing his fingers together. 'Money,' he said. 'For the room.'

'Tonight.'

The boy turned away in apparent disgust, and Christophe felt the angry humiliation the middle-aged feel when the young can dismiss them easily.

Out in the street, he began to be racked by jealousy. He was conscious of the loss of Antonieta as though each cell of his body was shrieking for her. He had never felt like this before, and believed it to be a by-product of his advancing age. This morning he knew that he had outlived his prime, and that Antonieta had abandoned him: the boy knew this, but had been told to tell him nothing. Perhaps the boy and Antonieta were in collusion to rob him.

It was another blinding, dusty day. Wherever he went he could not help looking for her face. In the Rua Chile, which is the chief street of Salvador, there are hotels with big windows, where respectable business men sit in white shark-skin suits, reading the newspapers and watching the women. Here she must often have passed, raising the plaudits of eyes: Antonieta was *mulata escura*, one of the dark ones who are the most desired.

At times it became impossible to believe that he would not find her round the next corner, or that, among the incomprehensible voices of the roadway, her voice was not calling his name. But after his heart had leapt with hope half a dozen times, he gave up the effort of concentration. He walked on.

He knew by now he was *cornudo, cocu*. His body began hurting again and he could not trust it with his feelings. He deliberately went away from the part of the city where he was most likely to find her, and spent the middle of the day, the hours of skull-cracking heat, sitting in a square full of carob-trees, not far from the big house he had visited the previous evening. The idea that the Civil Guards might be on the look out for him did not trouble him any more. The bit of his mind that reacted to danger was numb. He had even left the package in his valise at the hotel. It had become unimportant.

There were very few places in Salvador where you could sit down without spending money. Christophe realised that he was treating the city as an old man must do: an old man does not wander aimlessly, but with the knowledge that, before a certain time, he must reach a fountain with a tap of drinking water, a place to urinate, a bench to sit down on out of the sun. But even here, Christophe thought, the old men had a shelter they could return to by nightfall, where they were expected, though grudgingly and on sufferance.

Heat poured down out of the sky. The parakeets stopped screeching in the branches overhead and everything was held in the grip of noon. And then, at last, the shadows began to stretch. Bells rang. A flock of children in regulation orphanage uniforms were shepherded through the square by a couple of nuns. The whole line sparkled with noise, and Christophe saw the children cling to each other, rubbing their chins on each other's shoulders. Did they too foresee a future of loss? But compared with himself, even the most despised here were not alone; their consciousness was a part of the consciousness of the whole city, a part of it like the churches and the trees. Into this consciousness for him there was only one way, through women, through Antonieta, lost.

When the boy of the hotel came hurrying towards him, Christophe was still marching erect, his coat buttoned, his tie a tight knot, his face shaded by his Panama hat. Only the crumpled shirt collar, the thick dust on his shoes, could give anyone an idea that he wasn't still dominating his circumstances. But he was painfully stiff from his afternoon on the bench and his throat was sore with draughts of water from the public fountain. He knew that to quell the pangs of hunger he'd have to buy more cheap cigarettes, even though they fouled his mouth up and made him gape.

The boy sidled up to him and now his voice was soft and coaxing. He said the words twice before Christophe understood. 'You may stay in the room until Antonieta comes. My mother agrees.'

'And Antonieta?'

But again the boy shook his head. He walked back to the hotel beside Christophe, looking up at him and smiling, and greeting from time to time the women who already paraded the street. None of these tried to attract Christophe's attention. Before, he had imagined that the boy had told them he had no money, but now he wondered if he was considered to be Antonieta's property, and if she was expected back. Christophe tried to question the boy about this, but could not make him understand.

The boy gave Christophe his key and signed to him to go upstairs. A few minutes later he banged on the door, carrying a big sandwich of bread and meat. Christophe thanked him. 'You're a good boy,' he said.

But, next morning, there was still no news of Antonieta. Christophe closed the shutters against the torrent of sun, and wondered if he could survive another day.

He took the package out of his valise. Usually he returned to it with boredom, as one returns on a long train journey to a newspaper already leafed through four or five times. But today, for the first time, he saw it with an ordinary curiosity. The desolation of sexual jealousy that he had passed through had killed off the rest of his hopes. He had stopped telling himself that the package represented a place to live, the setting up of a studio with himself as the society portrait painter, complete with smock, Rembrandt hat and mahlstick. He did not think of his own survival with any interest at all.

Christophe cut away the brown paper and revealed a screw-topped bottle. The powder was shifting about inside. He had heard that people like Lemberg would divide it into small envelopes, possibly adulterating it with something else, and sell them one by one. Christophe was no longer interested; until he had freed himself of this thing, he was neither alive nor dead but suspended in anxiety.

Carefully, he unscrewed the bottle and took a very small amount, like a pinch of snuff. The world was suddenly silent.

He knew it would be some time before he felt anything, but he did not want the experience or illumination, or whatever it was, to happen here, on an iron bedstead behind the shutters of a dissolute hotel. He still possessed at least his sense of ceremony. He pushed the bottle into his pocket and hurried downstairs into the street.

Christophe clambered on to the first tram he saw and handed the conductor a small brown coin. Through the open sides of the tram he watched the whirling faces of the crowd fall back; he was leaving them on permanent holiday, his search was abandoned and his ambition forgotten.

The tram passed the big house, tree-hidden, of the rich girl. It stopped at the square where Christophe had endured the previous afternoon, then, rattling downhill, it gathered speed and he saw that it was going right out of the city. They were in the suburb of Rio Vermelho. Small houses alternated with patches of castor-oil plant or bamboo, and once the tram crossed a muddy creek fringed with brilliant-green grass, where washer-women were toiling over bundles of greyish clothing. The conductor came round on the outside of the tram, hand over hand like a tree-sloth, and collected another coin, and then, with its bells ringing, the tram lurched out on to the sea-coast at the Barra.

Here the road goes along a curved shore, until it reaches a headland crowned with a ruined Portuguese Colonial fortress. In the shelter of a rock, Christophe opened the bottle again and sniffed some more of the powder.

Cars approached him along the coast road and he knew for certain that his hand had only to go out, the wide palm smacking lightly on the windscreen, and they would stop. But later, there were no more cars. He returned to the shore, to an endless bed of sand, golden and softer than feathers, where, towards dusk, he slept.

The visions of the afternoon had been of extraordinary intensity, but when he woke it was with the usual sort of hangover. His body was back with him again, and he had fallen asleep on top of the bottle, which was pressed uncomfortably into his belly. While he was asleep the moon had risen; it stood, as if on a pillar of its own light, just above the rim of the sea.

Christophe took his life in his hands and looked at it. The long decline of his fortunes was over. His name would survive – his brother in England had a child – but Christophe himself had abdicated. He guessed that he would die quite soon and in misery but, as a concession to remembered beliefs, he wanted to be free to be chosen by death. Still, therefore, he had to get rid of the bottle.

The sea is untrustworthy: sooner or later its tides bring everything back. He crossed the road and looked at the low jungle stretching out ahead of him. Into it, as far as he could, he threw the bottle. He only imagined that he heard the noise of its fall among roots and swamp-water, three thousand dollars going into the eternal mud.

Then he slid back on to the shore and slept.

He fell asleep on some dry sand under the rocks, and when he awoke the sun was high in the sky. He had slept through the night and a large part of the day. At some time or other he had kicked off his shoes, and now, when he moved, he realised that his feet and his calves were horribly burnt: they had been in and out of the sun during the day. He had to throw away his socks because, if he wore them, his feet would no longer fit into the shoes. His mouth was seared dry and his head bursting with pain.

Christophe got off the tram and stumbled across the square by the cathedral. Nobody looked at him now. He had been brought up to believe that if you get dirty and drunk everyone will stare at you, but now he discovered this is the time when nobody does.

Near the hotel, he went into a bar to kill his thirst. Even here, where he was already well known, no one seemed to see him: it was as though at some time during the past twenty-four hours at the Barra he had become invisible. He crossed the street to the hotel. In his mind the small bedroom had become a well, a coffin, into which he had to throw and obliterate himself.

At the entrance, he almost fainted. His hand scrabbled wildly for the key on the hook. The boy heard him and came hurrying out of the back room.

'She is back! She is here!'

But when he looked at Christophe's white-stubbled face, his fatally-injured eyes, the boy retreated, respectful at the ruin which had overtaken his friend. He gave up any attempt at getting through to him. He pushed the key into Christophe's hand and then he ran out to fetch Antonieta.

Lying on the bed, Christophe became aware of someone moving near him, and then of the small, sub-verbal noises which must be the earliest things a man hears: the noises, not of disgust or horror but more of formal disapproval, which a woman makes in the presence of a physical disaster she knows she can cope with. He heard the little chimes of water in a tin basin, his forehead was sponged and his feet cooled almost miraculously with a soft cream. He was conscious too, without daring to observe it, of her sympathy all around him. He delivered himself to it and feared it might end if he once opened his eyes.

He was right.

'Christophe, I have looked for you all last night. Listen, please try to listen. I have found a man, a friend of mine – well, no friend – but I told him about this stuff you had and he is very interested. He will take it and sell it abroad and there will be no danger. Christophe, are you listening?'

He let her take his hand.

'Please speak to me.'

'It is no good.' His voice came dry and he coughed. 'I've thrown it away.'

He felt the emotion rushing through her body. 'Tell me where. We can get it back.'

'No, no.' Christophe felt cross at the idea. 'I threw it into a wild place and even I do not know where it is now. Having it was killing me.'

There was a silence. By now, the lights were on in the street outside and they shone pink through his closed eyelids.

He was the first to speak: 'Antonieta, where had you gone? Where had you gone?'

While he was waiting for her to answer, there was a knock at the door, and the boy came in with a plate of rice and black beans. He stayed talking to Antonieta. In the reddish twilight of the room Christophe watched them with half-open eyes, very conscious of their youth, the firmness of rounded limbs: the boy had the paler skin but the short cat-head of the Negro, and Antonieta's stillness now seemed a minor miracle, the gift of a peculiar grace.

When the boy had gone, Christophe said: 'He has been good to me.'

'He loves you too.'

She watched him eat the rice, stained with the dark gravy of the beans. She did not refer again to the loss of the package; it was one of those upheavals that shake life to its depths, then pass. Hers was the point of view of poverty: one is more likely to stay the same than to change, and one's life is too.

'He says we can keep this room and I will look after you. I still have some money the Portuguese gave me, before I met you. Later, when you are better, I can get work.'

He put the plate to one side, half-finished. She was helping him devotedly, without hesitation, and he did not want to damage this by asking questions.

Then, without him having to ask, she began to answer him. 'Poor boy, he knew where I was but he was too frightened to tell you.'

'Will you tell me?'

'Of course. I think you can understand. It is just that sometimes the police take all the girls they can find. It happened that night after we went to Albertinho.

You must have heard the sirens and the girls screaming. They always scream, because they want everyone to know what is going on.'

Ashamed, Christophe thought of his fear after leaving the big house, his hours of sanctuary in the crowded church – in flight from a terror that was not for him.

'The police have nothing against me. But there is one of them, a sergeant, who knows me. He used to play cards with Seu Silvio, my stepfather. He has been after me a long time, I think that is why I was arrested.'

Christophe flinched. The knowledge of suffering can make you close your eyes involuntarily, like too strong a light.

'They got what they wanted, he and his friends, there in the police station.'

'I understand.'

He had the truth now. He bit hard against it, as one tries to murder an aching tooth. When the truth came, it was always as bad as you could stand, far worse than you had expected, and so you could never really prepare yourself for it. And there was really no one to blame: Seu Silvio's friend had merely waited his opportunity; the poor girl had learned not to expect anything else from life. The horror, Christophe knew, was mostly in his own imagination.

He was grateful to Antonieta and she seemed fond of him. But in spite of the warm night, he felt cold. Later, he would open his eyes again, raise his hand and pat her with a comforting gesture. For the moment he could not bring himself to move.

Then he heard a sound and looked up astonished.

Antonieta was weeping as though she would die. He pulled her down and held her to him, his hands and head doing all they could to convince her of love.

DORIS LESSING

# Mrs Fortescue

THAT autumn he became conscious all at once of a lot of things he had never thought about before.

Himself, for a start. . . .

His parents . . . whom he found he disliked, because they told lies. He discovered this when he tried to communicate to them something of his new state of mind and they pretended not to know what he meant.

His sister who, far from being his friend and ally, 'like two peas in a pod' – as people had been saying for years – seemed positively to hate him.

And Mrs Fortescue.

Jane, seventeen, had left school and went out every night. Fred, sixteen, loutish schoolboy, lay in bed and listened for her to come home, kept company by her imaginary twin self, invented by him at the end of summer. The tenderness of this lovely girl redeemed him from the shame, the squalor, the misery of his loneliness. Meanwhile, the parents ignorantly slept, not caring about the frightful battles their son was fighting with himself not six yards off. Sometimes Jane came home first; sometimes Mrs Fortescue. Fred listened to her going up over his head, and thought how strange he had never thought about her before, knew nothing about her.

The family lived in a small flat over the liquor shop that Mr and Mrs Danderlea had been managing for Sanko and Duke for twenty years. Above the shop, from where rose, day and night, a sickly, inescapable reek of beer and spirits, were the kitchen and the lounge. This layer of the house (it had been one once) was felt as an insulating barrier against the smell, but it reached up into the bedrooms above. Two bedrooms – the mother and father in one; while for years brother and sister had shared a room, until recently Mr Danderlea had put up a partition making two tiny boxes, giving at least the illusion of privacy for the boy and the girl.

On the top floor, the two rooms were occupied by Mrs Fortescue, and had been since before the Danderleas came. Ever since the boy could remember, grumbling went on that Mrs Fortescue had the part of the house where the liquor smell did not reach; though she, if remarks to this effect came to her, claimed that on hot nights she could not sleep for the smell. But on the whole relations were good. The Danderleas' energies were claimed by buying and selling liquor, while Mrs Fortescue went out a lot. Sometimes another old woman came to visit her, and an old man, small, shrunken and polite, came to see her most evenings, very late indeed, often after twelve.

Mrs Fortescue seldom went out during the day, but left every evening at about

six, wearing furs: a pale, shaggy coat in winter, and in summer a stole over a
costume. She always had a small hat on, with a veil that was drawn tight over her
face and held with a bunch of flowers where the fur began. The furs changed
often: Fred remembered half a dozen blonde fur coats, and a good many little
animals biting their tails or dangling bright bead eyes and empty paws. From
behind the veil, the dark made-up eyes of Mrs Fortescue had glimmered at him
for years; and her small, old, reddened mouth had smiled.

One evening he postponed his homework, and slipped out past the shop where
his parents were both at work, and took a short walk that led him to Oxford
Street. The exulting, fearful loneliness that surged through his blood with every
heartbeat, making every stamp of shadow a reminder of death, each gleam of
light a promise of his extraordinary future, drove him around and around the
streets, muttering to himself, bringing tears to his eyes, or to his lips snatches of
song which he had to suppress. For, while he knew himself to be crazy, and
supposed he must have been all his life (he could no longer remember himself
before this autumn), this was a secret he intended to keep for himself and the
tender creature who shared the stuffy box he spent his nights in. Turning a corner
probably (he would not have been able to say) already turned several times
before that evening, he saw a woman walking ahead of him in a great fur coat
that shone under the street lights, a small veiled hat, and with tiny sharp feet that
took tripping steps towards Soho. Recognising Mrs Fortescue, a friend, he ran
forward to greet her, relieved that this frightening trap of streets was to be shared.
Seeing him, she first gave him a smile never offered him before by a woman; then
looked prim and annoyed; then nodded at him briskly and said as she always did:
'Well, Fred, and how are things with you?' He walked a few steps with her, said
he had to do his homework, heard her old woman's voice say: 'That's right, son,
you must work, your mum and dad are right, a bright boy like you, it would be a
shame to let it go to waste,' – and watched her move on, across Oxford Street,
into the narrow streets beyond.

He turned and saw Bill Bates coming toward him from the hardware shop, just
closing. Bill was grinning, and he said: 'What, wouldn't she have you then?'

'It's Mrs Fortescue,' said Fred, entering a new world between one breath and
the next, just because of the tone of Bill's voice.

'She's not a bad old tart,' said Bill. 'Bet she wasn't pleased to see you when
she's on the job.'

'Oh, I don't know,' said Fred, trying out a new man-of-the-world voice for the
first time, 'she lives over us, doesn't she?' (Bill must know this, everyone must
know it, he thought, feeling sick.) 'I was just saying hullo, that's all.' It came off,
he saw, for now Bill nodded and said: 'I'm off to the pictures, want to come?'

'Got to do homework,' said Fred, bitter.

'Then you've got to do it then, haven't you,' said Bill reasonably, going on his
way.

Fred went home in a seethe of shame. How could his parents share their house with an old tart (whore, prostitute – but these were the only words he knew), how could they treat her like an ordinary decent person, even better (he understood, listening to them in his mind's ear, that their voices to her held something not far from respect), how could they put up with it? Justice insisted that they had not chosen her as a tenant, she was the company's tenant, but at least they should have told Sanko and Duke so that she could be evicted and . . .

Although it seemed as if his adventure through the streets had been as long as a night, he found when he got in that it wasn't yet eight, and his mother said no more than that he shouldn't forget his homework.

He went up to his box and set out his school-books. Through the ceiling-board he could hear his sister moving. There being no door between the rooms, he went out to the landing, through his parents' room (his sister had to creep past the sleeping pair when she came in late) and into hers. She stood in a black slip before the glass, making up her face. 'Do you mind?' she said daintily. 'Can't you knock?' He muttered something and felt a smile come on his face, aggressive and aggrieved, that seemed to switch on automatically these days if he even saw his sister at a distance. He sat on the edge of her bed. 'Do you *mind?*' she said again, moving away from him some black underwear. She slipped over her still puppy-fatted white shoulders a new dressing-gown in cherry-red and buttoned it up primly before continuing to work lipstick on to her mouth.

'Where are you going?'

'To the pictures, if you've got no objection,' she chipped out, in this new, jaunty voice that she had acquired when she left school, and which, he knew, she used as a weapon against all men. *But why against him?* He sat, feeling the ugly grin apparently painted on his face, for he couldn't remove it, and he looked at the pretty girl with her new hair-do, putting thick black rings around her eyes, and he thought of how they had been two peas in a pod. *In the summer* . . . yes, that is how it seemed to him now, through a year's long summer of visits to friends, the park, the zoo, the pictures, they had been friends, allies, then the dark came down suddenly and in the dark had been born this cool, flip girl who hated him.

'Who are you going with?'

'Jem Taylor, if you don't have any objection,' she said.

'Why should I have any objection? I just asked.'

'What you don't know won't hurt you,' she said, very pleased with herself because of her ease in this way of talking. He recognised his recent achievement in the exchange with Bill as the same step forward as she was making, with this tone, or style; and, out of a quite uncustomary feeling of equality with her, asked: 'How is old Jem? I haven't seen him for ages.'

'Oh Fred, I'm *late.*' This bad temper meant she had finished her face and wanted to put on her dress, which she would not do in front of him.

Silly cow, he thought, grinning and thinking of her alter ego, the girl of his nights, does she think I don't know what she looks like in a slip, or even less?

Because of what went on behind the partition, in the dark, he banged his fist on it, laughing, and she whipped about and said: 'Oh Fred, you drive me crazy, you really do.' This being something from their brother-and-sister-past, admitting intimacy, even the possibility of real equality, she checked herself, put on a sweet contained smile, and said: 'If you don't *mind*, Fred, I want to get dressed.'

He went out, remembering only as he got through the parents' room and saw his mother's feathered mules by the bed, that he had wanted to talk about Mrs Fortescue. He realised his absurdity, because of course his sister would pretend she didn't understand what he meant . . . his fixed smile of shame changed into one of savagery as he thought: Well, Jem, you're not going to get anything out of her but *do you mind* and *have you any objection* and *please yourself*, I know that much about my sweet sister . . . In his room he could not work, even after his sister had left, slamming three doors and making so much racket with her heels that the parents shouted at her from the shop. He was thinking of Mrs Fortescue. But she was old. She had always been old, as long as he could remember. And the old women who came up to see her in the afternoons, were they whores (tarts, prostitutes, *bad women*) too? And where did she, they, do it? And who was the nasty, smelly old man who came so late nearly every night?

He sat with the waves of liquor smell from the ground floor rising past him, thinking of the sourish smell of the old man, and of the scented smell of the old woman, feeling short-breathed because of the stuffy reek of this room and associating it (because of certain memories from his nights) with the reek from Mrs Fortescue's room which he could positively smell from where he sat, so strongly did he create it.

Bill must be wrong: she couldn't possibly be on the game still, who would want an old thing like that?

The family had a meal every night when the shop closed. It was usually about ten-thirty when they sat down. Tonight there was some boiled bacon, and baked beans. Fred brought out casually: 'I saw Mrs Fortescue going off to work when I came out.' He waited the results of this cheek, this effrontery, watching his parents' faces. They did not even exchange glances. His mother pushed tinted bronze hair back with a hand that had a stain of grease on it, and said: 'Poor old girl, I expect she's pleased about the Act, when you get down to it, in the winter it must have been bad sometimes.' The words, *the Act* hit Fred's outraged sense of propriety anew; he had to work them out; thinking that his parents did not even apologise for the years of corruption. Now his father said (his face inflamed, he must have been taking nips often from the glass under the counter), 'Once or twice, when I saw her on Frith Street before the Act I felt sorry for her. But I suppose she got used to it.'

'It must be nicer this way,' said Mrs Danderlea, pushing the crusting remains of the baked beans towards her husband.

He scooped them out of the dish with the edge of his fried bread, and she said: 'What's wrong with the spoon?'

'What's wrong with the bread?' he returned, with an unconvincing whisky glare, which she ignored.

'Where's her place, then?' asked Fred, casual, having worked out that she must have one.

'Over that new club in Panton Street. The rent's gone up again, so Mr Spencer told me, and there's the telephone she needs now, well I don't know how much you can believe of what *he* says, but he's said often enough that without him helping her out she'd do better at almost anything else.'

'Not a word he says,' said Mr Danderlea, pushing out his big whisky stomach as he sat back, replete. 'He told me he was doorman for the Greystock Hotel in Knightsbridge, well it turns out all this time he's been doorman for that strip-tease joint along the street from her new place, and that's where he's been for years, because it was a night-club before it was strip-tease.'

'Well there's no point in that, is there?' said Mrs Danderlea, pouring second cups. 'I mean, why tell fibs about it, I mean everyone knows, don't they?'

Fred again pushed down protest: that yes, Mr Spencer (Mrs Fortescue's 'regular', but he had never understood what they had meant by the ugly word before) was right to lie; he wished his parents would lie even now; anything rather than this casual back-and-forth chat about this horror, years-old, and right over their heads, part of their lives, inescapable.

He ducked down his face and shovelled beans into it fast, knowing it was scarlet, and wanting a reason for it.

'You'll get heart-burn, gobbling like that,' said his mother, as he had expected.

'I've got to finish my homework,' he said, and bolting, shaking his head at the cup of tea she was pushing over at him.

He sat in his room until his parents went to bed, marking off the routine of the house from his new knowledge. After an expected interval Mrs Fortescue came in, he could hear her moving about, taking her time about everything. Water ran, for a long time. He now understood that this sound, water running into and then out of a basin, was something he had heard at this hour all his life. He sat listening with the ashamed, fixed grin on his face. Then his sister came in; he could hear her sharp sigh of relief as she flumped on the bed and bent over to take off her shoes. He nearly called out 'Good-night, Jane', but thought better of it. Yet all through the summer they had whispered and giggled through the partition.

Mr Spencer, her regular, came up the stairs. He heard their voices together; listened to them as he undressed and went to bed; as he lay wakeful; as he at last went off to sleep, feeling savage with loneliness.

Next evening he waited until Mrs Fortescue went out, and followed her, careful she didn't see him. She walked fast and efficiently, like a woman on her way to the office, not looking at people. Why then the fur coat, the veil, the make-up? Of course, it was habit, because of all the years on the pavement; for it was a sure thing she didn't wear that outfit to receive customers in her place. But it turned out that he was wrong. Along the last hundred yards before her door, she slowed her pace, took a couple of quick glances left and right for the police, then looked at a large elderly man coming towards her. This man swung around, joined her, and they went side by side into her doorway, the whole operation so quick, so smooth, that even if there had been a policeman all he could have seen was a woman meeting someone she had expected to meet.

Fred then went home. Jane was dressing for the evening. He followed her too. She walked fast, not looking at people, her smart new coat flaring jade, emerald, dark green, as she moved through varying depths of light, her black puffy hair gleaming. She went into the underground. He followed her down the escalators, and on to the platform, at not much more than arm's distance, but quite safe because of her self-absorption. She stood on the edge of the platform, staring across the rails at a big advertisement. It was a very large dark-brown gleaming revolver holster, with a revolver in it, attached to a belt for bullets; but instead of bullets each loop had a lipstick, in all the pink-orange-scarlet-crimson shades it was possible to imagine lipstick in. Fred stood just behind his sister, and examined her sharp little face examining the advertisement and choosing which lipstick she would buy. She smiled – nothing like the appealing shame-faced smile that was stuck, for ever it seemed, on Fred's face, but a calm, triumphant smile. The train came streaming in, obscuring the advertisement. The doors slid open, receiving his sister, who did not look around. He stood close against the window, looking at her calm little face, willing her to look at him. But the train rushed her off again, and she would never know he had been there.

He went home, the ferment of his craziness breaking through his lips in an incredulous raw mutter: a revolver, a bloody revolver . . . his parents were at supper, taking in food, swilling in tea, like pigs, pigs, pigs, he thought, shovelling down his own supper to be rid of it. Then he said: 'I left a book in the shop, Dad, I want to get it,' and went down dark stairs through the sickly rising fumes. In a drawer under the till was a revolver which had been there for years, against the day when burglars broke in and Mr (or Mrs) Danderlea frightened them off with it. Many of Fred's dreams had been spun around that weapon. But it was broken somewhere in its black-gleaming interior. He carefully hid it under his sweater, and went up, to knock on his parents' door. They were already in bed, a large double bed at which, because of this hideous world he was now a citizen of, he was afraid to look. Two old people, with sagging faces and bulging mottled fleshy shoulders lay side by side, looking at him. 'I want to leave something for Jane,' he said, turning his gaze away from them. He laid the revolver on Jane's pillow, arranging half a dozen lipsticks of various colours as if they were bullets coming out of it. His parents' bedroom was in darkness. His father was snoring and his mother did not answer his good-night.

He went back to the shop. Under the counter stood the bottle of Black and White beside the glass stained sour with his father's tippling. He made sure the bottle was still half-full before turning the lights out and settling down to wait. Not for long. When he heard the key in the lock he set the door open wide so Mrs Fortescue must see him.

'Why, Fred, whatever are you doing?'

'I noticed Dad left the light on, so I came down.' Frowning with efficiency, he looked for a place to put the whisky bottle, while he rinsed the dirtied glass. Then casual, struck by a thought, he offered: 'Like a drink, Mrs Fortescue?' In the dim light she focussed, with difficulty, on the bottle. 'I never touch the stuff, dear. . . .' Bending his face down past hers, to adjust a wine bottle, he caught the liquor on her breath, and understood the vagueness of her good nature.

'Well all right, dear,' she went on, 'just a little one to keep you company. You're like your Dad, you know that?'

'Is that so?' He came out of the shop with the bottle under his arm, shutting the door behind him and locking it. The stairs glimmered dark. 'Many's the time he's offered me a nip on a cold night, though not when your mother could see.' She added a short triumphant titter, resting her weight on the stair-rail as if testing it.

'Let's go up,' he said insinuatingly, knowing he would get his way, because it had been so easy this far. He was shocked it was so easy. She should have said: 'What are you doing out of bed at this time?' Or: 'A boy of your age, drinking, what next!'

She obediently went up ahead of him, pulling herself up.

The small room she went into, vaguely smiling her invitation he should follow, was crammed with furniture and objects, all of which had the same soft glossiness of her clothes, which she now went to the next room to remove. He sat on an oyster-coloured satin sofa, looked at bluish brocade curtains, a cabinet full of china figures, thick, creamy rugs, pink cushions, pink-tinted walls. A table in a corner held photographs. Of her, so he understood, progressing logically back from those he could recognise to those that were inconceivable. The earliest was of a girl with yellow collar-bone-length curls, on which perched a top-hat. She wore a spangled bodice, in pink; pink satin pants, long black lace stockings, white gloves, and was roguishly pointing a walking-stick at the audience – at him, Fred. 'Like a bloody gun,' he thought, feeling the shameful derisive grin come on to his face. He heard the door shut behind him, but did not turn, wondering what he would see: he never had seen her, he realised, without hat, veil, furs. She said, pottering about behind his shoulder: 'Yes, that's me when I was a Gaiety Girl, a nice outfit, wasn't it?'

'Gaiety Girl?' he said, protesting, and she admitted: 'Well that was before your time, wasn't it?'

The monstrousness of this second *wasn't it*, made it easy for him to turn and look: she was bending over a cupboard, her back to him. It was a back whose shape was concealed by thick, soft, cherry-red, with a tufted pattern of whirls and waves. She stood up and faced him, displaying, without a trace of consciousness at the horror of the fact, his sister's dressing-gown. She carried glasses and a jug of water to the central table that was planted in a deep pink rug, and said: 'I hope you don't mind my getting into something comfortable, but we aren't strangers.' She sat opposite, having pushed the glasses towards him, as a reminder that the bottle was still in his hand. He poured the yellow, smelling liquid, watching her face to see when he must stop. But her face showed nothing, so he filled her tumbler half-full. 'Just a splash, dear . . .' He splashed, and she lifted the glass and held it, in the vague tired way that went with her face, which, now that for the first time in his life he could look at it, was an old, shrunken face, with small black eyes deep in their sockets, and a small mouth pouting out of a tired mesh of lines. This old, rather kind face, at which he tried not to stare, was like a mask held between the cherry-red gown over a body whose shape was slim and young; and the hair, beautifully tinted a tactful silvery-blonde and waving softly into the hollows of an ancient neck.

'My sister's got a dressing-gown like that.'

'It's pretty isn't? They've got them in at Richard's, down the street, I expect she got hers there too, did she?'

'I don't know.'

'Well the proof of the pudding's in the eating, isn't it?'

At this remark, which reminded him of nothing so much as his parent's idiotic pattering exchange at supper-time, when they were torpid before sleep, he felt the ridiculous smile leave his face. He was full of anger, but no longer of shame.

'Give me a cigarette, dear,' she went on, 'I'm too tired to get up.'

'I don't smoke.'

'If you could reach me my handbag.'

He handed her a large crocodile bag, that she had left by the photographs. 'I have nice things, don't I?' she agreed with his unspoken comment on it. 'Well, I always say, I always have nice things, whatever else . . . I never have anything cheap or nasty, my things are always nice. . . . Baby Batsby taught me that, never have anything cheap or nasty, he used to say. He used to take me on his yacht, you know, to Cannes and Nice. He was my friend for three years, and he taught me about having beautiful things.'

'Baby Batsby?'

'That was before your time, I expect, but he was in all the papers once, every week of the year. He was a great spender, you know, generous.'

'Is that a fact?'

'I've always been lucky that way, my friends were always generous. Take Mr Spencer now, he never lets me want for anything, only yesterday he said: Your curtains are getting a bit *passé*, I'll get you some new ones. And mark my words, he will, he's as good as his word.'

He saw that the whisky, coming on top of whatever she'd had earlier, was finishing her off. She sat blinking smeared eyes at him; and her cigarette, secured between thumb and forefinger six inches from her mouth, shed ash on her cherry-red gown. She took a gulp from the glass, and nearly set it down on air: Fred reached forward just in time.

'Mr Spencer's a good man, you know,' she told the air about a foot from her unfocussed brown gaze.

'Is he?'

'We're just old friends now, you know. We're both getting on a bit. Not that I don't let him have a bit of a slap and a tickle sometimes to keep him happy, though I'm not interested, not really.'

Trying to insert the end of the cigarette inside her fumbling lips, she missed, and jammed the butt against her cheek. She leaned forward and stubbed it out. Sat back – with dignity. Stared at Fred, screwed up her eyes to see him, failed, offered the stranger in her room a social smile.

This smile trembled into a wrinkled pout, as she said: 'Take Mr Spencer now, he's a good spender, I'd never say he wasn't, but but but . . .' She fumbled at the packet of cigarettes and he hastened to extract one for her and to light it. '*But.* Yes. Well, he may think I'm past it, but I'm not, and don't you think it. There's a good thirty years between us, do you know that?'

'Thirty years,' said Fred, politely, his smile now fixed by a cold determined loathing.

'What do you think, dear? He always makes out we're the same age, now he's past it, but – well, look at that then if you don't believe me.' She pointed her scarlet-tipped and shaking left hand at the table with the photographs. 'Yes, that one, just look at it, it's only from last summer.' Fred leaned forward and lifted towards him the image of her just indicated which, though she was sitting opposite him in the flesh, must prove her victory over Mr Spencer. She wore a full-skirted, tightly-belted, tightly-bodiced striped dress, from which her ageing bare arms hung down by her sides, and her old neck and face rose shameless under the beautiful gleaming hair.

'Well it stands to reason, doesn't it?' she said, as it were indignant: 'Well what do you think then?'

'When's Mr Spencer coming?' he asked.

'I'm not expecting him tonight, he's working. I admire him, I really do, holding down that job, three, four in the morning sometimes, and it's no joke, those layabouts you get at those places, and it's always Mr Spencer who has to fix them up with what they fancy, if you know what I mean, dear, or get rid of them if they make trouble, and he's not a big man, and he's not young any more, I don't know how he does it. But he's got tact. Tact. Yes, I often say to him, you've got tact, I say, it'll take a man anywhere.' Her glass was empty, and she was looking at it.

The news that Mr Spencer was not expected did not surprise Fred; he had known it, because of his secret brutal confidence born when she had said: 'I never touch the stuff, dear.'

He now got up, went behind her, stood a moment steeling himself, because the embarrassed shame-faced grin had come back on to his face, weakening his purpose – then put two hands firmly under her armpits, lifted her and supported her.

She at first struggled to remain sitting, but let herself be lifted. 'Time for byebyes?' she said. But as he began to push her, still supporting her, towards the bedroom, she said, suddenly coherent: 'But Fred, it's Fred, Fred, it's Fred . . .' She twisted out of his grip, fell two steps back, and was stopped by the door to the bedroom. There she spread her two legs under the cherry gown, to hold her trembling weight, swayed, caught at Fred, held tight, and said: 'But it's *Fred*.'

'Why should you care,' he said, cold, grinning.

'But I don't work here, dear, you know that – no, let me go.' For he had put two great schoolboy hands on her shoulders.

He felt the shoulders tense, and then grow small and tender in his palms.

'You're like your father, you're the spitting image of your father, did you know that?'

He opened the door with his left hand; then spun her around by pushing at her left shoulder as she faced him; then, putting both hands under her armpits from behind, marched her into the bedroom, while she tittered, steadily.

The bedroom was mostly pink. Pink silk bedspread. Pink walls. A doll in a pink flounced skirt lolled against the pillow, its chin tucked into a white fichu over which it stared at the opposite wall where an eighteenth-century girl held a white rose to her lips. Fred pushed Mrs Fortescue over dark-red carpet, till her knees met the bed. He lifted her, dropped her on it, neatly moving the doll aside with one hand before she could crush it.

She lay, eyes closed, limp, breathing fast, her mouth slightly open. The black furrows beside the mouth were crooked; the eyelids shone blue in wells of black.

'Turn the lights out,' she tittered.

He turned out the pink-shaded lamp fixed to the head-board. She fumbled at her clothes. He stripped off his trousers, his underpants, pushed her hands aside, found silk in the opening of the gown that glowed cherry-red in the light from the next room. He stripped the silk pants off her so that her legs flew up, then flumped down. She was inert, he fumbled. Then her expertise revived in her, or at least in her tired hands, and he achieved the goal of his hot imaginings of these ugly autumn nights in one shattering spasm that filled him with no less disgust. Her old body stirred feebly under him, and he heard her irregular breathing. He sprang off her in a leap, tugged back pants, trousers. Then he switched on the light. She lay, eyes closed, her face blurred with woe, the upper part of her body nestled into the soft glossy cherry stuff, the white legs spread open, bare. She made an attempt to rouse herself, cover herself. He leaned over her, teeth bared in a hating grin, forcing her hands away from her body. They fell limp on the stained silk spread. Now he stripped off the gown, roughly, as if she were the doll. She whimpered, she tittered, she protested. He watched, with pleasure, tears welling out of the pits of dark and trickling crookedly down her face. She lay naked among the folds of cherry-colour. He looked at the grayish crinkles around the armpits, the small flat breasts, the loose stomach; then down, at the triangle of black hair where white hairs sprouted, obscene. She was attempting to fold her legs over each other. He forced them apart again, muttering: Look at yourself, look at yourself then . . . while he held his nausea, deepened by the miasmic smell which he had known was the air of this room. 'Filthy old whore, disgusting, that's what you are, disgusting. . . .' He let his grasp slacken on her thighs, saw red marks come up even as the legs flew together and she wriggled and burrowed to get under the cherry-red gown.

Then she opened her eyes and looked straight up at him. For the first time this evening she looked at him, straight in the eyes. He fell back a step, looking away from her, hearing his own breath coming in gasps of disgust.

She sat up, holding the gown around her – cherry-coloured gown, pink coverlet, pink walls, pink pink pink everywhere and the dark red carpet: he felt as if the whole room flamed with disgust.

'That wasn't very nice, was it?' she said, quavering, but reproachful. Her voice broke in a titter, but she brought her lips together at last and said again: 'That wasn't at all nice, Fred, it wasn't nice at all.' Without looking at him, she let her feet down (he could see them trembling) over the edge of the bed, and she peered over to fit them into pink-feathered mules.

He noted that he had a need to *help* her fit her pathetic feet into the fancy mules; and with a muttered exclamation of horror, fear and shame, he fled out, down the stairs, into his box, where he flung himself face down on the bed. Through the ceiling-board an inch from his ear he heard his sister move. She had been waiting for him.

She said, low, so the parents couldn't hear, all the flip jauntiness of her voice gone, breathless with accusation and hurt: 'Very clever, I *don't* think . . . very clever.' She waited, but he did not answer. 'I know you're there, don't pretend.' He kept silent, waiting for her to tire. 'If I was as clever as you I'd go and drown myself, when I saw that gun on my pillow I thought I'd faint, I suppose you think you're just too clever to live. . . .' He waited until she got tired, and he heard her turn over and away from him. Then he put the back of his hand against his clenched teeth, and pulled the pillow down over his head so that no one could hear him.

# Sister Imelda

THE NEW NUN walked around the convent grounds close to the laurel bushes and in the shade of the trees. She made her circuits with reverently bent head and eyes cast down. It was her first walk and no girl proved impudent enough to waylay her and look up under the black-and-white frame of her guimpe and veil, into her face. My friend Baba Brennan had reported to me that the new nun was tall, but slight, and I had gone into the front grounds to look at her.

The convent where we boarded was on the edge of a small town in the West of Ireland. The fees were low, and there were about eighty girls boarding, as well as a dozen or so day girls from the town.

We had returned from our long summer holiday. The convent, with high stone wall and great green iron gates, enclosed us again, seeming more of a prison than ever – for after our spell in the outside world we all felt very much older, and Baba and I were just that much nearer to final escape. And so, on that damp autumn evening when I first saw the new nun, I thought how she wanted to be alone, fating herself to be cut off with only God. Would I smile at her?

The next day the new nun, Sister Imelda, came into our class to take geometry. Her pale, slightly long face I saw as quite ordinary at first, though her eyes were blue-black, and she had a strong, pretty mouth.

Our Sister Imelda had spent the last four years – the same span of years that Baba and myself had spent in the convent as pupils – at the University in Dublin. And in time, when we learnt this about her, we felt baffled, unable to understand how she had resisted the temptations of that hectic world we believed existed somewhere 'out there'.

'Something wrong somewhere,' Baba said. 'With make-up she'd be marvellous.'

'She is a holy person,' I said. 'You forget about vocations. Even I might have a vocation.'

'I'll pray for you that you don't,' she said.

It seemed just possible to be a nun within the convent enclosure, with its think-of-nothing white-tiled walls, massive, frightening holy pictures of Christ bleeding in agony on the Cross, crowns of thorns and Sacred Hearts burning in gilt frames in every dark corner. Inside everything stayed for ever the same, like the bacon, the cabbage, the tough meat, the tapioca pudding, and the prayers on the stroke of the bell. Through the windows we saw the mournful conifer trees all around, against the wild, forbidding Irish sky. She was a right saint then, Baba said, having got into a university for four years for nix, and with hair on her head, to come back to our back of beyond, to poverty, chastity (which we thought meant simply no kissing of boys), and obedience. We visualised scenes of agony in some Dublin hostel, while a boy stood under her bedroom window throwing up clunks of clay, whistles, supplications.

What was even stranger was that Sister Imelda had attended this very convent, before our time; first as a pupil. She had distinguished herself by winning two scholarships; and straight away re-entered our convent as a postulant.

One story was that she had an atrocious temper when a postulant, and once during Christian Knowledge had used the leather strap on two girls. Someone also knew that her brother, a good-looking and famous hurley player, had been sued for breach of promise by some girl.

She was about twenty-five. Baba and I were just sixteen and in our last year at convent school.

Sister Imelda, when she came to our classroom, introduced herself by simply telling us her name and that she was going to take geometry. She talked first in a low voice of how valuable geometry could be to the enlargement of our minds, discipline of thought. One of her eyelids looked red and swollen, as if she were getting a sty. I wondered was she suffering self-mortification by not eating. Mamma said sties and boils were a sure sign of being run down.

The new nun absently held a stick of chalk between her first and second finger, as though it were a cigarette. I began to whisper to Baba that she might have been smoking when in Dublin. Sister Imelda looked sharply at me and said that I should pay attention, please. Her dark eyes showed such sudden authority that I prayed she would never have occasion to punish *me*.

The weeks went by. November came and the tiled walls of the recreation hall wept with damp. The gurgling warm-pipe 'central heating' (it lessened the chill if you could sit on a radiator) was not due to be turned on until December – November being the month of the Holy Souls in Purgatory we were advised to mortify our flesh.

Sister Imelda came quickly to recognise the girls capable of progress at geometry. It was my worst subject. She had not taken more than six or seven classes when she flung a blackboard duster at me in anger, and whitened me with chalk dust. The class became as silent as if everyone had stopped breathing. I went on standing and the nun's face reddened. She patted her eye with a handkerchief, the eye with the sty. It must have been hurting, throbbing. Noiselessly and still red in the face she fled from the room, leaving us ten minutes free until the next class. Had I the courage I would have run after her and said that she could slap me with the strap as long as she did not cry. A sort of speechless tenderness for her came to life in me.

Baba said that we could get her into serious trouble, 'Get her defrocked,' Baba said, dusting the chalk from my gym-frock.

That evening at chapel, in the dim light from the Benediction candles I discovered a holy picture in my prayer-book. Sister Imelda had put it there to atone for her temper, and on the back she had written a verse—

> Trust him when dark doubts assail thee,
> Trust Him when thy faith is small,
> Trust Him when to simply trust Him
> Seems the hardest thing of all.

There was no mistaking the fine, flowing handwriting and the green ink she used to correct our exercise books. She had located the compartment in the chapel where I kept my prayer-book and the next evening again had placed there for me a leather-bound book of French prayers, with 'For you' in green ink on the flyleaf.

When I thanked her, outside the chapel door she bowed, but did not speak. Mostly, the nuns were on silence and only talked during class.

Soon, I became publicly known as her 'pet'. I opened doors for her, raised the blackboard two pegs higher (she was taller than other nuns) and handed out the exercise books which she had corrected. Now, in the margins of my geometry propositions I would find 'Good', or 'Improving', where she used to dash 'Disgraceful'. Baba said it was sneaky being a nun's pet and that any girl who sucked up to nuns was not to be trusted as a friend.

About a month later I carried Sister Imelda's books up four flights of stairs to the cookery kitchen. She taught cookery to a junior class. As she walked ahead of me, up the stone stairs I thought 'How beautifully she walks in her black habit, swinging her beads in her hand as if going to strike someone with them.' On each landing she paused for breath and looked through the long, curtainless window at the street below. Outside two women in suede boots were chatting and smoking as they moved down the street with shopping baskets; inside, the cold air was raw with the smell of Jeyes Fluid. A working nun, kneeling, scrubbed the granite steps with intensity. Sister Imelda bowed to her, passed on, then put her finger in the earth of a potted plant to see if it were moist. I was happy in that stone prison then, happy to be near Sister Imelda, walking behind her as she twirled her beads and bowed to the servile nun. I no longer cried for my mother, or counted the days on a pocket calendar, until the Christmas holidays.

'Come back at five,' my nun said, taking the books on the threshold of the kitchen door.

When I returned an hour later the granite steps were still wet – things took a long while to dry in that place. Our underclothes felt so damp when they came back from the laundry, that I used to keep mine in the bed with me to dry them out.

My nun was sitting on the corner of a white, scrubbed table, looking out at the yew trees.

'I'd say you have a sweet tooth,' she said, unlocking one of the built-in wall presses and producing two jam tarts that were still warm from the oven.

'What will I do with them?'

'Eat them, you goose,' she said.

The smell of warm pastry, the taste of the sweet, sticky jam, gave me such pleasure that I felt we were doing something utterly forbidden. I was a tall girl at sixteen, somewhat grown out of my gym-frock, with thick auburn hair and large eyes in a round, pink face. (Baba said that I looked like 'Some kind of mad animal peeping through a hedge.') I looked at my nun and thought how peerless, how beautiful was her straight, aristocratic nose and her pale, thin face. She wore a white overall over her black habit, and it made her warmer and freer in speech, or so I thought.

'Had you a friend when you were in Dublin at University?' I asked daringly.

'I shared a desk with a sister from Howth and stayed in the same hostel,' she said.

'But what about boys?' I thought, 'and what of your life now and do you long to go out into the world?' But could not say it.

We knew something about the nuns' routine. It was rumoured that they wore itchy, wool underwear, ate dry bread for breakfast, rarely had meat, cakes or dainties, kept certain hours of strict silence with each other, as well as constant vigil on their thoughts; so that if their minds wandered to the subject of food or pleasure they would quickly revert to thoughts of God and their eternal souls. They slept on hard beds with rough sheets and black blankets. At four o'clock in the morning while we slept, each nun got out of bed in her habit – which was also her death habit – and, chanting, flocked down the wooden stairs to fling themselves on the tiled floor of the cold, unlit chapel. Each nun – even the Mother Superior – flung herself in total submission and said Latin prayers, offering up the day to God. Then, silently back to their cells for one more hour of rest. It was not easy to imagine Sister Imelda face downwards, arms outstretched, prostrate on the tiled floor.

I often heard their chanting when I wakened suddenly from a nightmare, because, although we slept in a different building, both adjoined and if one wakened for a moment one heard that monotonous chanting, long before the birds began, long before our own bell summoned us to rise at six.

'Do you eat nice food?' I asked.

'Of course,' she said and smiled. She sometimes broke into an eager smile which she did much to conceal.

'Have you ever thought of what you will be?' she asked.

I shook my head. My hopes changed from day to day.

She looked at her man's silver pocket watch, closed the damper of the range and prepared to leave. She checked that all the wall presses were locked by running her hand over them.

'Sister,' I called, gathering enough courage at last. We must must have some secret, something to join us together, 'What colour hair have you?'

We never saw the nuns' hair, or their eyebrows, or ears, as all that part was covered by a stiff, white guimpe.

'You shouldn't ask such a thing,' she said, getting pink in the face, and then she turned back and whispered, 'I'll tell you on your last day here, provided your geometry has improved.'

She had scarcely gone when Baba, who had been lurking behind some pillar, stuck her head in the door and said, 'Christ sake save me a bit.' She finished the second pastry, then went around looking in kitchen drawers. Because of everything being locked she found only some castor sugar in a china shaker. She ate a little and threw the remainder into the dying fire so that it flared up for a minute with a yellow flame. Baba showed her jealousy by putting it around the school that I was in the cookery kitchen every evening, gorging cakes with Sister Imelda and telling the shameful things which girls said about nuns and nuns' bosoms and things. The girls began to distrust me from then on.

I did not speak to Sister Imelda again privately until the Christmas concert, when she came to paint our faces and help us into our stage clothes. We were doing scenes from *Julius Caesar*. As Mark Antony I had been instructed by the head-nun to wear a purple nightdress, white knee-length socks and buckled shoes. Ten minutes before the curtain went up, I panicked because the socks were too tight and the nightdress too big. Calm Sister Imelda found a sequined belt for my waist, and tickled the soles of my bare feet as she stretched the shrunken socks, and got them on me somehow.

'It's the dye,' I said anxiously. My feet were black from the dye of my new cotton stockings and I worried that she might think I had not washed my feet. We bathed our feet twice weekly in cold water and it is easy to recall the shrieks and murmurs of the girls as their feet sank into the cold basins.

'Of course,' she said, smiling. Was it by accident that a little lipstick brightened her mouth? There was no doubt but that with make-up she would be beautiful.

Baba could say later that I bawled like 'A bloody butcher' as Mark Antony, but Sister Imelda stood in the wings and nodded emotionally during my big speech. That evening, before I left for the Christmas holiday, I gave her two half-pound boxes of chocolates – bought for me by one of the day girls – and she gave me a casket painted with gilt paint and covered on top with a cluster of minute shells.

On the cold, snowy afternoon four weeks later when we returned from our Christmas holiday, Sister Imelda stole up to the dormitory to welcome me back. All the other girls had gone to the recreation-hall to dance barn dances to piano music.

I was still unpacking as she came down the carpeted passage, between the rows of iron beds, without making a sound.

'And you've curled your hair,' she said, offended. I wished that she could have seen me in my blue pinafore frock, but as it was, I was once again wearing my navy gym-frock, navy wool jumper, black stockings and black, flat, laced shoes.

I offered her queen-cakes of Mamma's but she refused them and said she could only stay a second. She lent me a note-book of hers into which, as a pupil, she had written favourite poems and quotations from books that she liked. It had a soft, black leather cover and the pages smelt of carbolic soap. She must have kept it near her soap-dish.

'Are you well?' I asked. She looked pale. It may have been the reflection of the snow, or of the white cotton bedspreads on her face, but she appeared to be suffering. Her face looked more pinched too and her nose stuck out more. And still the same old black shoes, crinkled from years of wear and polishing.

'I've been thinking of you,' she said.

'Me too,' I said. At home, eating turkey and mince pies, I wished that she could be with us, sharing the fire and the lovely food.

'You know that it is not proper for us to be too friendly,' she said.

'Why not?' I asked. She was the only beautiful thing in the convent, she and the altar with its arrangements of fresh flowers, no matter what the season.

'Well, we mustn't get attached, it's not right,' she said. I could not ask what was not right about it, but I knew that she had never done more than tickle my toes the day of the concert, or shake hands with me before I left for my holidays. Nuns had a terrible life, there was no doubt about it.

From then on, she treated me as less of a favourite. Reading her note-book helped me over the first, deprived days. Into a like note-book I copied her chosen quotations.

But some little time later, when she supervised our studying – a different nun supervised each week – I had a smile from her, as she sat on the rostrum, bent over some exercise books. Having a problem with my geometry I plucked up courage and asked for help. Patiently she went over the theorem step by step. Standing close to her, and also because her guimpe was crooked, I saw one of her eyebrows for the first time. It was dark and bushy. Looking then at the smears of green ink on two of her fingers I recollected that probably she had never plucked her eyebrows, never thrown bath cubes into a hot bath and lolled in it, never had her hair permed and felt that twinge of piercing cold as the ammonia trickled down her neck. I'd had my first perm that Christmas, but she said that she was pleased to see my hair coming straight again.

As usual, at nine o'clock a tray of warm milk was brought for certain delicate girls. That night it was tepid; and I got the cracked cup. Drinking it slowly I could see specks of dust on the milk and I put it back unfinished. We went on with the private lesson, although now we had gone past geometry and Sister Imelda was telling me about the life of G. K. Chesterton and his absent-mindedness. G. K. Chesterton once put on his trousers backwards. I nearly burst trying to hold in my laughter.

The Mother Superior – a sharp-eyed woman with warts on her right cheek – came in, noiselessly.

'Would you please go back to your desk,' she said, 'And in future, kindly allow Sister Imelda to get on with her duties.'

I tiptoed back to my desk and saw my friendly enemy Baba smile with pleasure. Inspecting the empty milk cups on the aluminium tray the Mother Superior asked what girl had not finished her milk.

'Me, sister,' I said, raising my hand. She made me finish the dusty milk, and stand under the clock for the remainder of the study period as punishment for having 'yelled' with laughter in an 'unladylike' way.

For weeks I pined and tried to see my nun by waiting outside doors where I knew she was due. Each time she walked past with a cool nod. I wondered if the Mother Superior had asked her not to make such a favourite of me, or if she had decided so, herself. As time went on, she seemed to get more beautiful, the pale face I now saw as something resembling a saint's face carved out of stone, and she walked with such grace that I tried never to walk in front of her and be seen for the awkward lump I was.

It was not until one Sunday morning five weeks later that I had a private word with her.

One day in March the sun came out briefly, the broken clouds sailed across the sky, wind bent the convent trees, and (as a treat!) we were sent up to the playing-fields for a game of rounders, with Sister Imelda in charge. When my turn came to hit the ball with the long, wooden bat I crumbled into a state of panic and ducked, afraid the ball would hit me.

'Little Mo,' said Baba, jeering.

At length Sister Imelda crooked her finger and called me aside. We sat on a wooden bench and she told me that I must not give way to tears when humiliated, that life was a long succession of humiliations, and only through humility could the soul be perfected.

'What will you do when you're a nun?' she asked chidingly.

I had made up my mind to be a nun, and I felt that she guessed as much.

'When I'm a nun, will my bed be tossed just after I've made it, and will I have to eat liver and things I don't like as a punishment?' I asked.

'You'll see,' she said, and slipped a chocolate biscuit into my gym-frock pocket.

Walking down from the playing-field to our Sunday lunch of fat roast mutton and cabbage, we all chatted to Sister Imelda. The girls milled around her, linking her arms, trying to hold her hand, counting the various keys on her bunch.

'Sister, did you ever ride a motor bicycle?'

'Sister, did you ever wear seamless stockings?'

'Sister, what's your favourite food?'

'What do you do when you want to scratch your head?'

'If you had a wish, what would you choose?'

Yes, she said calmly, she had ridden a motor bicycle, but not worn seamless stockings. She liked bananas best, and if she had a wish it would be to go home for a few hours to see her parents and brother.

'Is he a smasher?' Baba asked, and got a real wink from the Sister, which made me jealous.

At lunch the mutton had a heavy gamey smell, but senior girls had come prepared with old envelopes or pieces of paper. I can still feel the damp heat from the warm meat as I put it inside my jumper, in order to sneak it out. The junior girls ate theirs diligently and Baba said that their insides would be crawling with maggots. Then, on our Sunday walk through the town and along the edge of the lake, we pulled out our damp lumps and threw them into the water.

After the walk we wrote home. We were allowed to write home once a week; our letters were always censored. I told my mother that I had made up my mind to be a nun, and asked if she could send me bananas, when and if they arrived at our local grocery shop.

That evening, perhaps as I wrote to my mother on the ruled white paper, a telegram arrived which said that Sister Imelda's brother had been killed on his motor bicycle, while on his way home from a hurling match. The Mother Superior announced it, and asked us to pray for his soul and write letters of sympathy to Sister Imelda's parents. We all wrote identical letters, because in our first year at school we had been given specimen letters for various occasions, and we all referred back to our specimen letter of sympathy.

Next day the town hire-car drove up to the convent and Sister Imelda, accompanied by another nun, went home for the funeral. She looked as white as a sheet with eyes redder than ever and a heavy knitted shawl over her shoulders. Although she came back that night (I stayed awake to hear the car) we did not see her for a whole week, except to catch a glimpse of her back, in the chapel.

When she resumed class she was peaky and distant, making no reference at all to her recent tragedy.

The day the bananas came I waited outside the door and gave her a bunch wrapped in tissue paper. Some were still a little green, and she said that Mother Superior would put them in the glasshouse to ripen. I felt that Sister Imelda would never taste them; they would be kept for a visiting priest or bishop.

'Oh, sister, I'm sorry about your brother,' I said, in a burst.

'It will come to us all, sooner or later,' Sister Imelda said dolefully.

I dared to touch her wrist to communicate my sadness. She went her way, with dutifully bent head.

Lent came and her suffering seemed to increase. Her face showed deathly white, and her eyes were small from crying. She grew irritable and had a boil on her cheek. She asked me to pray for her brother's soul and to avoid seeing her alone. Each time as she came down a corridor towards me I was obliged to turn the other way. Now, Baba or some other girl moved the blackboard two pegs higher and spread her shawl, when wet, over the radiator to dry.

Finally I got 'flu and was put to bed. Sickness took the same bleak course – a cup of hot senna delivered in person by the head-nun who stood there while I drank it, tea at lunch-time with thin slices of brown bread (because it was just after the war food was still rationed, so the butter was mixed with lard and had white streaks running through it and a faintly rancid smell), hours of just lying there surveying the empty dormitory, the empty iron beds with white counterpanes on each one, and convent Crucifixes laid on the white, frilled pillow-slips. I knew that she would miss me and hoped that Baba would tell her where I was. I counted the number of tiles from the ceiling to the head of my bed, thought of my mother at home on the farm mixing hen food, thought of my father, losing his temper perhaps, and stamping on the kitchen floor with nailed boots. I recalled the money owing for my school fees and hoped that Sister Imelda would never get to hear of it. During Christmas holiday I had seen a bill sent by the head-nun to my father which said, 'Please remit this week without fail'. I hated being in bed causing extra trouble and therefore reminding the head-nun of the unpaid liability. We had no clock in the dormitory, no way of guessing the time.

Marigold, one of the servants, came to take off the counterpanes at five and brought with her two gifts from Sister Imelda – an orange, and a little blue medal swinging on a small gold pin. I kept the orange peel in my hand, smelling it, and planning how I would thank her. Thinking of her I fell into a feverish sleep and was wakened when the girls came to bed at ten and switched on the various ceiling lights.

At Easter, Sister Imelda warned me not to give her chocolates so I got her a flash-lamp instead and two spare batteries. Pleased with such a useful gift (perhaps she read poems in bed), she put her arms round me and brushed her cheek against mine. It made up for the seven weeks of withdrawal, and as I drove down the convent drive with Baba she waved to me, as she had promised, from the window of her cell.

On the last term at school studying was intensive because of the State examinations which were to be held in June. Like all the other nuns Sister Imelda thought only of these examinations. She crammed us with knowledge, lost her temper every other day and gritted her teeth whenever the blackboard was too greasy to take the imprint of the chalk. If ever I met her on the corridor she asked if I knew such and such a thing, and coming down from Sunday games she went over various questions with us.

At last the examination day arrived and we sat at single desks supervised by some strange woman from Dublin. Opening a locked trunk she took out the pink examination papers and distributed them around. Geometry was on the fourth day. When we came out from it, Sister Imelda was in the hall with all the answers, so that we could compare our answers with hers. Then she called me aside and we went up towards the cookery kitchen and sat on the stairs while she went over the paper with me, question for question. I knew that I had three right and two wrong, but did not tell her so.

'It is black,' she said then, rather suddenly. I thought she meant the dark light where we were sitting.

'It's cool, though,' I said. Summer had come, our white skins baked under the heavy uniform and dark violet pansies bloomed in the convent grounds. Pansies like her eyes. She looked well again and her pale skin was once more unblemished.

'My hair,' she whispered, 'is black.' And she told me how she had spent her last night before entering the convent. She had gone out with a boy on a motor bicycle and ridden for miles, and they'd lost their way up a mountain and she became afraid she would be so late home that she would sleep it out next morning. It was understood between us that I was going to enter the convent in September and that I could have a last fling too. She let me fit on her silver ring – the ring all nuns wore on their marriage fingers.

Two days later we prepared to go home. There were farewells and outlandish promises, and autograph books signed, and girls trudging up the recreation hall, their cases bursting open with clothes and books. Baba scattered biscuit crumbs in the dormitory for the mice, and stuffed all her prayer-books under a mattress. Her father promised to collect us at four. I had arranged with Sister Imelda secretly, that I would meet her in one of the wooden chalets around the walks, where we would spend our last half-hour together. I expected that she would tell me something of what my life as a postulant would be like.

But Baba's father came an hour early. He had something urgent to do at four, and came at three instead. All I could do was ask Marigold to take a note to Sister Imelda. I wrote,

> Remembrance is all I ask,
> But if remembrance should prove a task,
> Forget me.

I hated Baba, hated her busy father, hated the thought of my mother standing in the doorway in her good dress, welcoming me home at last. I would have become a nun that minute if I could.

I wrote to my nun that night and again next day and then every week for a month. Her letters were censored so I tried to convey my feelings indirectly. In one of her letters to me (they were allowed one letter a month) she said that she looked forward to seeing me in September. But by September Baba and I had left for the University in Dublin.

I stopped writing to Sister Imelda then, reluctant to tell her that I no longer wished to be a nun.

In Dublin we enrolled at the same University as she had attended. I saw her maiden name on a list, for having graduated with special honours, and for days was again sad and remorseful. I rushed out and bought three batteries for the flash-lamp I'd given her, and posted them without any note enclosed. No mention of my missing vocation, no mention of why I had stopped writing.

One Sunday, on a summer afternoon, about two years later, Baba and myself travelled out to Howth on a bus. Howth is a seaside village near Dublin, favoured by students and all sorts of young people. The bus was full of mothers and babies, and older children in charge of younger children, as is found in Dublin, on their way to Dollymount Strand, which is on the way to Howth.

We were both what Baba called dressed up to the nines – red toe-nails, toeless sandals, bottled suntan on our legs, pancake on our faces and thick rims of dark mascara lining our eyes, and almost blinding us.

After a while I thought I smelled nuns in the bus – candles, incense, carbolic soap, camphor and a little of the scrubbed kitchen-table smell. But that would have been impossible on a bus full of poor children? We sat at the front. Whatever made me look around, I saw Sister Imelda and another nun sitting just inside the door at the back. They were looking towards the sea, not talking, but very interested in everything going on around them. I held the Sunday paper to the side of my face and said to Baba,

'Sister Imelda, in the back, keep your face down.'

'Why? There's nothing wrong with us. We'll go back and cut a great dash in front of her.'

'Oh please, please! I'll die if she sees me.'

'I'll just take a deck at her and see if she's changed.'

I gripped her arm and she must have felt me trembling. 'Oh, all right,' Baba said. 'If you're going to have a fit just because . . .'

But she kept her head down. We sat silent, while the bus stopped twice.

'Maybe they got off,' Baba said, and then, 'What would be the harm if we said hello?'

I couldn't explain it. It was as if I had betrayed Sister Imelda by not living as she did.

We passed a convent, and Baba said they might be going there. By then I had taken a desperate decision – to conquer myself, to stand up and speak to the person I had loved most in the world, after my mother. With my flushed face I stood up to go to the back of the bus.

The nuns had gone, the bus was moving again. I saw the backs of the two black, almost identical figures, on the pavement. I ran to the back of the bus, to see them, and see the last of my school-days being left behind.

# OLIVIA MANNING

# *A Romantic Hero*

HAROLD was up at dawn. The first light, coming through thin curtains that would not meet, had awakened him, but he would have wakened in any case. Indeed, he had scarcely slept. As he dressed, with noiseless cunning, he felt stiff and chilly and knew he was catching one of his colds, but he was too excited to give much thought to it.

The night before he had had to find his way by candle-light up the steep stair of the cottage where he was staying. The room had smelt musty. He suspected the bed might be damp, but he had to accept it. How like Angela not to give a thought to such a thing when arranging a room for him. Strong as a donkey herself, she treated his fear 'of damp as a superstition.

The three bedrooms of the cottage, one for the labourer, his wife and baby, one for Angela and one for Harold, were fitted into a space so small, the whole would not have made a reasonable room. Angela had pointed out that a whisper in one room could be heard in all of them, so Harold must not visit her bed. Much Harold cared. His only idea had been to get off to Seaham without her and he could be sure of doing that only if he left before she woke.

He made his way down the stairs by holding his breath. When he found himself outside the cottage, he felt like a volatile gas released from a bottle. With the downland turf pneumatic beneath his feet, the dew glinting in the tender sunlight, he could have burst into song from sheer happiness. He remembered that when they were squabbling yesterday, Angela had said he only sang when he was angry. Well, he wanted to sing now, and he was not angry. Far from it. His sense of triumph over Angela proved to him she had had her day. It was all over with Angela – and for him life was taking on meaning and joy.

By some quirk of nature, Harold, a tall man with a thin, constricted look, was impelled to prefer first the company of one sex, then of the other. Although nearly thirty-five years of age, he still saw himself as a young man, one for whom life had yet to burst into the flame of its beginning. And the beginning was now. He could put everything else behind him.

For the last few months he had spent most of his time with Angela. Angela, with a responsible secretarial job in the city, had been a pleasant enough companion at first, and after repeated failure to find satisfaction elsewhere, he had even begun to think of marrying her. Heaven help him if he had! What a risk he had run! What a pass loneliness could bring a man to!

And he had been saved, only yesterday, by a remarkable thing – the most remarkable thing that had ever happened to him. A wonderful thing; a thing that had restored his faith in himself and his future, and confirmed his belief that there awaited him, that there always had awaited him, a felicity so rare that only the exceptional few ever got a glimpse of it.

Angela was spending the first fortnight of her summer holiday walking on the South Downs. Harold had agreed to join her for the week-end. When he boarded the train, he found himself alone, on a non-stop run to Worthing, with the most perfect young man imaginable. Very young, fair, athletic and . . . beautiful. Yes, beautiful; with the sort of eyes that Harold described to himself as 'my sort of eyes'. Never before had Providence done such a thing for Harold.

For the first fifteen minutes Harold was sick with dread of some wretched bore coming down the corridor and joining them, but no one came. As he began to relax, he wanted to speak – to reach out, to make contact, to get things started without further delay. He desired so few people that anyone he found so eminently desirable seemed to belong to him as by a right. But experience had taught him caution. A too impetuous approach might cause misunderstanding and spoil things before they started. He held himself in check, but he could not keep himself from looking at the young man.

Conscious of Harold's stare, the young man raised his newspaper so that only his blond curls were visible above it. Harold noted the tight, shabby jeans that covered long lean legs, the old sandals that revealed the long, lean, sunburnt feet, the shirt of Madras cotton with buttons missing. It seemed to Harold a picture of casual hard-upness, but not of poverty. It was, he decided, exactly right.

Then, suddenly, the young man lowered the paper, stared back with amused blue eyes, and *smiled*.

Harold flushed painfully. He was furious with himself but at the same time his excitement was such it almost choked him. He dared not do anything. He looked out of the window and pretended interest in the London suburbs, then in the fields and cows. He was in a stupor and it was only when he recognised the first curves of the downland that he realised how time was rushing past. If nothing happened, it would soon be too late for anything to happen. He felt panic. He searched his mind for a remark that would be an invitation but not an intrusion. He must say something that without being in any way eccentric or outrageous, would mark him as the unusual, cultivated, interesting person he was – the sort of person that must appeal to a young man like this. He turned his head but before he could speak, the young man lent forward and offered him the newspaper. In his confusion, Harold accepted it, then realised he would have to do something with it. He retired behind it. The offer might be an approach, but what a waste of time! He leafed through the pages as quickly as the situation allowed then, handing the paper back, he spoke his thanks in his high, precise voice, adding after a suitable interval: 'Lovely day.'

'Yes, splendid,' the young man agreed in what Harold was relieved to hear was 'an educated voice'. Voices did not count for much these days. Some people even admired a touch of 'regional accent', but Harold had grown up over a small grocery shop in Bradford and he frankly loathed what he called 'all that kitchen sink stuff'. He had struggled out of it and now wanted no part of it. He often described his own voice as 'educated' and had been irritated recently when Angela had said that an elocutionist's voice was 'educated' in a sense quite different from that in which he used the world.

'Do you smoke?' the young man offered a squashed packet of cigarettes.

Harold shook his head: 'No, thank you. I have to preserve my voice.'

'Singer?'

'No. Elocutionist.'

The young man lit a cigarette then, lounging in his corner, blowing out smoke and narrowing his eyes against it, he smiled again.

*Well*! This was seduction if ever Harold had seen it. His *frisson* of response was such that he felt faint. He had never before had directed upon him such a significant and alluring smile. He glowed with gratitude. This wonderful young man was actually making the running. Had, indeed, made it from the first. He had offered Harold the paper, he had enquired if he were a singer, he had offered a cigarette. . . .

Seeing himself as the pursued, Harold felt more comfortable but not a whit less excited. Here at last was the answer to all his demands on life. He smiled. At once the young man smiled again. Now Harold had no doubt about it. The situation was his.

Harold was so assured now that as the houses of Worthing appeared, he took the situation in hand: 'Would you care for a cup of tea?'

'Might as well. I've half an hour to wait for the Seaham bus.'

They exchanged names. The young man was called David. They walked down the platform together. It was only as they reached the barrier that Harold remembered calamity: Angela was waiting on the other side. How awful she looked! And she would give David a wrong impression of Harold's interests. As for Angela – Harold saw her bright, bespectacled eyes grow brighter as she saw David and noted David's good looks. Her curiosity was roused. Harold willed her to go away, anywhere, on any excuse, but of course she did not go away. As though she read his thoughts, Angela grinned at Harold, then flicked a glance at David and back again to Harold. The silly little fool, what was she trying to convey? Introduced to her, David averted his gaze and Harold could not blame him. He must have seen, as Harold himself now saw only too clearly, that she was dumpy, badly dressed and lower middle class.

Harold was on edge until he managed, behind Angela's back, to catch hold of David's hand and give it a squeeze. David looked surprised but Harold felt sure he understood.

They went to the café beside the bus stop. Mercifully, Angela was keeping her mouth shut. She was observing them; no doubt gleefully, imagining that Harold was in for another disappointment. So long as she remained quiet, she could observe to her heart's content.

The café was hot, crowded and redolent of sweat and stale Indian tea. In precise, prim tones, Harold explained to the waitress that he wanted 'China' but either she did not know what he was talking about or pretended not to know.

David had become taciturn and Harold was certain that the presence of Angela had ruined their intimacy. He said he was 'a great walker' and asked David how far Seaham was from the village where he and Angela had their rooms. Here Angela had to chip in with the information that it was all of six miles. Did David walk much? Harold enquired. No, David preferred games and swimming. He went so far as to state that whenever he could, he spent his weekends at a Seaham bungalow.

'You stay there alone?' asked Harold.

'Usually. I'm cramming for the Oxford entrance. I hope to go up this autumn.'

'Lucky you!' For all his good will, Harold could not keep the hiss of envy out of his voice. There had never been any question of his going up to Oxford. His parents had spoiled him, they had given him every material comfort they could afford, but they would not waste money on higher education. They would not even let him try for a grant to one of the neighbouring Redbricks. They had sent him out at sixteen to serve his time in a gentlemen's outfitters and he had trained as an elocutionist after working hours. He had never forgiven them. It had taken him ten years to struggle out of his class. His father had left him three thousand pounds and, bitterly, he had seen it as the price of his youth.

David looked out of the window. His bus was about due. As he did not suggest their meeting again, Harold was forced to say: 'I was thinking of strolling over to Seaham tomorrow.'

'Some stroll!' giggled Angela.

Harold ignored her. Determined not to let her ruin his last chance of arranging something, he said desperately: 'Would you like me to call on you?'

'I don't mind,' David said but he gave no information.

By questioning him, Harold learnt that the bungalow was called 'St Chad's' and was by the sea.

'Anyone'll point it out,' David said as he rose and swung a rucksack up on to his shoulder. He said 'Cheerio', giving Harold a glimpse of his seductive, significant smile, and was gone. From their first introduction, he had not looked at or spoken to Angela, a fact that Harold found satisfactory. He gazed intently from the window to watch David's light, easy jump on to the Seaham bus, and he did not return to the realities about him until the bus had driven away.

Angela said: 'What's going on? And under my very nose, what's more!'

Harold, emulating David's aloofness, smiled to himself and said: 'Never you mind.' He was determined not to tell her a thing, not a thing, and he maintained his silence as their own bus took them to Findon and they walked up to the cottage where Angela was staying. But he could not keep it up. During their afternoon walk, she made him tell her everything and by the time he had finished, she was no longer laughing at him.

'I hope you're not making a mistake,' she said.

'I'm quite sure I'm not.'

'You've been mistaken before.'

'Perhaps I have, but this was different. A special sort of understanding existing between us from the start. I felt it at once. As soon as he smiled at me, I knew. I just knew.'

'I must say, he didn't seem very forthcoming in the café.'

'That's because you were there. You don't look your best in that yellow dress. Yellow's a colour that calls for a very good skin.'

'What a waspish creature you are, Harold! – or would be if you had more energy.'

Harold felt more flattered than not by being called waspish. His face in the glass looked to him pathetic rather than dangerous, a deprived face, as though he had as a child been underfed instead of stuffed with pastries, sweet biscuits, ice-creams and all the chocolates that lost their colour when on display in the grocery-shop window. 'Cossetted and spoilt,' he thought, 'Spoilt and cossetted,' as though some crime had been perpetrated against him. If his mother had not kept him wrapped up in cotton-wool, he would have learnt to resist the coughs and colds that now made his life a misery. Thinking of this, he began to sing to himself in protest and Angela said: 'You always do that when you're annoyed.'

'Do what?'

'Sing to yourself.'

He was suddenly furious and cried: 'You don't understand anything.'

'Poor Harold!' she sadly said.

He stopped in his tracks, turned on her and said: 'These days you are always going out of your way to annoy me. I wonder why?'

'I annoy *you!*' she gave an exaggerated gasp that disgusted him. Though she was getting on for thirty, she still had the silliness of the female adolescent. And God, how silly young women were! It was then that he realised that the feminine had become repulsive to him. It seemed to have happened in a moment, in the twinkling of an eye, but no doubt the change in him had been coming during these recent weeks of disagreement with Angela. It was almost impossible for him to understand how he had tolerated her for so long. Angela and he had met one wet Saturday afternoon in the Streatham public library. They had both put up their hands to take down the same copy of Maugham's *Writer's Note-book* and Harold had said impressively: 'I see we have similar tastes,' and Angela had giggled. She had then asked him what he thought of Maugham and had listened respectfully while he spoke his admiration and his reasons for it. They had walked together out of the library and after standing about talking for some time in the rain, had ended up in a tea-shop in Streatham Hill. He had been rather annoyed when Angela ordered a buck rarebit and relieved when she insisted on paying for it. Here was a girl whom it would be safe to see again. He found her to be no fool and not bad in bed, but what appealed to him and held him for so long was the abject humility that underlay her rather perky manner. He discovered soon enough that all the confidence had been kicked out of her by a bitch of a mother – a woman of cheap good looks, judging from the photograph that Angela kept beside her bed – who convinced Angela that she was too ugly ever to find herself a man. Angela was not ugly; just homely. She had a high-coloured bun of a face and glasses that she took off whenever possible, leaving a red rim on the bridge of her nose. She used no make up. 'What good would it do on a face like mine?' Gradually her admiration for Harold had deteriorated, and even her sympathy had faded. When she was not treating him as a joke, she was impatient of him and was capable at times of something not far from malice.

He felt that he had borne rather a lot from Angela. He thought of her giggle, her lack of looks and her refusal to attempt any sort of elegance. She said: 'What does it matter? Nobody looks at me,' but when she was with him, people looked at the pair of them and her dowdiness was a reflection upon him. He had tried to be tolerant. Angela was his friend – for terrible moments, it seemed she was his only friend. For terrible moments he had had to be grateful to her; had had to think of marrying her. Now he was released from all obligation to her.

As she gave her vulgar exaggerated gasp, he said: 'You know what you are – you're just an exhibitionist schoolgirl. You annoy people in order to get attention.'

That had stung her. She said: 'Indeed! Then let me tell you what I think about you. You're always saying you're an idealist – and what's the ideal? Someone who'll think you're wonderful, and who admires your voice and your piano playing and what you call your intellect; and put up with your self-centred conceit because they imagine you're sensitive and perceptive. Well, you may be sensitive where your own feelings are concerned, but you aren't even aware that other people have feelings.'

He shrugged this off: 'You don't understand. You've got no depths. You've never been clever enough – or wise enough, I ought to say – to understand how unhappy I've been. You aren't capable of understanding.'

'Everyone's unhappy.'

'Rubbish.'

'Yes, they are. Even if they don't parade their sorrows, they have them. People are full of anxiety; they don't know what hangs over them. It's not just the bomb – it's that life is so broken up and pointless. No one believes in anything, yet they want to believe. Oh, I don't know what it is, but it's the same for everyone. Your trouble is you're out of date. You want to be some sort of romantic hero lifted by your sufferings and your sensitive soul above the common run. Well, that's all over now. You've got to stop going round looking for a free gift of perfect love. You've got to try and understand how other people feel.'

He had listened to all this very patiently in order to show her how mistaken she was. He answered seriously: 'Whatever you say, individual relationships are the most important thing in life.'

'I don't deny it. But they're not given you on a plate. You have to earn them. It's no good thinking that every pretty boy you see is going to be the great love of your life. It's jolly unlikely, apart from anything else.'

He looked at her, the poor, plain, charmless girl, and smiled: 'You know your trouble?' he said, 'You're jealous.'

'You think so? Well, it doesn't matter. The truth is, I'd be jolly glad if you did find someone who adored you. I feel sorry for you. You're so miserably lonely.'

'Don't worry about me, my dear,' he answered lightly for he really felt now that he would never be lonely again.

As he walked towards Seaham, he could see the blue line of the sea, but it was further away than it looked. Angela had said the distance was six miles but Harold thought it must be eight or nine. He was not, as he had claimed, 'a great walker'. He occasionally took himself on solitary, reflective walks to Mitcham Common or Wimbledon or Richmond, but not much further, and there was always somewhere to stop for a cup of tea on the way. Harold would have been thankful for a cup of tea now as, sweating, exhausted and aware of his developing cold, he descended on Seaham, which was not, as he had hoped, an unspoilt fishing village, but a collection of seedy bungalows and bathing-huts. 'St Chad's' was one of the worst: a converted army hut. The front door stood ajar. Harold entered.

He had pictured himself arriving in time for breakfast – a late breakfast, but David would not get up very early. He might even find him still in bed and . . . but except for a couple of deck-chairs, a kitchen table, a cupboard, a sink, a camp-bed and a wireless set, the hut was empty. Harold tried to accept disappointment cheerfully. This interior was a part of David.

And David himself was not far away. He was lying on the beach, naked except for a sky-blue bathing slip, his shoulders propped against some rusty iron object left behind by the army. He had a text-book open beside him but was occupied in lazily throwing stones for a dog. As Harold's feet crunched on the shingle, he glanced round and said: 'Hallo. I'd forgotten about you.'

Even though he took this to be a coy untruth, Harold was stunned by the cruelty of such a greeting. He came to a stop and might have walked away had not David smiled and said: 'Sit down.'

Harold sat down, awkwardly, on the uncomfortable stones. Some minutes passed before he recovered his confidence and could look at David and see that he was even more handsome undressed than dressed. One direct glance at the beautifully smooth, muscled, sunburnt abdomen and chest, then Harold turned his gaze on the sea. He was near tears, caught between his hurt and his desire to stay until hurt was alleviated. For surely, if he did stay, David would make up for his brutality.

'Aren't you going to strip off?' David asked.

Harold, in an acute tone of distant refinement, said. 'I fear I have no bathing costume.'

'I've another slip on the line. Go and get it.'

'I'd rather not.'

'Oh, for Heaven's sake! You look too ridiculous here on the beach in that city gent's outfit.'

Harold forced a laugh: 'I'd look more ridiculous without it.'

'You couldn't.' David turned his back on Harold and called the dog to him. When it came, he caught it, rolled it over and pretended to wrestle with it. In the uproar that resulted, conversation was at a stop. Harold sat uneasily for a few minutes, then got to his feet and went back to the bungalow. The slip on the line was red. He took it inside the hut, undressed and put it on. He knew he was too thin and hated exposing himself. When he came out, he shivered not only from the fresh wind but from self-dislike. In the brilliant outdoor light, he felt like a shell-fish that had lost its shell. His skin was hideously white. When he appeared, walking painfully on the stones, David gave a howl of laughter then collapsed, his head buried in his arms, his whole body shaking.

Harold reproved him: 'I'm not at all well. I'm developing one of my colds.'

'Oh dear, oh dear!' David lay helplessly sobbing with laughter. When he at last managed to swallow his laughter back, he said: 'Why don't you run round a bit! It'll warm you up.'

In desolate obedience, Harold tried to run round in circles as he had seen athletes run on the screen, but the stones were agony and soon the dog, attracted by his activity, was bouncing about him, whoofing and snapping at his ankles. He found this intolerable and lost his temper in spite of himself: 'Get off; you brute,' he shouted.

It was evident that David could scarcely keep his laughter under. He called the dog and when it went to him, he cuffed it affectionately about the ears: 'I'll keep him busy,' he said and he began throwing stones again, but somehow Harold was always in the line of fire. The stones whanged round his feet and the dog, tearing after them, tripped him and sent him flying. He rose, rubbing a grazed elbow.

'Sorry!' David's shoulders were shaking again.

Very funny! Harold sat down. When the dog settled beside him, he pushed it irritably away.

'Don't you like animals?' asked David.

'They're all right in their proper place.'

'Isn't the beach a proper place? They seem right to me wherever they are.'

'Unlike human beings, you mean?'

'Well, human beings can look a bit silly at times. Aren't you going to bathe?'

'I don't think so. I've got a cold.'

'Then I'd get dressed if I were you. You look too awful like that.'

Harold, his eyes blurred by tears, stared out to sea for some minutes, then jumped up and returned to the bungalow and his clothing. David arrived while he was lacing up his shoes.

'How about something to eat?' David cheerfully asked.

'No, thank you. I'm going straight back.'

'Don't be an ass.' David turned on the wireless set and, without waiting to hear what noise would come from it, went to the cupboard and brought out bread, cheese, corned-beef and a tea-pot: 'Here!' he threw a bundle of knives and forks on the table, 'Put these straight.' He lit a spirit-stove and filled the kettle.

Harold was hungry and the thought of food cheered him. He saw the hospitality as a peace offering and decided he would feel better when he had had something to eat. He would stay, but not without protest. He said in suffering tones: 'You are so different from what I imagined: so different.'

'Sorry, but it's scarcely my fault.'

Harold adjusted the wireless and found a Beethoven symphony. He stood listening, his expression becoming entranced, until David said: 'Oke. All ready.'

While they were eating, Harold did his best to cross the barrier between them.

'So you'll be up at Oxford in the autumn! I sometimes go there for week-ends.'

David made no response. Harold asked: 'What do you intend to study?'

'Mathematics.'

'Good Lord!'

When the meal was over, David lit a cigarette and started clearing the table. Harold watched, making no move, while David poured water into a pan, stacked in the dishes, then threw a damp, dirty towel towards him: 'Let's get it over,' David said.

Harold rose unwillingly. He hated household chores, especially dish-washing. Dish-washing was the job his mother had imposed on him at home and he had always felt it an inferior activity. With a distasteful smile on his lips he took up the towel and said: 'I'm not in the habit of washing dishes, but I don't mind obliging you,' and as he spoke, he slid an arm round David's neck. David dodged away. Without turning or pausing in his work, he calmly said: 'Pull yourself together.'

Harold stood as though he had been slapped in the face, then threw the towel aside and walked out of the bungalow. He paused in the garden, his hands in his pockets, and sang to himself.

'He's a little flirt,' he thought, 'I'll call his bluff,' but he was not certain he could call David's bluff. He went to the wooden paling round the garden and leaning over it, pressed his hands against his eyes.

David came out to hang the towel on the line. He had put on his shirt and jeans. He said: 'At four o'clock I have to go to tea with friends.'

'Don't worry, I'm just leaving.'

'No need. How about a walk along the shore?'

Harold, looking at him, met the smile again and was more disturbed than before. They went together to the water's edge and along the sand strip.

'You don't like men that way?' Harold asked after long silence.

'I find I prefer women on the whole.'

'Do you mind my being attracted to you?'

'I suppose you can't help it,' David kept bending to pick up stones and skim them across the sea, 'I'd hoped it might be possible to have a friendship without that.'

Stung to an impolitic tartness, Harold asked: 'I can't say that was the impression you gave me.'

'No? Sorry for that. I'd better be getting back. They asked me to come early.' He glanced sideways at Harold and with his provoking smile said: 'Very pretty girl where I'm going.'

'Is there?' Harold was filled with resentment. The smile now seemed unforgivable. His cold was becoming worse. The undressing had done him no good. His hands in his pockets, his eyes on the ground, he began to feel really ill.

David stopped at the gate of one of the larger brick bungalows and held out a hand: 'This is where I leave you.' Harold, ignoring the hand, brushed past him without a word. He walked with a sense of purpose until he reached the brow of the downs, then his pace slowed, weariness came down on him. At the moment he felt only anger. Misery would come later. As he trudged along it seemed to him David had encouraged him simply to make a fool of him, then, bored, had simply dismissed him. But why should he get away with it? Why should Harold let himself be dismissed like that? He was not a fool or a weakling. He came to a stop, then, obstinately resolved, he turned in his tracks and walked back to 'St Chad's'. The door still stood ajar. He went in and, wrapping himself up in a blanket from the bed, sat down beside the wireless set and found some music. The music soothed him, then a sensuous tenderness and longing began to grow in him. He became aware of mysterious desires in himself and mysterious powers. He felt he had genius of a sort, though what sort he could not tell. Intoxicated by the sense of his own personality, he was certain that when David returned everything would be different. The hours passed. He lay entranced, waiting, filled with a delicious anticipation.

The room was completely dark when David returned. He switched on the light as he entered then saw Harold and stared at him blankly. Harold gave a weak titter.

'I couldn't go all that way back. I really didn't feel well enough.'

'What's the matter with you?'

'It's this cold. It's worse. My temperature's up. I must have got a chill down on the beach.'

'You'd better get into bed. I'll make you a hot drink.'

Harold took off his coat and trousers and lay on the bed in his shirt. He doubled the blanket over him. It was miserably thin. 'I'm highly susceptible to colds,' he said. Beneath him the canvas was hard and comfortless: 'I ought to have more covers.'

David took a woollen scarf from the cupboard and threw it to Harold. Wrapping it round his neck, Harold, with morose pleasure, smelt its scent of sweat and sand. He sat up in the bed, grinning wretchedly, and watched David heat in a pan some water, sugar and the end of a bottle of blackcurrant jam. He handed the drink to Harold by stretching from the bottom of the bed.

In silence they ate another meal of corned-beef and cheese. When it was finished and David was washing dishes again, Harold burst out: 'Why do you dislike me?'

'I don't dislike you – particularly.'

'You can't pretend that you like me: yet, at the station, you let me squeeze your hand: and you smiled at me on the train.'

'Doesn't everyone smile?'

'But not like that. You know there are smiles and smiles. You deliberately misled me.'

David went outside to hang the towel on the line.

Harold watched for him to reappear in the doorway, then accused him: 'If you didn't like me, you should have shown it straight away.'

'I suppose I made a mistake.'

'What do you mean – a mistake?' Harold sat upright in his eagerness to discuss himself, 'What is wrong with me?'

David laughed uncomfortably: 'How should I know?'

'Yesterday you were friendly. Today, straight away, you were cruel and cold. I felt you hated me. Why? For what reason? What did I do wrong? What made you change? Did you think I looked ridiculous?'

'Perhaps. A bit.'

'So that was it!' Having been given the answer he expected and dreaded, Harold sank back on to the bed with quivering lips. He said: 'I've found no one to understand me,' there was a pause before he could control himself sufficiently to add: '. . . or accept me.'

'Sorry about that.' David lit a candle. Switching off the light that hung naked, dim and fly-blown from the centre of the ceiling, he undressed in the obscurity of the candle's light. Watching him, Harold wondered what he would do when he was ready for bed.

To keep contact, any sort of contact, Harold asked: 'What's wrong with me?'

'How do I know? You're a bit difficult, I should say.'

'How? How am I difficult? In what way?'

'I'd call you artificial. You're not like other fellows.'

This statement of his difference filled Harold with a bleak satisfaction.

As David, in socks, pyjamas and overcoat, settled himself in one deck-chair and put his feet up on the other, Harold gave an anguished cry of disappointment. David ignored it. He blew out the candle and prepared for sleep. Harold protested out of the darkness: 'I quarrelled with my girl-friend for your sake.'

No reply came from David.

'She understands me. Why can't you understand me? She appreciates me. Why can't you? Tell me what prevents you? Tell me . . . tell me. . . .'

Silence.

'I'm only down for the week-end. I've got to go back tomorrow. I've got classes in the afternoon. Poor Angela won't see anything of me. I've left her alone all day. She'll be terribly upset. She may even decide to finish with me, and then I'll have no one. I'll have no one . . . no one.'

David gave a slight snore.

Tears slid from Harold's eyes and fell to the grimy pillow. He wondered if he had spoken the truth when he said Angela understood him? Did anyone understand him? Could they understand him? At the thought of his difference, he was comforted as though he were in some way ennobled by his separation from the rest of the human race, and he at last fell asleep.

He awakened again at first light and again got himself up and dressed silently, this time in order to escape without waking David. As he walked once more on the pneumatic turf of the downs and through the gleaming dew, his spirits rose, for he was returning to Angela. Whether she understood him or not, it seemed to him then that Angela with her feminine warmth and sympathy was the most desirable thing in the world.

ALAN SILLITOE

# Guzman, Go Home

BOUNCING and engine-noise kept the baby soothed, as if he were snug in the belly of a purring cat. But at the minute of feeding time, he screamed out his eight-week honeyguts in a highpowered lament, which nothing but the nipple could stop. Somewhere had to be found where he could feed in peace and privacy, otherwise his cries in the narrow car threatened the straight arrow of Chris's driving.

He often had fifty miles of road to himself, except when a sudden horn signalled an overtaking fast-driven Volkswagen loaded to the gills. 'Look how marvellously they go,' Jane said. 'I told you you should have bought one. No wonder they overtake you so easily, with that left hand drive.'

Open scrub fanned out north and west, boulders and olive trees, mountains combing the late May sky of Spain. It was sombre and handsome country, in contrast to the flat-chested fields of England. He backed into an orange grove, red earth newly watered, cool wind coming down from the fortress of Sagunto. While Jane fed the baby, he fed Jane and himself, broke off pieces of ham and cheese for a simultaneous intake to save time.

The car was so loaded that they looked like refugees leaving a city that the liberating army is coming back to. Apart from a small space for the baby the inside was jammed with cases, typewriter, tape-recorder, paint boxes, canvases, cleaning materials, baskets, flasks, coats, umbrellas and plastic bowls. On the luggage rack lay a trunk and two cases with, topping all, a folded pram-frame and collapsable bath.

It was a new car, but dust, luggage and erratic driving gave it a veteran appearance. They had crossed Paris in a hail and thunderstorm, got lost in the traffic maze of Barcelona, and skirted Valencia by a ring road so rotten that it seemed as if an earthquake had hit it half an hour before. Both wanted the dead useless tree of London lifted off their nerves, so they locked up the flat, loaded the car, and sailed to Boulogne, where the compass of their heart's desire shook its needle towards Morocco.

They wanted to get away from the political atmosphere that saturated English artistic life. Chris, being a painter, had decided that politics ought not to concern him. He would 'keep his hands clean' and get on with his work. 'I like to remember what happened in 1848 to Wagner,' he said, 'who fell in with the revolution up to his neck, helping the workers to storm the arsenal in Dresden, and organising stores for the defence. Then when the revolution collapsed he hightailed it to Italy to be "entirely an artist" again.' He laughed loud, until a particularly deep pothole cut it short in his belly.

Flying along the straight empty road before Valencia they realised freedom from the Sunday papers, those fat meaningless hulks spun out by middle-aged pundits of mediocrity. Nowadays, he imagined, more light came into their eyes at talk of good restaurants than it formerly had about socialism. The gallery owner advised Chris to go to Majorca, if he must get away, but Chris wanted to be near the mosques and museums of Fez, smoke *kif* at the tribal gatherings of Taroudant and Tafilalet, witness the rose-hip snake-green sunsets of Rabat and Mogador. The art dealer couldn't see why he wanted to travel at all. Wasn't England good enough for other painters and writers? 'They like it here, so why don't you? Travel broadens the mind, but it shouldn't go to the head. It's a thing of the past – old-fashioned. You're socially conscious, so you can't be away from the centre of things for long. What about the marches and sit-downs, petitions and talks?'

For ten hours he'd driven along the hairpin coast and across the plains of Murcia and Lorca, wanting to beat the previous day's run. They hadn't stopped for the usual rich skins of sausage-protein and cheese, but ate biscuits and bitter chocolate as they went along. He hardly spoke, as if needing all his concentration to wring extra m.p.h. from the empty and now tolerable road.

His impulse was to get out of Spain, to put that wide arid land behind them. He found it dull, its people too beaten down to be interesting or worth knowing. The country seemed a thousand years older than it had on his last visit. Then, he'd expected insurrection at any time, but now the thought of it was a big horse-laugh. The country smelt even more hopeless than England – which was saying a lot. He wanted to reach Morocco which, no matter how feudal and corrupt, was a new country that might be on the up and up.

So when the engine roared too much for good health at Benidorm, he chose to keep going in order to reach Almeria by nightfall. That extra roar seemed caused by a surcharge of rich fuel at leaving the choke out too long, that would right itself after twenty miles. But it didn't, and on hairpin bends he had difficulty controlling the car. He was careful not to mention this in case his wife persuaded him to get it repaired – which would delay them God knew how many days.

When the plains of Murcia laid a straight road in front of them, it wasn't much after midday. What did hunger matter with progress so good? The roaring of the engine sometimes created a dangerous speed, but maybe it would get them to Tangier. Nothing could be really wrong with a three-month-old car – so he drove it into the remotest part of Spain, sublime indifference and sublime confidence blinding him.

He shot through Villa Oveja at five o'clock. The town stood on a hill, so gear had to be changed, causing such a bellowing of the engine that people stared as if expecting the luggage-racked car to go up any second like the Bomb. The speed increased so much that Chris was ready to put his foot on the brake even when going uphill.

The houses looked miserable and dull, a few doorways opening into cobblestoned *entradas*. By one an old woman sat cutting up vegetables; a group of children were playing by another; and a woman with folded arms looked as if waiting for some fast car full of purpose and direction to take her away. Pools of muddy water lay around, though no rain had fallen for weeks. A petrol pump stood like a one-armed veteran of the Civil War outside an open motor workshop – several men busy within at the bonnet of a Leyland lorry. 'These Spanish towns give me the creeps,' he said, hooting a child out of the way.

He waved a farewell at the last house. Between there and Almeria the earth, under its reafforestation skin of cactus and weed, was yellow with sand, desert to be traversed at high speed with eyes half-closed. The road looped the hills, to the left sheer wall and to the right precipices that fell into approaching dusk. Earth and rocks generated a silence that reminded him of mountains anywhere. He almost expected to see snow around the next bend.

In spite of the faulty engine he felt snug and safe in his sturdy car, all set to reach the coast in a couple of hours. The road ahead looked like a black lace fallen from Satan's boot in heaven. No healthy tune was played by the sandy wind, and the unguarded drop on the right was enough to scare any driver, yet kilometres were a shorter measure than miles, would soon roll him into the comfort of a big meal and a night's hotel.

On a steep deserted curve the car failed to change gear. Chris thought it a temporary flash of overheated temper from the clutch mechanism, but, trying again – before the loaded car rolled off the precipice – drew a screech of igniting steel from within the gearbox.

He was stopped from trying the gears once more by a warning yell from Jane, pulled the hand brake firmly up. The car still rolled, its two back wheels at the cliff edge, so he pressed with all his force on the foot-brake as well, and held it there, sweat piling out on to the skin of his face. They sat, the engine switched off

Wind was the only noise, a weird hooting brazen hill-wind from which the sun had already extricated itself. 'All we can do,' he said, 'is hope somebody will pass, so that we can get help.'

'Don't you know *anything* about this bloody car? We can't sit here all night.' Her face was wound up like a spring, life only in her righteous words. It was as if all day the toil of the road had been preparing them for just this.

'Only that it shouldn't have gone wrong, being two months' old.'

'Well,' she said, 'British is best. You know I told you to buy a Volkswagen. What do you *think* is wrong with it?'

'I don't know. I absolutely don't bloody well know.'

'I believe you. My God! You've got the stupidity to bring me and a baby right across Europe in a car without knowing the first thing about it. I think you're mad to risk all our lives like this. You haven't even got a proper driving licence.' The wind too, moaned its just rebuke. But the honied sound of another motor on the mountain road filtered into the horsepower of their bickering. Its healthy and forceful noise drew closer, a machine that knew where it was going, its four-stroke cycle fearlessly cutting through the silence. While he searched for a telling response to her tirade, Jane put her arm out, waving the car to stop.

It was a Volkswagen (of course, he thought, it bloody-well had to be), a field-grey low-axelled turtle with windows, so fresh-washed and polished that it might just have rolled off the conveyor line. Its driver leaned out while the engine still turned: '*Que ha pasado?*'

Chris told him: the car had stopped, and it wasn't possible to change gear, or get it going at all. The Volkswagen had a Spanish number plate, and the driver's Spanish, though grammatical, was undermined by another accent. He got out, motioned Chris to do the same. He was a tall, well-built man dressed in khaki slacks, and a light-blue open-necked jersey-shirt a size too small: his chest tended to bulge through it and gave the impression of more muscle than he really had. His bare arms were tanned, and on one was a small white mark where a wrist watch had been. There was a more subtle tan to his face, as if it had done a slow change from lobster red to a parchment colour, oil-soaked and wind-worn after a lot of travel.

To Chris he seemed like a rescuing angel, yet there was a cast of sadness, of disappointment underlying his face that, with a man of his middle-age, was no passing expression. It was a mark that life had grown on him over the years, and for good reason since there was also something strong and ruthless in his features. As if to deny all this – yet in a weird way confirming it more – he had a broad forehead, and the eyes and mouth of an alert benign cat, with spectacles.

He sat in the driver's seat, released the brake, and signalled Chris to push. '*Harémos la vuelta.*'

Jane stayed inside, rigid from the danger they had been in, weary in every vein after days travelling with a baby that was feeding from herself. She turned now and again to tuck the sheet under the baby. The man beside her deftly manoeuvred the car to the safe side of the road, and faced it towards the bend leading back to Villa Oveja.

He started the engine. The turnover was healthy, and the wheels moved. Chris saw the car sliding away, wife, luggage, and baby fifty yards down the road. He was too tired to be afraid they would vanish for ever and leave him utterly alone in the middle of these darkening peaks. He lit a cigarette, in a vagrant slap-happy wind that, he had time to think, would never have allowed him to do so in a more normal situation.

The car stopped, then started again, and the man tried to change gear, which brought a further roaring screech from the steel discs within. He stopped the car, leaned from the window and looked with bland objective sadness at Chris. Hand on the wheel, he spoke English for the first time, but in an unmistakable German accent. He grinned and said, a high-pitched rhythmical rise and fall, a telegraphic rendering of disaster that was to haunt Chris a long time:

'England, your car has snapped!'

*

'Lucky for you, England, I am the owner of the garage in Villa Oveja. A towing rope in my car will drag you there in five minutes.

'My name is Guzman – allowing me to introduce myself. If I hadn't come along and seen your break-up you would perhaps have waited all night, because this is the loneliest Iberian road. I only come this way once a week, so you are double lucky. I go to the next town to see my other garage branch, confirm that the Spaniard I have set to run it doesn't trick too much. He is my friend, as far as I can have a friend in this country where, due to unsought-for happenings, I have spent nearly the same years as my native Germany. But I find my second garage is not doing too wrong. The Spaniards are good mechanics, a very adjustable people. Even without spare parts they have the genius to get an engine living – though under such a system it can't last long before being carried back again. Still, they are clever. I taught my mechanics all I know: I myself was once able to take tank engines into morsels, under even more trying conditions than here. I trained mechanics well, and one answered by taking his knowledge to Madrid, where I don't doubt he got an excellent job – the crooked ungrateful. He was the most brainful, so what could he do except trick me? I would have done the same in his place. The others, they are fools for not escaping with my knowledge, and so they will never get on to the summit. Likewise they aren't much use for me. But we will fix your car good once we get right back to the town, have no fear of it.

'You say it is only three months old? Ah, England, no German car would be such a bad boy after three months. This Volkswagen I have had two years, and not a nut and bolt has crawled out of place. I never boast about myself, but the Volkswagen is a good car, that any rational human being can trust. It is fast and hard, has a marvellous honest engine, that sounds to last a thousand years pulling through these mountains. Even on scorched days I like to drive with all my windows shut-closed, listening to the engine nuzzling swift along like a happy cat-bitch. I sweat like rivers, but the sound is beautiful. A good car, and anything goes wrong, so you take the lid off, and all its insides are there for the eye to see and the hand-spanner to work at. Whereas your English cars are difficult to treat with. A nut and bolt loose, a pipe snapped, and if you don't burn the fingers you surely sprain the wrist trying to get at the injured fix. It's as if your designers hide them on purpose. Why? It isn't rational why, in a people's car that is so common. A car should be natural to expose and easy to understand. On the other hand you can't say that because a car is new nothing should happen to it. Even an English car. That is unrealistic. You should say: This car is new, therefore I must not let anything happen to it. A car is a rational human being like yourself.

'Thank you. I've always had a wanton for English cigarettes, just as I have for the language. The tobacco is more subtle than the brutal odours of the Spanish. Language is our best lanes of communication, England, and whenever I meet travellers like yourself I take advantage from it.

'You don't like the shape of the Volkswagen? Ah, England! That is mistake number one in choosing a car. You English are so aesthetic, so biased. When I was walking through north Spain just after the war – before the ink was dry on the armistice signatures, ha, ha! – I was very poor and had no financial money – and in spite of the beautiful landscapes and marvellous towns with walls and churches, I sold my golden spectacles to a *bruto* farmer so that I can buy sufficing bread and sausage to feed me to Madrid. I didn't see the pleasant things so clearly, being minus them, but here I am today. So what does the shape of a car mean? That you like it? *Also!* That you don't wear spectacles yet, so you'll never have to sell them, you say? Oh, I am laughing. Oh, oh, oh! But England, excuse me wagging my finger at you, one day you may not be so fortunate.

'Ah! So! Marvellous, as you say: clever Guzman has flipped into second gear, and maybe I do not need my towing rope to get you back to town. I don't think you were so glad in all your life to meet a German, were you, England? Stray Germans like me are not so current in Spain nowadays?'

Shadows took the place of wind. A calm dusk slunk like an idling panther from the hips and peaks of the mountains. A few yellow lamps shone from the outlying white houses of Villa Oveja. Both cars descended on the looping road, then crept up to these lights like prodigal moths.

Chris remembered his ironic handwave of an hour ago, as he stopped outside Guzman's garage. A small crowd gathered: maybe they'd witnessed other motorists give that final handwave and draggle back in this forlorn manner. God's judgment, I suppose they think, the religious bastards. Guzman finished his inspection, sunlight seeming to shine on his glasses even in semi-darkness – which also hid what might be a smile: 'England, I will take you to a hotel where you can stay all night – with your wife and child.'

'All night!' Chris had expected this, so his exclamation wasn't so sharp.

'Maybe two whole nights, England.'

Jane's words were clipped with hysteria: 'I won't spend two nights in this awful dump.' The crowd recognised the livelier inflections of a quarrel, grew livelier themselves. Guzman's smile was less hidden: 'Rationally speaking, it must be difficult travelling with a family-wife. However, you will find the Hotel Universal modest but comfortable, I'm sure.'

'Listen,' Chris said, 'can't you fix this clutch tonight?' He turned to Jane: 'We could still be in Almeria by twelve.'

'Forget it,' she said. 'This is what . . .'

'. . . comes of leaving England with a car you know nothing about? Oh for God's sake!'

Guzman's heavy accent sometimes rose to an almost feminine pitch, and now came remorselessly in: 'England, if I might suggest . . .'

The hotel room smelled of carbolic and flit; it was scrupulously clean. Every piece of luggage was unloaded and stacked on the spacious landing of the second floor – a ramshackle heap surrounded by thriving able-bodied aspidistras. The room, dosed so heavily with flit, gave Jane a headache. Rooms with bath were non-existent, but a hand-basin was available, and became sufficient during their three days there.

Off the squalor of the main road were narrow, cobble-stoned streets. White-faced houses with overhanging balconies were neat and well cared for. The streets channelled you into a spacious square, where the obligatory church, the necessary townhall, and the useful *telegrafos*, emphasised the importance of the locality. While Guzman's tame mechanics worked on the car Chris and Jane sat in the cool dining-room and listened to Guzman himself:

'I come here always for an hour after lunch or dinner, to partake coffee and perhaps meet interesting people, by which I signify any foreigner who happens to be moving through. As you imagine, not many stay in our little God-forgotten town – as your charming and rational wife surmised on your precipitant arrival here. My English is coming back the more I talk to you, which makes me happy. I read much, to maintain my vocabulary, but speech is rare. I haven't spoken it with anyone for fourteen months. You express motions of disbelief? It's true. Few motorists happen to break up at this particular spot in Spain. Many English who come prefer the coasts. Not that the mosquitoes are any lesser there than here. Still, I killed that one: a last midnight blackout for the little blighter. Ah, there's another. There, on your hand. Get it, England. Bravo. You also are quick. They are not usually so bad, because we flit them to death.

'I suppose the English like Spain in this modern epoch because of its politics, which are on the right side – a little primitive, but safe and solid. Excuse me, I did not know you were speeding through to Africa, and did not care for political Spain. Not many visit the artistic qualities of Iberia, which I have always preferred. You are fed up with politics, you say, and want to leave them all behind? I don't blame you. You are wisdom himself, because politics can peril a man's life, especially if he is an artist. It is good to do nothing but paint, and good that you should come through this country. Why does an artist sit at politics? He is not used to it, tries his hand, and then all is explosioned in him. Shelley? Yes, of course, but that was a long time ago, my dear England. Excuse me again, yes, I will have a *coñac*. When I was in London, in 1932, somebody taught me a smart toast: health, wealth, and stealth! *Gesundheit!*

'Forgive my discretion, England, but I see from your luggage that you are an artist, and I must talk of it. I have a great opinion of artists, and can see why it is that your car broke down. Artists know little of mechanical things, and those that do can't ever be great artists. I myself began as a middling artist. It is a long story, which starts when I was eighteen, and I shall tell you soon.

'Your car is in good hands. Don't worry. And you, madam, I forbid you. We can relax after such a dinner. My mechanics have taken out the engine, and are already shaping off the spare necessary on the lathe. There are no spare parts for your particular name of car in this section of Spain, therefore we have to use our intelligent handicraft – to make them from nothing, from scrape, as you say. That doesn't daunt me, England, because in Russia I had to make spare parts for captured tanks. Ah! I learned a lot in Russia. But I wish I hadn't never been there. My fighting was tragical, my bullets shooting so that I bleed to death every night for my perpetrations. But bygones are bypassed, and are a long time ago. At least I learned the language. *Chto dyelaets?*

'Well, it is a pity you don't have a Volkswagen, which I have all the spare pieces for. Yet if you'd had a Volkswagen we wouldn't have been talking here. You would have been in Marrakech. Like my own countrymen: they overtake every traveller on the road in their fast Volkswagens, as if they departed Hamburg that morning and have to get the ferry ship for Tangier this evening, so as to be in Marrakech tomorrow. Then after a swift week-end in the Atlas Mountains they speed back to the office-work for another economic miracle, little perceiving that I am one of those that made that miracle possible. What do I mean? How?

'Ah, ah, ah! You are sympathetic. When I laugh loud, so, you don't get up and walk away. You don't stare at me or flinch. Often the English do that, especially those who come to Spain. Red-faced and lonely, they stare and stare, then walk off. But you understand my laugh, England. You smile even. Maybe it is because you are an artist. You say it is because I am an artist? Oh, you are so kind, so kind. I have been an artist and a soldier both, also a mechanic. Unhappily I have done too many things, fallen between cleft stools.

'But, believe it or not, I earned a living for longer years by my drawing than I have done as a garage man. The first money I earned in my life was during my student days in Konigsberg – by drawing my uncle who was a ship-captain. My father wanted me to be a lawyer, but I desired to be an artist. It was difficult to shake words with my father at that time, because he had just made a return from the war and he was very dispirited about Germany and himself. Therefore he wanted me to obey him as if I had lost the war for him, and he wouldn't let me choose. I had to give up all drawing and become a lawyer, nothing less. I said no. He said yes. So I departed home. I walked twenty miles to the railway station with all the money I'd saved for years, and when I got there, the next day, it transpires that the young fortune I thought I had wouldn't even take me on a mile of my long journey. All my banknotes were useless, yet I asked myself how could that be, because houses and factories still stood up, and there were fields and gardens all around me. I was flabbergasted. But I set off for Berlin with no money, and it took me a month to get there, drawing people's faces for slices of bread and sausage. I began to see what my father meant, but by now it was too late. I had taken the jump, and went hungry for it, like all rebellious youths.

'In my native home-house I had been sheltered from the gales of economy, because I saw now how the country was. Destituted. In Frankfurt a man landed at my foot because he had dropped from a lot of floors up. England, it was terrible: the man had worked for forty years to save his money, and he had none remaining. In such a confusion I decided more than ever that the only term one could be was an artist. Coming from Königsberg to Berlin had shown me a thrill for travel. But Berlin was dirty and dangerous. It was full of people singing about socialism – not national socialism, you understand, but communist socialism. So I soon left and went to Vienna – walking. You must comprehend that all this takes months, but I am young, and I like it. I do not eat well, but I do eat, and I have many adventures, with women especially. I think that it was the best time of my life. You want to go, madam? Ah, good night. I kiss your hand, even if you do not like my prattle. Good night, madam, good night. A charming wife, England.

'I didn't like Vienna, because its past glories are too past, and it was full of unemployed. One of the few sorts of people I can't like are the people without work. They make my stomach ill. I am not rational when I see them, so I try not to see them as soon as I can. I went to Budapest, walking along the banks of the Danube with nothing except a knapsack and a stick, free, healthy and young – while in every city there was much conflict where maybe people were finishing off what they had started in the trenches. I watched the steamers travelling by, always catching me up, then leaving me a long way back, until all I could listen to was their little toots of progress from the next switch of the river. The money crashed, but steamers went on. What else could Germany do? It was a good time though, England, because I never thought of the future, or wondered where I would reach in the years to be. I certainly didn't see that I should throw so much of my good years in this little Spanish town – in a country even more destituted than the one in Germany after I set off so easily from my birth-home. Excuse me, if I talk so much. It is the brandy, and it is also making me affectionate and sentimental. People are least intelligent when most affectionate, so forgive me if I do not always keep up the high standard of talk that two artists should kindle among them.

'No, I insist that it is my turn this time. Your wife has gone, no, to look after the baby? In fact I shall order a bottle of brandy. This Spanish liquid is hot, but not too intoxicating. Ah! I shall now pour. Say when. I have travelled a long way, to many places: Capri, Turkey, Stalingrad, Majorca, Lisbon, but I never forsaw that I should end up in the awkward state I am now in. It is unjust, my dear England, unjust. My heart becomes like a flitterbat when I think that the end is so close.

'Why? Ah! Where was I? Yes. In Budapest there was even more killing, so I went to Klausenburg (I don't know which country that town is in any more) and passed many of these beautiful clean Saxon towns, until I came to Constantinople. I walked through the mountains and woods of Transylvania, over the high Carpathians. The horizons changed every day: blue, purple, white, shining like the sun; and on days when there were no horizons because of rain or mist I stayed in some cowshed, or the salon of a farmhouse if I had pleased the family with my likenesses. I went on, walking, walking (I walked every mile, England, a German pilgrim), across the great plain, through Bucharest and across the Danube again, and into Bulgaria. I had left Germany far behind and my soul was free. Politics didn't interest me, and I was amazed, in freedom, at how my father had been sad at the war.

'How the brandy goes! But I don't get drunk. If only I could get drunk. But the more brandy I drink the colder I get, cool and icy on the heart. Even good brandy is the same. Health, wealth, and stealth! I got to Constantinople, and stayed for six months. Strangely, in the poorest city of all, I made a good living. In an oriental city unemployment didn't bother me: it seemed natural. I went around the terraces of hotels along the Bosporus making portraits of the clientels, and of all the money I made I gave the proprietors ten per cent. If they were modern I drew them or their wives also against the background of the Straits, and sometimes I would take a commission to portray a palace or historic house.

'One day I met a man who questioned if I would draw a building for him a few kilometres along the coast. He would give me five pounds now, and five pounds when we came back to the hotel. Of course, I accepted, and we drove in his car. He was a middle-aged Englishman, tall and formal, but he offered me a good price for the hour's drawing necessary. By now I had developed the quickness of draughtsmanship, and I sat on the headland easily sketching the building on the next cape. While I worked your Englishman, England, walked up and down smoking swiftly on a cigar, and looked nervous about something. I had ended, and was packing my sketches in, when two Turkish soldiers stood from behind a rock and came to us with rifles sticking out. "Walk to the car," the Englishman said to me, hissing, "as if you haven't done anything."

' "But," I said, "we've made nothing wrong, truly."

' "I should say not, my boy," he told me. "That was a Turkish fort you just sketch."

'We run, but two more soldiers stand in front of us, and the Englishman joked with them all four, patted them on the savage head, but he had to give out twenty pounds before they let us go, and then he cursed all the way back.

'It might have been worse, I realise at the hotel, and the Englishman is pleased, but said we'll have to move on for our next venture, and he asked me if I'd ever thought of hiking to the frontier of Turkey and Russia. "Beautiful, wild country," he told me. "You'll never forget it. You go there on your own, and make a few sketches for me, and it'll prove lucrative – while I sit back over my sherbet here. Ha, ha, ha!"

'So I questioned him: "Do you want me to sketch Turkish forts, or Soviet ones?"

' "Well," he said, "both."

'That, England, was my first piece of stealthy work, but it never made me wealthy and I already was healthy. Ah, ah, ah, ho, ho! You are strong, England. I cannot make you flinch when I hit you on the back like a friend. So! Before then I had been too naïve to feel dishonest. Once on the Turkish border I was captured, with my sketches, and nearly hanged, but my Englishman pays money, and I go free. Charming days. I wasn't even interested in politics. I hear your baby crying. England, your wife calls for you.'

'It is a fine night tonight, England, a beautiful star-dark around this town.

'I have travelled most of my life. Even during the war I was always voyaging. In my youth, after I was exported from Turkey by the soldiers (they took all my money before letting me go. If only we had conquered them during the war, then I would have met them again!) I travelled in innumerous countries of the Balkans and Central East, until I was so confused by the multiple currencies that I began to lose count of the exchange. I would recite my travellers' cataclysm as I crossed country limits: "Ten Slibs equals one Flap; a hundred Clackies makes one Golden Crud; four Stuks comes out at one Drek – but usually I went to the next nation with not Slib Flap Clackie or Golden Crud to my name, nothing except what I wear and a pair of worn sandals. I joke about the currencies, because there is no fact I cannot remember. Some borders I have crossed a dozen times, but even so far back I can memory the dates of them, and stand aside to watch myself at that particular time walking along, carefreed, towards the customs post.

'One of my adventures is that I get married, and my wife is a good German girl who also likes the walking life. Once we tramped from Alexandria, all along the coast of Africa to Tangier, but it was very hard because the Moslems do not like to have their faces drawn. However, there were many white people we met, and I also sketch a lot of buildings and interesting features – which were later found to be of much use to certain circles in Berlin. You understand, eh?

'We went back to Germany, and walked in that country also. We joined groups of young people on excursions to the Alps, and had many jolly times on the *hohewege* of the Schwarzwald. My wife had two children, both boys, but life was still carefreed. There were more young people like ourselves to enjoy it with. My art was attaining something, and I did hundreds of drawings, all of which I was very proud, though some were better than others, naturally. Most were burned to cinders by your aeroplanes, I am sad to say. I also lost many of my old walking friends in that war, good men . . . but that is all in the past, and to be soonest forgotten. Nowadays I have only a few comrades, in Ibiza. Life can be very sad, England.

'In that time before the war my drawings were highly prized in Germany. They hung in many galleries, because they showed the spirit of the age – were often of young people striving in all their purity to build the great state together, the magnificent corporation of one country. We were patriotic, England, and radical as well. Ah! It is good when all the people go forward together. You shouldn't think I liked the bad things though, about inferior races and so on. Because if you consider, how could I be living in Spain if I did? It was a proud and noble time when loneliness was forgotten. It contained sensations I often spend my nights thinking about, because it looked that after all the travels of my young days I was getting at last some look-on at my work, as well as finding the contentment of knowing a leader who pointed to me the fact that I was different from those people I had been through on my travels. He drew me together. Ah! England, at that you get more angry than if I had banged you on the shoulder like a jolly German! Well, I don't believe anything now, so let me tell you. Nothing, nothing . . . nothing. Everyone was joining something in those days, and I couldn't stop myself, even though I was an artist. And because I was an artist I went the whole way, to the extremes, right beyond the nether boundaries. I was carried along like this *coñac* cork, floating down a big river. I couldn't swim out of it, and in any case the river was so strong that I liked it, I liked being in it, a strong river, because I was as light as a cork and it would never carry me under. He . . . he made us as light as a cork, England. But politics are gone from my life's vision. I make no distinction any more between races or systems. One of my favourite own jokes is that of Stalin, Lenin and Trotsky playing your money game Monopoly together in the smallest back room of the Kremlin in 1922. Ha, ha, ha! You also think it is funny, England, no?

'No, you don't think it is funny, I can see that. I am sorry you don't. But listen to me though, you are lucky. So far you don't know what it is to belong to a nation that has taken the extreme lanes, but you will, you will. So I can see it coming because I read your newspapers. Up till now your country has been lucky, ours has been unlucky. We had no luck. You cut off the head of your King Karl; we didn't of our Karl. Ah, now you smile at my wit. You laugh. You have the laugh of the superior, England, but once on a time, if any foreigner laughed at me like that I could kill them. And I did! I did!

'Stop me if I shout. Forgive me. No, don't go, England. Your baby is not crying. Your wife does not call. Listen to me more. I don't believe anything except that I am able to repair your car and do it good. And that is something. It is a long way from my exhibitions of drawings, one of which, at Magdeburg, was opened and appreciated by You-know-who, a person who also knew about art. Yes, actually by him. He shook my own hand, this hand! Oh my God. I was reconciled to my father by then, and I can tell you that he was the proudest man in all Germany.

'Well, I will not ennui you any more about my adventures in those days. Let us skip a few years and talk about romantic Spain. Not that it was romantic. It can be a very dirty place, and annoying, unlike the cleaner countries, such as ours, my dear England. Just after crossing the mountains, on foot in 1945, I stayed in a shepherd's hut for two weeks of hiding. Someone paid the shepherd a terrible high rent for this stenching sty, and all the while I was attacked by ants, so that I go nearly mad. I looked mad – with my long beard and poor clothes. Ants came in the door and I start to kill them. Then I spare some lives in the hope that they would scuttle back and tell their friends that they had better not come near that hut because a crazy bone-German is conducting a proficient massacre. But it made no difference, and they kept coming to be killed. I went on and on killing them, for days, but they came on I suppose to see why it was that those before them were not coming back. There were thousands, but I got tired first. Ants are inhuman. Nowadays, if I see ants in my house or garage I use a flit gun – bacteriological warfare, if you like, and that is quicker. It stops them. I think of all those poor ants who get killed, and maybe the ants themselves have no option but to start this war on me. If only they were all individuals, England, like you – or me. Then maybe only one or two would have been killed before the others turned and ran. But no, they have their statues to the war, the Tomb of the Unknown Ant, who dies so that every ant could have his pebble of sugar, but died in vain. I have a sense of humour? Yes, I have. But it didn't protect me from doing great wrongs.

'How did I get to Spain? My life is full of long stories, but this time I came to Spain from necessity, from dire necessity. It was a matter of life and death. To get here I set out from Russia on a journeying much longer than the one I told you about already in my youth. Name a country, and I have been in it. Say a town and I can call the main street, because I have slept on it. I can tell you about the colour of the policeman's uniform, and where you can get the cheapest food; which is the best corner to stand and ask for money. I have done many things since the end of the war that I would not naturally do, that I should be ashamed of, except that it is man's duty to survive. During the war I thought it wasn't, but when the war started to end I taught myself that it was. How did I come to obtain my garage business? you ask. It takes much money to buy a garage, and I tell you something now that I wouldn't tell a walking soul, not even my wife, so that instead of forgiving me, you will try to understand.

'I got to Algeria. To say how would damage a few people, so I mustn't. Part of my time I was a teacher of English in Sétif, and passed myself as an Englishman. I imitated in every manner that man who was a spy back on the Turkish Bosporus until nobody in this new place spied the difference. I taught English to Moslems as well, but earned a bad living at it. To augment my in-money I made intricate maps of farmers' land in the area. I am a good reconnaissance man, and if a farmer had only a very poor and tiny square of land the map I drew made it look like a kingdom, and he was glad to have it square-framed, see something to fight for as he gazed at it hanging on the wall of his tin-roofed domicile, at night when the mosquitoes bit him mad, and he was double mad worrying about crops, money and drought – not to mention rebellion. Then I began selling plots of land in the *bled* that weren't accurately possessed by me – to Frenchmen who came straight out of the army from the mix-out in Indo-China – by telling people it was rich in oil. Nowadays I hear that it really is, but no matter. I sold the land only cheap, but I soon had enough good money to buy many passports and escape to Majorca. I got a fine work as travel-agent clerk in Palma, and worked good for a year, trying to save my money like an honest man. Spain was a stone country to make a living in then – things are much easier these days since the peseta is devalued. I couldn't save, because all the time I had before me the remembering of the man in Frankfurt who dropped at my feet completely dead because his life savings wouldn't buy a postal stamp. But then an Italian asks me to look after his yacht one winter, which was his huge mistake, because when I had sold it to a rich Englishman I took an aircraft to Paris.

'There I thought I had done such a deal of travelling that I should turn such knowledge into my own business. To commence, I announced in a good newspaper that ten people were desired for a trip around the world, that it would be a co-operative venture and that only little money would be needed, comparatively. When I saw the ten people I told that two thousand dollars each would be enough, but they had to be fed-up sufficiently with modern world-living to qualify for my expedition. I explained that out of our collective money we would comprise a lorry, and a moving-camera to take documentary films of strange places, that we would sell. Everybody said it was a shining brainwave, and I soon got the lorry and camera cheap. For two weeks we had map meetings while I planned each specific of the trip. They were all good people, so trusted me, even when I said that a supplementary cost would be laid because of the high price of film. No one would be leader of the expedition, I stipulated: it would be run by committee, with myself as the chairman. Much of the money I put in the bank, but the peril was I began to like the idea of this world-round journey so much that I couldn't make myself disappear. I kept on at it, obsessed at the plan. I wrote to many shops and factories and (even in France) they gave me equipment. I charged it all to my clients – as I called them in my secret self. Unfortunately the newspapers wrote stories about my scheme, and put my photo in the print.

'So our big lorry set out of Paris, and snapped on the road to Marseille. I repaired it, and from Marseille our happy gathering steamed to Casablanca on a packet-boat. I had moved battalions of men and tanks (and many prisoners) in every complication over Russia, but this was a happy situation, with these twenty people (by this time others had been entered to our committee). It was like being young again. Everyone loved me. I was *popular*, England, by total consent of all those dear, good friends. Tears fall into my eyes when I think of it – real tears that I can't bear the taste of. The further I gave in to my sentimental joining and went on with my dear international companions, the less was the money that I intended to go off and begin my garage within Spain. I had never had such a skirmish in my conscience. What could I do? Tell me, England, what could I do? Would you have done any better than such? No, you wouldn't, I know. My God! I am shouting again. Why don't you stop me?

'The lorry snapped awfully, at Colomb-Bechar, just before we intend to cross the real desert. But my talents triumph again, and I repaired it, and say I am going to try it out. They are still in the tents, eating some lunch, and I drive off, round and round in big circles. Suddenly I make a straight line and they never see me again. I don't know what became of them. They were nearly penniless. I took petrol and the cameras, everything expensive, as well as funds. It is too painful for me to speculate, so ask me nothing else, even if I tell you. From Casablanca I come to here, and when I have collected all from my banks I see there is enough to get my garage, and much to spare.

'And now I am in Spain, you think I have as much as a man could want? I have a Spanish wife, two children, and an interesting work. I have had several wives, and now a Spanish woman. She is dark, beautiful, and plump (yes, you have seen her) but in bed she doesn't act for me. My children go to the convent school, and kiss crosses, tremble at nuns and priests. These I cannot like at all, but what can I do? It has been a dull life, because there's not much to do here. Sometimes we go to a bullfight. But I don't like it. It is a good ritual, but not attractive to a rational human being like myself. All winter we see no travellers, and hug the fireplace like damp washing. Now and again I still do some drawings. Yes, that is one of them over there, that I presented to this hotel. You don't like it? You do? Ah, you make me very happy, England. Often I steer down the sealine to Algeciras, a short voyage in my dependable Volkswagen. It is a very pleasant port, and I make many sketches. I know some Russians who have a hotel and let me stay at cost rate. Gibraltar is a fascinating shape to make on paper, which I see from the terrace. I also go across to your famous English fort-rock to shopping, and maybe purchase one of those intellectual English Sunday newspapers there. One of them lasts me a month at least. I find them very good, exceptionally lively and interesting to a mind like mine.

'Ah, England, let us take a walk and I will tell you why my life is finished. That's better. The air smells fresh and good. Why, we have talked the whole night through. That green speck in the sky over there is the first dawn, a little light, a glow worm that the sun sends in front to make sure that all is dark for it. Your wife will never forgive you. But women are not rational human beings. Oh, oh, oh – England, you think they are? I can prove to you that they are not so, quicker than you can prove to me that they are. You say that the sun is a red sun? I can see that it will be. But I have been in Spain many times. In 1934 I came here, walking all through, sketching farmhouses and touristic monuments – later published as an album in Berlin. I surveyed the land. Spain I know exceedingly well. This beautiful land we saved from Bolshevism – though I sometimes wonder why. I am afraid of a communist government here, because if it comes, I am ended. The whole world gets dark for me. Maybe Franco will make a pact with communist Germany, and send me back to it. It has happened before. I feel my bed is not so safe to lie on.

'My life has been tragic, but I am not one of those who self-pities. It will be hot today. I sweat already. I must sell my garage and leave, go to another country. I am forced to abandon my wife and children, which is not a good fate. It gives me suffering in the heart that you cannot imagine. I am nearly sixty years. You will notice that I have not talked about the war, because it is too hurtful to me. My home was in East Prussia: but the Soviets took the family land. They enslaved and murdered my fellow countrymen. England, don't laugh. You say they should keep the Berlin Wall there for ever? Ah, you don't know what you are saying. I can see that my misfortune makes you glad. I was not there, of course, but I know what the Soviets did. My wife was killed in one of their air raids.

'England, please, do not ask me that question. I do not know who started such wicked bombings of the mass. A war begins, and many things happen. Much water flows under the bridge-road. Let me march on with my story. Please, patience. My two sons are in the communist party. As if that was why I fought, used in my body and soul the most terrible energies for one large Germany. I want to go back and beat them both, beat them without mercy, hit at them until they are dead.

'Once I had a letter from them, and they ask me to come back to my homeland. How the letter gets me I don't know, but a person in Toledo sends it. They beg me to come back and work for democratic Germany. Why do you think they ask me this? Innocent, because sons love and want their father? Ah! Because they know I shall be hanged when I get there. That is why they ask. They are devils, devils.

'I am leaving Villa Oveja, quitting Spain, because a Jew came to this town a few weeks ago. I think from my photo in the Paris paper and other photos issued by my enemies, he recognised me. They have fastened me down, hunted me like an animal, and know where I am now. I know they are leaving me for the time being, because perhaps there is a bigger job – someone more important before they concentrate on the small fish. This Jew wasn't like the others. He was tall, young and blond. He was browned by the sun, he was handsome, as if he'd been in Spain as much as I had, and one day he came to the door of my garage and looked in at me. He looked, to make sure. I could not compete his stare, and they could have used my face for the chalk of Dover. How did I know he was a Jew, you ask? Don't mock me, England, because I am no longer against them. I hardly look at his face, but I *knew* because his eyes were like sulphur, a nice young man who could have been a pleasant tourist, but I knew, I knew without knowing why I knew, that he was one of their soldiers. They have their own country now: if only they had their own country before the war, England. His eyes burned my heart away. I could not move. The next day he went off, but any time they will come for me. I am still young, even while sixty, yet think that perhaps I don't care, that I will let them carry me, or that I will kill myself before they come.

'It is not possible I stay here, because the people have turned. Maybe the Jew told something before he went away, but a man stopped me in one of the alley-streets and said: "Guzman, get out, go home." The man had been one of my friends, so you can imagine how it bit deep at me. And then, to hammer it harder, I have been seeing it written on walls in big letters: "Guzman, go home" – which makes my brains burst, because this is my home. No one understands, that I am wanting to be solitary, to have peace, to labour all right. When I make tears like this I feel I am an old man.

'I should not have killed those people. I sat down to eat. They were hungry in the snow, and I could not stop myself. I could not tolerate the way they stood and looked. They kept looking, England, they kept looking. People who couldn't work because they had no food to take into them. I fired my gun. My way went terrible after that, out of control. I was not rational.

'Look, don't go yet. Don't stand and leave me by. The sun is making that mountain drink fire. I shall always see mountains on fire, whenever I go and wherever else my feet tread, red mountains shaking flames out of their hat top. Even before the Jew came a dream was in me one night. I was a young scholar at the high school and circles were painted in the concrete groundspaces, for gymnasium games and drill. I stood in one, with a book in my hand to read. Everything changed, and the perfect circle was of white steel. A thin rod it was, a hot circle that glowed metal. I wanted to get out of it but I couldn't, because the heat from it was scorching my ankles. All the force of me was pressing against it, and though I was a highgrown man I couldn't jump out. I had a gun in my hand instead of a book and I was going to shoot myself, because I knew the idea that if I did I should get out and be able to walk off a freed man. I shot someone passing by, a silent bullet. But then I woke, and nothing had worked for me.

'In military life they say there is a marshal's rank in every soldier's kitbag. In peace-life I think there is a pair of worn sandals in every cupboard, because you don't ever know when the longest life-trudge is going to start – whether you are criminal or not. What shall I do? Your questions are pertinent, but I am practical. I am rational. I won't give in, because I am always rational. Maybe it is the best thing of quality obtained from my father. I look at my maps, and have the big hope of a hunted man. Do you have any dollars in currency that I could exchange? You haven't? Can you pay the repair bill on your car in dollars then? Ah, so. I have another Volkswagen I could sell you, only a year old and going like a spark, guaranteed for years on rough roads. The man I bought it from had taken it to Nyasaland – over earth, there and back. Pay me in pound-sterling then, in Gibraltar if you like. I can get the ferry there and back in a day, make my purchasing of necessaries for a long trek . . . no, you can't?

'It is going to be a cloudy day, good for driving because it will be not too hot. Your car is now in excellent order, and will run well for long hours. It is a reasonable car, with a stout motor and strong frame. It is not too logical for repairing, and will not have such long life as you thought when you bought it. Next time, if you want some of my best caution, you will purchase a Volkswagen. You won't regret it, and will always remember me for giving you such solid advice.

'I am tired after being up all night. Mind how you drive, on those mountain curves. Don't you see what it speaks in the sky over there? You don't? Your eyes are not good. Or perhaps you are deceiving me to save my feelings. It says: GUZMAN, GO HOME. Where can I go? I own two houses and my garage here. I own property, England, property. All my life I have wanted to own property. I shall have to sell it to them for nothing. So. Go home, they say to me, go home.

'I am light headed when I don't sleep the dark, but I must go to work, think some more while I am working. My name is not Guzman. That is a name the Spaniards gave me, because of my clever business ways. It has always surprised me that I could make my commercial career so well, when I started off life only as a poor hiker drawing faces. Now I am a wanderer, when I don't want to be.'

Chris, his face the grey-green colour of a living tree branch that had had the bark stripped from it, turned away and walked quickly through the quiet town to the hotel. His wife was feeding the baby. The day after tomorrow, they would be in Africa. Six months after that, he decided, back in London.

The car broke down again in Tangier. 'That crazy Nazi,' he thought, 'can't even mend a bloody car.'

# Suspense of Judgment

<hr>

At one o'clock in the morning on a warm, moonlit August night twenty years ago, I jumped from an American Dakota aircraft as it flew low over the English midlands. My parachute did not open, but I never reached the ground. Instead, I spent forty-five minutes alone in the night – waiting to die. For the first time in my life I really faced up to the aftermath of death, and I recoiled from what I had been taught.

D-day had come and gone. June and July had spent their long warm days, and the British 1st Airborne Division waiting in England felt they had been spent as slowly and reluctantly as a miser spends his coin.

They had been rushed to airfields for a drop behind the Falaise gap, only to have it cancelled when it became apparent that too many of the enemy had escaped to make the operation worthwhile, and the same reason was given for the cancellation of the landing at Rambouillet. And still the division waited, trained and rehearsed, and moaned as only the British soldier can moan.

But one August night a rehearsal took place that is destined to remain in my memory as clearly as if it had taken place yesterday, and not twenty years ago.

My platoon was the only part of our unit involved in the exercise and our task was to land and mark out the dropping-zone on which a parachute brigade was later to descend.

It might be as well to explain at this stage that parachute troops do not in fact parachute. They statachute. That is to say there is no question of rip-cords being pulled manually, since a static-line runs from the packed 'chute to a strongpoint in the aircraft. It is the weight of the soldier's body falling away from the plane that breaks a succession of 'ties' in the statachute. This means in effect, that although there is not a completely one hundred per cent guarantee that the canopy will develop, it must be pulled free of its pack and the aircraft – or must it?

As for most activities in the army, there is a drill for parachuting; not only for landing but also for quitting the aircraft. A correct exit should be made at 'attention' with the head held up and back, arms clamped rigidly to the side and legs together. This ensures a minimum risk of entanglement in the rigging lines caused by somersaulting with waving, uncontrolled limbs.

Jumping drill, like most drills, is disregarded by many who have found an easier or more agreeable way of carrying out the same task. My own particular method was quite simple, and I thought completely logical. As stick commander I always chose to jump first, and this entailed standing at the open door of the Dakota for about five minutes during the run-in. The red and green lights were in position immediately above the door: for the purposes of military discipline these constituted the cautionary and executive words of command, and non-compliance with their signals was naturally enough a court-martial offence. If you stand very close to the door you cannot see them; if you stand farther back in the plane you are that split second late in jumping. I chose to stand a pace back in the aircraft with my arms extended and my hands grasping the uprights of the door. By lifting my face slightly I could watch for the lights to change, and when they did I would pull myself forward with my hands and dive headfirst out of the plane. And that is exactly what I did on the most memorable night of my life.

But this time, instead of the normal breathtaking clutch of the slipstream, and the swift fall through the warm night air, followed by the reassuring strain on the harness as the 'chute developed, I felt as if some huge hand had seized my left foot and jerked me to a bone-breaking standstill.

I was spinning like a catherine-wheel beneath the aircraft's tail: the strong webbed static-line wrapped in one vice-like loop round my toecap. A sickening thud on my left shoulder stopped my spinning but swung me down under the aircraft. As I swung back again I sensed rather than saw the body of another parachutist flash by me on its downward journey. And then I was struck again, and another miss, and again and another miss, until the plane was emptied of its human cargo, and the pilot revved his engines, and with steadily increasing speed winged for home unaware that he was carrying an unwilling outside passenger.

I was floating through the air on my back with my limbs spreadeagled by the speed of the plane, and, as this increased I started to swoop up and down under the tail, but never quite touching it, until suddenly, either my vertical pendulum increased or the plane hit a succession of airpockets. Whichever it was, I struck the fuselage a series of stunning, resounding blows.

I have no idea how long this lasted, for the beating I received obliterated all recollection of time. I only knew it had stopped when an excruciating pain in my right groin forced its way through to my numbed brain, and I opened my eyes.

As my mind cleared I started to take stock of the situation. By raising my head slightly I could see my left leg held in traction by the line, and out of the corner of my eye I could glimpse its partner thrust out at an unnatural angle to my body and dangling from the knee down as if broken.

The static-line ran from the 'chute, over my left shoulder, and down to my boot, around which it was wrapped once. The line was double-anchored. Once to the strongpoint inside the plane, and once to my foot outside in the night. Beyond this it ran comparatively loosely to the parachute on my back. I realised that if I could in any way take the strain with my hands above my foot, I might kick free from the loop and drop normally.

I forced my arms in against the whip and pluck of the rushing air, and seizing the line below my waist I pulled myself into a half-sitting position. But as the area I presented to the backward thrust of the engines increased, the slipstream hit me like a wall, and it was only with the greatest difficulty I could breathe.

I groped down, one hand at a time, and obtained a fresh grip above my ankle, and then the real struggle began. I had to reach a few inches beyond my toe, and with the bulk of my equipment in front of me, this meant I had to bend my left leg against the traction of the line, the weight of my body, and the wind-tunnel-like thrust of the air. How long I fought to succeed in an effort which was doomed to failure from the start, I do not know, but eventually the combination proved too much for me and I was thrown violently back into my original position.

I realised I was very near death, but the pain in my groin had become so intense it appeared of more importance than my total eclipse. Straining with all my might I tried to draw my right leg towards my left. I could not move it a fraction. But, by forcing my arms down I managed to join my hands under my thigh, and another protracted struggle began. Slowly, inch by inch I drew and tugged my leg inwards until I could hook my right toe under and around my left ankle.

The feeling of relief and ease when I had succeeded was exhilarating but brief. My right leg had acted as a balancing outrider, and I found my arms alone were insufficient to maintain my balance. I started to rock. And then to spin. Slowly and gently at first, and in a fairly wide circle. But as the speed of spin increased, the circle narrowed to nothing and I whirled faster than any dervish had ever dreamed of. I spun until I could no longer distinguish the night or the plane or the stars – or the dark earth below.

Bright lights started to shoot through the blackness which enveloped me, and as I spun like a humming-top my mind sang and hummed in unison with my body until the two became inseparable and I slipped into unconsciousness.

When I came to I was back in my now familiar position, sailing through the night at nearly two hundred miles an hour, swinging and pitching beneath the belly of the aircraft; my left leg as straight and rigid as if held in surgical splints; my other three limbs splayed out and back by the force of the slipstream. It dawned on me that I had probably not been unconscious for very long, for the moment I had blacked out my ankles would have unlocked themselves and the spinning started to slow almost immediately.

My mind began to explore the possibilities before me, and I found it wandering freely through the many doors of martial death. But I quickly realised that my predicament had closed all but two or three of them, and these gaped hungrily before me.

I could cross the threshold a bloody, tattered, khaki doll, water-skiing on the smooth white lake of an airfield, or perhaps I should be cut loose from the plane flying as low as the pilot dared bring it over water. But at the speed I should strike it, the water would be as hard as a concrete runway. And then again, I could curtail the waiting and wondering. I could reach for my own knife and cut the webbed line, which, anchored inside the open doorway of the Dakota, held me suspended like a manikin on a giant's umbilical cord.

This cheerless contemplation of my end was abruptly interrupted by a hard stinging blow in the face, followed instantly by the sickly, salty taste of blood, and my arms fought against the slipstream in an instinctive effort to protect my head from further blows. Peering apprehensively through my crossed forearms I searched the Leviathan underside of the aircraft. I was certain this new unpleasantness was not in any way connected with the earlier buffeting I had experienced when we had hit a succession of small airpockets. Suddenly, an object flashed bird-like across my vision, struck me a solid blow on the chest, rested there for a brief moment and was gone. Almost in the same second my senses registered its departure I became conscious of a plucking at my right epaulette, and at once the mystery explained itself. As I, free of the aircraft's interior, was still held by the line to my foot, so my pistol, wrenched free of its holster, was still held by its lanyard to my right shoulder. My personal weapon, designed for my protection at close quarters, had become my enemy and was apparently intent on bludgeoning me to death. It struck me once more before I hauled it in like a reluctant trout. As I held it in my hand – it was a heavy .45 Canadian automatic – I began to appreciate how very tired my two battles with the slipstream had made me.

Apart from the pain in my groin I now felt quite comfortable, and except for my hands I felt warm with the pleasant, glowing, weary warmth one feels after a long hard game or a cross-country run.

The first confusing uncertainty had died down and been replaced by a stoical resignation. Born, not of courage, but of the inevitability of my death within – how long? half an hour? an hour? two hours? How much petrol had the aircraft? What would they decide to do when they found me, as find me they must when the Crew Chief pulled in the static-lines? I realised I had no idea when he did this. Would it be soon, or would he wait until just before landing? I supposed the entire aircrew were now sitting in a huddle drinking coffee, and I could not help envying them. I wondered too about my unit on the ground. What would they imagine had happened? Almost certainly that I had been injured and that I lay unconscious somewhere on the dropping-zone. Of course it was a clear moon-lit night and I might have been spotted silhouetted under the plane. Then I recollected the men who had hit me when they jumped. Had the impact been hard enough to be remembered by them later or would they confuse it with the initial shock of the slipstream? In any case what did it matter? There was nothing they or anyone else on the ground could do about it now.

For that matter what could the aircrew do about it? I had done *my* best but it had not been good enough, and I had little hope that their best would be any more successful. Had they had a hand-winch in the plane all would have been very easy. It was such an obvious answer to my predicament that I felt furious that the planners had never thought of it. I wondered if perhaps it had occurred to them, but that the idea had been discarded on the grounds of economy. It would hardly be worthwhile equipping thousands of transport aircraft with winches for the benefit of the few bloody fools who landed themselves in the fix I was in.

My mind turned reluctantly to the contemplation of my death and the form it would take.

It was not going to be as I had imagined it. Many years before I had overcome the fear of death and pain. I have always been proud of that victory, for it was my first, and I was only seven years old when I won it. Unfortunately it has proved a two-pronged victory, for although it has enabled me to do in cold blood many things that other men would have left undone, it has also led me into a number of quixotic actions which have landed me up to my neck in trouble. Because of this lack of fear, which is not to be confused with courage, I had always imagined that if I was to be killed in war it would be with troops and in action. And now it appeared I was to die dangling on the end of a line. For a moment a wave of anger swept over me. Anger at my own stupidity in disregarding the 'drill' of a correct parachute exit from the aircraft. However, my childhood philosophy quickly enabled me to suppress my anger as being a pointless emotion which could in no way solve my difficulty. I turned my mind to more practical things.

I was convinced the aircrew could not haul me into the aircraft against the pluck of the slipstream, for in addition to this terrific pull I weighed twelve stone, and I was wearing full operational battle-order complete with arms and ammunition: plus the now useless statachute on my back. I recalled that one man had been pulled back in. It had occurred in North Africa on a training jump. But on that occasion it had been daylight, and in addition to the aircrew there had been eight or ten parachute troops still in the plane who were able to lend their assistance, making a total of at least twelve. I made a quick calculation. Ruling out the pilot, there could only be four of the crew left to help me. I was sure nothing could be achieved by pulling. If I could not be hauled in, they must either cut me loose or land with me under the plane – there were no other alternatives. And since I could not conceive how I could survive a landing, this left only one way out. They would have to cut me loose. Where and when?

For a while my thoughts scattered. I pulled them together and concentrated on the problem. The R.E. officer they had cut loose over Poole harbour had been alive when they picked him up, but dead by the time the waiting motor launch had got him to the shore. I wondered how low the aircraft had flown on that occasion, and I could not see that it made much difference. For if the aircraft was very low I would strike at approximately the plane's stalling speed, and that was too fast. If on the other hand I was dropped into the water from about two hundred feet, my lateral speed would be considerably reduced, but of course I would go much deeper. I calculated again. Two hundred and fifty pound falling two hundred feet. I should go a long way down, and hampered by my ammunition, equipment and weapons, all of which were held in position by the parachute harness, I did not consider it likely I should reach the surface alive. The ideas suddenly started to flow. I may not have been afraid of death, but I got an awful lot of fun out of living.

If they hooked three or four static-lines together, joined one end to a strongpoint in the aircraft and the other end to my line, released that, and lowered me to the full length of the combined lines, I might then be about seventy feet under the plane. This would allow them to ease me on to the surface of the water before cutting me loose. One idea led to another. They could lower an observer-type 'chute out to me on one of the spare lines. If I was able to grasp it I might attach it in some way to my harness. Then, when they cut me loose, I could pull the rip-cord and make a reasonably orthodox descent although suspended by my midriff. I did not consider the ideas at all bad, but I doubted if they would occur to the crew. They would not be under quite the same pressure that I was. And then, the success of the second idea depended on my being conscious, and they would have no way of knowing if this was so. Very slowly it dawned on me that any ideas I might have were so much wasted thought. Good, bad, or indifferent, I had no means of communicating them to the plane or to the ground. I had better await their decision. One thing was certain. I should have to abide by it. It was not a question of it being the easiest thing to do, for it wasn't, it was the only thing left for me to do.

Once or twice, the thought of my family – my wife and baby son, my parents and my brother – had pushed itself to the forefront of my mind. Until now I had succeeded in fighting off their memory on the grounds that, in my position, although thinking of them might not in itself be a weakness, it could easily lead me to feel too sorry for myself. Resigned to the fact that if I was to survive, my survival depended upon the quick-thinking and action of others, I gave myself up to the contemplation of the future of my wife and son.

I had seen so little of my son that my love for him was, perforce, largely the dutiful love of a father for his heir. I did not really know him. I thought of my wife, a quiet calm-eyed girl whom I had married three years earlier. Until now I had always assumed that I knew her pretty well. I realised for the first time that I hardly knew anything about her. I had no conception of how her mind worked, of what she thought about, or how she spent the long lonely hours awaiting my periodic reappearances from the war. We had only once discussed the likelihood of my returning intact, or not at all, when it was all over. She had said then, and this I remembered very vividly, 'I have never tried to fool myself that you will not get hurt, but neither have I ever doubted for one moment that when the guns stop firing and the bombs stop bursting, you will emerge, a little battered perhaps, but I know you will come back to me. Somehow I always think of you as being indestructible.' My face fought a battle between tears and a wry smile at the memory of her faith. If I had wept at the recollection of her loving, misplaced judgement, I would not have been physically conscious of it. For some time past my eyes had been watering under the cut of a two hundred mile an hour slipstream.

The back of my neck and that part of my spine immediately above my hips were beginning to ache nearly as much as my right groin. From the side I must have looked like a letter in Arabic script. Straight from the toe to the hip; a deep hollowed bow to my shoulders; and then a short sharp bend where my head was forced back as far as it would go – my chin pointing at the stars. My right leg was at a right angle to my body and my left arm was flung back and out, and these two limbs maintained my balance as I sail-planed through the night. My right hand clutched my pistol, and to keep them on my chest I had hooked my thumb into the top of my camouflage smock. As the pain grew worse I thought more and more about the pistol. If the pain became unbearable I had a quick remedy. But once again my youthful conquest came to my aid. Pain cannot go on for ever no matter how bad it is. Either it stops or you die. Whatever happens, a time comes when you do not feel it any more. This being so, no matter what action I took, the pain would go or I should die first. There was no need for me to play an active part. I tucked the pistol into my smock and fumbled at my epaulette for some moments before my chilled fingers could undo the button. When they had achieved my object I freed the lanyard, reached inside my smock and threw the pistol down towards the Lincolnshire fields.

I was unable simply to drop the automatic. I had to make a very deliberate conscious effort and throw it. The action had the same kind of finality as letting the air out of a rubber dinghy in mid-Atlantic. I felt I had made my exit from the stage as a player. From now on I must watch from the wings, and see what others did to control the destiny of the swooping, swaying figure dancing puppet-like against the backcloth of the night.

I threw off the feeling of apathy which had followed swiftly in the wake of my renunciation of the chance of taking an active part in deciding my future. I tried to imagine what it would be like if they landed with me under the aircraft. Would it be one blinding flash and then oblivion, or would my limbs be broken first; singly or all together? How long could I remain on my back with my parachute to protect my spine until I was tossed and whirled about, and my helmet quit my head, and my skull bounced its way along the concrete runway till it squashed and scattered grey on grey? What did it matter if the experience lasted a breath of time or half a minute? I should die. And then – what then?

I had paid lip service to agnosticism for some years with the cynical insincerity of youth. I now realised that beneath the outward cynicism had always lain a firm conviction that we had but one life, and that life was lived here in the world we knew. To me death was finality. Beyond it there was nothing to look forward to, neither was there anything to fear.

The thought of dying and leaving those I loved filled me with regret. I felt a great sorrow for my family's unhappiness, and in thinking of them my thoughts turned to prayer and my childhood upbringing in the Church of England. I recalled my headmaster whom I had always held in awe and respect. He had been a clergyman with leanings towards the High Church, and I remembered the dogmatic confidence with which he had made his declarations of faith. Could he possibly be right? Was there really a good God who loved us all? For a moment I was tempted to offer up a prayer for assistance in my greatest hour of need.

Before any words could form themselves in my brain I realised I should have to begin, 'Please God, if there is a God . . .' I was filled with disgust at myself that eighteen years of propaganda directed at me by people who held convictions which were themselves the result of an earlier propaganda, should force its way through my reason simply because I was face to face with finality.

I started to talk aloud to myself although I could not hear a word with my ears. But something in my brain recorded the words I spoke that night in my long moments of truth. I have never forgotten them. They were my first honestly spoken creed, and I have never formulated another.

I said: 'I do not believe you are there God. I believe you to be a figment of the imagination of cowards. I believe you exist in men's thoughts, not because you are, but because they want you to be. Because they cannot exist without the hope of eternity. I believe that since they must have a God, they have dreamed up one who is benevolent, loving, and personal. But since I could be wrong and hundreds of millions could be right, I will offer you the only prayer I have ever been able to say with honest feeling.'

The wind had dried up the saliva and parched the inside of my mouth, but I struggled on with words I could not hear, and I recited John Galsworthy's 'Prayer' aloud.

> *If on a Spring night I went by*
> *And God were standing there,*
> *What is the prayer that I would cry*
> *To Him? This is the Prayer:*
> *O Lord of courage grave,*
> *O Master of this night of Spring!*
> *Make firm in me a heart too brave*
> *To ask thee anything!*

The last few words were hard struggle against an all-enveloping weariness that was creeping over my mind and body. I was becoming very tired. So tired that even the pain in my groin and spine had become detached, remote and of no consequence. I was near to the fatal sleep of exhaustion so dreaded by travellers in arctic and antarctic regions. I was reaching the stage where my body's cries for rest and peace were affecting my mind. I was beginning to care less and less what happened to me so long as it happened soon and quickly.

In a drowsy state bordering on unconsciousness I started to re-think my earlier thoughts. Was I, when confronted by certain death, defending a view I did not wholly believe? If I really believed everything I had just said, why had I said it?

And to whom had I said it? Could an act of bravado be carried out without an audience? Was it possible to defy a God one half believed in, when, if he did exist, one would be confronted by him within minutes? My glib agnosticism of the past had been easy, for nobody *knows*. But now I had moved a step beyond true agnosticism: I had come perilously near denying. When it came to an important issue I had always tried to be intellectually honest, but was I being so now? If I was not, who was I trying to deceive?

I thrashed the matter out to my satisfaction, but not then, I did it in the comfort of an American army hospital thirty-six hours later. For it was at this point in my reverie that I felt the nibbling at my left foot.

For a brief moment I felt myself fired by hope – perhaps the static-line was slipping off my toecap. I began to imagine myself falling away from the plane like a fish off the hook. I wondered where I should land, and hoped it would be near civilisation, for I realised I was in no condition to travel – probably not even able to walk.

The nibbling stopped, and I grabbed the static-line with both hands where it ran across my belly down to my foot. Pulling on the webbing I raised my head and saw framed in the open door the figure of the Crew Chief. With legs and arms braced he was peering back at me from the lighted interior of the aircraft. I sank back into my old posture and waited and wondered. Did my pulse beat a little faster now that I knew that I had been discovered? Yes – of course it did. Professor E. H. Erikson tells us that hope is the first emotional rung on the ladder of development. When all hope has gone, only hope remains.

I started once again to catalogue the possibilities, but before I had proceeded very far I felt a slow rhythmic pulling at my leg, and I heard the regular, thudding purr of the engines change. I lay back and mentally urged the American aircrew to greater efforts with but a faint belief that they could possibly succeed. Opening my eyes for a moment I was puzzled by something different about my position, but for a second I could not imagine what it was. And then it struck me in a flash and real hope surged through me like a blood transfusion – I was looking at a different part of the fuselage! – I watched intently, and at each heave on my leg the fuselage edged back a fraction. I strained my head forward and gauged the distance to the door. It was noticeably nearer, and I spotted that the propeller on my side of the plane was feathering gently in the night air. The pilot had cut his port engine to reduce the pull of the slipstream as much as possible. It was this action of his which inspired the first genuine feeling of hope I had experienced since I jumped. Largely, I think, because it was something I had not already thought of myself. They might have all kinds of tricks up their sleeves which had never occurred to me.

I crept inch by inch, foot by foot nearer to the open door and the warm comforting sanctuary of the aircraft's interior. And then I stuck. My body no longer parallel to the plane, but inclined at an angle of forty-five degrees; my left toecap jammed *under* the rounded step of the door, so that each time they heaved my ankle gave a little more, but still did not break. Never before or since have I wished for a broken limb. I felt that if it would only snap it must rubber its way over the step and into the grip of waiting hands.

It did not break: but the pain stopped when they started to let me out again. And as the line paid out and I drifted back through the night, I was filled with an abject despair I had not experienced earlier when I had been convinced there was no hope for me. My foot had arrived within inches of their hands, but now I was returning to my old position, and, I felt, a little farther from safety. For the crew's potential must have been reduced by what I knew had been a titanic struggle against so many odds.

I had kept my eyes closed as much as possible to protect them from the cut of the wind; only opening them for a specific purpose, but when I found myself no longer moving back towards the tail I opened them again – I suppose out of curiosity. It took me a moment to orientate myself, for I was not in my usual position. I had only returned about half-way. It occurred to me that the crew must have lashed the line round something in the plane, probably the bucket seats. At least, if they tried again they would have only half the initial work to do. I tried to visualise them inside the plane resting from their labours. I wondered how they felt about it all. No doubt they were cursing me as a bloody nuisance, and wishing me anywhere but where I was. But I felt sure they would try again – I had and have great faith in the human race. I imagine that in some way it compensates for my lack of a greater faith. I knew they would try again, and I racked my brains for a means whereby I could assist them in some way, and in so doing, help myself.

The idea came to me at precisely the moment they renewed their efforts, and as I once again drew near to the door it clarified in my mind. I considered that, all things being equal, I should arrive in the same position I had reached before. That is to say I should again be held at an angle of forty-five degrees to the aircraft; pulled there by the crew's efforts against the paralleling force of the slipstream. This meant that my right leg would in theory be nearer to the door than my left. In fact it would not be, since it was this leg's enforced position which had kept me continually in pain. However, I had succeeded in bringing my two legs together earlier on, albeit with disastrous consequences. Perhaps I could repeat what I had done before, but with happier results.

I arrived at what I was beginning to think of as my second fixed position much more quickly than the first time, and the crew returned to their task of attempting to pull my foot through the fuselage with a zeal I found far from comfortable. Such was their enthusiasm that I feared they would be successful before I had the opportunity of putting my own plan into operation.

Realising that it might well be my last chance of survival, I again seized my right thigh and started to tug and jerk it inwards; at the same time straightening it from the knee. Almost at once I felt the sole of my boot strike the fuselage, and I commenced to heel and toe it along the aircraft's side towards the rear upright of the door. By straining my head forward and up I could watch its progress, and simultaneously I saw for the first time the dim figures fighting to save me. I could only see two of them, and these were laying back on the line like the exhausted remnants of a tug-o-war team. And then my foot slid past the door's edge and into the aperture. At once it was seized by an eager pair of hands – I felt one great heave, and I was in the plane up to my knees – both of them. And there I stuck again. From my knees down I hung a dead weight, resisting every effort my rescuers could make.

I calculated that if they could hold me in my present position until they landed the plane, my head might just miss the runway – or it might not.

I did not consider it a good gamble, and I speculated on how I could reduce the odds. I had sat up once, much earlier when I was less tired. Could I do it again, and could I reach inside the aircraft? I considered that in my exhausted condition I would probably only manage it once, if at all.

I lay for a few seconds gathering my strength. And then, seizing the static-line at my waist with my left hand I threw myself up and forward, and my right hand entered the open door. And there, with stomach muscles torn by the effort, I hung for what seemed an eternity, until a strong hand grasped mine and another grabbed my wrist. But almost immediately my wrist was released, and the hand holding mine struggled to free itself, and the more it struggled the harder I gripped, until sanity prevailed and I reluctantly released his hand. There had to be a reason for his action – whoever it was. With every muscle in my body screaming for relief I somehow maintained my position; my hand extended, opening and closing in silent supplication. And then it was grasped again, and almost in the moment of contact I was in the aircraft, half-kneeling, half-lying on my right side. From where I lay I could see three of the crew stretched out, nearly as exhausted as I was, and their breathing was like the breathing of a beaten runner as he breasts the last hill. But whistling through and high above the noise they made I heard another sound I could not place. It was high-pitched and strident, and intermittent as a factory valve or a broken-winded horse. And then I placed it – close at home. It was my own breathing that rang and echoed through the plane. And as I breathed, I shuddered and shook like a man with St Vitus' dance. I had been breathing air which entered my mouth at two hundred miles an hour for so long that my lungs could not quickly adjust themselves to their new conditions.

The crew-member nearest to me groaned wearily to a sitting position; pulled off his flying jacket and flung it over me, and in a dazed way the others imitated his action until I was cloaked in their fur-lined warmth, but still I shivered under their comforting security.

Through half-shut lids I watched them pass a flask around between themselves, and I sent a message to my lungs to help me speak; to ask a little more from those to whom I owed my life. But my lungs had troubles of their own, and so my new request remained unasked.

At last one of them hitched himself lazily to his feet, and made his way forward to the pilot, and I closed my eyes and concentrated on controlling my breathing and the twitching of my limbs.

I must have dozed a little, for the next thing I remembered was a reassuring hand on my shoulder, shaking me gently, and a voice telling me, 'You'll be O.K. directly soldier, we're goin' in to land. We'll have you in hospital in two shakes of a . . .' I lay dreamily trying to make out his last few words. Two shakes of what had he said? A cat's whisker? A lamb's tail? A whore's hips? I never did decide what it was he said, and I only saw him once more, and there were so many other things to talk about I never got round to asking him, and so now I shall never know.

They turned me over on to my back and re-heaped their jackets about me, so that by turning my head slightly I could see out through the open door only three or four feet away from me. And once, when the plane banked before coming into land, I had a moment of panic. What if I should roll out through the ever-open aperture and be killed after all?

Long before the aircraft came to a standstill an ambulance was racing alongside; its lights blazing, and one of its crew leaning out of the offside window shouting unintelligible things into the night; and within seconds of the plane coming to rest the ambulance had backed up to the open door, and the aircrew were holding me up in a sitting position while they fumbled at my harness with unfamiliar hands. I found myself incapable of moving any part of my body except my arms, and these groped with almost senile impotence about my middle until my fingers found the release-box which held together the four straps of my parachute harness. Even after I found it, I had to make an effort of will to remember which way it had to be twisted before a blow released the restraining bands about my shoulders and thighs. To airmen, my very ordinary equipment offered difficulties, and it was only with my assistance that they could remove it. At last I was lifted on to a stretcher and a torch was shone into my face, and whatever they saw there caused the ambulance party to mutter among themselves, and then to unbutton my clothing, which, when freed to their liking, they wrenched back over my right shoulder, and I felt the keen bite of a hypodermic syringe as the needle entered my upper arm.

Minutes later I was being carried into a hospital, and just before we entered the room where I was to be examined, we passed an operating theatre, and through one of its half-open doors I saw a surgical team fitting masks. I was duly impressed by this example of American hustle.

The examination revealed no injury of any consequence, although it took some time and much washing before the caked blood was removed from my face, and two small cuts on my lip and cheek were laid bare to the disappointed gaze of the doctor.

During the examination I had carried on a conversation with him about how it had all happened, and where I ached, and why. Finding nothing wrong with me he very quickly lost interest, and this for some stupid reason annoyed me. He did not seem to appreciate that those who had suffered a similar experience had all been killed. Neither was he particularly interested in my praise of the aircrew for their extraordinary and sustained efforts on my behalf. And then – he played right into my hands.

Straightening up, he turned away from me and busied himself at a trolley which stood like a dumb-waiter behind him. Returning, he gave me an injection near to where I had received the earlier one fifteen minutes before. Airing my vast medical knowledge I enquired whether this injection was anti-tetanus.

'No,' he said, 'just a shot of morphia, it'll get you off to sleep, all you need is rest.'

'What then,' I asked, 'was the injection they gave me when I was on the stretcher?'

'Hell!' and his head jerked round as he said it, 'those goddamned fools said nothing about an injection.'

I amost raised myself up in my delighted excitement.

'In the British Army,' I said, and I spoke very slowly and ponderously, weighing each word before I let it fall, 'we teach even private soldiers that if they give a morphia injection they must mark the casualty quite clearly. If nothing else is available, they use the victim's blood and write a large M on his forehead.'

Having delivered myself of this broadside I sank back and closed my eyes with a self-satisfied sigh.

In no time at all they had me in bed; propped up by pillows; and an extremely attractive nurse was feeding me cups of strong black coffee. Before I had finished the first cup I was feeling ashamed of the cheap gibe I had made at the doctor's expense. Before I had finished the second cup I had passed out.

The next day was spent in dozing, silent self-congratulation, and in maintaining an air of nonchalance in the face of the eager questions showered on me by the other patients in the ward.

Later in the day I was unconsciously assisted in my act of hypocrisy by a visit from our second-in-command. He was quite the most casual man I have ever met. He sauntered into the ward as if he was entering his club; glanced languidly round till he caught my eye, and then, uttering a long soft 'ahh', he strolled over and sat down by my bed.

By this time you could have heard a pin drop anywhere in the ward. Every patient was apparently deeply immersed in a paper or magazine, but I could almost hear their ears twitch as they strained to hear what the two limeys would have to say to each other.

'Hallo.'

'Hallo.'

He looked curiously round the ward before he spoke again.

'Comfortable sort of dump, isn't it? Do themselves proud these Yanks What's grub like?'

I pointed out as briefly as possible that I had only had two meals, and that they had been pretty fair.

He sat in silence for a couple of minutes before he continued, and then he said:

'I've got to make out a preliminary report about this bloody nonsense. How did it happen?'

I limited my explanation to three or four sentences. It was difficult, but I managed.

He rose wearily to his feet.

'Oh well, I suppose that will do for now. They tell me you will be out in a day or two, and although leave is damned hard to get I might manage to wangle you a bit. I'll see what I can do.'

Strolling to the door he threw a 'cheerio' over his shoulder, and I muttered a reply before returning to my magazine. But, with my head lowered, I could not resist a surreptitious glance round the ward. Every head was turned, and on every face was a look of awed amazement as its owner watched our 2 i/c's departure.

It was on my second afternoon in a hospital bed that I allowed my mind for the first time seriously to review my nightmare experience, and the way in which the ordeal had channelled my vague, half-thought-out philosophy into a narrower, more sharply defined acceptance of the world I knew. In the face of death I had denied the existence of God, and this was something I had never considered doing before. Previously I had argued from a position of comparative strength. For I had merely asserted that I did not know, but that on available evidence I considered his existence unlikely.

I thought about it for a long time before I came up with the obvious truth. It was really quite simple. As a theist does not know – but believes and accepts, so I, also not knowing, disbelieved and refused to accept the teachings of those others who no more knew than I did.

I lost my tentative, child-like belief in God through the same medium that others have discovered him. By revelation. The majority of mankind is lazy in one or another degree, and most of them are apathetic when it comes to a question of faith. It is extremely difficult to hold steadfastly to a belief throughout one's life: it is even more difficult to eradicate the effects of a continual stream of propaganda delivered by those we love, trust, and respect. From a fairly early age doubts are continually cropping up, but there are only two ways of solving them. We either accept or reject through reason, and this would entail years of theological investigation and study, or we arrive at one conclusion or another by revelation. The true agnostic, if such an animal exists, simply states that he does not know, but then of course he has never really tried. It is hard to decide exactly how blameworthy he is in this respect, for very few arrive in a position where, on the one hand a decision is called for, and on the other, sufficient time is available to arrive at a conclusion. It may be argued that there is always time provided one starts thinking early enough, but if we accept the ingrained apathy of man; his reluctance to wrestle with a problem which has no immediate urgency, then we can appreciate why it is nearly always left until it is too late – until time has run out. But this is only of importance to the theist, and only if he is right. To the atheist, whether conscious or unconscious that he denies the existence of God, it only matters if he is wrong. By far the larger proportion of time-serving Christians have their doubts, but are unable to throw off the effects of the insidious propaganda directed at them over the years. They feel that so many people have believed for so many centuries, many of them learned and intelligent scholars, that there must be some truth in it. They are assisted to this end by a dream-like desire to perpetuate themselves through all eternity. If only it is true they will have achieved their wish-fulfilment. If it is not true, what do they lose?

I do not believe that, within the present sum of knowledge, anyone can arrive at either conclusion through reason.

How many times have we all heard a theist say, 'I cannot argue about it – I cannot prove it, but I know it to be so.' Sometimes, although not always, they add, 'It has to be so, otherwise life is pointless.' Of course it does not have to be so at all, it is simply that the wish for eternal life is strong in man because he has risen above the immediate and instinctive preoccupation with life practised by animals. Julian Huxley may discuss 'Religion without Revelation', but it is also possible to arrive in the atheistic camp, not by reason, but by the same kind of 'revelation' which has always been considered a weapon in the armoury of the theist.

I wondered when the roots of my near atheism had been planted, and I had to go back to my late childhood for the answer. I realised that, certainly by the time of my confirmation, I no more believed in God than I believed in Father Christmas. Both were something to be looked forward to; both were benevolent, personal and kind; the personification of love and giving; they represented a life or future which children and men wanted, and wanted desperately. But I could not see how wanting something, no matter how badly, could make it true. To me the whole thing was a gigantic, world-wide self-deception. It was rather like the faith the average man has in paper money. To be sure a pound note carries a promise of payment. But of payment with what? Gold? We are no longer on the gold standard, and if we were, what does one do with gold, eat it?

But the monetary system works, provided a sufficiently large number of people believe in it. When a majority of any country's population lose faith in the accepted form of exchange, that particular form will die; strangled by lack of faith – as religion is dying all over the world today. I had to go on using the monetary system whether I believed in it or not, for it affected the world I lived in. But I did not have to practice a faith in which I had no belief.

On the second afternoon I also had my second visit; the Dakota aircrew came to see me, and as they walked through the door at the end of the ward the question of how I had been saved was answered for me by their appearance. Collectively, they were the biggest group of men I had seen in a long, long time. I should not imagine that one of them weighed less than fifteen stone.

After the usual greetings and exchanging of names we excitedly talked over the whole episode.

The thing which had astonished them most was, when first my foot, and then my hand appeared through the doorway. They had been absolutely convinced that I must be unconscious if not dead. The question I had been dying to ask was – who had first gripped my hand, and why had he been forced to leave go? The answer was surprisingly ordinary.

It had been the Crew Chief who had first seized my hand and wrist, and he declared that I had gripped his so hard in return that I had driven into his hand a large ornamental ring he was wearing, and that the pain had been so intense he had to free his hand to remove the ring before pulling me into the plane.

I was flabbergasted: I had considered myself so weakened at the time as to be incapable of the physical effort he described. It seems the desire for self-preservation can tap unsuspected reservoirs of strength even when the body has been subjected to prolonged punishment.

I was fortunate enough to be granted fourteen days' leave before returning to my unit, and when I did rejoin them I was at once struck by the studied kindness with which I was treated by everybody from the Commanding Officer downwards. Of course they made caustic remarks about the devil looking after his own. And they were interested in the technicalities of my experience and rescue. But the one thing they never asked me about was the next jump, although at briefings, when dropping-zones were being pointed out and rendezvous indicated, I felt their eyes dwell a little longer on me than on any one else. They did not know how I was going to feel during the two or three hours' flight to the objective – nor did I.

The next time our unit jumped was on 17 September 1944. We landed north of the Neder Rhine at Arnhem, and on that day the unit maintained its unrivalled record of never having had one of its members refuse to jump since the day the unit was formed. Ten days later there were very few of them left with whom I should ever be able to discuss how I felt during the long flight across England, over the North Sea, and into Holland.

MALCOLM LOWRY

# The Element Follows You Around, Sir!

## CALLED TO THE BAR ONCE TOO OFTEN

### BARRISTER BEATS BASTILLE

Captain Ethan Llewelyn, famed criminal lawyer, was called to the bar once again last Saturday night. But evidently he stayed there too long. The ceremony enacted in the Courthouse Monday resulted in suspension of his licence to drive for one month and a fine of $50. Alcohol impairment charges against him were dropped. The lawyer fell afoul of the law himself on the Toronto–St Catherines turnpike where he was questioned in his stalled auto by a passing prowl car officer.

### TRUE TO FORM

Long noted as the 'helper of the little man', Captain Llewelyn, who admitted having had two drinks 'at a farewell party for myself,' explained that, true to form, he had stopped five minutes before to give a push to a carful of youths who had also stalled on the road, then in restarting had 'conked out' himself. Asked to explain why on the wrong side of the road, he replied that his car, of English make, had 'apparently run dry too' and had no doubt stopped on the left side 'out of habit' or 'as a protest' or 'simply because it preferred it'.

### NOT SOZZLED SAMARITAN

This explanation apparently being received dimly he was hauled to the Toronto bastille but later released under his own recognisance without bail. Later he explained to newsmen, 'I must have been suffering from belated shock, and thought I was still in Europe. Anyway don't call me the sozzled Samaritan.' Captain Llewelyn has only recently returned from France. The noted lawyer's house, the Barkerville Arms, in Niagara-on-the-Lake, and long an attraction for tourists, was completely gutted by fire weekend before last, threatening surrounding potential industrial property valued at over $500,000.

Elephants may be fed whisky and warm water in limited quantity on ocean voyages.

The pile-dwellings of the Nicobar Islanders in the Bay of Bengal are among the world's most ancient type of homes.

No, he had not forgotten that little item in the Toronto *Tribune*, nor was likely ever to forget, now, that last filler. Nor their towing the MG away – it was still the same one (and one of the few of its kind, that special 1932 four-seater convertible MG Magna 'University' model), like the sporting hearse – and taking him to gaol in that very unsporting hearse, the Black Maria; nor the gaol itself, so familiar to him from the outside looking in, nor the friendly cop, who knew him, who said, 'Don't worry, Mr Llewelyn, we've had some of the best people in Toronto down here, as *you* should know, sir.' Nor the unfriendly one, who didn't, and who, when he kept on talking about the fire, had shoved him in the urine-smelling 'tank' for a while. 'And what's *your* name?' he asked another fellow sufferer there . . . 'Oh, I'm just an old murderer.'

'Somehow not to go mad . . .' Yes, but now it was as if the subjective world within, in order to combat that threat, had somehow turned itself inside out: as if the objective world without had itself caught a sort of hysteria. Caught it, maybe, from poor darling Jacqueline, who, though she'd been magnificently sporting about his arrest, indignant on his behalf, tender, even managing to be humorous, now became subject to occasional hysterical fits herself, into which she could be startled more and more easily. And there appeared to be no febrifuge against this double sickness, this interpenetrating fever of madness, where effect jostled cause in a wrong dimension and reality itself seemed euchred. As (or was it by reversal?) in those plays where the players mingling with the audience make their exits and entrances over the orchestra pit (as once in those days perhaps when Niagara-on-the-Lake's old cinema had been an experimental theatre) and watching them you abruptly discover your companion not to be the girl you brought to the show but the Hairy Ape himself – or Claude Rains, in 'From Morn Till Midnight' – insanity and nightmare seemed to flow into life and back again without hindrance, to the frenzied infection of both.

During the previous fortnight at the Prince of Wales, between their fire and Ethan's arrest, there had been a succession of violent thunderstorms, and it seemed to them they heard the fire-engine wailing almost every night. Yet curiously, because there'd been no fires at all in Niagara-on-the-Lake for many years, three more fires, following their own, *had* broken out in those two weeks, two probably caused by lightning, one quite inexplicable, all three occurring at night, though all, unlike their own, minor. These fires all struck on the side of the Old Barkerville ruins remote from the Prince of Wales. But now, on his return from his week-end in Toronto which had ended so ignominiously (a trip, however, which already had as its object the eventual severing of his connections with the Toronto branch of his firm, the farewell party for himself had been no joke), now, four more fires, suddenly, terrifyingly, struck close to the Prince of Wales itself. Fatigued and tight, Ethan and Jacqueline, who was also under doctor's orders fairly heavily sedated, actually slept through the first of these fires, started by lightning striking a woodshed behind the old stables with the cobwebbed coaches, though it wasn't fifty yards away. On the second occasion,

Ethan woke to find the red conflagration raging right outside their bedroom window and Jacqueline already in a frenzy. Shrieking – imagining, she said later, the Prince of Wales itself in flames – she half dragged and carried Tommy from his room out into the street. Fortunately it wasn't the hotel, only another woodshed that was burning. Having, with the aid of the understanding Madame Grigorivitch (*née* Dovjhenko! – who, an exiled Ukrainian, was no stranger to such sufferings), succeeded in calming Jacqueline, Ethan helped the firemen put out the blaze, tripped over the hose, gave himself a black eye.

Jacqueline greeted him back in the hotel with a mocking smile and half a bottle of gin, where earlier there had been none.

'Hoot. So we have to keep ourselves in balance, eh mon?' she said gaily.

'—'

'My poor lamb, that really is a first-class shiner.'

'How's Tommy?'

'Sleeping like an angel. Now. He kicked and screamed of course and wanted to go to the fire.'

Ethan observed after a time, eyeing her as well as he could over his glass – she was holding a compress over the other eye: 'If Francesca was a girl anything like you, I don't see that Paolo can have had such a grim time after all.'

'Did you save anything?'

'Apart from the surrounding potential industrial property valued at more than $500,000, since you ask, yes. We – we shot a bear – saved L'Hirondelle's woodshed. Part of it . . . But it was pretty damned funny.'

'What was funny?'

'No one knows how it started. No lightning tonight. No explanation at all, the firemen said.'

'Ah, hoot man, have a drop of the creature!'

She woke him up later: 'Did anyone have anything more to say about *our* fire?'

'Nothing new. No one apparently saw it till it was too late,' he said deliriously. 'God damn it!'

After five hours of towering nightmares, Ethan woke in sunlight, determined to go on the wagon forever and pull them both together. This determination lasted until midday, when the liquor store caught fire. Nothing was lost save a few old packing cases and a bottle of whisky *blanc vieux Canadien*, which exploded. Once more the pyrenewielding grocer, who'd been talking to the manager of the cinema next door (outside which it said COMING! 'THE WANDERING JEW'), was the hero.

There wasn't any explanation for this fire either, though the fourth one, occurring the next night, in a cottage on the lakeward side of the Prince of Wales, was caused by an overturned kerosene lamp. A terrific thunderstorm shook Niagara-on-the-Lake after this, though lightning did no damage locally that was reported. It would have been uncomfortable, under normal circumstances, despite the minimal damage from these outbreaks, to realise that in this way, living in the Prince of Wales, they had been surrounded by an actual ring of fire. As it was, the effect of the knowledge was devastating. Jacqueline, exhausted and sedated, and often tight, seemed to him to be only partly aware of what was happening. And what *was* happening? (How much of it actually *had* happened, he wondered later. Yes, but all of it had happened, he thought, from some bloodshot sphere behind his closed eyes in the bus. And happened to *them*.) After all, it hadn't been called the Storm Country for nothing, had it? Storms were to be expected. Yet the besetting sense of the unnatural, of *cauchemar*, penetrated even Jacqueline's wall of defences. For such storms were not to be expected in May. They were almost unheard of. They were the properties and effects, the *klangmalerei*, of the lakeside dramas of July and August. And the conclusion, in Ethan's state of mind, grossly exaggerated by alcohol, seemed inescapable: not satisfied with having taken their home, it was exactly as if something, some 'intelligence', was searching for them *personally*, or *him* personally, all over the town, and preparing to strike again.

But now its strategy became confused, dispersed. Though storms continued to break overhead, some force seemed to have abduced the lightning, as well as the plague of fires themselves, in the opposite direction, in fact every other direction. Phenomena went galloping and gambolling over the whole countryside, though now and then, as if to show it had not forgotten after all, the 'intelligence' would strike a chord again in Niagara-on-the-Lake itself. Now they really did hear the fire-engine clanging rebelliously after fires nearly every night; but distantly, those of Queenston, and perhaps St Catherines and Hamilton as well. Now more than ever, on country roads, the lightning was 'peeling the poles and biting the wires', the lake must more than ever have tasted of sulphur, though Ethan had not the heart to sample it again.

This was sad, because between storms the weather was very hot.

Sometimes the 'intelligence' expressed itself almost benignly. The barber and his wife limped home one Saturday evening from an outlying pub, took refuge under an elm, were struck by lightning and came home at the double, forever cured of all rheumatisms from that day forward. They had need of their new-won agility because that night their own house, on Niagara-on-the-Lake's outskirts, took fire. A fireball went bouncing solemnly across their lawn and in through their kitchen window from which Mrs McTavish sprang screaming, though landing unhurt. The fireball set a few curtains ablaze, then the flames died out of their own accord.

More of the Chief's famous 'ground lightning' felled more trees, or half-felled them, or was reported to have felled them, across the road bordering the golf course. The 'intelligence' was coming back. One night, Niagara-on-the-Lake rocked with the celestial tumult overhead as in the grip of an earthquake. Bangs and crashes sounded across the fields shuddering with lightning where Jacqueline and Ethan had gathered sumac and teazle to decorate the Barkerville. An abandoned farmhouse five miles away went up in flames. And a little tree house, without the tree being even scorched. On top of this, apparitions, or 'mysterious lights', were reported to have been seen moving in the many overgrown and neglected graveyards of Niagara-on-the-Lake. Thunder returned to Niagara with redoubled violence as of huge aerial battles above the lake. And now the whole town itself (or all but the most level-headed members, among whom should have been included, relatively, Jacqueline herself and even Ethan himself) became involved in this tumult, this tempest, this kind of celestial disorder of the kinesthesia. Rumours of every kind started, grew, swelled and, like fireballs themselves, having bounced in through a few kitchen windows, were dissipated. A phantom sailing-ship with all its topmasts blazing with corposants was observed sailing in an easterly direction. A sea monster, with horns like a goat, 119 feet long, was reported cavorting down the Niagara River. Psychic investigators investigated. People left their doors open for Jesus to walk in. The priest sprinkled holy water on the threshold of Jix Gleason's 'Osteopathy and Manipulative Treatment'. And, it was said, 'in many homes'. And lastly, M. Grigorivitch's setter gave birth to a blue dog.

Meantime, Ethan, in order not to remember the exact date of their fire, for in that way he saw himself acquiring another obsession, or perhaps not to have to think of 'May' at all, found himself each night in bed trying to think back instead over all the October ninths he could recall for the last seventeen years, and it seemed to him since Peter Cordwainer's death there had always been a misfortune, or the beginning of a misfortune, at or near that date. And this, that at least it wasn't the first fortnight in October – was, apart from gin, one of the few consolations he had at this time.

In the meanwhile, too, he had finally, or almost finally, severed connections with the Toronto branch of his firm, though it wasn't as yet clear whether he would be able, as he hoped, to join another branch of it in Vancouver. As he hoped? The truth was Ethan did not hope for anything at this period. To go west seemed simply a blind solution, about as good as death. He did not work, had none to do, but hung around the town, himself like some earthbound phantom, haunting the place of his nativity and earthly disaster. Occasionally it would occur to him he was not meeting his ordeal as he should. Yet he really did nothing about it, despite repeated half-hearted attempts.

Jacqueline, for her part, was alternately sporting and mean. That she might be waiting for him to take a sterner and more decisive attitude himself towards both their lives scarcely ever occurred to him. One night, having upbraided him for not 'going on the wagon', as he had several times promised, when he announced once more he *would* do just this, she upbraided him instead for his blatant hypocrisy in daring to pretend anything of the kind, so that, in no time at all, he found it convenient to imagine that he was being 'driven to drink' by her. While Jacqueline equally, having made similar resolutions, would see herself as 'driven to drink' by Ethan. At other times Ethan would suddenly find himself alcoholically unable to comprehend why Jacqueline, having lamented for so long her lack of exposure to anything convincingly supernatural, should now, with the evidence, as he saw it, right under her nose, reject all interest in it. That she might actually be scared half to death by terror she couldn't or wouldn't, give name to he couldn't see either. Nor could he see – or see seriously – that his own entertainment of such thoughts at such a crisis might be a presage of almost as complete a breakdown in himself as, complementarily, these very phenomena might seem to indicate in the world of causes about him. Yes, he said to himself, again, it's as though nature herself is having a kind of nervous breakdown. Why not? Human beings have them. Perhaps Jacqueline is having one.

He went to talk to the pyrenewielding grocer about it: this indeed – to talk to any human being – was a relief: first, he'd confined himself to talking only about their own fire: then there was the second fire, the third fire, the four new fires: now God knows how many fires there were to talk about.

The grocer thought a long time, then he said: 'H'm. It's like the element follows you around, sir.'

'How do you mean it follows you around? . . . You're damn right, of course.'

'Like when you get worms,' said the grocer, wrapping Ethan's purchase of two tins of orange juice. (It was extremely important that the grocer should think of him drinking that orange juice, as if he had no eyes in his head to watch him marching off afterwards straight across the street to the liquor store.) 'Missis gets worms – fortunately she's a very smart woman – preserves the worm. Damn big worm. Doctor congratulates her. Then he says: "Funny thing. I haven't had a case of worms in five years and then – bingo! – five cases, all this afternoon, all different families. You're the fifth," he says.'

'Worms!' said Ethan. 'God damn it, man, having your house burn down's not like worms!'

'No, I meant all these crazy fires, coming after yours – same damn thing, Mr Llewelyn . . . We were burned out once, in Whiskey Creek, Saskatchewan. Moved to Swift Current, Manitoba. Place where there'd been no fires for donkey's years. Soon as we get there – bang! five fires, all in the same month . . .'

'What's that? *Three* bottles of gin? I can't give you three,' said the man in the fire-scarred liquor store. 'I will give you three though, since it's you . . . Yes, fire,' he sighed. 'Well, we were lucky. Compared with you, I'll say . . . Don't know how ours happened either . . . Hell, it's like they say . . . It's like the element follows you around, sir.'

'Thank you – would you mind saying that again?'

'Worst damn thing that can happen to a man.'

COMING! 'THE WANDERING JEW.'

It had not been so unwise after all, insofar as anything he did could be said to be wise those days, and whatever his ulterior motives, to have insisted they stay at the Prince of Wales. Not only did the racket downstairs in the evenings help to drown the increasing noise of their own dissensions, or poor Jacqueline's conniptions, when there were no thunderstorms to drown it, but the kindhearted

Madame Grigorivitch proved a tower of refuge and a sadly needed mother to
Jacqueline, and Tommy, too (who since his father's arrest had not ceased to be
the corpse's mate, but now in a more literal sense; and was even in a kind of half
disgrace, persecuted by his former friends, while supported by newer wilder
factions, good or bad for him as it happened to be), who otherwise must have got
completely out of hand. She was a mother on occasion to Ethan also, feeding him
bottled beer in the kitchen on those nights he found it impossible to sleep, no
matter how tight he was. Their conversation always ran as follows:

'Are you by any chance related to a Russian movie director called Dovjhenko,
Madame Grigorivitch?'

'I tink I muzz have know him as a little boy. Tink he is my cousin, maybe.'

'I saw this film he made and it was wonderful, when you forgot the
propaganda. There's this scene where someone has to kill his brother in a
forest—'

'Dovjhenko Ukrainian peoples . . . Here, drink your beer.'

'Now Dostoevsky . . .'

Then, comforted in some sort, he would return to Jacqueline, uneasily
sleeping under her sedative, and lie quietly beside her in the dark. . . .

As one device to send himself to sleep he tried reciting the Lord's Prayer.
Rarely did he get so far as 'And deliver us from evil', though when he did, he
repeated this phrase many times. Starting again, the prayer became dislocated.
For 'Our Father which art in heaven', he would find himself saying something
like: 'Our fire which art in fear.' And out of the word fear, instantly, would *grow*
fears; fears of the next day, fears of seeing advertisements, which he now seemed
to in almost every newspaper, for Mother Gettle, at almost every street corner –
in fact there were two hoardings on the main street, including the new one, and
he could scarcely avoid seing *them* – and there were always the tins of soup, in
the grocery, to be reckoned with; fears of the next day's ordeal, with people
looking at him queerly on the street as if he'd been responsible for all the fires (or
still loathsomely snickering over his arrest), fears of yet another day darkening to
its end with a sense of guilt. And out of the fears grew wild hatreds, great
unreasoning esemplastic hatreds: hatred of people who looked at him so
strangely in the street: long-forgotten hatreds of schoolmates who'd persecuted
him about his eyes at school; hatred of the day that ever gave him birth to be the
suffering creature he was, hatred of a world where your house burned down with
no reason, hatred of himself, and out of all this hatred did not grow sleep.

In order to combat the mental sufferings of the day, and perhaps also to
distract attention from his black eye, Ethan had now let his beard grow. So in
daytime his anguish was swallowed up by another sort of self-consciousness, that
excruciating consciousness of the beard. Indeed he *was* the beard. Even now in
bed he was the beard. Our beard which art in beard walking down the beard.
Give us this day our daily beard. And deliver us from beard.

'You don't think you'll fool the Mounted Police with that foliage do you,

Captain Llewelyn?' the Chief of Police greeted him heartily on the library steps, where they led down to the basement of the police station. 'Ha, ha, ha!'

'I wasn't fixing to fool the Mounted Police, I was fixing to fool *you*, ha, ha, ha,' answered Ethan, always delighted at so much attention from the 'Law', at least when it was as avuncular as this. 'How goes the ground lightning? Have you caught the roving arsonist?' He wasn't so sure, now, on second thoughts, he would have liked what the Chief of Police had just said, had he not addressed him as 'Captain'.

'God damn. There is no arsonist, far as I can see. Oh, in cases like this, nearly always some crazy firebug springs up, takes advantage of the situation. Oh, we'll catch someone setting fire to a house one of these fine days, all right . . . Yeah, but I seen nearly as bad as this too one time . . . Antigonish.'

'—?'

'It's the name of my home town,' said the Chief indignantly. 'Now you take these here polterghosts . . . Oh, I've been called out on them things too in my day.'

Ethan lit a cigarette. It was important that the Chief should not smell his breath, or think he had a hangover. He had acquired a cigarette holder now, perhaps for analogous reasons to the beard, but he didn't fit the cigarette into it, just left it in his pocket. He hadn't lit the cigarette either, for that matter, but now he did.

'Poltergeists! Are you meaning to suggest my damn house was haunted?'

'I don't say that, Captain Llewelyn. No. But now take these here polterghosts. In Antigonish, say. I've had experience of these damn things. Bolts of fire, pianos jumping around, weights sprung out of the grandfather clock at my detective sergeant one time, and I don't know what all. The priest sometimes seems to fix it up. Only you can't pin this stuff down. Can't arrest anybody you know.'

Ethan glanced round him nervously and seemed to hear himself saying: 'Well, it couldn't have been us, could it? Doesn't there always have to be a little girl in the family when there's a poltergeist?' Now what had he done with his cigarette? What if he should set fire to the police station? But there it was, smoking away on the steps. And the Chief set his boot on it, as if absently. 'Anyhow, what can lightning have to do with poltergeists?' he said. 'Lightning's responsible for half these fires, isn't it?'

'What do you make of it yourself?' the Chief of Police enquired, 'as a Captain of Intelligence?' with, Ethan thought, a suddenly searching look. 'You're right. There's no sense to it . . . There *is* usually a little girl, well, *some*times a little boy, connected with these things, too, to begin with, now I think about it. That's what that book I read said too. Some little girl suffering from this here shizo-frenzia; what you call it. And then the whole town catches this here shizo-frenzia, goes haywire – and God knows, Captain Llewelyn, *this* whole town's got it too, if you ask me . . . Talking mongoose too, I read about . . . What they used to call witches is just polterghosts too,' he added more formally.

Ethan asked severely, feeling, however, a sense of horripilation, his hair prickling along his scalp: 'It wasn't a poltergeist or a witch short-circuited the battery of that car over there three weeks ago, was it?'

'Aw, hell's bells!' The Chief, as though reciprocally, removed his cap and scratched his head. 'It's just one of them things. But I'll be frank. I've got these polterghosts on the brain a bit, having had experience of them before like, in Antigonish. It's them fires that don't burn things up proper that get me down,' he went on, with unintentional cruelty. 'Well, you might call it a kind of cower-dice. (The Chief pronounced it to rhyme with price.) Now you're a reading man, Captain Llewelyn, and I shouldn't say this, because I'm a Catholic, but there's a book in the library down there tells you all about it. One of these sickic investigators put me on to it. Oh yeah, I go down there to the library sometimes, when there's nothing doing, chew the fat with Miss Braithwaite. You wouldn't believe me, that damn place used to be a regular meeting place for drug operators. Smuggling the stuff across the border. Made me feel uneasy too, this goddam book . . . I ran in a husband and wife once for conspiring to commit arson for their insurance,' he went on, as Ethan shuddered, 'and now sometimes I feel I did wrong. Put the little girl in a detention home too . . . It sure as hell upset me, this book . . . Me and the Missis were all set to win at the police whist drive that night, and after I read it I couldn't keep my mind on the game.'

'Who wrote it?'

The Chief assumed a literary air. 'Just go down there and ask Miss Braithwaite for *Ten Talents*. That's the name. She'll fix you up. And tell her I sent you.' He hesitated. But seeing that Ethan was still waiting for an answer he added, in a slightly aggrieved voice, 'Booth Tarkington.'

'Booth *Tark*ington?'

'I was real surprised myself. Used to read his "Penrod" stories when I was a lad. You ever read "Penrod"?'

Ethan, shaking his head, reflected that all he knew of Booth Tarkington was the wonderful if mutilated, movie of 'The Magnificent Ambersons', made by Orson Welles. 'But I read somewhere a while ago the poor fellow was going blind,' he said.

'Is that so? Well, that's too bad . . . I was real surprised that he should have written such a book. Of course I couldn't read it all, just glanced at it, like. Very different style from "Penrod". Real deep stuff. But it sure gives you the lowdown on all them polterghosts. Well—'

'See you in Antigonish!'

Ethan, in fact, had been in the act of going down to the library too, not to read anything, or to get a book out, but simply to give the good impression locally that he had, so to speak, 'gone down to the library'. Now the thought of the Chief's book deterred him: a bit too near the knuckle . . .

COMING! 'THE WANDERING JEW.'

At the Prince of Wales he traversed the lonely Men's side of the beer parlour and dropped into the kitchen to have a look at M. Grigorivitch's dog. It was blue, all right.

That night the bandstand went up in smoke.

'Christ! You begin to think you must walk in your sleep and do it yourself,' Ethan told the grocer.

'Well, you just don't want to let yourself get that way, Captain Llewelyn,' counselled the other in a kind tone, placing Ethan's cans of orange juice in a brown-paper parcel. 'Two tins of Mother Gettle's soup, you said?'

God knows why he had bought them! He wasn't going to insult Madame Grigorivitch by asking her to warm the tins up, and Jacqueline and he had no gas ring. Presumably it had been his idea of, for once, 'facing reality'. He dropped them into a garbage can.

'There's the devil in it,' he told the man in the liquor store, cautiously looking round for the Mounted Police. *Fear may only be defeated by defiance or faith.* The comfortingly crafty thought was also in his mind that if these fires really *could* be conceived of as being produced for 'them personally', then, perversely, they might be construed as the work of some really well-meaning intelligence, who had chosen this relatively harmless method of making him 'rationalise' what had happened to the Barkerville. But his friend did not contradict him. In more senses than one: gin, since the day before, was unrationed.

So, after a period of comparative restraint, were the recurring phenomena. A dirt-laden fog settled over the whole area of Niagara-on-the-Lake and Queenston, causing hydroelectric poles to catch fire through short circuits and, as the papers said, 'knocking out some electricity', while even hydroelectric officials termed this fog a 'strange phenomenon'. And seventy-nine-year-old Mrs Annie McMorran, the mother of the golf professional, who lived opposite the club house, watched with fear as a lightning bolt appeared to flash down her chimney and send a red-hot ball of fire rolling across her living-room. Then Tommy dropped his own thunderstone down the chimney.

'I know who did it, Daddy,' he announced delightedly one day, out of breath, having run all the way back from school to make this disclosure.

'Who did what, son?'

'Burned our house down, of course!'

'*What!* – Who?' stammered Ethan, aghast.

'Oh,' said Tommy airily, 'Small boys. They think you're a Communist *spy*.'

Ethan carefully and controlledly stubbed out the cigarette he'd been smoking in an ashtray beside him. 'You know what W. C. Fields said when he was asked how he liked small boys, don't you?' he asked.

'No, what?'

Now, confound it, Ethan had to search in all the other ashtrays in the bedroom for a smoking cigarette and on finding the cigarette he'd put out even feel the end of that to find if it was hot before he was sure it was the one he *had* put out.

'No, what, Daddy?' Tommy repeated. 'Don't keep me waiting!'

*'Boiled.'*

Though Ethan was instantly remorseful about this harsh jest, Tommy thought it the funniest thing he'd ever heard in his life, and after that their relations improved considerably. 'We get on just like a house on—' Ethan said to Jacqueline.

'Yes. Just like a house on.'

That night, lightning knocked out electrical power all the way from Niagara-on-the-Lake to St Catherines. Electric company emergency crews worked all night restoring it. The fog, however, a gentleman, had moved away. Nonetheless, the postmaster's wife, she of the banana sandwiches and the Grape-up, reported that the lightning had knocked a telephone from her hand at 8:15 the same evening. She spent the night with friends and when she returned found another bolt of lightning had smashed a wall plug to pieces. Jacqueline went to St Catherines to see an aunt; the lightning burned out the motor on the 8 p.m. tram she was taking, delaying service for one hour while the crippled vehicle was towed off the line. Flashes of lightning blasted the local radio station off the air and damaged a service station. New, violent, unexpected storms began now at all hours of the day and night with rain, hail and loud claps of thunder. Then the Brigadier General 'got his', as he termed it, in much the same way as the postmaster's wife. Only he received such a paralysing shock from the telephone he was hospitalised for three days. Towering thunderheads appeared in the sky, lightningless, went away again. Then, just as everything seemed normal once more, something stranger still happened, considering the comparative flatness of the land: a giant mud slide oozed down and buried one end of a power station between Niagara-on-the-Lake and Queenston, which, according to the papers, would keep industrial plants normally served by the station on staggered working 'for a considerable time'.

It was true these last peripheral events did not directly affect Ethan and Jacqueline. They were more affected by a decision Ethan took at this point. Though his driver's licence was now once more valid, having consulted Jacqueline when she was off guard, he sold the car. He wasn't going to drive again, or let her drive either, while alcohol remained a problem. Unfortunately, this sad, commendable decision – for they loved the car – whose motive had really involved the final severing of their connections with Niagara-on-the-Lake itself, regarding which he'd felt his will to act becoming more and more sapped, had the opposite of its intended effect. Instead of helping to free them, it was as if now he'd neatly imprisoned them. He couldn't indeed have erected a more formidable obstacle to the final winding up of their affairs here. There was no bus to Toronto. Telephone service was often impaired. In order to go by train, it was necessary first to take a bus to St Catherines; two hours' drive, then another three to Toronto itself. But there never seemed to be a bus to St Catherines. A seaplane could have made the trip in five minutes, but there was no plane service; while the *Noronic* was tied up at the dock, 'pending greater safety provisions'. There wasn't even the old troop train any longer. Jacqueline now saw herself deliberately trapped in the Prince of Wales. She was; so was he. He saw it himself. He couldn't take a hint. Obviously something more than the loss of their own house by fire, fireballs, the all-dreaded thunderstone, the very disorder of the heavens themselves and whole divisions of polterghosts was going to be necessary to drive them out of Niagara-on-the-Lake.

One evening, after a bitter quarrel with Jacqueline on the subject, and walking with averted head through the beer parlour downstairs (they were both pretending they were trying to cut down on their drinking), he went off by himself to the local cinema to see 'The Wandering Jew'. Or his beard went off by *it*self. It was the first show, the feature already half over. Nonetheless he had become so obsessed with the notion that, with his beard, he might have been taken for some figure advertising the movie itself, it was at least ten minutes before he began to concentrate on the film. (Worse still, what if someone in the cinema should imagine he really was The Wandering Jew? Or, in some yet more complicated manner, imagine that Ethan thought himself the Wandering Jew had dropped in – and what if The Wandering Jew was a Communist spy too! – to see a film about himself?) 'Subjectively' – it was a variation of the old idea which rode him – Ethan wondered if this wasn't an almost universal experience, when life was going desperately, and you dropped into some lousy movie to get an hour away from yourself, only to discover that, lo and behold, this movie might as well have been a sort of symbolic projection, phantasmagoria, of that life of yours, into which you'd come half-way through. This old film, with its menacing, almost inaudible characters and clanking machinery of which you half knew the plot, and bad, sad, music, its hero (oh, that beard on the screen didn't fool the Mounted Police in Ethan, he knew who *he* was) going to his predetermined ruin, when to evade ruin was now your only hope, or you hoped it was: in fact you'd thought you were fractionally evading it by coming to the movie in the first place. And against such a predetermined doom, as against one's fate in the nightmare, finally you rebel! How? when the film will always end in the same way anyhow?

Yet perhaps it was at such moments, with hangovers in movies – as in pubs, hamburger stalls, lavatories, on ferryboats, in addled but profound prayer, in drunken dreams themselves – that the real decisions that determined one's life were often made, that lay behind its decisive actions, at moments when the will, confronted with its own headlong disease, and powerless to save, yet believes in grace. . . .

Much good that was doing poor old Buttadeaus, or Caragphilus, or Ahasuerus, the striker of Jesus, at the moment, either to believe in it, or appeal to it! – 'A fugitive and a wanderer shalt thou be in the earth, ran the curse of the Lord,' someone was saying in a crackling voice on the screen. 'And as with Cain, the Lord appointed a sign for him, lest any finding should smite him.' It was a flaming cross on his brow, that he covered with a velvet ribbon. Altogether worse than Ethan's black eye. And it was not, at the moment, saving him from being smitten. So The Wandering Jew was in a sense Cain too, ghastly notion; especially since (apart from that little matter of Abel) Cain appeared to Ethan one of the few humane people in the Old Testament. But what else was it The Wandering Jew – not the legend, simply the words, the phrase – reminded him of? Inner Circle. Inner Temple. (The Inner Temple had provided Ethan's own admission to the bar.) 'From Morn Till Midnight.' London. Somehow London.

No. It was Niagara-on-the-Lake's cinema itself, which had something in common with his own first approach to the arts, that had reminded him of 'From Morn Till Midnight'. The cinema in which he sat (he remembered again) had been built as an experimental theatre; a quarter of a century ago, in those days of the early O'Neill in Province-town, of 'The Long Voyage Home', in fact. Where The Wandering Jew now bemoaned his fate, the Hairy Ape had once beaten his breast, though without, unfortunately, attracting any attention from across the border, as had been the idea. It had closed for some years and reopened as a cinema, still privately owned, and following a policy somewhat similar to the one in Toronto where Jacqueline and he had first met, and all this he knew because his father, who had never seen a decent play or film in his life, but who liked a finger in every pie, had long been one of its directors. This project failing, as well as other more conventional policies, it had now become a movie house apparently showing anything so long as the piece was at least ten years old, and in this way, with still a fair sprinkling of English and foreign films, it occasionally put on something interesting. 'The Wandering Jew' – too theatrical, too slow, poorly directed, lighted, portentously acted – still showed no signs of being among their number. And he recognised none of the actors, though the Jew himself, an excellent part, was effectively played.

Ah, now he knew what he was reminded of. It was of a play he had never seen, or the advertisement for a play, that had been running in London, years and years and years ago, when he was a boy. MATHESON LANG IN 'THE WANDERING JEW'. He remembered the advertisements for it now, along the upper sides of the red two-decker buses, but mostly it was a huge poster in the London tube stations that had fascinated him. The poster, shaped to the concave tunnel, and half the length of the underground station, showing the wretched Jew, his eternal sea-gown scarfed about him, struggling against the wind, in thunder and lightning, among riven trees; yes, he saw the hoarding again now plainly, as if once more before his eyes. Because it had been just after his eyes got better. What wild romance it had denoted for him! That was what life was: to see – even to *be* – MATHESON LANG IN 'THE WANDERING JEW'! . . . NEW THEATRE. NIGHTLY 8:30. MATINEES WEDNESDAYS AND SATURDAYS. A PLAY IN THREE ACTS BY – by whom? Inner Circle. Inner Temple. The tube was known as the Inner Circle and there was an underground station, the 'Temple'. By F. Temple: – No, J. Temple Thurston! That was it. 'The Wandering Jew', a play in three acts by J. Temple Thurston. Most likely this was a movie made from that play, and if he hadn't been so upset by his quarrel with Jacqueline, and self-conscious about his beard, he probably would have noticed that Mr Thurston – whether the playwright would have been grateful for this or not – had been given credit in small letters on some placard outside the cinema.

Just the same, the dreadful story of the poor Jew cursed by Christ never to die through the centuries – as if Christ could have been, *be* Christ, and put a curse on any man, least of all one who struck Him (had he, Ethan, struck Him? he, Ethan had struck Him) – the legend must have stemmed from some anti-Semitic source – could not lose all its force, or its power to move even to tears. 'Isn't Death Wonderful?' it should have been called. For it was death that was all the Wanderer's longing; death precisely what no one was going to give him; death, the thought of which filled him with the same euphoria, meant the same thing as life for the lovers in that other, never-to-be-forgotten, Griffith film, like that illness which is said to possess deep-sea divers, who cannot resist going lower and lower, until they drown, 'the rapture of the depths' – not that the Jew, alas, ever seemed allowed to approach that close to drowning . . .

'I plunge into the ocean; the waves throw me back with abhorrence upon the shore,' here he was saying, and, in a flashback, suiting the action to the word. And now reporting no better luck with other, recently more familiar, methods. 'I rush into fire; the flames recoil at my approach; I oppose myself to the banditti, their swords become blunted against my breast.' Bloody woe, it was as bad as the tank in Toronto. Yet that was nothing to the unkind treatment he was receiving from the volcano he'd just hurled himself into, from which he was now being spurned on an angry stream of lava. And all he got out of this was to be suspected of witchcraft.

'He is looked upon as an alien, but no one knows whence he hails, he has not a single friend in the town: he speaks but rarely, and never smiles; has neither servants nor goods, but his purse is well-furnished, and is said to do much good among the townspeople. Some regard him as an Arabian Astrologer, others declare him to be Doctor Faustus himself . . . He is of majestic appearance, with powerful features and large, black, flashing eyes. . . . His hair hangs in disarray over his forehead . . .'

H'm. Not unlike Sergeant-Major Edgar Poe, in fact, late of the American Army, and points south. Or what about a large flashing black *eye*? So now, my God – and couldn't one escape fire even at the movies? – they had got him, were going to burn the poor devil at the stake as a sorcerer. They were burning him. The flames shot up. But it was as one might have expected. Ahasuerus had proved, once more, incombustible. Not even his beard was singed. Some of his lower garments appeared scorched, otherwise he was unharmed. Yet instead of taking this sportingly as evidence of his innocence (as, say, the English might in Joan of Arc's case) – innocence by this time, heaven knows, of everything – his captors had to turn him loose, with further maledictions on his head, to begin his wanderings afresh, coming through thunder, the film ending now, to sombre crepitant chords, with a windswept lightning-crackling landscape, the tableau exactly like that of the old hoarding of Matheson Lang in the whistling London underground. (And what more than a lonely Wandering Jew was not he, Ethan, at last, to whom figures on hoardings had begun to have more validity than human beings!) But he was just lonely without Jacqueline. Together they could have enjoyed the film, bad as it was. She would have closed her eyes at the moment they set the torches to the stake, as she always too dramatically did when any character was being maltreated on the screen, opened them to see – perhaps – Donald Duck . . . It was not until Ethan had sat half-way through the cartoon following the feature that he began to perceive, with fear, a certain horrible relevance in that fire which had burned, yet not consumed . . . Or did he mean irrelevance, when he thought how completely their own house had been burned? Bah! Really, he must get hold of himself, go and look at the Kokoschka in the art gallery for a while (where first the image of the troop train as an evil spirit feeling its way into a human brain must have occurred to him). But with these reflections Donald Duck himself became horrible, and he watched the antics of the ill-tempered bird with gloom, as though seeing upon the screen his own passions hideously caricatured...There is no worse place than a cinema, either, in which to be conscious of the too many drinks you've had too many hours before, especially when in combination with the drinks you are proposing not to have afterwards.

The feature began again: 'THE WANDERING JEW' – yes – *From the play by J. Temple Thurston* . . .

Ethan stayed to verify that much, then, like someone plunging headlong into a bar, sought refuge in the little public library, which stayed open till 9:30 p.m.

'Good evening, Miss Braithwaite. Do you have a book here called *Ten Talents?*'

'Who is the author, Mr Llewelyn?'

'Booth Tarkington.'

Miss Braithwaite, with puzzled politeness, and a half smile, called her assistant. 'Do you know anything about these *Ten Talents*, Kitty? By Booth Tarkington, Captain Llewelyn says.'

' . . . We have *Seventeen*, "Alice Adams" . . .'

After some discussion it was decided by Miss Braithwaite, politely (and correctly), that Booth Tarkington had written no such book, and by Kitty, that it was out.

Ethan, as reluctant to provide a further clue by mentioning the Chief of Police had recommended it as he was publicly to pursue further interest at this time in a work about poltergeists, asked could he 'browse' awhile.

It was an interesting little library, in the old toll booth, beneath the Police Station; the volumes mostly of the Victorian era; with complete sets of Howells, Meredith, Mark Twain, Mark Rutherford and a startling array of translations from the nineteenth-century French Classics: the Goncourt Brothers, Zola,

Flaubert; *Crime and Punishment* was there, in Constance Garnett's translation; so was Lawrence's *Aspects of American Literature*; but twentieth-century fiction seemed scarcely represented save by the seven-day books, current best-sellers, lying on a shelf above Miss Braithwaite's head. Ethan felt a despair that, out of all these books, he had possibly not read four straight through; and of the current books, none; even though of recent years he'd been trying to read more.

There existed a separate section for 'religious and occult' volumes, and aware of a certain ratification, even admiration, for his beard in this place, he browsed awhile without undue anguish. The section was well stocked with a surprising number of recently printed works of this nature, for which, one surmised, the war had been the invisible salesman. Ethan almost immediately – so immediately it was as though the volume had been waiting for him – found what he was looking for, took the book over to a table and sat down.

Booth Tarkington had not indeed written *Ten Talents*. And *Ten Talents* was clearly not the name of the book the Chief had in mind. Booth Tarkington had written an appreciation for a book named *Lo!* by Charles Fort, and a piece of its cover, with a quotation, was pasted inside an omnibus volume of works by the same author, among them *Lo!* itself, and a book called *Wild Talents*. It was this inclusive volume Ethan was glancing through – A writer whose pen is dipped in earthquake and eclipse – Booth Tarkington. The Chief's mistake was complicated, but it wasn't difficult to see how he'd made it, especially if he'd had one eye on Miss Braithwaite. While the name Charles Fort probably meant as little to him as to Ethan.

But *Wild Talents* hadn't much concerning actual poltergeist phenomena, though there seemed other large sections throughout the omnibus dealing with that subject. Fort, an American who had died in 1932, obviously a genius if ever there was one, the possessor, together with the appalling insight, of all the scotomas and quirks of such dedicated powers, had obviously also been a pioneer in his approach to this type of research: one felt much intelligent opinion had come closer in recent years to accepting some of his views on such phenomena – in so far as he had any, for dogma in any form seemed his principal foe – accepting them even as a possible cause of otherwise inexplicable fires, and it must have been these parts the psychic investigator had referred the Chief to, under the impression their content was strictly 'psychical'. The joke, to some extent, was on the investigator. But then the whole book, wherever you opened it, was so compulsively entertaining on the surface, even with all its enormous weight of documentation, it was easy to be deceived, so hard was it to concentrate on a given spot. The immediate thesis of *Wild Talents* (which must be *Ten Talents*) in so far as one could take it in so rapidly, was as logically compelling as it must have been acutely discomforting to Ethan, had not the author's personality everywhere provided such robust assurance one soon forgot oneself. In no time at all one had been pleasantly convinced that certain unexplained fires (apart from those that seemed the undoubted work of poltergeists, whatever *they*, finally, were) had acutally been *feared* into existence: that, on occasion, feelings of sheer hatred or revenge towards other human beings had been sufficient to cause, without admixture of purposive 'magic', disaster, otherwise inexplicable, to others. (So why not to oneself, Ethan thought, as psychiatry implied, by hatred of onself?) Moreover, that motives, not acted upon, could produce the same result as those same motives had they been translated into action . . . It was one thing to have felt this instinctively, quite another to see it in cold print. For what criminal lawyer could not recall some instance in his own experience, where a confessed crime of murder or theft had offered the only conceivable motive and explanation for some secondary collateral, apparently covering crime, the criminal could not, in either the physical or legal sense, possibly have committed?

None of this formed the main thesis of the whole work – Ethan was skipping back and forth in the omnibus from book to book by this time – into another book called *The Book of the Damned*, into yet another called *New Worlds* – all of so obviously extraordinary a kind one felt astonishment that its author's name had not long since become a household word. Surely few writers were ever capable so swiftly and convincingly of disaffecting a reader from the regular bounds of his cosmos. Although in one sense Fort didn't widen them, he narrowed them. In ten minutes more, Ethan had become convinced that the sources of Niagara-on-the Lake's black fog – for here, by gosh, was *their* black fog, and the mud, and the fireballs, and not only these but rains of periwinkles and frogs too – were perhaps unknown lands situated at relatively no great distance in the dark nebulae, that celestial visitors of all kinds were no uncommon occurrence, that the object shaped like a man seen passing over Vicksburg, Pennsylvania, the report of which had once so perplexed him, was possibly no less than he seemed to be. And now, on every page he turned to, he seemed to see examples of the kinds of phenomena which had plagued them so frequently of late, cited as having been reported innumerable times before throughout history, or at least the last hundred years; everywhere in the work they were given veridicity – yes, everywhere Ethan was looking, as if once more those pages had wanted, were demanding to be looked at tonight – here they all were again, the black fog, the mud, the unexplained fires, the fires that burned, the fires that did not burn, or went out, or did not wholly consume, the wandering mysterious lights in churchyards in rural places and now again the fireballs, the auxiliary prodigies, in fact everything save M. Grigorivitch's blue dog, though no sooner had he thought that, than here was an example cited of a dog who had said good morning and vanished in a 'greenish vapour'. Mr Fort had drawn the line at the dog who said good morning.

The cumulative effect was terrifying: yet, for all that, Ethan thought to himself again, oddly reassuring. It was all something like going into a house reputed to be – that one had always thought was haunted, in the company of some amiable Don Quixote, and perhaps a barrel of Amontillado. Or a hogshead of gin. But haunted by spirits? Not a bit of it. Such notions were really the work of romantics. The only haunted house was the human mind. And the human mind was that of a magician – how the McCandless would have liked this bit – who had forgotten the use of his powers, but from time to time could not help using them. All of which by no means discounted the possibility of other 'intelligences' inhabiting those regions so much nearer than were supposed, those near those – now he thought of it – far too near regions. Only nothing was *super*natural. Everything would be explained when the time came. Even those 'imperfect' conflagrations could be explained, were not really supernatural – and it was perhaps almost a disappointment after all – could be Jesus.

*The man of one of our stories, J. Temple Thurston – alone in his room – and that a pictorial representation of his death by fire was enacting in a distant mind—*

Suddenly Ethan's eye fell on a passage that almost made him drop dead with fright. What? – J. Temple Thurston? death by fire . . . *The man of one of our stories – J. Temple Thurston* (he read, thunderstruck) *– alone in his room – and that a pictorial representation of his death by fire was enacting in a distant mind – and that into the phase of existence that is called 'real' stole the imaginary – scorching his body, but not his clothes, because so was pictured the burning of him – and that, hours later, there came into the mind of the sorcerer a fear that this imposition of what is called the imaginary upon what is called the physical bore quasi-attributes of its origin, or was not realistic, or would be, in physical terms, unaccountable, and would attract attention – and that the fire in the house was visualised, and was 'realised', but by a visualisation that in turn left some particulars unaccounted for.*

Ethan glanced yet again at the passage, saw that was what it said – almost incomprehensible when so isolated, but God knows it said enough – noted the page and the end of the preceding paragraph: 'It was during a thunderstorm and the woman had been killed by lightning,' which seemed irrelevant (though another storm was at this moment beginning), took out the book and ran up the steps leading from the basement of the police station.

The knowledge, in any case, could scarcely be borne alone. He'd narrowly escaped having to bear it too, being locked up in the darkening public library that, as he hurried out, had been on the point of closing, himself forgotten, to be bailed out perhaps, at the frantic sounds of his knocking, only by old Chief Toll Booth Tarkington himself, in cautious search of subayuntamiento polterghosts.

HELD OVER. 'THE WANDERING JEW.' Cameo Cinedrome. Ethan's feeling of panic was now succeeded by a mysterious sense of elation, even self-congratulation, flooding through his being as he hurried through the hot lightning-flickering dusk under the few remaining elms thrashing overhead in concussive gusts (he wondered later if Mr Fort was right, and this sensation perhaps an atavistic one, common to all men, who suddenly seem to feel, if only for an instant, and on a sub-human plane, their own lost magical powers restored), hurried past the clock tower – over which a frantic homing seaplane was flying soundlessly, like a bird with long shoes, into a patch of hyacinthine sky in the west – hurried home to the Prince of Wales Hotel . . . *King Storm whose Sheen is Fearful.*

He found Jacqueline, who had previously announced with fury she was going to bed, after having seen to Tommy for the night, wickedly drinking beer and talking to M. Grigorivitch in the almost deserted Ladies and Escorts. She greeted him with a radiant and friendly smile while M. Grigorivitch went off to get them one on the house.

'What's the book?' she said cheerfully.

But Ethan's calm had left him, and having tried to tell her his story about the cinema, The Wandering Jew, and the library, his hands trembling, he couldn't find anywhere the passage in *Wild Talents* about Temple Thurston.

'Give the book to me . . .'

*Upon the night of April 6, 1919* [Jacqueline found immediately these words, which she read aloud] – *see the Dartford [Kent] Chronicle, April – Mr J. Temple Thurston was alone in his home, Hawley Manor, near Dartford. His wife was abroad.*

'But Jacqueline – !'

*Particulars of the absence of his wife, or of anything leading to the absence of his wife, are missing. Something had broken up this home. The servants had been dismissed. Thurston was alone.*

'But that wasn't the passage—'

*At 2:40 o'clock, morning of April 7, the firemen were called to Hawley Manor. Outside Thurston's room, the house was blazing, but in his room there was no fire. Thurston was dead. His body was scorched: but upon his clothes there was no trace of fire.*

'But Jacqueline!' Ethan interposed again, with horror.

*From the story of J. Temple Thurston I pick up that this man, with his clothes on, was so scorched as to bring on death by heart failure, by a fire that did not affect his clothes. This body was fully clothed, when found, about 3 a.m., Thurston hadn't been sitting up drinking. There was no suggestion that he had been reading. It was commented upon, at the inquest, as queer, that he should have been up and fully clothed at about 3 a.m. The scorches were large red patches on the thighs and lower parts of the legs. It was much as if, bound to a stake, the man had stood in a fire that had not mounted high.*

'Great *God*!' Ethan felt a tightening of his throat at the roots of his tongue. 'But Jacqueline. The *end* of The Wandering Jew, in the movie—'

'All right, Ethan. I get it.' She looked up at him with frightened eyes. 'All right. But wait – let me finish . . .

*In this burning house nothing was afire in Thurston's room. Nothing was found, such as charred fragments of nightclothes, to suggest that, about 3 o'clock, Thurston, awakened by a fire elsewhere in the house, had gone from his room, and had been burned and had returned to his room, where he had dressed, but had then been overcome. It may be that he had died hours before the house was fired.*

'But that's absolutely inconceivable! That isn't the passage I read at all!' Ethan burst out.

*It has seemed to me* [Jacqueline pursued, calmly reading on] *most fitting to regard all accounts in this book as 'stories'. There has been a permeation of the fantastic, or whatever we mean by 'untrueness'. Our stories have not been realistic. And there is something about the story of J. Temple Thurston that, to me, gives it the look of a revised story. It is as if, in an imagined scene, an author had killed off a character by burning, and then, thinking it over, as some writers do, had noted inconsistencies, such as a burned body, and no mention of a fire anywhere else in the house – So then, as an afterthought, the fire in the house – but, still such an amateurish negligence in the authorship of this story, that the fire was not explained. To the firemen, this fire in the house was as unaccountable as, to the Coroner, was the burned body in the unscorched clothes. When the firemen broke into Hawley Manor, they found the fire raging in Thurston's room. It was near no fireplace, near no electric wires that might have crossed. No odour of paraffin, nothing suggestive of arson. No robbery.*

*The fire, of unknown origin, seemed directed upon Thurston's room, as if to destroy, clothes and all, this burned body in unscorched clothes. Outside, the door of this room was blazing when the firemen arrived.*

In the same way he had felt himself flooded by that strange sense of elation after leaving the library, Ethan now felt the fright this had cancelled coming back, but in a far more powerful form, as though now he were being overwhelmed by a sea, a huge breaker of primeval terror – and as if the obsessive thought of fire itself had produced the compensatory image, the opposite symbol of water – or it was like an incoming wave from the burning lake of fire in his nightmare – and now, as the feeling receded, he were left sprawling in a titanic undertow.

At the same time he saw clearly the blazing door, the unscorched clothes, the imperfectly burned body of the poor playwright alone in his room, saw the closing scenes of the movie again, The Wandering Jew bound to the stake; 'It was much as if, bound to a stake, the man had stood in a fire that had not mounted high'; the imperfectly burned undying Ahasuerus, his imperfectly burned dead 'creator', 'in a fire that had not mounted high, as if bound to the stake'; and fearing to see these things too clearly, found himself remembering too some words of the passage he had been unable to find again in *Wild Talents*: 'that the fire was visualised by a visualisation that in turn left some particulars unaccounted for'; 'that a pictorial representation of his death by fire was enacting in a distant mind': 'that into the phase of existence that was real, stole the imaginary': then . . . !

But he now became conscious of something more frightening still taking place in his mind. It was a feeling that permeated the high, ill-lit mustard-yellow walls of the hotel beer parlour, the long dim corridor between the two beer parlours, on which the door was opened by an invisible hand (revealing, lying flat on her back, a good woman weighing 350 pounds, from Gravesend, London, who had so far resisted all efforts to be lifted – it was fruitless, as Ethan well knew, had tried before: she went through this performance almost every night about this time, and then, at 10:45, just before closing time, would get up of her own accord and go home, as though nothing had happened), a feeling which seemed a very part of the very beer-smelling air, as if – the feeling perhaps someway arising, translated to this surrounding scene, from the words themselves – there were some hidden correspondence between these words and this scene, or between some ultimate unreality and meaninglessness he seemed to perceive adumbrated by them (by these words, under their eyes, in the book on the table – and yet for an instant what meaning, what terrifying message flashed from all this meaninglessness), and his inner perception of this place – no, it was as if this place were suddenly the exact outward representation of his inner state of mind: so that, shutting his eyes for a long moment of stillness (in which he imagined he could hear, distantly, pounding, the tumultuous cataract of Niagara Falls twenty miles away), he seemed to feel himself merging into it, while equally there was a fading of it into himself: it was as though, having visualised all this with his eyes shut now he *were* it – these walls, these tables, that corridor, with the huge woman from Gravesend, flat on her back motionless in it, obdurate as the truth, this beer parlour, this place of garboons hard by the Laurentian Shield! But in this new reality not even the goodness of its landlords served to redeem it. Nor any other benevolence of fellowship, gaiety, the relatively innocent drink it purveyed. For his visualisation included also everything that was ordinarily invisible too, Sergeant-Major Poe's 'unparticled matter' rendered palpable to the gaze, so that it was like *seeing* all the senseless trickeries and treacheries alcohol had here imposed on the mind; all the misery, mischief, wretchedness, illusions: yes, the sum of all the hangovers that had been acquired here, and quite overlooking those that had been healed. Ethan now held this collective mental image for an instant completely, unwaveringly, on the screen of his mind. Image or state of being that, finally appeared to imply, represent, an unreality, a desolation, disorder, falsity that was beyond evil. Satan was in a sense perhaps a realised figure in the human psyche. But even such a Satan could not, and for that reason, dwell in this region: or if this were in his domain, he held no sway; or, by some more than legal fiction, so far beneath the abysmal, was it, his law sounded here faint, unheard, confused – like the recurrent sounds of the engine in the refrigerator. Yet this seemed the home also of more conscious mental abortions and aberrations; of disastrous yet unfinished thoughts, half hopes and half intentions, and where precepts, long abandoned, stumbled on. Or the home of a half-burned man, himself an imperfect visualisation, at the stake; this place where neither death nor suicide could ever be a solution, since nothing here had been sufficiently realised ever to possess life.

Ethan opened his eyes. What was he saying to himself? Had he really *had* some sort of vision – the feeling had not altogether departed – some kind of 'mystical' experience 'reversed'? Some form, less of an illumination than a *disillumination*, a kind of minor St Paul's vision upside down; certainly it had arisen, if in an unorthodox manner, from an almost complete and mysterious identification of subject with object: and had been accompanied, paradoxically, by such an astonishing sense of ecstasy, one felt one could never begin to describe it, even to

Jacqueline, even to her father, who, if anyone, should be equipped to understand it, without somehow leading to the propagation of a lie, an ecstasy which still persisted, though diminished, an icy ecstasy now, like that, while far more intense, which sometimes grips the drinker, not yet quite sober, waking in half-delirium after a prolonged debauch, before 'reality' asserts itself – and waking indeed you discover your clothes to be neatly folded up in the icebox where, alas, no drink has been providently left. Ethan came to his senses abruptly. Grace had at least penetrated to this more immediate mundane region in the shape of another beer, and he drank it hungrily.

What had it all meant? Was he not real himself? Were *they* not, either of them, Jacqueline or himself, real, but imperfect, creatures of someone else's imperfect imagination? Was this all mankind's lot on this earth, that he, man, had no intrinsic reality to himself, that reality was a thing to be striven for, else he remained in limbo? It wasn't that there was anything particularly original about such thoughts, any more than there had been, he now saw, in the form of his 'disillumination' (on the contrary, as to aesthetic content it had perhaps hardly more merit than a parody based on a misreading of T. S. Eliot or, for that matter, Swinburne), yet the intensity, the conviction, was still there, this impression as of something overwhelmingly important that had just occurred. And he saw something important *had* occurred. What was important was that he was now convinced there must be some complete triumphant counterpart, hitherto based on hearsay or taken on trust, of that experience he had had, or almost had: as there must be of that abyssal region – some spiritual region maybe of unborn divine thoughts beyond our knowledge . . . So why, then, should he have rushed to the conclusion that the extraordinary thing that had happened tonight with The Wandering Jew and Temple Thurston and Charles Fort, that this collision of contingencies, was in its final essence diabolical, or fearful, or meaningless? Why, to the conclusion that he had somehow magically produced it himself, than that any message in it for *them* was necessarily terrifying? Mightn't he equally well consider that he'd been vouchsafed, was so being vouchsafed, a glimpse into the very workings of creation itself – indeed with this cognition Ethan seemed to see before his eyes whole universes eternally condensing and recondensing themselves out of the 'immaterial' into the 'material', and as at the continued visualisation of their Creator, being radiated back again. While meantime here on earth the 'material' was only cognisable through the mind of man! What was real, what imaginary? Yes, but couldn't the meaning, the message, for *them*, be simply that there *had* been a message at all? Yes, could he not just as well tell himself – as Cyprian of Antioch – that here God had beaten the devil at his own game, that magic was checkmated by miracle! Ethan drank half another beer. Gone was his fright. In its stead was awe. In the beginning was the Word. But what unpronounceable Name had visualised the Word?

'Nothing mysterious at all,' Jacqueline was saying calmly. 'I simply looked up your Temple Thurston in the index, since it didn't seem to occur to you.'

'I didn't know there *was* an index,' Ethan almost shouted, as thunder, a single colossal explosion, struck overhead.

Other more distant thunderclaps crashed and banged around the peninsula; then all the lights in the Prince of Wales Hotel went out.

Outside of war, there is no noise on land or sea as shattering and extreme as that of a thunderstorm in the storm country, the Great Lakes basin, and it seemed useless, with this going on, which possessed its own peculiar uneasy exhilaration, in the intermittent dark and blaze, to attempt to explain to Jacqueline, as if she needed any further explanation, the significance of poor Temple Thurston's unscorched clothes, his scorched body, the Jew at the stake.

M. Grigorivitch drifted in, carrying candles, their gold flames wavering in the draught. 'The lightning is peeling the poles and biting the wires, Captain Llewelyn,' he moved on with his candles to the other tables.

Then there was dead silence and the lightning started again soundlessly on its own accord and the impression was of a child playing with an electric torch, switching it on and off in the hotel garden. 'I must say Fort didn't show much pity for poor old Temple Thurston,' he heard Jacqueline saying, though it was the kind of thing he might have said himself, and perhaps indeed he had said it: 'It's an inconceivably horrible world, why does anyone bother to live in it?'

'Have you ever heard of Charles Fort before?' Ethan almost certainly had asked.

'No.'

'Your father never spoke of him?'

'No . . . Not that I know of . . . I think he's writing of the Qliphoth, though; the world of shells and demons.'

'Do you suppose Tommy's sleeping through *this?*'

'Like an angel.'

Suddenly, just the same, cobalt lightning filled the room, and he saw Jacqueline's face across the table, eyes staring widely at him.

'But you *must* have read this passage,' all at once she cried through the thunder. Then, as the lights came on again: 'Here. Look for yourself – Thurston, J. Temple. 912ff. It's the only page reference it gives in the index.'

'But I told you – I didn't *look* in the index. Why the devil *should* I?'

'Well, try to remember the number of your page then.'

'It added up to 7 . . . 1051. Let's try that.'

There, sure enough, was the passage, and Ethan read it to her:

*The man of one of our stories, J. Temple Thurston – alone in his room – and that a pictorial representation of his death by fire was enacting in a distant mind –*

'Very well then! It was an oversight of the person who made the index,' Jacqueline said stubbornly.

Thunder sounded like a single plane, high, in windy cloudy weather, that, going fast downwind invisibly overhead (the wind blowing in the opposite direction below), sounds like forty planes, as they sat looking at each other with scared eyes across the table.

And though they searched till closing time, in candle-light, and under electric light, and with candles again, all through that omnibus of Charles Fort's works, nowhere did they find any further reference to J. Temple Thurston; there was no hint that Fort had ever heard of him as an author at all, and certainly not the author of the play *The Wandering Jew*, at the end of which 'bound to a stake, the man had stood in a fire that had not mounted high . . .'

And perhaps indeed it had been another Temple Thurston.

That night, a house, on the lakeside of the Prince of Wales, took fire, and Ethan felt himself being borne solemnly homeward on a litter to the Prince of Wales Hotel, with its triple signature of feathers over the door: a cage of lovebirds, lofting slowly out of a window, and floating down towards him, had struck him on the head.

He had gone to the rescue with the volunteer fire brigade at 2 a.m., clad in his pyjamas and an army greatcoat. Not that this was a serious fire either, even for the lovebirds, or himself, but it did the trick. They went west. And one of his last memories of Niagara-on-the-Lake was of the lurid vitrified lake itself, reflecting the fire: and of the grocer, one of his pall bearers, who had nobly arrived with his fire-extinguisher, of the grocer saying, 'H'm. It's just like I said. The element follows you around, sir!'

And Saskatchewan and Saskatchewan and Saskatchewan: said the train: and Saskatchewan and Saskatchewan and Saskatchewan. And Manitoba and Manitoba and Manitoba. Five thousand miles at thirty miles an hour. Five hundred miles of prairie were ablaze. Beyond the Great Divide, they looked down on the wild beauty of lakes and ravines and pastures of British Columbia with all the boundless and immeasurable longing in their gaze of two children of Israel shading their eyes before a vision of the Promised Land. And when from the Rockies they had descended through the Fraser valley, the first thing they saw of Vancouver was, from the train window at Port Moody – across the water on their right, a swift-flowing inlet – a fisherman's shack, built on piles, burning. . . .

FRANK O'CONNOR
# *Variations on a Theme*

I

KATE MAHONEY was sixty when her husband died. After that, she had, like many another widow, to face the loss of her little house. It was a good house in a good lane. There was a sandstone quarry behind, so that no one could overlook them except from a great distance, and though there was a terrace of really superior houses between them and the road, and it had no view and little or no sunlight, it was quiet and free of traffic any hour of the day or night – a lovely place for children, as she often said.

Her two daughters, Nora and Molly, were married, one in Shandon Street and the other on the Douglas Road, but even if either of them had been in a position to offer her a home she would have had doubts about accepting it. What she said was that the people in Shandon Street were uncivilised and the people on the Douglas Road had no nature, but what she really thought was that her daughters shouted too much. The truth was that Kate shouted enough for a regimental sergeant-major, and the girls – both gentle and timid – had learned early in life that the only way of making themselves heard was to shout back. Kate did not shout all the time: she had another tone, reserved for intimate occasions, which was low-pitched and monotonous and in which she tended to break off sentences as though she had forgotten what she was saying. But, low-pitched or loud, her talk was monumental, like headstones. Her hands and legs were twisted with rheumatics, and she had a face like a butcher's block in which the only really attractive feature was the eyes, which looked astonishingly young and merry.

She loved the lane and the neighbours – so different from the nasty strange people you met in Shandon Street and the Douglas Road – but mostly she longed to die in the bed her husband had died in. With the rheumatics she could not go out and do a day's work as other widows did to stretch out their couple of halfpence. It was this that turned her mind to the desperate expedient of taking in a foster child – this and the realisation that the lane was a lovely place for children. She could hardly help feeling that it would be a good influence on a child.

It was a terrible thing to descend to, more particularly for a woman who had brought up two children of her own, but there didn't seem to be any alternative. Motherhood was the only trade she knew. She went with her problem to Miss Hegarty, the nurse, who owned one of the bigger houses between her and the road. Miss Hegarty was a fine-looking woman of good family, but so worn out by the endless goings-on of male and female that she admitted to Kate that most of the time she could not be bothered to distinguish between honest and dishonest transactions. 'Aha, Mrs Mahoney!' she said triumphantly. 'They all start out in a laugh and all end up in a cry.' Even to women in labour she would call out joyously, 'Last year's laugh is this year's cry, Mrs Mahoney.' The funny thing about Miss Hegarty was that though nobody had ever mentioned a man's name in connection with her, she seemed to know of every girl within fifty miles who was in trouble.

Kate, however, found her a good counsellor. She advised her against taking foster children from the local council because they paid so badly that you would have to take three or four to make a living out of them. The thing to do was to take a child of good family whose mother would be able to support it. Even then you couldn't rely on vagabonds like that because they were all unstable and might skip off to foreign parts without warning, but you would still have the grandparents to fall back on. 'Oh, Mrs Mahoney, if they have it they'll pay to keep their precious daughter's name out of the papers. Fitter for them to keep her off the streets!'

Miss Hegarty knew of a girl of that kind from Limerick who was going to England to have her baby and would probably be glad of a good home for it in Ireland but not too close to her family. When Mrs Mahoney told Nora and Molly, Molly didn't seem to mind but Nora got very dramatic and said that personally she'd choose the poorhouse – a remark Kate did not like at all, though it was only what you'd expect from a giddy creature like Nora.

From Nora she borrowed back the old family perambulator, and one spring morning it appeared outside the door in the lane with a baby boy asleep inside while Kate herself sat on the window-sill to explain her strange position. 'My first!' she shouted gaily, and then went on in the monotonous voice she used for solemn occasions to explain that this was no ordinary child such as you would get from the workhouse, but the son of a beautiful, educated girl from one of the wealthiest, best-bred families in Limerick, who herself was manageress of a big shop there. Of course, the neighbours smiled and nodded and groaned, and agreed it was a sad case but that times were changing; and did not believe a word that Kate told them because they knew a girl like that must have the bad drop and the bad drop was bound to be passed on. All the same they were sorry for Kate, an old neighbour and a respectable one who had no choice but to put the best face she could on it. The young married women who, as they said themselves, had paid for their titles, were not so charitable and said that you could not allow decent children to grow up in an atmosphere like that, and that the priest or the landlord should stop it because it was lowering the value of morality and property in the lane. They did not say it too loud, because, however humiliated she might be, Kate was a very obstinate old woman, and a vulgar one as well if she was roused.

So Jimmy Mahoney was permitted to grow up in the lane along with the honest transactions and turned into a good-looking, moody kid, cheerful and quarrelsome, who seemed to see nothing wrong in his mother's being so old. On the contrary, he seemed to depend on her more than the other children did on their real mothers, and sometimes when she left him alone and went off to see Nora or Molly he refused to play and sat and sulked on the doorstep till she got home. Even that ended one day when he simply went after her, without as much as the price of the tram, and walked to the other side of the city to Molly's on the Douglas Road.

'Oh, you divil you!' Kate shouted when she looked round and saw him staring accusingly at her from the front door. 'I thought you were a ghost. A nice position I'd be in if you went and got yourself killed on me!' Then she grinned and said, 'I suppose you couldn't get on without me.' Molly, a beautiful, haggard woman, gave him a smile of mortification and said quietly, 'Come in, Jimmy.' It was a thing she would not have wished for a pound because she knew it would have to be explained to the neighbours as well as her own children. But afterwards, whatever she or Nora might think, Kate brought him with her wherever she went. They might imagine that he had no such claim on their mother but Jimmy thought otherwise.

But by the time he was five or six things were again going hard with Kate. Money wasn't what it had been and her little margin of profit was contracting. She paid another visit to Miss Hegarty, and this time the nurse had an even more staggering story. It seemed there was this well-to-do girl in Bantry who was engaged to a rich Englishman and then went and had an affair with a married man she had known from the time she was twelve.

'A married man!' exclaimed Kate. 'Oh, my, the things that go on!'

'Don't talk to me, Mrs Mahoney!' Miss Hegarty cried dramatically. 'Don't talk to me. If you knew the half of what was going on, 'twould make you lose your religion.'

Kate felt it her duty to warn Jimmy that he was getting a little brother. Miss Hegarty herself advised that, but whatever Miss Hegarty knew about flighty girls she seemed to know very little about small boys. When Mrs Mahoney told him he began to roar and kick the furniture till she was sure the whole lane was listening. He said that he didn't want any little brother. He said if she brought one into the house that he'd walk out. He said she was too old to be having babies and that she'd have everyone talking about them. As she sighed afterwards, a husband wouldn't have given her such dogs' abuse. And what Jimmy said was nothing to what her daughters said.

'Ah, mammy, you're making a holy show of us!' Nora cried when she came to call.

'I'm making a show of ye?' Kate cried wonderingly, pointing at her bosom with the mock-innocent air that maddened her daughters. 'I do my business and I don't cost ye a penny – is that what ye call making a show of ye?'

'Ah, you'd think we were something out of a circus instead of an old respectable family,' stormed Nora. 'That I can hardly face the neighbours when I come up the lane! Ahadie, 'tis well my poor daddy doesn't know what you're making of his little house.' Then she put her hands on her hips like a common market woman and went on. 'How long do you think you'll be able to keep this up, would you mind us asking? You think you're going to live forever, I suppose?'

'God is good,' Kate muttered stiffly. 'I might have a few years in me yet.'

'You might,' Nora said mockingly. 'And I suppose you imagine that if anything happens to you, Molly and myself will keep up the good work, out of Christian charity?'

'Aha, God help the innocent child that would be depending on Christian charity from the likes of you!' Kate retorted with sudden anger. 'And their people have plenty, lashings of it – more than you'll ever be able to say with your husband in a steady job in the Brewery! How sure you are of yourself! My goodness, that we'd never do anything at all if we were to be always thinking of what was round the next corner. And what about my rent? Are you going to pay it?'

'Ah, 'tisn't the rent with you at all, and it never was,' Nora said with growing fury. 'You only do it because you like it.'

'I like it?' her mother asked feebly as though she were beginning to doubt Nora's sanity. 'An old woman like me that's crippled with the rheumatics? Oh, my!' she added in a roar of anguish, 'that 'tis in a home I ought to be if I had my rights. In a home!'

'You and your home!' Nora said contemptuously. 'That's enough of your lies now, mammy! You love it! Love it! And you care more for that little bastard than you ever did about Molly or me.'

'How dare you?' Kate cried, rising with as much dignity as the rheumatics permitted. 'What way is that to speak to your mother? And to talk about a poor defenceless child like that in my house, you dirty, jealous thing! Yes, jealous,' she added in a wondering whisper as though the truth had only dawned on her in that moment. 'Oh, my! Ye that had everything!'

All the same, Kate was a bit shaken, not because of the row, because the Mahoneys had always quarrelled like that, as though they all suffered from congenital deafness, and they got the same pleasure out of the mere volume of sound they could produce that certain conductors get out of Wagner. What really mortified her was that she had given herself away in front of Nora, whose intelligence she despised. Now if it had been Molly she wouldn't have minded so much, for though Molly was apparently serving her time to be a saint, she had the intelligence to see through Kate's little dodges. It was true that Kate had taken Jimmy in for perfectly good mercenary reasons, and that without him she would have no home at all; and it was very wrong under the circumstances for Nora to impute sentimental motives to her; but all the same she wasn't so far wrong. Motherhood was the only trade Kate knew, and she liked to practise it as her poor husband had liked to make little chairs and tables in the last year of his life, when no one cared whether he made them or not; and though her rheumatics were bad and her sight wasn't all it used to be, she felt she practised it better, the older she got. It was also true enough to say that she enjoyed Jimmy more than she had enjoyed her own children, and if you had pressed her about it, she would have said that in those days she had been young and worried about everything. But if you had pressed her hard enough you would also have discovered that there wasn't a boy on the whole road that she thought was a patch on Jimmy. And what was wrong with that? she might have added. You might say what you like but there was a lot in good blood.

She would not have understood at all if you had accused her of being an old dreamer who was attracted to Jimmy by the romance and mystery of his birth – the sort of thing she had missed in her own sober and industrious youth, but just the same, Jimmy gave her the chance of sitting over the fire in the evening with some old crony and discussing like a schoolgirl things she would scarcely have known existed.

'Oh, when I seen Jimmy's mother that day in the solicitor's office she was like something you'd see in a shop window, Mrs Sunners,' she would chant. 'She was beautiful, beautiful! And I could see by that set face of hers that she had a month of crying all bottled up inside her. Oh, Mrs Sunners, if you seen her the way I did you'd know that nothing she could do would be bad.'

And later, when she had tucked Jimmy in for the night and lay awake in the other room, saying her rosary, she would often forget her prayers and imagine how she would feel if one stormy night (for some reason she made it stormy) there came a knock at the door and Kate saw Jimmy's father standing in the lane, tall and handsome with a small black moustache and the tears in his eyes. 'Mr Mulvany,' she would say to the teacher (she was always making up names and occupations for Jimmy's unknown father), 'your son wants nothing from you,' or (if she was in a generous mood) 'Senator MacDunphy, come in. Jimmy was beginning to think you'd never find him.'

But dreamers are forever running into degrading practicalities that they have failed to anticipate, and there was one thing about her extraordinary family that really worried Kate. Before she had even laid eyes on him, the second boy had also been christened James and because she was terrified of everything to do with the law she did not dare to change his name. But so that Jimmy should not be too upset, she left his name as it was, plain James – an unnatural name for any child as she well knew.

James was a very different sort of child from Jimmy. He was a baby with a big head, a gaping mouth and a cheerless countenance that rarely lit up in a smile. Even from the first day it was as though he knew he was there only on sufferance and resigned himself to the fact.

Fortunately, Jimmy took to him at once. He liked being left in charge, and was perfectly happy to change and entertain him. He explored the neighbourhood to study all the other babies and told Kate that James was cleverer than the whole lot of them. He even got Kate's permission to wheel the old perambulator up and down the main road so that people could see for themselves what James was like and came back with great satisfaction to report any approving remarks he happened to elicit. As he had a violent temper and would fight anyone up to twice his weight, the other kids did not make any public remarks about this sissified conduct.

2

A couple of times a year Jimmy's mother, whom he knew only as Aunt Nance, came to stay with friends in Cork, and Jimmy visited her there and played with the two children who were called Rory and Mary. He did not like Rory and Mary because they ganged up on him at once and he only went on his aunt's account. She was tall and good-looking with a dark complexion and dark, dark hair; she talked in a crisp nervous way, and was always forgetting herself and saying dirty words like 'Cripes!' and 'Damn!' which delighted Jimmy because these were words that were supposed to be known only to fellows.

When he got home Kate asked him all sorts of questions about his visit, like how many rooms there were in the house, what he ate there, what sort of furniture there was and what size was the garden – things that never interested Jimmy in the least.

When James began to grow up he too asked questions. He wanted to know what school Rory and Mary went to, what they learned there and whether or not Mary played the piano. These too were questions that did not interest Jimmy, but it dawned on him that James was lonely when he was left behind like that and wanted to see the Martins's place for himself. It seemed an excellent idea to Jimmy because James was a steady, quiet kid who would get on much better with Rory and Mary than he did, but when he suggested it Kate only said James was too young and Aunt Nance said she'd see.

It ended by his suspecting that there was something fishy about James. There had always been something fishy about him, as though he didn't really belong to the family. Jimmy wasn't clear how you came to belong to the family but he knew it had to happen in a hospital or in the house, and he couldn't remember anything of the sort happening to James. One evening, when Kate was complaining of her rheumatics he asked her casually if she hadn't gone to hospital with it.

'Ah, how would the likes of me go to hospital?' she asked sourly. 'I was never in a hospital in my life and I hope I never am.'

James was in the room and Jimmy said no more for the time being. Later that night he returned to the subject.

'You're not James's mother, are you, mammy?'

'What's that you say?' she cried in astonishment.

'I said you're not James's mother, that's all.'

'Oye, what queer things you think of!' she said crossly.

'But you're not,' he said with a shrug. 'You only took him in because his own mother didn't want him, isn't that it?'

'You inquisitive puppy!' she hissed. 'Don't let the child hear you saying things like that.'

'But it's true, isn't it? She's the one you get the money from.'

Kate threatened him into silence, but she was terrified. 'Oh, my, the cunning of him!' she said next day to Mrs Sunners. 'The way he cross-hackled me – that poor Jack Mahoney never did the like all the long years we were married! And what am I to say to him? Who will I get to advise me?' The neighbours could not advise her, and even if they tried it would be useless because they had no more experience than herself. Miss Hegarty might have been able to advise her but Kate felt that asking her advice would be a sort of admission that she had failed in the job.

And all the time Jimmy's behaviour grew worse. At the best of times it wasn't very good. Though occasionally he got into high spirits and entertained herself and James by the hour, telling funny stories, the high spirits rarely lasted long and he sulked on his bed with a comic. After this he would go out with other, rougher kids, and return late with a guilty air she could spot from the end of the lane and which meant he had broken a window or stolen something from a shop. She watched him from the back door when she saw him in the quarry because she was sure he had a hidey hole there where he kept the things he stole, but when she poked round there by herself she could never find anything. At times like these she was never free of anxiety, because she knew it imperilled the sufferance the neighbours extended to him and if ever a policeman – which God forbid! – came to her door, they would be the first to say it was all you could expect of a boy like that. But this was the worst bout yet.

Finally, she decided to tell him the truth about James, or as much of it as she thought he could understand, and one night when James was asleep she sat with him in the darkness over the kitchen fire and told him in her monotonous voice about this beautiful, beautiful girl in Bantry and how as a girl she was in love with this nice young man, and his cruel parents made him marry a girl he did not love at all, and then the girl's parents persuaded her to marry this rich Englishman with motor cars and yachts and big houses in all parts of the world, but at the last moment the poor girl's heart misgave her and she tried to be reunited to the one she truly loved. She told it so movingly that by the end she was in tears herself, but Jimmy's first words startled her out of her daydream.

'All the same, mammy, James should be with his own mother,' he said.

She was astonished and dismayed at the maturity of his tone. This was no longer any of the Jimmys she had known but one who spoke with the sort of authority poor Jack had exercised on the odd occasions when he called his family to order. She even found herself apologising in the way she might have apologised to poor Jack.

'Ah, wisha, how could she without that husband of hers knowing?'

'Then she ought to tell him,' Jimmy said, and again it was like her dead husband's voice speaking to her.

'Tell him? Tell him what?'

'Everything.'

'Is it to be upsetting the child?' she asked complainingly.

'If she doesn't upset him, somebody else will,' he said with his brooding old-mannish air.

'They will, they will, God help us!' she sighed. 'People are bad enough for anything. But the poor child may as well be happy while he can.'

But it was Jimmy, not James, she was concerned about. James might get by, a colourless, studious, obedient boy like him, without giving much offence to anyone, but one day Jimmy would beat another boy or steal something from a shop and the whole truth would come out. For a few moments she was tempted to tell him but she was afraid of what his mother would say when she knew.

Meanwhile, she saw to her surprise that she seemed to have given Jimmy a purpose in life, though it was something she might have expected. Jimmy was always like that, up or down, full of initiative and independence or shiftless and dependent. Now he took over James personally. He announced that it was bad for the kid to be so much alone and took him with him when he went down the Glen or up the river with bigger boys. It was not James's notion; he didn't like bigger boys and didn't in the least mind being left alone with the bits of clean paper he managed to pick up for his writings and drawings, but Jimmy said it was for his good and anything anyone said was good for James he would give a fair trial to. When he came home he repeated his adventures to Kate in the literal gloomy manner of a policeman making a report.

'Jimmy took me down the Glen with Bobby Stephens and Ted Murtagh. I don't like Ted Murtagh. He says dirty words. Jimmy and me fished for thorneybacks. Then he showed me a blackbird's nest. You can't touch a bird's nest because the bird would know and leave the young ones to die. Ted Murtagh robs birds' nests. I think that's wrong, don't you, mammy?'

James collected bits of information, right and wrong, apparently under the impression that they would all come in handy one day, and to each of them he managed to attach a useful moral lesson. No wonder he sometimes made Jimmy smile.

But Jimmy still continued to brood on James's future. He waited until Aunt Nance came to Cork again, and when he got her to himself he poured it all out on her. He had managed a convince himself that Kate had not understood but that Aunt Nance who was cleverer would only have to hear the facts to do something about it. Before he had even finished his story she gave him a queer hurt look and cut him off.

'You'll know what it's all about one of these days,' she said.

'But don't you think he should be with his mother?' he asked.

'I don't know,' she said with her boldest air, and then took out a cigarette.

'And even if I did I wouldn't criticise,' she added.

'Well, I think it's wrong,' he said sullenly. 'The poor kid has no one to play with. Couldn't I bring him over here tomorrow?'

'Begod, you couldn't, Jimmy,' she said. 'Too many blooming kids they have on this place already, if you ask me.'

He left her in one of his mutinous, incoherent fits of rage. He did not take the bus home, even though he had the money, but walked and stood on the river's edge, flinging stones. It was late when he got home but he told Kate the whole story. 'Ah, what business had you to be interfering?' she asked miserably. He went to bed, and she heard him tossing and muttering to himself. Finally she lit the candle and went into the little attic room that he shared with James. He sat up in bed and looked at her with mad eyes.

'Go away!' he whispered fiercely. 'You're not my mother at all.'

'Oye!' she whimpered, sleepy and scared. 'You and your mother!'

'You're not, you're not, you're not!' he muttered. 'I know it all now. I'm like James only you wouldn't tell me. You haven't the decency. You tell me nothing only lies.'

'Whisht, whisht, whisht and don't wake the child!' she whispered impatiently. 'Come into the other room.'

He stumbled out ahead of her in his nightshirt, and she sat on the edge of her bed and put her arm round him. He was shivering as if he had a fever, and she no longer felt capable of controlling the situation. She felt old and tired and betrayed.

'What made you think of it, child?' she asked wearily.

'Aunt Nance,' he said with a sob.

'Was it she told you?' She knew she didn't even sound surprised.

'No. She wouldn't tell me anything, only I saw she was afraid.'

'Who was she afraid of?'

'I asked her to get James's mother to bring him home with her and she got frightened.'

'Oh, oh, oh, you poor desolate child, and you only did it for the best!' she wailed.

'I want to know who my mother is,' he cried despairingly. 'Is it Aunt Kitty?' (Kitty was the mother of Rory and Mary.)

'Why then, indeed, it is not.'

'Is it Aunt Nance so?'

'Wisha, child, lie down here and you can sleep with Mammy.'

'I don't want to sleep,' he said frantically. 'How can I sleep? I want to know who my mother is and you won't tell me.' Then, turning suddenly into a baby again, he put his head on her lap and wept. She patted his fat bottom under his nightshirt and sighed. 'You're perished,' she said. 'What am I going to do with you?' Then she lifted him into her bed and pulled up the clothes.

'Will I get you a cup of tea?' she asked with feigned brightness and, as he shook his head, she added 'I will, I will.' A cup of tea in the middle of the night was the greatest luxury she could think of. She put on an old coat and went downstairs to the kitchen where the oil lamp was turned low. There was still a spark of fire left and she blew on it and boiled the big iron kettle. When she climbed awkwardly back up the stairs with the two mugs of tea she heard him still sobbing and stopped. 'God direct me!' she said aloud. Then she sat on the edge of the bed and shook him. 'Drink this, my old *putog*!' she said humorously. It had always made him laugh to be called a sausage.

'I don't want it,' he said. 'I want to know who my mother is.'

'Drink it, you dirty little caffler!' she said angrily. 'Drink it or I won't tell you at all.'

He raised himself in the bed and she held the mug to his mouth, but he could not stop shivering and the tea spilled over his nightshirt and the bedclothes. 'My good sheet!' she muttered. Then she took her own cup and looked away into a corner of the room as though to avoid his eyes. 'She is your mother, your Aunt Nance,' she said in a harsh expressionless voice, 'and a good mother she is, and a good woman as well, and it will be a bad day for you when you talk against her or let anyone else do it. She had the misfortune to meet a man that was beneath her. She was innocent. He took advantage of her. She wasn't the first and she won't be the last.'

'Who was it?' he asked.

'I don't know and I don't want to know.'

'Who was it? Because I'm going to find out and when I do I'm going to kill him.'

'Why then, indeed, you're going to do nothing of the sort,' she said sharply. 'He's your father, and he's there inside you, and the thing you will slight in yourself will be the rock you'll perish on.'

The dawn came in the window, and she still rambled on, half dead with sleep. Later, when she reported it to her cronies, she said with a sour laugh that it was nothing but lies from beginning to end and what other way could it be when she hadn't a notion how a girl like that would feel, but at the time it did not seem to be lies. It seemed rather as though she were reporting a complete truth that was known only to herself and God. And in a queer way it steadied Jimmy. The little man came out in him again. Once she had persuaded him of the truth of his mother's being a victim, he had no further thought for his own trouble.

'Mammy, why didn't she bring me to live with her?' he asked earnestly. 'I could look after her.'

'Oye, you will child, you will one of these days,' she said sourly. Though later it seemed funny to think of Jimmy looking after his mother, at the time it only hurt her because she would never have a son who would feel that way about her. Daughters were a poor thing for a mother to be relying on.

'Mammy, does this mean that there's something wrong with James and me?'

he asked at last, and she knew that this was the question that preoccupied him above all others.

'Indeed, it means nothing of the sort,' she cried, and for the first time it seemed to herself that she was answering in her own person. 'It is nothing only bad, jealous people would say the likes of that. Oh, you'll meet them, never fear,' she said, joining her hands, 'the scum of the earth with their marriage lines and their baptismal lines, looking down on their betters! But mark what I say, child, don't let any of them try and persuade you that you're not as good as them. And better! A thousand times better!'

Strange notions from a respectable old woman who had never even believed in love!


3

When Jimmy was fourteen and James between eight and nine, Jimmy's mother decided it was time for him to come and live with her. At first things seemed to have turned out well for her. After Jimmy's birth she had met a very nice young man who fell in love with her. She had told him the whole story, and unlike the general run of fellows in her neighbourhood, who sheered away from her the moment they caught a whiff of scandal, he accepted it as a normal event that might have happened to any decent girl. This seemed to her much too good to be true, and she had held off marrying him for years. The irony of it was that when she knew he was really in love with her and she with him it was too late. After long years of marriage they had no children of their own. Even before this became obvious he had wanted to adopt Jimmy and bring him up as their own child, but she had put it off and off. First, she said, she wanted them to have the pleasure of a normal child in normal surroundings; Jimmy would come later. But now there was little chance of that and she had begun to blame herself, to feel, even, that it was a sort of judgement on her for having given Jimmy up originally. Finally, her husband had laid down the law. They were having Jimmy to live with them and the neighbours could say what they pleased.

It was a terrible shock to Kate, though why it should have been so she didn't know, since for years it was she who had argued with her neighbours that the time had come for Jimmy to have a proper education and mix with the right class of people. Now she realised that she was just as jealous and possessive as anyone else. She had never criticised Jimmy's mother or allowed anyone else to do so, but now she hadn't a good word to say for her. 'She neglected him when it suited her, and now when it suits her she wants him back,' she complained to Mrs Sunners. 'Ah, now you have to be fair, ma'am,' Mrs Sunners replied philosophically. 'Fair? Why have I to be fair?' Kate retorted angrily. 'Let them that have it be fair. Them that are without it are entitled to their say.'

Besides, Jimmy provoked her. He was always up or down, and now he was up all the time, thinking only of the marvellous new world that was opening before him and without a thought for herself and James. He told her blithely that he would always come back for the holidays and comforted James by saying that his turn would come next and he'd be going to London. 'He will, he will,' she said and began to weep. 'And neither of ye will care what happens to me.' At this he grew frantic and shouted 'All right, I won't go if you don't want me to.' Then she turned the full force of her malice on him and shouted, 'Who said I didn't want you to go? How could I keep you here and me with nothing? Go to the ones with the cars and the fur coats! Go to the ones that can look after you!'

And yet when his step-father came and took him away she had a feeling of immense relief. She realised that she was not the one to look after him. He was too wild; too big and noisy and exacting; he needed a man to keep him in order, and besides, now that she had become old and stiff and half-blind, the housekeeping was more of a strain. She would decide to give himself and James a treat and go to town for the good stewing beef, and suddenly realise when she got back to the house that she had forgotten how to make stew. 'God direct me!' she would say aloud, closing her eyes. 'How was it I used to make it when I was younger? "Delicious" poor Jack used to say it was.'

James was an easier proposition altogether, a boy who wouldn't notice whether you gave him stew or a can of soup or a mug of tea so long as he got the occasional penny for his exercise books. It was music with him now, and he spent hours carefully ruling over the exercise books and making marks that he said were operas and singing them over to her in a tuneless sort of voice. Signs of it; he had almost ruined his eyes and she had to get black glasses for him. He was having trouble in school as well, for the headmaster, who lived up the road, knew who he was and disliked having such a boy in his good clean Catholic school.

One day James came home and said in his unemotional way, 'Mammy, Mr Clancy said to me today "James Mahoney, or whatever your name is." I don't think it was very nice of him to say that, mammy, do you?' Kate went a little mad. Her first notion was to complain about Mr Clancy to the Dean, but she had a suspicion that the Dean and Clancy were hand in glove and that any justice she got she would have to take for herself. So she donned her old hat and coat, took her umbrella by way of a walking stick and went up the road to the headmaster's big house. When he appeared at the door she asked him what he meant by insulting her child and he called her 'an impudent old woman' and slammed the door in her face. Then she banged on the knocker, beat the door with the handle of her umbrella and read and spelt him for two generations back. She saw by the way that the curtains along the road were being twitched that she had an audience, and she recounted how his mother, known to the Coal Quay as 'Norry Dance Naked' had owned slum property and refused to supply doors for the conveniences. It must be admitted that she was a very vulgar old woman, and after that, James had to go to the monks. The monks did not mind who his mother was because they soon satisfied themselves that James was a born examination-passer who was worth good money to them.

But the loss of Jimmy showed her how precarious was her hold on James, and in the evenings when they were alone she encouraged him to talk about what he would do when he was grown-up. James, it seemed to her, had only one ambition and that was to become a statue. He knew all the statues in town, and for a while had been rather depressed because it had seemed to him that the only way to become a statue was to be a martyr for Ireland, a temperance reformer or the founder of a religious order, none of which attracted him. But then he discovered from a library book that you could also be a statue for writing books or composing music, which was why he worked so hard making up operas. Looking at his big solemn face in the firelight, Kate thought that there was something of the statue about it already.

Jimmy had been a great boy to raise a laugh, particularly against himself, and James, who knew the way she felt about him, tried to be funny too; but if she was to be killed for it, she could not raise a laugh at James's jokes. At yet she knew that James was gentler, steadier and more considerate. 'Jimmy have the fire but James have the character,' was how she summed them up.

Then early one morning she heard a hammering on the front door and started up in a panic, feeling sure something had happened to Jimmy. He had been on her mind for a week and she had been scolding James to stop blinding himself over his old books and write to his brother to see was he all right. It was a queer way for a woman to behave who had been congratulating herself on having got rid of him, but Kate's mental processes were never very logical. Without even waiting to ask who was there she opened the door and saw Jimmy outside. Instantly she was light-headed with a relief and joy.

'Oh, child, child!' she sobbed, throwing her arms round his neck. 'Sure, I thought you'd never come home. How did you get here at all?'

'I walked most of it,' he said with a characteristic dash of boastfulness.

'You did, you did, you divil you, you did!' she muttered impatiently and then her voice rose to a squeal of anguish. 'Are them your good trousers?'

'Who is it, mammy?' James shouted petulantly from upstairs.

'Come down and see, can't you?' she retorted, and went to tinker with the fire while James came downstairs in his nightshirt.

'Sorry I'm back, James?' Jimmy said with a grin, holding out his hand.

'No, Jimmy, I'm very glad you're back,' James said in a small voice.

'Put on your topcoat, you little devil!' cried Kate. 'How often have I to be telling you not to go round. in your shirt. Out to the yard, and everything. . . . That fellow!' she sighed to Jimmy. 'He have the heart scalded in me. I'd want ten eyes and hands, picking things up after him.'

They had breakfast together just as the sun was beginning to pick out the red quarry behind the house, and it tinged Jimmy's face with fresh colour as he told them of his all-night trip. It was a marvel to Kate how she had managed to listen to James all that time, remembering how Jimmy could tell a story. Whatever James told you always seemed to begin or end with something like 'Mammy, wasn't I clever?' but Jimmy began by revealing himself a fool and ended by suggesting something worse but it never crossed your mind that he was a fool at all.

'And what did you do with the money for the fare?' Kate asked suspiciously. 'Spent it, I suppose?'

'What fare?' he asked, blushing.

'I suppose she gave you the money for the train at any rate?'

'Oh, I didn't tell her.'

'You didn't what?' Kate asked slowly. 'Oh, my! I suppose you had a fight with her and then walked out of the house without a word to her or anybody? I declare to God you're never right.'

'She doesn't mind what I do,' Jimmy said with a defiant shrug.

'She doesn't, I hear!' Kate said ironically. 'I suppose she didn't pay you enough attention? And now she'll be blaming it all on me. She'll be saying I have you ruined. And she'll be right. I have you ruined, you little caffler!' She opened the back-door and looked up at the great sandstone face of the quarry reflecting the morning light. 'Oh, my! There's a beautiful morning, glory be to God!'

A half an hour later she heard the unfamiliar sound of a car turning into the lane and cocked her head in alarm. It stopped immediately in front of the cottage. She spun round on Jimmy, who was now as white as she felt herself. 'Is that the police?' she asked in an angry whisper. She knew it was the wrong thing to say, but Jimmy did not appear to hear her. All the glow seemed to have gone out of him. 'If that's Uncle Tim I'm not going back with him,' he said dully. Kate went to the front door and saw Nance's husband, a good-looking young man with the sort of pink and white complexion she called 'delicate'.

'Here we are again, Mrs Mahoney,' he said without rancour.

'Oh, come in, sir, come in,' she said obsequiously, wiping her hands on her sack apron, and now she was no longer the proud possessive mother but the old hireling caught in possession of property that was not rightly hers. The young man strode into the kitchen as if it was his own and stopped dead when he saw Jimmy sitting by the window.

'Now, what made me come here first?' he asked good-naturedly. 'Mrs Mahoney, I have the makings of a first-class detective in me. Tim the Tracer, that's my name. Criminals shudder when they hear it.' When Jimmy said nothing he cocked his head reproachfully. 'Well, Jimmy?' he asked. Kate could see that Jimmy both liked and dreaded him.

'I'm not going back with you, Uncle Tim,' he said with an indignation that was half an appeal.

'Begor, you are, Jimmy,' his stepfather said but still with no trace of resentment. 'It wouldn't be much use me going back to Limerick without you. And if you think I'm going to spend the rest of my days chasing you round Ireland, you're wrong. This last jaunt was enough for me.' He sat down, and Kate saw he was exhausted.

'Wisha, you'll have a cup of tea,' she said.

'I will, and a whole teapot-full, Mrs Mahoney,' he replied. 'I didn't even have time to get my breakfast with this fellow.'

'I don't want to go back, Uncle Tim,' Jimmy said furiously. 'I want to stop here.'

'Listen to that, ma'am,' Tim said, cocking his head at Kate. 'Insulting Limerick, and in Cork of all places!'

'I'm not saying anything about Limerick,' Jimmy cried despairingly, and again he was a child and defenceless against the dialectic of adults. 'I want to stop here.'

Screwing up her eyes as she filled the teapot again and put it on the table, Kate tried to intervene on his behalf.

'Wisha, 'tis only a little holiday he wants, sir,' she said humbly, but this only made Jimmy madder than ever.

'It isn't a holiday I want,' he shouted. 'I want to stop here for good. This is my home, and I told my mother so.'

'And don't you think that was a pretty hard thing to say to your mother, Jimmy?' his stepfather asked dryly.

'It's true,' Jimmy said angrily.

'Come on and have your cup of tea, sir,' Kate said, trying to smooth things down. 'Will you have another, Jimmy?'

'I will not,' Jimmy said, beginning to cry. 'And it isn't that I'm not fond of her, but she left it too late. She shouldn't have left it so late, Uncle Tim.'

'You might be right there, son,' his stepfather said wearily, pulling his chair up to the table. 'You can let things like that go too far, and maybe you are too old to get used to your mother. But you're not going the right way about it either.'

'All right then,' Jimmy cried, at the end of his tether. 'What should I do?'

'Don't run out of a situation whenever it gets too hard,' his stepfather said, going on with his skimpy breakfast of bread and tea. 'People's feelings are hurt when you do things like that. Talk to her and tell her how you feel. Maybe the best thing would be for you to come back and go to a proper school here, but leave it to her to make the arrangements. You see, you don't seem to understand what it cost your mother to bring you home at all. It may have been the wrong thing to do; it may have been a failure, but you don't want to leave her feeling that her life is nothing but failures.'

'He's right, Jimmy, boy, he's right,' Kate said, recognising the deep feeling in his tone. 'If you don't go back now you could never go back with all the old talk there would be. But if you go back now you can always come home for the holidays.'

'Oh, all right,' Jimmy said with despair.

And it was real despair as she well knew, not play-acting. Of course, he indulged in a bit of that as well. He would not kiss her when he was leaving, and when James said cheerfully 'You'll be back with us in a couple of weeks', Jimmy took a deep breath and said 'I may or I may not', leaving it to be understood that he did not rule out the possibility of suicide. But she knew that he did not want to go, that he looked on her house as the only home he knew, and she had great boasting about it among the neighbours. 'A boy of fourteen, ma'am, that was never away from home all the days of his life, travelling back like that through the night, without food or sleep – oh, my, where would you find the likes of him?'

And at the end of his stay with his mother they resumed their existence together more or less where it had been broken off. There was only one major change in their relationship. A couple of days after his return Jimmy said 'I'm not going to call you "mammy" any more.' 'Oye, and what are you going to call me?' she asked with sour humour. 'I'm going to call you "granny",' he said. 'The other sounds too silly.' After a few weeks, James, who had continued to call her by the old name, said 'granny' too, as though by mistake, and she suddenly lost her temper and flew at him. 'Glad enough you were of someone to call "mammy"!' she shouted. Though she knew it was only fair, she did not like it. Like the young married women who had objected to Jimmy and himself in the first place, she felt she had paid for her title.

4

A year later, what with the rheumatics and the bronchitis, Kate had to go to hospital, and Nora and Molly each agreed to take one of the boys, but when it was put up to them neither of them would agree. They stayed on in the little house by themselves, and each week one of the girls came up a couple of times to clear up after them. They reported that the mess was frightful, though you could always tell which of the boys was responsible, because Jimmy was a conscientious messer, who piled everything into one enormous heap, apparently in the hope that Santa Claus would find it, while James left things wherever he happened to be whenever an idea struck him. As a result Kate left hospital too soon, but even then she was too late to prevent mischief, for while she was away Jimmy had quietly left school and got himself a job in a packers.

'Oh, you blackguard!' she sighed fondly. 'I knew you'd be up to something the minute my back was turned. Oh, my, that I'd want a hundred eyes! But back to school you go tomorrow, my fine gentleman, if I have to drag you there myself. And 'twouldn't the first time.'

'How can I go back to school?' Jimmy asked indignantly. 'They could have the law on me unless I gave a month's notice.' Jimmy knew that she was terrified of policemen, lawyers and inspectors, and even at her advanced age was always in dread of being marched off to gaol for some crime she never committed.

'I'll talk to the manager myself,' she said. 'Who is he?'

'You can't talk to the manager,' said Jimmy. 'He's away on holidays.'

'Oh, you liar!' she muttered happily. 'There's no end to the lies you tell. Who is it, you scamp?'

'Anyway, I have to have a job,' Jimmy said in a grown-up voice. 'If anything happens to you who's going to look after James?'

'Oh, you divil out of hell!' she said, because it was something that had worried her a lot and she knew now that Jimmy realised it. She knew that Jimmy was the sort of bossy kid who would take on a responsibility like that because he could show off about it, but at the same time he would have his own good reasons which you wouldn't see until later.

'A lot he have to hope for if 'tis you he's relying on!' she shouted. 'Did you tell your mother?'

'That's right,' he said bitterly, confounded by her injustice. 'What time have I to write to my mother?'

'Plenty of time you have to write to her when 'tis money you want,' Kate said with a knowing air. 'Sit down there and write to her now, you vagabond! I suppose you want me to take the blame for your blackguarding.'

Jimmy with his usual martyred air sat at the table and agonised over a note to his mother.

'How do you spell "employment", James?' he asked.

'Aha!' she exclaimed malevolently. 'He wants to give up school and he don't know how to spell a simple word.'

'All right, spell it you, so!' he retorted.

'In my time, for poor people, the education was not going,' she replied with great dignity. 'People hadn't the chances they have now, and what chances they had, they respected, not like the ones that are going today. Go on with your letter, you thing!'

And again his stepfather came and argued with him. He explained patiently that without a secondary education of some sort, Jimmy would never get into a college and would probably never rise above being a common labourer. Jimmy knew his stepfather liked him and began to cry, but he was in one of his obstinate moods and would not give in. He said again and again that he wanted to be independent. When his stepfather left, he accompanied him to the car, and they had a long conversation that made Kate suspicious.

'What were ye talking about?' she asked.

'Oh, nothing,' Jimmy said lightly. 'I only asked him who my father was. He says he doesn't know.'

'And if he says it, he means it,' snapped Kate. 'How inquisitive you're getting.'

'He said I was entitled to know,' Jimmy replied angrily. 'He told me I should ask Nance.' (Sometimes he called his mother 'mother' and sometimes 'Nance', and whichever he said sounded awkward.)

'You should,' Kate said ironically. 'I'm sure she's dying to tell you.'

But when next he came back from a visit to his mother he had a triumphant air, and late in the evening he said boastfully, 'Well, I found out who my father was anyway.'

'It didn't take you long.' said Kate. 'How did you do it?'

'It was Uncle Tim, really,' he admitted. 'I was arguing with Nance when he walked in. He was mad! He just said "Get out, Jimmy!" and I did. Half an hour later he came into me and said "Now go and talk to your mother!" She was crying.'

'Small wonder!' Kate said with a shrug. 'Who was it?'

'Nobody in particular, actually,' Jimmy admitted with a defeated air. 'The name was Creedon. He had some sort of grocery shop in North Cork, but he's left that for years. She thinks he's in Birmingham, but I'm going to find out.'

'For what?' she asked. 'What good will it do you to find out?'

'I can go to see him, can't I?' he asked defiantly.

'You can what?'

'Go and see him,' he grumbled with some doubt in his voice. 'Why wouldn't I?'

'Why wouldn't you, indeed, and all the attention he paid you!' she retorted. 'You're never right.'

And, indeed, there were times when she thought he wasn't. For months on end he seemed not to think at all of his parentage, and then he began to day-dream till he worked himself into a fever of emotion. In a fit like that she never knew what he might do. He was capable of anything, and even though it might never come to violence, she did not know from day to day what deep and irreparable hurt some casual remark might inflict on him.

One day he went off. A sailor on the Fishguard boat had arranged for him to travel free. While he was away she fretted, and, of course, being Jimmy, he did not even send a card to say where he was. She nursed the vague hope that Jimmy would not be able to locate his father; that he would have moved; but, knowing Jimmy's obstinacy in pursuit of an obsession, she had little confidence in this. She tried to imagine what their meeting would be like and hoped only that his father would not say anything to provoke him.

'Oh, my!' she sighed to James. 'If Jimmy took it into his head he'd kill him.'

'Oh, no, granny!' James said in his bored way. 'Jimmy isn't going to England just to kill him. He has more sense than you think.'

'Oye, and what is he going for?' she asked. 'Since you know so much about him?'

'It's only curiosity,' James said. 'Jimmy is always looking for something that was never there.'

Then, one autumn morning, after James had left for school at the other side of the city, Jimmy walked in, looking dirty and dishevelled. He had had no breakfast, and she fumbled blindly about the kitchen, trying to get it for him in a hurry, and cursing old age that made it such a labour. But her heart was light. She had only been deceiving herself, thinking that Jimmy and his father might quarrel when all that could have happened that would have made a difference to her was that they might have got on too well.

'Oh, you blackguard!' she said fondly, leaning on the kitchen table and grinning into his face, to see him better. 'Where were you?'

'Everywhere.'

'And did you find him?'

'Of course I found him. I had to follow him to London.'

'And what do you think of him now you have him?' she asked too jovially to be true.

'Ah, he's all right,' Jimmy said casually, and his tone didn't sound true either. 'I don't think he has long to live though. He's drinking himself to death.'

Instantly she was ashamed of her own jealousy and pettiness – she could afford to be, now that she had him back.

'Ah, child, child, why do you be upsetting yourself about them?' she cried miserably. 'They're not worth it. Nobody is worth it.'

She sat in the kitchen with him for two hours. It was just as when he had run away from his mother's house, as though he had been saving it all up for her – the tramp across Wales and England, the people who had given him lifts, and the lorry-driver who had given him dinner and five bob when Jimmy had told his story. She felt she could see it all, even the scene when he knocked at the door in the shabby London lodging-house and an unshaven man with sad red eyes peered out suspiciously at him, as though no one ever called except to harass him further.

'And what did you say?' Kate asked.

'Only "Don't you know me?"' Jimmy recited, as though every word of it was fixed in his memory. 'And he said "You have the advantage of me." So I said, "I'm your son."'

'Oh, my!' Kate exclaimed, profoundly impressed and a little sorry for Jimmy's father though she had resolved to hate everything she learned about him. 'And what did he say then?'

'He just started to cry.'

'Fitter for him do it fifteen years ago!' Kate shouted in a sudden access of rage.

'I said "Well, it's all over and done with now", and he said "'Tisn't, nor 'twill never be. Your mother missed nothing when she missed me. I was a curse to others, and now I'm only a curse to myself."'

'How sorry he is himself!' himself!' said Kate.

'He has reason,' said Jimmy, and went on to describe the squalid room where he had stayed for a week with his father, sleeping in the same unmade bed, going out with him to the pub to put a few shillings on a horse, yet Kate felt a little touch of pride in the way Jimmy described the sudden outbursts of extravagant humour that lit up his father's maudlin self-pity. And then, being Jimmy, he could not help laughing outright at the good advice which was all his father had to give him    warnings against drink and betting but mostly against being untrue to himself.

'The cheek of him!' cried Kate, who could see nothing in the least humorous in it. 'Oh, that 'tis me he should have had! I'd soon give him his answer, the night-walking vagabond!'

'I don't care,' Jimmy said with a defiant shrug of his shoulders. 'I like him.'

Kate could scarcely reply to this, it was so unjust. She was furious at the thought that after all her years with Jimmy she might have lost him in a single day to the man who had never raised a finger to help him, nor asked whether he was living or dead. But she knew, too, that it was fear that made her angry, because she had gone closer to losing Jimmy than she had ever done before.

## 5

At first, when Jimmy got a girl of his own, Kate paid no attention. She thought it was only foolishness, but when it went on for more than six months, and Jimmy took the girl out every Friday night, she began to grow nervous. She told Mrs Sunners that she was afraid Jimmy might marry 'beneath him'. When this got back to the girl's people, they were outraged because they were afraid that Mary was going to do the same thing. 'A boy that nobody knows who he is or where he comes from!' they went around saying. 'Or is she in her right mind at all?'

Kate dreaded Friday evenings on that account. Jimmy would come in from work, and shave and strip and wash under the tap in the backyard. Then he would change into his best blue suit and put brilliantine on his hair, and she watched every move he made with gloom and resentment.

'You're not going to be late again?' she would ask.

'Why wouldn't I be late?' Jimmy would ask.

'You know I can't sleep while you do be out.' (This was true; any other night of the week she had no trouble in sleeping.)

Finally James himself ticked her off. One Friday evening he closed his book, raised his glasses on his forehead and said 'Granny, you worry too much about Jimmy and that girl. Jimmy is steadier than you give him credit for.'

'He is, I hear,' she retorted rudely. 'He have as much sense as you have, and that's not much, God knows. Wouldn't you go out and have a game of handball like a natural boy?'

'That has nothing to do with it,' James said equably. 'I know Jimmy better than you do. There's nothing wrong with Jimmy only that he has very little confidence in himself, and he's too easily influenced. That's why he prefers to go with stupid people instead of clever ones. They make him feel superior. But he has a very good intelligence if ever he tries to make use of it.'

At the same time Kate wondered often if Jimmy would ever outgrow his attitude to his family. So far as his immediate neighbours were concerned, the whole thing was forgotten except to his credit. He was as much one of themselves as any of the honest transactions brought up in the locality. But it was as if Jimmy himself could never really forget that he was an outsider; again and again the old fever broke out in him and each time the form it took came as a surprise to Kate. Once he took off on his bicycle to a little town eighty miles away where his uncle ran a grocery store. His uncle had kept his father supplied with small money orders that promptly went on horses. Jimmy didn't get much of a welcome because his uncle quite unjustly suspected that Jimmy wanted money orders as well and besides, he did not want the job of explaining his nephew to the townspeople. In spite of his tepid welcome, Jimmy came home in high spirits and gave Kate and James a really funny description of his uncle; a frightened, cadaverous, clever little man who lectured Jimmy on the way the country was going to the dogs, with people neglecting religion, working less and expecting more. Jimmy felt he had the laugh on his uncle, but at Christmas it was his uncle who had the laugh on Jimmy, because he sent him a small money order as well. Jimmy was deeply touched by it; once or twice they saw him take it out of his pocket and study it with a smile as though it were a long and intimate letter.

Worse still, there was the summer when he took his bicycle and, with the help of his sailor friend, stowed away again on the Fishguard boat. This time he cycled through Southern England to the little Dorset town where his mother had lodged while she was having him, all alone, without husband, lover, or friend to encourage her. Kate thought this whole expedition very queer and grumbled again that he was 'never right' but somewhere inside herself she realised that it was part of his way of getting to belong. And she knew, whatever anyone said, he would go on like that to the end of his days, pursued by the dream of a normal life that he might have lived and a normal family he might have grown up with.

James observed it too with considerable interest but with a fundamental disapproval. He had never shown much curiosity about his own blood-relations, though he knew he had brothers and sisters who went to expensive English schools, and he let it be seen that he thought Jimmy cheapened himself by the way he sought out his own.

'Ah, that's only because I always had to live too close to them,' Jimmy said. 'Boy, if I was like you, I'd never have anything to do with any of them again.'

'Oh, I don't know,' James grumbled. 'I don't see why I should avoid them. I'd like to meet my mother and my brothers and sisters. It's only natural, but I don't want to meet them yet.'

'You're right, boy,' Jimmy said with sudden depression. 'Because all they'd do is look down on you. Oh, they'll be polite and all the rest of it, but they'll look down on you just the same.'

'Oh, you always take things to the fair,' James said petulantly. 'You think people look down on you because you haven't enough confidence in yourself. You always think there's something wrong with you, and it's not that at all. It's something wrong with them. They're people who pay far too much attention to what other people think. If I meet them when I'm a civil servant or a teacher in the university they'll be delighted to know me. People like that never neglect anyone who may be of use to them.'

Kate, amused by James's juvenile lecturing, knew that there was a sad wisdom in what he said. While Jimmy, who had something of his father's weakness and charm, might prove a liability, James would work and save, and it would be his curiosity about his family that would be satisfied, not theirs about him. And James would make perfectly certain that no member of it patronised him. She was very old, and her grip on life had slackened, but she did very much long to see how James would deal with his family.

All the same, she knew she wouldn't see it. She fell ill again and Molly came to the house to nurse her while Nora and usually one or both of their husbands came to relieve her in the evenings. Her presence made an immediate change in the house. She was swift and efficient; she fed the boys and made conversation with callers, leaning against the door-post with folded arms, and then would slip away into the front room or out the yard and weep savagely to herself for a few minutes, as another woman might do for a quick drink. The priest came, and Molly chatted with him about the affairs of the parish as though she had no other thought in mind, and then dashed up to her mother's room again. Kate asked to see Jimmy and James. The two boys went quietly up the stairs and stood at either side of the big bed. Each of them took one of her hands.

'Don't upset yeerselves too much, boys,' she said. 'I know ye'll miss me, but ye need have no regrets. Ye were the two best sons a mother ever reared.' She thought hard for a moment and added something that shocked them all. 'I'm proud of ye, and yeer father is proud of ye.'

'Mammy!' Molly whispered urgently. 'You forget. 'Tis Jimmy and James.'

Kate opened her eyes for a few moments and looked straight at her.

'I know well who it is,' she said. Then her eyes closed again and she breathed noisily for some minutes as though she were trying to recollect herself. 'Don't do anything he'd be ashamed of. He was a good man and a clean-living man, and he never robbed anyone of a ha'penny. Jimmy, look after your little brother for me.'

'I will, mammy,' Jimmy said through his tears.

Something about that sudden reversion to the language of childhood made Molly break down. She took refuge in the front room to weep. Nora scolded her as all the Mahoneys had always scolded one another.

'Ah, have a bit of sense, girl!' she said lightly. 'You know yourself poor mammy's mind is wandering.'

'It is not wandering, Nora,' Molly said hysterically. 'I saw her and you didn't. She knew what she was saying, and Jimmy knew it too. They were her real children all the time and we were only the outsiders.'

That night, when Kate was quiet at last in her brown shroud, clutching the rosary beads on her breast, the neighbours came in and sat round her in the candlelight. They were asking the same question that Molly had already asked herself: how it was that a woman so old could take the things the world had thrown away and from them fashion a new family, dearer to her than the old, and better than any she had known. But Kate had taken her secret with her.

ANTHONY POWELL

# A Reference for Mellors

A LONG, low house in brown stone. Wragby Hall looked much as one had been
led to expect. It was set among trees from which the rain still dripped forlornly on
to tangled undergrowth. The oaks stood silent and tired, like old, worn-out
seekers after pleasure, unable to keep up in this grimy, mechanised world of ours.
The weather was sultry, and from where Tevershall pit-bank was burning, a
scent of coal-dust and sulphur charged the atmosphere; while lowering
macintosh-coloured clouds gave warning that another heavy downpour might at
any moment take place. Away beyond the park at the far end of the drive a
hooter gave three short blasts, and there came the noise of shunting trucks, the
whistle of colliery locomotives, and the voices of men, bitter and discontented;
loud rasping voices raised in conflict. Ashes had been thrown down in front of the
entrance to the house to fill the cavities of the gravel in which pools of brackish
water had accumulated. He rang an iron bell and waited, trying to remove from
one eye a small piece of grit, blown down-wind from the furnaces. After some
minutes the door was opened by a good-looking, middle-aged woman, dressed in
black.

'Lady Chatterley?'

She smiled slowly, sphinxlike.

'Her Ladyship is expecting you.'

She took the hat and overcoat.

'Her Ladyship is in her own sitting-room. She said I was to show you straight
up.'

Some concealed implication of enquiry seemed to rest in those rather defiant
grey eyes. No doubt it was a little uncommon for a guest to be given access to that
intimate, inviolate apartment; or some hint such as this was at least conveyed by
her look, a questioning of the favoured stranger's credentials it might be.
Turning on her heel, she led the way up the main staircase, and along a passage
hung with stark oil-paintings and then up more stairs. On one of the landings, the
door of a lumber-room was ajar and behind a pile of hat-boxes, suitcases, vestry
chests, rosewood cradles, and engravings from Landseer's works, was the glimpse
of a contraption which seemed at first sight an unusual form of mowing-machine,
but declared itself almost immediately as Sir Clifford Chatterley's wheel-chair.
It was rusty and covered with dust; and piled high with riding-boots and old golf
clubs. Clearly it had lain unused for years.

'Sir Clifford won't be back for some weeks?'

'He's in London, sir. He often has to go there now on business.'

'He has become an important figure in coal.'

224

'He has indeed, sir.'

'I suppose he is – perfectly all right now.'

'Oh yes, sir. Absolutely.'

She laughed quietly to herself as if this was a rather foolish question to have asked, and she knew the answer all right. She was a thick-set, healthy-looking woman, speaking with a broad Derbyshire burr, with keen eyes and a strong supple body, like a tigress, moving through some dark, thick undergrowth.

'Oh yes. Sir Clifford is absolutely all right now.'

She gave another of those secretive, excludatory laughs as she opened a door on the third floor and showed him into a small room decorated in pink and yellow distemper, upon the walls of which hung huge German reproductions of paintings by Renoir and Cézanne. He had the impression of entering a bright, up-to-date schoolroom where lessons are enjoyed.

Constance Chatterley was standing by the window, looking down on to the park. She turned slowly, and held out her hand with a movement that carried with it a challenge of hidden energies; fair, blue-eyed, with some occasional freckles. A faint fragrance of Coty's Woodviolet was wafted across the room.

'So you found your way here in spite of the rain.'

The other woman paused at the door.

'Will you have tea here or in the drawing-room, m'Lady?'

'In the drawing-room, Mrs Bolton.'

'At five o'clock or earlier, m'Lady?'

'I will ring when we are ready for it.'

'Very good, m'Lady.'

Lingering, almost rebelling, Mrs Bolton left the room hesitantly, as if unwilling to submit to this assertion of a subtler will than her own. Lady Chatterley was certainly handsome. Not in a too demure or dull way. On the contrary she had put on plenty of lipstick, and her clothes looked almost over-smart for the country. At the same time she gave an impression of a person at ease with herself and her surroundings, a person not easily embarrassed. This was a relief because it might be necessary to make enquiries that would sound – in the ordinary way – inquisitive. She held out a box of gold-tipped cigarettes.

'Do sit down,' she said. 'You wanted to see me about a reference?'

Best to go straight to the point. There was nothing to be gained by beating about the bush; especially with someone so unaffected.

'A friend of mine is looking for a suitable man for a post in one of the national game-preserves of the Dominions. He has had an applicant who seems to be the right type and who gave your name as a reference. Hearing that I was staying with neighbours of yours my friend suggested that you wouldn't mind if I came over, and had a talk about this man.'

'But of course—'

'There were certain points my friend wanted to make sure about before he engages anyone. It is quite an important position, you know, and – coming under the Government – you will appreciate that one has to make the fullest enquiries. The man is a former employee of your husband's I understand. Mellors. I take it he gave your name as he knew Sir Clifford was away from home.'

For a moment she frowned, as if at a loss.

'Mellors?'

'Mellors,' I said, 'Oliver Mellors. A gamekeeper.'

'Mellors, it was Parkin. Wasn't it Parkin? Or was it Mellors? I dimly recall the name Parkin, and yet Mellors is familiar too. Anyway, I remember the man you mean, I'm sure. I am so glad he is in the way of getting a good job. He never seemed somehow very happy here. But such a nice man.'

'My friend says he appears to be an excellent type. I believe he had a commission in India during the war.'

'Yes, a quartermaster, I think, or do they call it the Army Service Corps? Clifford told me, but I forget. Clifford says he always laughs when he thinks of Mellors handing out stores. You'd have had to have been a real old soldier to have got by Mellors, Clifford always says.'

'That sounds promising. He will be able to deal with the clerical side.'

'Oh yes, Mellors started in an office – but I think he liked to remember his army days. He always saluted if one came across him in the grounds.'

'I suppose he has the usual formal requirements – honest, sober, hard-working, an early riser – I mean he won't be too much of an old soldier?'

'Honest to a fault. An absolutely reliable man. Sober too – and didn't at all mind getting up early. I believe as a matter of fact he had rather a weak head.'

She pouted archly.

'Was there some trouble? Tipsy at the tenants' dance or something of the sort.'

'Really I have only the vaguest reason for saying he had a weak head. Perhaps I shouldn't have mentioned it. Only after he left us, my father happened to run into Mellors in the street in London. They had seen a good deal of each other because Papa has a passion for the rough shooting around here.'

'Your father is Sir Malcolm Reid, R. A., of course.'

'Like most artists he is a bit of an eccentric. He took Mellors to a sort of Bohemian club he belongs to in Soho and gave him lunch. Papa always likes to do himself well – and he said that by the end of the meal poor Mellors got rather red in the face and kept on telling the same story over and over again about how when he was in the army in India he would have been a captain if it hadn't been for the dark gods.'

'I suppose the Indians had been getting on his nerves.'

'Visits to temples or something, I expect. Perhaps he had seen queer oriental carvings – I myself have been shown some that might easily upset a highly strung person. Anyway it was all rather a shame to my mind – but Papa is quite shameless where it's a question of having too many liqueurs after luncheon.'

'This was obviously a most exceptional occasion. But he is a hard worker – Mellors?'

'As far as he goes, he is a very hard worker. Of course, you realise that he is not a strong man. I remember in the days when my husband used a wheel-chair, the engine that drove the chair went wrong. Mellors tried to push it as if it were a bath-chair, and really got quite breathless, poor fellow. That breathlessness was really why Clifford's father had arranged for him to have the job in the first place.'

'So he dates back to your father-in-law's time?'

'Oh, he was quite an old retainer.'

'And knew his job well?'

'There was not a great deal to do, you see, as we couldn't afford big parties – just an occasional old friend like Mr Michaelis, the novelist, for a night or two. In fact Clifford always said it was a terrible piece of extravagance employing a gamekeeper at all these days, but he went on because he thought it would give Mellors time to himself for reading and so on.'

'Why reading?'

'Mellors was quite a highbrow in his way. He was a scholarship boy at Sheffield Grammar School and always had the air of having come down in the world a bit. We wanted to do anything we could for him.'

'His father was a local blacksmith, wasn't he?'

'Oh, surely not? A schoolmaster, I think. On second thoughts, I believe he did shoe horses for a time – to demonstrate the dignity of manual labour. Mellors had a lot of those rather William Morris-y ideas too, you know.'

'But I understand that he described himself as of "mining stock"?'

'His grandfather – or possibly his great-grandfather – had something to do with the mine – surface work of some sort. It's quite true. Mellors was very proud of being "mining stock" – all the more because he himself was a bit of a highbrow. In fact I believe he even had something published in the *New Statesman* once – a little piece of verse, or his impressions, or something of the sort.'

'I had no idea . . .'

'He had quite a small library of books in the cottage he lived in here – we might have gone to see it if it hadn't begun to rain so hard, it's rather snug. There were books about the causes of earthquakes, and electrons, and curious Indian customs – the "dark gods", perhaps – and Karl Marx, Freud, every sort of thing.'

'He sounds an out-of-the-way fellow.'

'Oh, Mellors was a real character. And then he loved dressing up. That was why he always wore a sort of green velveteen uniform and gaiters. Clifford made rather a fuss about the expense of getting it for him, but in the end he gave in, and Mellors got his way – as he usually did in things he had his heart on.'

'He must have looked quite picturesque.'

'He did say to me once that he thought men ought to wear close red trousers and little short white jackets – but really we had to draw the line there. Unfortunately, the Chatterley livery is a rather sombre affair of black and drab so there was nothing much to be done for him in that direction. However, I think he was fairly happy with his green velveteens.'

There was a pause. Lady Chatterley looked out again towards the park, as if trying to recall more information about Mellors that might be of assistance to his new employers. Now the rain was coming down in sheets, thudding like artillery against the window panes.

'There was another – rather delicate question.'

'Yes?'

'A considerable female staff is employed on certain clerical and other duties connected with the scientific observation of the habits of the animals within the preserve in question. Mellors, I am sure, could be trusted not . . . not to make a fool of himself . . . Only there was a rumour about some sort of a scandal in connection with his wife – that is only why I ask. No doubt gossip and much exaggerated.'

'I am sure it was. That was certainly our impression here. I should say he was entirely trustworthy – unless some quite unusual circumstances were to arise.'

'Excellent.'

'In fact your question would make our housekeeper, Mrs Bolton – who let you in – laugh a great deal.'

'She had a poor opinion of Mellors?'

'I'm afraid she used to laugh about him sometimes.'

'Then we need to go no further into the matter of his wife?'

'I don't think the trouble about Mrs Mellors was to be taken too seriously – although, of course, there was a certain amount of talk in the village at the time. The Mellors had all sorts of what were then thought to be rather "advanced" ideas. For example, he always used to refer to her by her maiden name as "Bertha Coutts".'

'No relation to the banking family?'

'If so, very distant. There were endless – and I believe rather unnecessarily public – discussions as to whether or not, for example, it was better for husband and wife to have separate rooms, whether companionate marriage was a prudent preliminary; how large families should be, and if it was desirable for a married couple to spend a certain time apart from one another in the course of the year.'

'She was rather a highbrow too?'

'She had lived in Birmingham. I think moved in circles on the outskirts of the Repertory Theatre.'

'One can understand that all this was not wholly appreciated in the neighbourhood.'

'It was during one of Mellors' temporary separations from his wife that he returned to his situation with us.'

'You say "temporary" – did he go back to his wife then?'

'In the end they decided in favour of a divorce – but without any hard feelings on either side.'

'Were there any children?'

'A little girl. Mrs Mellors held rather decided views as to how her daughter should be brought up, and was very anxious that no early harm should be done by frustration. I understand there were signs of – well – a bit of a father fixation. Besides Mrs Mellors was conscientiously opposed to blood sports, which created difficulties vis-à-vis her husband's profession.'

'There would be no question of Mrs Mellors wanting to accompany him if he took up this post?'

'On the contrary. During their periods apart Mrs Mellors found herself increasingly influenced by the personality of one of the colliers at Stack's Gate – a prominent figure in local Chapel circles. They used to discuss social and economic questions with others in the village interested in such matters. In the end they married.'

'So Mellors is entirely without encumbrances.'

'It is a long time since I have seen him – but this talk of ours has made me remember a lot of things about him. When he finally parted company with his wife there was some vague question of his getting married again – to someone younger than himself and in rather a different walk of life.'

'Indeed.'

'It would not, I think, have been particularly suitable!'

'A local girl?'

'I believe . . . It was after he left us. They used to meet in London.'

'Did anything come of it?'

'Very sensibly, the understanding was broken off by mutual consent.'

'No doubt all for the best.'

'After that, Mellors let it be known that he very definitely intended to remain single. He was quite happy, he used to say, with his wild flowers and his animals – and the wonderful imitations he used to give – when he had an audience – of the local dialect, in the origins of which he was keenly interested.'

'Why did he actually leave your service, finally?'

Lady Chatterley considered for a moment.

'Temperament,' she said at last. 'It was a question of temperament. And, after all, most of us want a change at times. I suppose Mellors was like the rest of the world and enjoyed a little variety at intervals. He used to say, "There are black days coming for all of us and for everybody." In some ways he was a very moody man. An unusually moody man.'

There was another pause.

'I am really most grateful to you. I think you have told me quite enough to assure me that he would fill the vacancy admirably – that is if his health holds up.'

'That is the question,' she said very quietly, 'if his health holds up.'

She swung her feet on to the sofa, and lay back, stretching towards an ashtray to extinguish the stub of her cigarette. One of her suede slippers fell to the ground. She did not bother to recapture it. Outside the rain had ceased and a dull sun showed through the heavy cloudbanks. Below the window the hazelbrake was misted with green, and under it the dark counterpane of dog's mercury edged the velvet of the sward. Still the breeze bore on its wings the scent of tar, and all the time came the thud, thud, thud of industrial afternoon in the Midlands; while the gentle perfume of Coty's Woodviolet was more than ever apparent above the insistent incense of the undying furnaces.

PATRICK WHITE

# A Woman's Hand

THE wind was tearing into the rock-plants, slashing reflections out of the leaves of the mirror-bush, torturing those professional martyrs the native trees. What must originally have appeared an austere landscape, one long rush of rock and scrub towards the sea, was prevented from wearing its natural expression by the parasite houses clinging to it as obstinately as wax on diseased orange branches. Not that the houses weren't, nearly all of them, technically desirable, some of them even Lovely Homes worth breaking into. Although the owners of the latter were surely aware of this, they had almost completely exposed their possessions behind unbroken plate-glass. To view the view might have been their confessable intention, but they had ended, seemingly, overwhelmed by it. Or bored. The owners of the lovely seaside homes sat in their worldly cells playing bridge, licking the chocolate off their fingers, in one case copulating, on pink chenille, on the master bed.

Evelyn Fazackerley looked away. It was, in any case, what she would have called a heavenly day. She was breathless with it, from the pace at which Harold was walking, as much as from the biting air.

'You should walk more slowly,' she suggested, because it was time she asserted herself. 'That is what retirement is for.'

It was the kind of remark Harold ignored. Their marriage was strewn with such. It was not unagreeable that way.

Perhaps because he had been thrown into retirement so unexpectedly, so abruptly, he had difficulty in believing in it, and had taken refuge in perpetual motion, though they kept the flat as a pied-à-terre.

Evelyn was squinting back at the glass faces of the huddled houses. In the general dazzlement of the landscape and the physical exhaustion of an unnecessary but virtuous walk, she felt that warm surge of desire which only material things can provoke.

'How vulgar they all are!' she said.

And was automatically absolved.

'Nothing wrong in being well-lined.'

If he sounded tired, it was not from their walk – he had remained a physically active man – but from remembering the ganglion of plumbing on the neo-Tudor wall across from their neo-Tudor flat.

'Oh, come!' Evelyn said. 'There are certain standards the ones who know can't afford to drop.'

Evelyn was one who knew. Harold knew too. Only he didn't care enough.

Harold was again involved with the mystical problem of his own retirement.

Before it had happened he used to say: Retirement will be the time of life when I read the books I have bought and never read, when I shall re-read *War and Peace*, and perhaps understand Dostoevski. Probably write something myself, something solid and factual about cotton in Egypt, or a travel book. Perhaps one or two articles for *Blackwood's*. Whereas retirement had, in fact, meant nothing of this. If anything, it was more than ever a prolonged waiting for some moment of revelation or fulfilment, independent of books, of other minds, while depending only partly on himself.

He was lucky to have Evelyn.

'Do you think this road is going to lead anywhere?' she asked, and smiled at space.

Although she could have been mistaken for a delicate woman, and liked to think of herself as threatened, she was less fragile than wiry, or stringy. Certainly she experienced the odd headache, on occasions when her sensibility was taxed, but she almost never suffered from physical fatigue. Her weakness, she claimed, was in never being able to find enough on which to exercise her over-active mind. Nor was she capable of simply sitting. She would really have to see about taking up a charity, like Meals on Wheels. She was good at talking to the aged, and it was so gratifying to see in their old faces the appreciation of advice.

'Why shouldn't it lead somewhere?' Harold asked.

'I beg your pardon?'

'The road. This is a day's outing, isn't it?'

'Yes,' she said. 'That was the intention.'

They had eaten a rather nasty lunch – charred chops and fried banana lumped together on a lettuce leaf – in a cemented rockery beside the highway. There was nothing after that but to follow one on the side roads.

Evelyn picked a bunch of shivery-grass, and breathed deep, too deep, on returning momentarily to the years before she knew the answers.

'Yes,' she said. 'We're lucky to have enough to eat. And the climate. The Australian climate. Fancy if we'd been the Burds. Running that awful service station. Quite apart from anything else, the Thames Valley is so damp.'

Harold continued crunching springily ahead. She could smell the acceptable smell of his pipe. Evelyn preferred the company of men for the simple reason that she enjoyed being liked back. Women did not like her honesty.

'In the long run,' she said, 'Australian nationality paid.'

But again Evelyn experienced a little twinge of guilt. She plunged her chin into the bunch of pale-silvery shivery-grass.

'Do you think Win Burd really works in their service station?' she asked, but only casually. 'Sticking a petrol hose into strangers' cars?'

'If that's what she wrote you.'

'Some women are not strictly truthful,' Evelyn said. 'And you know Win' – she gave the laugh she kept for those whose faults she had to accept '– she always loved to dramatise.'

It did not seem to bother Harold.

'Anyway, whether she works the hose, or not, it's too dreadful to think about –' Evelyn continued, 'Win and Dudley reduced to a service station!'

Her mouth grew thin and appalled, as though the disaster had been her own.

'Most of them in the same boat – most of them English –' Harold said, 'after Suez.'

'But the Burds,' Evelyn protested, 'could have bought and sold the lot. That staircase they brought from Italy must have cost more than most of the others *had*.'

She was careful not to include themselves.

'Wasn't it lovely!' She sighed. 'Rose marble.'

The guests resumed mounting the rosy stairs to be received, those the Burds had invited, with professional affection, the others, with irony disguised as tact, Evelyn – she was an intelligent woman – had seen through it all, and had always felt glad she was on the right side of Win and Dudley's irony. Harold's managing the business for them in a country of the wrong colour made her almost one of the family.

Win Burd had delighted in parties. She could not resist fancy dress. Her long lovely thighs and legs were made for display, and she always took advantage of them. That gold lamé Knave of Hearts the year the Fat Boy showed too warm an interest. Scandal notwithstanding, Win must have derived enormous satisfaction from snubbing a king. The summer the Fazackerleys spent an extended leave in Australia, Win had insisted on Evelyn's packing the Knave of Hearts: so useful on the ship, throw it overboard afterwards. Evelyn had only accepted because she couldn't very well refuse. Though of course she hadn't worn anything so daring, not to say disgraceful, as Win's tinkling tunic. Both during the voyage, and after, Evelyn had brooded over their employer's generosity, while trying not to relate it to the image of her own, always rather skinny, thighs. She had sold the costume soon after landing.

'Perhaps Win can *put up with* the service station,' she said to Harold. 'She had a streak of something. Not exactly vulgarity. Toughness. It was probably true what people said.'

'What?'

'Oh, you know. About the chorus.'

'Can't remember,' said Harold, though she was sure he did.

'Poor Win! She had a heart of gold. But, my God, wasn't she plain!'

'The face of a goat and the body of a statue. Not all women are as lucky as that.'

'Oh, Harold! You shouldn't.'

'What's wrong? There are men who are partial to goats – even to statues, I'm told.'

'Oh, Harold! How dreadful! How *sick*!'

But she loved it. She loved the opportunity to use the with-it word.

The houses of success strung out along the ridge seemed to leap in approval of her knowing mirth. The houses strung out, though, no longer piled, she had to observe. The thinning process, together with the wind down her cleavage, turned her cold. Her laughter flickered and was extinguished.

Evelyn said: 'I do hope there won't be a war.'

'What put that into your head?'

'My few investments, naturally. Where should we be without them?'

'In the soup like anybody else.'

Evelyn wasn't prepared to argue. She wasn't just *anybody*, whatever Harold decided for himself.

The road had faded to a faint sandstone scar beneath the persisting razor-back.

'There,' she said, 'I told you it wouldn't come to anything. Nobody would be mad enough to build in such a barren spot as this. Nobody but a suicide.'

When the little, attenuated, clinging weatherboard offered itself at the last flick of the vanishing road.

Harold said: 'It suited somebody to build.'

'What? That! That *hutch*!'

Certainly the wooden house couldn't pretend to be much more. Clamped to what was practically a cliff, there was nothing to suggest ease or skill in its execution. It was the defenceless amateurishness of the house which roused Evelyn's dark-red scorn. It was a kind of honesty in its painfully achieved proportions, in its out-of-plumb match-stick stairway and exposed seaward balcony which moved Harold and filled him with a longing for something he could never accomplish. Perhaps it was just as well to see the house as a hutch, to imagine large soft animals turning on straw, or enormous satiny birds contemplating the ocean from behind wooden bars. Although he would never have confessed it to Evelyn, his imagination had often helped him out.

But just then Harold Fazackerley was confounded by reality.

The head, the face, the solid shoulders of a man appeared on the out-of-plumb outside stairway, rising above the level of the roof, the road, to look inside the letter-box for one of those letters, Harold could see, the man did not expect to find.

In the same manner, the expression on the anonymous face was directed towards the strangers on the road: doubting, but hopeful.

Then Evelyn Fazackerley heard her husband, not exactly call, bleat, rather, from unpreparedness. It was disconcerting, coming from such a man.

'Clem! Clem, isn't it? Dowson?'

From beneath his stubbly hair, the man's red, large-pored face very diffidently admitted to the name. It infuriated Evelyn. She knew too much about him in advance. Slow people drew from her an irritation almost as visible as blood. Oh yes, she knew!

Excitement was making Harold's mouth lose control.

'You remember Clem, Evelyn!'

He turned.

Harold, she saw with a shock, had been rejuvenated. She would take her time.

'Clem Dowson?'

She might have been proud of her inability to remember.

'The *Simla*. The *Nepal*.' Harold helped.

Then she did begin, faintly, sighingly, allowing herself to recall a heavy engineer, in one liner, and in a second. Since then, she noticed, sun and wind had made him more transparent. In those days the steam and sweat of the engine-room had kept him the colour and texture of suet. Opaque. Afterwards, on land, when she had been given the opportunity of getting to know him better, she hadn't succeeded.

'Ah yes why of course *yes*!'

Whatever your feelings, there were always the social obligations, so Evelyn was turning on what she knew to be her charm. But she had never cared for engineers. Pursers, now, were almost always jolly, first officers sometimes capable of fascinating, but engineers, even when shouting you a white lady, seemed to remain below with their engines, or whatever the things were called.

'And this is where you've hidden yourself away!' She would make it sound a charming joke.

'Yes,' said Dowson.

He did not attempt to excuse himself, though his solid body, attached to the frail railings for support, trembled slightly. It might have been the wind buffeting him, if he had not been protected from the wind by his comic house. He had stood, she allowed herself to realise, on another still occasion, in an almost identical position, holding on to a mango tree.

So now, as she looked at him, she said: 'I wonder exactly how long it is since we took you with us to the Delta?'

'Long enough,' Dowson mumbled, getting a fresh grip of the rail with his coarse, bristly fingers.

He had made himself look even cruder by wearing his hair shorn to a stubble, no doubt attempting to disguise his baldness. It made his eyes look bluer, his face more enormous and open to attack.

For that matter all three of them were temporarily somewhat exposed, unable to rely on the disguise of words, as they stood amongst the stones and silence, arrested in their moment of statuary.

Till Harold broke away with that candour which Evelyn had deplored before putting it down to his innocence and his sex.

'Anyway, Clem,' he said, 'isn't it about time you showed us over your hide-out? I take it you built the house yourself.'

Dowson laughed. He turned. He was hanging his head and still heaving slightly as he went down the wooden stairs. If he did not reply to Harold, it was clearly because he was giving him the answers to his questions.

The Fazackerleys followed, as it was intended.

'But how *clever*!'

Even before crossing the threshold Evelyn knew which line to take. It was so easy. She was so expert. With shy, boring men.

'You don't mean to tell me you made *this*? This cunning little cupboard with revolving shelves!'

Dowson reached out with his hand and held her for a moment, firmly, even hurtfully, through her glove.

'Only with a finger,' he warned. 'It only needs a touch of the finger.'

Evelyn might have felt offended if the incident hadn't been so significant. In the circumstances she simply passed on.

'And what is this?' she asked. 'This *surrealistic* contraption in wire?'

'That is one of my own inventions. That's to turn the egg out – automatically,' he explained, 'as soon as it's boiled.'

'But how amusing!'

Or how pathetic.

'If only Harold had half your talent. Now that we're retired, he only threatens to read books, and never gets around to that.'

She looked at her husband, though, asking forgiveness for the slight wound she had been moved to inflict. But he did not seem aware of it. There was so much. men failed to notice.

The kitchen was all very well. The living-room – she could not hope to see the bedroom – ought to be more rewarding, because more personal, revealing. But it was, in fact, a disappointment. Too bare, too glary. The two armchairs, their covers too tight. The desk: on it one or two instruments, in which she could not take an interest, bottles of coloured inks, what was probably a dictionary. Not even a photograph. Evelyn loved to be able to relate photographs to the owners of them, or better still, she loved the photographs which could not be explained.

But, on a little, ugly, yellow table, there was a basket of wools. And a sock stretched on a darning egg. It put the moisture back into Evelyn's drying lips.

In time they were sitting over Dowson's tea, the kind of dark red brew you might have expected, in thick white common cups, which showed a rime of tannin as the tide receded. Harold was leaning forward very seriously above his tilted cup, his grey eyes – she had always been proud of their honesty – for the moment rather irritatingly abstracted, as his mouth struggled to convey an awkward preoccupation.

'And what do you *do* with yourself?' he asked when finally he dared.

It was almost as though he were embarrassed to discuss anything so personal in front of his wife.

Dowson sat pulling at the tufts of hair on the backs of his fingers. Then he drew in his mouth, and focused his shockingly blue eyes.

'I sit and watch the ocean,' he answered Harold straight.

Harold appeared to find it a perfectly normal reply, and a gust of breath rose in Evelyn's throat as though to protest against an immoral act.

'But it's so empty. Most of the time, anyway. Except for some uninteresting ship. Ships are only interesting when you're in them,' she managed to gasp.

Neither of the men noticed her.

'You're lucky to know how,' Harold continued.

Evelyn mightn't have been in the room.

Dowson laughed – for Harold. It sounded unexpectedly gentle.

'I don't say you don't need to practise. In the beginning.'

'Yes,' said Harold. 'But the beginning – that's the difficulty.'

Then Dowson leaned forward and said: 'What about those poems you used to write?'

Evelyn raised her head.

'Poems?' Harold could have been afraid.

'At school.'

'Oh, yes. That was at school.'

Evelyn was swaying slightly.

'That was a beginning,' Dowson suggested.

Evelyn had a headache. Of course, she knew, she had heard, but long ago, Clem Dowson and Harold had been together at that preparatory school. It was the wind giving her a head, or the atmosphere of boredom their host created just by his physical presence.

'Fancy your remembering about those poems,' Harold said, and laughed. 'I had forgotten.'

He hadn't.

Harold Fazackerley, the little leggy boy with protruding ears and blue, chilblained hands, used to write poems and things in his peculiar screwed-up writing on scraps of paper he was always terrified might blow about and have to be explained to someone. When he couldn't have explained half of what came out. But the poems were necessary to him at that stage. At a later date, when his reason had sorted things out, he related those creative skirmishes of his boyhood to a hot shower on a cold afternoon or a smooth stool on a warm morning. Often as a boy he had suffered from constipation for stretches of several days. The poems seemed to ease his fears.

All winter the school buildings had been victimised by the winds. But in the summer, when the Virginia creeper was again in residence, and the dust thickened amongst tired laurels, and the smell of disinfectant rose piercingly from oversodden urinals, small boys were fairly trampled by the possibilities of living.

There were the scandals. Harold Fazackerley had not understood them quite. And was frightened by all that. He would not have liked to hear it explained, so he avoided those who were on the point of telling.

Clem Dowson was that silent, slightly older, much thicker boy: thick ankles in heather-mixture stockings, knees out-grown from knickerbockers. Clem would probably have started shaving early on. He did not go with anybody much, yet survived his isolation. He was not averse to anyone or anything, though it was hard to know whom or what he liked, beyond birds' eggs and grass-chewing and fried bread. He was probably, in fact he *was*, a funny sort of fish you would have been ashamed of meeting in the holidays.

Then Harold Fazackerley went up to Clem Dowson on an afternoon smelling of smoke and showed him two of those poems he had written. And Clem had read and handed them back. He smiled. He had broad teeth with grooves down them.

He said: 'They won't ever understand. Your writing's too hard to read.'

And at once Harold Fazackerley was reassured. They had a secret between them, besides, which was perhaps what he had wanted.

There was nothing between Clem and Harold, nothing you could be ashamed of. Harold had never done anything like that, or not that you could count. Nothing reprehensible, as he might have expressed it later, in his report-writing days. Not with Clem, anyway.

Sometimes they mucked around the paddocks looking for nests. How Clem shone, blowing a maggie's egg for Harold on a clear morning of spring, ankle-deep in dead grass, against the huge stringy-bark. Held to his more-than-friend's lips the speckled eggshell increased in transparency, and reddish, palpitating light.

'My intellectual husband has kept the secrets you apparently share.'

Pleating her mouth, lowering her eyelids, Evelyn Fazackerley made an exquisite irony of it.

In abeyance for a short space out of respect for memory, the wind had begun again to torment the little room in which they sat. The tenure of the house perched above the sea was more than ever insecure.

Evelyn looked at Harold and forgave him any hurt he might have caused her. Forgiveness had always come easily to her.

She even turned to Dowson and asked: 'Shall we see you again?'

Though here she only half-forgave. She was putting the man in an awkward position. She knew. She wanted to. It was the best way of cutting a knot. And he shuffled slightly, his rubber soles, and gave a congested smile, not even to Harold, but the room.

Harold said: 'I don't expect we could ever tempt Clem inside our horrible flat.'

Although feeling it was unnecessarily sincere, Evelyn played up to it.

'With my cooking! No *suffragis* now, you know!'

She could enjoy the faint bitterness of it.

'I'll look in. Some time. Perhaps,' Dowson suggested, mastering each word except the last.

Nobody seemed to think of offering or receiving an address.

Harold Fazackerley could have been muddling again over some problem the elusiveness of which had become a worry. He was greyer than Evelyn knew him, as though bleached by the blazing ocean, shrunken and brittle in the presence of Dowson's resilient stillness. Could it be that Harold's manhood would desert him before the end?

Although the possibility did not bear investigating to any depth because of the terror in it, Evelyn often dared wish she might outlive her husband, whose virility still attracted other women. She could not complain really, herself contributing to this in choosing his more exciting clothes, and in many little, more personal ways, such as taking her own nail-scissors to clip back an independent hair of his moustache, or those which were sprouting beyond his nostrils.

'I mean,' Harold was saying, or harping, 'Clem has come out of it with so much more than most of us. I mean, he has learnt to sit still. He has learnt to think.'

Not a thought in his head. You only had to look. Or did men, especially men together, experience something women couldn't?

She examined Dowson particularly closely, and disliked more than ever what she saw. If she had prodded him hard she imagined he would have felt of hard rubber.

'Certainly Mr Dowson has made himself very comfortable. Charming. This cosy little house. All the inventions. That egg-boiling thing alone. But a bit lonely at times, I should have thought.'

There, she knew, she had put her finger on it.

Then Dowson looked at her – it was for the first time, she realised, for the first time, at least, since they had stood beneath the mango tree years ago in the steaming Delta – Dowson said:

'A spell of loneliness never did anybody any harm.'

Evelyn got up, sweeping out of her lap the non-existent crumbs, because there hadn't been even a bought biscuit.

'If you are convinced,' she said.

They had all, in fact, got up.

'It's been fine seeing you, Clem,' Harold Fazackerley was saying. 'We must write. We must keep in touch.'

Although, to emphasise it, Harold had taken him by the elbow, Dowson hung his head, not believing it possible. Dowson, the elder, more stomachy, congested, preparing for a lonely stroke, had been transformed into the younger, Evelyn saw. She did not know whether she was pleased. The sight of Harold's youthful back often inclined her to invent youth for herself. Now his back was the wrong side.

As they clung to the rickety outside stairway, above the supine rock-plants and the unfortunate, spinning fuchsias, she was battered into charity.

'How shall we find,' she began to ask through the veered wind, 'how can we get in touch with you?'

'Just put "Dowson",' Dowson answered incredibly. 'Dowson,' he repeated, '"Bandan Beach".'

Standing on the friable road, the wind spiralling round his legs inside the stuff of his trousers, Harold Fazackerley again visualised those large primeval animals and enormous satiny birds gravely observing the ocean from behind wooden bars. It was not possible to communicate with such removed creatures, except through silences, of which there were never enough.

Yet he had communicated a little, he thought, or hoped, with Dowson.

All the way, and especially in the bus, Evelyn kept repeating they had had a lovely day.

'Yes,' he agreed, at one stage, because it was expected of him, 'and I was particularly glad to come across old Clem.'

'I like him,' she said, firmly, holding up her chin.

He ignored it. Perhaps he thought nobody else appreciated Dowson.

'I envy Clem,' Harold said.

'How?' she asked, drawing in her breath.

'He's happy.'

'Oh, come!' said Evelyn. 'You can't say *we* aren't happy.'

'No,' he agreed. 'Is the window too much for you?'

She shook her head, giving him her dreamy look, one of those relics of her girlhood.

'The air is so lovely,' she said; she would not let it be otherwise.

They were being jolted past the litter of matchbox houses waiting on that sweep of the coast for the tidal wave which hadn't yet materialised.

'I would have said,' she said, 'he wasn't all that happy. In his do-it-yourself house. With those unnecessary gadgets.'

'Why?'

Although he did not move, except as thrown by their onward motion, she could sense him rearing inside his constraining body beside her on the lumpy public-transport seat.

'Because,' she said, 'well – it lacks a woman's hand.'

She looked down at her own formally gloved hands. Whatever her other deficiencies she could afford to be proud of her hands. During the almost endless stretch between Colombo and Fremantle an artist had once asked to paint them, and she had been persuaded – with Harold's knowledge.

But now Harold was invisibly rearing, finally actually heaving and altering position, rather too uncomfortably, aggressively, on the bus seat.

'But you don't understand,' he blurted, 'a man like Clem Dowson.'

'Then I don't,' she decided to agree.

Because, to submit in a crisis, was to subscribe to her own reasonableness.

Harold appeared convinced, and rightly. Nobody could have questioned her loyalty to him, in the larger sense, either in the squalid present, or the good old plushier days of power and respect. When Egypt had gone to so many women's heads.

Harold Fazackerley had returned to Egypt after the First War. His friend Dudley Burd had kept his promise. First Dudley's father, then Dudley himself, became Harold Fazackerley's employer. Friends more than employers, although Evelyn always maintained the idea of friendship was not as elastic as Harold liked to think. Anyway, he was in the habit of calling his employer 'Dud' to his face, and of helping himself to drink before he had been invited. It seemed to entertain Dudley Burd to employ an 'Aussie'. He even used the word 'Dink'. It was all very well, and amusing, and English, after mentioning the names of people, Evelyn confirmed, the Burds had actually met, to season his conversation with crude colonial salt.

Evelyn detested that. For a long time she couldn't avail herself of the familiarity the Burds appeared genuinely to be offering. Her hand trembled holding gin. She was nervous, she supposed, in the beginning: it was agony to imagine the colours she had chosen did not go, or that she was making mistakes at dinner parties, or that her accent might be showing through. 'Oh no, Sir Dudley,' she might say. 'Thank you. Really. I'd rather not. Well, you see, not every Australian girl is at home on a horse. Just as,' she added with a little giggle, 'not every Australian speaks with an accent.' She hated to hear her own giggle. But the scent of gin was anaesthetising her gaucherie, giving her courage. She liked, she had to admit, the faint scent of leather and sweat, of horse, and the men who had been riding them.

Or Win: the trailing, the devastating, interchangeable scents of Win Burd.

'Ev, darling, what a bloody bore those Rockliffes proposed to barge in for lunch! It would be much more fun to get ginned up a little together, and enjoy a siesta afterwards. But you're not *drink*-ing! Evelyn?'

'Oh yes, Lady Burd! Thank you. I'm doing nicely.'

Again that giggle. When she wasn't stupid. Probably less so than Lady Burd.

Early on, the Burds had suggested she drop the Sir and Lady. But she couldn't bring herself to it. If she hadn't done it in her own time it might have seemed unnatural, and she would have felt embarrassed.

Also, perhaps, she did enjoy the sound of the title.

'That's so terribly kind of you, Lady Burd . . . Yes, Lady Burd . . . We'd be thrilled.'

Because Win used to telephone sometimes in that slurry, half-ginned voice, and suggest that Evelyn and Harold might like to spend the week-end in the Delta, which meant: use the house on what was referred to by the Burds' British dependants as the Estate. Evelyn was delighted for a time to receive its freedom, but she had to be so careful not to give anything like a display of girlish or vulgar enthusiasm, and she had to take particular care over her enunciation. She couldn't afford to throw accent and grammer over her shoulder like Win Burd. The upper class English could get away with murder.

Sometimes when Harold had leave the Fazackerleys might spend a week or fortnight at the house on the Estate. The Burds found it a bit of a bore; they preferred the Aegean and the elaborately simple luxury of their converted caique. But in spite of the Egyptians and the flies Evelyn decided to love the Delta. She became the chatelaine. Of the Burd's certainly rather spartan, but cool, shuttered, whitewashed house. With lands stretching between canals. And mango trees, heavy with nauseating fruit.

'You'd think they'd introduce some upholstery, at least, and a few modern conveniences,' Evelyn complained once. 'The mattresses are like lying on the ground.'

Harold had to make excuses for the Burds.

'They like to rough it now and again.'

'Oh, I suppose so,' Evelyn agreed, 'if you have something as smooth as rose marble to return to.'

But even without benefit of staircase, Evelyn Fazackerley came into her own, as chatelaine, standing, for instance, in the doorway which separated dining-room from kitchen quarters, frowning, shouting:

'*Gibbou wahed foutah, Mohammed!*'

To the slave.

Harold might say: 'Darling – why do Anglo-Saxons have to shout at foreigners?'

'But I wasn't shouting,' Evelyn replied. 'I was making myself understood. And surely if you classify Arabs as "foreigners" it raises them to the level of Europeans? Not that I'm sticking up for Europeans! They're there – we know – but I don't know any, and don't particularly want to.'

'Aren't you being narrow-minded?'

She looked at him. Because he was in love with her he was making it sound a virtue. So she was reassured.

'I am accused!' she said softly, looking down at the rather greasy bean soup.

Evelyn Fazackerley was slim. She wore a lot of white. In the reflective dark of the old Delta house, surrounded by a steamy, indolent landscape, she saw herself as the spirit of cool. If only her arms hadn't been quite so thin, or the pores hadn't stood so wide open in her otherwise immaculate skin.

But her power allowed her to forget such details. She was amazed, even shocked by the passion she seemed to inspire in her husband during those steamy summer months.

'By the time October is here,' Win Burd used to say, 'I'm destroyed, I'm any Alexandrian whore.'

Win, of course, was extravagant in every way. She could afford to be.

One summer while they were all still comparatively young the Burds had lent the house in the Delta for the Fazackerleys to take a week's leave. The prospect no longer pleased Evelyn: the mango trees, the dark rooms, the smell, and worse, the taste of primus, Egyptian women afloat in black along the paths of the canals, laughing at what she was never going to discover – all would be the same as before, except that Mohammed had been replaced by Mustapha, and Mustapha by Osmin.

Moreover, Evelyn brooded, the Burds only lent the house in summer when the Delta was at its steamiest.

It was two nights to their departure. Harold had come in, she realised.

'You remember that man, that Dowson, the engineer from the *Nepal*? The one I was at school with. Well he's in Alex, Evelyn. Been sick. He's just discharged from hospital.'

It was far too sticky and undignified a night. Having to remember that engineer was to remember only irritably.

'I'd have taken him for a Scot,' she said. 'But he wasn't.'

Harold was in his kind mood. Its feelers were gently reaching out.

'I think he's hard up for something to do. A bit lonely, I'd say. He's got another ten days before joining his ship. I told him he'd better come out to Kafr el Zayat with us.'

'Oh, darling! That means I've got to set to and buy a whole lot of extra *stuff*! You're most unreasonable at times.'

'You've only got to ring the Nile Cold in the morning,' Harold said.

She laughed rather high. She was wearing a lime sash.

'You do show me up, darling,' she said. 'And more often than not you're perfectly right.'

It was the sort of moment which made their relationship such a special one.

Harold kissed her. He had been drinking, but only the way everyday did. It added to his masculinity.

'Dowson has a friend,' he said.

'A friend? Then how can he be lonely?'

Harold was slowed down.

'Well, I mean. A manner of speaking. And anyway, the friend's a Greek. It isn't the same as your own kind.'

'A Greek? I've never met a Greek,' said Evelyn.

'It may be an interesting experience. This one has just come from an archaeological dig somewhere in Upper Egypt.'

'*You don't mean to say you* . . .' Evelyn could only break off.

'Couldn't very well avoid it. He's a stranger, and Dowson's friend. I asked the Greek too.'

'I ask *you*! You sit drinking in some bar, and before you know, you've invited all the rag-tag in the bar! Darling, I do think you might have considered the position you're putting us in. Bad enough the stodgy engineer. I know he's honest, if uncouth in almost every way. But a Greek. In Win and Dudley's home.'

'Win and Dudley have been known to invite Armenians, and I never heard the silver was missing.'

'That is different. The Burds are responsible to themselves.'

Nothing was spoken at dinner, except when Evelyn said: '*Esh, Khalil. Gawam!*'

The drought from which she was suffering had grown so intense it was surprising such plentiful tears gushed over the coffee.

'Oh, darling, I am silly! I am silly!' she said, making it sillier.

When he came and sat against her, the familiar outline of his body through the wringing shirt robbed her of her last control. She kissed his hands through the mess of tears. She and Harold were melting together in a scent of jasmine and moist flower-beds.

So next morning he promised to ring Dowson after Evelyn had rung the Nile Cold Storage. Reason had decided against the Greek. Evelyn said such a very simple man as Dowson would be easily persuaded. Harold said he hoped he would.

On the morning of the day, when Evelyn had just discovered the Nile Cold had forgotten the *pâté* she had specially ordered, the police were beating up a beggar in the street, the heavy man she remembered as Dowson the engineer appeared in the driveway. At his heels a second man. Evelyn froze inside her perspiration. Not, possibly, the Greek? Each of the men was carrying a small case.

Dowson shook hands much too firmly. The Greek, it was, pronounced his own name. Evelyn, determined not to listen, knew only that it went off like fireworks.

Then Evelyn, not with the assistance of her will, but in a gust of dizzying, and equally pyrotechnical, inspiration, began to say her piece:

'Oh, but what an embarrassing, such a terribly distressing mistake! Oh, but Harold surely, Mr Dowson? Or can it be another instance of the appalling Alexandrian telephone system? Harold explained to me how he explained that, much as we'd have liked it *ourselves*, we're hardly the masters in a *lent* house. It is kind of Sir Dudley and Lady Burd to allow us *our* friends—' here she turned with evident graciousness to the engineer '—but for us to go farther would, I feel, only be to impose on the Burds. Will Mr Dowson explain?' she appealed to Harold. 'More clearly? To his friend?'

In a morning which had already grown merciless enough to allow no shadows, she had stood the solid Dowson, like a wall, between herself and the situation.

Evelyn was smiling. Everyone was smiling. Harold was making noises as though somebody had punched him in the ribs. The Greek was smiling most of all. He was a small and, in every way, insignificant man. His necktie, which he had been in the habit of knotting always lower, and tried to restore for the occasion to even lengths, was looking chewed and stringy.

Evelyn turned away after that, but did just glance back once. Dowson had retreated along the drive with his friend, to where the hedge of blue plumbago was broken by the gateway. They were standing together in the white dust. Dowson's hand was on the Greek's shoulder.

'We've behaved rottenly,' Harold was saying. 'I expect we've hurt both of them.'

'Nonsense,' she said. 'People are thicker-skinned than you think.'

All the same, she was determined to be particularly nice to the Dowson man during his few days in the Delta.

She began already on the way. As Harold drove she would turn round towards the engineer, who was sitting on the edge of the rear seat, his hands firmly grasping the back of that in front of him. It made them an intimate trio. Such a very simple man could only, she was certain, have forgiven her. Even so, she felt her face flicker with light and wind, also possibly with remembrance of a recent, if unimportant, 'scene'.

However she might look in the Egyptian glare, at least she would not see, nor probably, would Dowson. Though she half-closed her eyes – a trick learnt from the mirror – whenever she turned to address their guest. Confidence seduced her mouth, the face she turned full on at him.

She was making that kind of conversation for visitors passing through: the water buffalo and ibises, together with some of the cotton jargon and statistics picked up from listening interminably to experts.

When suddenly she was forced to remark: 'I do hope your friend wasn't hurt by the stupid mistake Harold – we, all of us, made.'

Dowson smiled his sandy smile.

'I don't think he's one who ever expects too much.'

Evelyn did not expect that.

'I've always been told the Greeks, the modern Greeks, that is, not the real ones,' she said, 'are practically orientals.'

'Protosingelopoulos is real enough,' Dowson said.

The windborne sun had set fire to his suety face.

'You should know,' Evelyn said. 'He's your friend. Have you known him long?'

'Three and a half days,' said Dowson.

'Oh, but really – are you always so sure?'

Dowson answered: 'Yes.'

She realised then that his sitting forward on the edge of the seat and clutching the back of theirs, had not been to bring them all more closely together, but to help him coil more tightly inside his secretive mind. How repulsive the backs of his fingers were, with their tufts of reddish-blond hair. She had turned after that and watched the long, straight, boring road.

Dowson, surprisingly, seemed at home in the Burds' house. When he was not listening to, or out driving with, Harold, the thick-walled rooms provided him with a silence the equivalent of his own, their rough proportions might have been designed to contain his crude form. As he strolled about the grounds, the landscape was perhaps more indifferent to his presence, though he appeared unaware of it, planting his heels firmly as he walked, in no particular direction but the one in which his thoughts were leading him.

She had to admit she was put out by what Dowson was becoming, so she looked for any weakness which might compensate for his rejecting the mould she had decided must be his. As in the case of so many visitors passing through from other climates, his clothes were quite unsuitable. When Dowson abandoned his blue serge coat, and walked in his wrong shirt and serge trousers, she was more than amused, she was glad to see him look so out of place, hence vulnerable.

Sometimes as he wove thumping through the mango grove, or past the beds of reedy carnations, he would be carrying a book under his arm. There were occasions when she came across him, a core in the shadow of one of the closely shuttered rooms, at least sitting with, if not actually reading, the open book.

At last she reached the point where she couldn't resist taking it from him. To satisfy her curiosity.

'You'll ruin your eyes,' she said, not ungently, 'reading in such a dim light.'

It was a translation from the Greek, she discovered. Poems. By someone called Cavafy.

'Surely you're not an intellectual!' she said, and smiled a healing smile.

'Not exactly,' Dowson said.

'Harold has moments of fancying himself as an intellectual. Oh, I'm not trying to belittle him. He's much cleverer than I. I'm only a scatter-brained woman.'

She waited for him to handle that, but he didn't.

'What very difficult-looking, not to say peculiar, poems!' she said, handling back something she would have to make up her mind about. 'If you understand those, then it makes you most horribly intellectual, and I shall have to adopt a different attitude towards you.'

Dowson sat rubbing his hands together as if working tobacco for a pipe. The head on the bull-shoulders was averted, so that she found herself looking at his clumsy profile. Though she had been wrong in her assessment of his character, it was gratifying to know that his physical coarseness could not dissolve, and that his shirt, in keeping, smelled slightly of sweat.

'You don't have to understand,' she realised he was saying, 'not everything, not every word. I don't pretend to. It's something the Professor gave me,' he added.

'Which professor?'

'Protosingelopoulos.'

'That little man a professor? You amaze me! Though I wonder why. When life is all surprises.'

Their talk was almost making her feel intellectual herself. But Dowson didn't seem aware of it, or was sensitive only to his own problems and reactions.

'I fancy I'm causing you trouble by being here,' he said suddenly.

'Whatever put that into your head?' she asked. 'I'm only afraid you may be bored. I think I know what forced unemployment must feel like to an active man. At least today Harold will be driving over to Mansoura, to look at a crop he's interested in. You'll be able to go with him. And talk about all the things you have in common.'

'What are those?' he asked unexpectedly, and tried to make it sound less strange by laughing.

She wondered whether he was cunning.

'If I knew,' she answered, 'then you might trust me more.'

Just then Harold flung open the door, and said: 'That idiot of an Arab tells me only now the pump stopped working yesterday, and that we're practically without water. Instead of going to Mansoura I'll have to drive over and fetch de Boisé. Do you want to come with me, Clem, on this errand, not that it's an interesting one?'

'No, Harold,' said Dowson. 'I'll stay and see what can be done about the pump. It's probably something just in my line. Then you can drive to Mansoura as arranged.'

A practical man, he was again happy, she saw, at the prospect of making himself useful. She was only scornful of the ease with which he and Harold called each other by their Christian names. What should have strengthened seemed to make them weak.

After Harold left, and Dowson had started tinkering with the pump, there was nothing to fill the morning but the steam which rose from the Delta. She sat down and again began looking through the book of poems, from which an occasional carved image formed glittering in her mind. First a word here and there, then whole phrases, breathed disconcertingly. Love was exchanged on terms she knew existed in theory, and which now in the half-light of poetry were too palpably fleshed, too suffocatingly scented. She remembered hearing of an English-woman raped by an Arab in Nouzha Gardens. Evelyn put the book down. There was no rape, she felt, which could not be avoided.

But the perfume persisted, of overblown words, sweat, and the dark red roses growing outside the shutters from Delta silt.

In the course of the morning Dowson came and asked her for some rags. He looked so content and unselfconscious.

'What a mess you've made of your shirt,' she said, but completely detached.

'I'll give it a wash,' he said, 'afterwards.'

'Oh, no!' she said. '*They* will give it a wash.'

As she went to rummage for a suitable rag, her self-possession sat most agreeably on her. She came back with an old silk slip of Lady Burd's.

'Isn't it too good?' he asked.

'I shouldn't think so,' she replied, and laughed. 'Or if it is, it won't be missed.'

Not by Win. Who flew a hat from Paris for a wedding, and sent it back, and flew another.

'How is the *pump*?' she asked, deliberately impaling the word on her tongue.

'We'll fix it,' he said earnestly.

But she had not listened for his answer. She was fascinated by Win's silk slip hanging from his bare arm, and the skin of his arms dribbled with black machine oil and daubed with greyer grease.

They met only briefly at lunch.

When she lay down for her siesta she could hear the intermittent sound of metal, tinny in competition with the dead weight of heat. He had been ill, he might get a sunstroke, she thought, but you could not persuade a man against what he wanted. How glad she was she had married Harold, whose wanting had less conviction in it. She wondered how she had found Harold, and where in sleep she would find him again.

For an instant she came across him or, no, Dowson, seated at a round, iron, slanted table. Dowson was stuffing his mouth with a mouse-trap variety of cheese. Why must you eat like that? she asked. Because, he said through his bread, you are starving, aren't you, Mrs Fazackerley? She particularly resented the use of her name, as well as the rain of crumbs steadily falling.

On waking up, her right cheek was creased, and she was feeling irritable, but by the time she had bathed and powdered herself, she could have felt sorry for someone else. Old tangos persisted in her head, and the smell of a liner's decks at night. It was only natural. Half the life of so many Australians was spent at sea, getting somewhere, she reflected.

When she met Dowson she asked through her brightest lipstick: 'Hasn't my old Harold got back?'

'No,' said Dowson.

He was looking a caricature of himself, in a fresh shirt, and those blue serge trousers which, apparently, were the only ones he had with him.

'What a bore!' she said. 'The dinner will be awful. It would have been awful anyway.'

After pouring his whisky she asked: 'Are you glad to be an Australian?'

'I'd stopped thinking about it.'

'I'm glad I am,' she said, whether he believed it or not.

She was truly glad, though, for the reality of her healthy Australian girlhood. She was thankful for the apple she had bitten into, but thrown away extravagantly.

'Do you think Harold could have had an accident?' she asked.

'No. Why?' he said. 'There are too many reasons why he shouldn't have. People usually get back even when you're expecting them not to.'

It was the gin, she suspected, giving her morbid ideas. Although normally it was not the kind of thing she did, she had another one to quell them.

'You don't understand,' she said, 'what Harold means to me. Although,' she said, '*you* can talk to him, or not talk, and arrive at something I can never get at.'

Dowson looked puzzled and stupid.

He said: 'But, but?'

She suggested they stroll a bit. It was healthier than sitting drinking and having morbid ideas about car accidents and marriage.

'We didn't mention marriage,' said Dowson.

He was that kind of a man.

Anyway, they began to tread the darkness down. Though the magic slide of the Delta had been withdrawn, the smell of it was there: exhausted clover and dung fires. When they told her it was dung, when she was newly arrived in Egypt, it had been one of the things to resent. Till by degrees it became a comfort of the nomadic existence, which was what the life of any foreigner in Egypt remained. Tonight there were also the stars, at which she used to look in the beginning, before she got into the habit of taking them for granted.

'Didn't we,' she continued, tripping over something in the darkness, 'discuss marriage? I thought we were discussing it practically continuously.'

She could not help limping at first from the momentary pain in her ankle, but he did not attempt to support her.

'Not to my knowledge, Mrs Fazackerley,' he said, 'although I gather you're pretty obsessed by it.'

'Then *you* have never been married!' She shot it out.

'No,' he agreed.

She wondered whether the darkness would disguise the shape her mouth was taking.

'They say that if a man isn't married by the age of thirty, he's either very selfish, or very immoral. I wonder which you are!'

That at least convinced her she need not limp.

'Married or single,' Dowson said, 'I'd say most men were moderately selfish and moderately immoral.'

'But you don't want to see!' she cried. 'It's the immoderate bachelors I'm talking about.'

'I don't see, Mrs Fazackerley,' he said, 'why it should interest you all that much. When you have what you want.'

'Oh, I know! I know!'

Her face bumped against a mango in the dark. She was spattered with leaves and her own protests.

'But we are talking, aren't we,' she persisted, 'to keep our spirits up? And to get to know each other. Why don't I know you?'

'That I can't answer,' he said. 'If we are meant to know a person, then we do.'

In a glitter of starlight she saw a little of his face, and the expression had nothing for her. It was frightening.

'You are a man who strikes me as never being frightened,' she said. 'That in itself is frightening to anyone who is frightened.'

'What are you frightened of?' he asked.

'Almost everything. Living in this country.' Her mind lurched. 'English accents. *Scorpions!*' She pounced on the scorpions. 'Even now, after years in

Egypt, I'm terrified I shall forget to think, and step into a shoe which has a scorpion inside.'

And her hand, surprising to herself, seized his rough arm. It was as though she had never touched a man before, and the experience drew her towards him, closer still, to further experience of night and horror. Lurid and unconvincing in themselves, the scorpions had been necessary as a starting point. Just as Dowson's coarse and clumsy body might prove the kind of debasement she would return to in sober moments with all the drunkenness of remorse.

They had come out on the edge of the plantation, where a black water flowed through the greenish silver light, and the raised Arab voices were splintering the cubes of village houses. Only Dowson remained solid.

'Did you ever find one?' he asked, still anchored in what they had been discussing.

'What?' she uttered.

'A scorpion.'

He laughed like a boy. With his free arm he was holding on to the trunk of a young mango tree.

'No,' she said. 'But it isn't any less frightening to expect.'

Although in the several light-years of their journey she had flattened, plastered herself against him according to the instructions she had somehow learnt, they both remained curiously objectiveless, Dowson might have withdrawn from his solid body, except, she realised, he was very slightly trembling.

'You expect *death*, don't you?' he was chattering, 'without even putting on your shoe. But you stop thinking about it. You'd never get on with living.'

'Oh yes, I'm silly, I know! It's my fate always to be reminded of it!'

She was retreating by shivers of self-mortification.

'I know!' She gulped repeatedly.

She was standing crying beside him in the green Egyptian night. Now that her lust, it had not been lust, was no more than a tingling of coarse hair against her memory, she badly wanted him to believe in something more than her sterility.

'I'm sorry.' From a great distance she was listening to herself. 'I'm upset. Our little boy. You know we lost our child.'

'*No!*' said Dowson, with the full weight of his astonishment.

He was looking at her too heavily, too.

'Fell into one of the canals.' She was whimpering helplessly by now. 'You see, Mr Dowson? You *will* understand?'

Still the desire spurted in her to embrace her child's great stubbly head. Her lost child.

'What age was the little boy?'

It might have made her shriek with laughter if she herself hadn't created the solemnity. The green light was glittering in Dowson's earnest eyes.

'Five,' she calculated.

But he did not notice it was dragged out of her, and for a moment she got possession of his blunt, sweating fingers, which she no longer very much wanted, of which, in fact, she had a horror, as of herself.

'You must never,' she commanded, she remembered how to, 'never bring this up with Harold, who was more upset than I can tell,' she continued very rapidly. 'We never talk about it ourselves.'

Dowson the fish was still goggling, and she still dissolved in the misery of deceit.

Shortly after, the headlights were approaching down the long straight road.

'Sorry, Evelyn darling,' Harold said, 'there's no excuse I can offer. I'm just late.'

She couldn't even feel badly used.

'We were beginning to worry about you,' Dowson said.

'Why?' asked Harold.

Neither could answer.

'No harm is done,' said Evelyn. 'Except in the kitchen. I can't be responsible for the dinner.'

Sweeping a spider out of her hair, she went into the house to restore her face.

In the morning Harold came to her and said: 'Dowson has decided to return to Alex. He wants to send for a car. But I told him I'd drive him over.'

'Oh?' she said. 'How peculiar he is! When he still has several days to put in.'

'Perhaps he wants to see something more of his friend before joining his ship at Port Said.'

When she went out to the front, Dowson was trying to refasten one of the locks of his suitcase.

'I'm so sorry you have to rush off,' she began. 'But I understand your wanting to see something of Professor Proto before you leave. I shall always feel he may have a grudge against me because it wasn't possible to invite him too.'

It was easier to sound sincere when obligations had been removed.

Dowson could have been mystified by the obviously broken lock of his cheap suitcase. He continued fiddling with the rusty hasp.

'Protosingelopoulos?' he said. 'I expect he'll have left for Greece by this.'

'But Harold said . . .'

Harold was calling to the Arab to wipe the windscreen of the car. His back was turned. It was impossible to tell if he was aware of the snippet of conversation she was left holding with his friend. Harold was permanently pre-occupied with the upkeep of cars. With cotton. Or, she admitted with a twinge, his wife.

And Dowson, she realised, was not at all mystified. He was looking away to hide what he knew, and would go off in possession of her secret. Fortunately the man was too stupid or too honest to make use of it.

'Good-bye, Mr Dowson,' she said. 'I hope you'll soon feel perfectly strong.'

He laughed oddly, and, looking at his large feet, replied: 'I never felt sick. Nothing you could put your finger on. Only they told me I was.'

Then Harold was driving his friend or nuisance away. Dowson waved, or put up a blunt hand. Harold waved, and it was Harold on whom she focused, as he signalled that soon they would be uninterruptedly together. Sometimes she found herself wishing Harold might go down with a serious illness so that she could demonstrate a devotion which her surface concealed. She saw him lying by shielded light, in haggard, waxen profile, inside a mosquito net. While she drained the fever from him, into her own body.

But it was she who suffered illnesses, unimportant, fretful ones. It was humiliating.

At sixty Evelyn Fazackerley was tolerably preserved. Although she had looked skinny as a girl, by sixty her skinniness had become a figure, and she reinforced herself with hats. She was fortunate, the glass had told her, in having taste. Windows, the windows of buses, returned her conviction, as she allowed the motion of the bus to throw her lightly against her husband's shoulder, because in his retirement, Harold was almost always at her side.

Sometimes she wondered how much a man, a really masculine man like Harold, was aware of the part a woman's softness played in his life. She wondered on the afternoon they were being carried back from that beach. She had on her coat with the smoky-fox collar, less fashionable than timeless, like something worn by the Queen Mother.

'There's the ironing,' Harold was saying. 'That'd be a bit of a problem. But you could pay a woman to do it. I expect that's how old Clem gets round it. There's still the shopping, though. I can't stand the sight of a man with a string bag.'

'You surprise me,' Evelyn said, 'thinking yourself into a situation that, with luck, you'll never find yourself in – and taking an interest in a person so uninteresting as Mr Dowson.'

'Clem interests me tremendously,' Harold said.

'There's no accounting for tastes, I suppose. Some of those books you buy, for instance. From page to page, I can never remember the *names* in a Russian novel.'

She laughed tolerantly, however. She often did the most boring things if Harold showed he wanted her to.

'That Dowson,' she returned to it from behind half-closed eyes, 'I remember seeing him with a book in his hands. But I wonder whether he can really read.'

'Don't expect he needs to.'

'Oh, come, darling!'

Harold was so magnanimous she completely closed her eyes.

'Clem strikes me as being as self-contained as – as some object – take,' said Harold, straining awkwardly, 'take a chunk of glass.'

Evelyn opened her eyes. Harold was positively sweating, as though from embarrassment.

'But what was he?' she asked. 'A ship's engineer! Who retired to an Australian beach. And what? And nothing!'

'He probably hasn't lived a life of any interest himself. But absorbs – and reflects – experience.'

Harold was chewing on the words. In the end he took out his pipe.

Evelyn felt most disturbed.

'What was that illness he had?' she asked. 'When his ship dropped him off in Egypt.'

'I believe it was a nervous breakdown.'

Evylyn moistened her lips.

'You didn't tell me,' she said.

'Didn't I? I don't suppose I tell everything. Do you?'

'I try to,' she said.

The bus was carrying them into the city. Now that they were looking at it again each vaguely wondered whether they had chosen to live in it.

'What I admire most in Dowson,' Harold Fazackerley said abruptly, 'is his ability to choose.'

'You can't say we don't do practically everything we choose,' Evelyn murmured, drowsy from the bus.

But turned suddenly on her husband, and asked with the utmost earnestness, which was unusual for her, even when she felt earnest: 'Harold, do you think Dowson is queer?'

'What on earth makes you ask that?'

'I don't know,' she said, shrugging. 'The sea, they say, turns them queer.'

'It wasn't the Navy. On a liner the women don't give them much opportunity.'

'No!'

She giggled. She liked the way he put things. How glad she was to be married to Harold, who seldom ignored the openings she offered for a slightly oblique exchange. He respected in her the subtlety which lots of men might have pinched out on recognising.

They were soon shut in the lift of the block in which they lived. Dust had settled on the branches of the iron roses, on the stems of originally gilded lilies, of the door that sometimes stuck. At different levels the same landing sank in striations of brown pine to meet the slowly rising lift. The Fazackerleys tried to count their lift among their blessings. But Evelyn always stood clear of its thicket of metal flowers, for fear of coming into contact with their slight fur, their greasy dew.

On going inside tonight she said: 'At least there's nothing like your own home.'

At least it was a relief to relieve. Harold eased himself sideways into the lavatory's narrow stall, and himself stood like a horse gone at the knees. From down the well the sounds of night began exploding in Hungarian. The iron veins of neo-Tudor wall outside became for Harold Fazackerley, on an empty bladder, the arteries of life.

'I expect even Mr Dowson feels attached,' Evelyn said, resuming, as often, a dialogue with which he failed to reconnect. 'To that lonely little rickety house,' she added.

Evelyn his wife was doing something to her hair. She had already, it appeared, attended to that first necessity, her mouth. Her lips dripped with light and crimson. He couldn't have done without Evelyn, of course. The vision of her death-mask on the last of the Egyptian pillow-slips made him switch on the radio.

Actors were acting out a play to which neither of them listened.

Because, when Evelyn had brought the sherry, which neither of them really liked, she turned towards him, flickering her eyelids, and began: 'You will probably think it peculiar, but I suddenly had an idea.'

Harold rejected the idea that his necessary but dear wife looked like a thin clown.

'What idea?' he asked, knocking back the Amontillado Dry.

Evelyn at first continued flickering her eyelids.

'Well,' she said, 'I don't want to meddle. But I suddenly thought of Nesta Pine, well, in connection with – now don't laugh – the Dowson man.'

But Evelyn did, exactly, laugh, tilting back her head, and twiddling the last of her pearls.

'Nesta Pine? Good God! Whatever made you? Nesta Pine!'

He could not join in Evelyn's laughter.

'There!' said Evelyn complacently. 'I knew you'd find it most peculiar, but I'm prepared to persuade you it makes sense.'

Then she sat down, exposing those parts of her which had always been much too thin, but he loved her. Only Harold knew how Evelyn had envied Win Burd her legs.

'Surely Nesta,' Evelyn was arguing, 'deserves in the end a few of the good things of life?'

'But in your opinion Clem Dowson is far from being a good thing.'

'Oh, my *opinion*!' She lowered her eyes. 'What do you care about *my* opinion?'

He was by now too interested to contradict.

'Nesta's too quiet,' he said.

'Isn't *he*?'

'Yes.'

Although the situation was grave she did not seem to notice it. Nor would he have expected her to. It was his concern. He had observed Clem very closely, right down to that ingrown hair which, Matron said, had caused the boil. Matron gave it her Aberdonian squeeze, and Clem stood it. But could he stand the kindliest, the cotton-wooliest intentions of a Nesta Pine?

'She's a jolly good cook,' Evelyn said.

If he allowed her to continue, it was because he had dropped into the habit, from their being together so long. They still slept together, perhaps once a fortnight. He did love her.

'I know,' Evelyn said. 'Because I had lunch with them once when she was with Mrs Boothroyd.'

'I wonder Nesta put up with that old bitch.'

'I don't know that the old thing was such a bitch,' said Evelyn. 'Nesta can be trying, too, in her own way. But it would be different with a man. Anyhow, I was considering her cooking. And that is most important to an elderly man. A nice cook. The digestion is so important.'

'Mm,' said Harold.

'Her mother trained her,' Evelyn said. 'I do feel sorry for Nesta. Once upon a time there was a place for a well-trained, practical, unmarried woman of good family and no income. Today there's simply no call for them – like parlour maids.'

'She did pretty well with the Princess. No cooking in those days.'

Evelyn kicked up her feet and giggled.

'She had it good with the Princess!'

Evelyn loved it. They had been through it all before. After the second sherry Harold, too, quite enjoyed it.

'Lived on the fat of the land,' Evelyn said. 'Many lands!'

She nursed her refilled glass.

'And not a sign of it,' she said.

'You wouldn't expect it,' said Harold. 'Half those Australian women come back looking as though they hadn't been farther than Leura.'

Evelyn smiled, and nodded her head.

'They were related, weren't they? Harold asked. 'Nesta and the Princess?'

'What?' said Evelyn, really angry. 'But you knew Harold, you *knew!*'

It was one of those games they played.

'Nesta Pine and Addie Woolcock were sort of cousins. On the mother's side. Melbourne. Old Mother Woolcock was most determined. Nobody was exactly surprised when Fernandini Lungo jumped at Addie their first season in Europe. A horrid little man, I believe, but he left her alone. Addie was happy with the title, and the Prince with her sausages.'

'I remember about the sausages.'

'Oh, yes. Very popular at one time. There was one variety had bits of tomato mixed with the beef. Horrid,' Evelyn said.

The Fazackerleys sipped their sherry and forgot the spirits it had replaced. They were themselves the spirits of a certain age.

'I should go and get dinner,' Evelyn sighed.

Harold didn't encourage her. Experience had taught him to lose interest in food. Besides, he was filled with his vision of Nesta Pine: a large, white cloudy woman, usually carrying parcels. The parcels hung from her fingers like clusters of brown, bursting fruit. People allowed her to shop for them.

Evelyn was growing dreamier.

'I can see her knitting—' she would have rocked if it had been possible '—in that funny room on top of the sea. Such a comfort. Nesta was always a great knitter. She took to it at school, I seem to remember. None of the girls at Mt. Palmerston liked her much. And I suppose the knitting was some kind of compensation. She used to offer to teach us stitches. It didn't appeal to us at all. Nasty little things we were!'

'I thought you liked Nesta.'

'Oh, but I do! You get to like people like Nesta. Life wouldn't be livable unless.'

'I shan't collaborate in any way.' Harold might have been rejecting a knife.

'I shan't ask you to,' Evelyn said. 'I don't propose to do an awful lot myself. You don't have to push men and women. Only assist nature a little. See they drift together. Mingle.'

She made it look like mist, and the remorselessly unconscious grey fingered coldly at Harold Fazackerley's joints.

While Evelyn sat forward, holding the points of her elbows. Smiling. A more purposeful future had made the lines of her face more distinct.

'Now I must really see about getting our dinner,' she said rather breathlessly.

And went out into the kitchen to open a tin of salmon.

It was the name, obviously, which helped Evelyn see Nesta sitting at the foot of one of the enormous pine trees which grew on the windy side of Mt. Palmerston, or at least the tree had appeared enormous to the girls playing on the slippery needles under foot. The scent, the sound of pine trees haunted Evelyn terribly as soon as she became involved again. She was haunted too, by Nesta. Curiously, though, Nesta seated beneath the tree was not the older girl she had been at school, but the largebreasted woman she had finally become, almost always in grey, straight, knitted dresses. Or twin-sets, with plaid skirts in other greys. Although time had had its way with her face, her hair had remained aggressively black without assistance from the bottle. Beneath the heavily-spiked branches her hair still glowed with startling colours, light accoutred her thickening body with the greyish-brown armour of bark. As she sat, her smile was filtering through her thoughts, rather than directed at a face approaching.

On one occasion, though, in Evelyn's mind, Nesta was wearing her older-girl's hair and body. The other children had drifted away. The long dark fall of hair was gathered at the back of Nesta's head by a thin brown velvet ribbon. Or was it a snood? Evelyn couldn't quite see. Nesta sat holding the knitting-needles as though preparing for a rite.

'Why are you always knitting?' Evelyn asked.

Nesta did not seem to hear, though her broad face was begining to offer itself from behind the web of her private smile. Evelyn noticed the fawn circles, of flannel, or shammy leather, in the whiter face. As Nesta suddenly leaned forward.

'I've only just started,' she said, fluffing out the frill of knitting. 'I haven't decided. It could be for you, Evie,' she said.

She applied the frill to Evelyn's bare, prickling neck.

'I'm not called "Evie",' Evelyn protested.

She was both fascinated and disgusted to see that Nesta's breasts were already almost fully formed. Like milk buns.

So she ran away. Through the scent of resin and the sound of pines. Her own footsteps chasing her over the slippery needles.

'Hold hard!' Harold was protesting from the other bed. 'You're shaking the wall!'

'Ohhh,' she replied. 'I must have been dreaming.'

'Whatever about?' Harold asked from the dry ground of wakefulness.

'I don't know,' she said pitifully. 'Or was it about the Burds and their horrible service station?'

Her neck felt stiff. After a certain age there was really little more rest in sleep than in waking. The great difference, or doubtful advantage, was that in sleep you were planned for, in life you planned.

Whether she had dreamed about the Burds or not, and she was inclined to think she hadn't, Evelyn returned to a plan she was forming: for sending Win the blue dress she was about to discard. After all, it was a nice dress, certainly nothing in gold lamé, but so much wear left in it. Evelyn hadn't told Harold yet. She proposed to enjoy, to embroider her plan a little longer. Over and over again she visualised Win receiving the parcel, fiddling with the knots on a damp-cold morning in Surrey. She saw Win's face, as she remembered it: that of a shrewd goat nibbling at gossip, jabbing seldom, but with skill. Win would be old by now, though. A Nellie Wallace smelling of petrol.

Evelyn shievered on her corrugated bed.

'They're too short,' she grumbled, pulling the sheet up.

'Who?'

Harold could sound so dry at night, and distant, hinting at other allegiances joined in sleep. In the days when they had shared a bed his toe-nails used to make a dry, scraping, almost a tearing sound, as he turned.

'Cheap sheets,' she said bitterly. 'When all the good Egyptian ones wear out we'll have to decide which to sacrifice – our chests, or our feet.'

Harold was escaping her. She turned her head.

'Harold,' she said, 'I was dreaming about Nesta Pine. I suddenly remember.'

Her voice filled the room with the hopelessness, the helplessness of honesty in darkness.

'I thought I ought to tell you,' she said.

He was buzzing. His voice made an attempt, but remained disintegrated.

'Do you think Nesta is a Lesbian?' she asked.

Harold was bundling, scraping the sheet.

'I don't believe there's any such thing. I don't believe it's possible,' he said. He laughed. Evelyn did too.

'They say there are ways and means.' She yawned rather crooked. 'I was only wondering,' she managed between yawns. 'All those women she lived with. Most of them pretty harmless. But Addie Woolcock – the Princess – she was taken to Europe so early. And moved in more unconventional circles. She had the body of a boy. I can remember she had on a dress. Handpainted by a famous artist, they said. A Futurist, I believe he was called. He was a kind of Movement. Well, he had done a hunting scene on Addie's dress. Some goddess or other. If you could fool yourself. They explained it to me. With Addie inside the dress. Like any common mannequin. She enjoyed that sort of thing. And took up with poor old boring Nesta. Who used to make the hotel reservations, and book the tours.'

Evelyn yawned.

'Of course it was only a matter of convenience. And even those who are successful cling to bits of the past.'

The room had filled with thickest darkness. Evelyn Fazackerley would have liked to wash her hot hands. And anoint them with Dreaming Lotus. A nice drink of Alka-Seltzer.

'Are you awake, Harold?'

She slept.

On mornings when she left him to buy their chops and look round David Jones, Harold Fazackerley used to go to the parks, until suspecting that the elderly men seated on benches presented the more negative aspect of retirement. He must get a job, at least a part-time job. Until he made up his mind – strange, when so many had depended so long on his immediate decisions – he sometimes tried staying behind in the flat. He took down a book. Or he simply sat in the creaking silence of shoddy woodwork, in the suffocating silence of Evelyn's blazing blue cushions.

Above the blaze of sea Harold would distinguish Clem Dowson clambering animal-wise amongst the flat rock-plants and combed-out scrub. Or Clem, similarly silent and intent, in the bare room built of silence. There were definitely those who could make use of silence, just as there were those who knew how to use tools. Harold had never made anything with his hands, and silence only used him up.

Half-embarrassed he wondered whether Dowson believed in God. Probably didn't need to. He, Harold, had never needed, or when he had begun faintly to need, was diffident about embarking on a relationship of such large demands.

Instead he took down *War and Peace*, and although appalled by its half-remembered riches, was on several occasions about to begin. On the morning when he came closest, or at least had glanced through the list of characters involved, Evelyn burst in on him with that string bag which tried not to look like a string bag.

'You'll never guess!' Haste and excitement had turned her pale under her complexion. 'I ran into Nesta – Nesta – Pine – in the haberdashery at Jones's. She's living at – oh, some boarding house. She's promised to look in. So, *all that* looks more or less pre-ordained!'

Perhaps it was her happy choice of a word which gave her a look of triumph.

'You don't believe you're going to foist that woman on poor Dowson, do you?'

'Not really,' Evelyn said, and laughed. 'I'm not so presumptuous.'

Then she emptied out of the string bag the reel of silk which had been her morning's mission, and went to put it away.

On the afternoon Nesta looked in on them it was fortunate they weren't away on one of their expeditions. Too vague, or too discreet, she had not been persuaded to choose a date. However, when she did appear, she came in almost with the air of being expected, and when she had arranged her parcels within sight, settled down as though the friendship had been a deeper and unbroken one.

Nesta, stirring her tea, said to Evelyn in that dead quiet voice which some remote part of her released: 'That day you lunched at Mrs Boothroyd's there was quite a little scene after you left.'

Nesta laughed to re-live it in the depths of her inward-looking eyes.

'When you had gone, she said: "Do you think she liked me?" She attached great importance to being liked.'

'Isn't that natural?' Evelyn said. 'To me it's important. Though I don't imagine many people do like me,' she added expectantly.

Nesta continued since she had begun.

'I forget what I said to reassure her. In any case one never could. She started on the pork. You remember we had pork.'

Evelyn did not remember.

'Mrs Boothroyd said: "Anyway, your pork didn't turn out too well. Your crackling. A *cuirass*! When it's usually one of your star turns".'

Harold Fazackerley was about to yawn, but stopped himself, to be incensed.

'Wonder you didn't walk out on her.'

'After all,' said Evelyn, 'it was you who were doing the favour.'

The rather horrid little cakes in paper cups, all she had for Nesta Pine – it was Nesta's fault – looked, she hoped, better than they were.

'Oh, she *needed* me! Nesta protested. 'And when you are needed.'

Evelyn looked up as though she had found the scent again.

Nesta was lighting a cigarette. They had forgotten about Nesta and the cigarettes. She had taken to a pair of tweezers in the days of their fashion, and had continued to smoke her cigarette with tweezers long after the fashion had passed. Evelyn remembered how strangers used to nudge one another as Nesta sat smoking in public places. Always oblivious of her silver tweezers. Now she sat, at a deliberate distance, the tweezers attached by their ring to an index finger, the cigarette slightly quivering, like a hawk on the falconer's wrist. As Nesta, the mistress of her cigarette, sat fastidiously smoking. Quietly absorbed. The smoke flowing, wreathing, through every crevice, it seemed, of her large face, white against white, except where the fawn circles round the eyes broke or emphasised the scheme.

Evelyn looked at Harold. She was so delighted with the apparition she had conjured up.

'How wonderful to be needed,' she said. 'Not only by Mrs Boothroyd. By all of them.'

Nesta looked as though Evelyn might have gone too far, but did not deny that ministering to the needs of others was her profession. She continued smoking. Only the cigarette quivered slightly at the end of the little silver tweezers.

'Even by the Princess,' Evelyn persisted.

Nesta's stomach rumbled from its distance.

'Addie didn't need anybody,' she said. 'But imagined she did from time to time.'

Harold should have felt sorrier for this large woman, all in black, whose hips were filling the narrow scuttle of a creaking rosewood chair. But Nesta's turnip flesh had not craved for sympathy.

'To imagine you need somebody is surely the same thing as to need.' The frills of the property cakes twitched as Evelyn manipulated them. 'And Addie was so fond of you besides.'

Then Nesta released her half-smoked cigarette from the silver tweezers. She got up. She was turning, searching for her only too obvious heap of parcels so that at moments she presented her broad black hips, at others her full white, goitrous throat. Evelyn could not remember ever having seen Nesta in black.

'She was not fond.' Nesta wrenched it out. 'I irritated. I irritated Addie.'

Her throat was swallowing, her white cheeks were munching on the words, as she quickly bound her fingers to the parcels with the string which cut.

Harold did not want to look.

Evelyn was made so nervous she laughed.

'That too,' she giggled, 'can be a kind of necessity. Perhaps Addie needed someone to irritate her.'

Nesta was again composed. She stood smiling for the long comforter life had knitted, unevenly, but acceptably enough.

'Next time you come,' Evelyn said, 'you must warn us, and we shall be better prepared.'

She rubbed her cheek against Nesta's for an instant, as though ratifying something secret.

Evelyn was glowing, Harold saw, when they were alone.

'Next time I won't be caught,' he said.

Evelyn was laughing in little chugging bursts.

'Don't be silly, Harold dear. Dowson isn't a rabbit. And you see what a victim poor Nesta's always been.'

'You wouldn't do it!'

'No! No! No!' She threw back her head. 'Hasn't Dowson a will of his own? No man is *compelled*.'

She was looking at her husband whom she needed as much as any of those women had needed Nesta Pine. She could feel herself perspiring round the eyes.

'Not compelled,' Harold was saying. 'Compulson is easier to resist.'

Unlike smoke. Smoke would drift in, suffocatingly at times, where the windows stood innocently open.

'You forget,' he said, 'that Addie Woolcock, on at least two known occasions, slashed her own wrists.'

'Addie – what?' Evelyn was horrified. Then she mumbled: 'Well – I did, I suppose. I'd forgotten.'

To Evelyn Fazackerley, suicide, even of the half-hearted kind, was one of the great immoralities. Why, murder was more pardonable; murder showed guts.

'But all this,' she said, 'is beside the point and my few harmless words.'

'All right, darling!' he said, laughingly kissing her.

She was reassured by his moustache.

That night while cleaning her teeth she called across the expanse of their intimate flat:

'I do remember now about Addie – on one of the occasions. They said she did it with a little mother o'pearl penknife which had been a present from somebody. There was a picture of her in one of the papers, waving from the deck of a liner, leaving Southampton. There was a bandage round her wrist, under the bracelets. Nesta had come back. She was standing beside her.'

Evelyn had cut some remarkably thin, for once remarkably professional, cucumber sandwiches. When not too wet, they tasted so cool and refined. There was also one of those old-fashioned tea-cakes, extravagant with melted butter, made by Evelyn, as well as a really expensive Viennese *Torte*, which she had brought in, and admitted to it. She couldn't apologise enough for not having made the *Torte*.

Evelyn did the talking. Harold looked for the most part coerced, and began at once to get indigestion from the cucumber. Dowson and Nesta Pine addressed their hosts from time to time, and once Miss Pine, through these intermediaries, her fellow-guest.

'Does Mr Dowson know,' she asked, averting her face, lowering her beige eyelids, 'does he know, living as he does in an exposed position, that geraniums stand up to wind better than pelargoniums?'

Dowson moved, and moaned, it sounded – low, however.

Nesta Pine blew the smoke through her nose.

'Pelargoniums,' she said, 'are far too brittle.'

But Evelyn did not allow any more. Everyone should remain in character. She was doing her virtuoso stuff, and on such occasions Harold Fazackerley couldn't help admiring his wife.

'The little exquisite flowers of the Dolomites' – they made her close her eyes as though in exquisite pain – 'the year we went there on leave from Egypt. One felt frustrated, not being able to transplant such masses of vivid, but *pure*, colour. Fatal in Egypt. Australia would be almost as bad. Almost all alpine flowers wither up in the Australian sun.' Acceptance of the fact made it appear, if anything, more brutal. 'Mr Dowson,' she said, 'I shan't *force*, but *suggest*, another piece of this soggy tea-cake. Of course I'm not an expert cook.' Here she glanced at Nesta. 'But get away with it at times. And know what men like. Unless Harold is chivalrous. Or dishonest.'

Dowson had dressed himself up in clothes which did not belong to his body, but which were obviously his best. He looked orange inside them, except for his eyes, which might have blazed if they hadn't been so innocent.

They were so intensely blue, it was this, probably, which prevented Nesta looking at them.

She had been persuaded to take off her hat, and was sitting the coils and mats of dark, fern-root hair, the brooding, shammy-leather eyelids, separated from the rest of her by a vagary of smoke from her fastidiously held cigarette. Today she was dressed in grey. To Evelyn's satisfaction. Grey was in keeping.

But Harold would have felt uneasy even without cucumber. He wished he was alone, like Clem Dowson knew how to be.

Dowson sat with his thick fingers stacked together, the orange tufts visible on the backs of them.

Then Evelyn Fazackerley, drawing down her mouth, asked: 'And what have you been doing with yourself lately, Mr Dowson?'

Because she had felt the thread of continuity sagging.

Dowson hoisted himself up and replied: 'As a matter of fact, I've been making cumquat jam.'

Suddenly Nesta Pine was writhing, yes, writhing, in Harold's mother's rosewood chair, which she had continued to favour although it was scarcely able to contain her.

'Not cumquat?' she rasped.

Evelyn had forgotten Nesta's eyes. They were topaz colour, glistening, even glittering.

'I have had failures with cumquat,' Nesta gasped.

The Fazackerley's realised Nesta Pine and Clem Dowson were addressing each other directly, as well as publicly.

'I almost always burn it,' Nesta was confessing.

'Not if you throw in three two-shilling pieces.'

'Ah!' She breathed out smoke. 'If you can remember. My Aunt Mildred Todhunter taught me the trick with the two-shilling pieces.'

Then they sat looking at each other a while. When they realised they were being observed, they composed their clothes. Nesta's cigarette-tweezers ejected the extinct butt. Dowson's eyes dispensed with practically the entire room.

The chill had come too soon into a hitherto humid day.

Evelyn was saying: 'Of all the things these Egyptian devils think of, the submerging of temples is the most difficult to accept.'

Evelyn allowed several weeks to elapse before sitting down to a letter she had spent most of that time composing.

She wrote:

*Dear Mr. Dowson,*
   *To my mind, we who have reached a certain age are very dependent on our friends, and should foregather more frequently under the roof-tree—*

she paused to admire it

   *—of one or another of us. Actually, I am writing to suggest you come here to a little informal lunch—*

those she feared and admired would have written 'luncheon', but on giving it thought she rejected the word on psychological grounds

   *—if the prospect of deserting your beloved house and planned routine does not altogether bore you . . .*

'What are you doing, Evelyn?' Harold asked.

'Writing a letter.'

He did not enquire further because he knew.

Evelyn was disgusted on receiving no reply to her letter, while telling herself it was foolish to expect civilities from anyone so uncouth.

When a note arrived:

*Dear Madam,*
   *I am writing for Mr. Dowson who is sick. I go there Tuesdays for the ironing and he asked me to write the letter. He is real sick. It is his heart sort of. They say he will reoover and he will, because he is not going not to. I am only writing because he asked me and you are a person he respect. But he does not want you or anyone else to come. It is such a long way.*

*Your sincerely,*
E. PERRY (*Mrs.*)

Evelyn said: 'Dowson is seriously ill. His heart.'

Poor old Clem,' said Harold, working his knuckles. 'We'd better go down to him.'

'No,' she said. 'That kind of man, when sick, can't bear people pouring in. But he's got to eat. To live. Perhaps I could take him something.'

They both saw him trussed on the bed of sickness in that house of the winds. So Harold agreed. Evelyn was, after all, the woman.

She bought a boiler, and took the soup in a little billy-can which slopped over on her blue skirt in the bus. It was in the best cause, she had to remind herself all the way down that road as her heels went over on the stones.

The gangway through the wind, down the side of the cliff, over the passive succulents and nervous, wiry clumps of thyme, led her at last to a still house. In the kitchen she heard the drip of a tap, and regretted Harold's absence. The egg-boiling invention stood out far too sculpturally.

And Clem Dowson lying on his bed. He opened his eyes very briefly but distinctly under the orange brows.

He said: 'I didn't expect anybody.'

The wind off the sea howled amongst the mauve-fleshed rock-plants.

Her hair no doubt was looking terrible.

'But we can't *desert* you. Look, I've brought you some good nourishing soup.'

He did not look, however. He had resumed lying with his eyes closed, probably one of those men who sulk when they are ill, and must be wooed.

'Would you like me to warm some up?'

'No,' he said.

'Well, then,' she said, her charity refusing to be extinguished, 'I'll put it in the refrigerator, and you can take some when you feel inclined.'

She went back into the kitchen, which she knew well enough by now. It was the bedroom she longed to examine. On the first occasion its owner had not taken them there.

The refrigerator was neither too well nor too poorly stocked. Evelyn stood her soup amongst the usual necessities after pouring it into a bowl. There was a fish pudding, she noticed, then, of rather too professional a texture, delved into, as you might have expected by a sick, clumsy man.

'That looks a jolly appetising fish pudding,' she said on returning with her brightness to the bedroom. 'It looks so light. And such a creamy sauce. I expect your Mrs Perry, who wrote to us, made you that, didn't she?'

Dowson blew down his nose.

'Never cooked anything eatable in her life. Judging by what she brings me to try.'

He spoke with such vehemence Evelyn found it hard to believe he was seriously ill.

'No,' he said. 'Miss Pine brought the pudding,' he said.

'*Ohhh?*'

She was quite put out. But as she had started the thing it was logical to follow it through.

'I am so glad you have found something in common,' she said. 'Food, anyway. Most important. Nesta,' she said, 'is such an excellent person. So reliable.'

As she sat on her upright, hospital-visitor's chair, intent on her wedding and engagement rings, she heard herself sound as though recommending a brand of goods from a store.

'Miss Pine's all right,' said Dowson, his eyes still closed, his nose swivelling to escape a non-existent fly.

Evelyn Fazackerley could imagine Nesta's visit. She could hear their joint silence. Yet, why should it not seem natural? Mushrooms congregate. And spawn together. Horrid expression.

In her unbalance and distaste she glanced round the room, which she had looked forward to exploring before this unpleasant discovery. Pathetic the inner rooms of solitary males. Chaster even than the cupboards of elderly virgin women. The darning egg, naked today. An almost used up carpenter's pencil. Saved string, wound in impeccable hanks. A kerosene lamp, with opalescent shade, still in use. *The Conquest of Peru*. A pair of mittens which on winter mornings by the sea would half-cover the raw, the knotty hands of Dowson.

The name, she saw, could have been carved into him by a knife.

Then he opened his eyes, and looked at her, and said: 'Miss Pine is a good sort.'

Evelyn Fazackerley sat moistening her lips. She had intended to offer to take on the mending. Instead she coughed and looked at her watch.

'I mustn't forget my bus.'

On the way back through the kitchen to collect her billy she reopened the refrigerator door, and gouged out with her index finger a little of Nesta's fish pudding. It tasted most delicate, faintly flavoured with something she couldn't identify.

She went back into the bedroom and took him by that meaty hand.

'O, Clem, dear' – she had never called him by his first name before – 'Harold and I would do anything for you – *anything* – for the sake of old times – if only you would tell us.'

Dowson half-smiled – he might have been falling asleep – turning his face to the wall, which had been washed a flat white.

She left him then, with the suspicion that she was the innocent one. As she stumbled back along the unmade road the forms of the yellow furniture remained solidly with her, together with the knowledge that on neither occasion had she managed to unlock anything in that ostensibly open house, and that she had felt not the slightest recognition in his hand.

Evelyn put off telling Harold about Nesta Pine's visit to Dowson, and soon it was rather too late to tell. She waited instead for Nesta to give some shape to her intentions. The rules of friendship demanded it. But Nesta did not come. She has used us just enough, Evelyn began to see, and now that she has met this man she is off to the races on the sly. Well, if she wished to humiliate herself. The mystery of the woman's face, behind the smoke, the uneven powder and web of sentimental loyalties, or of the precociously mature girl in the ugly Mt Palmerston tunic, knitting up wool at the foot of the armoured tree, was a mystery no longer; it was the expression of congenital cunning.

On an incongruous occasion – but the whole business was incongrous – Evelyn Fazackerley allowed herself a vision of the elderly Nesta in one of the more convulsive attitudes of love: a great jack-knife of sprung flesh, the saucered rump, breasts heaving and plopping like a pot of porridge come to the boil.

'How revolting!' she said out loud.

And her breath snapped back elastically.

Harold Fazackerley turned from the urgent operations of a gang of men tunnelling into a mountainside, towards the state of rapt unreality his wife had trailed with her into the open, out of their neo-Tudor cocoon. For the Fazackerleys were off on one of their 'jaunts', as Evelyn used to refer to them. They were doing the Snowy Scheme by coach.

'What is revolting?' Harold shouted.

Competing against a passage for men's raised voices and splitting rock, he sounded angrier than normally.

'I forgot to tell you,' Evelyn shouted back, at the same time looking over her shoulder to see whether she could trust the landscape, 'the day I went down to Dowson, I found that Nesta had taken him a fish – a fish *pudding!*'

She had eaten off her lipstick, and her lips looked pale. For an isolated moment Harold Fazackerley would have liked not to have been married to his wife.

'I often wonder, Evelyn,' he continued shouting, his voice as wobbly as an old man's, 'how you ever experience anything fresh for remembering what has happened already.'

But the drills, he realised, were silent, and he regretted his voice, his crankiness.

That night at the hotel he ordered a bottle of claret to accompany their not so mixed grill. To make a little occasion.

'Well, it isn't much chop, is it?' he apologised. 'None of it!'

'What did you expect?'

She smiled at him out of the worldliness which had returned to her with a change of dress. Glancing round the room at the other couples, thin and fat, moist and dry, their fellow-passengers from the coach, she tried to create the impression that she and Harold at their own little table – she always insisted on their own table – were brilliant lovers who had sailed the Nile.

When he shattered her attempt.

'That fish pudding of Nesta's,' he said, 'I wonder if it was any good.'

Her mouth, blossoming again with the glamour of their past, wilted abruptly on her face.

Then she said: 'Actually, I did taste it, and have to admit, it wasn't at all bad.'

At least it cracked the ice which had frozen her relationship with Nesta Pine and Clem Dowson. She began to refer to them again. Both during what she remembered as 'that *ghastly* trip', and after, Evelyn found she was able to make jokes at her own expense, especially with the assistance of the fish pudding, the soft white ludicrous substance of which clogged Nesta's cunning and diminished its power.

With melancholy reserve Harold talked about going down to see 'poor old Clem'. Evelyn said yes they must, both of them, it was their duty, however touchy and impatient his illness might have made him. But they were overcome by a paralysis. They would go when it was cooler, warmer, or when the patient would be sufficiently recovered to enjoy their visit. They did not go. That woman, that Mrs Perry, Evelyn said, no doubt came in to do for him, and sounded an excellent person.

Their debate might have continued if Harold hadn't received Clem's letter:

*Dear Harold,*

*This is to let you know Nesta Pine and I decided to make a go of it. We were married last month. We came straight home, because we both felt, at our age, it would have looked foolish to trip off somewhere on a honeymoon. Our habits have formed, I shan't go as far as to say 'set'! Neither of us expects too much.*

*You know I have never been a great hand at expressing myself, Harold, but can't let this opportunity pass without wondering how different it might have been if we had met more often – or if we hadn't met in the beginning. I suppose I have always been most influenced by what can never be contained. The sea, for instance. As for the human relationships of any importance, what is left of them after they have been sieved through words?*

*Funny sort of letter, I can hear you say! But you can forget about it, and next time we meet, nothing will be changed.*

*Miss Pine –* he had crossed it out *– Nesta, sends her regards to your wife, for whom she seems to have a deep affection.* . . .

If the Fazackerleys weren't stunned, at least their ears rang.

'How grotesque!' said Evelyn.

She kept returning to the letter, as though in search of a window through which she might catch sight of recognisable attitudes. It *was* grotesque. If she did not say 'obscene', that would have been going too far. When she herself was, however innocently, involved. For Evelyn Fazackerley affection meant something, not exactly material, but demonstrable. And Nesta Pine, of cloudy features and brooding breasts, had begun to demonstrate. She was reaching out a shade farther, from under the giant trees, offering the frill of grey knitting. Evelyn wondered, poundingly, how she felt about it. But she would not allow herself for long, or not after her skin began to prickle. As in childhood she was again running away, over the slippery needles, back into the living-room.

'I don't know *what* they "expect",' she said, hitting the letter and laughing hoarsely. 'Only they *may* find,' she added hopefully, 'that it is more than they imagined. Most people do.'

But Harold Fazackerley had become a sieve through which the words ran like water, and experience, or more specifically, that which has not been experienced. The little boy crying in the fetor of disinfected latrines. *What's up, young Fazack?* The square, warty hand gently thumping his sorrows. *Nothing.* Then the exquisite bliss even of maggots seething through the dusk and urine-sodden sawdust. The wind at sea, scouring the skin, sweeping out all but the farthest corners of the mind. The burning-glass of a blue eye. The stationary question-mark of a white ibis amongst the papyrus. Dreams and prophecies beating on jerry-built pitch-pine doors.

But of course the implications of the letter with which he was vibrating as he sat in his appointed box, were also the tremblings, the thunderings of age.

They were all, not what you would call old, but elderly, when, not so very long afterwards, the Fazackerleys were summoned to the house on the cliff. (*They couldn't very well avoid it*, as Evelyn put it.) They were all either scraggy or bulging. Clothes of a past elegance and cut hung too loosely on the scraggy ones. Whereas Clem, as well as Nesta Dowson (yes, Dowson) appeared stuffed inside what should have been the appropriate loose, practical garments.

The Dowsons were terribly alike, and unlike, Evelyn saw.

What Harold saw he wasn't sure, beyond the sea still blazing through the windows. The wind blowing, of course. Through the windows of the Dowson's house the wind was always visible.

The Fazackerleys had been invited to a cup of tea.

'I must say, Harold, it's pretty mean of Nesta, considering she's such a dab at cooking.'

'Perhaps it didn't suit Clem. Nesta's not the only one – not now – to be considered.'

'Oh, Clem!' Evelyn's head might have been mounted on ball bearings. 'She's a fool if she doesn't make a stand.'

The Fazackerleys had taken them a plated toast-rack, though Evelyn was afraid it might shame them to receive a present after their neglect and deceit.

Anyway, there they all were, cups precariously positioned, bread-and-butter plates balanced uncomfortably. Evelyn noticed the crockery was no longer Clem's common white, but a service Nesta had most probably inherited from one of the old ladies, her mother, or even Mrs Boothroyd.

The light touched the rather delicate cups and turned them into transparent eggshell from which the life was still only half-blown.

Harold's cup was rattling in its saucer. The wind was rattling the loose-fitting windows.

'Oh, what a lovely little brooch!' Evelyn's voice could not resist pouncing.

For Nesta had pinned a little bunch of mosaic flowers, most vivid on its black marble background, against the grey jumper of her twin-set, below the thick white goitre of her throat. Certainly not a wedding present. Evelyn could not visualise that man's meaty hands offering anything Italianate.

'Is it something the Princess – did she leave it to you?' she asked.

'Oh, no!' Nesta, lowering those beige eyelids, sounded shocked. 'Addie had nothing Italian to leave. She only *wore* the jewels. They belonged to the Fernandini Lungos. Besides,' she said, softening the rest of her reply, 'this little brooch is of no importance. Something I picked up. A souvenir shop. On the Ponte Vecchio.'

Her hands were suddenly too full of china.

'But it is pretty,' she apologised.

'Lovely,' Evelyn emphasised, though there was no cause for further interest.

There was no reason why she should feel screwed-up inside. The incident was far too trivial. Nesta herself had admitted to the ordinariness of her brooch while correcting a mistake anybody might have made. But Evelyn could have screamed for her gaffe – if any of those present would have known how to slap her.

Nesta broke one of the inherited cups. Her distress froze her above it a fraction too long, in an attitude of knock-knees. She was wearing grey ribbed stockings, no doubt knitted by herself. Her legs, beneath the shaggy skirt, looked like those of a born misfit on the hockey field.

'That was very clumsy of you,' Dowson complained.

(During the whole afternoon he did not once call her by name.)

'But you know I am clumsy,' she said, well, clumsily.

As he got down on his knees, on the boards, he was behaving as though the cup had been his, not his wife's. Watching the hands deal with the fragments, Harold was again reminded of the maggie's egg Clem had blown for him when they were boys.

'Don't forget – in the bin for the dump,' Dowson warned. 'We have three bins,' he was explaining to guests, 'one for the dump, one for the compost, and a third for the incinerator.'

Then they were silent for a little, except for the slither and chatter of the remains of Nesta's cup, as she swept them into, presumably, the right bin.

That afternoon Nesta made no attempt to smoke. She brought out her knitting instead, and as she coaxed the grey, or faintly sage, feelers of wool, it provided something of the same effect.

Dowson sat frowning, listening perhaps to the sound of the needles. They were both listening.

Evelyn felt herself drowning in a situation the shore of which was concealed from her.

Battered by her ear-rings, she turned towards the view, and began in her high, light, deliberately superficial voice: 'How perfectly *marvellous* the sunsets must look from up here. Out to sea.'

Dowson cleared his throat.

'The sun sets in the west, the other side of the ridge.'

Nesta was smiling rather painfully at her knitting.

'We watch the sun*rise*,' she said, 'most mornings. That is wonderful.'

'You must be early risers!' Evelyn gobbled her reply, turning annoyance with herself into a comic disapproval of others.

'Oh, yes. We are up early,' said Nesta, with a proud inclination of her head. 'Both of us.'

Dowson got up. He moved away from his wife, and stood by the window looking out. The sun had already abandoned the sea for a world the other side of the ridge, leaving a distillation of perfectly white light on the corrugated water.

The Fazackerleys were left to listen to Nesta's knitting-needles, the sound of which she accompanied with her head and a just visible motion of her pale lips. For Evelyn who had always hated, not to say feared, the silences in empty rooms, the sound of the bone needles was another kind of silence, and she began to gather herself and Harold.

They looked back. It was extraordinary to see the Dowsons standing *together*, at the gate below road level, in the drained evening light.

Harold and Evelyn did not speak on the way home, blaming it on the sea air.

Evelyn should have written a letter of thanks on the thick white note-paper which was one of her extravagances. She was expert at such letters, dashing them off in a gallant hand. But this time she hesitated. It was the arthritis in her thumb.

Although she had never received more than one or two letters from Nesta, she recognised this one immediately it came, and saved it up till Harold should return. Then when he did, she thought better of it, and kept the letter until she was again alone.

*Dear Evelyn,*
[Evelyn herself would have written *Dearest.*]

*I don't know why I am writing except to say how fond I am of you. Clem is fond of you, I believe, but would never admit. Neither of us says much, which is the strangest part of it — for I have lived with peacocks all my life!*

*Most people do not know the peacock also redeems. I began to realise when we visited that church above Salonika — or convent was it? — so deserted we could not decide — when the evening was suddenly filled with silent peacocks — never before had I seen them in the air — then settling to roost, their tails turned to branches of cedar.*

*Clem, I think, does not believe in redemption because he has no need of it. His eyes are perfectly clear. You couldn't flaw them in competition with a crystal. Although he and I are in so many ways the same, there we differ.*

*Well, my poor Evelyn, you did not see the sunset! Let me tell you it mostly shrieks with the throats of peacocks — though sometimes it will open its veins, offering its blood from love rather than charity.*

NESTA PINE.

The signature alone was a hammer blow to Evelyn Fazackerley. She did not know what to do with Nesta's letter. If there had been an open fire she could have reduced the thing immediately. In the absence of one, she put the letter in a box, and there it burned, but continued burning.

Evelyn had never been so frightened. The dreadful part was: she would never be able to tell Harold, she had never told him anything, nothing of importance. If it had been possible to ring the police, or better still, the fire brigade, they might have carried her down out of her panic. But it was not possible, in spite of the telephone book, and the numbers she had drawn circles round. Instead of the clangour of approaching engines, what she had to listen to was the frightened clapper of her dry heart.

Harold came in only to say: 'See somebody about my back. At our age I suppose we must expect a certain number of aches.'

He sat pinching up the skin on the backs of his hands.

'Although I have rung the last three mornings,' Evelyn said, looking at the ridges of his blue skin, 'the Gas Company doesn't seem to realise it is under obligation.'

She continued watching the hands with which she had been familiar.

'Harold? It's the front left burner. If only you were handier.'

Harold said – at times he sounded like leather: 'Ought to send for old Clem Dowson. Clem could fix it.'

She shied away from what was less easy to avoid on a morning in one of the canyons progress had worn into their city. She would not be allowed, it seemed, to sidestep the Dowsons. Though it was only Clem present in the flesh. Under his coat he was wearing one of those tweed waistcoats she had not noticed for years. At least it gave her a certain advantage. And the face. Something had been subtracted from it.

'You're the last person, Clem, I'd imagine meeting in the city,' Evelyn said in the rakish voice she put on for masculine but harmless men.

He mumbled about his solicitor. Or was it Nesta's solicitor.

'I must tell you,' she said. 'I am so happy to know Nesta is in your hands.' She looked away from them at once, however, the red fingers plaited helplessly against the tweed waistcoat. 'Poor Nesta has made so many homes for others, to say nothing of the suitcase life she led round Europe with Addie Woolcock, it's a joy to see her make a home of her own.'

It was a neat, even pretty touch, and Evelyn felt she could be proud of it.

'She didn't make it. The home was there already,' said Dowson.

'But a woman adds those little touches.'

A wind, not the one which rocked the houses on the cliff, had sprung up the concrete canyon, and was creaking between them.

'She was not that kind of woman,' he said. 'No frills. Just as I'm not the kind of man who enjoys a fuss.'

'It has turned out perfectly! I'm so relieved.' Evelyn was glad to be sincere.

Till realising Dowson had related Nesta to the past. She got the gooseflesh then.

Dowson's lips seemed to reach out, the tendons were stretched like wire in the contraption of his neck. He was like, she saw, one of his own inventions, or a piece of that disturbing modern sculpture. A piece which moved, without escaping by its own motion.

'Nesta is ill,' he was saying.

His lips still reaching for words under the bristly orange moustache gave the whole situation a permanent look.

She was the one who must make an attempt.

'There is so much sickness about,' she agreed. 'The virus 'flu. What did we suffer from, I sometimes wonder, before they discovered the viruses? The wind,' she said, casting down her eyes, 'is so treacherous at this time of the year to anybody in any way bronchial.'

'She couldn't remember whether Nesta was. But she gave a cough for all those who were bronchially afflicted. While sympathising, she was determined to keep her sympathy general. She wouldn't look at Dowson's fixed, watery eye.

'What I would like you to understand—' he was begging for something '—Nesta herself asked to go into the home. For treatment. The treatment alone must be hellish. I would never have put her there – not otherwise – although we had the argument on the way to the pit – she'd put the pieces in the wrong bin. That, I suppose, was the last touch. For both of us. Both too conscientious. And quiet. Two silences, you know, can cut each other in the end.'

Again she was staring at his hands. He was not peacock enough to have thought of slashing his wrists. He was suffering instead in some more corrosive, subterranean way.

'I am so – so – sorry,' Evelyn said. 'Which hospital – home is it?'

He told her the name. Which she would forget. In fact, she had already forgotten.

If only Harold had been there. Harold was useless in a crisis, but somehow gave her the power to act more brilliantly.

As for Dowson, his grief, remorse, whatever it was, had grown embarrassing in its crude importunity. The rims of his eyes might have been touched up, to glitter as they did, with such an intensity of raw red.

As there was nothing she could do, Evelyn left him. She trod very softly down the street, as though it were carpeted, as though all the doors were locked, as though the unfortunate, though fortunately helpless patients were sitting the other side, listening, in their trussed or shocked condition, for further reprisals.

When she got in she announced: 'I met Dowson. Nesta is suffering from some kind of nervous collapse. She is in the – he told me the name, but I forget.'

She gabbled it, not to make it unintelligible, but to get it over.

Harold, who was usually astounded, wasn't.

'Don't you think it odd?' she asked when she could bear it no longer.

'No,' he said slowly. 'I suppose not.'

'I hope you are right,' Evelyn said. 'So many people have breakdowns today. It's the strain we live under – always the threat of war – the pace,' she said, 'and no servants.'

Harold sat pinching up his skin.

'Dowson himself,' she said, 'had that breakdown, when they dropped him off in Egypt.'

It was about this time that Harold Fazackerley took to going farther afield, on his own, without telling Evelyn where. Perhaps if she hadn't had a fright she might have grown peevish, cross-questioned him, wondered whether he had started a mistress. Because she had had the fright and didn't want another, she kept quiet. So Harold was able, for the time being, to make these solitary expeditions. He would turn up on deserted parts of the coast, amongst rocks and lantana. Once he came across a rubbish dump and got his breath back sitting in a burst armchair on the edge of a gully. He was greatly moved by the many liberated objects he discovered, in particular a broken music-box from an age of more elegant subterfuges. Sometimes sunsets overtook him, and their impersonal rage did him good.

None of it meant there was any question of his being disloyal to Evelyn. She was his wife. If long association had turned that into an abstract term, it had not prevented the abstract from eating in as unwaveringly as iron.

He was attracted also to those iron-coloured evenings which bring out the steel and oyster tones in the sea. He was drawn to the wind which swells a sea while coldly slicing the flesh off human bones. With motion not direction his motive, he liked to take a ferry in the late afternoon. The wind-infested waters of the harbour matched his grey, subaqueous thoughts. Nor would any other mind intrude. Of the race of ferry passengers, one half was too dedicated to its respectability and evening papers, the other sidled instinctively after those it recognised as fellow rakes.

Often as an older man Harold Fazackerley had been embarrassingly told he was 'distinguished-looking'. If he had been less conscious of his inadequacies, he might have basked in the flattery of it. As things were, he had to laught it off. There was even a tract of disgust in the gesture of protest with which he drew the no longer fashionable overcoat of English tweed closer to his 'distinguished' figure. The mannerism became finally a tic, which would break out on his solitariness, as on the afternoon when, without any reason, he remembered the ridiculous tweezers Nesta Pine had used for holding her cigarette.

He was standing alone on the deck of the plunging ferry, above waves drained of their normally extrovert colours. It was too blustery, too rough, for the majority. They preferred to huddle, coddling their mushroom skins behind glass. Some of them had evidently looked to drink for additional protection. The only other venturesome or possessed human being besides Harold Fazackerley himself was hanging over the rail at the bows. This large, spread character, staring monotonously at the waves, was probably bilious, Harold decided, until, as he passed behind the leaning figure, he realised they were responding in much the same way to the motion of the ferry, that they were sharing the smell of ships at sea, and that the stranger was no stranger, but his friend Dowson.

Dowson looked round. He was dishevelled by the head-on wind, but not drunk. Like a schoolboy he had rolled up his hat and crammed it into the pocket of his coat, which was straining to break free of the single button holding it. His fiery stubble stared in the blast. His mouth looked loose, from the draughts of air he must have swallowed.

The meeting was too unexpected. Harold would not have chosen it. In spite of his long, and delicately intimate relationship with Dowson, he could not think how to open a convincing conversation.

'I've been over to see my wife,' Dowson plunged straight in, as though he had been waiting for the opportunity to tell.

'She must have been pleased,' Harold said, and at once heard how fatuous it sounded.

'I don't think she was,' said Dowson. 'She was in a pretty bad temper. And she never used to be bad-tempered. That was one of the things we were up against. But today she was, I won't say – spiteful. She kept complaining about the screech of peacocks. Of course the traffic does make a hell of a noise out there. And to anyone in her condition. She must have meant the traffic.'

Harold Fazackerley would have liked to enquire into the peacocks, if only of his own mind, but this wasn't the time. What he did understand was that Dowson had shrivelled inside his indestructible body. It was a shocking discovery, the more so because he could feel himself the stronger for it.

Such a state of affairs would, he hoped, have become repulsive if it hadn't been so temporary. Dowson, or the genius of his fleshy body, had decided to resume the wrestling match. He who had turned round to face an accusation, locking his arms through the rail, exposing his chest, his belly, to whatever thrust, his unguarded face to the fist, had heaved himself back in the direction they were headed. And at that moment the sun struck, slashing the smudgy drifts of cloud, opening the underbelly of the waves, so that the peacock-colours rose again in shrill display out of the depths.

'My God –' Dowson was gasping and mouthing '– one day, Harold, when we meet – in different circumstances – I must try to tell you all I have experienced.' He was speaking from behind closed eyes. 'That was the trouble between us. Between myself and that woman. We had each lived at the same level. It was too great shock to discover there was someone who could read your thoughts.'

Harold Fazackerley did not look but knew the tears were running from under the red, scaly eyelids, the orange, salt-encrusted brows.

'That put an end to what should never have happened in the first place.'

Soon after, they were received into a calm, into a striped marquee of light. Passengers were walking up the gangways of gently swaying matchwood. Somewhere a brass band was rather tackily playing.

Habit made the two men shake hands. One of them went on, to catch the bus, to the house which was ostensibly his, the other returning in the same ferry, as he could not remember having any further plan.

Harold began by not mentioning he had met Dowson on the ferry, and once he had begun, it was easy enough not to mention; it was his own very private experience.

'Have a good walk?' Evelyn asked on his return, and bit through the silk with which she had just threaded the needle.

Needlework had been considered one of her accomplishments as a girl, but she had soon put away something which might have made others doubt her capacity for sophistication. Until latterly, in what she was amused to refer to as her 'old age', she would start, half-ironic, half-nostalgic, some piece of elaborate embroidery to occupy herself on occasions of neglect.

Seeing his wife at her work Harold felt appropriately guilty. All that evening his eye was on her needle rather than on what he was trying to read. He would have liked to be able to talk to her, but couldn't. At least winter was not far off, when they were due to leave for Cairns.

The following evening he bought her a bunch of roses.

'Oh, dearest, how *sweet!*' Evelyn said with a spontaneity which overlooked the fact that the roses were mostly leaf and rather bruised.

Harold grew guiltier than ever on seeing he had chosen such a bad bunch, and to realise he had been swindled again.

He had also brought her the evening newspaper.

'I don't know why we waste our money,' Evelyn Fazackerley always said.

But she read the evening papers. She liked to look at the horoscope, 'just for fun', and she enjoyed – you couldn't say 'enjoyed' because it would have sounded too sick – it was because she took an interest in the 'quirks of human nature' that she read, or at least glanced through, the murders.

'Any good murders tonight?' Harold asked as a matter of course.

'No,' she said. 'Murderers,' she said, in that voice she used to put on to make them laugh on board ship, 'murderers are running out of ideas.'

When Evelyn's paper began to rustle.

'Harold,' she said, 'Clem – Clem Dowson is dead.'

It ripped into Harold Fazackerley.

'What?' he said stupidly. 'How – *Clem?*'

'An accident – it appears,' said Evelyn, holding the paper as far away from her as possible. 'How shocking!'

She was determined to make it anybody's death, and Harold should have felt grateful.

' "Clement Perrotet Dowson," ' Evelyn read aloud, ' "walking from the direction of the ferry, was struck down by a bus yesterday evening and instantly killed . . ." '

But the muted voice did not save Harold from it.

'Instantly! What a mercy!' Evelyn said.

It was incredible to him the strength some women had, or the convention they obeyed, which could transform an apocalypse into a platitude.

'Apparently,' said Evelyn, still dealing with it, 'the driver put on his brakes, and at least two pedestrians tried to prevent poor – Clem, who didn't seem to realise. Apparently — ' she clung to the word she had recently discovered – 'he walked on, stumbled, they say, and fell under the bus.'

She put the paper away.

'Crushed!'

'Did they write "crushed"?' Harold asked.

Because he wanted to visualise Clem's great fiery head, glaring, blaring its final illumination, not rubbed out like a rotten melon on the tarred road.

'No,' said Evelyn. 'Not precisely.'

The walls of the flat were threatening them.

'Oh dear, the poor man, what can we do?' Evelyn protested.

She was wiping her hands on the little guest towel she had been embroidering so exquisitely.

'Is there any family?' she asked.

'I don't know.'

Evelyn was desolate, because who would break it to Nesta, in the cell to which her absence of vocation had withdrawn her.

' "Perrotet" ,' Evelyn said. 'Did you know, Harold, that he was called "Perrotet"?'

It was the hour when night began to take over in foreign tongues.

'Harold?'

Harold had not known, nor did they hear how Clem Dowson's remains were tidied up.

Or not until Evelyn received a note from the Perry woman:

*Dear Mrs. Ferzackly,*

*I have been in and done all I could do, all clothes to Salvation Army and such like, because the poor thing is too sick and will stay there they say. The young solicitor has been lovely. He and Mr. Tompson have arranged, so now the house is shut up till Mr. Tompson finds a buyer, it may take long, because the house isn't everybody's cup of tea. ( Mr. Tompson is Estate Agent Bandana.) So that is how it is, and if you would like to take a look, thought I had better inform you where to find the key.*

*Knowing of the long friendship with the late Mr. D. I am enclosing a snap I took after they was married. I would be happy for you to keep the snap. Sorry if the snap is blurred, I think the camera isn't up to much, but it is always a bit of a gamble.*

*Yours as ever,*

E. PERRY *(Mrs.)*

Evelyn would have preferred to ignore the snapshot, but took a quick disapproving look. The badly developed photograph was already discoloured.

The figures of two large and shapeless people were arrested in the middle of nowhere. Although they might have been connected they were standing rather apart, undecided whether they should face each other or the camera. At least the photographer acted as some kind of focus point for smiles which might otherwise have remained directionless. Blur and all, she had caught her subjects wearing that expression of timeless innocence approaching imbecility, of those on whom the axe has still to fall. Like the photographs of murdered people in the papers.

Evelyn could not have kept Mrs Perry's snap. She would have torn it up immediately if Harold hadn't been there, not exactly watching, but knowing.

'A letter from that woman,' she said, because there was no way out, 'from Mrs Perry. She doesn't add anything – or nothing of importance – to what we knew.'

How could she? They had never known so much.

Harold, Evelyn suspected as she made for the bathroom cupboard, was going to settle down to a prolonged, sentimental-morbid session with Mrs Perry's snapshot. Well, men were less sensitive.

Harold did, in fact, allow himself to be drawn into Mrs Perry's haze. Read the letter, too, several times. If he had had the courage – he realised late in life he was no more than physically brave – he might have gone down to Bandana, collected the key from that estate agent, and had a last look over the house.

But – Evelyn might have got to know. He couldn't have borne that. Any more than his entry into the still warm, the gently creaking house – or hutch, they had perhaps rightly called it, in which some soft but wise primeval animal used to turn gravely on its straw, absorbing from between the wooden bars a limitless abstraction of blue, and giant satiny bird had settled and resettled its wings, its uncommunicative eye concentrated on some prehistory of its own.

Fur and feather never lie together.

Harold Fazackerley made that noise with the mucus in his nose which his wife Evelyn deplored. He put the letter, together with the snap, inside his wallet, where the heat of his body had united many other documents by the time they were forgotten.

When Harold announced he had booked a room at the Currawong Palace for a week Evelyn felt it her duty to disapprove and produce reasons why he shouldn't have, while secretly aware how relieved she would be to escape from the little box which contained too many confused emotions.

'But isn't that extravagant,' she protested, 'to say the least? When we are leaving for Cairns in July. And autumn,' she said, 'in the Mountains, can be depressing. Besides, nobody I can think of ever stayed at the Currawong Palace. Well, perhaps one person – a typist – though quite a decent girl.'

Harold said: 'Anyhow, I've done it, so we'll leave on Thursday.'

The weeks left to their departure for Cairns would be easily countable after their return from Currawong.

The Currawong Palace was one of those follies built in the shape of a castle by somebody who went broke from it. Business enterprise had extended the castle by trailing more practical wings through a conflicting landscape, and by dotting pavilions amongst the evergreens intended to daunt the native scrub. There were guests who patronised Currawong in Spring, briefly to admire rhododendrons, or in autumn to be dazzled by a splendour of lit maples. But such individuals were too few and discreet to count as clientèle: the honeymoon couples who stared speechless over food, gathering strength for the next clinch, the young lady typists (typistes was perhaps nearer the mark) who perched on gilt in the ballroom while the business executives stalked up and down, rigid in their dark-suits-for-evening, and the foreigners, the foreigners were everywhere, lamenting Vienna and Budapest, filling all the most comfortable chairs.

After one glance the first evening Evelyn knew what a mistake Harold had made.

'We shall just have to put up with it,' she sighed, 'and close our eyes – and ears – and enjoy each other's company.'

She gave him one of those consuming looks she sometimes managed to construct when she was feeling consumed.

'Do you suppose there will be *anyone?*' she asked as they were changing into fresh things for dinner. 'There must be *someone.*'

'I expect so,' Harold said.

His thinning shanks ached as he pulled on the too expensive socks he still bought out of habit.

As they prepared to go down she patted his back. Harold's back, she was pleased to think, would be the most presentable in a roomful of riffraff. Out of modesty she did not dwell on her own donkey brown under the musquash stole – once a coat – jolly smart – she only glanced obliquely at the wardrobe door in passing.

Downstairs, antlers presided; the velvet had worn off by now. The melon was terrible. There were some splinters of fish done in sawdust. She refused to wrestle with her cartilage of mutton. Over their helpings of marshmallow and tinned pineapple-ring the honeymoon couples were beginning to uncoil.

But afterwards, in the longue, during the rite of coffee essence – ugh! – Evelyn discovered that old Mrs Haggart, the widow of a grazier.

'Delicious coffee,' said Mrs Haggart, fitting her mouth to the space above the cup.

'*Yes!*' Evelyn gnashed a smile.

But found the old lady innocent.

She was one of those elderly Australian ladies innocent of a great deal, even of her own Cadillac and any other manifestation of her wealth. (Evelyn became at once passionately devoted to what she recognised as the Kolinsky cape.) Mrs Haggart had the skin of a lizard, yellowed by the sun. Her voice, as though thinned by drought, persisted not much above a whisper in the same dusty monotone. But she was kind. She would smile at the rudest waiter, asking, it seemed, for his forgiveness. Mrs Haggart was so kind it was a wonder she had managed to hang on to the Cadillac.

'We used to drive out of the city,' she told Evelyn, after first clearing her throat of dust, 'always – while my husband was alive – and even now, I drive out with Bill—' Evelyn did not think she would have liked to call her chauffeur 'Bill', but Mrs Haggart was so democratic '—we drive around the outskirts, looking for a fresh cabbage, or any other vegetable. I do enjoy a fresh-picked vegetable.'

Evelyn was entranced by the strangeness of it. She held her head brightly on one side, and gurgled for her new friend.

'Don't you?' asked Mrs Haggart, turning quite vehement.

'Oh, indeed, vegetables are so important!'

Evelyn was fascinated by the string of naked diamonds hanging innocently round Mrs Haggart's slack neck.

The old lady looked down, and was reassured by the sight of her own interlock cutting across the V of velvet.

Then she raised her head and said: 'My husband was not so fond of vegetables.'

Suddenly for no reason Evelyn felt very angry.

'Harold – my husband and I,' she said, 'have more or less similar tastes. Where,' she asked, 'where is Harold?'

Mrs Haggart glanced over the arm of the sofa at the floor. She almost toppled. But recovered herself. At once it became obvious she had contributed enough to the search.

'Perhaps he isn't feeling well,' she said.

'It would be most unusual,' said Evelyn. 'Harold is never ill. I am the one.'

Mrs Haggart couldn't stop looking at Evelyn's arms. Then she suggested something quite horrid, but senile of course.

'Perhaps he's looking over the partners for the dance.'

'Oh, but there's only dancing on Saturday. I understood.'

'I thought there was dancing *every* night at Currawong,' said Mrs Haggart, introducing slight colour into her monotone. '*Every* night,' she repeated. 'But I can't say for *sure*, as I don't know where I put the prospectus.'

She resigned herself to the Kolinsky cape.

'Now, my husband,' she sat twangling faintly.

'Ah, there he is!' Evelyn said.

Some kind of expectation was making her tremble.

'Who?'

'Harold. My husband.'

Mrs Haggart's washed-out curiosity flickered behind her thickish glasses, investigating the cause of her new acquaintance's agitation. Mrs Fazackerley was sitting on the edge of the sofa trembling like a young girl.

Then Mrs Haggart made out the husband – there was no other possible candidate in sight – a cut above most in more distinguished company, still plenty of wear in him too, advancing on them in no hurry. While Mrs Fazackerley waved those gold bracelets. Egyptian, hadn't she said?

'There, you see, you didn't lose him,' Mrs Haggart consoled. 'And probably won't. Unless in an accident. If an accident has been arranged there's nothing you can do about it.'

But Mrs Fazackerley didn't hear, or had perhaps heard too much. Her neck had grown stringier. Now that she had attracted his attention, and he was picking his way through the Jewesses, she sat forward farther still, gathering her knees into her arms, her throat straining red.

Mrs Haggart was not a woman who cultivated undue luxury, but did enjoy a good stare.

'I'd begun to worry. Where on earth have you been?' Mrs Fazackerley almost called.

'Nowhere,' he said.

Staringly luxuriously out of her moon-shaped glasses Mrs Haggart saw that he was smiling at his wife as though he only half-remembered her.

'Just wandering,' Mr Fazackerley said.

He had not, in fact, wandered any distance. Why he had not gone farther, he would have been too embarrassed to admit. Nor could he bring himself to accept Evelyn's girlish intensity as she craned up at him from the sofa, trying to penetrate his thoughts. A nonchalance protected him, which he found rather agreeable.

The hotel, which should have desolated, mildly pleased. As he strolled, it had muted his footsteps with enormous flesh-coloured roses. He had easily navigated the gilt islands on which stranded typists sat, plumping out their mouths in anticipation, combing their hair with opalescent fingernails. There had been no sign that a chunk of the ornamental mouldings, which had obviously crumbled over the years, would be aimed at him deliberately if it should happen again.

Only when he stepped outside into the still more impersonal dark, with its solider, blacker rhododendrons, and the disembodied voices, did Harold Fazackerley begin to have doubts for his safety. Or not exactly his safety. To feel he might be in danger, without having earned the right to regret it. Evelyn had been sensible enough to advise against autumn in the Mountains. The mist, for one thing, had begun to finger between himself and his clothes.

Not all the ritual passion of lovers could warm the beds of rotten leaves or humanise the undergrowth as he advanced towards the line of native scrub. Where, on the edge, he knew he still wasn't ready for disclosures which might be made. To his shame, he felt he had been gone too long, and that his wife would be waiting for him. So he went back to the lounge, stepping over any bodies which lay in the way.

Evelyn had turned to the old lady beside her on the sofa.

'It has been so charming,' his wife was saying. 'But the journey has given me a headache. I think it is time we went to bed.'

With as much interest as she seemed capable of Mrs Haggart examined the man who had been included in her friend's decision. Well, it had never been altogether unusual to include. Which perhaps decided Mrs Haggart to smile one of those filtered smiles, less for the present than for the past.

'I shall watch the people enjoying themselves,' she announced. 'I shall listen to the community singing.'

Then the Fazackerleys became aware that *Click Go the Shears* had started up at the end of one of the spokes which radiated from the hub of the lounge. A plaster shell, encrusted with coloured electric bulbs, increased the volume and fanned it outwards.

Enclosed in their varnished bedroom Evelyn could let herself go.

'As I expected,' she said. 'It's all perfectly ghastly.'

She took off her imitation pearl ear-rings, the increased weight of which was threatening to pull her under. Her string of *real* pearls she wore day and night for safety.

'Even the old lady.' She sighed. 'Although to some extent refined. Wasn't it a gorgeous Kolinsky cape?'

She allowed her own tired musquash to draggle across the ottoman.

'Can't you see Nesta – Nesta Pine,' said Evelyn Fazackerley, creaming herself at the dressing-table, 'sitting with an old creature like that in a whole series of ghastly hotels.' In its gulf the mirror was breeding other mirrors. 'Mrs Haggart is straight out of Nesta's stable. Nesta would have been just the thing for Mrs Haggart.' Evelyn could have been working it up, a fresh phase, in Elizabeth Arden, on her own face. 'If Nesta were ever to recover. Lots of people do, you know, from nervous disorders. Nesta – now she's a widow – Oh, no, Harold, don't please! Not when I'm all covered with cream.'

In any case passion with lights on, she had always found it embarrassing.

But Harold's hands, she realised, were heavy cold outside the film of warm grease with which she had been reviving her neck.

'Why must you start on Nesta?'

As she sat at the flimsy dressing-table he was addressing her reflection in the glass.

'She was our friend, wasn't she?' Evelyn replied, also in reflection. 'It's natural that she should crop up. Never more natural than in a place like this.'

'But Nesta is suffering,' Harold said, 'we can't begin to guess, in what kind of hell.'

Because his hands were so gentle in the angles of her neck it made Evelyn angry.

'It isn't my fault, is it, that Nesta Pine went round the bend? It was you – your – that man – that dead weight – that *Dowson*. I caught him reading a book once when he was staying with us at Kafr el Zayet. A book – oh, I can't explain it. Did it ever occur to you that red-haired men have a most distinctive smell? Oh, there's nothing I can accuse him of. Nothing of which you can say; that was the root of the trouble. He sort of seeped. We had several talks – you couldn't call them conversations because he was incapable of expressing himself. On one occasion we were strolling, I remember – one evening – through that mango grove – I can never see, let alone smell the beasty fruit, without getting the horrors – Dowson was not exactly telling but hinting. Poor old Nesta! I can just imagine! With that orange orangutang! And after all she'd gone through with someone as cold and egotistical, as delicately destructive as Addie Woolcock Fernandini Thingummy.'

'Don't shriek,' he advised. 'They'll think a peacock – Yes, Addie and Nesta,' he said, 'must have burnt each other up. But what does it matter, provided you blaze together – *blaze*,' he was searching, '—in peacock-colours.'

He ended up sounding ashamed.

It made Evelyn turn round.

'Harold, how loathsome! And why peacocks? It means,' she said, 'you must have been reading my private – my private papers!'

It was no longer a matter of reflections. They were facing each other in the flesh.

'Ever since the day we read how Clem Dowson died I think I've been trying to forgive you, Evelyn.'

'Oh,' she shouted, 'indeed! I suppose *I* pushed Dowson under the bus! As well as putting Nesta where she is. Blame me, my dear. After all, I'm your wife.'

'No,' he said, 'I'm to blame. We never got a child. But *I* got *you*. I made you – more than likely! My only creative achievement!'

She looked at him.

'Oh, my darling,' she said, coughing up a noise which normally would have worried her in case anybody heard, 'my darling,' she spluttered, coughing, 'if you wanted to kill me, you couldn't have done it more effectively!'

But in front of this scraggy woman, his wife, death, he felt, was no longer of any importance.

He hated what he was looking at, what he had caused. He took hold of the string of pearls, which, in the beginning, when there had been several strands, had given joy out of proportion. To both of them. He took the pearls, and twisted and jerked. And jerked. The string broke easily enough. He listened to the pearls scamper skittishly away against and behind lacquered veneer.

Evelyn didn't resist. She was too terrified. Not to recognise her husband. She had never known Harold. Was there also, possibly, ultimately, something hitherto unsuspected to recognise in herself? That was far more terrifying.

So she could not stop her dry cough, or retching. If she had been more supple she would have flung herself on the floor, but as she wasn't she got down groggily, on all fours. She found herself, like some animal, on the hotel carpet.

It could have been that death no longer appeared so very important to Evelyn either.

'The pearls,' she whimpered, and it was a relief to admit her practical nature.

He looked down at her. Inside the slip her breasts continued shrivelling. The hotel lamp, rose-shaded to assist the diffident, couldn't help Evelyn's breasts. They remained a shabby yellow.

Nor himself: an old brittler man.

Or animal down beside the other rootling and grovelling after pearls.

'Poor Evelyn!' he found himself beginning again, to encourage them both in a predicament. 'We'll find the pearls. It was my fault. Perhaps when it's daylight. Move the furniture. So that the maid won't sweep them up. Mistake them for beads. Throw them out. Or tread on them.'

They were at times kneeling, at times trampling on the pearls themselves, in the indiscriminate business of picking their way through what remained of their life together.

When she finally got to bed, the grit was still in Evelyn's knees, but she could not bother about it.

She said: 'I could do with a good stiff brandy. If I could face the staff. If they would come at this hour of night. Anyway it would cost the earth.'

He fondled her breasts a little, but suspected she didn't realise it was happening, just as it wasn't happening to him.

So he went out, unable, besides, to embrace the ritual of undressing. Evelyn did not protest. She was lying on the bed, half revealed by the hotel linen. She had started to give a performance of sleep, looking, he noticed, like a badly-carved serving of steamed fowl.

Harold heard the beige roses responding to his footsteps in the passages. Although life was being lived spasmodically, at times even violently, behind closed doors, the passages were deserted and only economically lit.

In an open doorway Mrs Haggart in a black kimono was putting out her shoes as though she believed something would be done about them.

'In Harrogate,' she said to the one guest who offered himself, 'we used to see bottles of spa-water standing outside the doors with the boots. We had gone there, my husband and I, for our health.'

Something shook her.

'Melon,' she said, 'is the worst gas-maker of all.'

Her neck still flickering with blue fire, Mrs Haggart covered up her combinations with the rather elusive black kimono before withdrawing.

The whole hotel was beginning to subside into a detritus of pleasure: the stuffed egg someone had trodden into the carpet, shreds of lettuce and mauve Kleenex, the click of slow ping-pong balls, last phrases of 'The Little Brown Jug'. None of it held Harold up. Reaching for the glass doors. Bursting out. Finally running. He couldn't help hearing himself: youth would have given it a sound of cattle, whereas age transposed it into the dry scuttle of a cockroach.

His movements emphasised the intense stillness of the shrubberies. Moisture was dripping from the rhododendrons. The animal intruder scattering gravel and tearing beaded spider-web did not interrupt the dripping bushes. He was the least of that cavern of dark which night was filling with the stalactites of silence. Realisation spurred him to blunder deeper in, to try to shake off something which, by light, could only have appeared an exhibition of panic.

Harold Fazackerley's teeth confessed: *I am an old man with the wind up looking for what.*

And then he began to come across it. Where the overstuffed shrubberies gave out, he plunged across the boundary into the scrub. In which the whips lashed. In which the rocks sprang up under his papery soles. A rapier was raised to slash his cheek. He could feel the flesh receding. Or he was freed of some inessential part of him as he blundered on, no longer troubling to tear off the cold webs of mist. The mist clothed his fingers, and clung to his bared cheekbone.

As he stumbled through the mists, they were beginning, he saw, as though for his special benefit, to give up the moon. He was standing on the edge of a great gorge, into which there was no need to throw himself because he had experienced every stone of it already. He was the black water trickling, trickling, at the bottom of it. He was the cliffside pocked with hidden caves. He was the deformed elbows of stalwart trees.

And all the time in the gorge, the mists were lying together, dreaming together, fur and feather gently touching, on which the healing moon rode. It was not that any of them had abandoned their material forms, but that night and mist had melted those broad faces, making more accessible the disturbing similar features, to which he had never dared demonstrate his love.

He went back presently. There was a single voice singing in the kitchens, and a clash of late crockery. In the fuzzy half-light of the hotel there was nobody to notice that Harold Fazackerley's kneecap was showing through his dark suit. Evelyn was sleeping, really sleeping, under a glitter of tears and cold cream. Her mouth was sucking at life with the desperation of rubber.

When Harold had undressed his somewhat unfamiliar body, and scrubbed his teeth, and put them back, he got into the other bed.

The rest of their stay at the Currawong Palace was agreeable enough, thanks chiefly to Mrs Haggart, who had taken a fancy to Evelyn. And you couldn't deny the old thing her little pleasures.

Evelyn and Mrs Haggart would be driven most afternoons, in the Cadillac, by Mrs Haggart's Bill, to look-outs, waterfalls, and the entrances to caves. (If they didn't venture inside the latter, it was because all caves are much alike.) The two women most enjoyed pulling up in front of a view, where Evelyn would tell about the Nile, and Mrs Haggart remember the vegetables she had bought. They would sit there until a swirl of mist warned them.

Sometimes Mr Fazackerley was persuaded to accompany the ladies, in his tweed cap set straight, and the English overcoat which wouldn't wear out. Mrs Haggart made him sit beside Bill, and her world was once again orderly and masculine.

'When he was younger,' she remarked, 'my husband had a leather coat. It smelled most delicious.'

Evelyn continued to worship the Kolinsky cape, which its owner wore only at night, and the string of naked diamonds, which sometimes overlapped with day, because Mrs Haggart forgot to take it off.

Once Evelyn Fazackerley began: 'Nesta Pine—' and stopped.

'Who?' Mrs Haggart asked, although she wasn't interested.

'A friend,' said Mrs Fazackerley, noticing how the changed light was carving the sandstone into other shapes.

And soon the week was up. The two women exchanged addresses, which even Mrs Haggart suspected they would never use.

It had all been so agreeable, however.

'I have so much enjoyed', Mrs Haggart said.

Looking at the husband, she wove one of those smiles over her almost colourless lips.

'I envy you,' she added as colourlessly. 'Anyone can see you are such mates.'

Harold had learnt, no doubt in the Army, to hold himself erect. It made Evelyn proud.

The Fazackerleys continued making their trips. That winter they went to Cairns. You couldn't expect them to sit at home listening to their creaking cupboards and the leaking tap. They went twice to the Barrier Reef. They were lucky that, as age increased, their mechanism seemed to have been built for life. They flew to the Adelaide Festival, once only, because Evelyn cracked her ribs in the shower at that motel. She suffered perfect agonies, but the toughest moment was always when, hats held down, they walked into the wind across the tarmac. One year they did that cruise round the Pacific, beyond their means, and a mistake in other ways besides: for the scent of mangoes, and the drowned thoughts the sea kept throwing up at them. They flew to New Zealand, but really it was antiquated. (On the way back, one of the engines conked out.) The winter Evelyn's arthritis played up – her hands were pretty twisted by now – and Harold's turn gave her a scare, they started earlier than usual; they visited the Dead Heart.

Harold always arranged her rug.

He would ask: 'You're sure you're feeling comfortable, dear?'

Couples from Coff's Harbour and Hay, Wollongong and Peak Hill, never stopped asking one another who those people could possibly be.

As the Fazackerleys continued to enjoy their retirement, preferably in the front seats, so that nothing might obstruct.

Only on one occasion, above an aerial landscape of lashing trees, Harold Fazackerley, his limbs again fleshed, straddling the globe, returned for an instant to the solitary condition he remembered as normal, to the faces of those who were missing, the faces he had never touched.

But he was quick to enquire: 'You're sure you're comfortable, darling?'

As they sat out their travelogue, they became so sodden with technicolor, it was hoped they might not jump at the final flack flacker of transparent film.

# STEPHEN VIZINCZEY
## Crime and Sentiment

I N the anti-semitic folklore of Eastern Europe, it is the wicked habit of the Jews to eat Christian babies at Passover. This vile practice is never exposed in the newspapers (*they* have seen to that) but the facts will out now and then. Everyone knows what Moses did to the innocents of ancient Egypt, and in modern times there were the pogroms. The pogroms exposed the Israelites to the whole world. For what else, what else but the sight of monstrous cannibalism, could have driven peaceful peasants to killing their own Jews? There is no smoke without fire.

Such information is vital to a factory hand in Hungary – or rather it may turn out to be so, as in the case of the young man who knew nothing of religious diets and consequently had his skull broken with twelve-inch angle-irons.

Endowed perhaps with clairvoyance (and most certainly with a horror of physical exertion) Peter didn't want to go to the factory in the first place. He planned to spend the summer by one of the famous swimming pools of Budapest, lounging on the grass and occasionally jumping feet first from the diving board, an accomplishment which made him feel strong and sporty. In fact, he was a pale and spindly boy, the kind who is at the top of his class in every subject except gymnastics and stays clear of rough games. In the gym he would stand by the climbing rope, fiddling with it earnestly while the other boys were high up in the air, touching the ceiling; and as for leaping over the wooden horse or tumbling on the mats, he had been excused from those exercises at an early age. 'I'm an individualist,' he declared when his classmates tried to make fun of him, adding with quick condescension, 'not that you'd know what "individualist" *means*.' Which was perhaps the oddest thing about Peter: either very shy or very arrogant, he blushed when someone spoke to him or else looked straight through the other person, depending on his mood. An only child, he kept his parents at arm's length and at home spent most of his time in his bedroom, studying, reading or playing chess with himself, to the loud accompaniment of Beethoven's violin concerto or The Highlights of Verdi, his two favourite records, which his parents couldn't help overhearing for years on end but tolerated in silent rage. He intended to study medicine at the University of Budapest, hoping eventually to specialise in cancer research (he had given up smoking at sixteen) or, if all else failed, to become a gynaecologist like his father.

The factory was a grave surprise for Peter, a new continent that lay only a streetcar ride from his home. As soon as he arrived he was taken to one of the courtyards, which served as an open-air warehouse for ten-feet-high angular iron rods standing against giant racks – all of them covered with rust, dust and smut, and all vibrating slightly but eerily from the movement of the machines rumbling away far and near. His job was to carry the rods to one end of the long courtyard and through a side door, where they would be cut into twelve-inch lengths and passed on to undergo various other operations, for what final purpose nobody seemed to know. A conspicuous newcomer in his bright blue overalls, all bones, freckles and sweat, he staggered back and forth between the racks and the door, carrying three or four rods at a time in a vain effort to keep up with the operator of the cutting machine. Although each flange was only two inches wide and a few millimetres thick, the length of the rods gave them weight, and as they slid apart on his shoulder they swung violently in different directions. Apparently blinded by fear that they would fall and crush him, he advanced in a wavering line, gaping with wide-open mouth as if he needed all the air he could swallow. Workmen passing by stopped to observe the spectacle: there was something nauseating, something indecent in the sight of a young man so incapable of a little hard work, so evidently not the master of his own body; it was like watching a man in a bar getting dead drunk on one glass of beer.

'Who's that scarecrow?' one of them asked the operator of the cutting machine, who had moved to the doorway, since he had nothing else to do.

'Now you can see for yourselves what kind of help I have to put up with,' he seethed. 'A high school graduate! Jesus Mary! I already told the boss to give me somebody else, but he says it's Party policy and the kid's here for the summer.'

'If he lasts the day I'll kiss Lenin's ass.'

'Yeah. They make the poor rich boys sweat a little before they let them into the university. Not a bad idea, but I wish they'd leave me out of it.'

'The poor bugger,' another said, shaking his head in sympathy. 'He must be a Jew.'

Peter had no notion of being watched and found wanting: his heart was thudding, loud and wild like a whole army of mad drummers, beating the blood up into his ears and eyes, and after a while he could see nothing but the sharp edges of the rods hovering over him. Through all this, he felt oddly elated, as if he were staggering not between two points in space but towards the meaning of life. He hadn't chosen this test of his adaptability, the fright, the wrenching of muscles, the shower in his own sweat, the pain in his shoulders; but once they were forced upon him, he wanted to find out how long he could endure, how much he could take. There is a trait of the drug addict in each of us: we crave new experiences and some part of our body welcomes every unfamiliar sensation, even pain, as if our nerves had a curiosity of their own. And don't we all share a vague belief that affliction is both ennobling and enlightening? Even the feeblest illiterate feels virtuous and clever after a vicious toothache. Lurching across the courtyard, his legs shaking and his eyes glazed, Peter somehow felt that he was gaining in wisdom what he lost in equilibrium.

Growing up in a liberal home and communist schools, he had always been taught to respect the proletariat, and now he was joining their ranks. Just a few days earlier, his school principal, sending the students off to their compulsory summer jobs, had exhorted them to remember that 'It is the Workers, their courage, their dedication, their labour, that assure mankind of a glorious future – you should be grateful for this opportunity to share their task, you must get to know them and learn from them.' The fact that the principal was bald and dotty in a solemn sort of way, and that they all knew the student work programme had been set up to ameliorate the permanently temporary crisis of the economy, in no way diminished the impact of the speech on Peter. Dr Horvath, an intellectual who had acquired his political convictions in the thirties, often told his son that the workers and peasants were braver, wiser, nobler men than the landowners and capitalists, fascists and commissars who had oppressed them through their long and bitter history. Observing that his father and the school officials, although they were on the opposite sides of every issue, shared a profound admiration for the proletariat, Peter was convinced that the superiority of the People was beyond dispute, a simple fact. But ideas such as these are just accidental signals of deeper and more universal responses than reasoning. A child is both repelled and challenged by the dark room and the night outside, by the lurking monsters of sickness, hunger and loneliness, and grows up to hope that the wretched of the earth know the answers to the questions he cannot even ask. Now that he was among the workers and actually becoming one of them, Peter was eager to prove himself and to learn. At any rate, there was the possibility: although he was still unable to hold the rods together and stop them from swaying and swinging, he floundered through to lunch break without an accident.

'I'm not doing so badly, boss, am I?' he declared by way of boast and apology to the operator of the cutting machine.

'You don't have to call me "boss",' the other said, twisting his mouth to express his contempt for the freak – just in case he tried to behave with the insolence of his kind. 'My name's Josef. Here we call each other by our *Christian* names.'

'Mine's Peter – Peter Horvath.'

'They even take over our names,' Josef thought sourly.

They sat in the doorway with legs outstretched, turning their backs to the oily, airless belly of the plant but keeping their heads out of the sun. It was late June and though the morning still belonged to spring, by noon it was high summer. Josef was watching the student's legs, which resting on the ground, still shook violently as if their owner had a fever. Josef's own legs were solid and firm, but he was below average height and had a peculiarly long, narrow face, as if his head had been pressed when he was born. 'That short fellow with the long head' was the way most people described him; but to the student he appeared formidably strong and tough.

'How long have you been working here?' Peter asked him wistfully.

Josef raised his head: his brown eyes shone with a strange, unchanging gaze. 'What's the matter – are you nosey?'

'I was just wondering.'

'Let's wonder about *you*. I bet this is the first day you ever worked in your life – right? Just went to school, eh?'

'Yes.'

'Well, I couldn't live off my rich daddy.' He jerked his head upward with the dark pride of a man who was about to be shot for being a Christian factory worker but couldn't care less. The veins and muscles streaking the skin on his neck, he gazed off into the distance, far beyond the plant, towards the horizon, seemingly oblivious of his companion. 'I bet that freak has a room of his own,' he thought.

'I've been making my living since I was fourteen. That's six years now. Started out packing crates and loading them on trucks – it wasn't an easy job like you've got.

'What was it like?'

Josef jerked his head again. 'I'm not complaining.'

Peter made an extra effort of will to control his legs. However, no sooner had his limbs stopped trembling than his eyelids began to droop, so that he had to concentrate on keeping them open. In Josef's sullen anger he sensed only a kind of aggressive vitality, a wide-awake alertness, which humbled him.

'Do you have far to come to work, Josef?'

'Where do you come from? A nice big house on Rose Hill, I bet. You don't get much smoke and dirt up there.'

'No, we just live in an apartment building downtown,' Peter was glad to say.

'Well, I've lived ten blocks from here all my life. These days there's a lot of queer riff-raff around – here today and gone tomorrow. But not me. I'm still sleeping in the same room I was born in.' Again he turned his unchanging gaze on the student. 'What about you? I bet you were born in a hospital.'

'Yes,' Peter confessed, blushing, and added by way of excuse, 'My father's a doctor.'

Josef nodded knowingly. 'In a hospital. I thought so.'

Still wondering what question to ask next and how he should ask it, Peter fell asleep, with food in his mouth.

'He'll do, considering,' Josef decided. 'One of these days I'll get him talking about Jewish girls.'

During work they had little opportunity for conversation. As the former air-raid sirens sounded and the old machines began to shake, they had to pick themselves up in a hurry, and the factory patrol made sure that no time was wasted on the job. The afternoon was worse for Peter, because the sun had heated the rods and soon his hands were covered with blisters; and even though he brought his winter gloves to work the next day, his hands continued to torment him, impairing whatever dexterity he might have gained from practice. Several times the long rods swung away from his shoulder, but he was scared enough to jump clear as they crashed to the ground.

The two young men spent most of their lunch breaks together, sitting in the doorway. For a while Josef's fixed stare unnerved the student, but he soon noticed the others straining their eyes in the same way, and at home Dr Horvath explained that it was a symptom of chronic lack of sufficient sleep. The fact that Josef wasted little time in bed only made him more impressive: eight hours at the factory drained all of Peter's strength, emptied him of all desire for any amusement but eating and sleeping, and he envied Josef's ability to watch soccer games after work or drop into the nearby tavern in the evening and get involved in fights.

As the student gave him due respect and listened attentively to his stories (unless overcome by drowsiness) Josef began to think of him as 'my weakling' and no longer cursed about the slow delivery of the rods. Several times he went out for them himself, showing the novice how to carry them so that they wouldn't swing around. 'Don't worry about it too much,' he said, wanting to encourage the boy. 'After all, it isn't your fault that you were born into a queer race. You can't choose your parents, can you?' He called 'queer' everything he disliked, and Peter thought this was another reference to his bourgeois background as a rich doctor's son. Their friendship, based on mutual misunderstanding, grew undisturbed for nearly two weeks, until Josef finally got around to the subject of the family and women.

'I'm a family man. I'm big on the family. Still with my father and mother – I don't even mind my sisters. As my old man says, the home is the place for everything.'

'Don't you think about getting married?'

Josef twisted his mouth to express his opinion of marriage. (He had once seen this grimace in a film and had taken to it.) 'Not me, brother, I won't get married until I knock up a girl. And believe me, I watch it. Girls come better by the dozen, they say.'

'He isn't shy, he isn't afraid of them,' Peter thought.

'But you know more about that than I do,' the other continued. 'They say Jewish girls are hotter than ours.'

'I guess so,' Peter agreed evasively, as he wasn't anxious to confess that he had never gone farther with the opposite sex than a movie house.

'Yeah, they say Jewish girls know how to abandon their pride with real style. You know what a girl's pride is?'

'No.'

'Her underwear. That's what we call her pride around here. Good, eh? When she gives up her pride, brother, you're home. But what am I talking for? You're the one who should be teaching me.' He added with involuntary, almost unconscious severity, 'Everybody knows you Jews are promiscuous.'

'Why should they be more promiscuous than other people? That's just fascist propaganda.' As the other turned his gaze on him, Peter became more conciliatory. 'Anyway, I don't really know. You're wrong – I'm not Jewish.'

This made Josef angry. 'Listen, I don't like that. I don't like it at all. You shouldn't be ashamed to own up who you are, even if you're the Devil himself.'

'I'd tell you if I was,' Peter insisted. 'Why shouldn't I tell you? But I happen to be a Catholic. At least, my grandparents are Catholics. I wasn't baptised, we're atheists. Besides, what does it matter?'

'What do you mean, you're "atheists"?'

'Well, we don't believe in God.'

'Sure, godless, that's part of it. But if you admitted that much, you might as well go all the way.'

'But I did! I told you, I'm telling you, I'm not Jewish.'

This time, Josef pointed an accusing finger at the student's freckled nose. 'Listen, kid, I'm a hundred per cent Christian blood, but even if I was a Tartar or a Turk or even a Jew, I'd have the guts to admit it. So don't make me mad.'

'You're just not listening to what I'm saying!' To escape from the menacing forefinger, Peter rose to his feet. 'Besides, how could I be Jewish?' he asked, nonplussed by the absurdity of their argument. 'I even have an uncle who's an anti-semite.'

'You talk too much!' For a moment, however, Josef was assailed by doubts: had he been mistaken? was the Jew trying to make a fool of him? Oh, he knew the type who always told him he was wrong, that he didn't understand – that was how he got the worst of every deal. Slowly he raised himself from the ground, as if preparing to knock down his opponent. 'Just don't get on your high horse, kid,' he said in a threatening voice, shaking and bitter as if someone had kicked him. 'Just don't try to act like you were a cut above ordinary people!'

'It's just that you happen to be wrong,' Peter protested, his chest heaving in a kind of reflex reaction to the other's sudden fury.

'Are you trying to tell me I'm stupid?'

'All I'm trying to tell you is that I happen to know who I am better than you do.'

'Just don't act like you think you're superior!'

As the sirens signalled the end of the lunch break, each went back to his work, relieved that they didn't have to resolve the issue. Peter walked quickly and even ran for short distances with the rods, not wanting to give the machinist an opportunity to complain of delays. Even so, he had by this time mastered the job too well to be engrossed by it. 'Why can't Josef believe what I say,' he fumed. 'Why does he tell me I'm conceited, just because he's wrong? And why is he so hung up on the Jews?' Finding no answers to these questions, Peter tried to remember his mother's brother, the anti-semite, usually referred to by the rest of the family as 'that poor idiot'. He had gone to America after the war, and Peter could recall nothing of him but a postcard he had sent years ago, a picture of palm trees and the blue sea. Wondering what the Pacific Ocean might be like, Peter calmed down sufficiently to consider Josef's miseries.

Though the factory bore the up-to-date name of Red Flag Metal Works (adopted when the Russians took over the country from the Germans in 1945) it was in fact a remnant from the first decade of the century, a random assortment of long, low, decrepit brick sheds with machinery that would have been the pride of any industrial museum. The whole smoke- dirt- and heat-ridden complex sprawled over two and a half square miles of rumbling junkyard – two and a half square miles of rusting metal, sagging roofs, cracks in the walls, cracks in the concrete floors, cracks in the windows offering no better view than their own abstract patterns of dirt and the patches of earth between the cracked paving stones in the courtyards. It was a wilderness of deserted objects, by the evidence of these objects, yet it was inhabited twenty-four hours a day by people doing various jobs that were always the same – men and women, young and old, all of them different, but what difference did it make, since they were all confined to this place? The air they breathed was black with soot and despair. The Red Flag employed over ten thousand workers in three shifts: those who escaped the morning had to come in for the afternoon, those who escaped the day had to come in for the night; the misery had to be inflicted without interruption. Out of this land laid low by rust and the plague that spreads from wasted lives rose a tall new American-style office block, the Administration Building, symbolising the government's determination to modernise industry; and from this building a woman broadcast to the workers at irregular but frequent intervals, numbing their hearts with the indifference of the powers that controlled their fate. Her voice boomed at them through innumerable loudspeakers, citing production figures, giving the latest news from the Korean War, and always ending with the same cheery reminder: 'Remember, comrades, the factory belongs to you, the country belongs to you!'

Hearing the voice again, the student was seized by rage and began to wonder, not for the first time, how Josef could stand it day after day. What was the secret of his fortitude, what sustained him as he pushed the rods under the blades and presses of his machine, one after the other, for hours, years, perhaps forever? 'What else could keep him going but hate?' Peter asked himself. 'For all he gets out of living, why shouldn't he hate me, or the Jews, or his own mother for that matter? In his place I'd hate the whole world.' Josef was all right, after all. 'He's noble, because he goes on living,' Peter decided.

Nevertheless, he didn't want to run the risk of continuing their argument. When the sirens signalled the end of the morning shift, he was half-way down the courtyard, but to avoid talking to his companion he turned around and carried the rods back to their place at the rack. Racing to the exit, he was among the first to queue up at the punch clocks, breathing heavily and attracting the attention

of an old man in front. 'Anxious to get out, eh?' The old man had a blushy yellow
moustache and only two front teeth, but he was chuckling and his small bright
eyes were rolling with curiosity like a child's. 'Say, aren't you the boy who's only
with us for the summer?'

'Yes, that's me,' Peter assented eagerly, bursting with gratitude for this token
of sympathetic interest.

In fact, old Toth was interested in everybody and everything. Now past sixty,
he had always been one of those people who sustain themselves not so much on
food and drink as on private information. Having no direct involvement in the
world, Toth was dying to hear all about it. He never went to see a film, for
instance, but would hang about you for days to find out what it was like. If you
wanted to talk about a family row or a disappointing Sunday excursion and to
listen in turn to all the secret events of someone else's life, he was the man to turn
to. Ever since the student's arrival at the plant, Toth had been looking forward to
running into him. 'I recognised you,' the old man said, his frail head trembling
with excitement and the saliva flowing profusely by his two teeth. 'I noticed you
tussling with those rods in the courtyard.'

'They're heavier than they look, but I'm getting better.'

'And you say,' Toth continued with his friendly chuckle, 'you say you aren't
a Jew, eh?'

Several of the men broke from the queue and came closer: it seemed that they
had all heard a funny story in the afternoon.

'Yes, that's what I say,' Peter answered listlessly. But as he saw that his
embarrassment was taken for an admission that he was lying, he added defiantly,
'Any objection, grandpa? If not, I'd appreciate it if you'd mind your own
business.'

Visibly hurt, the old man drew back. 'You don't have to snarl at me. I only
asked you a question. As far as I'm concerned, you may be a Turk, just like
you say.' Then he turned to the others: 'They can only be civil to their own
kind.'

Josef might have forgiven anything, even the weakling's cowardly attempt to
deny his racial origin, but brazen lying was another matter. 'Not only does that
scarecrow tell lies to my face, he's mad at *me* for not swallowing them. He acts like
I was letting him down or something,' the machinist told the workmen with
whom he was eating lunch the following day. Josef abhorred nothing so much as
lying: it was indecent, unchristian; whenever he had to lie to a girl, to the
foreman or to his mother, he felt so guilty about it that he had to curse himself. He
didn't claim to be perfect, but at least his heart was in the right place – as the
student's clearly was not. 'But I'm telling you,' he concluded, 'I'll break that
punk, I won't let him get away with it.'

Adopting the psychological approach, he began to catch the smart-alec
youngster off guard by asking innocent questions such as 'How do you say "good

morning" in Yiddish?' When Peter reacted by arguing and shouting, Josef would smile disarmingly, retreating to confuse his antagonist. 'What's wrong with asking you if you know a couple of words in a foreign language? You've been at school all your life – I thought you might have learned something there. You said you studied Latin, didn't you? I bet you can't tell me "good morning" in Latin either. And you call me a stupid fascist!' The strategy worked: as the days went by, the suspect's denials became less and less confident and emphatic. 'He knows the score,' Josef thought, 'he knows that I see through him.'

A week after their first argument, Peter confessed. It was at six in the morning, when he went inside to pick up his gloves, which he always left overnight on the shelf behind the cutting machine. 'Last night I was talking to my old man about you,' Josef said. 'Afterwards for some reason or other we got into an argument about Jewish holidays – we couldn't agree which was the biggest one. I said Passover, is that right?'

'Right. Passover is the biggest.'

The other grinned as if he had just caught a running rabbit with one hand. 'How do you know? I mean how can you be sure?'

'I ought to know – I'm a Jew, I always go to church on Saturdays. Satisfied?'

Josef's grin turned into a grimace; then his face grew solemn and he waved the confession away. 'Listen, I couldn't care less whether you're a Jew or not. It's all the same to me. I just don't like it when somebody lies to me and then calls me names just because I won't fall for his stories. But I guess you're too young yet to know any better, so we'll forget all about it.'

And all would have been well, except that now it was Peter who began to act strangely. His submission for the sake of peace brought out his arrogance and belligerence: he couldn't forgive Josef for forcing him to give in, and although he still tried to be mindful of his companion's bad luck in life, it was no longer any use. In trying to find excuses for Josef, he began hating him, and his reverence for the People gradually turned into the bitter conviction that mankind was a pack of idiots and brutes. He felt betrayed. No doubt his violent reactions had also (as Dr Horvath frequently observed to no effect) a great deal to do with going to bed late. After a few weeks at the factory, his body had adjusted to the rough work, so that he no longer fell asleep right after supper but began to stay up until eleven o'clock or midnight again, as he did while going to school – with the difference that he had to get up at a quarter to five in the morning to be at the factory by six. Consequently, he was just as exhausted as he had been at the beginning of the summer, but this exhaustion didn't reveal itself in drowsiness: he was wide-awake now, perpetually tense and keyed-up. At first, he was only angry with himself, for having accepted the role of a sissy, of the weakling who couldn't climb or fight. After all, didn't he work just as hard as anybody else in the world? Throbbing with resentful pride, he dreamed of taking on all the bullies who had made him run; he didn't even have to close his eyes to see them all knocked to the ground, bleeding their life away through their noses. After capitulating to Josef, however, he had no time to think of anyone else's blood. He stared back at the enemy with a fixed gaze of his own.

'You sure are smart,' he said one day. 'How did you know I was a Jew, even when I said I wasn't?'

'Listen, kid, I'm not the type to rub in anything, so don't worry about it. It was just that I didn't like you lying to me.'

'But don't forget, I was *taught* to lie.' The high school intellectual had worked out a vengeance of great subtlety: he imagined that attributing more and more preposterous opinions to Josef would force him to recognise the depths of his stupidity, so that he would never have another moment's peace for the rest of his life. 'You know as well as I do, lying is a Jewish habit. It's hard to shake off, believe me.'

Josef took the statement as a further attempt on the kid's part to come clean, and shook his hand with truly felt sympathy. 'Don't ride yourself so hard – what could you do if you never had a chance? Besides, who's a saint?'

He decided to take the penitent over to join the group in the shower hut, which had damp stone walls and floors and was favoured as the coolest place to eat lunch. Since there were twenty-four men who worked the 'morning shift' in the same building (from six a.m. to two-thirty p.m., with half an hour off at noon) there were enough of them at the showers to make a crowd and greet the newcomer with as much goodwill as if he were a guest from outer space. No longer the arrogant s.o.b. trying to pass himself off as a Christian, Peter was treated with as much consideration as if he were one of themselves – with more consideration, in fact, on account of his misfortune in being a Jew.

Old Toth with his yellow moustache and wet chin was at hand, offering a cardboard box to the guest. 'Here, have one of these cookies, my lady's real clever at them.'

'Thank you very much,' Peter said piously, 'but I'm orthodox – our rabbi forbids us to eat cookies.'

Reflecting that he'd never seen another Jew in the flesh, except in '44 when he'd watched the soldiers herding them away to do some honest work in Germany, and that he should know more about their customs, old Toth withdrew the box of cookies, his jowls shaking with approbation and righteousness. 'Forgive me, my boy, far be it from me to encourage you to go against your religion. That wouldn't be proper at all.'

They were all kind-hearted fellows, and if they despised Peter it was not out of malice but out of a compulsion to give vent to their better feelings. After all, how often could they practise the Christian virtue of forgiving their enemies, of humbling themselves to their inferiors? Hadn't Christ himself allowed a Jewish whore to wash his feet and dry them with her hair? The opportunity to emulate the son of God filled them with a new wave of benevolence and even gratitude towards the newcomer – and doesn't all love spring from a desire to transcend ourselves? In that moment, had there been a need, they would have laid down their lives to protect the Jew from any harm.

But the student couldn't discern their tender sentiments; he thought that anti-semites had no hearts. Worse: having made up his mind that they were all unfeeling morons, he still persisted in believing that he could teach them a lesson. 'My dad is so greedy,' he confessed histrionically, 'he sometimes steals my pocket money that he gives me himself.'

'Don't ride yourself, kid,' Josef countered, 'that even happens in Christian families. What else can the old man do when he runs out of beer money?'

'Your father is your father. You must honour your parents, no matter what.'

'And my mother, she's a typical Jewess,' Peter continued doggedly, deter-mined to jolt them back to reality with the most ludicrous, most incredible story he could fabricate. 'My mother has a lover!'

'Never mind, son, you must honour her no matter what she does.'

Everyone concurred and, as the air-raid sirens sounded, the men went back to work in a cheerful, friendly mood.

After a few days, however, they began to be annoyed, as the kid went on pestering them with his Jewishness and Jewish vices, and no longer with an air of remorse but with unaccountable impatience and hostility. When he complained one morning that it was going to be too hot a day even for the descendant of a desert tribe, Josef decided he had heard enough.

'Jews aren't *that* different from other people,' he growled while cleaning his cutting machine. The parts had to be oiled to work properly, but the oil collected all the iron dust and particles of dirt, forming a thick mud which it was a nerve-racking job to remove, especially from the joints and screws. 'They suffer from the heat just like anybody else. You sound like you're worried we'll forget who you are!' He always left the machine spotless, but the night man never bothered to clean it – an injustice which riled Josef each morning as he confronted the unholy mess. 'I used to think you pretended you weren't a Jew because you had the decency to be ashamed of it, but you're just a nervy bastard like all the rest.'

'A Jew is a Jew is a Jew,' Peter announced triumphantly as he stepped out to the courtyard.

Josef walked over to the next man to impart this new turn of events. The first half-hour of the day was given over to tinkering with the machinery, and discipline wasn't taken seriously before six-thirty a.m. 'That weakling of mine, he's getting too smart. He never stops blabbing about his race.'

'Maybe he's trying to ease his conscience.'

'He has no conscience, that freak. He's bragging, I tell you. He's *proud* of it.'

As soon as Josef had stated the phenomenon, it became immediately obvious to the others as something they had already detected themselves. Only Toth was taken by surprise. 'I heard many things in my life,' said the old gossip, his head trembling with excitement, 'but that beats all. Proud of it! And I was just saying to my lady last night that there's nice ones among them, once you get to know them.'

'Before you leave us, kid,' Josef said in as hostile a voice and as casual a manner as he could possibly manage, 'you should tell us what you eat at Passover. I've always wondered about that.'

The two young men had come to treat each other with intense revulsion, but the student scored more points, feverishly baiting his workmate (and anybody else who would listen) with his racial superiority in evil-doing. Though the others had grown tired even of despising him, Josef remained fair game.

'Why, we eat the traditional orthodox food, of course – you'd probably throw it up.' He couldn't be more precise as he wasn't quite sure whether the answer should be goose or lamb; besides, lamb sounded too ordinary to send Josef into a fit.

'I'd throw up, that's for sure,' answered the other, as if he were indeed about to do so, but then buried his nose in the paper cup and loudly slurped his coffee. Between one and two a.m. an old woman rolled a trolley through the building, dispensing hot drinks to all those who asked for them; but many of the men wouldn't eat or drink anything during the night, even though it was now their daytime. To give them a break from the heat, the management had switched around the first and last shifts at the beginning of August, and they now spent their rest period inside the building to keep warm. Also, the cavernous interior of the long, narrow shed looked more inviting at night: the rickety and rather small machines had a greater presence, their bulk looming larger and brighter with the metallic dust glittering on their surfaces in the light of the bare overhead bulbs. Not that Josef gave a thought to his surroundings: he was straining his eyes on the floor to conceal his agitation. He had enquired about Passover meals to embarrass the arrogant s.o.b. with the crimes of his ancestors, but as soon as he heard his own question, he had a foreboding of the answer. Why should the Jews have changed? Suddenly his eyes were filled with the image of the body he had seen lying on the pavement during the war: it was a small boy, and his bowels were hanging outside his shirt. No, the Jews weren't the only ones without mercy, but who else would murder infants for food? Though Josef kept opening and closing his eyes, he couldn't erase the image of the entrails and the shirt. His throat was thick with rage and he had to drink the rest of his coffee before he could speak. 'And how do you get hold of a baby?'

'What baby?' asked Peter, who seemed to have lost the thread of the conversation.

'They couldn't get babies these days,' interjected the foreman. A tall, blond man in his late forties, slightly stooped under the weight of his authority, he had kept his distance from the men while they were on the morning shift, but seemed to have settled down among them since they had come on night duty. 'It's impossible to abduct babies now.'

'What do you mean, impossible? How many grown men disappeared just from this place?'

'That's different – that was politics.'

'You mean to tell me that the Jews can't do as much for their religion as others do for politics? Anyway, did you ever hear of a secret police man who wasn't a Jew?'

'That's just what I mean – you go after hearsay, not facts. You talk like a reactionary,' the foreman said, without much conviction.

The two continued arguing for some time before Peter realised that they actually suspected him of eating babies; but if he was slow to catch on, he made up for it with enthusiasm. 'You can abduct anybody for gold,' he assured them. 'And especially babies. We buy a baby every year from one of the hospitals. They'll only sell them for gold or U.S. dollars, but you can get them.'

Some of the men sitting by their machines got up from their stools and drifted closer. Though lately they had lost interest in the student and his big talk, the mention of U.S. dollars gave this story the ring of truth. As Peter worked outside in the courtyard and had no stool of his own, he happened to be sitting on top of a huge pile of angle-irons, and it's possible that being physically above the others and literally looking down on them contributed to his heedless mood. 'If you have hard currency,' he went on matter-of-factly, 'you can eat as many babies as you want.'

'Why don't you shut up?' asked the exasperated foreman. 'What's got into you? You're practising to be an actor or something?'

'I just wanted to enlighten you,' Peter answered pertly, though by now he wanted to shock and annoy the company for the sheer joy of it.

'It had to be the hospital,' Josef said in a low, shaking voice, thinking that the same fate might have befallen him had he been born in a hospital instead of in the safety of his home. He had a horror of those quiet, sinister buildings, and what was a huge joke to the doctor's son appeared entirely plausible to him. 'That's the easiest place to pinch babies from. I should have guessed that much.'

'We get them from the maternity ward. It's really very simple. My mother just phones the head nurse and asks for a healthy newborn baby.'

'A Christian child, you mean!' protested a man farther back.

'Naturally. You wouldn't think we'd eat our own kind, would you?'

'Holy Mary,' sighed old Toth, the saliva suddenly flooding his cheek. 'I would never have believed it if you hadn't told me.'

'Go on, tell us!' Josef demanded. 'Tell us!'

'Well, the head nurse and my mother haggle over the price for a while on the phone, and then the baby is put into an ambulance, it screams through the streets with its sirens going full blast, and before you can say a prayer the baby is in our kitchen. Why, after Passover there are some maternity wards without a single infant left in them. They have to send home all the mothers.' Complacently, Peter looked down at his audience, giving them time to visualise the hospital nursery with its rows of empty cots, the hysteria of hundreds of mothers, the mass conspiracy of nurses, doctors, orderlies, ambulance drivers, porters, police, officials and newspapermen, all of them willing to act as accessories to infanticide. Assuming an air of relaxed indifference, he contemplated the moment of triumph when the men would wake up with a start and curse him shamefacedly for their own gullibility. 'When it's there, my father cuts the head off and then we roast the thing in the electric stove at a moderate temperature,' he added for final measure.

However, no one started shaking his fist at the student. The men were silent and kept looking at the floor. They were too stunned to consider the petty mechanics of the crime – indeed, who could be so unfeeling as to worry about nurses, doctors and policemen, with the story of an innocent child's slaughter still ringing in his ears? Their hearts were gripped by the helpless infant's terror in its last moments, that terror was all that they could possibly hold, as their faces distended and darkened to the colour of frozen blood.

Only the foreman had the presence of mind to reason at all. 'Come on boys, break it up, let's get back to work.' To show a good example, he walked away.

'You just think that one over,' said Peter. Climbing down from the pile of angle-irons and knocking a few pieces to the floor in the process, he walked out to the courtyard with the sense of a job well done.

No one else moved or said anything for some time. Then old Toth decided to shuffle back to his place, mumbling weakly on the way. 'I wouldn't have believed it could still happen, not in these days.'

'There's a woman in our street,' Josef said, recovering enough to crush the paper cup in his fist. 'She was taken to a hospital to have her baby, but she never saw it. They told her it was born dead.'

For a moment the student reappeared in the doorway, dropping his load of rods on the floor, then turned around smartly.

'He doesn't give a damn how we feel,' Josef thought, 'and why should he? What could we do about it? I touch him and they fix me up in prison.' In fact, it is conceivable that nothing would have happened that night if he had *expected* himself to avenge the children; he might then have reflected long enough about the whole business to suspect its improbability. But Josef had listened to the student's story – just as he always listened to stories concerning Jews – with the willing credulity one might accord to a description of the customs of the aborigines in Australia. Why should he have bothered to wonder whether the story was true or not? It had nothing to do with him. What he wanted to do was to forget the whole thing. But once he had allowed the idea to enter his head, by a forged passport as it were, once the thought was inside, it made no difference how it had got there; he believed it just as much as if he had seen photographs of the babies. He was overcome with pity for the children and shame for not lifting a finger against the butchers.

The student returned with another load of rods and threw them on top of the others. The clanging of the metal startled Josef, who went back to his machine; but he couldn't start the motor, his hands were shaking, he thought he heard a child crying – or thought he *should* hear it. 'They know we won't hit back,' he thought. 'They can kill our children, they can even brag about it, they know we can't do a thing, just swallow and forget.' The more he tried to forget, the more his mind turned on his own shame; was there anything in life he wouldn't put up with? He looked about him as wildly as if the shed had been a closed grave and he had awakened to find himself buried alive.

'They can do what they want to us!' he cried out. 'We're just a bunch of sheep, it's a wonder they don't eat every one of us!'

The words carried to most of his workmates and there was an approving murmur. The building was in fact uncannily quiet: only a few of the machines were going, the men were just fiddling about disconcertedly, and the foreman couldn't be seen anywhere.

'He might be just pulling our legs, you know,' one man said doubtfully. 'The last person I heard tell that kind of story was my grandfather, and he was crazy as a mad parrot, God rest his soul. It might be just an old wives' tale.'

'Good,' Josef commented, jerking his head upward. He was beyond hate now: one hates a person, and the Jew was no longer a person but simply the accidental subject of this matter between his conscience and God. 'You just stick to that line. If anybody wants to accuse us of anything we can laugh at them and say they must think we're all off our heads.' Nevertheless, he went back to his machine and tried to work.

Though the air was cold outside, Peter preferred working at night. The sunlight was too sharp, it showed the true and worst side of each piece of junk, made the oil waste and the men themselves stink, and burned into everything the sense of unending and universal disintegration. But at night the bare electric bulbs that swayed over the courtyard, hanging on wires strung between the roofs of the buildings, blurred the sharpest edges of squalor, and the surrounding dark and silence lent everything that moved or gave a sound a degree of uniqueness. During the day the chimneys spewed only smoke and soot, but at night there were sparks flashing in the smoke, so many signs of life in a world dead in sleep. As Peter walked back and forth between the wavering circles of light, shouldering his rods with practised ease, he whistled an aria from The Highlights of Verdi.

Hearing the whistling, Josef let out a cry, snatched a piece of angle-iron and ran out to the courtyard, and two of the men followed him. The rest later testified that they hadn't noticed what was happening. The student was found when the sun came up, several courtyards away from his post, with a fractured skull but still alive. Eventually he recovered from his injuries, though he never quite got over his surprise.

WILLIAM TREVOR

# The Mark-2 Wife

STANDING alone at the Lowhrs' party Anna Mackintosh thought about her husband Edward, establishing him clearly for this purpose in her mind's eye. He was a thin man, forty-one years of age, with fair hair that was often untidy. In the seventeen years they'd been married he had changed very little: he was still nervous with other people, and smiled in the same abashed way, and his face was still almost boyish. She believed she had failed him because he had wished for children and she had not been able to supply any. She had, over the years, developed a nervous condition about this fact and in the end, quite some time ago now, she had consulted a psychiatrist, a Dr Abbatt, at Edward's pleading.

In the Lowhrs' rich drawing-room, its walls and ceiling gleaming with a metallic surface of ersatz gold, Anna listened to dance music coming from a tape-recorder and continued to think about her husband. In a moment he would be at the party too, since they had agreed to meet there, although by now it was three-quarters of an hour later than the time he had stipulated. The Lowhrs were people he knew in a business way, and he had said he thought it wise that he and Anna should attend this gathering of theirs. She had never met them before, which made it more difficult for her, having to wait about, not knowing a soul in the room. When she thought about it she felt hard done by, for although Edward was kind to her and always had been, it was far from considerate to be as late as this. Because of her nervous condition she felt afraid and had developed a sickness in her stomach. She looked at her watch and sighed.

People arrived, some of them kissing the Lowhrs, others nodding and smiling. Two dark-skinned maids carried trays of drinks among the guests, offering them graciously and murmuring thanks when a glass was accepted. 'I'll be there by half-past nine,' Edward had said that morning. 'If you don't turn up till ten you won't have to be alone at all.' He had kissed her after that, and had left the house. I'll wear the blue, she had thought, for she liked the colour better than any other: it suggested serenity to her, and the idea of serenity, especially as a quality in herself, was something she valued. She had said as much to Dr Abbatt, who had agreed that serenity was something that should be important in her life.

An elderly couple, tall twig-like creatures of seventy-five, a General Ritchie and his wife, observed the lone state of Anna Mackintosh and reacted in different ways. 'That woman seems out of things,' said Mrs Ritchie. 'We should go and talk to her.'

But the General gave it as his opinion that there was something the matter with this woman who was on her own. 'Now, don't let's get involved,' he rather tetchily begged. 'In any case she doesn't look in the mood for chat.'

His wife shook her head. 'Our name is Ritchie,' she said to Anna, and Anna, who had been looking at the whisky in her glass, lifted her head and saw a thin old woman who was as straight as a needle, and behind her a man who'was thin also but who stooped a bit and seemed to be cross. 'He's an old soldier,' said Mrs Ritchie. 'A General that was.'

Strands of white hair trailed across the pale dome of the old man's head. He had sharp eyes, like a terrier's, and a grey moustache. 'It's not a party I care to be at,' he muttered, holding out a bony hand. 'My wife's the one for this.'

Anna said who she was and added that her husband was late and that she didn't know the Lowhrs.

'We thought it might be something like that,' said Mrs Ritchie. 'We don't know anyone either, but at least we have one another to talk to.' The Lowhrs, she added, were an awfully nice, generous couple.

'We met them on a train in Switzerland,' the General murmured quietly. 'Quite suitable, really.'

Anna glanced across the crowded room at the people they spoke of. The Lowhrs were wholly different in appearance from the Ritchies. They were small and excessively fat, and they both wore glasses and smiled a lot. Like two balls, she thought.

'My husband knows them in a business way,' she said. She looked again at her watch: the time was half-past ten. There was a silence, and then Mrs Ritchie said:

'They invited us to two other parties in the past. It's very kind, for we don't give parties ourselves any more. We live a quiet sort of life now.' She went on talking, saying among other things that it was pleasant to see the younger set at play. When she stopped, the General added:

'The Lowhrs feel sorry for us, actually.'

'They're very kind,' his wife repeated.

Anna had been aware of a feeling of uneasiness the moment she'd entered the golden room, and had Edward been with her she'd have wanted to say that they should turn round and go away again. The uneasiness had increased whenever she'd noted the time, and for some reason these old people for whom the Lowhrs were sorry had added to it even more. She would certainly talk this over with Dr Abbatt, she decided, and then, quite absurdly, she felt an urge to telephone Dr Abbatt and tell him at once about the feeling she had. She closed her eyes, thinking that she would keep them like that for only the slightest moment so that the Ritchies wouldn't notice and think it odd. While they were still closed she heard Mrs Ritchie say:

'Are you all right, Mrs Mackintosh?'

She opened her eyes and saw that General Ritchie and his wife were examining her face with interest. She imagined them wondering about her, a woman of forty whose husband was an hour late. They'd be thinking, she thought, that the absent husband didn't have much of a feeling for this wife to be as careless as that. And yet, they'd probably think, he must have had a feeling for her once since he had married her in the first place.

'It's just,' said Mrs Ritchie, 'that I had the notion you were going to faint.'

The voice of Petula Clark came powerfully from the taperecorder. At one end of the room people were beginning to dance in a casual way, some still holding their glasses in their hands.

'The heat could have affected you,' said the General, bending forward so that his words would reach her.

Anna shook her head. She tried to smile, but the smile failed to materialise. She said:

'I never faint, actually.'

She could feel a part of herself attempting to bar from her mind the entry of unwelcome thoughts. Hastily she said, unable to think of anything better:

'My husband's really frightfully late.'

'You know,' said General Ritchie, 'it seems to me we met your husband here.' He turned to his wife. 'A fair-haired man— he said his name was Mackintosh. Is your husband fair, Mrs Mackintosh?'

'Of course,' cried Mrs Ritchie. 'Awfully nice.'

Anna said that Edward was fair. Mrs Ritchie smiled at her husband and handed him her empty glass. He reached out for Anna's. She said:

'Whisky, please. By itself.'

'He's probably held up in bloody traffic,' said the General before moving off.

'Yes, probably that,' Mrs Ritchie said. 'I do remember him well, you know.'

'Edward did come here before. I had a cold.'

'Completely charming. We said so afterwards.'

One of the dark-skinned maids paused with a tray of drinks. Mrs Ritchie explained that her husband was fetching some. 'Thank you, madam,' said the dark-skinned maid, and the General returned.

'It isn't the traffic,' Anna said rather suddenly and loudly. 'Edward's not held up like that at all.'

The Ritchies sipped their drinks. They can sense I'm going to be a nuisance, Anna thought. 'I'm afraid it'll be boring,' he had said. 'We'll slip away at eleven and have dinner in Charlotte Street.' She heard him saying it now, quite distinctly. She saw him smiling at her.

'I get nervous about things,' she said to the Ritchies. 'I worry unnecessarily. I try not to.'

Mrs Ritchie inclined her head in a sympathetic manner; the General coughed. There was a silence and then Mrs Ritchie spoke about episodes in their past. Anna looked at her watch and saw that it was five to eleven. 'Oh God,' she said.

The Ritchies asked her again if she was all right. She began to say she was but she faltered before the sentence was complete, and in that moment she gave up the struggle. What was the point, she thought, of exhausting oneself being polite and making idle conversation when all the time one was in a frightful state?

'He's going to be married again,' she said quietly and evenly. 'His Mark-2 wife.'

She felt better at once. The sickness left her stomach; she drank a little whisky and found its harsh taste a comfort.

'Oh, I'm terribly sorry,' said Mrs Ritchie.

Anna had often dreamed of the girl. She had seen her, dressed all in purple, with slim hips and a purple bow in her black hair. She had seen the two of them together in a speedboat, the beautiful young creature laughing her head off like a figure in an advertisement. She had talked for many hours to Dr Abbatt about her, and Dr Abbatt had made the point that the girl was simply an obsession. 'It's just a little nonsense,' he had said to her kindly, more than once. Anna knew in her calmer moments that it was just a little nonsense, for Edward was always kind and had never ceased to say he loved her. But in bad moments she argued against that conclusion, reminding herself that other kind men who said they loved their wives often made off with something new. Her own marriage being childless would make the whole operation simpler.

'I hadn't thought it would happen at a party,' Anna said to the Ritchies. 'Edward has always been decent and considerate. I imagined he would tell me quietly at home, and comfort me. I imagined he would be decent to the end.'

'You and your husband are not yet separated then?' Mrs Ritchie enquired.

'This is the way it is happening,' Anna repeated. 'D'you understand? Edward is delayed by his Mark-2 wife because she insists on delaying him. She's demanding that he should make his decision and afterwards that he and she should come to tell me, so that I won't have to wait any more. You understand,' she repeated, looking closely from one face to the other, 'that this isn't Edward's doing?'

'But, Mrs Mackintosh—'

'I have a woman's intuition about it. I have felt my woman's intuition at work since the moment I entered this room. I know precisely what's going to happen.'

Often, ever since the obsession had begun, she had wondered if she had any rights at all. Had she rights in the matter, she had asked herself, since she was running to fat and could supply no children? The girl would repeatedly give birth and everyone would be happy, for birth was a happy business. She had suggested to Dr Abbatt that she probably hadn't any rights, and for once he had spoken to her sternly. She said it now to the Ritchies, because it didn't seem to matter any more what words were spoken. On other occasions, when she was at home, Edward had been late and she had sat and waited for him, pretending it was a natural thing for him to be late. And when he arrived her fears had seemed absurd.

'You understand?' she said to the Ritchies.

The Ritchies nodded their thin heads, the General embarrassed, his wife concerned. They waited for Anna to speak. She said:

'The Lowhrs will feel sorry for me, as they do for you. "This poor woman," they'll cry, "left all in the lurch at our party! What a ghastly thing!" I should go home, you know, but I haven't even the courage for that.'

'Could we help at all?' asked Mrs Ritchie.

'You've been married all this time and not come asunder. Have you had children, Mrs Ritchie?'

Mrs Ritchie replied that she had had two boys and a girl. They were well grown up by now, she explained, and between them had provided her and the General with a dozen grand-children.

'What did you think of my husband?'

'Charming, Mrs Mackintosh, as I said.'

'Not the sort of man who'd mess a think like this up? You thought the opposite, I'm sure: that with bad news to break he'd chose the moment elegantly. Once he would have.'

'I don't understand,' protested Mrs Ritchie gently, and the General lent his support to that with a gesture.

'Look at me,' said Anna. 'I've worn well enough. Neither I nor Edward would deny it. A few lines and flushes, fatter and coarser. No one can escape all that. Did you never feel like a change, General?'

'A change?'

'I have to be rational. I have to say that it's no reflection on me. D'you understand that?'

'Of course it's no reflection.'

'It's like gadgets in shops. You buy a gadget and you develop an affection for it, having decided on it in the first place because you thought it was attractive. But all of a sudden there are newer and better gadgets in the shops. More up-to-date models.' She paused. She found a handkerchief and blew her nose. She said:

'You must excuse me: I am not myself tonight.'

'You mustn't get upset. Please don't,' Mrs Ritchie said.

Anna drank all the whisky in her glass and lifted another glass from a passing tray. 'There are too many people in this room,' she complained. 'There's not enough ventilation. It's ideal for tragedy.'

Mrs Ritchie shook her head. She put her hand on Anna's arm. 'Would you like us to go home with you and see you safely in?'

'I have to stay here.'

'Mrs Mackintosh, your husband would never act like that.'

'People in love are cruel. They think of themselves: why should they bother to honour the feelings of a discarded wife?'

'Oh, come now,' said Mrs Ritchie.

At that moment a bald man came up to Anna and took her glass from her hand and led her, without a word, on to the dancing area. As he danced with her, she thought that something else might have happened. Edward was not with anyone, she said to herself: Edward was dead. A telephone had rung in the Lowhrs' house and a voice had said that, en route to their party, a man had dropped dead on the pavement. A maid had taken the message and, not quite understanding it, had done nothing about it.

'I think we should definitely go home now.' General Ritchie said to his wife. 'We could be back for *A Book at Bedtime*.'

'We cannot leave her as easily as that. Just look at that poor creature.'

'That woman is utterly no concern of ours.'

'Just look at her.'

The General sighed and swore and did as he was bidden.

'My husband was meant to turn up,' Anna said to the bald man. 'I've just thought he may have died.' She laughed to indicate that she did not really believe this, in case the man became upset. But the man seemed not to be interested. She could feel his lips playing with a strand of her hair. Death, she thought, she could have accepted.

Anna could see the Ritchies watching her. Their faces were grave, but it came to her suddenly that the gravity was artificial. What, after all, was she to them that they should bother? She was a wretched woman at a party, a woman in a state, who was making an unnecessary fuss because her husband was about to give her her marching orders. Had the Ritchies been mocking her, she wondered, he quite directly, she in some special, subtle way of her own?

'Do you know those people I was talking to?' she said to her partner, but with a portion of her hair still in his mouth he made no effort at a reply. Passing near to her, she noticed the thick, square fingers of Mr Lowhr embedded in the flesh of his wife's shoulder. The couple danced by, seeing her and smiling, and it seemed to Anna that their smiles were as empty as the Ritchies' sympathy.

'My husband is leaving me for a younger woman,' she said to the bald man, a statement that caused him to shrug. He had pressed himself close to her, his knees on her thighs, forcing her legs this way and that. His hands were low on her body now, advancing on her buttocks. He was eating her hair.

'I'm sorry,' Anna said. 'I'd rather you didn't do any of that.'

He released her where they stood and smiled agreeably: she could see pieces of her hair on his teeth. He walked away, and she turned and went in the opposite direction.

'We're really most concerned,' said Mrs Ritchie. She and her husband were standing where Anna had left them, as though waiting for her. General Ritchie held out her glass to her.

'Why should you be concerned? That bald man ate my hair. That's what people do to used-up women like me. They eat your hair and force their bodies on you. You know, General.'

'Certainly, I don't. Not at all.'

'That man knew all about me. D'you think he'd have taken his liberties if he hadn't? A man like that can guess.'

'Nonsense,' said Mrs Ritchie firmly. She stared hard at Anna, endeavouring to impress upon her the errors in her logic.

'If you want to know, that man's a drunk,' said the General. 'He was far gone when he arrived here and he's more so now.'

'Why are you saying that?' Anna cried shrilly. 'Why are you telling me lies and mocking me?'

'Lies?' demanded the General, snapping the word out. 'Lies?'

'My dear, we're not mocking you at all,' murmured Mrs Ritchie.

'You and those Lowhrs and everyone else, God knows. The big event at this party is that Edward Mackintosh will reject his wife for another.'

'Oh now, Mrs Mackintosh—'

'Second marriages are often happier, you know. No reason why they shouldn't be.'

'We would like to help if we could,' Mrs Ritchie said.

'Help? In God's name, how can I be helped? How can two elderly strangers help me when my husband gives me up? What kind of help? Would you give me money – an income say? Or offer me some other husband? Would you come to visit me and talk to me so that I shouldn't be lonely? Or strike down my husband, General, to show our disapproval? Would you scratch out the little girl's eyes for me, Mrs Ritchie? Would you slap her brazen face?'

'We simply thought we might help in some way,' Mrs Ritchie said. 'Just because we're old and pretty useless doesn't mean we can't make an effort.'

'We are all God's creatures, you are saying. We should offer aid to one another at all opportunities, when marriages get broken and decent husbands are made cruel. Hold my hands then, and let us wait for Edward and his Mark-2 wife. Let's all three speak together and tell them what we think.'

She held out her hands but the Ritchies did not take them.

'We don't mean to mock you, as you seem to think,' the General said. 'I must insist on that, madam.'

'You're mocking me with your talk about helping. The world is not like that. You like to listen to me for my entertainment value: I'm a good bit of gossip for you. I'm a woman going on about her husband and then getting insulted by a man and seeing the Lowhrs smiling over it. Tell your little grandchildren that sometime.'

Mrs Ritchie said that the Lowhrs, she was sure, had not smiled at any predicament that Anna had found herself in, and the General impatiently repeated that the man was drunk.

'The Lowhrs smiled,' Anna said, 'and you have mocked me too. Though perhaps you don't even know it.'

As she pushed a passage through the people, she felt the sweat running on her face and her body. There was a fog of smoke in the room by now, and the voices of the people, struggling to be heard above the music, were louder than before. The man she had danced with was sitting in a corner with his shoes off, and a woman in a crimson dress was trying to persuade him to put them on again. At the door of the room she found Mr Lowhr. 'Shall we dance?' he said.

She shook her head, feeling calmer all of a sudden. Mr Lowhr suggested a drink.

'May I telephone?' she said. 'Quietly somewhere?'

'Upstairs,' said Mr Lowhr, smiling immensely at her. 'Up two flights, the door ahead of you: a tiny guest room. Take a glass with you.'

She nodded, saying she'd like a little whisky.

'Let me give you a tip,' Mr Lowhr said as he poured her some from a nearby bottle. 'Always buy Haig whisky. It's distilled by a special method.'

'You're never going so soon?' said Mrs Lowhr, appearing at her husband's side.

'Just to telephone,' said Mr Lowhr. He held out his hand with the glass of whisky in it. Anna took it, and as she did so she caught a glimpse of the Ritchies watching her from the other end of the room. Her calmness vanished. The Lowhrs, she noticed, were looking at her too, and smiling. She wanted to ask them why they were smiling, but she knew if she did that they'd simply make some polite reply. Instead she said:

'You shouldn't expose your guests to men who eat hair. Even unimportant guests.'

She turned her back on them and passed from the room. She crossed the hall, sensing that she was being watched. 'Mrs Machintosh,' Mr Lowhr called after her.

His plumpness filled the doorway. He hovered, seeming uncertain about pursuing her. His face was bewildered and apparently upset.

'Has something disagreeable happened?' he said in a low voice across the distance between them.

'You saw. You and your wife thought fit to laugh, Mr Lowhr.'

'I do assure you, Mrs Mackintosh, I've no idea what you're talking about.'

'It's fascinating, I suppose. Your friends the Ritchies find it fascinating too.'

'Look here, Mrs Mackintosh—'

'Oh, don't blame them. They've nothing left but to watch and mock, at an age like that. The point is, there's a lot of hypocrisy going on tonight.' She nodded at Mr Lowhr to emphasise that last remark, and then went swiftly upstairs.

'I imagine the woman's gone off home,' the General said. I dare say the husband's drinking in a pub.'

'I worried once,' replied Mrs Ritchie, speaking quietly for she didn't wish the confidence to be heard by others. 'That female, Mrs Flynn.'

The General roared with laughter. 'Trixie Flynn,' he shouted. 'Good God, she was a free-for-all!'

'Oh, do be quiet.'

'Dear girl, you didn't ever think—'

'I didn't know what to think, if you want to know.'

Greatly amused, the General seized what he hoped would be his final drink.

He placed it behind a green plant on a table. 'Shall we dance one dance,' he said, 'just to amuse them? And then when I've had that drink to revive me we can thankfully make our way.'

But he found himself talking to nobody, for when he had turned from his wife to secrete his drink she had moved away. He followed her to where she was questioning Mrs Lowhr.

'Some little tiff,' Mrs Lowhr was saying as he approached.

'Hardly a tiff,' corrected Mrs Ritchie. 'The woman's terribly upset.' She turned to her husband, obliging him to speak.

'Upset,' he said.

'Oh, there now,' cried Mrs Lowhr, taking each of the Ritchies by an arm. 'Why don't you take the floor and forget it?'

They both of them recognised from her tone that she was thinking that the elderly exaggerated things and didn't always understand the ways of marriage in the modern world. The General especially resented the insinuation. He said:

'Has the woman gone away?'

'She is upstairs telephoning. Some silly chap upset her apparently, during a dance. That's all it is, you know.'

'You have got the wrong end of the stick entirely,' said the General angrily, 'and you're trying to say we have. The woman believes her husband may arrive here with the girl he's chosen as his second wife.'

'But that's ridiculous!' cried Mrs Lowhr with a tinkling laugh.

'It is what the woman thinks,' said the General loudly, 'whether it's ridiculous or not.' More quietly, Mrs Ritchie added:

'She thinks she has a powerful intuition when all it is is a disease.'

'I'm cross with this Mrs Mackintosh for upsetting you two dear people!' cried Mrs Lowhr with a shrillness that matched her roundness and her glasses. 'I really and truly am.'

A big man came up as she spoke and lifted her into his arms, preparatory to dancing with her. 'What could anyone do?' she called back at the Ritchies as the man rotated her away. 'What can you do for a nervy woman like that?'

There was dark wallpaper on the walls of the room: black and brown with little smears of muted yellow. The curtains matched it; so did the bedspread on the low single bed, and the covering on the padded head-board. The carpet ran from wall to wall and was black and thick. There was a narrow wardrobe with a door of padded black leather, and brass studs and an ornamental brass handle. The dressing-table and the stool in front of it reflected this general motif in different ways. Two shelves, part of the bed, attached to it on either side of the pillows, served as bedside tables: on each there was a lamp and a book, and on one of them a white telephone.

As Anna closed and locked the door, she felt that in a dream she had been in a dark room in a house where there was a party, waiting for Edward to bring her terrible news. She drank a little whisky and moved towards the telephone. She dialled a number and when a voice answered her call she said:

'Dr Abbatt? It's Anna Mackintosh.'

His voice, as always, was so soft she could hardly hear it. 'Ah, Mrs Mackintosh,' he said.

'I want to talk to you.'

'Of course, Mrs Mackintosh, of course. Tell me now.'

'I'm at a party given by people called Lowhr. Edward was to be here but he didn't turn up. I was all alone and then two old people like scarecrows talked to me. They said their name was Ritchie. And a man ate my hair when we were dancing. The Lowhrs smiled at that.'

'I see. Yes?'

'I'm in a room at the top of the house. I've locked the door.'

'Tell me about the room, Mrs Mackintosh.'

'There's black leather on the wardrobe and the dressing-table. Curtains and things match. Dr Abbatt?'

'Yes?'

'The Ritchies are people who injure other people, I think. Intentionally or unintentionally, it never matters.'

'They are strangers to you, these Ritchies?'

'They attempted to mock me. People know at this party, Dr Abbatt; they sense what's going to happen because of how I look.'

Watching for her to come downstairs, the Ritchies stood in the hall and talked to one another.

'I'm sorry,' said Mrs Ritchie. 'I know it would be nicer to go home.'

'What can we do, old sticks like us? We know not a thing about such women. It's quite absurd.'

'The woman's on my mind, dear. And on yours too. You know it.'

'I think she'll be more on our minds if we come across her again. She'll turn nasty, I'll tell you that.'

'Yes, but it would please me to wait a little.'

'To be insulted,' said the General.

'Oh, do stop being so cross, dear.'

'The woman's a stranger to us. She should regulate her life and have done with it. She has no right to bother people.'

'She is a human being in great distress. No, don't say anything, please, if it isn't pleasant.'

The General went into a sulk, and at the end of it he said grudgingly:

'Trixie Flynn was nothing.'

'Oh, I know. Trixie Flynn is dead and done for years ago. I didn't worry like this woman if that's what's on your mind.'

'It wasn't,' lied the General. 'The woman worries ridiculously.'

'I think, you know, we may yet be of use to her: I have a feeling about that.'

'For God's sake, leave the feelings to her. We've had enough of that for one day.'

'As I said to her, we're not entirely useless. No one ever can be.'

'You feel you're being attacked again, Mrs Mackintosh. Are you calm? You haven't been drinking too much?'

'A little.'

'I see.'

'I am being replaced by a younger person.'

'You say you're in a bedroom. Is it possible for you to lie on the bed and talk to me at the same time? Would it be comfortable?'

Anna placed the receiver on the bed and settled herself. She picked it up again and said:

'If he died, there would be a funeral and I'd never forget his kindness to me. I can't do that if he has another wife.'

'We have actually been over this ground,' said Dr Abbatt more softly than ever. 'But we can of course go over it again.'

'Any time, you said.'

'Of course.'

'What has happened is perfectly simple. Edward is with the girl. He is about to arrive here to tell me to clear off. She's insisting on that. It's not Edward, you know.'

'Mrs Mackintosh, I'm going to speak firmly now. We've agreed between us that there's no young girl in your husband's life. You have an obsession, Mrs Mackintosh, about the fact that you have never had children and that men sometimes marry twice –'

'There's such a thing as the Mark-2 wife,' Anna cried. 'You know there is. A girl of nineteen who'll delightedly give birth to Edward's sons.'

'No, no –'

'I had imagined Edward telling me. I had imagined him pushing back his hair and lighting a cigarette in his untidy way. "I'm terribly sorry," he would say, and leave me nothing to add to that. Instead it's like this: a nightmare.'

'It is not a nightmare, Mrs Mackintosh.'

'This party is a nightmare. People are vultures here.'

'Mrs Mackintosh. I must tell you that I believe you're seeing the people at this party in a most exaggerated light.'

'A man—'

'A man nibbled your hair. Worse things can happen. This is not a nightmare, Mrs Mackintosh. Your husband has been delayed. Husbands are always being delayed. D'you see? You and I and your husband are all together trying to rid you of this perfectly normal obsession you've developed. We mustn't complicate matters, now must we?'

'I didn't run away, Dr Abbatt. I said to myself I mustn't run away from this party. I must wait and face whatever was to happen. You told me to face things.'

'I didn't tell you, my dear. We agreed between us. We talked it out, the difficulty about facing things and we saw the wisdom of it. Now I want you to go back to the party and wait for your husband.'

'He's more than two hours late.'

'My dear Mrs Mackintosh, an hour or so is absolutely nothing these days. Now listen to me please.'

She listened to the soft voice as it reminded her of all that between them they had agreed. Dr Abbatt went over the ground, from the time she had first consulted him to the present moment. He charted her obsession until it seemed once again, as he said, a perfectly normal thing for a woman of forty to have.

After she had said good-bye, Anna sat on the bed feeling very calm. She had read the message behind Dr Abbatt's words: that it was ridiculous, her perpetually going on in this lunatic manner. She had come to a party and in no time at all she'd been behaving in a way that was, she supposed, mildly crazy. It always happened, she knew, and it would as long as the trouble remained: in her mind, when she began to worry, everything became jumbled and unreal, turning her into an impossible person. How could Edward, for heaven's sake, be expected to live with her fears and her suppositions? Edward would crack as others would, tormented by an impossible person. He'd become an alcoholic or he'd have some love affair with a woman just as old as she was, and the irony of that would be too great. She knew, as she sat there, that she couldn't help herself, and that as long as she lived with Edward she wouldn't be able to do any better. 'I have lost touch with reality,' she said. 'I shall let him go, as a bird is released. In my state how can I have rights?'

She left the room and slowly descended the stairs. There were framed prints of old motor-cars on the wall, and she paused now and again to examine one, emphasising to herself her own continued calmness. She was thinking that she'd get herself a job. She might even tell Edward that Dr Abbatt had suggested that their marriage should end since she wasn't able to live with her thoughts any more. She'd insist on a divorce at once. She didn't mind the thought of it now, because of course it would be different: she was doing what she guessed Dr Abbatt had been willing her to do for quite a long time really: she was taking matters into her own hands, she was acting positively – rejecting, not being rejected herself. Her marriage was ending cleanly and correctly.

She found her coat and thanked the dark-skinned maid who held it for her. Edward was probably at the party by now, but in the new circumstances that was neither here nor there. She'd go home in a taxi and pack a suitcase and then telephone for another taxi. She'd leave a note for Edward and go to a hotel, without telling him where.

'Goodnight,' she said to the maid. She stepped towards the hall door as the maid opened it for her, and as she did so she felt a hand touch her shoulder. 'No,

Edward,' she said. 'I must go now.' But when she turned she saw that the hand
belonged to Mrs Ritchie. Behind her, looking tired, stood the General. For a
moment there was a silence. Then Anna, speaking to both of them, said:

'I'm extremely sorry. Please forgive me.'

'We were worried about you,' said Mrs Ritchie. 'Will you be all right, my
dear?'

'The fear is worse than the reality, Mrs Ritchie. I can no longer live with the
fear.'

'We understand.'

'It's strange,' Anna said, passing through the doorway and standing at the top
of the steps that led to the street. 'Strange, coming to a party like this, given by
people I didn't know and meeting you and being so rude. Please don't tell me if
my husband is here or not. It doesn't concern me now. I'm quite calm.'

The Ritchies watched her descend the steps and call out to a passing taxi-
cab. They watched the taxi drive away.

'Calm!' said General Ritchie.

'She's still in a state, poor thing,' agreed his wife. 'I do feel sorry.'

They stood on the steps of the Lowhrs' house, thinking about the brief glance
they had had of another person's life, bewildered by it and saddened, for they
themselves, though often edgy on the surface, had had a happy marriage.

'At least she's standing on her own feet now,' Mrs Ritchie said, 'I think it'll
save her.'

A taxi drew up at the house and the Ritchies watched it, thinking for a
moment that Anna Mackintosh, weak in her resolve, had returned in search of
her husband. But it was a man who emerged and ran up the steps in a manner
which suggested that, like the man who had earlier misbehaved on the dance-
floor, he was not entirely sober. He passed the Ritchies and entered the house.
'That is Edward Mackintosh,' said Mrs Ritchie.

The girl who was paying the taxi-driver paused in what she was doing to see
where her companion had dashed away to and observed the thin figures staring
at her from the lighted doorway, murmuring to one another.

'Cruel,' said the General. 'The woman said so: we must give her that.'

'He's a kind man,' replied Mrs Ritchie. 'He'll listen to us.'

'To us, for heaven's sake?'

'We have a thing to do, as I said we might have.'

'The woman has gone. I'm not saying I'm not sorry for her—'

'And who shall ask for mercy for the woman, since she cannot ask herself?
There is a little to be saved, you know: she has made a gesture, poor thing. It must
be honoured.'

'My dear, we don't know these people; we met the woman quite in
passing.'

The girl came up the steps, settling her purse into its right place in her
handbag. She smiled at the Ritchies, and they thought that the smile had a hint

of triumph about it, as though it was her first smile since the victory that Anna Mackintosh had said some girl was winning that night.

'Even if he'd listen,' muttered the General when the girl had passed by, 'I doubt that she would.'

'It's just that a little time should be allowed to go by,' his wife reminded him. 'That's all that's required. Until the woman's found her feet again and feels she has a voice in her own life.'

'We're interfering,' said the General, and his wife said nothing. They looked at one another, remembering vividly the dread in Anna Mackintosh's face and the confusion that all her conversation had revealed.

The General shook his head. 'We are hardly the happiest choice,' he said, in a gentler mood at last, 'but I dare say we must try.'

He closed the door of the house and they paused for a moment in the hall, talking again of the woman who had told them her troubles. They drew a little strength from that, and felt armed to face once more the Lowhrs' noisy party. Together they moved towards it and through it, in search of a man they had met once before on a similar occasion. 'We are sorry for interfering,' they would quietly say; and making it seem as natural as they could, they would ask him to honour, above all else and in spite of love, the gesture of a woman who no longer interested him.

'A tall order,' protested the General, pausing in his forward motion, doubtful again.

'When the wrong people do things,' replied his wife, 'it sometimes works.' She pulled him on until they stood before Edward Mackintosh and the girl he'd chosen as his Mark-2 wife. They smiled at Edward Mackintosh and shook hands with him, and then there was a silence before the General said that it was odd, in a way, what they had to request.

# Johnny Panic and the Bible of Dreams

EVERY day from nine to five I sit at my desk facing the door of the office and type up other people's dreams. Not just dreams. That wouldn't be practical enough for my bosses. I type up also people's daytime complaints: trouble with mother, trouble with father, trouble with the bottle, the bed, the headache that bangs home and blacks out the sweet world for no known reason. Nobody comes to our office unless they have troubles. Troubles that can't be pinpointed by Wassermanns or Wechsler-Bellvues alone.

Maybe a mouse gets to thinking pretty early on how the whole world is run by these enormous feet. Well, from where I sit I figure the world is run by one thing and this one thing only. Panic with a dog-face, devil-face, hag-face, whore-face, panic in capital letters with no face at all – it's the same Johnny Panic, awake or asleep.

When people ask me where I work, I tell them I'm assistant to the secretary in one of the out-patient departments of the clinics' building of the City Hospital. This sounds so be-all, end-all they seldom get around to asking me more than what I do, and what I do is mainly type up records. On my own hook though, and completely under cover, I am pursuing a vocation that would set these doctors by their ears. In the privacy of my one-room apartment I call myself secretary to none other than Johnny Panic himself.

Dream by dream I am educating myself to become that rare character, rarer, in truth, than any member of the Psycho-analytic Institute, a dream connoisseur. Not a dream-stopper, a dream-explainer, an exploiter of dreams for the crass practical ends of health and happiness, but an unsordid collector of dreams for themselves alone. A lover of dreams for Johnny Panic's sake, the Maker of them all.

There isn't a dream I've typed up in our record books that I don't know by heart. There isn't a dream I haven't copied out at home into Johnny Panic's Bible of Dreams.

This is my real calling.

Some nights I take the elevator up to the roof of my apartment building. Some nights, about three a.m. Over the trees at the far side of the common the United Fund torch flare flattens and recovers under some witchy invisible push and here and there in the hunks of stone and brick I see a light. Most of all, though, I feel the city sleeping. Sleeping from the river on the west to the ocean on the east, like some rootless island rockabying itself on nothing at all.

I can be tight and nervy as the top string on a violin and yet by the time the sky begins to blue I'm ready for sleep. It's the thought of all those dreamers and what they're dreaming wears me down till I sleep the sleep of fever. Monday to Friday what do I do but type up those same dreams. Sure, I don't touch a fraction of them the city over, but page by page, dream by dream, my intake books fatten and weigh down the bookshelves of the cabinet in the narrow passage running parallel to the main hall, off which passage the doors to all the doctors' little interviewing cubicles open.

I've got a funny habit of identifying the people who come in by their dreams. As far as I'm concerned, the dreams single them out more than any Christian name. This one guy, for example, who works for a ball-bearing company in town, dreams every night how he's lying on his back with a grain of sand on his chest. Bit by bit this grain of sand grows bigger and bigger till it's big as a fair-sized house and he can't draw breath. Another fellow I know of has had a certain dream ever since they gave him ether and cut out his tonsils and adenoids when he was a kid. In this dream he's caught in the rollers of a cotton mill, fighting for his life. Oh, he's not alone, although he thinks he is. A lot of people these days dream they're being run over or eaten by machines. They're the cagey ones who won't go on the subway or the elevators. Coming back from my lunch hour in the hospital cafeteria I often pass them, puffing up the unswept stone stairs to our office on the fourth floor. I wonder, now and then, what dreams people had before ball-bearings and cotton mills were invented.

I've got a dream of my own. My one dream. A dream of dreams.

In this dream there's a great half-transparent lake stretching away in every direction, too big for me to see the shores of it, if there are any shores, and I'm hanging over it, looking down from the glass belly of some helicopter. At the bottom of the lake – so deep I can only guess at the dark masses moving and heaving – are the real dragons. The ones that were around before men started living in caves and cooking meat over fires and figuring out the wheel and the alphabet. Enormous isn't the word for them; they've got more wrinkles than Johnny Panic himself. Dream about these long enough and your feet and hands shrivel away when you look at them too closely; the sun shrinks to the size of an orange, only chillier, and you've been living in Roxbury since the last ice age. No place for you but a room padded soft as the first room you knew of, where you can dream and float, float and dream, till at last you actually are back among those great originals and there's no point in any dreams at all.

It's into this lake people's minds run at night, brooks and gutter-trickles to one borderless common reservoir. It bears no resemblance to those pure sparkling-blue sources of drinking water the suburbs guard more jealously than the Hope diamond in the middle of pine woods and barbed fences.

It's the sewage farm of the ages, transparence aside.

Now the water in this lake naturally stinks and smokes from what dreams have been left sogging around in it over the centuries. When you think how much room one night of dream props would take up for one person in one city, and that city a mere pinprick on a map of the world, and when you start multiplying this space by the population of the world, and that space by the number of nights there have been since the apes took to chipping axes out of stone and losing their hair, you have some idea what I mean. I'm not the mathematical type: my head starts splitting when I get only as far as the number of dreams going on during one night in the State of Massachusetts.

By this time I already see the surface of the lake swarming with snakes, dead bodies puffed as blowfish, human embryos bobbing around in laboratory bottles like so many unfinished messages from the great I Am. I see whole storehouses of hardware: knives, paper cutters, pistons and cogs and nut-crackers; the shiny fronts of cars looming up, glass-eyed and evil-toothed. Then there's the spider-man and the web-footed man from Mars, and the simple, lugubrious vision of a human face turning aside forever, in spite of rings and vows, to the last lover of all.

One of the most frequent shapes in this large stew is so commonplace it seems silly to mention it. It's a grain of dirt. The water is thick with these grains. They seep in among everything else and revolve under some queer power of their own, opaque, ubiquitous. Call the water what you will, Lake Nightmare, Bog of Madness, it's here the sleeping people lie and toss together among the props of their worst dreams, one great brotherhood, though each of them, waking, thinks himself singular, utterly apart.

This is my dream. You won't find it written up in any casebook.

Now the routine in our office is very different from the routine in Skin Clinic, for example, or in Tumour. The other clinics have strong similarities to each other; none are like ours. In our clinic treatment doesn't get prescribed. It is invisible. It goes right on in those little cubicles, each with its desk, its two chairs, its window and its door with the opaque glass rectangle set in the wood. There is a certain spiritual purity about this kind of doctoring. I can't help feeling the special privilege of my position as assistant secretary in the Adult Psychiatric Clinic. My sense of pride is borne out by the rude invasions of other clinics into our cubicles on certain days of the week for lack of space elsewhere: our building is a very old one, and the facilities have not expanded with the expanding needs of the time. On these days of overlap the contrast between us and the other clinics is marked.

On Tuesdays and Thursdays, for instance, we have lumbar punctures in one of our offices in the morning. If the practical nurse chances to leave the door of the cubicle open, as she usually does, I can glimpse the end of the white cot and the dirty yellow-soled bare feet of the patient sticking out from under the sheet. In spite of my distaste at this sight, I can't keep my eyes away from the bare feet, and I find myself glancing back from my typing every few minutes to see if they are still there, if they have changed their position at all. You can understand what a distraction this is in the middle of my work. I often have to reread what I have typed several times, under the pretence of careful proof-reading, in order to memorise the dreams I have copied down from the doctor's voice over the audiograph.

Nerve Clinic next door, which tends to the grosser, more unimaginative end of our business, also disturbs us in the mornings. We use their offices for therapy in the afternoon, as they are only a morning clinic, but to have their people crying, or singing, or chattering loudly in Italian or Chinese, as they often do, without break for four hours at a stretch every morning, is distracting to say the least. The patients down there are often referred to us if their troubles have no ostensible basis in the body.

In spite of such interruptions by other clinics, my own work is advancing at a great rate. By now I am far beyond copying only what comes after the patient's saying: 'I have this dream, doctor.' I am at the point of creating dreams that are not ever written down at all. Dreams that shadow themselves forth in the vaguest way, but are themselves hid, like a statue under red velvet before the grand unveiling.

To illustrate. This woman came in with her tongue swollen and stuck out so far she had to leave a party she was giving for twenty friends of her French-Canadian mother-in-law and be rushed to our emergency ward. She thought she didn't want her tongue to stick out and, to tell the truth, it was an exceedingly embarrassing affair for her, but she hated that French-Canadian mother-in-law worse than pigs, and her tongue was true to her opinion, even if the rest of her wasn't. Now she didn't lay claim to any dreams. I have only the bare facts above to begin with, yet behind them I detect the bulge and promise of a dream.

So I set myself to uprooting this dream from its confortable purchase under her tongue.

Whatever the dream I unearth, by work, taxing work, and even by a kind of prayer, I am sure to find a thumbprint in the corner, a malicious detail to the right of centre, a bodiless mid-air Cheshire cat grin, which shows the whole work to be got up by the genius of Johnny Panic, and him alone. He's sly, he's subtle, he's sudden as thunder, but he gives himself away only too often. He simply can't resist melodrama. Melodrama of the oldest, most obvious variety.

I remember one guy, a stocky fellow in a nail-studded black leather jacket, running straight in to us from a boxing match at Mechanics Hall, Johnny Panic hot at his heels. This guy, good Catholic though he was, young and upright and all, had one mean fear of death. He was actually scared blue he'd go to hell. He was a piece-worker at a fluorescent light plant. I remember this detail because I thought it funny he should work there, him being so afraid of the dark as it turned out. Johnny Panic injects a poetic element in this business you don't often find elsewhere. And for that he has my eternal gratitude.

I also remember quite clearly the scenario of the dream I had worked out for this guy: a gothic interior in some monastery cellar, going on and on as far as you could see, one of those endless perspectives between two mirrors, and the pillars and walls were made of nothing but human skulls and bones, and in every niche there was a body laid out, and it was the Hall of Time, with the bodies in the foreground still warm, discolouring and starting to rot in the middle distance, and the bones emerging, clean as a whistle, in a kind of white futuristic glow at the end of the line. As I recall, I had the whole scene lighted, for the sake of accuracy, not with candles, but with the ice-bright fluorescence that makes skin look green and all the pink and red flushes dead black-purple.

You ask, how do I know this was the dream of the guy in the black leather jacket? I don't know. I only believe this was his dream, and I work at belief with more energy and tears and entreaties than I work at re-creating the dream itself.

My office, of course, has its limitations. The lady with her tongue stuck out, the guy from Mechanics Hall – these are our wildest ones. The people who have really gone floating down towards the bottom of that boggy lake come in only once, and are then referred to a place more permanent than our office which receives the public from nine to five, five days a week only. Even those people who are barely able to walk about the streets and keep working, who aren't yet half-way down in the lake, get sent to the out-patient department at another hospital specialising in severer cases. Or they may stay a month or so on our own observation ward in the central hospital which I've never seen.

I've seen the secretary of that ward, though. Something about her merely smoking and drinking her coffee in the cafeteria at the ten o'clock break put me off so I never went to sit next to her again. She has a funny name I don't ever quite remember correctly, something really odd, like Miss Milleravage. One of those names that seem more like a pun mixing up Milltown and Ravage than anything in the city phone directory. But not so odd a name, after all, if you've ever read through the phone directory, with its Hyman Diddlebockers and Sasparilla Greenleafs. I read through the phone book once, never mind when, and it satisfied a deep need in me to realise how many people aren't called Smith.

Anyhow, this Miss Milleravage is a large woman, not fat, but all sturdy muscle and tall on top of it. She wears a grey suit over her hard bulk that reminds me vaguely of some kind of uniform, without the details of cut having anything strikingly military about them. Her face, hefty as a bullock's, is covered with a remarkable number of tiny macula, as if she'd been lying under water for some time and little algae had latched on to her skin, smutching it over with tobacco-browns and greens. These moles are noticeable mainly because the skin around them is so pallid. I sometimes wonder if Miss Milleravage has ever seen the wholesome light of day. I wouldn't be a bit surprised if she'd been brought up from the cradle with the sole benefit of artificial lighting.

Byrna, the secretary in Alcoholic Clinic just across the hall from us, introduced me to Miss Milleravage with the gambit that I'd 'been in England too .

Miss Milleravage, it turned out, had spent the best years of her life in London hospitals.

'Had a friend,' she boomed in her queer, doggish basso, not favouring me with a direct look, 'a nurse at Bart's. Tried to get in touch with her after the war, but the matron had changed, everybody'd changed, nobody'd heard of her. She must've gone down with the old matron, rubbish and all, in the bombings.' She followed this with a large grin.

Now I've seen medical students cutting up cadavers, four stiffs to a classroom about as recognisably human as Moby Dick, and the students playing catch with the dead men's livers. I've heard guys joke about sewing a woman up wrong after a delivery at the charity ward of the Lying-In. But I wouldn't want to see what Miss Milleravage would write off as the biggest laugh of all time. No thanks and then some. You could scratch her eyes with a pin and swear you'd struck solid quartz.

My boss has a sense of humour too, only it's gentle. Generous as Santa on Christmas Eve.

I work for a middle-aged lady named Miss Taylor who is the head secretary of the clinic and has been since the clinic started thirty-three years ago – the year of my birth, oddly enough. Miss Taylor knows every doctor, every patient, every outmoded appointment slip, referral slip and billing procedure the hospital has ever used or thought of using. She plans to stick with the clinic until she's farmed out in the green pastures of social security benefits. A woman more dedicated to her work I never saw. She's the same way about statistics as I am about dreams: if the building caught fire she would throw every last one of those books of statistics to the firemen below at the serious risk of her own skin.

I get along extremely well with Miss Taylor. The one thing I never let her catch me doing is reading the old record books. I have actually very little time for this. Our office is busier than the stock exchange with the staff of twenty-five doctors in and out, medical students in training, patients, patients' relatives, and visiting officials from other clinics referring patients to us, even when I'm covering the office alone, during Miss Taylor's coffee break and lunch hour, I seldom get time to dash down more than a note or two.

This kind of catch-as-catch-can is nerve-racking, to say the least. A lot of the best dreamers are in the old books, the dreamers that come in to us only once or twice for evaluation before they're sent elsewhere. For copying out these dreams I need time, a lot of time. My circumstances are hardly ideal for the unhurried pursuit of my art. There is, of course, a certain derring-do in working under such hazards, but I long for the rich leisure of the true connoisseur who indulges his nostrils above the brandy snifter for an hour before his tongue reaches out for the first taste.

I find myself all too often lately imagining what a relief it would be to bring a briefcase into work big enough to hold one of those thick, blue, cloth-bound record books full of dreams. At Miss Taylor's lunch time, in the lull before the doctors and students crowd in to take their afternoon patients, I could simply slip one of the books, dated ten or fifteen years back, into my briefcase, and leave the briefcase under my desk till five o'clock struck. Of course odd-looking bundles are inspected by the doorman of the Clinics Building and the hospital has its own staff of flatfeet to check up on the multiple varieties of thievery that go on, but for heaven's sake, I'm not thinking of making off with typewriters or heroin. I'd only borrow the book overnight and slip it back on the shelf first thing the next day before anybody else came in. Still, being caught taking a book out of the hospital would probably mean losing my job and all my source material with it.

This idea of mulling over a record book in the privacy and comfort of my own apartment, even if I have to stay up night after night for this purpose, attracts me so much I become more and more impatient with my usual method of snatching minutes to look up dreams in Miss Taylor's half-hours out of the office.

The trouble is, I can never tell exactly when Miss Taylor will come back to the office. She is so conscientious about her job she'd be likely to cut her half hour at lunch short and her twenty minutes at coffee shorter, if it weren't for her lame left leg. The distinct sound of this lame leg in the corridor warns me of her approach in time for me to whip the record book I'm reading into my drawer out of sight and pretend to be putting down the final flourishes on a phone message or some such alibi. The only catch, as far as my nerves are concerned, is that Amputee Clinic is around the corner from us in the opposite direction from Nerve Clinic and I've got really jumpy due to a lot of false alarms where I've mistaken some peg-leg's hitching step for the step of Miss Taylor herself returning early to the office.

On the blackest days, when I've scarcely time to squeeze one dream out of the old books and my copywork is nothing but weepy college sophomores who can't get a lead in 'Camino Real', I feel Johnny Panic turn his back, stony as Everest, higher than Orion, and the motto of the great Bible of Dreams, 'Perfect fear casteth out all else', is ash and lemon water on my lips. I'm a wormy hermit in a country of prize pigs so corn-happy they can't see the slaughter house at the end of the track. I'm Jeremiah vision-bitten in the Land of Cockaigne.

What's worse: day by day I see these psyche-doctors studying to win Johnny Panic's converts from him by hook, crook, and talk, talk, talk. Those deep-eyed, bush-bearded dream-collectors who preceded me in history, and their contemporary inheritors with their white jackets and knotty-pine-panelled offices and leather couches, practised and still practise their dream-gathering for worldly ends: health and money, money and health. To be a true member of Johnny Panic's congregation one must forget the dreamer and remember the dream: the dreamer is merely a flimsy vehicle for the great Dream-maker himself. This they will not do. Johnny Panic is gold in the bowels, and they try to root him out by spiritual stomach pumps.

Take what happened to Harry Bilbo. Mr Bilbo came into our office with the hand of Johnny Panic heavy as a lead coffin on his shoulder. He had an interesting notion about the filth in this world. I figured him for a prominent part in Johnny Panic's Bible of Dreams, Third Book of Fear, Chapter Nine on Dirt, Disease and General Decay. A friend of Harry's blew a trumpet in the Boy Scout band when they were kids. Harry Bilbo'd also blown on this friend's trumpet. Years later the friend got cancer and died. Then, one day not so long ago, a cancer doctor came into Harry's house, sat down in a chair, passed the top of the morning with Harry's mother and, on leaving, shook her hand and opened the door for himself. Suddenly Harry Bilbo wouldn't blow trumpets or sit down on chairs or shake hands if all the cardinals of Rome took to blessing him twenty-four hours around the clock for fear of catching cancer. His mother had to go turning the TV knobs and water faucets on and off and opening doors for him. Pretty soon Harry stopped going to work because of the spit and dog droppings in the street. First that stuff gets on your shoes and then when you take your shoes off it gets on your hands and then at dinner it's quick trip into your mouth and not a hundred Hail Mary's can keep you from the chain reaction. The last straw was, Harry quit weight-lifting at the public gym when he saw this cripple exercising with the dumb-bells. You can never tell what germs cripples carry behind their ears and under their fingernails. Day and night Harry Bilbo lived in holy worship of Johnny Panic, devout as any priest among censers and sacraments. He had a beauty all his own.

Well, these white-coated tinkerers managed, the lot of them, to talk Harry into turning on the TV himself, and the water faucets, and to opening closet doors, front doors, bar doors. Before they were through with him, he was sitting down on movie house chairs, and benches all over the Public Garden, and weight-lifting every day of the week at the gym in spite of the fact another cripple took to using the rowing machine. At the end of his treatment he came in to shake hands with the Clinic Director. In Harry Bilbo's own words, he was 'a changed man'. The pure Panic-light had left his face; he went out of the office doomed to the crass fate these doctors call health and happiness.

About the time of Harry Bilbo's cure a new idea starts nudging at the bottom of my brain. I find it hard to ignore as those bare feet sticking out of the lumbar puncture room. If I don't want to risk carrying a record book out of the hospital in case I get discovered and fired and have to end my research forever, I can really speed up work by staying in the Clinics Building overnight. I am nowhere near exhausting the clinic's resources and the piddling amount of cases I am able to read in Miss Taylor's brief absences during the day are nothing to what I could get through in a few nights of steady copying. I need to accelerate my work if only to counteract those doctors.

Before I know it I am putting on my coat at five, and saying good night to Miss Taylor who usually stays a few minutes overtime to clear up the day's statistics, and sneaking around the corner into the ladies' room. It is empty. I slip into the patients' john, lock the door from the inside, and wait. For all I know, one of the clinic cleaning ladies may try to knock the door down, thinking some patient's passed out on the seat. My fingers are crossed. About twenty minutes later the door of the lavatory opens and someone limps over the threshold like a chicken favouring a bad leg. It is Miss Taylor, I can tell by the resigned sigh as she meets the jaundiced eye of the lavatory mirror. I hear the click-cluck of various touch-up equipment on the bowl, water sloshing, the scritch of a comb in frizzed hair, and then the door is closing with a slow-hinged wheeze behind her.

I am lucky. When I come out of the ladies' room at six o'clock the corridor lights are off and the fourth floor hall is empty as church on Monday. I have my own key to our office; I come in first every morning, so that's no trouble. The typewriters are folded back into the desks, the locks are on the dial phones, all's right with the world.

Outside the window the last of the winter light is fading. Yet I do not forget myself and turn on the overhead bulb. I don't want to be spotted by any hawk-eyed doctor or janitor in the hospital buildings across the little courtyard. The cabinet with the record books is in the windowless passage opening on to the doctors' cubicles which have windows overlooking the courtyard. I make sure the doors to all the cubicles are shut. Then I switch on the passage light, a sallow twenty-five watt affair blackening at the top. Better than an altarful of candles to me at this point, though. I didn't think to bring a sandwich. There is an apple in my desk drawer left over from lunch, so I reserve that for whatever pangs I may feel about one o'clock in the morning, and get out my pocket notebook. At home every evening it is my habit to tear out the notebook pages I've written on at the office during the day and pile them up to be copied in my manuscript. In this way I cover my tracks so no one idly picking up my notebook at the office could ever guess the type or scope of my work.

I begin systematically by opening the oldest book on the bottom shelf. The once-blue cover is no-colour now, the pages are thumbed and blurry carbons, but I'm humming from foot to topknot: this dream book was spanking new the day I was born. When I really get organised I'll have hot soup in a thermos for the dead-of-winter nights, turkey pies and chocolate eclairs. I'll bring hair-curlers and four changes of blouse to work in my biggest handbag Monday mornings so no one will notice me going downhill in looks and start suspecting unhappy love affairs or pink affiliations or my working on dream books in the clinic four nights a week.

Eleven hours later. I am down to apple core and seeds and in the month of May, nineteen thirty-four, with a private nurse who has just opened a laundry bag in her patient's closet and found five severed heads in it, including her mother's.

A chill air touches the nape of my neck. From where I am sitting cross-legged on the floor in front of the cabinet, the record book heavy on my lap, I notice out of the corner of my eye that the door of the cubicle beside me is letting in a little crack of blue light. Not only along the floor, but up the side of the door too. This is odd since I made sure from the first that all the doors were shut tight. The crack of blue light is widening and my eyes are fastened to two motionless shoes in the doorway, toes pointing towards me.

They are brown leather shoes of a foreign make, with thick elevator soles. Above the shoes are black silk socks through which shows a pallor of flesh. I get as far as the grey pinstriped trouser cuffs.

'Tch, tch,' chides an infinitely gentle voice from the cloudy regions above my head. 'Such an uncomfortable position! Your legs must be asleep by now. Let me help you up. The sun will be rising shortly.'

Two hands slip under my arms from behind and I am raised, wobbly as an unset custard, to my feet, which I cannot feel because my legs are, in fact, asleep. The record book slumps to the floor, pages splayed.

'Stand still a minute.' The Clinic Director's voice fans the lobe of my right ear. 'Then the circulation will revive.'

The blood in my not-there legs starts pinging under a million sewing machine needles and a vision of the Clinic Director acid-etches itself on my brain. I don't even need to look around: fat pot-belly buttoned into his grey pinstriped waistcoat, woodchuck teeth yellow and buck, every-colour eyes behind the thick-lensed glasses quick as minnows.

I clutch my notebook. The last floating timber of the Titanic.

What does he know, what does he know?

Everything.

'I know where there is a nice hot bowl of chicken noodle soup.' His voice rustles, dust under the bed, mice in straw. His hand welds on to my left upper arm in fatherly love. The record book of all the dreams going on in the city of my birth at my first yawp in this world's air he nudges under the bookcase with a polished toe.

We meet nobody in the dawn-dark hall. Nobody on the chill stone stair down to the basement corridors where Jerry the record room boy cracked his head skipping steps one night on a rush errand.

I begin to double-quickstep so he won't think it's me he's hustling. 'You can't fire me,' I say calmly. 'I quit.'

The Clinic Director's laugh wheezes up from his accordion-pleated bottom gut. 'We mustn't lose you so soon.' His whisper snakes off down the whitewashed basement passages, echoing among the elbow pipes, the wheelchairs and stretchers beached for the night along the steam-stained walls. 'Why, we need you more than you know.'

We wind and double and my legs keep time with his until we come, somewhere in those barren rat-tunnels, to an all-night elevator run by a one-armed Negro. We get on and the door grinds shut like the door on a cattle car and we go up and up. It is a freight elevator, crude and clanky, a far cry from the plush passenger lifts I am used to in the clinics building.

We get off at an indeterminate floor. The Clinic Director leads me down a bare corridor lit at intervals by socketed bulbs in little wire cages on the ceiling.

Locked doors set with screened windows line the hall on either hand. I plan to part company with the Clinic Director at the first red Exit sign, but on our journey there are none. I am in alien territory, coat on the hanger in the office, handbag and money in my top desk drawer, notebook in my hand, and only Johnny Panic to warm me against the ice-age outside.

Ahead a light gathers, brightens. The Clinic Director, puffing slightly at the walk, brisk and long, to which he is obviously unaccustomed, propels me around a bend and into a square, brilliantly lit room.

'Here she is.'

'The little witch!'

Miss Milleravage hoists her tonnage up from behind the steel desk facing the door.

The walls and the ceiling of the room are riveted metal battleship plates. There are no windows.

From small, barred cells lining the sides and back of the room I see Johnny Panic's top priests staring out at me, arms swaddled behind their backs in the white ward nightshirts, eyes redder than coals and hungry-hot.

They welcome me with queer croaks and grunts as if their tongues were locked in their jaws. They have no doubt heard of my work by way of Johnny Panic's grapevine and want to know how his apostles thrive in the world.

I lift my hands to reassure them, holding up my notebook, my voice loud as Johnny Panic's organ with all stops out.                                                 .

'Peace! I bring to you. . . .'

The Book.

'None of that old stuff, sweetie.' Miss Milleravage is dancing out at me from behind her desk like a trick elephant.

The Clinic Director closes the door to the room.

The minute Miss Milleravage moves I notice what her hulk has been hiding from view behind the desk – a white cot high as a man's waist with a single sheet stretched over the mattress, spotless and drumskin tight. At the head of the cot is a table on which sits a metal box covered with dials and gauges.

The box seems to be eyeing me, copperhead-ugly, from its coil of electric wires, the latest model in Johnny-Panic-Killers.

I get ready to dodge to one side. When Miss Milleravage grabs, her fat hand comes away a fist full of nothing. She starts for me again, her smile heavy as dog-days in August.

'None of that. None of that. I'll have that little black book.'

Fast as I run around the high white cot, Miss Milleravage is so fast you'd think she wore roller-skates. She grabs and gets. Against her great bulk I beat my fists, and against her whopping milkless breasts, until her hands on my wrists are iron hoops and her breath hushabyes me with a love-stink fouler than Undertaker's Basement.

'My baby, my own baby's come back to me. . . .'

'She,' the Clinic Director says, sad and stern, 'has been making time with Johnny Panic again.'

'Naughty, naughty.'

The white cot is ready. With a terrible gentleness Miss Milleravage takes the watch from my wrist, the rings from my fingers, the hairpins from my hair. She begins to undress me. When I am bare, I am anointed on the temples and robed in sheets virginal as the first snow. Then, from the four corners of the room and from the door behind me come five false priests in white surgical gowns and masks whose one lifework is to unseat Johnny Panic from his own throne. They extend me full-length on my back on the cot. The crown of wire is placed on my head, the wafer of forgetfulness on my tongue. The masked priests move to their posts and take hold: one of my left leg, one of my right, one of my right arm, one of my left. One behind my head at the metal box where I can't see.

From their cramped niches along the wall, the votaries raise their voices in protest. They begin the devotional chant:

> The only thing to love is Fear itself.
> Love of Fear is the beginning of wisdom.
> The only thing to love is Fear itself.
> May Fear and Fear and Fear be everywhere.

There is no time for Miss Milleravage or the Clinic Director or the priests to muzzle them.

The signal is given.

The machine betrays them.

At the moment when I think I am lost the face of Johnny Panic appears in a nimbus of arc lights on the ceiling overhead. I am shaken like a leaf in the teeth of glory. His beard is lightning. Lightning is in his eye. His Word charges and illumines the universe.

The air crackles with his blue-tongued, lightning-haloed angels.

His love is the twenty-storey leap, the rope at the throat, the knife at the heart.

He forgets not his own.

HAROLD ACTON

# The Gift Horse

'EVERARD is the most munificent of men. Few confirmed bachelors are – in my experience. He's always loading me with lovely presents.'

'He must have a crush on you, darling. Though he is always ready to come round for a meal, he has never given me a thing.'

'Perhaps you make him feel like an extra man. Everard has his pride. He doesn't care to be exploited.'

'An invitation to dine is hardly exploitation.'

'That all depends. A meal may have invisible strings attached to it. Everard realises his entertainment value. Without apparent effort he makes things crackle. And everybody knows his taste is exquisite.'

'You mean his appetite. Last time he helped himself to so much asparagus that there wasn't enough to go round.'

'Surely that's rather flattering?'

Everard had in fact confided to Hilda that he only went to Rosemary's on account of her cook. 'I'd put up with a lot of boredom for a perfect *blini*,' he added.

Rosemary wore an aggrieved expression. 'I can't deny that my cook has merits. But one resents being treated like a restaurant. I don't think I'll ask him again.'

Hilda tittered. 'You'll change your mind when you need another extra man.'

'Darling, how well you understand my foibles. Tell me more about the presents he showers on you. Are they practical or merely decorative? Let's have a peep.'

'The odd thing is that he's morbidly shy about them. He begs me not to show them. "I got this just for you," he always tells me. "I don't want to make other girls jealous."'

It was Rosemary's turn to titter. 'Jealous of that old bag of bones?'

'At least they are bones of contention. Two opulent widows have been running after him for years.'

'Amazing! That throws a new light on him. Do you know these widows? Who are they?'

'One is a Mrs Hibbard of Cap Ferrat. The other is our country neighbour Grace Fotheringham whose husband was an ambassador to I forget where. Everard divides his summers between them. They're wildly jealous of each other.'

'Why doesn't he marry one of them and settle down? There's something so dreary about old bachelors.'

'Everard can live off his friends, and most of them can well afford to keep him.'

'He has never even offered me a cup of tea. It's high time he gave me something. What has he given you now?'

Hilda led her towards a cabinet filled with bric-à-brac, such as ivory netsukes, snuff-boxes and snuff-bottles. 'Nearly all these,' she remarked, 'were presents from Everard.'

'My word, quite a little museum! I can see I shall have to cultivate him more often. He's certainly a connoisseur. Why, that's Meissen, or is it Dresden? And I've always had a penchant for Fabergé.'

Hilda picked up a jade frog with ruby eyes. 'Everard brought me this the other day.'

Rosemary fancied she had seen it before, she couldn't think where. Loretta Perkins collected Fabergé: perhaps she had seen one like it in her menagerie of chi-chi animals? Its familiarity continued to nag at her but she said nothing except: 'Aren't you lucky! Obviously he's mad about you, darling.' Her eyes skimmed the shelves and rested on a snuff-box in the shape of a butterfly. For a moment she caught her breath. Surely it couldn't be a replica of hers? She turned it over in her hand and stroked its wings as if to question it. Could she be mistaken? She recalled with a pang that she had not noticed it lately. 'Was this another of Everard's gifts?' she asked.

Hilda nodded coyly. Rosemary resolved to rush home and investigate. 'You've not done too badly,' she observed. 'I must see what I can do, turn on the charm before it is too late. Did Everard inherit these bibelots?'

'I've no idea. More likely he picked them up in antique shops.'

Picked them up was the operative expression, Rosemary reflected. 'Somehow one doesn't connect him with a family. He seems to have sprung from nowhere.'

'I know nothing of his antecedents. He never mentions them.'

'One longs to discover more. These objects prove that he has considerable flair. I'll ring him up this evening.'

'He's in the South of France with widow Hibbard.'

'How tiresome. I need an extra man for *Norma*. Ralph has refused to sleep through another opera.'

'Rosemary, you're incorrigible.' The rivals parted gaily, each brushing the other's cheek with varnished lips. But Rosemary was inwardly apprehensive, for she could not banish a suspicion that the butterfly snuff-box belonged to her. In all her visits to sale-rooms she had never spotted its equal. She tried to recall the last occasion when Everard had come to dinner. Had it been a week or a fortnight ago? He had been a frequent guest but she had never liked him. She remembered with distaste that he was apt to stroke her furniture and turn her plates upside down. Yet it was difficult to believe that he would go so far . . . And if he had taken it, what was the point of giving it to a mutual friend? She could hardly wait to solve the teasing riddle.

On her way home she wondered about Everard's relations with Hilda. What on earth did they see in each other? Big bouncing Hilda and wizened Everard: they formed an incongruous pair. She tried to analyse her attitude towards them. It all boiled down to their serviceability. Everard was a useful fourth at bridge, and he put Ralph in a good temper. She was suddenly reminded that he had given Ralph a repeater watch by Bréguet which he prized so highly that he wore it on a platinum chain. Evidently he preferred Ralph to herself. Could Everard be queer? Her feminine instinct decided that he was sexless – except when he gazed at articles of virtu (which he pronounced with an exasperating French accent). Then a covetous gleam would moisten his slate-grey eye, and his fingers became predatory claws. She had noticed this when she had shown him her *famille verte* parrots. He had clutched them with quivering hands and broken into a sweat. 'Staggering,' he had muttered. 'I hope you'll leave them to me in your will.' As if he had the faintest chance of surviving her!

While she was running upstairs the telephone tinkled. Hilda again. 'Everard has been on my conscience,' she explained. 'I shouldn't have shown you his things. Please forget and say no more about them. He's so sensitive I'd hate to hurt his feelings.'

Rosemary was inclined to answer that the presents might equally be on Everard's conscience. 'Of course I won't breathe a word,' Rosemary assured her insincerely. She raced into her sitting-room, followed by yapping Ming and Ching, the white Pekinese she called her guardians. Usually she greeted them in pidgin English which they pretended to understand, but this evening she was too flurried to notice them.

One glance at her rosewood console table proved that they had been unable to guard her butterfly snuff-box. She stood gazing at the vacant spot where it had rested as on a flower and a pang of misery shot through her like neuralgia. It was as if she had lost a dear cousin whom she might have overlooked now and then but who had remained a familiar presence, a permanent comfort in the background of her over-organised existence. Gone! For a moment its image flickered before her. She stretched out a hand to grasp it and realised with a sob that it was no longer there. The butterfly had taken wing and flown out of the window, all the way to Hilda's flat. Tears welled into her eyes. Then she stamped her foot defiantly. 'No, this can't happen to me. I'll get it back even if it means a rumpus.'

After the first shock of anger and disappointment she thought: 'Hilda's bound to return it when I prove it's mine. Everard must have swiped it, the old brute.'

There could be no other explanation. Marshall, her maid, was completely above reproach. Rosemary dashed to the telephone but Hilda was out. Fortunately perhaps, for in her actual state of nerves she might talk recklessly. Supposing Hilda refused to surrender it? She might be convinced that Everard had offered it in good faith. Rosemary would have to consult Ralph when he returned from the City. His advice was occasionally sound.

Ralph rang up to inform her that he had been detained at the office: she need not keep any dinner for him, he would sup at the club. How typical: he was never available when he was needed. At other times he was apt to blunder in her way. Then a bright idea occurred to her. She telephoned Loretta Perkins, who also belonged to Everard's circle of hostesses.

'I was wondering only this morning at the hairdresser's, whatever has happened to Rosemary?' Loretta replied. 'And now that you have rung up I can see that something *has* happened. Is Ralph being naughty again, or is it one of the boys? I'm so lucky to be free as air. No worries of that kind.'

'Gracious, how you jump at conclusions! You're wide off the mark this time. What I wanted to ask in strict confidence was have you been missing things?'

'Missing what? I don't follow you, dear.'

'I mean items from your collection.'

'Now that you mention it I can't find my Fabergé frog. It's the least valuable of my pets, but that is no consolation.'

'I'm almost sure I've spotted it as well as a snuff-box of mine.'

'Darling, how thrilling. Where?'

'You'd never guess. At Hilda's.'

'How on earth did she get hold of them?'

'In perfect innocence. They were presents from a man.'

'That doesn't sound so innocent to me. I've always suspected that Hilda had a lover. Who is he?'

The overworked telephone revolted and they were cut off. Having found another clue, Rosemary did not care. When the instrument rang again she failed to reply. Presuming that it must be Loretta, she chuckled to herself, for it amused her to keep her inquisitive friend in suspense. While the telephone tinkled on and on she gazed at the console table where her butterfly box had rested – how many years? – without any interference. She had taken its presence so much for granted that she had ceased to notice until today when it had appeared to flutter its wings at her in Hilda's cabinet. She mixed herself a Bloody Mary and as she sipped it her longing to recover the treasure afflicted her like a toothache. She had no appetite for dinner, nor could she concentrate on the latest Simenon. The radio merely irritated her: those complacent voices jarred on her jangled mood.

Forlornly she sat waiting for Ralph with Ming and Ching snuffling beside her on the sofa. She was dozing off when Ralph lurched into the room and kissed her with brandy breath. The dogs yapped in protest against the disturbance. At once Rosemary related the details of her visit to Hilda.

'You and Loretta had better stake your claims,' he said. 'I'm sure Hilda won't make any fuss about returning the loot.'

'I wish I could feel sure. People often grow more attached to trifles than to their friends. I do myself.'

'Come, come, you never noticed its absence any more than I did. Hilda will deliver the goods but it's dashed awkward for Everard. A professional thief wouldn't behave like that. To pinch them and give them away to a mutual friend – it doesn't make sense.'

'He's always the first to arrive at a party, usually before the host. Quite a haul can be made in those few minutes.'

'Before challenging him you must be cautious. Yours may not be the only snuff-box of that type, or Loretta's the only frog.'

'To me the case is crystal-clear. I'm convinced.'

'Let me round him up for a chin-wag before you take action. Kleptomania's a disease. Not being a psychiatrist I'll ask Dr Cooper to collaborate.'

'If the snuff-box was yours I believe you'd do nothing about it.'

'I've always had a soft spot for old Everard. He gave me my Bréguet repeater, like the one the Iron Duke gave his A.D.C. after Waterloo.'

'You'd better look out or you'll be had up for receiving.'

'Righto, I'll keep it under my waistcoat. I don't intend to part with it.'

'And I don't intend to part with my butterfly.'

'Don't worry, dear. I'm sure you'll get it back.'

But Rosemary did worry. The distinct image of Everard snatching her treasure kept her awake at night: she resented it more than if it had been stolen by an ordinary burglar. The impudence of his presenting it to Hilda, who hadn't the slightest notion of its value. You only have to lose a thing to appreciate its rarity, she mused.

While Everard was tanning himself in the South of France there was little she could do. Rosemary decided reluctantly that she would have to bide her time.

'Everard dear, you shouldn't. I don't expect such presents and you can't afford them. I read in the paper that one was sold for several thousand guineas the other day. Do keep it and I'll be much happier. All I want is your company and you ration it too severely.'

'You know how deeply I'm attached to you, Nesta. Haven't I proved it again and again? Lady Catersham was furious with me for leaving her.'

Nesta Hibbard gazed at him with sad spaniel eyes. She saw him as Horace Walpole, herself as Madame du Deffand. Though she was not yet blind she was older than Everard – at an age when every additional year counts as double. She regarded him as an arbiter of taste. He had selected and arranged her furniture; he had helped to choose her dresses, hats and shoes; he advised her on food and wine. She seldom went shopping without him, and how she revelled in those expeditions! He imparted the last touch of refinement to her receptions and she was flattered when he was mistaken for her husband. With his languid air of distinction he impressed her friends.

'When will Everard be arriving?' they asked her. 'We must throw a party for him.'

And to those who celebrated his regular visits to Cap Ferrat he brought some trinket from England in token of gratitude. And they all exclaimed: 'Dear Everard, how you pamper us!'

'It's a homeless heirloom,' he replied. 'I'm delighted it has found a home with you.'

Nesta's friends called him her beau and quizzed her on the subject: 'When shall we hear the chime of wedding bells?'

These friends were scattered along the coast in Marzipan villas and hotels where they tried to prolong the *dolce vita* of good King Edward's heyday, turning a deaf ear and a blind eye to the antics of astronauts and other futuristic phenomena. Everard introduced a spice of variety into the routine of these voluntary exiles who periodically shared Browning's nostalgia: 'Oh to be in England, now that April's here!' But it was another England they remembered.

When he was in London Everard's gossipy letters about social events, which seemed far more vivid than the newspaper columns from which they were culled, were recited by Nesta to a spellbound group of cronies. A legend had gained credence that he was the offspring of a duke. Nesta never denied it, and Everard remained reticent though he hinted that the trinkets he bestowed were relics of an ancestor's collection. Their output, however, never seemed to dry up, and each had some subtle *rapport* with the recipient.

On this occasion he had offered Nesta an eighteenth-century Staffordshire figure of a rosy-cheeked lass whose crinoline might have been designed by Miró with suggestive dots and squiggles. It looked surprisingly modern, yet Nesta, who considered herself an authority on Staffordshire salt-glazed stoneware, knew it was authentic. In the past he had presented her with a miniature attributed to Hilliard, a diamond spray-brooch, a fan by Conder, a Battersea enamel snuff-box with Corydon playing bagpipes to Amaryllis (Everard and Nesta), a Chinese cloisonné phoenix, a Meissen Harlequin and Columbine (Everard and Nesta again), a Chelsea ink-stand, a small bronze dancing figure from Tibet, a minute painting on copper of a Dutch carousal and, less appropriate, despite its quaintness, a Lambeth delftware barber's bowl adorned with scissors, comb, razor, leeches and other instruments of his trade: the assortment was rich, original and varied.

'I wonder you get them through the Customs free of duty,' Nesta remarked.

'They are only trifles,' Everard replied. 'The Customs are after bigger game – or cigarettes. By the way, I haven't forgotten your Harem Puffs, the amber-scented ones.'

'You absolute angel. I must kiss you for that.'

With a grimace that was comically demure Everard permitted himself to be moistened on the cheek by his infatuated hostess. Dante, her Florentine majordomo, glimpsed them over his cocktail tray and thought: 'Ridiculous, at their age! But it cannot go much further.'

Dante disliked and distrusted Everard. He disliked him because his tips were so niggardly that he had to refuse them out of self-respect. He distrusted him since he had caught sight of him creeping out with a parcel when the old lady's silver coffee-pot had vanished. Fearing that he as an alien servant might fall under suspicion, he had immediately reported its disappearance to the Signora and proposed to summon the police.

'I bear an honoured name, and I would not have it tarnished by reason of a coffee-pot,' he declared. 'I keep a strict eye on the staff, but I cannot spy on the Signora's guests.'

'Are you suggesting that one of my friends would walk off with a coffee-pot?' Nesta retorted indignantly.

'Why not, Signora? You are so hospitable and the Riviera abounds in sharks.'

'Be more precise, Dante. Give me an example.'

Dante smiled at her compassionately. 'I could give you many, Signora. There's the Countess who crams her bag with your cakes after your bridge-teas, pretending they are for her poodle. She also empties the chocolates from their panniers after dinner. And the Marquise fills her case with your scented cigarettes. And only yesterday I saw Mr Gifford leave the house with a big parcel. I could not presume to inspect the contents, but it had the same dimensions as your coffee-pot.'

'Not a word against Mr Gifford. He is one of my closest friends.'

'With your permission I must vindicate myself. In the matter of missing silver all fingers will point at your major-domo. The responsibility is mine.'

'I trust you completely, Dante. Surely that ought to suffice.'

'A day may come when you will cease to trust me. A tea-pot may follow the coffee-pot, spoons may follow knives and forks – and I repeat I feel responsible, Signora. I desire my character to be cleared in advance.'

'I'm sure my coffee-pot will turn up,' said Nesta. 'In any case I forbid you to call the police.'

'Then I shall demand an affidavit that you absolve me from blame.'

'Won't it do just as well if I raise your wages?'

The prospect of more emolument induced Dante to relax, and a smile effaced his frown of discontent. Nesta knew that smile which signified: 'I'm at your service so long as I'm rewarded.' She sighed with relief. Dante was a necessary luxury but she wanted no truck with the French police. She, too, had noticed the rapacity of certain guests, but she bore them no resentment. On the contrary, it wrung her heart-strings when Daisy made a clean sweep of her cakes and Natasha bagged her cigarettes, for it meant that they must be poor in spite of their veneer of affluence. Most of them lived on and at the casino. When in luck they made a splash, especially the White Russians, with *zakuski* and vodka all round and music, music, music. Their vicissitudes provided Nesta with distraction during Everard's absence. Often they brought equivocal partners to her house, but one had to be tolerant in a cosmopolitan clique. Dante was not exaggerating their peccadilloes, but Nesta was annoyed with him for daring to cast a slur on her favourite.

Dante must be jealous; only that could account for his outrageous innuendo.

Since Dante had sleuthed him into a boudoir where Nesta kept her Old Dresden (her generic term for porcelain), Everard grew wary of the prying butler. Though he had spotted several figurines that would appeal to Grace Fotheringham he was never given a chance to remove them. His padded suitcase was still empty after a fortnight's stay. On previous visits he had never failed to fill it.

There were, however, other possibilities among the expatriate community. Maggie McGrew had enough Dutch and Georgian silver to fill a shop-window. And Natasha had not yet parted with all her icons. While the others were absorbed in bridge he might unhood a pocket-sized one on his way to the loo. A weakness of the bladder – 'excuse me if I powder my nose' – had often served him as a plausible pretext. Perhaps in aiming at the coffee-pot, which was larger than his usual quarry, he had been over-ambitious. If nothing else materialised he would have to try again, and if Dante caught him he would say that its handle needed soldering.

In the meantime he accompanied Nesta to luncheons and dinners where he met the same futile people, and to dress-makers and other shops along the Riviera. As Nesta was slow to make up her mind he spent many a wearisome hour in shops exclusively feminine. But he seldom departed without a souvenir.

As a reward for his counsel Nesta would say: 'Now I must get you something nice. Your clothes are far too conservative for the Côte d'Azur. Let me find you something gay.' It gave her additional pleasure to renew his wardrobe. 'They'll imagine I'm being kept by you,' Everard murmured.

'That's what I'd love to do, dear, if you'd only let me,' she replied, squeezing his limp hand.

At Maggie McGrew's he had to compete with Captain Gutteridge. After a few dry Martinis Maggie's drooping eye began to rove towards other males, including Everard, whose friendship with Nesta tickled her curiosity. Everard's manner with her was formal yet flirtatious. He kept her guessing. Under the table at dinner her foot pressed his and he returned the pressure, but her drooping eyelid signalled that she was already half-seas-over. She invariably wore white kid gloves to conceal her knobbly hands. Yet she chain-smoked through meals, dropping ashes over the lobster mayonnaise, burning holes in the table-cloth and sometimes in her gown. While the men sat over their port Everard excused himself 'to spend a penny'.

'Spend tuppence for me,' one of them chortled with a wink and continued to discuss recent golf scores.

The bathroom adjoined Maggie's bedroom. Seeing that the coast was clear Everard tiptoed in to reconnoitre. The accumulation of silver on her dressing-table made his mouth water. Everard made a lightning inventory. All this for the toilet of a raddled old dipsomaniac! There was an *embarras de choix*, and he had to decide which were the most manoeuvrable. There was an irresistible cigarette case of platinum and gold which fitted his breast pocket. The boxes might make his dinner jacket bulge. However, he decided to take that risk with two of the smallest. One was shaped like a high-heeled shoe – just the thing for Grace's collection. Maggie would be too squiffy to notice their absence before tomorrow. A lingering appraisal of the remnants – perhaps he could return for them later – and he rejoined one other male guest in the dining-room. On his way out to join the ladies, he slipped a salt-cellar into his trousers. Otherwise it was an evening of conventional pattern. They played bridge till one o'clock with copious 'night-caps' in between. Everard was the only sober member of the party.

A couple of days later Maggie confided to Nesta that she was going to sack her maid. 'We can't prove it yet but I'm positive that she's been pilfering. I've lost several bits of old silver recently and the cigarette case given me by King Fuad. I miss that most of all: it brought back blissful memories. The police are watching her movements, but it's an uncomfortable feeling to keep a maid one cannot trust.'

'How I agree,' cooed Nesta. 'Maids bother me so that I'd sooner fend for myself. I'm lucky to have Dante; it's like having a private detective in the house. Everard calls him Cerberus.'

'I envy you,' sighed Maggie. She had attempted to bribe Dante into her service with a promise to double his wages but he had declined. He disapproved of drunken dowagers on the loose.

The news that Maggie's maid was under suspicion would have encouraged Everard to capture more silver had not Maggie mentioned that she had locked it up, except the candelabra, too heavy to manipulate. He would have to be content with his paltry percentage. Yet something in the air of Cap Ferrat made his fingers itch for booty.

Natasha possessed a glowing Madonna of the Novgorod School in a jewelled frame which would fit his 'special' pocket like a glove. But she told him candidly that she could not organise a party for him as her luck at roulette had failed her.

'Don't dream of it. A tête-à-tête over tea would be much nicer. I'll bring the tea-leaves myself, a packet from Fortnum's. Your native samovar will do the rest.'

Broke though she was, Natasha would not take him at his word. She provided enough *pâté de foie gras* sandwiches and chocolate éclairs for a school treat and arranged half a dozen tables for bridge and poker. Her bed-sitting room was packed with greedy gamblers. The icons beside her bed were hidden by a Japanese screen so that it was not difficult for Everard to glide behind it while his hostess was attending to her other guests.

Maggie was still maundering about her maid and the cigarette case which King Fuad had given her on board the royal dahabeeyah. 'So far the police haven't been able to trace the stolen goods. I'm afraid I won't see them again.'

'You console me for not having a maid,' said Natasha. 'In Petersburg I used to have dozens but I never lost anything before the Revolution. And here I have nothing to lose except my family icons, and I'm told they are *démodés* whenever I try to sell them.'

'Do show them to me,' said Nesta. Everard could have slapped her at that moment.

'Let's finish our rubber first,' he said testily.

When the game was over and the losses were subtracted from the gains it was time for everybody to dress for yet another party. To Everard's vexation Nesta offered to fetch Natasha in her limousine. When he returned an hour later he found her in floods of tears.

'I shall not go, I'm too *angoissée*,' she wailed. 'The most precious of my icons has disappeared. It has been in my family for generations. Somebody must have taken it while we were playing bridge this afternoon. I have had to give a list of my guests to the police.'

Everard urged her to attend the party, though she broke down and cried 'Who could be so heartless as to steal one of my last heirlooms, the one I valued most of all? It is a complete mystery. The police are not interested in helping a poor refugee. Besides, they do not understand what a Russian icon signifies. They laugh in my face and suggest that I keep *louche* lovers. I shall never see my holy relic again.'

'I promise to find you another,' said Everard soothingly. 'There's a little shop near the British Museum which specialises in Oriental antiques.'

'Thank you for the generous thought. But it is the sentiment attached to my icon, the prayers that have been said before it by my parents and grandparents, which make it so dear to me.'

Everard commiserated with her, as if unaware that the object was in his handbag. His conscience did not prick him in the least. He knew that Nesta would provide compensation.

Natasha was too typical a Slav to behave like a wet blanket, so that she soon recovered her ebullience at the party, whereas Everard and Nesta grew more phlegmatically Anglo-Saxon. Everard could see nothing to tempt him and Nesta was depressed at the prospect of his departure.

'I wish you could stay here for ever,' she told him.

Everard's mask froze into Horace Walpole's, impassive and aloof.

'I should like nothing better,' he replied, 'but I can't disappoint the old folks at home. I have my faults but I have never let anyone down.'

'Except me,' said Nesta bitterly. 'I love you more than all the others put together. And life is so short. Haven't you been happy here? You know there is nothing I would not do for you . . .'

Nesta's whole face quivered and her elaborate make-up seemed in danger of cracking.

'You are the dearest of women,' Everard replied, 'and you have given me a marvellous time. Unfortunately I have my social obligations.'

In spite of his remarkable staying power Everard had begun to long for

England. Even Nesta complained of the Riviera now and then: 'I don't know what society is coming to.' Everard considered that it had come to a stagnant pond where a family of frogs, neither French nor by Fabergé, croaked continually: 'I ask you to lunch (or dinner), You ask me to lunch (or dinner), I owe you a lunch (or dinner), You owe me a lunch (or dinner), I wonder why So-and-So hasn't asked me to lunch or dinner lately.'

In England, perhaps on account of the cooking, people were less concerned with filling their bellies. Everard became abstemious by reaction. But since Nesta called him cruel he was forced to relent. He might yet add a souvenir or two to his collection.

Parting from Nesta had always been sticky and this time she made it worse by a hysterical fit of weeping. The scene left a disagreeable after-taste. Everard's social round was meticulously planned – a week here, a fortnight there – but his longest visits were reserved for Nesta Hibbard and Grace Fotheringham. These ladies were coevals, but whereas Nesta was superficially cosmopolitan Grace was proud of being 'county' to the backbone.

'I sink or swin with Britain even if the Commies take over,' Grace asserted. 'Let others cry stinking fish and emigrate. Here I am and here I stay.'

So comfortable was her house, so sylvan her park, that her immobility entailed no sacrifice. Not even Everard could have inveigled her abroad, and Everard, as she often proclaimed, was her favourite man. His visits to Fotheringham Hall were no less eagerly expected than his visits to *Mon Repos*.

Owing to a frugal diet, regular hours and abundant fresh air, Grace had preserved a big round baby face without the aid of cosmetics. She devoured several newspapers but read little else: she had no Madame du Deffand delusions and Horace Walpole was hardly â name to her. But her affection for Everard was a steady flame. All her neighbours remarked that her eyes were brighter when he came to stay: he flattered and amused her simultaneously. His accounts of society on the Azure coast were as good as a play and she was delighted with the unpredictable souvenirs he brought her.

Everard enjoyed more freedom with Grace than with Nesta. There was no snooping Dante at Fotheringham Hall. He could prowl all over the place to his heart's content. If one of Grace's bibelots disappeared he never heard it mentioned. And the house was crammed with small, choice, portable objects. The late Sir Geoffrey had had a penchant for jade; his forebears had collected miniatures; and Grace had amassed a singular assemblage of tiny shoes in porcelain, ivory, silver and other materials. The rooms were gay, with pink as the predominant colour. The furniture was sprawling Edwardian. The sofas could have been converted into beds; chests of drawers were scented with lavender and pot-pourri filled bowls of *famille rose*. It was the ideal setting for an old-fashioned musical comedy. The food was wholesome and suited Everard better than the flesh-pots of Cap Ferrat.

Grace met him at the little railway station and held out both her chubby hands in welcome. Under a huge picture hat her whole face beamed at him.

'Dear Everard, at last!' she exclaimed. 'It has seemed such a long, long time. I was afraid you'd been seduced by one of those sirens you described in your delicious letters from the Riviera.'

'I was there for business rather than pleasure,' he replied not untruthfully.

'I hope it was a success. You're looking splendid.'

'So are you, Grace. Honey and flowers – the same fresh Gainsborough beauty. By Jove, it's a tonic to set eyes on you again.'

Though Grace lacked a Dante, she possessed a bull terrier called Pongo which growled at Everard with peculiar animosity – peculiar because it was so amiable with her other guests. Once it had given him a nasty bite so Grace deemed it advisable to leave her pet at home on this occasion. As if it blamed Everard for depriving it of a drive in the car, Pongo growled at him so viciously that Grace had to expel it from the room. Everard was slightly unnerved by the incident but Grace's cucumber sandwiches restored his equanimity.

'I've been looking forward to this like a schoolboy to his hols,' he said. 'The Riviera's all very well in small doses but I've had enough of it. Business apart, I can't think why I wasted so much time there.'

'Nor can I, Everard. Anyhow better late than never. I'm delighted you could tear yourself away from so many temptations. Hilda Betterton was inquiring about you yesterday. She has had a tiff with Rosemary Filson and wants your advice.'

'What about, I wonder?'

'Oh, some present you gave her which Rosemary declares was stolen from her drawing-room.'

Everard grinned uncomfortably. 'Shall we be seeing Hilda?'

'She asked us over for dinner tonight but I'm afraid I was selfish. I wanted to keep you all to my wee self.'

'Perfect, that was just what I was hoping. Hilda would be *de trop*. Do you often see Rosemary Filson?'

'Not since she stayed with Hilda last year. Frankly I couldn't bear her, and I'm not the least bit interested in all the names she drops.'

'I agree. Her social success is entirely due to her cook.'

'I'm afraid you'll find mine very plain after the French cuisine.'

'I'd sooner eat mutton with you than foie gras at Cap Ferrat.'

'Flatterer. Another sandwich? There's also some gentleman's relish. You must be famished after your journey.'

Everard did not need to be asked. He had had no luncheon in anticipation of this tea.

While he dressed for dinner Everard wondered whether he should present Grace with the icon as well as the shoe-shaped box or reserve the former for a later visit. The icon might look barbaric among the English miniatures. He cursed his folly for giving the snuff-box to Hilda: he had done so when he had felt unwanted and unloved. She had kissed him and told him how popular he was, and she had scolded him for his reckless generosity.

The shoe-shaped box seemed more appropriate. He always chaffed Grace about her 'shoe-fetish': it was one of their private jokes. 'You ought to be psycho-analysed,' he told her.

'For loving you?' she retorted.

His gift evoked gurgles of delight. 'I'd lost hope of finding another,' she explained. 'But how can I accept such a rarity?'

The usual friendly squabble ensued. Everard forbore from answering that she would pay for it in other ways.

His remarkable staying power was best exemplified at Fotheringham Hall. Between croquet in the afternoon and backgammon in the evening he did a little gardening with Grace to stimulate his appetite for her solid meals. He always took two helpings of the boiled silverside of beef and the maids encouraged him to eat more. 'Another dumpling, sir? Cook will be disappointed unless you finish them off.'

The only fly in his ointment was the weekly letter, page after rambling page from Nesta who continued to bewail his absence and beseech him to return. 'Life is meaningless without you,' she wrote. 'I'm unutterably bored. *C'est une maladie de l'âme.*'

Madame du Deffand again! And like Horace Walpole, Everard threatened to stop writing unless she pulled herself together. It was absurd to pretend that she didn't have loads of fun. Wasn't she the virtual Queen of Cap Ferrat? Why couldn't she send him the latest news of her court? Had Maggie's missing silver turned up, and had her maid been arrested? Had Natasha recovered her icon? He smiled at his cynicism as he scribbled his moral lecture. Nesta should count her blessings. The woes that afflicted the rest of humanity had spared Cap Ferrat.

Not at all, she replied. Forest fires had been raging in the neighbourhood and now there were thunderstorms like hurricanes; the airport at Nice had been flooded and Communism was on the rampage; the lower classes were ruder than ever, even the shopkeepers and waiters in restaurants were apt to be uncivil.

'You have Dante to protect you,' he retorted. 'And with so many congenial friends – how's Jim Gutteridge by the way? – you need never spend a dull moment.'

But Nesta's cronies were failing fast: Maggie had gone to Vichy for her spleen, Jim Gutteridge had had a stroke, Natasha was suffering from blood pressure and had fainted in the Casino just when she was winning at roulette. Nesta herself was worried about her palpitations: she was trying a saltless diet which destroyed her appetite. Everard was reminded of the salt-cellar he held in reserve: perhaps he would give it to Hilda.

Health was the one subject banned at Fotheringham Hall. Grace never mentioned it and she discouraged others from doing so. Hilda came over to dine as soon as Grace decided she could no longer monopolise Everard. When he presented her with Maggie's salt-cellar Hilda thanked him less effusively than usual. 'How pretty,' she remarked, 'and how sweet of you to call me the salt of the earth, but I can't go on depriving you of family heirlooms.'

'I thought it would brighten your breakfast tray. I'm getting on in years you know, though I keep my age a secret. This will remind you of me when I am gone.'

'Do take it,' said Grace. 'Everard chose it specially for you. He'll be hurt if you refuse it.'

'It's much too grand for me.'

'What rot. Why look a gift horse in the mouth?' Grace prompted her.

'Perhaps Rosemary will claim it like that snuff-box which she swears is hers.'

'You shouldn't have shown it to her,' said Everard. 'I particularly asked you not to. She's the most grasping woman I know. Of course she'll try to extract it from you.'

'Rosemary and I were at school together. I can see that she wants the snuff-box desperately.'

'Her behaviour doesn't sound very friendly to me,' said Grace. 'Spreading horrid lies about the kindest of mortals. Never mind what she says, Everard. We'll stand up for you, won't we?'

'It's not agreeable to be libelled by a woman who pesters one to dine with her,' said Everard gloomily.

'You should never have gone,' said Grace.

Everard was inclined to agree but he blamed Hilda's indiscretion. He couldn't remember if he had given her anything else of Rosemary's.

Hilda lacked the courage to add that Loretta Perkins had also put in a claim for her Fabergé frog. Since Grace and Everard were both so insistent she accepted the salt-cellar, but she wondered if it would lead to further friction.

Far from spoiling his dinner this episode stimulated Everard's appetite and he helped himself twice to the treacle pudding. Hilda's reluctance to accept the salt-cellar had amused him. 'Next week you must dine with me,' she said.

Everard luxuriated in the placid routine of Fotheringham Hall. The weather was autumnal for August and frequent showers drove him indoors but even the climate was exhilarating after the pitiless glare of the Riviera. Everard was as happy indoors as in the garden for he could browse to his heart's content among Grace's bric-à-brac. Chimney-pieces, cabinets and tables were so cluttered that it was easy to camouflage the displacement of an object. A spell of wet weather revived his acquisitive instincts. He picked up an assortment of Christmas presents which more than compensated for his losses at backgammon, since it was his policy to let Grace win. A meal with the vicar was unexpectedly remunerative though the apostle spoons were more manageable than the Victorian tobacco jars, always acceptable to pipe-smoking cronies. One must take what comes one's way, he reflected, furtively slipping a couple of spoons in his pocket while the vicar was saying grace.

As the weeks went by he began to think it strange that he heard nothing more from Hilda. If he rang her up it would look like fishing. He mentioned this to Grace who telephoned with the gymkhana as a pretext. Her maid replied that Hilda had gone to bed with a chill. Grace had no patience with illness which she suspected was imaginary in nine cases out of ten. However, she called on Hilda with a basket of nectarines from her greenhouse. Somewhat to her surprise it was Hilda who opened the front door.

'My daily's out shopping,' she explained. 'Fortunately my temperature's down. Anyhow it was nothing serious. The fact is I'm shy of meeting Everard since Rosemary Filson and Loretta Perkins are both dunning me for the return of the presents he gave me. Though I'm not possessive I hesitate to send the things back. It would seem an admission that Everard pinched them. I simply don't know what to do. It's all so unpleasant that it has given me nightmares.'

'Snap out of it, Hilda. Those women are taking advantage of your gullibility. You only have to look at Everard to see that his conscience is clear. Though he hasn't said as much I suspect he's offended by your neglect. I told him you were seedy and he wanted to send you a Russian icon which he says has healing properties. Isn't that typical?'

'Once bitten twice shy. I want no more of his presents. They're getting too hot to hold.'

'That's quite enough. I thought you had more gumption.'

Grace sailed out of Hilda's cottage like a proud ambassadress after the failure of an important mission. She said nothing about it to Everard, whom she found playing patience in the library after extracting an inscribed first edition of *Alice's Adventures in Wonderland* from one of the shelves. He had searched in vain for *Through the Looking-Glass* but perhaps that was asking too much: he knew 'The Walrus and the Carpenter' by heart and felt a certain affinity with the Walrus, who was 'a *little* sorry for the poor oysters.' Lewis Carroll's classic, which was lost on Grace, would cheer up Nesta in the midst of her palpitations.

Dear Grace! Her house was incomparably pleasanter than Nesta's and there were fewer hospitable houses at Everard's disposal since the war. If Grace should ask him to marry her – and she often seemed on the verge of doing so – he was prepared to accept, but alas, it was only Nesta who made the advances. Perhaps he should exert a little pressure and withdraw his countenance when it was most desired.

With every semblance of regret he told Grace one morning that he would have to shorten his visit. 'I've had an SOS from Lady Catersham,' he announced, 'who implores me to help her with a charity bazaar. The date had to be altered on account of the rector's retirement.'

'Where do I come in?' Grace exclaimed peevishly. 'I was expecting you to stay at least another fortnight.'

'Please don't put it that way. Of all my friends you are the dearest. But poor Lady Catersham is eighty-five and looks it. As she's Martyr to sciatica she has been more helpless than usual since the death of Miss Murchison, her lady companion. I'm one of the executors, you know.'

'It's too bad,' said Grace tearfully. 'To throw me over for an old hag with one foot in the grave.'

'If you think I'm letting you down, I'll put her off.'

'Yes do, for my sake. Tell her I also have my charity bazaars. I'm sure she has plenty of nurses to cope.'

'We ought to be married,' said Everard with a weary smile. 'You treat me as if we were.'

'At our age that would be silly. I'm not so young as I look.'

'You are too young, that's the snag. I'm the antique.'

Grace pressed his hand. 'Aren't things marvellous as they are? Two friends enjoying the autumn of life together in perfect freedom. Wedlock is a padlock, my dear. I'll be a wife to you in all but name.'

'Thank you,' he muttered. 'I shouldn't demand more as I have so little to offer . . .' He gazed at her sentimentally.

'You silly boy. If you want me to pop into bed I'm ready to do so, but it wouldn't be much fun for either of us. One must be realistic.'

'That I've never been. I'm a hopeless romantic.'

Grace pressed his hand again. 'Well, it is my duty to rescue you from Lady Catersham. She's becoming a bad habit.'

But after dilly-dallying another week Everard grew restive. It was obvious that Grace had no intention of proposing. In a mood of acute frustration he sent himself a telegram saying that Lady Catersham had taken a turn for the worse. Showing this to Grace, 'I'm afraid I've got to go,' he said glumly. 'I'd never forgive myself if I deserted my old friend on her death-bed.'

'She'll probably be unconscious by the time you reach her,' Grace replied. But he wore so dismal an expression that she had to relent. 'I'll let you go on condition you return within a week.'

A few days later Everard called on Lady Catersham from the village inn where he was staying. Having borrowed some of her crested writing paper he composed a fictitious account of his visit.

He alleged that Lady Catersham had begun to recover as soon as she set eyes on him. Now that she was well enough to be wheeled in the park he was at liberty to return in every sense to Grace. It this were convenient, would she kindly send an answer to his London address.

The reply, when it came, left him stupefied. Grace advised him to leave the country before he was charged with larceny on several counts. He could keep the purloined souvenirs of Fotheringham Hall but he must not suppose that he would be welcomed there again. Further communication with her was superfluous.

Though the shock was intense Everard decided to bluff it out. He regarded Hilda as a rock of loyalty. To her he telephoned in his distress. Had Grace taken leave of her senses, he asked? He could not imagine why she had written him such a letter. They had parted amicably; she had even begged him to return.

Hilda spoke to him gently but firmly. She, too, advised him to disappear until Rosemary and Loretta had forgotten and forgiven the losses they had suffered. At present they were so delighted to recover their treasures that they had withdrawn their threats to prosecute him. They had visited Grace together and insisted on her checking her inventory of heirlooms. She had done so reluctantly, and the proof of his duplicity had made her blow up. Hilda had had much ado to dissuade her from denouing him to Scotland Yard. 'I've never seen her in such a rage,' she said. 'You had better return to Cap Ferrat, at any rate till the eruption dies down. But I implore you to curb your too-generous instincts.'

Everard did not wait for further advice. He packed up his traps and caught the next plane for Nice. After some deliberation he kept his relics from Fotheringham Hall. Nesta would appreciate the miniatures. One of them might plausibly be described as a portrait of Madame Deffand before she went blind. He would tell her that it had belonged to Horace Walpole.

Nesta was at the airport to welcome him. 'What a wonderful answer to my prayers,' she exclaimed.

The sunlight accentuated her myriad wrinkles coated with a pale pink powder which clung like hoarfrost to the fuzz on her double chin.

'Your letters worried me,' he said, 'especially those palpitations you wrote of. So I've descended on you like a bolt out of the blue.'

'More like the Archangel Gabriel,' she gushed. 'How well you're looking, but you've lost weight. You must sunbathe on the terrace. I'll get Dante to spread a lilo for you.'

Everard's thin lips twitched into a mechanical grin. Already the prospect of an indefinite sojourn at *Mon Repos* depressed him.

Dante noticed that his luggage was heavier than usual and that there was more of it. A born diplomat, he greeted Everard with an exaggerated bow. But he watched Everard more closely than before. He seemed to dog his footsteps. 'Anything I can do for you, Monsieur?' he would enquire, peeping round the door of whichever room Everard chanced to occupy.

'When I need you I shall ring the bell,' Everard answered huffily.

From his room he could hear Nesta telephoning to all the Toms, Dicks and Harrys of her acquaintance. He saw himself condemned to a ruthless routine of bridge and cocktail parties. Perhaps he should have returned the miniatures, but that would have been equivalent to an admission of weakness. He had refrained from answering Grace's ultimatum. Her anger was bound to subside: after a few months she would only remember the rosier features of their twenty year old friendship.

As time went on it was Everard who nursed the grievance. Grace's resentment was out of all proportion to his offence, if offence it could be called. His nostalgia for Fotheringham Hall made *Mon Repos* all the more intolerable.

Nesta's cocktails dulled the palate for good wine, but they enabled one to face the interminable evenings. Her coterie vegetated in the same vacuum. Natasha had a bright new wig but in other respects she was down on her luck.

'We Slavs are superstitious,' she told Everard. 'Since losing my icon I have never won at roulette.'

Everard was reminded that her icon was upstairs in his dispatch-case.

'I've brought you a lucky talisman from London,' he said.

He went to fetch the Novgorod icon, carefully wrapped in tissue paper, and handed it to Natasha. She opened it in a flash.

'A miracle!' she cried. 'My heart overflows with joy.' She kissed the holy image and then kissed Everard. 'A million thanks, most chivalrous of friends! But where oh where did you discover it?'

'In a curio shop near the British Museum.'

'Poor Serge must have sold it for his dope, but I'll say nothing. I'm too happy to see it again.'

While she dabbed her tears Nesta slipped a few thousand francs inside the icon's frame.

'Now, Natasha, run off to the Casino and try your luck. If it fails you this time . . .' She left the sentence unfinished. Natasha would gamble as long as she breathed.

'No, I'd rather give a party for you and Everard.'

'You'll do no such thing – until you've broken the bank.'

'I'll break it yet', said Natasha.

Never before had Everard been so certain that it was more blessed to give than to receive. But he could not help regretting Grace. Whether she could endure life without him remained to be seen. He would not be so easy to replace as her miniatures. He even – in his few moments of optimism – pictured her imploring his forgiveness. She would cry a little on his shoulder, and he would assure her that bygones were bygones. A grand and glorious reconciliation would follow at Fotheringham Hall.

In the meantime he enjoyed a minor satisfaction when he presented her miniatures to Nesta as well as the inscribed first edition of *Alice's Adventures in Wonderland*, the loss of which Grace had failed to notice.

'What a heavenly book. It takes me back to my age of innocence.'

For Nesta it was as if an eternal spring had dawned. Everard would quicken the languid pulse of her existence. Very gracefully they would grow old together.

For Everard it was like entering a golden cage, watched by a circle of predatory cats. He felt he was being punished undeservedly for his tenderness of heart.

SUSAN HILL

# The Custodian

AT five minutes to three he climbed up the ladder into the loft. He went cautiously, he was always cautious now, moving his limbs warily, and never going out in bad weather without enough warm clothes. For the truth was that he had not expected to survive this winter, he was old, he had been ill for one week, and then the fear had come over him again that he was going to die. He did not care for his own part, but what would become of the boy? It was only the boy he worried about now, only he who mattered. Therefore he was careful with himself, for he had lived out this bad winter, it was March, he could look forward to the spring and summer, could cease to worry for a little longer. All the same he had to be careful not to have accidents, though he was steady enough on his feet. He was seventy-one. He knew how easy it would be, for example, to miss his footing on the narrow ladder, to break a limb and lie there, while all the time the child waited, panic welling up inside him, left last at the school. And when the fear of his own dying did not grip him, he was haunted by ideas of some long illness, or incapacitation, and if he had to be taken into hospital, what would happen to the child, then? *What would happen?*

But now it was almost three o'clock, almost time for him to leave the house, his favourite part of the day, now he climbed on hands and knees into the dim, cool loft and felt about among the apples, holding this one and that one up to the beam of light coming through the slats in the roof, wanting the fruit he finally chose to perfect, ripe and smooth.

The loft smelled sweetly of the apples and pears laid up there since the previous autumn. Above his head, he heard the scrabbling noises of the birds, house martins nesting in the eaves, his heart lurched with joy at the fresh realisation that it was almost April, almost spring.

He went carefully down the ladder, holding the chosen apple. It took him twenty minutes to walk to the school but he liked to arrive early, to have the pleasure of watching and waiting, outside the gates.

The sky was brittle blue and the sun shone, but it was very cold, the air smelled of winter. Until a fortnight ago there had been snow, he and the boy had trudged back and forwards every morning and afternoon over the frost-hard paths which led across the marshes, and the stream running alongside of them had been iced over, the reeds were stiff and white as blades.

It had thawed very gradually. Today, the air smelled thin and sharp in his nostrils. Nothing moved. As he climbed the grass bank on to the higher path, he looked across the great stretch of river, and it gleamed like a flat metal plate

346

under the winter sun, still as the sky. Everything was pale, white and silver, a gull came over slowly, and its belly and the undersides of its wings were pebble grey. There were no sounds here except the sudden chatter of dunlin swooping and dropping quickly down, and the tread of his own feet on the path, the brush of his legs against grass clumps.

He had not expected to live this winter.

In his hand, he felt the apple, hard and soothing to the touch, for the boy must have fruit, fruit every day, he saw to that, as well as milk and eggs which they fetched from Maldrun at the farm, a mile away. His limbs should grow, he should be perfect.

Maldrun's cattle were out on their green island in the middle of the marshes, surrounded by the moat of steely water, he led them across a narrow path like a causeway, from the farm. They were like toy animals, or those in a picture, seen from this distance away, they stood motionless, cut-out shapes of black and white. Every so often, the boy was still afraid of going past the island of cows, he gripped the old man's hand and a tight expression came over his face.

'They can't get at you, don't you see? They don't cross water, not cows. They're not bothered about you.'

'I know.'

And he did know – and was still afraid. Though there had been days, recently, when he would go right up to the edge of the strip of water and stare across at the animals, he would even accompany Maldrun to the half-door of the milking parlour, and climb up and look over, would smell the thick, sour, cow-smell, and hear the plash of dung on to the stone floor. Then he was not afraid. The cows had great, bony haunches and vacant eyes.

'Touch one,' Maldrun had said. The boy had gone inside and put out a hand, though standing well back, stretched and touched the rough pelt, the cow had twitched, feeling the lightness of his hand as if it were an irritation, the prick of a fly. He was afraid, but getting less so, of the cows. So many things were changing, he was growing, he was seven years old.

Occasionally the old man woke in the night and sweated with fear that he might die before the boy was grown, and he prayed, then, to live ten more years, just ten, until the boy could look after himself. And some days it seemed possible, seemed indeed most likely, some days he felt very young, felt no age at all, his arms were strong and he could chop wood and lift buckets, he was light-headed with the sense of his own youth. He was no age. He was seventy-one. A tall, bony man with thick white hair, and without any spread of spare flesh. When he bathed, he looked down and saw every rib, every joint of his own thin body, he bent an arm and watched the flicker of muscle beneath the skin.

As the path curved round, the sun caught the surface of the water on his right, so that it shimmered and dazzled his eyes for a moment, and then he heard the familiar faint, high moan of the wind, as it blew off the estuary a mile and more away. The reeds rustled dryly together like sticks. He put up the collar of his coat.

But he was happy, his own happiness sang inside his head, that he was here, walking along this path with the apple inside his pocket, that he would wait and watch and then, that he would walk back this same way with the boy, that none of those things he dreaded would come about.

Looking back, he could still make out the shapes of the cows, and looking down, to where the water lay between the reed-banks, he saw a swan, its neck arched and its head below the surface of the dark, glistening stream, and it too was entirely still. He stopped for a moment, watching it and hearing the thin sound of the wind, and then, turning, saw the whole, pale stretch of marsh and water and sky, saw for miles, back to where the trees began, behind which was the cottage and then far ahead, to where the sand stretched out like a tongue into the mouth of the estuary.

He was amazed that he could be alive and moving, small as an insect, across this great, bright, cold space, amazed that he should count for as much as Maldrun's cows and the unmoving swan.

The wind was suddenly cold on his face. It was a quarter past three. He left the path, went towards the gate, and began to cross the rough, ploughed field which led to the lane, and then, on another mile to the village, the school.

Occasionally he came here not only in the morning, and back again in the afternoon, but at other times when he was overcome with sudden anxiety and a desire to see the boy, to reassure himself that he was still there, was alive. Then he put down whatever he might be doing and came, almost running, stumbled and caught his breath, until he reached the railings and the closed, black gate. If he waited there long enough, if it was dinner or break time, he saw them all come streaming and tumbling out of the green painted doors, and he watched desperately until he saw him, and he could loosen the grip of his hands on the railings, the thumping of his heart eased inside his chest. Always, then, the boy would come straight down to him, running over the asphalt, and laughed and called and pressed himself up against the railings on the other side.

'Hello.'

'All right, are you?'

'What have you brought me? Have you got something?'

Though he knew there would be nothing, did not expect it, knew that there was only ever the fruit at home time, apple, pear or sometimes, in the summer, cherries or a peach.

'I was just passing through the village.'

'Were you doing the shopping?'

'Yes. I only came up to see . . .'

'We've done reading. We had tapioca for pudding.'

'That's good for you. You should eat that. Always eat your dinner.'

'Is it home time yet?'

'Not yet.'

'You will be here, won't you? You won't forget to come back?'

'Have I ever?'

Then, he made himself straighten his coat, or shift the string shopping-bag over from one hand to the other, he said, 'You go back now then, go to the others, you play with them,' for he knew that this was right, he should not keep the child standing here, should not show him up in front of the rest. It was only for himself that he had come, he was eaten up with his own concern, and fear.

'You go back to your friends now.'

'You will be here? You will be here?'

'I'll be here.'

He turned away, they both turned, for they were separate, they should have their own ways, their own lives. He turned and walked off down the lane out of sight of the playground, not allowing himself to look back; perhaps he went and bought something from the shop, and he was calm again, no longer anxious. He walked back home slowly.

He did not mind all the walking, not even in the worst weather. He did not mind anything at all in this life he had chosen, and which was all-absorbing, the details of which were so important. He no longer thought anything of the past. Somewhere he had read that an old man has only his memories, and he had wondered at that, for he had none, or rather they did not concern him, they were like old letters which he had not troubled to keep. He had, simply, the present, the cottage, and the land around it, and the boy to look after. And he had to stay well, stay alive, he must not die yet. That was all.

But he did not often allow himself to go up to the school like that, at unnecessary times, he would force himself to stay and sweat out his anxiety and the need to reassure himself about the child, in some physical job, he would beat mats and plant vegetables in the garden, prune or pick from the fruit trees or walk over to see Maldrun at the farm, buy a chicken, and wait until the time came so slowly around to three o'clock, and he could go, with every reason, could allow himself the pleasure of arriving there a little early, and waiting beside the gates, which were now open, for the boy to come out.

'What have I got today?'

'You guess.'

'That's easy. Pear.'

'Wrong!' He opened his hand, revealing the apple.

'Well, I like apples best.'

'I know. I had a good look at those trees down the bottom this morning. There won't be so many this year. Mind, we've to wait for the blossom to be sure.'

'Last year there were hundreds of apples. *Thousands*.' He took the old man's hand as they reached the bottom of the lane. For some reason he always waited until just there, by the whitebeam tree, before doing so.

'There were *millions* of apples!'

'Get on!'

'Well, a lot anyway.'

'That's why there won't be so many this year. You don't get two crops like that in a row.'

'Why?'

'Trees wear themselves out, fruiting like that. They've to rest.'

'Will we have a lot of pears instead, then?'

'I dare say. What have you done at school?'

'Lots of things.'

'Have you done your reading? That's what's the important thing. To keep up with your reading.'

He had started the boy off himself, bought alphabet and word picture-books from the village, and, when they got beyond these, had made up his own cut-out pictures from magazines and written beside them in large clear letters on ruled sheets of paper. By the time the boy went to school, he had known more than any of the others, he was 'very forward', they said, though looking him up and down at the same time for he was small for his age.

It worried him that the boy was still small, he watched the others closely as they came out of the gates and they were all taller, thicker in body and stronger of limb. His face always looked old.

The old man concerned himself even more, then, with the fresh eggs and cheese, milk and fruit, watched over the boy while he ate. But he did eat.

'We had meat and cabbage for dinner.'

'Did you finish it?'

'I had a second helping. Then we had cake for pudding. Cake and custard. I don't like that.'

'You didn't leave it?'

'Oh no. I just don't like it, that's all.'

Now, as they came onto the marshes, the water and sky were even paler and the reeds beside the stream were bleached, like old wood left out for years in the sun. The wind was stronger, whipping at their legs from behind.

'There's the swan.'

'They've a nest somewhere about.'

'Have you seen it?'

'They don't let you see it. They go away from it if anybody walks by.'

'I drew a picture of a swan.'

'Today?'

'No. Once. It wasn't very good.'

'If a thing's not good you should do it again.'

'Why should I?'

'You'll get better then.'

'I won't get better at drawing.' He spoke very deliberately, as he so often did, knowing himself, and firm about the truth of things, so that the old man was silent, respecting it.

'He's sharp,' Maldrun's wife said. 'He's a clever one.'

But the old man would not have him spoiled, or too lightly praised.

'He's plenty to learn. He's only a child yet.'

'All the same, he'll do, won't he? He's sharp.'

But perhaps it was only the words he used, only the serious expression on his face, which came of so much reading and all that time spent alone with the old man. And if he was, as they said, so sharp, so forward, perhaps it would do him no good?

He worried about that, wanting the boy to find his place easily in the world, he tried hard not to shield him from things, made him go to the farm to see Maldrun, and over Harper's fen by himself, to play with the gamekeeper's boys, told him always to mix with the others in the school playground, to do what they did. Because he was most afraid, at times, of their very contentment together, of the self-contained life they led, for in truth they needed no one, each of them would be entirely happy never to go far beyond this house; they spoke of all things, or of nothing, the boy read and made careful lists of the names of birds and moths, and built elaborate structures, houses and castles and palaces out of old matchboxes, he helped with the garden, had his own corner down beside the shed, in which he grew what he chose. It had been like this from the beginning, from the day the old man had brought him here at nine months old and set him down on the floor and taught him to crawl, they had fallen naturally into their life together. Nobody else had wanted him. Nobody else would have taken such care.

Once, people had been suspicious, they had spoken to each other in the village, had disapproved.

'He needs a woman there. It's not right. He needs someone who knows,' Maldrun's wife had said. But now, even she had accepted that it was not true, so that, before strangers, she would have defended them more fiercely than anyone.

'He's a fine boy, that. He's all right. You look at him, look. Well, you can't tell what works out for the best. You can never tell.'

By the time they came across the track which led between the gorse bushes and down through the fir trees, it was as cold as it had been on any night in January, they brought in more wood for the fire and had toast and the last of the damson jam and mugs of hot milk.

'It's like winter. Only not so dark. I like it in winter.'

But it was the middle of March now, in the marshes the herons and redshanks were nesting, and the larks spiralled up, singing through the silence. It was almost spring.

So, they went on as they had always done, until the second of April. Then, the day after their walk out to Derenow, the day after they saw the kingfisher, it happened.

From the early morning, he had felt uneasy, though there was no reason he could give for his fear, it simply lay, hard and cold as a stone in his belly, and he was restless about the house from the time he got up.

The weather had changed. It was warm, and clammy, with low, dun-coloured clouds and, over the marshes, a thin mist. He felt the need to get out, to walk and walk; the cottage was dark and oddly quiet. When he went down between the fruit trees to the bottom of the garden, the first of the buds were breaking into green, but the grass was soaked with dew like a sweat, the heavy air smelled faintly rotten and sweet.

They set off in the early afternoon. The boy did not question, he was always happy to go anywhere at all, but when he was asked to choose their route, he set off at once, a few paces ahead, on the path which forked away east, in the opposite direction from the village and leading, over almost three miles of empty marsh, towards the sea. They followed the bank of the river, and the water was sluggish, with fronds of dark green weed lying below the surface. The boy bent, and put his hand cautiously down, breaking the skin of the water but when his fingers came up against the soft, fringed edges of the plants he pulled back.

'Slimy.'

'Yes. It's out of the current here. There's no freshness.'

'Will there be fish?'

'Maybe there will. Not so many.'

'I don't like it.' Though for some minutes he continued to peer between the reeds at the pebbles which were just visible on the bed of the stream.

'He asks questions,' they said. 'He takes an interest. It's his mind, isn't it – bright – you can see, alert, that's what. He's forever wanting to know.'

Though there were times when he said nothing at all, his small, old-young face was crumpled in thought, there were times when he looked and listened with care and asked nothing.

As they went on, the air around them seemed to close in further, it seemed harder to breathe, and they could not see clearly ahead to where the marshes and mist merged into the sky. Here and there, the stream led off into small, muddy pools and hollows, and the water in them was reddened by the rust seeping from some old can or metal crate thrown there and left for years, the stains which spread out looked like old blood. Gnats hovered in clusters over the water.

'Will we go on to the beach?'

'We could.'

'We might find something on the beach.'

Often they searched among the pebbles for pieces of amber or jet, for old buckles and buttons and sea-smooth coins washed up by the tides: the boy had a collection of them in a card-board box in his room.

'You could die here. You could drown in the water and never, never be found.'

'That's not a thing to think about. What do you worry over that for?'

'But you could, you could.'

They were walking in single file, the boy in front. From all the secret nests down in the reed-beds, the birds made their own noises, chirring and whispering, or sending out sudden cries of warning and alarm. The high, sad call of a curlew came again and again, and then ceased abruptly. The boy whistled in imitation.

'Will it know it's me? Will it answer?'

He whistled again. They waited. Nothing. His face was shadowed with disappointment.

'You can't fool them, not birds.'

'You can make a blackbird answer you. You can easily.'

'Not the same.'

'Why isn't it?'

'Blackbirds are tame, blackbirds are garden birds.'

'Wouldn't a curlew come to the garden?'

'No.'

'Why wouldn't it?'

'It likes to be away from things. They keep to their own places.'

They walked on, and then, out of the thick silence which was all around them came the creaking of wings, nearer and nearer and sounding like two thin boards of wood beaten slowly together. A swan, huge as an eagle, came over their heads, flying very low, so that the boy looked up for a second in terror at the size and closeness of it, caught his breath. He said urgently, 'Swans go for people, swans can break your arm if they hit you, if they beat you with their wings. Can't they?'

'But they don't take any notice, so come on, you leave them be.'

'But they *can* can't they?'

'Oh, they might.' He watched the great, grey-white shape go awkwardly away from them, in the direction of the sea.

A hundred yards further on, at the junction of two paths across the marsh there was the ruin of a water-mill, blackened after a fire years before, and half broken down, a sail torn off. Inside, under an arched doorway, it was dark and damp, the walls were coated with yellowish moss and water lay, brackish, in the mud hollows of the floor.

At high summer, on hot, shimmering blue days they had come across here on the way to the beach with a string bag full of food for their lunch, and then the water-mill had seemed like a sanctuary, cool and silent, the boy had gone inside and stood there, had called softly and listened to the echo of his own voice as it rang lightly round and round the walls.

Now, he stopped dead in the path, some distance away.

'I don't want to go.'

'We're walking to the beach.'

'I don't want to go past that.'

'The mill?'

'There are rats.'

'No.'

'And flying things. Things that are black and hang upside-down.'

'Bats? What's to be afraid of in bats? You've seen them, you've been in Maldrun's barn. They don't hurt.'

'I want to go back.'

'You don't have to go into the mill. Who said you did? We're going on to where the sea is.'

'*I want to go back now.*'

He was not often frightened. But standing there in the middle of the hushed stretch of fenland, the old man felt again disturbed himself, the fear that something would happen, here, where nothing moved and the birds lay hidden, only crying out their weird cries, where things lay under the unmoving water and the press of the air made him sweat down his back. Something would happen to them, something . . .

What could happen?

Then, not far ahead, they both saw him at the same moment, a man with a gun under his arm, tall and black and menacing as a crow against the dull horizon, and as they saw him, they also saw two mallard ducks rise in sudden panic from their nests in the reeds, and they heard the shots, three shots that cracked out and echoed for miles around, the air went on reverberating with the waves of terrible sound.

The ducks fell at once, hit in mid-flight so that they swerved, turned over, and plummeted down. The man with the shotgun started quickly forward and the grasses and reeds bent and stirred as a dog ran, burrowing, to retrieve.

'I want to go back, *I want to go back.*'

Without a word, the old man took his hand, and they turned, walked quickly back the way they had come, as though afraid that they, too, would be followed and struck down, not caring that they were out of breath and sticky with sweat, but only wanting to get away, to reach the shelter of the lane and the trees, to make for home.

Nothing was ever said about it, or about the feeling they had both had walking across the marshes, the boy did not mention the man with the gun or the ducks which had been alive and in flight and then so suddenly dead. All that evening, the old man watched him, as he stuck pictures in a book, and tore up dock leaves to feed to the rabbit, watched for signs of left-over fear. But he was only, perhaps, quieter than usual, his face more closed up; he was concerned with his own thoughts.

In the night, he woke, and got up, went to the boy and looked down through the darkness, for fear that he might have had bad dreams and woken, but there was only the sound of his breathing; he lay quite still, very long and straight in the bed.

He imagined the future, and his mind was filled with images of all the possible horrors to come, the things which could cause the boy shock and pain and misery, and from which he would not be able to save him, as he had been powerless today to protect him from the sight of the killing of two ducks. He was in despair. Only the next morning, he was eased, as it came back to him again, the knowledge that he had, after all, lived out the winter, and ahead of them lay only light and warmth and greenness.

Nevertheless, he half-expected that something would still happen to them, to break into their peace. For more than a week, nothing did, his fears were quieted, and then the spring broke, the apple and pear blossom weighed down the branches in great, creamy clots, the grass in the orchard grew up as high as the boy's knees, and across the marshes the sun shone and shone, the water of the river was turquoise, and in the streams, as clear as glass; the wind blew warm and smelled faintly of salt and earth. Walking to and from the school every day, they saw more woodlarks than they had ever seen, quivering on the air high above their heads, and near the gorse bushes, the boy found a nest of leverets. In the apple loft, the house martins hatched out, and along the lanes, dandelions and buttercups shone golden out of the grass.

It was on the Friday that Maldrun gave the boy one of the farm kittens, and he carried it home close to his body beneath his coat. It was black and white, like Maldrun's cows. And it was the day after that, the end of the first week of spring, that Blaydon came, Gilbert Blaydon, the boy's father.

He was sitting outside the door watching a buzzard hover above the fir copse when he heard the footsteps. He thought it was Maldrun bringing over the eggs, or a chicken – Maldrun generally came one evening in the week, after the boy had gone to bed, they drank a glass of beer and talked for half an hour. He was an easy man, undemonstrative. They still called one another, formally 'Mr Bowry', 'Mr Maldrun'.

The buzzard roved backwards and forwards over its chosen patch of air, searching.

When the old man looked down again, he was there, standing in the path. He was carrying a canvas kitbag.

He knew, then, why he had been feeling uneasy, he had expected this, or something like it, to happen, though he had put the fears to the back of his mind with the coming of sunshine and the leaf-breaking. He felt no hostility as he looked at Blaydon, only extreme weariness, almost as though he were ill.

There was no question of who it was, yet above all he ought to have expected a feeling of complete disbelief, for if anyone had asked, he would have said that he would certainly never see the boy's father again. But now he was here, it did not seem surprising, it seemed, indeed, somehow inevitable. Things had to alter, things could never go on. Happiness did not go on.

'Will you be stopping?'

Blaydon walked slowly forward, hesitated, and then set the kitbag down at his feet. He looked much older.

'I don't know if it'd be convenient.'

'There's a room. There's always a room.'

The old man's head buzzed suddenly in confusion, he thought he should offer a drink or a chair, should see to a bed, should ask questions to which he did not want to know the answers, should say something about the boy.

*The boy.*

'You've come to take him . . .'

Blaydon sat down on the other chair, beside the outdoors-table. The boy looked like him, there was the same narrowness of forehead and chin, the same high-bridged nose. Only the mouth was different, though that might simply be because the boy's was still small and unformed.

'You've come to take him.'

'Where to?' He looked up. 'Where would I have, to take him to?'

But we don't want you here, the old man thought, we don't want anyone: and he felt the intrusion of this younger man, with the broad hands and long legs sprawled under the table, like a violent disturbance of the careful pattern of their lives, he was alien. *We don't want you.*

But what right had he to say that? He did not say it. He was standing up helplessly, not knowing what should come next, he felt the bewilderment as some kind of irritation inside his own head. He felt old.

In the end, he managed to say, 'You'll not have eaten?'

Blaydon stared at him. 'Don't you want to know where I've come from?'

'No.'

'No?'

'I've made a stew. You'll be better for a plate of food.'

'Where is he?'

'Asleep in bed; where else would he be? I look after him, I know what I'm about. It's half-past eight, gone, isn't it? What would he be doing but asleep in his bed, at half-past eight?'

He heard his own voice rising and quickening, as he defended himself, defended both of them, he could prove it to this father or to anyone at all, how he'd looked after the boy. He would have said, what about you? Where have you been? What did you do for him? But he was too afraid, for he knew nothing about what rights Blaydon might have – even though he had never been near, never bothered.

'You could have been dead.'

'Did you think?'

'What was I to think? I knew nothing. Heard nothing.'

'No.'

Out of the corner of his eye, the old man saw the buzzard drop down suddenly, straight as a stone, on to some creature in the undergrowth of the copse. The sky was mulberry coloured and the honeysuckle smelled ingratiatingly sweet.

'I wasn't dead.'

The old man realised that Blaydon looked both tired and rather dirty, his nails were broken, he needed a shave, and the wool at the neck of his blue sweater was unravelling. What was he to say to the boy then, when he had brought him up to be so clean and tidy and careful, had taken his clothes to be mended by a woman in the village, had always cut and washed his hair himself. What was he to tell him about this man?

'There's hot water. I'll get you linen, make you a bed. You'd best go up first, before I put out the stew. Have a wash.'

He went into the kitchen, took a mug and a bottle of beer and poured it out, and was calmed a little by the need to organise himself, by the simple physical activity.

When he took the beer out, Blaydon was still leaning back on the old chair. There were dark stains below his eyes.

'You'd best take it up with you.' The old man held out the beer.

It was almost dark now. After a long time, Blaydon reached out, took the mug and drank, emptying it in four or five long swallows, and then, as though all his muscles were stiff, rose slowly, took up the kitbag, went towards the house.

When the old man had set the table and dished out the food, he was trembling. He tried to turn his mind away from the one thought. That Blaydon had come to take the boy away.

He called and when there was no reply, went up the stairs. Blaydon was stretched out on his belly on top of the unmade bed, heavy and motionless in sleep.

While he slept, the old man worried about the morning. It was Saturday, there would not be the diversion of going to school, the boy must wake and come downstairs and confront Blaydon.

What he had originally said was, your mother died, your father went away. And that was the truth. But he doubted if the boy so much as remembered; he had asked a question only once, and that more than two years ago.

They were content together, needing no one.

He sat on the straight-backed chair in the darkness, surrounded by hidden greenery and the fumes of honeysuckle, and tried to imagine what he might say.

'This is your father. Other boys have fathers. This is your father who came back, who will stay with us here. For some time, or perhaps not for more than a few days. His name is Gilbert Blaydon.

'Will you call him "father", will you? . . .'

'This is . . .'

His mind broke down before the sheer cliff confronting it and he simply sat on, hands uselessly in front of him on the outdoors table, he thought of nothing, and on white plates in the kitchen the stew cooled and congealed and the new kitten from Maldrun's farm slept, coiled on an old green jumper. The cat, the boy, the boy's father, all slept. From the copse, the throaty call of the nightjars.

'You'll be ready for breakfast. You didn't eat the meal last night.'

'I slept.'

'You'll be hungry.' He had his back to Blaydon. He was busy with the frying-pan and plates over the stove. What had made him tired enough to sleep like that, from early evening until now, fully clothed on top of the bed! But he didn't want to know, would not ask questions.

The back door was open on to the path that led down between vegetable beds and the bean canes and currant bushes, towards the thicket. Blaydon went to the doorway.

'Two eggs, will you have?'

'If . . .'

'There's plenty.' He wanted to divert him, talk to him, he had to pave the way. The boy was there, somewhere at the bottom of the garden.

'We'd a hard winter.'

'Oh, yes?'

'Knee-deep, all January, all February, we'd to dig ourselves out of the door. And then it froze – the fens froze right over, ice as thick as your fist. I've never known anything like it.'

But now it was spring, now outside there was the bright, glorious green of new grass, new leaves, now the sun shone.

He began to set out knives and forks on the kitchen table. It would have to come, he would have to call the boy in, to bring them together. What would he say? His heart squeezed and then pumped hard, suddenly, in the thin bone-cage of his chest.

Blaydon's clothes were creased and crumpled. And they were not clean. Had he washed himself? The old man tried to get a glimpse of his hands.

'I thought I'd get a job,' Blaydon said.

The old man watched him.

'I thought I'd look for work.'

'Here?'

'Around here. Is there work?'

'Maybe. I've not had reason to find out. Maybe.'

'If I'm staying on, I'll need to work.'

'Yes.'

'It'd be a help, I dare say?'

'You've a right to do as you think fit. You make up your own mind.'

'I'll pay my way.'

'You've no need to worry about the boy, if it's that. He's all right, he's provided for. You've no need to find money for him.'

'All the same . . .'

After a minute, Blaydon walked over and sat down at the table.

The old man thought, he is young, young and strong and fit, he has come here to stay, he has every right, he's the father. He is . . .

But he did not want Blaydon in their lives, did not want the hands resting on the kitchen table, and the big feet beneath it.

He said, 'You could try at the farm. At Maldrun's. They've maybe got work there. You could try.'

'Maldrun's farm?'

'It'd be ordinary work. Labouring work.'

'I'm not choosy.'

The old man put out eggs and fried bread and bacon on to the plates, poured tea, filled the sugar basin. And then he had no more left to do, he had to call the boy.

But nothing happened as he had feared it, after all.

He came in. 'Wash your hands.' But he was already half way to the sink, he had been brought up so carefully, the order was not an order but a formula between them, regular, and of comfort.

'Wash your hands.'

'I've come to stay,' Blaydon said at once, 'for a bit. I got here last night.'

The boy hesitated in the middle of the kitchen, looked from one to the other of them, trying to assess this sudden change in the order of things.

'For a week or two,' the old man said. 'Eat your food.'

The boy got on to his chair. 'What's your name?'

'Gilbert Blaydon.'

'What have I to call you?'

'Either.'

'Gilbert, then.'

'What you like.'

After that, they got on with eating; the old man chewed his bread very slowly, filled, for the moment, with relief.

Maldrun took him on at the farm as a general labourer, and then their lives formed a new pattern, with the full upsurge of spring. Blaydon got up, and ate his breakfast with them and then left, there was a quarter of an hour which the old man had alone with the boy before setting off across the marsh path to school, and in the afternoon, an even longer time. Blaydon did not return, sometimes, until after six.

At the weekend, he went off somewhere alone, but occasionally, he took the boy for walks; they saw the heron's nest, and then the cygnets, and once a peregrine, flying over the estuary. The two of them were at ease together.

Alone the old man tried to imagine what they might be saying to each other, he walked distractedly about the house, and almost wept, with anxiety and dread. They came down the path, and the boy was sitting up on Blaydon's shoulders, laughing and laughing.

'You've told him.'

Blaydon turned, surprised, and then sent the boy away. 'I've said nothing.'

The old man believed him. But there was still a fear for the future, the end of things.

The days lengthened. Easter went by, and the school holidays, during which the old man was happiest, because he had so much time with the boy to himself, and then it was May, in the early mornings there was a fine mist above the blossom trees.

'He's a good worker,' Maldrun said, coming over one evening with the eggs and finding the old man alone. 'I'm glad to have him.'

'Yes.'

'He takes a bit off your shoulders, I dare say.'

'He pays his way.'

'No. Work, I meant. Work and worries. All that.'

What did Maldrun know? But he only looked back at the old man, his face open and friendly, and drank his bottled beer.

He thought about it, and realised that it was true. He had grown used to having Blaydon about, to carry the heavy things and lock up at night, to clear out the fruit loft and lop off the overhanging branches and brambles at the entrance to the thicket. He had slipped into their life, and established himself. When he thought of the future without Blaydon, it was to worry. For the summer was always short and then came the run down through autumn into winter again. Into snow and ice and cold, and the north-east wind scything across the marshes. He dreaded all that, now that he was old. Last winter, he had been ill once, and for only a short time. This winter he was a year older, anything might happen. He thought of the mornings when he would have to take the boy to school before it was even light, thought of the frailty of his own flesh, the brittleness of his bones, he looked in the mirror at his own weak and rheumy eyes.

He had begun to count on Blaydon's being here to ease things, to help with the coal and wood and the breaking of ice on pails, to be in some way an insurance against his own possible illness, possible death.

Though now it was still only the beginning of summer, now he watched Blaydon build a rabbit hutch for the boy, hammering nails and sawing wood, uncoiling wire skilfully. He heard them laugh suddenly together. This was what he needed, after all, not a woman about the place, but a man, the strength and ease of a man who was not old, did not fear, did not say, 'Wash your hands', 'Drink up all your milk', 'Take care'.

The kitten grew, and spun about in quick, mad circles in the sun.

'He's a good worker,' Maldrun said.

After a while, the old man took to dozing in his chair outside, after supper, while Blaydon washed up, emptied the bins and then took out the shears, to clip the hedge or the grass borders, when the boy had gone to bed.

But everything that had to do with the boy, the business of rising and eating, going to school and returning, the routine of clothes and food and drink and bed, all that was still supervised by the old man. Blaydon did not interfere, scarcely seemed to notice what was done. His own part in the boy's life was quite different.

In June and early July, it was hotter than the old man could ever remember. The gnats droned in soft, grey clouds under the trees, and over the water of the marshes. The sun shone hard and bright and still, the light played tricks so that the estuary seemed now very near, now very far away. Maldrun's cows tossed their heads, against the flies which gathered stickily in the runnels below their great eyes.

He began to rely more and more upon Blaydon as the summer reached its height, left more jobs for him to do, because he was willing and strong, and because the old man succumbed easily to the temptation to rest himself in the sun. He still did most of the cooking, but he would let Blaydon go down to the shops, and the boy often went with him.

He was growing, his limbs were filling out and his skin was berry-brown. He lost the last of the pink-and-whiteness of babyhood. He had accepted Blaydon's presence without question and was entirely used to him, though he did not show any less affection for the old man, who continued to take care of him day by day. But he became less nervous and hesitant, more self-assured, he spoke of things in a casual, confident voice, learned much from his talks with Blaydon. He still did not know that this was his father. The old man thought there was no reason to tell him – not yet, not yet, they could go on as they were for the time being, just as they were.

He was comforted by the warmth of the sun on his face, by the scent of the roses and the tobacco-plants in the evening, the sight of the scarlet bean-flowers clambering higher and higher up their frame.

He had decided right at the beginning that he himself would ask no questions of Blaydon, would wait until he should be told. But he was not told. Blaydon's life might have begun only on the day he had arrived here. The old man wondered if he had been in prison, or else abroad, working on a ship, though he had no evidence for either. In the evenings they drank beer together and occasionally played a game of cards, though more often Blaydon worked at something in the garden, and the old man simply sat watching him, hearing the last cries of the birds from the marshes.

With the money Blaydon brought in they bought new clothes for the boy and better cuts of meat, and then, one afternoon, a television set arrived with two men in a green van to erect the aerial.

'For the winter,' Blaydon said. 'Maybe you won't bother with it now. But it's company in the winter.'

'I've never felt the lack.'

'All the same.'

'I don't need entertainment. We make our own. Always have made our own.'

'You'll be glad of it, once you've got the taste. I told you – it's for the winter.'

But the old man watched it sometimes very late in the evenings of August, and discovered things of interest to him, new horizons were opened, new worlds.

'I'd not have known that,' he said, 'I've never travelled. Look at what I'd never have known.'

Blaydon nodded. He himself seemed little interested in the television set. He was mending the front fence, staking it all along with old wood given to him by Maldrun at the farm. Now the gate would fit closely and not swing and bang in the gales of winter.

It was on a Thursday night towards the end of August that Blaydon mentioned the visit to the seaside.

'He's never been,' he said, wiping the foam of beer from his top lip.

'He told me. I asked him. He's never been to the sea.'

'I've done all I can. There's never been the money. We've managed as best we could.'

'You're not being blamed.'

'I'd have taken him, I'd have seen to it in time. Sooner or later.'

'Yes.'

'Yes.'

'Well – I could take him.'

'To the sea?'

'To the coast, yes.'

'For a day? It's far enough.'

'A couple of days, I thought. For a weekend.'

The old man was silent. But it was true. The boy had never been anywhere and perhaps he suffered because of it, perhaps at school the others talked of where they had gone, what they had seen, shaming him. If that was so, he should be taken, should go everywhere, he must not miss anything, must not be left out.

'Just a couple of days. We'd leave first thing Saturday morning and come back Monday. I'd take a day off.'

He had been here three months now, and not missed a day off work.

'You do as you think best.'

'I'd not go without asking you.'

'It's only right. He's at the age for taking things in. He needs enjoyment.'

'Yes.'

'You go. It's only right.'

'I haven't told him, not yet.'

'You tell him.'

When he did, the boy's face opened out with pleasure, he licked his lips nervously over and over again in his excitement, already counting until it should be time to go. The old man went upstairs and sorted out clothes for him, washed them carefully and hung them on the line, he began himself to anticipate it all. This was right. The boy should go.

But he dreaded it. They had not been separated before. He could not imagine how it would be, to sleep alone in the cottage, and then he began to imagine all the possible accidents. Blaydon had not asked him if he wanted to go with them. But he did not. He felt suddenly too tired to leave the house, too tired for any journeys or strangers, he wanted to sit on his chair in the sun and count the time until they should be back.

He had got used to the idea of Blaydon's continuing presence here, he no longer lived in dread of the coming winter. It seemed a long time since the days when he had been alone with the boy.

They set off very early on the Saturday morning, before the sun had broken through the thick mist that hung low over the marshes. Every sound was clear and separate as it came through the air, he heard their footsteps, the brush of their legs against the grasses long after they were out of sight. The boy had his own bag, bought new in the village, a canvas bag strapped across his shoulders. He had stood up very straight, eyes glistening, already his mind was filled with imaginary pictures of what he would see, what they would do.

The old man went back into the kitchen and put the kettle on again, refilled the teapot for himself and planned what he was going to do. He would work, he would clean out all the bedrooms of the house and sort the boy's clothes for any that needed mending; he would polish the knives and forks and wash the curtains and walk down to the village for groceries, he would bake a cake and pies, prepare a stew, ready for their return.

So that, on the first day, the Saturday he scarcely had time to think of them, to notice their absence and in the evening, his legs and back ached, he sat for only a short time outside, after his meal, drunk with tiredness, and slept later than usual on the Sunday morning.

It was then that he felt the silence and emptiness of the house. He walked about it uselessly, he woke up the kitten and teased it with a feather so that it would play with him, distract his attention from his own solitude. When it slept again, he went out, and walked for miles across the still, hot marshes. The water between the reed beds was very low and even dried up altogether in places, revealing the dark, greenish-brown slime below. The faint, dry whistling sound that usually came through the rushes was absent. He felt parched as the countryside after this long, long summer, the sweat ran down his bent back.

He had walked in order to tire himself out again but this night he slept badly and woke out of clinging nightmares with a thudding heart, tossed from side to side, uncomfortable among the bedclothes. But tomorrow he could begin to count the strokes of the clock until their return.

He got up feeling as if he had never slept, his eyes were pouched and blurred. But he began the baking, the careful preparations to welcome them home. He scarcely stopped for food himself all day, though his head and his back ached, he moved stiffly about the kitchen.

When they had not returned by midnight on the Monday, he did not go down to the village, or across to Maldrun's farm to telephone the police and the hospitals. He did nothing. He knew.

But he sat up in the chair outside the back-door all night with the silence pressing in on his ears. Once or twice his head nodded down onto his chest, he almost slept, but then jerked awake again, shifted a little, and sat on in the darkness.

He thought, they have not taken everything, some clothes are left, clothes and toys and books, they must mean to come back. But he knew that they did not. Other toys, other clothes, could be bought anywhere.

A week passed, and the summer slid imperceptibly into autumn, like smooth cards shuffled together in a pack, the trees faded to yellow and crinkled at the edges.

He did not leave the house, and he ate almost nothing, only filled and refilled the teapot, and drank.

He did not blame Gilbert Blaydon, he blamed himself for having thought to keep the boy, having planned out their whole future. When the father had turned up, he should have known what he wanted at once, should have said, 'Take him away, take him now,' to save them this furtiveness, this deception. At night, though, he worried most about the effect it would have on the boy, who had been brought up so scrupulously, to be tidy and clean, to eat up his food, to learn. He wished there was an address to which he could write a list of details about the boy's everyday life, the routine he was used to following.

He waited for a letter. None came. The pear-trees sagged under their weight of ripe, dark fruit and after a time it fell with soft thuds into the long grass. He did not gather it up and take it to store in the loft, he left it there for the sweet pulp to be burrowed by hornets and grubs. But sometimes he took a pear and ate it himself, for he had always disapproved of waste.

He kept the boy's room exactly as it should be. His clothes were laid out neatly in the drawers, his books lined on the single shelf, in case he should return. But he could not bother with the rest of the house, dirt began to linger in corners. Fluff accumulated greyly beneath beds. The damp patch in the bathroom wall was grown over with moss like a fungus when the first rain came in October.

Maldrun had twice been across from the farm and received no answer to his questions. In the village the women talked. October went out in fog and drizzle, and the next time Maldrun came the old man did not open the door. Maldrun waited, peering through the windows between cupped hands, and in the end left the eggs on the back step.

The old man got up later and later each day, and went to bed earlier, to sleep between the frowsty, unwashed sheets. For a short while he turned on the television set in the evenings and sat staring at whatever was offered to him, but in the end he did not bother, only stayed in the kitchen while it grew dark around him. Outside, the last of the fruit fell on to the sodden garden and lay there untouched. Winter came.

In the small town flat, Blaydon set out plates, cut bread and opened tins, filled the saucepan with milk.

'Wash your hands,' he said. But the boy was already there, moving his hands over and over the pink soap, obediently, wondering what was for tea.

# Parthenope

MY UNCLE ARTHUR had red hair that lay close to his head in flat, circular curls, and a pointed red beard, and his blue-green eyes were at once penetrating and bemused. He was the object of mingled derision and respect in our family. He was a civil servant who had early attracted attention by his brilliance; but the chief of his department, like so many English civil servants, was an author in his spare time and, when he published a history of European literature, my uncle reviewed it in the leading weekly of the day, pointing out that large as was the number of works in the less familiar languages that his chief supposed to be written in prose, though in fact they were written in verse, it was not so large as the number of such works that he supposed to be written in verse, though in fact they were written in prose. He wrote without malice, simply thinking his chief would be glad to know. My uncle never connected this review with his subsequent failure to gain a promotion that had seemed certain, or to have the day as snug as civil servants usually had it in the nineteenth century. But in the course of time his chief died, and my uncle rose to be an important official. However, he did a Cabinet Minister much the same service he had rendered his chief, and he never received the title that normally went with his post.

So he seesawed through life, and I liked his company very much when he was an old man and I was a young girl, for it was full of surprises. When I asked him a question, I never knew if his answer would show that he knew far less than I did or far more; and though he was really quite old, for he was my father's elder by many years, he often made discoveries such as a schoolchild might make, and shared them with an enthusiasm as little adult. One day he gave me no peace till I had come with him to see the brightest field of buttercups he had ever found near London; it lay, solid gold, beside the great Jacobean mansion Ham House, by the River Thames. After we had admired it he took me to nearby Petersham Church, to see another treasure, the tomb of Captain Vancouver, who gave his name to the island; my uncle liked this tomb because he had spent some years of his boyhood in Canada and had been to Vancouver Island when it was hardly inhabited. Then we had tea in an inn garden, and it happened that the girl who waited on us was called away by the landlord as she set the china on the table. His voice came from the kitchen: 'Parthenope! Parthenope!' My uncle started, for no very good reason that I could see. There had been a time when many ships in the British Navy were called after characters in Greek history and mythology, male and female, and therefore many sailors' daughters had been given the names of nymphs and goddesses and Homeric princesses and heroines of Greek tragedy. The only strange thing was that it was a long time since British ships had been christened so poetically, and most of the women who had acquired these Classical names by this secondary interest were by now old or middle-aged, while our little waitress was very young. She had, as she told us when she came back, been called after a grandmother. But my uncle was plainly shaken by hearing those four syllables suddenly borne on the afternoon air. His thin hand plucked at the edge of the tablecloth, he cast down his eyes, his head began to nod and shake. He asked me if he had ever told me the story of the Admiral and his seven daughters, in a tone that suggested that he knew he had not and was still trying to make up his mind whether he wanted to tell it now. Indeed, he told me very little that day, though I was to hear the whole of it before he died.

The story began at the house of my grandmother's sister, Alice Darrell, and it could hardly have happened anywhere else. When her husband, an officer in the Indian Army, died of fever, her father-in-law had given her a house that he had recently and reluctantly inherited and could not sell because it was part of an entailed estate. He apologised for the gift, pleading justly that he could not afford to buy her another, and she accepted it bravely. But the house lay in a district that would strain anybody's bravery. To reach it, one travelled about eight miles out of London along the main Hammersmith Road, the dullest of highways, and then turned left and found something worse. For some forgotten reason, there had sprung up at this point a Hogarthian slum, as bad as anything in the East End, which turned into a brawling hell every Saturday night. Beyond this web of filthy hovels lay flatlands covered by orchards and farmlands and market gardens, among which there had been set down three or four large houses. There was nothing to recommend the site. The Thames was not far distant, and it was comprehensible enough that along its bank there had been built a line of fine houses. But at Alice Darrell's there was no view of the river, though it lay near enough to shroud the region in mist during the winter months. It was true that the gardens had an alluvial fertility, but even they did not give the pleasure they should have done, for the slum dwellers carried out periodical raids on the strawberry beds and raspberry canes and orchards.

These stranded houses had been built in Regency times and were beautiful, though disconcerting, because there was no reason why they should be there, and they were so oddly placed in relation to each other. They all opened off the same narrow road, and Aunt Alice's house, Currivel Lodge, which was the smallest of them, lay at the end of a drive, and there faced sideways, so that its upper windows looked straight down on the garden of the much bigger house beside it, as that had been built nearer the road. This meant that my grand-aunt could not sit on the pretty balcony outside her bedroom window without seeming to spy on her neighbours, so she never used it. But when my Uncle Arthur went to stay with her as a little boy, which was about a hundred years ago, nothing delighted him more than to shut himself in his bedroom and kneel on his window seat and do what his Aunt Alice could not bear to be suspected of doing.

Currivel Lodge should have been a dreary place for the child. There was nowhere to walk and nowhere to ride. There was no village where one could watch the blacksmith at his forge and the carpenter at his bench. In those days, nobody rowed on the Thames anywhere but at Oxford, unless they were watermen earning their living. There was little visiting, for it took a good hour to an hour and a half to drive to London, and my needy grand-aunt's horses were old crocks. Her children were all older than little Arthur. But he enjoyed his visit simply because of the hours he spent on that window seat. I know the setting of the scene on which he looked, since I often stayed in that house many years later; for of course my grand-aunt's family never left it. When the entail came to an end and the property could have been sold, there were the Zulu Wars, the South African War, the First World War, and all meant that the occupants were too busy or too troubled to move; and they were still living there when the house was swept away in a town-planning scheme during the twenties. What Arthur in his day and I in mine looked down on was a croquet lawn framed by trees, very tall trees – so tall and strong, my uncle said with approval, that though one could not see the river one knew that there must be one not far away. Born and reared in one of the wettest parts of Ireland, he regarded dry weather and a dry soil as the rest of us regard dry bread.

To the left of this lawn, seen through foliage, was a stone terrace overgrown with crimson and white roses. Behind the terrace rose the mellow red rectangle of a handsome Regency house with a green copper cupola rising from its roof. What my uncle saw there that was not there for me to see was a spectacle that gave him the same sort of enjoyment I was to get from the ballet *Les Sylphides*. When the weather was fine, it often happened that there would come down the broad stone steps of the terrace a number of princesses out of a fairy tale, each dressed in a different pale but bright colour. Sometimes there were as few as four of these princesses; occasionally there were as many as seven. Among the colours that my uncle thought he remembered them wearing were hyacinth blue, the green of the leaves of lilies of the valley, a silvery lilac that was almost grey, a transparent red that was like one's hand when one holds it up to a strong light, primrose yellow, a watery jade green, and a gentle orange. The dresses were made of muslin, and billowed in loops and swinging circles as their wearers' little feet carried them about in what was neither a dance nor the everyday motion of ordinary people. It was as if these lovely creatures were all parts of a brave and sensitive and melancholy being, and were at once confiding in each other about their griefs, which were their common grief, and giving each other reassurance.

Some carried croquet mallets and went on to the lawn and started to play, while the others sat down on benches to watch them. But sooner or later the players would pause and forget to make the next stroke, move toward each other and stand in a group, resting their mallets on the ground, and presently forget them and let them fall, as the spectators rose from their seats to join them in their exchange of confidences. Though they appeared in the garden as often as three times a week, they always seemed to have as much to say to one another as if they met but once a year; and they were always grave as they talked. There was a wildness about them; it was impossible to tell what they would do next; one might suddenly break away from the others and waltz round the lawn in the almost visible arms of an invisible partner; but when they talked they showed restraint; they did not weep, though what they said was so plainly sad, and they rarely laughed. What was true of one of them was true of all, for there seemed very little difference between them. All were golden-headed. The only one who could be told apart was the wearer of the lilac-grey dress. She was taller than the rest, and often stood aloof while they clustered together and swayed and spoke. Sometimes a woman in a black gown came down from the terrace and talked to this separate one.

The girls in the coloured dresses were the seven daughters of the Admiral who owned the house. My uncle saw him once, when he called on Alice Darrell to discuss with her arrangements for repairing the wall between their properties; a tall and handsome man with iron-grey hair, a probing, defensive gaze, and a mouth so sternly compressed that it was a straight line across his face. The call would never have been made had there not been business to discuss. The Admiral would have no social relations with his neighbours; nobody had ever been invited to his house. Nor, had such an invitation been sent, would Aunt Alice have accepted it, for she thought he treated his daughters abominably. She could not help smiling when she told her nephew their names, for they came straight off the Navy List: Andromeda, Cassandra, Clytie, Hera, Parthenope, Arethusa, and Persephone. But that was the only time she smiled when she spoke of them, for she thought they had been treated with actual cruelty, though not in the way that might have been supposed. They were not immured in this lonely house by a father who wanted to keep them to himself; their case was the very opposite.

The Admiral's daughters were, in effect, motherless. By Aunt Alice my Uncle Arthur was told that the Admiral's wife was an invalid and had to live in a mild climate in the west of England, but from the servants he learned that she was mad. Without a wife to soften him, the Admiral dealt with his daughters summarily by sending each of them, as she passed her seventeenth birthday, to be guided through the London season by his only sister, a wealthy woman with a house in Berkeley Square, and by giving each to the first man of reasonably respectable character who made her an offer of marriage. He would permit no delay, though his daughters, who had inheritances from a wealthy grandfather, as well as their beauty, would obviously have many suitors. These precipitate marriages were always against the brides' inclinations, for they had, strangely enough, no desire but to go on living in their lonely home.

'They are', Aunt Alice told her nephew, hesitating and looking troubled, 'oddly young for their ages. I know they are not old, and that they have lived a great deal alone, since their mother cannot be with them. But they are really very young for what they are.' They had yielded, it was said, only to the most brutal pressure exercised by their father. It astonished my uncle that all this was spoken of as something that had happened in the past. They did not look like grown-up ladies as they wandered in the garden, yet all but two were wives, and those two were betrothed, and some of them were already mothers. Parthenope, the one with most character, the one who had charge of the house in her father's absence, had married a North Country landowner who was reputed to be a millionaire. It was a pity that he was twice her age and had, by a dead wife, a son almost as old as she was, but such a fortune is a great comfort; and none of her sisters was without some measure of that same kind of consolation. Nevertheless, their discontent could be measured by the frequency with which they returned to the home of their childhood.

The first time my uncle visited Currivel Lodge, the Admiral's seven daughters were only a spectacle for his distant enjoyment. But one day during his second visit, a year later, his aunt asked him to deliver a note for Miss Parthenope at the house next door. Another section of the wall between the properties was in need of buttresses, and the builder had to have his orders. My uncle went up to his bedroom and smoothed his hair and washed his face, a thing he had never done before between morning and night of his own accord, and when he got to the Admiral's house he told the butler, falsely but without a tremor, that he had been told to give the note into Miss Parthenope's own hands. It did not matter to him that the butler looked annoyed at hearing this: too much was to stake. He followed the butler's offended back through several rooms full of fine furniture, which were very much like the rooms to which he was accustomed, but had a sleepy air, as if the windows were closed, though they were not. In one there were some dolls thrown down on the floor, though he had never heard that there were any children living in the house. In the last room, which opened on the stone terrace and its white and crimson roses, a woman in a black dress with a suggestion of a uniform about it was sitting at an embroidery frame. She stared at him as if he presented a greater problem than schoolboys usually do, and he recognised her as the dark figure he had seen talking with the tallest of the daughters in the garden.

She took the letter from him, and he saw that the opportunity he had seized was slipping out of his grasp, so he pretended to be younger and simpler than he was, and put on the Irish brogue, which he never used at home except when he was talking to the servants or the people on the farms, but which he had found charmed the English. 'May I not go out into the garden and see the young ladies?' he asked. 'I have watched them from my window, and they look so pretty.'

It worked. The woman smiled and said, 'You're from Ireland, aren't you?' and before he could answer she exclaimed, as if defying prohibitions of which she had long been weary, 'What is the harm? Yes, go out and give the note to Miss Parthenope yourself. You will know her – she is wearing grey and is the tallest.' When he got out on the terrace, he saw that all seven of the Admiral's daughters were on the lawn, and his heart was like a turning wind-mill as he went down the stone steps. Then one of the croquet players caught sight of him – the one who was wearing a red dress, just nearer flame colour than flesh. She dropped her mallet and cried, 'Oh, look, a little boy! A little red-haired boy!' and danced toward him, sometimes pausing and twirling right round, so that her skirts billowed out round her. Other voices took up the cry, and, cooing like pigeons, the croquet players closed in on him in a circle of unbelievable beauty. It was their complexions that he remembered in later life as the marvel that made them, among all the women he was ever to see, the non-pareils. Light lay on their skin as it lies on the petals of flowers, but it promised that it would never fade, that it would last forever, like a pearl. Yet even while he remarked their loveliness and was awed by it, he was disconcerted. They came so close, and it seemed as if they might do more than look at him and speak to him. It was as if a flock of birds had come down on him, and were fluttering and pecking about him; and they asked so many questions, in voices that chirped indefatigably and were sharper than the human note. 'Who are you?' 'You are Mrs Darrell's nephew?' 'Her brother's child or her sister's?' 'How old are you?' 'What is your name?' 'Why is your middle name Greatorex?' 'Oh, what lovely hair he has – true Titian! And those round curls like coins!' 'Have you sisters?' 'Have they hair like yours?' Their little hands darted out and touched his hands, his cheeks, his shoulders, briefly but not pleasantly. His flesh rose in goose pimples, as it did when a moth's wing brushed his face as he lay in bed in the dark. And while their feathery restlessness poked and cheeped at him, they looked at him with eyes almost as fixed as if they were blind and could not see him at all. Their eyes were immense and very bright and shaded by lashes longer than he had ever seen; but they were so light a grey that they were as colourless as clear water running over a bed of pebbles. He was glad when the woman in the black dress called from the terrace, 'Leave the boy alone!' He did not like anything about the Admiral's daughters, now he saw them at close range. Even their dresses, which had looked beautiful from a distance, repelled him. If a lady had been sitting to a portrait painter in the character of a wood nymph, she might have worn such draperies, but it was foolish to wear them in a garden, when there was nobody to see them. 'Leave the boy alone!' the woman in black called again. 'He has come with a letter for Parthenope.'

She had not been one of the circle. Now that the others fell back, my uncle saw her standing a little way off, biting her lip and knitting her brows, as if the scene disturbed her. There were other differences, beyond her height, that distinguished her from her sisters. While they were all that was most feminine, with tiny waists and hands and feet, she might have been a handsome and athletic boy dressed in woman's clothes for a school play. Only, of course, one knew quite well that she was not a boy. She stood erect, her arms hanging by her sides, smoothing back the muslin billows of her skirt, as if they were foolishness she would be glad to put behind her; and, indeed, she would have looked better in Greek dress. Like her sisters, she had golden hair, but hers was a whiter gold. As my uncle and she went toward each other, she smiled, and he was glad to see that her eyes were darker grey than her sisters', and were quick and glancing. He told her who he was, speaking honestly, not putting on a brogue to win her, and she smiled and held out her hand. It took her a little time to read the letter, and she frowned over it and held her forefinger to her lips, and bade him tell his aunt that she would send over an answer later in the day, after she had consulted her gardeners, and then she asked him if he would care to come into the house and drink some raspberry vinegar. As she led him across the lawn to the terrace, walking with long strides, he saw that her sisters were clustered in a group, staring up at a gutter high on the house, where a rook had perched, as if the bird were a great marvel. 'Should I say goodbye to the ladies?' he asked nervously, and Parthenope answered, 'No, they have forgotten you already.' However, one had not. The sister who wore the light-red dress ran after him, crying, 'Come back soon, little boy. Nobody ever comes into this garden except to steal our strawberries.'

Parthenope took him through the silent house, pausing in the room where the dolls lay on the floor to lift them up and shut them in a drawer, and they came to a dining-room, lined with pictures of great ships at war with stormy seas. There was no raspberry vinegar on the top of the sideboard – only decanters wearing labels marked with the names of adult drinks he was allowed only at Christmas and on his birthday, and then but one glass, and he always chose claret. So they opened the cupboard below, and sat down together on the carpet and peered into the darkness while he told her that he did not really want any but if it had gone astray he would be pleased to help her find it. But when the decanter turned up at the very back of the shelf (and they agreed that that was what always happened when one lost anything, and there was no doubt that objects can move) they both had a glass, talking meanwhile of what they liked to eat and drink. Like him, she hated boiled mutton, and she, too, liked goose better than turkey. When he had finished and the talk had slowed down, he rose and put his glass on the sideboard, and offered her a hand to help her up from the floor, but she did not need it; and he gave a last look round the room, so that he would not forget it. He asked her, 'Why is your chandelier tied up in a canvas bag? At home that only happens when the family is away.' She answered, 'Our family is away,' speaking so grimly that he said, 'I did not mean to ask a rude question.' She told him, 'You have not asked a rude question. What I meant was that all but two of us have our own homes, and those two will be leaving here soon.' It would not have been right to say that she spoke sadly. But her tone was empty of all it had held when they had talked about how much better chicken tastes when you eat it with your fingers when you are out shooting. He remembered all the sad things he had heard his aunt say about her family, the sadder things he had heard from the servants. He said, 'Why don't you come back with me and have tea with my aunt?' She said, smiling, 'She has not asked me.' And he said, 'Never think of that. We are not proper English, you know; we are from Ireland, and friends come in any time.' But she thanked him, sighing, so that he knew she would really have liked to come, and said that she must go back to her sisters. As the butler held the front door open for my uncle, she gave him a friendly slap across the shoulders, as an older boy might have done.

After that, my uncle never watched the Admiral's daughters again. If a glance told him that they were in the garden, he turned his back on the window. He had not liked those staring eyes that were colourless as water, and it troubled him that, though some of them had children, none had said, 'I have a boy, too, but he is much younger than you,' for mothers always said that. He remembered Parthenope so well that he could summon her to his mind when he wished, and he could not bear to see her with these women who made him feel uneasy, because he was sure that he and she felt alike, and therefore she must be in a perpetual state of unease. So when, the very day before he was to go back to Ireland, he looked out of his bedroom window and saw her alone on the lawn he threw up the sash and called to her; but she did not hear him.

She was absorbed in playing a game by herself, a game that he knew well. She was throwing a ball high into the air, then letting her arms drop by her sides, and waiting to the last, the very last moment, before stretching out a hand to catch it. It was a strange thing for a grown-up lady to be doing, but it did not distress him like the playground gambolling and chattering of her sisters. They had been like children as grown-ups like to think of them, silly and meaningless and mischievous. But she was being a child as children really are, sobered by all they have to put up with and glad to forget it in play. There was currently some danger that his own father was going to get a post in some foreign place and that the whole family would have to leave County Kerry for years and years; and when he and his brothers and sisters thought of this they would go and, each one apart, would play this very same game that Parthenope was playing.

He did not want to raise his voice in a shout, in case he was overheard by his aunt or his mother. They would not understand that, although Parthenope and he had met only once, they knew each other quite well. He got up from the window seat and went out of his room and down through the house and out into the garden. There was a ladder in the coach house, and he dragged it to the right part of the wall and propped it up and stopped it with stones, and climbed to the top and called 'Miss Parthenope!' When she saw him, she smiled and waved at him as if she really were glad to see him again.

'Where are your sisters?' he asked cautiously.

'They have all gone away. I am going home tomorrow.'

'So am I.'

'Are you glad?'

'Papa will be there,' he said, 'and my brothers and sisters, and Garrity the groom, and my pony.'

She asked him the names of his brothers and sisters, and how old they were, and where his home was; and he told her all these things and told her, too, that his father was always being sent all over the world, and that of late he and his brothers and sisters had heard talk that someday, and it might be soon, he would be sent to some foreign place for so long that they would have to go with him, and they didn't want this to happen; for, though they loved him and wanted to be near him, they loved County Kerry, too. At that, she stopped smiling and nodded her head, as if to say she knew how he must feel. 'But perhaps it won't happen,' he said, 'and then you must come and stay with us for the hunting.'

He thought of her in a riding-habit, and at that he noticed that she was wearing a dress such as his own mother might have worn – a dress of grey cloth, with a tight bodice and a stiffened skirt, ornamented with braid. He said, 'How funny to see you dressed like other ladies. Don't you usually wear that lilac-grey muslin dress?'

She shook her head. 'No. My sisters and I only wear those muslin dresses when we are together here. My sisters like them.'

'Don't you?' he said, for her tone had gone blank again.

'No,' she answered, 'not at all.'

He was glad to hear it, but it seemed horribly unfair that she should have to wear clothes she did not like, just because her sisters did; nothing of the sort happened in his own family. 'Then don't wear them!' he said passionately. 'You mustn't wear them! Not if you don't like them!'

'You're making your ladder wobble,' she said, laughing at him, 'and if you fall down I can't climb over the wall and pick you up.' She started across the lawn toward the house.

'Garrity says that you're lost if you let yourself be put upon,' he cried after her, his brogue coming back to him, but honestly, because he spoke to Garrity as Garrity spoke to him. He would have liked to have the power to make her do what she ought to do, and save her from all this foolishness.

'Goodbye, goodbye,' she called across the growing distance. 'Be a good boy, and come back to see us next year.'

'You will be here for sure?' he asked eagerly.

'Oh, yes,' she promised. 'We will always be back here for some time in the summer. My sisters would rather be here than anywhere in the world.'

'But do you like it yourself?' he asked angrily.

It was no use. She had run up the steps to the terrace.

My uncle did not come back the next year, because his fears were realised and his father was appointed to a post in Canada. But from his aunt's letters to his mother he learned that, even if he had returned to Currivel Lodge, he would not have seen Parthenope, for the Admiral sold the house later that year, as soon as his two remaining daughters went to the altar, which they did with even greater reluctance than their elder sisters. Alice Darrell's maid happened to be at the window one winter day and saw the two of them walking up and down the lawn, dressed in those strange, bright muslin gowns and wearing no mantles, though the river mist was thick, while they wept and wrung their hands. Aunt Alice felt that, even if the Admiral had felt obliged to bundle all his daughters into matrimony, he should at least not have sold the house, which was the one place where they could meet and have a little nursery happiness again.

In the course of time, Uncle Arthur came back to Ireland, and went to Trinity College, Dublin, and passed into the English Civil Service, and was sent to London. The first time he went back to Currivel Lodge, he stood at his bedroom window and stared out at the croquet lawn of the house next door, and it looked very much like other croquet lawns. Under the trees two men and two women were sitting round a tea table, all of them presenting the kind of appearance, more common then than now, that suggests that nothing untoward happens to the human race. It occurred to him that perhaps his boyish imagination had made a story out of nothing, but Aunt Alice gave him back his version intact. The Admiral had really hectored his daughters into early and undesired marriages, with the most brutal disregard for their feelings, and the daughters had really been very strange girls, given to running about the garden in a sort of fancy dress and behaving like children – all except Parthenope, who was quite remarkable. She had made her mark in society since then. Well, so they all had, in a way. Their photographs were always in the papers, at one time, and no wonder, they were so very pretty. But that seemed over now, and, indeed, they must all be out of their twenties by now, even the youngest. Parthenope's triumphs, however, had been more durable. It was said that Queen Victoria greatly approved of her, and she was often at Court.

My uncle always thought of Parthenope when he was dressing for any of the grander parties to which he was invited, and he soon found his way to the opera and ascertained which was her box, but she was never at the parties, and, unless she had changed out of all recognition, never in her box at Covent Garden either. My uncle did not wish to approach her, for he was a poor young man, far below her grandeur, and they had belonged to different generations; at the least, she was twelve years older than he was. But he would have liked to see her again. Soon, however, he received an intimation that that would not be possible. One morning at breakfast he unfolded his newspaper and folded it again almost immediately, having read a single paragraph, which told him that Parthenope had met a violent death.

He had failed to meet her at parties and to see her in her opera box because she had been spending the winter abroad, taking care of two of her sisters who had both been the victims of prolonged illness. Originally, they had settled at Nice, but had found it too urban, and had moved to a hotel at Grasse, where they spent some weeks. Then a friend had found them a pleasant villa at Hyères, and the party had started off from Grasse in two carriages. Parthenope and her sisters and a lady's maid had travelled in the first, and another maid and a courier had followed in the second. The second carriage had dropped far behind. Afterwards, the coachman remembered that he had been oddly delayed in leaving the inn where they had stopped for a midday meal; he had been told that a man was looking for him with a letter for his employers, and failing to find him had gone to a house some way down the village street. The coachman sought him but there was nobody there; and on his return to his horses he discovered that a harness strap was broken, and he had to mend it before they could resume their journey. After a sharp turn in the road, he had found himself driving into a felled tree trunk, and when the courier and the maid and the coachman got out they could see no sign of the first carriage. It was found some hours later, abandoned on a cart track running through a wood to a river. There was no trace of any of its occupants. Later that same day the maid crawled up to a farmhouse door. Before she collapsed, she was able to tell the story of an attack by masked men, who had, she thought, killed the three sisters outright because they refused to tell in which trunk their jewel cases were packed. She had escaped during the struggle, and while she was running away through the woods she had heard terrible prolonged screaming from the riverbank. As the river was in flood, there was no hope of recovering the bodies.

After my uncle had read all the accounts of the crime that appeared in the newspapers, and had listened to all he could hear from gossiping friends, there hung, framed on the wall of his mind, a romantic picture of a highway robbery, in the style of Salvator Rosa, with coal-black shadows and highlights white on hands lifted in imploration, and he felt no emotion whatsoever. When he had opened *The Times* at breakfast, his heart had stopped. But now he felt as if he had been stopped before an outmoded and conventional picture in a private gallery by a host who valued it too highly.

A year or so later, Alice Darrell mentioned to him an odd story she had heard. It appeared that Parthenope had been carrying a great deal more jewellery than would seem necessary for a woman travelling quietly with two invalid sisters. To be sure, she had not taken all the jewellery she possessed, but she had taken enough for the value to be estimated at fifty thousand pounds; and of this not a penny could be recovered, for it was uninsured. Her husband had left the matter for her to handle, because she had sold some old jewellery and had bought some to replace it just about the time that the policy should have been renewed, but she had failed to write the necessary letter to her lawyers till the very night before the journey to Hyères, and it was found, unposted, at the hotel in Grasse.

'Parthenope!' my uncle said. 'Let an insurance policy lapse! Parthenope! I'll not believe it.'

'That's just what I said,' Alice Darrell exclaimed. 'Any of the others, but not Parthenope. She had her hand on everything. Yet, of course, she may have changed. They are a queer family. There was the other one, you know – the one who disappeared. That was after the accident.'

It seemed that another sister – Hera, Aunt Alice thought it was – had also suffered ill health, and had gone to France with a nurse, and one day her cloak and bonnet were found on the bank of a river.

'I wish that things turned out better,' Aunt Alice remarked sadly. 'They do sometimes, but not often enough.'

This was the only criticism of life he had ever heard her utter, though she had had a sad life, constantly losing the people she loved, to tropical diseases or to wars against obscure tribes that lacked even the interest of enmity. What she uttered now made him realise that she had indeed thought Parthenope remarkable, and he said, smiling, 'Why, we are making ourselves quite miserable about her, though all we know for sure is that she let an insurance policy lapse.'

He did not hear of the Admiral's daughters again until after a long space of time, during which he had many other things to think about: his career, which was alternately advanced by his brilliance and retarded by his abstracted candour; a long affair with a married woman older than himself, some others that were briefer; and his marriage, which, like his career, and for much the same reason, was neither a success nor a failure. One day when he was reading the papers at his club, he heard two men speaking of a friend who was distressed about his mother, whose behaviour had been strange since she had been left a widow. She had rejected the dower house and gone off to the Continent to travel by herself, and now refused to come back to see her family or to meet them abroad. The mother had an old Greek name, and so had a sister, who had got herself murdered for her jewels in the South of France. My uncle went on staring at his newspaper, but it was as if a door in his mind were swinging backward and forward on a broken hinge.

Many years later, when Aunt Alice was dead and my uncle was a middle-aged man, with children who were no longer children, he broke his journey home from a conference in Spain at a certain town in the south-west of France, for no other reason than that its name had always charmed him. But it proved to be a dull place, and as he sat down to breakfast at a café in the large and featureless station square it occurred to him to ask the waiter if there were not some smaller and pleasanter place in the neighbourhood where he could spend the rest of the day and night. The waiter said that, if Monsieur would take the horse-bus that started from the other side of the square in half an hour, it would take him to the village where he, the waiter, was born, and there he would find a good inn and a church that people came all the way from Paris to see. My uncle took his advice; and, because his night had been wakeful, he fell asleep almost as soon as the bus started. He woke suddenly to find that the journey had ended and he was in a village which was all that he had hoped it would be.

A broad, deliberate river, winding among low wooded hills, spread its blessings at this point through a circular patch of plain, a couple of miles or so across, which was studded with farm houses, each standing beside its deep green orchard. In the centre of this circle was a village that was no more than one long street, which looked very clean. The houses were built of stone that had been washed by the hill rains, and beside the road a brook flowed over a paved bed. There were bursts of red valerian growing from the cracks in the walls and in the yard-long bridges that crossed the brook. The street ended in a little square, where the church and the inn looked across cobblestones, shaded by pollarded limes, at the *mairie* and the post office. At the inn, my uncle took a room and slept for an hour or two in a bed smelling of the herbs with which the sheets had been washed. Then, as it was past noon, he went down to lunch, and ate some potato soup, a trout, some wood strawberries, and a slice of cheese. Afterward, he asked the landlord how soon the church would be open, and was told that he could open it himself when he chose. The priest and his housekeeper were away until vespers, and had left the church keys at the inn.

When he went to the church, it was a long time before he unlocked the door, for there was a beautiful tympanum in the porch, representing the Last Judgement. It was clearcut in more than one sense. There was no doubt who was saved and who was damned: there was a beatific smile on the faces of those walking in Paradise, which made it seem as if just there a shaft of sunlight had struck the dark stone. Also the edges of the carving, though the centuries had rubbed them down, showed a definition more positive than mere sharpness. Often my uncle played games when he was alone, and now he climbed on a wooden stool which was in the porch, and shut his eyes and felt the faces of the blessed, and pretended that he had been blind for a long time, and that the smiles of the blessed were striking into his darkness through his fingertips.

When he went into the church, he found, behind an oaken door, the steps that led to the top of the tower. He climbed up through darkness that was transfixed every few steps by thin shafts of light, dancing with dust coming through the eyelet windows, and he found that, though the tower was not very high, it gave a fine view of an amphitheatre of hills, green on their lower slopes with chestnut groves, banded higher with fir woods and bare turf, and crowned with shining rock. He marked some likely paths on the nearest hills, and then dropped his eyes to the village below, and looked down into the oblong garden of a house that seemed larger than the rest. At the farther end was the usual, pedantically neat French vegetable-garden; then there was a screen of espaliered fruit-trees; then there was a lawn framed in trees so tall and strong that it could have been guessed from them alone that not far away there was a river. The lawn was set with croquet hoops, and about them were wandering four figures in bright dresses – one hyacinth blue, one primrose yellow, one jade green, one clear light red. They all had croquet mallets in their hands, but they had turned from the game, and as my uncle watched them they drew together, resting their mallets on the ground.

Some distance away, a woman in black, taller than the others, stood watching them.

When one of the croquet players let her mallet fall on the grass, and used her freed hands in a fluttering gesture, my uncle left the top of the tower and went down through the darkness and shafts of light and locked the church door behind him. In the corner of the square, he found what might have been the château of the village – one of those square and solid dwellings, noble out of proportion to their size, which many provincial French architects achieved in the seventeenth century. My uncle went through an iron gateway into a paved garden and found that the broad door of the house was open. He walked into the vestibule and paused, looking up the curved staircase. The pictures were as old as the house, and two had been framed to fit the recessed panels in which they hung. The place must have been bought as it stood. On the threshold of the corridor beyond, he paused again, for it smelled of damp stone, as all the back parts of his father's house in County Kerry did, at any time of the year but high summer. It struck him as a piece of good fortune for which he had never before been sufficiently grateful that he could go back to that house any time he pleased; he would be there again in a few weeks' time. He passed the open door of a kitchen, where two women were rattling dishes and pans and singing softly, and came to a closed door, which he stared at for a second before he turned the handle.

He found himself in a salon that ran across the whole breadth of the house, with three French windows opening on a stone terrace overlooking the garden. As he crossed it to the steps that led down to the lawn, he came close to a bird cage on a pole, and the scarlet parrot inside broke into screams. All the women on the lawn turned and saw him, and the tall woman in black called, 'Que voulez-vous, monsieur?' She had put her hand to her heart, and he was eager to reassure her, but could not think how, across that distance, to explain why he had come. So he continued to walk toward her, but could not reach her because the four others suddenly scampered toward him, crying 'Go away! Go away!' Their arms flapped like bats' wings, and their voices were cracked, but, under their white hair, their faces were unlined and their eyes were colourless as water. 'Go away!' shrilled the one in light red. 'We know you have come to steal our strawberries. Why may we not keep our own strawberries?' But the figure in black had come forward with long strides, and told them to go on with their game, and asked again, 'Que voulez-vous, monsieur?'

Her hair was grey now, and her mouth so sternly compressed that it was a straight line across her face. She reminded my uncle of a particular man – her father, the Admiral – but she was not like a man, she was still a handsome and athletic boy, though a frost had fallen on him; and still it was strange that she should look like a boy, since she was also not male at all. My uncle found that now he was face to face with her it was just as difficult to explain to her why he had come. He said, 'I came to this village by chance this morning, and after I had luncheon at the inn I went to the top of the church tower, and looked down on this garden, and recognised you all. I came to tell you that if there is anything I can do for you I will do it. I am a civil servant who has quite a respectable career, and so I can hope that I might be efficient enough to help you, if you need it.'

'That is very kind,' she said, and paused, and it was as if she were holding a shell to her ear and listening to the voice of a distant sea. 'Very kind,' she repeated. 'But who are you?'

'I am the nephew of your neighbour, Mrs Darrell,' said my uncle. 'I brought you a letter from her, many years ago, when you were all in your garden.'

Her smile broke slowly. 'I remember you,' she said. 'You were a fatherly little boy. You gave me good advice from the top of a ladder. Why should you have found me here, I wonder? It can't be that, after all, there is some meaning in the things that happen. You had better come into the house and drink some of the cherry brandy we make here. I will get the cook to come out and watch them. I never leave them alone now.'

While she went to the kitchen, my uncle sat in the salon and noted that, for all its fine furniture and all its space and light, there was a feeling that the place was dusty, the same feeling that he had noticed in the Admiral's house long ago. It is the dust of another world, he thought with horror, and the housemaids of this world are helpless against it. It settles wherever these women live, and Parthenope must live with them.

When she came back, she was carrying a tray with a slender decanter and very tiny glasses. They sat sipping the cherry brandy in silence until she said, 'I did nothing wrong.' He looked at her in astonishment. Of course she had done nothing wrong. Wrong was what she did not do. But she continued gravely, 'When we all die, it will be found that the sum I got for the jewellery is intact. My stepson will not be a penny the worse off. Indeed, he is better off, for my husband has had my small inheritance long before it would have come to him if I had not done this.'

'I knew you would have done it honestly,' said my uncle. He hesitated. 'This is very strange. You see, I knew things about you which I had no reason to know. I knew you had not been murdered.'

Then my uncle had to think carefully. They were united by eternal bonds, but hardly knew each other, which was the reverse of what usually happened to men and women. But they might lapse into being strangers and nothing else if he showed disrespect to the faith by which she lived. He said only, 'Also I knew that what you were doing in looking after your family was terrible.'

She answered, 'Yes. How good it is to hear somebody say that it is terrible, and to be able to answer that it is. But I had to do it. I had to get my sisters away from their husbands. They were ashamed of them. They locked them up in the care of strangers. I saw their bruises.' My uncle caught his breath. 'Oh,' she said, desperately just, 'the people who looked after them did not mean to be cruel. But they were strangers; they did not know the way to handle my sisters. And their husbands were not all bad men either. And, even if they had been, I could not say a word against them, for they were cheated; my father cheated them. They were never told the truth about my mother. About my mother and half her family.' She raised her little glass of cherry brandy to her lips and nodded, to intimate that that was all she had to say, but words rushed out and she brought her glass down to her lap. 'I am not telling the truth. Their husbands cheated, too. . . . No, I am wrong. They did not cheat. But they failed to keep their bond. Still, there is no use talking about that.'

'What bond did your sisters' husbands not keep?' my uncle asked.

'They married my sisters because they were beautiful, and laughed easily, and could not understand figures. They might have considered that women who laugh easily might scream easily, and that, if figures meant nothing to them, words might mean nothing either, and that, if figures and words meant nothing to them, thoughts and feelings might mean nothing too. But these men had the impudence to feel a horror of my sisters.'

She rose, trembling, and told him that he must have a sweet biscuit with his cherry brandy, and that she would get him some; they were in a cupboard in the corner of the room. Over her shoulder, she cried, 'I cannot imagine you marrying a woman who was horrible because she was horrible, and then turning against her because she was horrible.' She went on setting some wafers out on a plate, and he stared at the back of her head, unable to imagine what was inside it, saying to himself, 'She realises that they are horrible; there is no mitigation of her state.'

When she sat down again, she said, 'But it was my father's fault.'

'What was your father's fault?' he asked gently, when she did not go on.

'Why, he should not have made us marry; he should not have sold our house. My sisters were happy there, and all they asked was to be allowed to go on living there, like children.'

'Your father wanted his daughters to marry so that they would have someone to look after them when he was dead,' my uncle told her.

'I could have looked after them.'

'Come now,' said my uncle, 'you are not being fair. You are the same sort of person as your father. And you know quite well that if you were a man you would regard all women as incapable. You see, men of the better kind want to protect the women they love, and there is so much stupidity in the male nature and the circumstances of life are generally so confused that they end up thinking they must look after women because women cannot look after themselves. It is only very seldom that a man meets a woman so strong and wise that he cannot doubt her strength and wisdom, and realises that his desire to protect her is really the same as his desire to gather her into his arms and partake of her glory.'

Moving slowly and precisely, he took out his cardcase and was about to give her one of his cards when a thought struck him. She must have the name of his family's house in County Kerry as well as his London address, and know that he went there at Christmas and at Easter, and in the summer too. She would be able to find him whenever she wanted him, since such bootblack service was all he could render her.

She read the card and said in an astonished whisper, 'Oh, how kind, how kind.' Then she rose and put it in a drawer in a *secrétaire*, which she locked with a key she took from a bag swinging from the belt of her hateful black gown. 'I have to lock up everything,' she said, wearily. 'They mean no harm, but sometimes they get at papers and tear them up.'

'What I have written on that card is for an emergency,' said my uncle. 'But what is there that I can do now? I do not like the thought of you sitting here in exile, among things that mean nothing to you. Can I not send you out something English – a piece of furniture, a picture, some china or glass? If I were in your place, I would long for something that reminded me of the houses where I had spent my childhood.'

'If you were in my place, you would not,' she said. 'You are very kind, but the thing that has happened to my family makes me not at all anxious to remember my childhood. We were all such pretty children. Everybody always spoke as if we were bound to be happy. And in those days nobody was frightened of Mamma – they only laughed at her, because she was such a goose. Then one thing followed another, and it became quite certain about Mamma, and then it became quite certain about the others; and now I cannot bear to think of the good times that went before. It is as if someone had known and was mocking us. But you may believe that it is wonderful for me to know that there is someone I can call on at any time. You see, I had supports, which are being taken away from me. You really have no idea how I got my sisters out here?'

My uncle shook his head. 'I only read what was in the newspapers and knew it was not true.'

'But you must have guessed I had helpers,' she said. 'There was the highway robbery to be arranged. All that was done by somebody who was English but had many connections in France, a man who was very fond of Arethusa. Arethusa is the one who spoke to you in the garden; she always wears red. This man was not like her husband; when she got worse and worse, he felt no horror for her, only pity. He has always been behind me, but he was far older than we were, and he died three years ago; and since then his lawyer in Paris has been a good friend, but now he is old, too, and I must expect him to go soon. I have made all arrangements for what is to happen to my sisters after my death. They will go to a convent near here, where the nuns are really kind, and we are preparing them for it. One or other of the nuns comes here every day to see my sisters, so that they will never have to be frightened by strange faces; and I think that, if my sisters go on getting worse at the same rate as at present, they will by then believe the nuns when they say that I have been obliged to go away and will come back presently. But till that time comes I will be very glad to have someone I can ask for advice. I can see that you are to be trusted. You are like the man who loved Arethusa. My poor Arethusa! Sometimes I think,' she said absently, 'that she might have been all right if it had been that man whom she had married. But no,' she cried, shaking herself awake, 'none of us should have married, not even me.'

'Why should you not have married?' asked my uncle. 'That the others should not I understand. But why not you? There is nothing wrong with you.'

'Is there not?' she asked. 'To leave my family and my home, to stage a sham highway robbery, and later to plot and lie, and lie and plot, in order to get my mad sisters to a garden I had once noted, in my travels, as something like the garden taken from them when they were young. There is an extravagance in the means my sanity took to rescue their madness that makes the one uncommonly like the other.'

'You must not think that,' my uncle told her. 'Your strange life forced strangeness on your actions, but you are not strange. You were moved by love; you had seen their bruises.'

'Yes, I had seen their bruises,' she agreed. 'But', she added, hesitantly, 'you are so kind that I must be honest with you. It was not only for the love of my sisters that I arranged this flight. It is also true that I could not bear my life. I was not wholly unselfish. You do not know what it is like to be a character in a tragedy. Something has happened which can only be explained by supposing that God hates you with merciless hatred, and nobody will admit it. The people nearest you stand round you saying that you must ignore this extraordinary event, you must – what were the words I was always hearing? – "keep your sense of proportion", "not brood on things". They do not understand that they are asking you to deny your experiences, which is to pretend that you do not exist and never have existed. And, as for the people who do not love you, they laugh. Our tragedy was so ridiculous that the laughter was quite loud. There were all sorts of really quite funny stories about the things my mother and sisters did before they were shut up. That is another terrible thing about being a character in a tragedy; at the same time you become a character in a farce. Do not deceive yourself,' she said, looking at him kindly and sadly. 'I am not a Classical heroine, I am not Iphigenia or Electra or Alcestis, I am the absurd Parthenope. There is no dignity in my life. For one thing, too much has happened to me. One calamity evokes sympathy; when two calamities call for it, some still comes, but less. Three calamities are felt to be too many, and when four are reported, or five, the thing is ludicrous. God has only to strike one again and again for one to become a clown. There is nothing about me which is not comical. Even my flight with my sisters has become a joke.' She sipped at her glass. 'My sisters' husbands and their families must by now have found out where we are. I do not think my husband ever did, or he would have come to see me. But there are many little indications that the others know, and keep their knowledge secret, rather than let loose so monstrous a scandal.'

'You say your husband would have to come to see you?' asked my uncle, wanting to make sure. 'But that must mean he loved you.'

At last the tears stood in her eyes. She said, her voice breaking, 'Oh, things might have gone very well with my husband and myself, if love had been possible for me. But of course it never was.'

'How wrong you are,' said my uncle. 'There could be nothing better for any man than to have you as his wife. If you did not know that, your husband should have made you understand it.'

'No, no,' she said. 'The fault was not in my husband or myself. It was in love, which cannot do all that is claimed for it. Oh, I can see that it can work miracles, some miracles, but not all the miracles that are required before life can be tolerable. Listen: I love my sisters, but I dare not love them thoroughly. To love them as much as one can love would be to go to the edge of an abyss and lean over the edge, farther and farther, till one was bound to lose one's balance and fall into the blackness of that other world where they live. That is why I never dared let my husband love me fully. I was so much afraid that I might be an abyss, and if he understood me, if we lived in each other, he would be drawn down into my darkness.'

'But there is no darkness in you,' said my uncle, 'you are not an abyss, you are the solid rock.'

'Why do you think so well of me?' she wondered. 'Of course you are right to some extent – I am not the deep abyss I might be. But how could I be sure of that when I was young? Every night when I lay down in bed I examined my day for signs of folly. If I had lost my temper, if I had felt more joy than was reasonable, I was like one of a tuberculous family who has just heard herself cough. Only the years that had not then passed made me sure that I was unlike my sisters and, until I knew, I had to hold myself back. I could not let the fine man who was my husband be tempted into my father's fault.'

'What was your father's fault?' asked my uncle, for the second time since he had entered that room.

Again her disapproval was absolute, her eyes were like steel. But this time she answered at once, without a moment's hesitation: 'Why, he should not have loved my mother.'

'But you are talking like a child!' he exclaimed. 'You cannot blame anyone for loving anyone.'

'Did you ever see him?' she asked, her eyes blank because they were filled with a distant sight. 'Yes? You must have been only a boy, but surely you saw that he was remarkable. And he had a mind, he was a mathematician, he wrote a book on navigation that was thought brilliant; they asked him to lecture to the Royal Society. And one would have thought from his face that he was a giant of goodness and strength. How could such a man love such a woman as my mother? It was quite mad, the way he made us marry. How could he lean over the abyss of her mind and let himself be drawn down into that darkness?'

'Do not let your voice sink to a whisper like that,' my uncle begged her. 'It – it—'

'It frightens you,' she supplied.

'But have you', he pressed her, 'no feeling for your mother?'

'Oh, yes,' she said, her voice breaking. 'I loved my mother very much. But when she went down into the darkness I had to say goodbye to her or I could not have looked after my sisters.' It seemed as if she was going to weep, but she clung to her harshness and asked again, 'How could my father love such a woman?'

My uncle got up and knelt in front of her chair and took her trembling hands in his. 'There is no answer, so do not ask the question.'

'I must ask it,' she said. 'Surely it is blasphemy to admit that one can ask questions to which there are no answers. I must ask why my father leaned over the abyss of my mother's mind and threw himself into it, and dragged down victim after victim with him – not only dragging them down but manufacturing them for that sole purpose, calling them out of nothingness simply so that they could fall and fall. How could he do it? If there is not an answer—'

He put his hand over her lips. 'He cannot have known that she was mad when he begot his children.'

Her passion had spent itself in her question. She faintly smiled as she said, 'No, but I never liked the excuse that he and my sisters' husbands made for themselves. They all said that at first they had simply thought their wives were rather silly. I could not have loved someone whom I thought rather silly. Could you?'

'It is not what I have done,' said my uncle. 'May I have some more cherry brandy?'

'I am so glad you like it,' she said, suddenly happy. 'But you have given me the wrong glass to fill. This is mine.'

'I knew that,' he told her. 'I wanted to drink from your glass.'

'I would like to drink from yours,' she said, and for a little time they were silent. 'Tell me,' she asked meekly, as if now she had put herself in his hands, 'do you think it has been wrong for me to talk about what has happened to me? When I was at home they always said it was bad to brood over it.'

'What nonsense,' said my uncle. 'I am sure that it was one of the major misfortunes of Phèdre and Bérénice that they were unable to read Racine's clear-headed discussions of their miseries.'

'You are right,' said Parthenope. 'Oh, how kind Racine was to tragic people! He would not allow for a moment that they were comic. People at those courts must have giggled behind their hands at poor Bérénice, at poor Phèdre. But he ignored them. You are kind like Racine.' There was a tapping on the glass of the French window, and her face went grey. 'What has happened now? Oh, what has happened?' she murmured to herself. It was the cook who had tapped, and she was looking grave.

Parthenope went out and spoke with her for a minute, and then came back, and again the tears were standing in her eyes. 'I thought I might ask you to stay all day with me,' she said. 'I thought we might dine together. But my sisters cannot bear it that there is a stranger here. They are hiding in the raspberry

canes, and you must have heard them screaming. Part of that noise comes from
the parrot, but part from them. It sometimes takes hours to get them quiet. I
cannot help it; you must go.'

He took both her hands and pressed them against his throat, and felt it swell as
she muttered, 'Goodbye.'

But as he was going through the paved garden to the gateway he heard her call
'Stop! Stop!' and she was just behind him, her skirts lifted over her ankles so that
she could take her long strides. 'The strangest thing,' she said, laughing. 'I have
not told you the name by which I am known here.' She spelled it out to him as he
wrote it down in his diary, and turned back toward the house, exclaiming, 'What
a thing to forget!' But then she swung back again, suddenly pale, and said, 'But
do not write to me. I am only giving you the name so that if I send you a message
you will be able to answer it. But do not write to me.'

'Why not?' he asked indignantly. 'Why not?'

'You must not be involved in my life,' she said. 'There is a force outside the
world that hates me and all my family. If you wrote to me too often it might hate
you, too.'

'I would risk that,' he said, but she cried, covering her eyes, 'No, no, by being
courageous you are threatening my last crumb of happiness. If you stay a
stranger, I may be allowed to keep what I have of you. So do as I say.'

He made a resigned gesture, and they parted once more. But as she got to the
door he called to her to stop and hurried back. 'I will not send you anything that
will remind you of your home,' he said, 'but may I not send you a present from
time to time – some stupid little thing that will not mean much but might amuse
you for a minute or two?'

She hesitated but in the end nodded. 'A little present, a very little present,' she
conceded. 'And not too often.' She smiled like the saved in the sculpture in the
church, and slowly closed the door on him.

But when he was out in the square and walking toward the inn he heard her
voice crying again, 'Stop! Stop!' This time she came quite close to him and said,
as if she were a child ashamed to admit to a fault, 'There is another thing that I
would like to ask of you. You said that I might write to you if I wanted anything,
and I know that you meant business things – the sort of advice men give women.
But I wonder if your kindness goes beyond that; you are so very kind. I know all
about most dreadful things in life, but I know nothing about death. Usually I
think I will not mind leaving this world, but just now and then, if I wake up in the
night, particularly in winter, when it is very cold, I am afraid that I may be
frightened when I die.'

'I fear that, too, sometimes,' he said.

'It seems a pity, too, to leave this world, in spite of the dreadful things that
happen in it,' she went on. 'There are things that nothing can spoil – the spring
and the summer and the autumn.'

'And, indeed, the winter, too,' he said.

'Yes, the winter, too,' she said and looked up at the amphitheatre of hills round the village. 'You cannot think how beautiful it is here when the snow has fallen. But, of course, death may be just what one has been waiting for; it may explain everything. But, still, I may be frightened when it comes. So if I do not die suddenly, if I have warning of my death, would it be a great trouble for you to come and be with me for a little?'

'As I would like to be with you always, I would certainly want to be with you then,' he said. 'And, if I have notice of my death and you are free to travel, I will ask you to come to me.'

My uncle found that he did not want to go back to the inn just then, and he followed a road leading up to the foothills. There he climbed one of the paths he had remarked from the top of the church tower, and when he got to the bare rock, he sat down and looked at the village beneath him till the twilight fell. On his return to London, he painted a watercolour of the view of the valley as he recollected it, and pasted it in a book, which he kept by his bedside. From time to time, some object in the window of an antique shop or a jeweller's would bring Parthenope to his mind, and he would send it to her. The one that pleased him as most fitting was a gold ring in the form of two leaves, which was perhaps Saxon. She acknowledged these presents in brief letters; and it delighted him that often her solemn purpose of brevity broke down and she added an unnecessary sentence or two, telling him of something that had brightened her days – of a strayed fawn she had found in her garden, or a prodigious crop of cherries, which had made her trees quite red. But after some years these letters stopped. When he took into account how old he was, and by how many years she had been the elder, he realised that probably she had died. He told himself that at least she had enjoyed the mercy of sudden death, and presently ceased to think of her. It was as if the memory of her were too large to fit inside his head; he felt actual physical pain when he tried to recollect her. This was the time when such things as the finest buttercup field near London and the tomb of Captain Vancouver seemed to be all that mattered to him. But from the day when he heard the girl at the inn called by the name of his Parthenope he again found it easy to think of her; and he told me about her very often during the five years that passed before his death.

# Town and Country Lovers

I

DR FRANZ-JOSEF VON LEINSDORF is a geologist absorbed in his work; wrapped up in it, as the saying goes – year after year, the experience of this work enfolds him, swaddling him away from the landscapes, the cities and the people, wherever he lives – Peru, New Zealand, the United States. He's always been like that, his mother could confirm from their native Austria. There, even as a handsome small boy he presented only his profile to her: turned away to his bits of rock and stone. His few relaxations have not changed much since then. An occasional skiing trip, listening to music, reading poetry – Rainer Maria Rilke once stayed in his grandmother's hunting lodge in the forests of Styria and the boy was introduced to Rilke's poems while very young.

Layer upon layer, country after country, wherever his work takes him – and now he has been almost seven years in Africa. First the Côte d'Ivoire, and for the past five years, South Africa. The shortage of skilled manpower brought about his recruitment there. He has no interest in the politics of the countries he works in. His private preoccupation-within-the-preoccupation of his work has been research into underground water-courses, but the mining company that employs him in a senior though not executive capacity is interested only in mineral discovery. So he is much out in the field – which is the veld, here – seeking new gold, copper, platinum and uranium deposits. When he is at home – on this particular job, in this particular country, this city – he lives in a two-roomed flat in a suburban block with a landscaped garden, and does his shopping at a supermarket conveniently across the street. He is not married – yet. That is how his colleagues, and the typists and secretaries at the mining company's head office, would define his situation. Both men and women would describe him as a good-looking man, in a foreign way, with the lower half of the face dark and middle-aged (his mouth in thin and curving, and no matter how close-shaven his beard shows like fine shot embedded in the skin round mouth and chin) and the upper half contradictorily young, with deep-set eyes (some would say grey, some black), thick eyelashes and brows. A tangled gaze; through which concentration and gleaming thoughtfulness perhaps appear as fire and languor. It is this that the women in the office mean when they remark he's not unattractive. Although the gaze seems to promise, he has never invited any one of them to go out with him. There is the general assumption he probably has a girl who's been picked for him, he's bespoken by one of his own kind, back home in Europe where he comes from. Many of these well-educated Europeans have no intention of becoming permanent immigrants; colonial life doesn't appeal to them.

One advantage, at least, of living in under-developed or half-developed countries is that flats are serviced. All Dr von Leinsdorf has to do for himself is buy his own supplies and cook an evening meal if he doesn't want to go to a restaurant. It is simply a matter of dropping in to the supermarket on his way from his car to his flat after work in the afternoon. He wheels a trolley up and down the shelves, and his simple needs are presented to him in the form of tins, packages, plastic-wrapped meat, cheeses, fruit and vegetables, tubes, bottles. . . . At the cashiers' counters where the customers must converge and queue there are racks of small items uncategorised, for last-minute purchase. Here, as the coloured girl cashier punches the adding machine, he picks up cigarettes and perhaps a packet of salted nuts or a bar of nougat. Or razor blades, when he remembers he's running short. One evening in winter he saw that the cardboard display board was empty of the brand of blades he preferred, and he drew the cashier's attention to this. These young coloured girls are usually pretty unhelpful, taking money and punching their machines in a manner that asserts with the time-serving obstinacy of the half-literate this limit of any responsibility towards customers, but this one ran an alert glance over the selection of razor blades, apologised that she was not allowed to leave her post, and said she would see that the stock was replenished 'next time'. A day or two later she recognised him, gravely, as he took his turn before her counter – 'I ahssed them, but it's out of stock. You can't get it. I did ahss about it.' He said this didn't matter. 'When it comes in, I can keep a few packets for you.' He thanked her.

He was away with the prospectors the whole of the next week. He arrived back in town just before nightfall on Friday, and was on his way from car to flat with his arms full of briefcase, suitcase and canvas bags when someone stopped him by standing timidly in his path. He was about to dodge round unseeingly on the crowded pavement but she spoke. 'We got the blades in now. I didn't see you in the shop this week, but I kept some for when you come. So. . . .'

He recognised her. He had never seen her standing before, and she was wearing a coat. She was rather small and finely-made, for one of them. The coat was skimpy but no big backside jutted. The cold brought an apricot-graining of warm colour to her cheekbones, beneath which a very small face was quite delicately hollowed, and the skin was smooth, the subdued satiny colour of certain yellow wood. That crêpey hair, but worn drawn back flat and in a little knot pushed into one of the cheap wool chignons that (he recognised also) hung in the miscellany of small goods along with the razor blades, at the supermarket. He said thanks, he was in a hurry, he'd only just got back from a trip – shifting the burdens he carried, to demonstrate. 'Oh shame.' She acknowledged his load. 'But if you want I can run in and get it for you quickly. If you want.'

He saw at once it was perfectly clear that all the girl meant was that she would go back to the supermarket, buy the blades and bring the packet to him there where he stood, on the pavement. And it seemed that it was this certainty that made him say, in the kindly tone of assumption used for an obliging underling, 'I live just across there – *Atlantis* – that flat building. Could you drop them by for me – number seven-hundred-and-eighteen, seventh floor—'

She had not before been inside one of these big flat buildings near where she worked. She lived a bus and train-ride away to the West of the city, but this side of the black townships, in a township for people her tint. There was a pool with ferns, not plastic, and even a little waterfall pumped electrically over rocks, in the entrance of the building *Atlantis*; she didn't wait for the lift marked GOODS but took the one meant for whites and a white woman with one of those sausage-dogs on a lead got in with her but did not pay her any attention. The corridors leading to the flats were nicely glassed-in, not draughty.

He wondered if he should give her a twenty-cent piece for her trouble – ten cents would be right for a black; but she said, 'Oh no – please, here—' standing outside his open door and awkwardly pushing back at his hand the change from the money he'd given her for the razor blades. She was smiling, for the first time, in the dignity of refusing a tip. It was difficult to know how to treat these people, in this country; to know what they expected. In spite of her embarrassing refusal of the coin, she stood there, completely unassuming, fists thrust down the pockets of her cheap coat against the cold she'd come in from, rather pretty thin legs neatly aligned, knee to knee, ankle to ankle.

'Would you like a cup of coffee or something?'

He couldn't very well take her into his studio living-room and offer her a drink. She followed him to his kitchen, but at the sight of her pulling out the single chair to drink her cup of coffee at the kitchen table, he said, 'No – bring it in here—' and led the way into the big room where, among his books and his papers, his files of scientific correspondence (and the cigar boxes of stamps from the envelopes), his racks of records, his specimens of minerals and rocks, he lived alone.

It was no trouble to her; she saved him the trips to the supermarket and brought him his groceries two or three times a week. All he had to do was leave a list and the key under the doormat, and she would come up in her lunch hour to collect them, returning to put his supplies in the flat after work. Sometimes he was home and sometimes not. He bought a box of chocolates and left it, with a note, for her to find; and that was acceptable, apparently, as a gratuity.

Her eyes went over everything in the flat although her body tried to conceal its sense of being out of place by remaining as still as possible, holding its contours in the chair offered her as a stranger's coat is set aside and remains exactly as left until the owner takes it up to go. 'You collect?'

'Well, these are specimens – connected with my work.'

'My brother used to collect. Miniatures. With brandy and whisky and that, in them. From all over. Different countries.'

The second time she watched him grinding coffee for the cup he had offered her she said, 'You always do that? Always when you make coffee?'

'But of course. Is it no good, for you? Do I make it too strong?'

'Oh it's just I'm not used to it. We buy it ready – you know, it's in a bottle, you just add a bit to the milk or water.'

He laughed, instructive: 'That's not coffee, that's a synthetic flavouring. In my country we drink only real coffee, fresh, from the beans – you smell how good it is as it's being ground?'

She was stopped by the caretaker and asked what she wanted in the building? Heavy with the *bona fides* of groceries clutched to her body, she said she was working at number 718, on the seventh floor. The caretaker did not tell her not to use the whites' lift; after all, she was not black; her family was very light-skinned. There was the item 'grey button for trousers' on one of his shopping lists. She said as she unpacked the supermarket carrier, 'Give me the pants so long, then,' and sat on his sofa that was always gritty with fragments of pipe tobacco, sewing in and out through the four holes of the button with firm, fluent movements of the right hand, gestures supplying the articulacy missing from her talk. She had a little yokel's, peasant's (he thought of it) gap between her two front teeth when she smiled that he didn't much like, but, face ellipsed to three-quarter angle, eyes cast down in concentration with soft lips almost closed, this didn't matter. He said, watching her sew, 'You're a good girl'; and touched her.

She remade the bed every late afternoon when they left it and she dressed again before she went home. After a week there was a day when late afternoon became evening, and they were still in bed.

'Can't you stay the night?'

'My mother,' she said.

'Phone her. Make an excuse.' He was a foreigner. He had been in the country five years, but he didn't understand that people don't have telephones in their houses, where she lived. She got up to dress. He didn't want that tender body to go out in the night cold and kept hindering her with the interruption of his hands; saying nothing. Before she put on her coat, when the body had already disappeared, he spoke. 'But you must make some arrangement.'

'Oh my mother!' Her face opened to fear and vacancy he could not read.

He was not entirely convinced the woman could think of her daughter as some pure and unsullied virgin. . . . 'Why?'

The girl said, 'S'e'll be scared. S'e'll be scared we get caught.'

'Don't tell her anything. Say I'm employing you.' In this country he was working in now there were generally rooms on the roofs of flat buildings for tenants' servants.

She said: 'That's what I told the caretaker.'

She ground fresh coffee beans every time he wanted a cup while he was working at night. She never attempted to cook anything until she had watched in silence while he did it the way he liked, and she learned to reproduce exactly the simple dishes he preferred. She handled his pieces of rock and stone, at first admiring the colours – 'It'd make a beautiful ring or a necklace, ay.' Then he showed her the striations, the formation of each piece, and explained what each was, and how, in the long life of the earth, it had been formed. He named the mineral it yielded, and what that was used for. He worked at his papers, writing, writing, every night, so it did not matter that they could not go out together to public places. On Sundays she got into his car in the basement garage and they drove to the country and picnicked away up in the Magaliesberg, where there was no one. He read or poked about among the rocks; they climbed together, to the mountain pools. He taught her to swim. She had never seen the sea. She squealed and shrieked in the water, showing the gap between her teeth, as – it crossed his mind – she must do when among her own people. Occasionally he had to go out to dinner at the houses of colleagues from the mining company; she sewed and listened to the radio in the flat and he found her in the bed, warm and already asleep, by the time he came in. He made his way into her body without speaking; she made him welcome without a word. Once he put on evening dress for a dinner at his country's consulate; watching him brush one or two fallen hairs from his shoulders in the dark jacket that sat so well on him, she saw a huge room, all chandeliers and people dancing some dance from a costume film – stately, hand-to-hand. She supposed he was going to fetch, in her place in the car, a partner for the evening. They never kissed when either left the flat; he said, suddenly, kindly, pausing as he picked up cigarettes and keys, 'Don't be lonely.' And added, 'Wouldn't you like to visit your family sometimes, when I have to go out?'

He had told her he was going home to his mother in the forests and mountains of his country near the Italian border (he showed her on the map) after Christmas. She had not told him how her mother, not knowing there was any other variety, assumed he was a medical doctor, so she had talked to her mother about the doctor's children and the doctor's wife who was a very kind lady, glad to have someone who could help out in the surgery as well as the flat.

She remarked wonderingly on his ability to work until midnight or later, after a day at work. She was so tired when she came home from her cash register at the supermarket that once dinner was eaten she could scarcely keep awake. He explained in a way she could understand that while the work she did was repetitive, undemanding of any real response from her intelligence, requiring little mental or physical effort and therefore unrewarding, his work was his greatest interest, it taxed his mental capacities to their limit, exercised all his concentration, and rewarded him constantly as much with the excitement of a problem presented as with the satisfaction of a problem solved. He said later, putting away his papers, speaking out of a silence: 'Have you done other kinds of work?' She said, 'I was in a clothing factory before. Sportbeau shirts, you know? But the pay's better in the shop.'

Of course. Being a conscientious newpaper reader in every country he lived in, he was aware that it was only recently that the retail consumer trade in this one had been allowed to employ coloureds as shop assistants; even punching a cash register represented advancement. With the continuing shortage of semi-skilled whites a girl like this might be able to edge a little further into the white-collar category. He began to teach her to type. He was aware that her English was poor, even though, as a foreigner, in his ears her pronunciation did not offend, nor categorise her as it would in those of someone of his education whose mother tongue was English. He corrected her grammatical mistakes but missed the less obvious ones because of his own sometimes exotic English usage – she continued to use the singular pronoun 'it' when what was required was the plural 'they.' Because he was a foreigner (although so clever, as she saw) she was less inhibited than she might have been by the words she knew she misspelled in her typing. While she sat at the typewriter she thought how one day she would type notes for him, as well as making coffee the way he liked it, and taking him inside her body without saying anything, and sitting (even if only through the empty streets of quiet Sundays) beside him in his car, like a wife.

On a summer night near Christmas – he had already bought and hidden a slightly showy but nevertheless good watch he thought she would like – there was a knocking at the door that brought her out of the bathroom and him to his feet, at his work table. No one ever came to the flat at night; he was not at home to friends; during the day it might have been a canvasser or hawker. The summons was an imperious banging that did not pause and clearly would not stop until the door was opened.

She stood in the bathroom doorway gazing at him across the passage into the livingroom; her bare feet and shoulders were free of a big bath towel. She said nothing, did not even whisper. The flat seemed to shake with the strong unhurried blows.

He made as if to go to the door, at last, but now she ran and clutched him by both arms. She shook her head wildly; her lips drew back but her teeth were clenched, she didn't speak. She pulled him into the bedroom, snatched some clothes from the clean laundry laid out on the bed, and got into the wall cupboard, thrusting the key at his hand. Although his arms and calves felt weakly cold he was horrified, distastefully embarrassed at the sight of her pressed back crouching there under his suits and coat; it was horrible and ridiculous. *Come out!* he whispered. *No! Come out!* She hissed: *Where? Where can I go?*
*Never mind! Get out of there!*

He put out his hand to grasp her. At bay, she said with all the force of her terrible whisper, baring the gap in her teeth: *I'll throw myself out the window.*

She forced the key into his hand like the handle of a knife. He closed the door on her face and drove the key home in the lock, then dropped it among coins in his trouser pocket.

He unslotted the chain that was looped across the flat door. He turned the serrated knob of the yale lock. The three policemen, two in plain clothes, stood there without impatience although they had been banging on the door for several minutes. The big dark one with an elaborate moustache held out in a hand wearing a plaited gilt ring some sort of identity card.

Doctor von Leinsdorf said quietly, the blood coming strangely back to legs and arms, 'What is it?'

The sergeant told him they knew there was a coloured girl in the flat. They had had information; 'I been watching this flat three months, I know.'

'I am alone here.' Dr von Leinsdorf did not raise his voice.

'I know, I know who is here. Come—' And the sergeant and his two assistants went into the livingroom, the kitchen, the bathroom (the sergeant picked up a bottle of after-shave cologne, seemed to study the French label) and the bedroom. The assistants removed the clean laundry that was laid upon the bed and then turned back the bedding, carrying the sheets over to be examined by the sergeant under the lamp. They talked to one another in Afrikaans, which the Doctor did not understand. The sergeant himself looked under the bed, and lifted the long curtains at the window. The wall cupboard was of the kind that has no knobs; he saw that it was locked and began to ask in Afrikaans, then politely changed to English, 'Give us the key.'

Dr von Leinsdorf said, 'I'm sorry, I left it at my office – I always lock and take my keys with me in the mornings.'

'It's no good, man, you better give me the key.'

He smiled a little, reasonably. 'It's on my office desk.'

The assistants produced a screwdriver and he watched while they inserted it where the cupboard doors met, gave it quick, firm but not forceful leverage. He heard the lock give.

She had been naked, it was true, when they knocked. But now she was wearing a long-sleeved t-shirt with an appliquéd butterfly motif on one breast, and a pair of jeans. Her feet were still bare; she had managed, by feel, in the dark, to get into some of the clothing she had snatched from the bed, but she had no shoes. She had perhaps been weeping behind the cupboard door (her cheeks looked stained) but now her face was sullen and she was breathing heavily, her diaphragm contracting and expanding exaggeratedly and her breasts pushing against the cloth. It made her appear angry; it might simply have been that she was half-suffocated in the cupboard and needed oxygen. She did not look at Dr von Leinsdorf. She would not reply to the sergeant's questions.

They were taken to the police station where they were at once separated and in turn led for examination by the District Surgeon. The man's underwear was taken away and examined, as the sheets had been, for signs of his seed. When the girl was undressed, it was discovered that beneath her jeans she was wearing a pair of men's briefs with his name on the neatly-sewn laundry tag; in her haste, she had taken the wrong garment to her hiding place.

Now she cried, standing there before the District Surgeon in a man's underwear.

He courteously pretended not to notice. He handed briefs, jeans and t-shirt round the door, and motioned her to lie on a white-sheeted high table where he placed her legs apart, resting in stirrups, and put into her where the other had made his way so warmly a cold hard instrument that expanded wider and wider. Her body opened. Her thighs and knees trembled uncontrollably while the doctor looked into her and touched her deep inside with more hard instruments, carrying wafers of gauze.

When she came out of the examining room back to the charge office, Dr von Leinsdorf was not there; they must have taken him somewhere else. She spent what was left of the night in a cell, as he must be doing; but early in the morning she was released and taken home to her mother's house in the coloured township by a white man who explained he was the clerk of the lawyer who had been engaged for her by Dr von Leinsdorf. Dr von Leinsdorf, the clerk said, had also been bailed out that morning. He did not say when, or if, she would see him again.

A statement made by the girl to the police was handed in to Court when she and the man appeared to meet charges of contravening the Immorality Act in a Johannesburg flat on the night of – December, 19 – . *I lived with the white man in his flat. He had intercourse with me sometimes. He gave me tablets to take to prevent me becoming pregnant.*

Interviewed by the Sunday papers, the girl said, 'I'm sorry for the sadness brought to my mother.' She said she was one of nine children of a female laundry worker. She had left school in Standard Three because there was no money at home for gym clothes or a school blazer. She had worked as a machinist in a factory and a cashier in a supermarket. Dr von Leinsdorf taught her to type his notes.

Dr Franz-Josef von Leinsdorf, described as the grandson of a baroness, a cultured man engaged in international mineralogical research, said he accepted social distinctions between people but didn't think they should be legally imposed. 'Even in my own country it's difficult for a person from a higher class to marry one from a lower class.'

The two accused gave no evidence. They did not greet or speak to each other in Court. The Defence argued that the sergeant's evidence that they had been living together as man and wife was hearsay. (The woman with the dachshund, the caretaker?) The magistrate acquitted them because the State failed to prove carnal intercourse had taken place on the night of – December, 19–.

The girl's mother was quoted, with photograph, in the Sunday papers: 'I won't let my daughter work as a servant for a white man again.'

2

The farm children play together when they are small; but once the white children go away to school they soon don't play together any more, even in the holidays. Although most of the black children get some sort of schooling, they drop every year further behind the grades passed by the white children; the childish vocabulary, the child's exploration of the adventurous possibilities of dam, koppies, mealie lands and veld – there comes a time when the white children have surpassed these with the vocabulary of boarding-school and the possibilities of inter-school sports matches and the kind of adventures seen at the cinema. This usefully coincides with the age of twelve or thirteen; so that by the time early adolescence is reached, the black children are making, along with the bodily changes common to all, an easy transition to adult forms of address, beginning to call their old playmates 'miss' and '*baasie*', little master.

The trouble was Paulus Eysendyck did not seem to realise that Thebedi was now simply one of the crowd of farm children down at the kraal, recognisable in his sisters' old clothes. The first Christmas holidays after he had gone to boarding-school he brought home for Thebedi a painted box he had made in his woodwork class. He had to give it to her secretly because he had nothing for the other children at the kraal. And she gave him, before he went back to school, a bracelet she had made of thin brass wire and the grey-and-white beans of the castor oil crop his father cultivated. (When they used to play together, she was the one who had taught Paulus how to make clay oxen for their toy spans.) There was a craze, even in the *platteland* towns like the one where he was at school, for boys to wear elephant hair and other bracelets beside their watchstraps; his was admired, friends asked him to get similar ones for them. He said the natives made them on his father's farm and he would try.

When he was fifteen, six feet tall, and tramping round at school dances with the girls from the 'sister' school in the same town; when he had learnt how to tease and flirt and fondle quite intimately these girls who were the daughters of prosperous farmers like his father; when he had even met one who, at a wedding he had attended with his parents on a nearby farm, had let him do with her in a locked storeroom what people did when they made love – when he was as far from his childhood as all this, he still brought home from a shop in town a red plastic belt and gilt hoop earrings for the black girl, Thebedi. She told her father the *missus* had given these to her as a reward for some work she had done – it was true she sometimes was called to help out in the farmhouse. She told the girls in the kraal that she had a sweetheart nobody knew about, far away, away on another farm, and they giggled, and teased, and admired her. There was a boy in the kraal called Njabulo who said he wished he could have bought her a belt and earrings.

When the farmer's son was home for the holidays she wandered far from the kraal and her companions. He went for walks alone. They had not arranged this;

it was an urge each followed independently. He knew it was she, from a long way off. She knew that his dog would not bark at her. Down at the dried-up river-bed where five or six years ago the children had caught a leguaan one great day – a creature that combined ideally the size and ferocious aspect of the crocodile with the harmlessness of the lizard – they squatted side by side on the earth bank. He told her traveller's tales: about school, about the punishments at school, particularly, exaggerating both their nature and his indifference to them. He told her about the town of Middleburg, which she had never seen. She had nothing to tell but she prompted with many questions, like any good listener. While he talked he twisted and tugged at the roots of white stinkwood and Cape willow trees that looped out of the eroded earth around them. It had always been a good spot for children's games, down there hidden by the mesh of old, ant-eaten trees held in place by vigorous ones, wild asparagus bushing up between the trunks, and here and there prickly pear cactus sunken-skinned and bristly, like an old man's face, keeping alive sapless until the next rainy season. She punctured the dry hide of a prickly pear again and again with a sharp stick while she listened. She laughed a lot at what he told her, sometimes dropping her face on her knees, sharing amusement with the cool shady earth beneath her bare feet. She put on her pair of shoes – white sandals, thickly Blanco-ed against the farm dust – when he was on the farm, but these were taken off and laid aside, at the river-bed. One summer afternoon when there was water flowing there and it was very hot she waded in as they used to do when they were children, her dress bunched modestly and tucked into the legs of her pants. The schoolgirls he went swimming with at dams or pools on neighbouring farms wore bikinis but the sight of their dazzling bellies and thighs in the sunlight had never made him feel what he felt now, when the girl came up the bank and sat beside him, the drops of water beading off her dark legs the only points of light in the earth-smelling, deep shade. They were not afraid of one another, they had known one another always; he did with her what he had done that time in the storeroom at the wedding, and this time it was so lovely, so lovely, he was surprised . . . and she was surprised by it, too –he could see in her dark face that was part of the shade, with her big dark eyes, shiny as soft water, watching him attentively: as she had when they used to huddle over their teams of mud oxen, as she had when he told her about detention week-ends at school.

They went to the river-bed often through those summer holidays. They met just before the light went, as it does quite quickly, and each returned home with the dark – she to her mother's hut, he to the farmhouse – in time for the evening meal. He did not tell her about school or town any more. She did not ask questions any longer. He told her, each time, when they would meet again. Once or twice it was very early in the morning; the lowing of the cows being driven to graze came to them where they lay, dividing them with unspoken recognition of the sound read in their two pairs of eyes, opening so close to each other.

He was a popular boy at school. He was in the second, then the first soccer team. The head girl of the 'sister' school was said to have a crush on him; he didn't particularly like her, but there was a pretty blonde who put up her long hair into a kind of doughnut with a black ribbon round it, whom he took to see films when the schoolboys and girls had a free Saturday afternoon. He had been driving tractors and other farm vehicles since he was nine years old, and as soon as he was eighteen he got a driver's licence and in the holidays, this last year of his school life, he took neighbours' daughters to dances and to the drive-in cinema that had just opened twenty kilometres from the farm. His sisters were married, by then; his parents often left him in charge of the farm over the weekend while they visited the young wives and grandchildren. When Thebedi saw the farmer and his wife drive away on a Saturday afternoon, the boot of their Mercedes filled with the fresh-killed poultry and vegetables from the garden that it was part of her father's work to tend, she knew that she must come not to the river-bed but up to the house. The house was an old one, thick-walled, dark against the heat. The kitchen was its lively thoroughfare, with servants, food supplies, begging cats and dogs, pots boiling over, washing being damped for ironing, and the big deep-freeze the missus had ordered from town, bearing a crocheted mat and a vase of plastic irises. But the diningroom with the bulging-legged heavy table was shut up in its rich, old smell of soup and tomato sauce. The sittingroom curtains were drawn and the polished cabinet of the combination radio-record player silent. The door of the parents' bedroom was locked and the empty rooms where the girls had slept had sheets of plastic spread over the beds. It was in one of these that she and the farmer's son stayed together whole nights – almost: she had to get away before the house servants, who knew her, came in at dawn. There was a risk that someone would discover her or traces of her presence if he took her to his own bedroom, although she had looked into it many times when she was helping out in the house and knew well, there, the row of silver cups he had won at school.

When she was eighteen and the farmer's son nineteen and working with his father on the farm before entering a veterinary college, the boy Njabulo asked her father for her. The boy's parents met with hers and the money he was to pay in place of the cows it is customary to give a prospective bride's parents was settled upon. He had no cows to offer; he was a labourer on the Eysendyck farm, like her father. A bright youngster; old Eysendyck had taught him brick-laying and was using him for odd jobs in construction, around the place. She did not tell the farmer's son that her parents had arranged for her to marry. She did not tell him, either, before he left for his first term at the veterinary college, that she thought she was going to have a baby. Two months after her marriage to Njabulo, she gave birth to a daughter. There was no disgrace in that; among her people it is customary for a young man to make sure, before marriage, that the chosen girl is not barren, and Njabulo had made love to her then. But the infant was very light and did not quickly grow darker as most African babies do. Already at birth there was on its head a quantity of straight, fine floss, like that which carries the seeds of certain weeds in the veld. The unfocused eyes it opened were grey flecked with yellow. Njabulo was the matt, opaque coffee-grounds colour that has always been called black; the colour of Thebedi's legs on which beaded water looked oyster-shell blue, the same colour as Thebedi's face, where the black eyes, with their interested gaze and clear whites, were so dominant.

Njabulo made no complaint. Out of his farm labourer's earnings he bought from the Indian store a cellophane-windowed pack containing a pink plastic bath, six napkins, a card of safety pins, a knitted jacket, cap and bootees, a dress, and a tin of Johnson's Baby Powder, for Thebedi's baby.

When it was two weeks old Paulus Eysendyck arrived home from the veterinary college for the holidays. For the first time since he was a small boy he came right into the kraal. It was eleven o'clock in the morning. The men were at work in the lands. He looked about him, urgently; the women turned away, each not wanting to be the one approached to point out where Thebedi lived. Thebedi appeared, coming slowly from the hut that Njabulo had built in white man's style, with a tin chimney and a proper window with glass panes, set in as straight as walls made of unfired bricks would allow. She greeted him with hands brought together and a token movement representing the respectful bob with which she was accustomed to acknowledge she was in the presence of his father or mother. He lowered his head under the doorway of her home and went in. He said, 'I want to see. Show me.'

She had taken the bundle off her back before she came out into the light to face him. She moved between the iron bedstead made up with Njabulo's checked blankets and the small wooden table where the pink plastic bath stood among food and kitchen pots, and picked up the bundle from the snugly-blanketed grocer's box where it lay. The infant was asleep; she revealed the closed, pale, plump tiny face, with a bubble of spit at the corner of the mouth, the spidery pink hands stirring. She took off the woollen cap and the straight fine hair flew up after it in static electricity, showing gilded strands here and there. He said nothing. She was watching him as she had done when they were little, and the gang of children had trodden down a crop in their games or transgressed in some other way for which he, as the farmer's son, the white one among them, must intercede with the farmer. She disturbed the sleeping face by scratching or tickling gently at a cheek with one finger, and slowly the eyes opened, saw nothing, were still asleep, and then, awake, no longer narrowed, looked out at them, grey with yellowish flecks, his own hazel eyes.

He struggled for a moment with a grimace of tears, anger and self-pity. She could not put out her hand to him. He said, 'You haven't been near the house with it?'

She shook her head.

'Never?'

Again she shook her head.

'Don't take it out. Stay inside. Can't you take it away somewhere? You must give it to someone—'

She moved to the door with him.

He said, 'I'll see what I will do. I don't know.' And then he said: 'I feel like killing myself.'

Her eyes began to glow, to thicken with tears. For a moment there was the feeling between them that used to come when they were alone down at the river-bed.

He walked out.

Two days later, when his mother and father had left the farm for the day, he appeared again. The women were away on the lands, weeding, as they were employed to do as casual labour in summer; only the very old remained, propped up on the ground outside the huts in the flies and the sun. The child had not been well; it had diarrhoea. He asked her where its food was. She said, 'The milk comes from me.' He stood a moment and then went into Njabulo's house, where the child lay; she did not follow but stayed outside the door and watched without seeing an old crone who had lost her mind, talking to herself, talking to the fowls who ignored her.

She thought she heard small grunts from the hut, the kind of infant grunt that indicates stirring within a deep sleep. After a time, long or short she did not know, he came out and walked away with plodding stride (his father's gait) out of sight, towards his father's house.

The baby was not fed during the night and although she kept telling Njabulo it was sleeping, he saw for himself in the morning that it was dead. He comforted her with words and caresses. She did not cry but simply sat, staring at the door. Her hands were cold as dead chicken's feet to his touch.

Njabulo buried the little baby where farm workers were buried, in the place in the veld the farmer had given them. Some of the mounds had been left to weather away unmarked, others were covered with stones and a few had fallen wooden crosses. He was going to make a cross but before it was finished the police came and dug up the grave and took away the dead baby: someone – one of the other labourers? their women? – had reported that the baby that was almost white had died very soon after a visit by the farmer's son. Pathological tests on the infant corpse showed intestinal damage not always consistent with death by natural causes.

Thebedi went for the first time to the country town where Paulus had been to school, to give evidence at the preparatory examination into the charge of murder brought against him. She cried hysterically in the witness box, saying yes, yes (the gilt hoop earrings swung in her ears), she saw the accused pouring liquid into the baby's mouth. She said he had threatened to shoot her if she told anyone.

More than a year went by before, in that same town, the case was brought to trial. She came to Court with a new-born baby on her back. She wore gilt hoop earrings; she was calm; she said she had not seen what the white man did in the house.

Paulus Eysendyck said he had visited the hut but had not poisoned the child.

The Defence did not contest that there had been a love relationship between the accused and the girl, or that intercourse had taken place, but submitted there was no proof that the child was the accused's.

The judge told the accused there was strong suspicion against him but not enough proof that he had committed the crime. The Court could not accept the girl's evidence because it was clear she had committed perjury either at this trial or at the preparatory examination. There was the suggestion in the mind of the Court that she might be an accomplice in the crime; but, again, insufficient proof.

The judge commended the honourable behaviour of the husband (sitting in court in a brown-and-yellow-quartered golf cap bought for Sundays) who had not rejected his wife and had 'even provided clothes for the unfortunate infant out of his slender means.'

The verdict on the accused was 'not guilty'.

The young white man refused to accept the congratulations of press and public and left the Court with his mother's raincoat shielding his face from photographers. His father said to the press, 'I will try and carry on as best I can to hold up my head in the district.'

Interviewed by the Sunday papers, who spelled her name in a variety of ways, the black girl, with photograph, was quoted: 'It was a thing of our childhoold, we don't see each other any more.'

FAY WELDON

# *Alopecia*

It's 1972.

'Fiddlesticks,' says Maureen. Everyone else says 'crap' or 'balls', but Maureen's current gear, being Victorian sprigged muslin, demands an appropriate vocabulary. 'Fiddlesticks. If Erica says her bald patches are anything to do with Brian, she's lying. It's alopecia.'

'I wonder which would be worse,' murmurs Ruthie in her soft voice, 'to have a husband who tears your hair out in the night, or to have alopecia.'

Ruthie wears a black fringed satin dress exactly half a century old, through which, alas, Ruthie's ribs show even more prominently than her breasts. Ruthie's little girl Poppy (at three too old for playgroup, too young for school) wears a long white (well, yellowish) cotton shift which contrasts nicely with her mother's dusty black.

'At least the husband might improve, with effort,' says Alison, 'unlike alopecia. You wake up one morning with a single bald patch and a month or so later there you are, completely bald. Nothing anyone can do about it.' Alison, plump mother of three, sensibly wears a flowered Laura Ashley dress which hides her bulges.

'It might be quite interesting,' remarks Maureen. 'The egg-head approach. One would have to forgo the past, of course, and go all space-age, which would hardly be in keeping with the mood of the times.'

'You are the mood of the times, Maureen,' murmurs Ruthie, as expected. Ruthie's simple adulation of Maureen is both gratifying and embarrassing, everyone agrees.

Everyone agrees, on the other hand, that Erica Bisham of the bald patches is a stupid, if ladylike, bitch.

Maureen, Ruthie and Alison are working in Maureen's premises off the Kings Road. Here Maureen, as befits the glamour of her station, the initiator of Mauromania, meets the media, expresses opinions, answers the phone, dictates to secretaries (male), selects and matches fabrics, approves designs and makes, in general, multitudinous decisions – although not, perhaps, as multitudinous as the ones she was accustomed to make in the middle and late sixties, when the world was young and rich and wild. Maureen is forty but you'd never think it. She wears a large hat by day (and, one imagines, night) which shades her anxious face and guards her still pretty complexion. Maureen leads a rich life. Maureen once had her pubic hair dyed green to match her fingernails – or so her husband Kim announced to a waiting (well, such were the days) world. She divorced him not long after, having lost his baby at five months. The head of the

402

foetus, rumour had it, emerged green, and her National Health Service GP refused to treat her any more, and she had to go private after all – she with her Marxist convictions.

That was 1968. If the state's going to tumble, let it tumble. The sooner the better. Drop out, everyone! Mauromania magnifique! And off goes Maureen's husband Kim with Maureen's *au pair* – a broad-hipped, big-bosomed girl, good breeding material, with an ordinary coarse and curly bush, if somewhat reddish.

Still, it had been a good marriage as marriages go. And as marriages go, it went. Or so Maureen remarked to the press, on her way home (six beds, six baths, four recep., American kitchen, patio, South Ken) from the divorce courts. Maureen cried a little in the taxi, when she'd left her public well behind, partly from shock and grief, mostly from confusion that beloved Kim, Kim, who so despised the nuclear family, who had so often said that he and she ought to get divorced in order to have a true and unfettered relationship, that Maureen's Kim should have speeded up Maureen's divorce in order to marry Maureen's *au pair* girl before the baby arrived. Kim and Maureen had been married for fifteen years. Kim had been Kevin from Liverpool before seeing the light or at any rate the guru. Maureen had always been just Maureen from Hoxton, east London: remained so through the birth, rise and triumph of Mauromania. It was her charm. Local girl makes good.

Maureen has experience of life: she knows by now it is wise to watch what people do, not listen to what they say. Well, it's something to have learned. Ruthie and Alison, her (nominal) partners from the beginning, each her junior by some ten years, listen to Maureen with respect and diffidence.

And should they not? After the green pubic hair episode, after the *au pair* and divorce incident, Maureen marries a swinging professor of philosophy, a miracle of charm and intelligence who appears on TV, a catch indeed. Maureen's knowledge of life and ideas is considerable: it must be: lying next to a man all night, every night, wouldn't you absorb something from him? Sop up some knowledge, some information, some wisdom?

Someone, somewhere, surely, must know everything? God help us if they don't.

Maureen and the professor have a son. He's dyslexic – the professor tries to teach him English at two, Latin at three, and Greek at four – and now, away at a special boarding-school, is doing well on the sports field and happy. She and the professor are divorced. He lives in the South Ken home, for reasons known only to lawyers. All Maureen wants now (she says, from her penthouse) is another chance: someone familiar, trustworthy, ordinary. A suburban house, a family, privacy, obscurity. To run Mauromania from a distance: delegating: dusting, only pausing to rake in the money.

Mauromania magnifique!

'Mind you,' says Maureen now, matching up purple feathers with emerald satin to great effect, 'if I was Brian I'd certainly beat Erica to death. Fancy having to listen to that whining voice night after night. The only trouble is he's become too much of a gentleman. He'll never have the courage to do it. Turned his back on his origins, and all that. It doesn't do.'

Maureen has known Brian since the old days in Hoxton. They were evacuees together: shared the same bomb shelter on their return from Starvation Hall in Ipswich – a boys' public school considered unsafe for the gentry's children but all right for the East Enders'. (The cooking staff nobly stayed on; but, distressingly, the boys, it seems, had been living on less than rations for generations, hence Starvation Hall.)

'It's all Erica's fantasy,' says Ruthie, knowledgeably. 'A kind of dreadful sexual fantasy. She *wants* him to beat her up so she trots round London saying he does. Poor Brian. It comes from marrying into the English upper classes, old style. She must be nearly fifty. She has this kind of battered-looking face.'

Her voice trails away. There is a slight pause in the conversation.

'Um,' says Alison.

'That's drink,' says Maureen, decisively, 'Poor bloody Brian. What a ball-breaker to have married.' Brian was Maureen's childhood sweetheart. What a romantic, platonic idyll! She nearly married him once, twice, three times. Once in the very early days, before Kim, before anyone, when Brian was selling books from a barrow in Hoxton market. Once again, after Kim and before the professor, by which time Brian was taking expensive photographs of the trendy and successful – only then Erica turned up in Brian's bed, long-legged, disdainful, beautiful, with a model's precise and organised face, and the fluty tones of the girl who'd bought her school uniform at Harrods, and that was the end of that. Not that Brian had ever exactly proposed to Maureen; not that they'd ever even been to bed together: they just knew each other and each other's bed partners so well that each knew what the other was thinking, feeling, hoping. Both from Hoxton, east London: Brian, Maureen; and a host of others, too. What was there, you might ask, about that particular acre of the East End which over a period of a few years gave birth to such a crop of remarkable children, such a flare-up of human creativity in terms of writing, painting, designing, entertaining? Changing the world? One might almost think God had chosen it for an experiment in intensive talent-breeding. Mauromania, God-sent.

And then there was another time in the late sixties, when there was a short break between Brian and Erica – Erica had a hysterectomy against Brian's wishes; but during those two weeks of opportunity Maureen, her business flourishing, her designs world-famous Mauromania a label for even trendy young queens (royal, that is) to boast, rich beyond counting – during those two special weeks of all weeks Maureen fell head over heels classically in love with Pedro: no, not a fisherman, but as good as – Italian, young, open-shirted, sloe-eyed, a designer. And Pedro, it later transpired, was using Maureen as a means to laying all the models, both male and female (Maureen had gone into menswear). Maureen was the last to know, and by the time she did Brian was in Erica's arms (or whatever) again. A sorry episode. Maureen spent six months at a health farm, on a diet of grapes and brown rice. At the end of that time Mauromania Man had collapsed, her business manager had jumped out of a tenth-floor window, and an employee's irate mother was bringing a criminal suit against Maureen personally for running a brothel. It was all quite irrational. If the employee, a runaway girl of, it turned out, only thirteen, but looking twenty, and an excellent seamstress, had contracted gonorrhoea whilst in her employ, was that Maureen's fault? The judge, sensibly, decided it wasn't, and that the entire collapse of British respectability could not fairly be laid at Maureen's door. Legal costs came to more than £12,000: the country house and stables had to be sold at a knock-down price. That was disaster year.

And who was there during that time to hold Maureen's hand? No one. Everyone, it seemed, had troubles enough of their own. And all the time, Maureen's poor heart bled for Pedro, of the ridiculous name and the sloe eyes, long departed, laughing, streptococci surging in his wake. And of all the old friends and allies only Ruthie and Alison lingered on, two familiar faces in a sea of changing ones, getting younger every day, and hungrier year by year not for fun, fashion, and excitement, but for money, promotion, security, and acknowledgement.

The staff even went on strike once, walking up and down outside the workshop with placards announcing hours and wages, backed by Maoists, women's liberationists and trade unionists, all vying for their trumpery allegiance, puffing up a tiny news story into a colossal media joke, not even bothering to get Maureen's side of the story – absenteeism, drug addiction, shoddy workmanship, falling markets, constricting profits.

But Ruthie gave birth to Poppy, unexpectedly, in the black and gold ladies' rest-room (customers only – just as well it wasn't in the staff toilets where the plaster was flaking and the old wall-cisterns came down on your head if you pulled the chain) and that cheered everyone up. Business perked up, staff calmed down as unemployment rose. Poppy, born of Mauromania, was everyone's favourite, everyone's mascot. Her father, only seventeen, was doing two years inside, framed by the police for dealing in pot. He did not have too bad a time – he got three A-levels and university entrance inside, which he would never have got outside, but it meant poor little Poppy had to do without a father's care and Ruthie had to cope on her own. Ruthie of the ribs.

Alison, meanwhile, somewhat apologetically, had married Hugo, a rather straight and respectable actor who believed in womens' rights; they had three children and lived in a cosy house with a garden in Muswell Hill: Alison even belonged to the PTA! Hugo was frequently without work, but Hugo and Alison manage, between them, to keep going and even happy. Hugo thinks Alison should ask for a rise, but Alison doesn't like to. That's the trouble about working for a friend and being only a nominal partner.

'Don't let's talk about Erica Bisham any more,' says Maureen now. 'It's too draggy a subject.' So they don't.

But one midnight a couple of weeks later, when Maureen, Ruthie and Alison are working late to meet an order – as is their frequent custom these days (and one most unnerving to Hugo, Alison's husband) – there comes a tap on the door. It's Erica, of course. Who else would tap, in such an ingratiating fashion? Others cry 'Hi!' or 'Peace!' and enter. Erica, smiling nervously and crookedly; her yellow hair eccentric in the extreme; bushy in places, sparse in others. Couldn't she wear a wig? She is wearing a Marks & Spencer nightie which not even Ruthie would think of wearing, in the house or out of it. It is bloodstained down the back. (Menstruation is not yet so fashionable as to be thus demonstrable, though it can be talked about at length.) A strong smell of what? alcohol, or is it nail-varnish? hangs about her. Drinking again. (Alison's husband, Hugo, in a long period of unemployment, once veered on to the edge of alcoholism but fortunately veered off again, and the smell of nail-varnish, acetone, gave a warning sign of an agitated, overworked liver, unable to cope with acetaldehyde, the highly toxic product of alcohol metabolism.)

'Could I sit down?' says Erica. 'He's locked me out. Am I speaking oddly? I think I've lost a tooth. I'm hurting under my ribs and I feel sick.'

They stare at her – this drunk, dishevelled, trouble-making woman.

'He,' says Maureen finally. 'Who's he?'

'Brian.'

'You're going to get into trouble, Erica,' says Ruthie, though more kindly than Maureen, 'if you go round saying dreadful things about poor Brian.'

'I wouldn't have come here if there was anywhere else,' says Erica.

'You must have friends,' observes Maureen, as if to say, Don't count us amongst them if you have.

'No.' Erica sounds desolate. 'He has his friends at work. I don't seem to have any.'

'I wonder why,' says Maureen under her breath; and then, 'I'll get you a taxi home, Erica. You're in no state to be out.'

'I'm not drunk, if that's what you think.'

'Who ever is,' sighs Ruthie, sewing relentlessly on. Four more blouses by one o'clock. Then, thank God, bed.

Little Poppy has passed out on a pile of orange ostrich feathers. She looks fantastic.

'If Brian does beat you up,' says Alison, who has seen her father beat her mother on many a Saturday night, 'why don't you go to the police?'

'I did once, and they told me to go home and behave myself.'

'Or leave him?' Alison's mother left Alison's father.

'Where would I go? How would I live? The children? I'm not well.' Erica sways. Alison puts a chair beneath her. Erica sits, legs planted wide apart, head down. A few drops of blood fall on the floor. From Erica's mouth, or elsewhere? Maureen doesn't see, doesn't care. Maureen's on the phone, calling radio cabs who do not reply.

'I try not to provoke him, but I never know what's going to set him off,' mumbles Erica. 'Tonight it was Tampax. He said only whores wore Tampax. He tore it out and kicked me. Look.'

Erica pulls up her nightie (Erica's wearing no knickers) and exposes her private parts in a most shameful, shameless fashion. The inner thighs are blue and mottled, but then, dear God, she's nearly fifty.

What does one look like, thigh-wise, nearing fifty? Maureen's the nearest to knowing, and she's not saying. As for Ruthie, she hopes she'll never get there. Fifty!

'The woman's mad,' mutters Maureen. 'Perhaps I'd better call the loony wagon, not a taxi?'

'Thank God Poppy's asleep.' Poor Ruthie seems in a state of shock.

'You can come home with me, Erica,' says Alison. 'God knows what Hugo will say. He hates matrimonial upsets. He says if you get in between, they both start hitting you.'

Erica gurgles, a kind of mirthless laugh. From behind her, mysteriously, a child steps out. She is eight, stocky, plain and pale, dressed in boring Ladybird pyjamas.

'Mummy?'

Erica's head whips up; the blood on Erica's lip is wiped away by the back of Erica's hand. Erica straightens her back. Erica smiles. Erica's voice is completely normal, ladylike.

'Hallo darling. How did you get here?'

'I followed you. Daddy was too angry.'

'He'll be better soon, Libby,' says Erica brightly. 'He always is.'

'We're not going home? Please don't let's go home. I don't want to see Daddy.'

'Bitch,' mutters Maureen, 'she's even turned his own child against him. Poor bloody Brian. There's nothing at all the matter with her. Look at her now.'

For Erica is on her feet, smoothing Libby's hair, murmuring, laughing.

'Poor bloody Erica,' observes Alison. It is the first time she has ever defied Maureen, let alone challenged her wisdom. And rising with as much dignity as her plump frame and flounced cotton will allow, Alison takes Erica and Libby home and installs them for the night in the spare room of the cosy house in Muswell Hill.

Hugo isn't any too pleased. 'Your smart sick friends,' he says. And, 'I'd beat a woman like that to death myself, any day.' And, 'Dragging that poor child into it: it's appalling.' He's nice to Libby, though, and rings up Brian to say she's safe and sound, and looks after her while Alison takes Erica round to the doctor. The doctor sends Erica round to the hospital, and the hospital admit her for tests and treatment.

'Why bother?' enquires Hugo. 'Everyone knows she's mad.'

In the evening, Brian comes all the way to Muswell Hill in his Ferrari to pick up Libby. He's an attractive man: intelligent and perspicacious, fatherly and gentle. Just right, it occurs to Alison, for Maureen.

'I'm so sorry about all this,' he says. 'I love my wife dearly but she has her problems. There's a dark side to her nature – you've no idea. A deep inner violence – which of course manifests itself in this kind of behaviour. She's deeply psychophrenic. I'm so afraid for the child.'

'The hospital did admit her,' murmurs Alison. 'And not to the psychiatric ward, but the surgical.'

'That will be her hysterectomy scar again,' says Brian. 'Any slight tussle – she goes quite wild, and I have to restrain her for her own safety – and it opens up. It's symptomatic of her inner sickness, I'm afraid. She even says herself it opens to let the build-up of wickedness out. What I can't forgive is the way she drags poor little Libby into things. She's turning the child against me. God knows what I'm going to do. Well, at least I can bury myself in work. I hear you're an actor, Hugo.'

Hugo offers Brian a drink, and Brian offers (well, more or less) Hugo a part in a new rock musical going on in the West End. Alison goes to visit Erica in hospital.

'Erica has some liver damage, but it's not irreversible: she'll be feeling nauseous for a couple of months, that's all. She's lost a back tooth and she's had a couple of stiches put in her vagina,' says Alison to Maureen and Ruthie next day. The blouse order never got completed – re-orders now look dubious. But if staff haven't the loyalty to work unpaid overtime any more, what else can be expected? The partners (nominal) can't do everything.

'Who said so?' enquires Maureen, sceptically. 'The hospital or Erica?'

'Well,' Alison is obliged to admit, 'Erica.'

'You are an innocent, Alison.' Maureen sounds quite cross. 'Erica can't open her poor sick mouth without uttering a lie. It's her hysterectomy scar opened up again, that's all. No wonder. She's a nymphomaniac: she doesn't leave Brian alone month in, month out. She has the soul of a whore. Poor man. He's so upset by it all. Who wouldn't be?'

Brian takes Maureen out to lunch. In the evening, Alison goes to visit Erica in hospital, but Erica has gone. Sister says, oh yes, her husband came to fetch her. They hadn't wanted to let her go so soon but Mr Bisham seemed such a sensible, loving man, they thought he could look after his wife perfectly well, and it's always nicer at home, isn't it? Was it *the* Brian Bisham? Yes, she'd thought so. Poor Mrs Bisham – what a dreadful world we live in, when a respectable married woman can't even walk the streets without being brutally attacked, sexually assaulted by strangers.

It's 1973.

Winter. A chill wind blowing, a colder one still to come. A three-day week imposed by an insane government. Strikes, power-cuts, black-outs. Maureen,

Ruthie and Alison work by candlelight. All three wear fun-furs – old stock, unsaleable. Poppy is staying with Ruthie's mother, as she usually is these days. Poppy has been developing a squint, and the doctor says she has to wear glasses with one blanked-out lens for at least eighteen months. Ruthie, honestly, can't bear to see her daughter thus. Ruthie's mother, of a prosaic nature, a lady who buys her clothes at C & A Outsize, doesn't seem to mind.

'If oil prices go up,' says Maureen gloomily, 'what's going to happen to the price of synthetics? What's going to happen to Mauromania, come to that?'

'Go up the market,' says Alison, 'the rich are always with us.'

Maureen says nothing. Maureen is bad-tempered, these days. She is having some kind of painful trouble with her teeth, which she seems less well able to cope with than she can the trouble with staff (overpaid), raw materials (unavailable), delivery dates (impossible), distribution (unchancy), costs (soaring), profits (falling), re-investment (non-existent). And the snow has ruined the penthouse roof and it has to be replaced, at the cost of many thousands. Men friends come and go: they seem to get younger and less feeling. Sometimes Maureen feels they treat her as a joke. They ask her about the sixties as if it were a different age: of Mauromania as if it were something as dead as the dodo – but it's still surely a label which counts for something, brings in foreign currency, ought really to bring her some recognition. The Beatles got the MBE; why not Maureen of Mauromania? Throw-away clothes for throw-away people?

'Ruthie,' says Maureen. 'You're getting careless. You've put the pocket on upside-down, and it's going for copying. That's going to hold up the whole batch. Oh, what the hell. Let it go through.'

'Do you ever hear anything of Erica Bisham?' Ruthie asks Alison, more to annoy Maureen than because she wants to know. 'Is she still wandering round in the middle of the night?'

'Hugo does a lot of work for Brian, these days,' says Alison carefully. 'But he never mentions Erica.'

'Poor Brian. What a fate. A wife with alopecia! I expect she's bald as a coot by now. As good a revenge as any, I dare say.'

'It was nothing to do with alopecia,' says Alison. 'Brian just tore out chunks of her hair, nightly.' Alison's own marriage isn't going so well. Hugo's got the lead in one of Brian's long runs in the West End. Show business consumes his thoughts and ambitions. The ingenue lead is in love with Hugo and says so, on TV quiz games and in the Sunday supplements. She's under age. Alison feels old, bored and boring.

'These days I'd believe anything,' says Ruthie. 'She must provoke him dreadfully.'

'I don't know what you've got against Brian, Alison,' says Maureen. 'Perhaps you just don't like men. In which case you're not much good in a fashion house. Ruthie, that's another pocket upside-down.'

'I feel sick,' says Ruthie. Ruthie's pregnant again. Ruthie's husband was out of prison and with her for exactly two weeks; then he flew off to Istanbul to smuggle marijuana back into the country. He was caught. Now he languishes in a Turkish jail. 'What's to become of us?'

'We must develop a sense of sisterhood,' says Alison, 'that's all.'

It's 1974.

Alison's doorbell rings at three in the morning. It is election night, and Alison is watching the results on television. Hugo (presumably) is watching them somewhere else, with the ingenue lead – now above the age of consent, which spoils the pleasure somewhat. It is Erica and Libby. Erica's nose is broken. Libby, at ten, is now in charge. Both are in their night-clothes. Alison pays off the taxi-driver, who won't take a tip. 'What a world,' he says.

'I couldn't think where else to come,' says Libby. 'Where he wouldn't follow her. I wrote down this address last time I was here. I thought it might come in useful, sometime.'

It is the end of Alison's marriage, and the end of Alison's job. Hugo, whose future career largely depends on Brian's goodwill, says, you have Erica in the house or you have me. Alison says, I'll have Erica. 'Lesbian, dyke,' says Hugo, bitterly. 'Don't think you'll keep the children, you won't.'

Maureen says, 'That was the first and last time Brian ever hit her. He told me so. She lurched towards him on purpose. She *wanted* her nose broken; idiot Alison, don't you understand? Erica nags and provokes. She calls him dreadful, insulting, injuring things in public. She flays him with words. She says he's impotent: an artistic failure. I've heard her. Everyone has. When finally he lashes out, she's delighted. Her last husband beat hell out of her. She's a born victim.'

Alison takes Erica to a free solicitor, who – surprise, surprise – is efficient and who collects evidence and affidavits from doctors and hospitals all over London, has a restraining order issued against Brian, gets Libby and Erica back into the matrimonial home, and starts and completes divorce proceedings and gets handsome alimony. It all takes six weeks, at the end of which time Erica's face has altogether lost its battered look.

Alison turns up at work the morning after the alimony details are known and has the door shut in her face. Mauromania. The lettering is flaking. The door needs re-painting.

Hugo sells the house over Alison's head. By this time she and the children are living in a two-room flat.

Bad times.

'You're a very destructive person,' says Maureen to Alison in the letter officially terminating her appointment. 'Brian never did you any harm, and you've ruined his life, you've interfered in a marriage in a really wicked way. You've encouraged Brian's wife to break up his perfectly good marriage, and turned Brian's child against him, and not content with that you've crippled

Brian financially. Erica would never have been so vindictive if she hadn't had you egging her on. It was you who made her go to law, and once things get into lawyers' hands they escalate, as who better than I should know? The law has nothing to do with natural justice, idiot Alison. Hugo is very concerned for you and thinks you should have mental treatment. As for me, I am really upset. I expected friendship and loyalty from you, Alison; I trained you and employed you, and saw you through good times and bad. I may say, too, that your notion of Mauromania becoming an exclusive fashion house, which I followed through for a time, was all but disastrous, and symptomatic of your general bad judgement. After all, this is the people's age, the sixties, the seventies, the eighties, right through to the new century. Brian is coming in with me in the new world Mauromania.'

Mauromania, meretricious!

A month or so later, Brian and Maureen are married. It's a terrific wedding, somewhat marred by the death of Ruthie – killed, with her new baby, in the Paris air crash, on her way home from Istanbul, where she'd been trying to get her young husband released from prison. She'd failed. But then, if she'd succeeded, he'd have been killed too, and he was too young to die. Little Poppy was at the memorial service, in a sensible trouser-suit from C & A, brought for her by Gran, without her glasses, both enormous eyes apparently now functioning well. She didn't remember Alison, who was standing next to her, crying softly. Soft beds of orange feathers, far away, another world.

Alison wasn't asked to the wedding, which in any case clashed with the mass funeral of the air-crash victims. Just as well. What would she have worn?

It's 1975.

It's summer, long and hot. Alison walks past Mauromania. Alison has remarried. She is happy. She didn't know that such ordinary everyday kindness could exist and endure. Alison is wearing, like everyone else, jeans and a T-shirt. A new ordinariness, a common sense, a serio-cheerfulness infuses the times. Female breasts swing free, libertarian by day, erotic by night, costing nobody anything, or at most a little modesty. No profit there.

Mauromania is derelict, boarded up. A barrow outside is piled with old stock, sale-priced. Coloured tights, fun-furs, feathers, slinky dresses. Passers-by pick over the stuff, occasionally buy, mostly look, and giggle, and mourn, and remember.

Alison, watching, sees Maureen coming down the steps. Maureen is rather nastily dressed in a bright yellow silk shift. Maureen's hair seems strange, bushy in parts, sparse in others. Maureen has abandoned her hat. Maureen bends over the barrow, and Alison can see the bald patches on her scalp.

'Alopecia,' says Alison, out loud. Maureen looks up. Maureen's face seems somehow worn and battered, and old and haunted beyond its years. Maureen stares at Alison, recognising, and Maureen's face takes on an expression of half-apology, half-entreaty. Maureen wants to speak.

But Alison only smiles brightly and lightly and walks on.

'I'm afraid poor Maureen has alopecia, on top of everything else,' she says to anyone who happens to enquire after that sad, forgotten figure, who once had everything – except, perhaps, a sense of sisterhood.

SHIRLEY HAZZARD

# A Crush on Doctor Dance

WHEN Rupert Thrale was thirteen and had trouble with his back, his mother took him to a new hospital across the river. After the X-rays had been studied, it was again Grace Thrale who sat beside him in a waiting-room while he turned pages of a book on marsupials and tested a loose green rubber tile with the toe of his school boot. When, at the name of Thrale, they got up together to be shown to a doctor's empty office, they walked with arms touching. And, as they sat alone beside a desk, Mrs Thrale leaned forward out of her anxiety and kissed the boy; and the door opened.

The man who came in saw the mother bending forward, her arm extended on a chair-back, her throat curved in helpless solicitude, her lips to her son's hair which palely mingled with her own. In the next instant she turned and looked; and Rupert, getting to his feet, disowned her caress.

What Grace Thrale saw was a solid man of about thirty in Nordic colours – high-complexioned, blue-eyed, bright-haired, and dressed in white – standing at an open door.

The tableau was brief; but even the boy remembered it.

The three of them sat at the desk, and the young doctor said, 'Don't worry.' He put a row of photographs up on a metal rack and lit them: the notched segments, the costal arcs, the grey knuckled frame of a bare existence with its deathly omen. 'These are what we call the dorsal vertebrae.' He pointed with a pencil; and Grace Thrale looked at her son's mortality – all the respiring tissue blazed away, all that was mobile or slept, could resent or relish. It was as if she stared at an ossified remnant in a child's grave.

There was to be a corrective operation – which was delicate, infrequently performed, and involved a rod of stainless steel. It did not affect growth. 'You'll be better than new, I promise.' The doctor addressed himself in this way to the boy, without heartiness, in a low clear voice and slight Scots accent, including the mother by a filament of experience which was almost tender. His face, in its revealing colour and kindness, might in another era have been beautiful. His hair glowed, gold enough to be red.

When they were leaving, he told Grace she should make an appointment to come with her husband. 'We should talk it over with the surgeon.'

The boy's father, Christian Thrale, was about his country's business, conferring at Dar es Salaam. Grace would come alone on Thursday.

At the door there was a projecting sign: *Angus Dance, MD.*

On Thursday he lit the photographs and showed with the pencil. He said it was tricky but would be all right. They had the best man in London to do the job.

Grace Thrale sat side by side with Angus Dance to look at the plates, and, handling one of them, left a tremulous print of humid fingers. When the surgeon arrived, Dance got up and stood in the sun by the window, where he was white and gold, a seraph, a streak of flame.

Grace told him that her husband was coming home, to be present for the operation.

'You'll be seeing my colleague. I'll be on leave that week.' He saw she was disturbed. 'Just for a few days.' When the surgeon left them, Dance sat to fill out his portion of a form. He told her he was going to his parents' house, near Inverness.

'What's Inverness like these days?'

'Oh – like everywhere – full of Japanese.' Reading over the form, he said, 'We're neighbours. I see you're in the Crescent. I live around the corner, in the place that's painted blue.'

They agreed they did not like the shade. Grace said she often walked past the building, taking the short cut through the brick passage – which, originally reserved for pedestrians, was now abused. She knew he said conventional things to calm her; and was calmed by his humane intention.

The Doctor said, 'Rupert will run me down there one day on his bike and I'll be a cot case.' He gave her back the form and touched her sleeve. 'You'll be anxious. But there is no need.'

The operation went so well that Christian Thrale was back at Dar es Salaam in a matter of days. The boy would be in hospital a month or so. Grace came every morning and afternoon, bringing comic books, a jigsaw, clean pyjamas. There was a cafeteria where she had lunch.

'How was Inverness?'

Doctor Dance was carrying a tray. 'The gateway to the Orient. I'm glad Rupert's doing so well.' His upright body gave a broad impression, both forcible and grave. He had short muscular arms, on which the hair would be red.

They sat down together and Grace conveyed Christian's gratitude all the way from Tanzania, even bringing out a letter. Relief gushed from her in forms of praise: the nurses were so kind, the surgeon, the therapist from Karachi. Sister Hubbard was a saint, and Rupert would be spoiled beyond repair. She then said, 'Well – why should you hear this in your time off?'

Her light hair was sculpted down from a central parting and fell in wings over her ears. Once in a while she would touch it, a ring glinting on her raised hand. Her nails were of a housewifely length, unvarnished. 'What about your journey?'

He said he always took the train. His parents lived an isolated life, but now had the telly. The house, which was in the Black Isle, was always cold, not only from heatlessness but from austerity. 'They like it bare. Predictably enough, my sister and I tend to clutter.' There was only one picture in the house: 'A framed photograph of the *Tirpitz*, which was sunk the day I was born. Or at least the news came that forenoon that they had sunk it.' His sister was also a doctor, and lived in Edinburgh.

Grace pictured the old crofters in the stark house uttering monosyllables like 'aye' and 'wee' and 'yon'; the maiden sister, a ruddy, tweedy pediatrician called, in all likelihood, Jean. 'They must miss the two of you.'

'My father still does consultant work. He's an engineer. Then, I run up fairly regularly. And Colette is going to them for Easter. It's really harder for her, since she's married, with a family.'

That evening Grace asked at a dinner-party, 'Does anyone remember what year we sank the *Tirpitz*?'

It happened that Grace Thrale and Doctor Dance spoke every day. There were the X-rays to light up and look at – each of these tinged with the bloom of deliverance; there was Rupert's bedside, there were the corridors and the cafeteria. Once they stayed ten minutes talking on a stair. They soon dispatched the neighbourhood topics – the abused brick passage, the hideous new hotel nearby that took groups – and Grace found out that Angus Dance was divorced from a student marriage, voted Liberal, had spent a year in Colombia on an exchange programme, and kept a small sailing boat at Burnham-on-Crouch. He had done prison visiting at Wormwood Scrubs, but now lacked the time. One day he had a book on his desk, about the Brontës.

Mentioning his marriage, he said, 'Young people aren't doing that so much now.' Younger than she, he already considered himself an elder.

Grace told him how her parents had died in the wreck of a ferry when she was four. Next – so it seemed, as she came to relate it – there had been Christian. Recounting these things, she felt her story was undeveloped, without event; years were missing, as from amnesia, and the only influential action of her life had been the common one of giving birth. The accidental foundering of her parents had remained larger than any conscious exploit of her own, and was still her only way to cause a stir.

This vacancy might have affected growth. Compared with his variousness, she was fixed, terrestrial; landlocked, in contrast to his open sea.

These exchanges with Doctor Dance were Mrs Thrale's first conversations. With Christian there was the office, there were the three children, there the patterns and crises of domestic days. She had not often said, 'I believe', 'I feel'; nor had felt the lack. Now beliefs and feelings grew delightful to her, and multiplied. Between visits to the hospital, she rehearsed them: she held imaginary discourse with Angus Dance, phantasmal exchanges in which Grace was not ashamed to shine. There was a compulsion to divulge, to explain herself, to tell the simple truth. The times when she actually sat by him and looked at X-ray plates generated a mutual kindliness that was the very proof of human perfectibility. After these occasions there was consciousness of exertion – a good strain such as the body might feel from healthful unaccustomed action.

One day, passing a paper from hand to hand, their fingers touched; and that was all.

'I suppose', said Grace Thrale, 'that Angus was always a Scots name.'

'It's a version of Aeneas.'

She could not recall what Aeneas had done, and thought it better not to ask.

He was changing her. She wished more than anything to match his different level of goodness – his sensibility that was precise as an instrument, yet with a natural accuracy; his good humour that was a form of generosity; his slight and proper melancholy. It was virtue she most desired from him, as if it were an honour he could confer. He could make an honest woman of her.

The bare facts of Mrs Thrale's love, if enumerated, would have appeared familiar, pitiful and – to some – even comical. Of this, she herself was conscious. It was the sweetness that was unaccountable.

Because the condition struck her as inborn, she raked her experience for precedent. She dwelt on a man she had known long ago, before her marriage – a moody schoolteacher who often broke appointments or came late, and over whom she had suffered throughout a cold summer. Only the year before, she had heard he was now farming in Dorset, and had looked up his name in the telephone directory. He provided no prologue to Angus Dance. In contrast to the schoolteacher, on the other hand, Christian had appeared a model of consideration, a responsible lover whose punctuality had from the start prefigured matrimony. Angus Dance had no precursor.

Grace put the end of a pen between her lips. Hugh, her middle son, said, 'Why do you look that way?'

'I'm thinking what to tell Daddy.'

At night she was alone with Angus Dance when she lay down solitary in the dark with her arm half-clasped about her body. She thought that Christian would soon return from Dar es Salaam. The knowledge that he would at once make love to her brought mere acceptance.

The week after Rupert came home from hospital, Mrs Thrale ran into Doctor Dance in the street. They met at a site of road repairs, and could hardly hear each other for the pneumatic drill. Grace stared at his clear, hectic skin and tawny head, his noonday colours, while concrete particles exploded and the pavement thrilled. Consciousness shivered also, on some inward Richter scale.

'Let's get out of this.' Dance went through a motion of taking her elbow but did not in fact do so. They were both going to the cake-shop, and agreed that the woman there was grumpy but the *croissants* good. When they crossed at the corner Grace said, 'We all miss you.' She heard this speech turn coy with trepidation, and a little tic started up in her cheek. He smiled: 'Now, that's going too far.' But added, 'I miss you all, too.' Saying 'all' both made it possible and detracted: a pact, scrupulously observed.

In the shop Grace had to wait for the seedcake. Angus Dance shook hands. 'Doctors are always overdue somewhere. I hope we meet again.'

When he had gone out, the grim woman behind the counter said, 'So he's a doctor, is he? He has a lovely face.'

When Christian praised the seedcake, Grace said, 'I got it from that nice woman at the corner.'

Every spring the Thrales gave a party – drinks and little things to eat. They called this decorous event 'our smash'. Grace went over her question in silence: I would like to invite that young doctor. We might ask Rupert's doctor, who lives practically next door. What about asking that Doctor Dance, who was super with Rupert?

To the question as ultimately phrased, Christian responded, 'Good idea.' He had it in mind to ask someone very senior from his department, and supposed a doctor would mix.

Grace telephoned the hospital. Dance knew her voice: 'Hello.' He did not say 'Mrs Thrale', and had never done so. He wrote the date of the party, and six to eight. 'Is it a special occasion?'

'It's my birthday. Not that we tell people.'

She had a new dress that displayed her breasts. Christian said, 'Isn't it a bit bare?' He traced the outline of black silk with his finger on her flesh. 'Happy birthday, Grace darling.'

Although they had a couple from Jamaica to do the drinks, it was Grace who opened the door to Angus Dance. Before entering, he bent and kissed her cheek, murmuring 'Birthday.' He gave her a little packet, which was later found to contain lavender water. Grace trembled under the astonishing kiss, from which she turned away with the male impress of jacket indelible on her silk and female arms. When Christian came over from the foot of the stairs, discarding his party face for the serious theme of Rupert, she moved back into the curve of the piano, where Dance soon joined her.

'Who plays?'

'I do.' For once she did not add, 'My sole accomplishment.' He leaned to look at stacked music. She had put the Chopin on top to impress. She saw him turn the sheets with deliberate large hands; she watched his almost spiritual face. Authority had passed from him in this amateur setting, and his youth was a blow, a disappointment. Authority had in fact passed to her. She presided, a matron, over her household, her associates, her charming children: mistress of the situation.

She did not know how to address him now that he was disestablished. At the hospital the nurses had called him 'Doctor', as women with a family will call their own husbands 'Father' or 'Daddy'.

They spoke about the community centre, and Grace told him the art show would open on Sunday. Dance said, 'I might look in.'

Rupert appeared with Dance's whisky, and other guests were introduced. In an oval mirror they had bought in Bath she saw the room, tame with floral charm and carpeted, like England, wall to wall in green. And herself, in this field of flowers – practically indistinguishable from cushions and curtains, and from ornaments that, lacking temperament, caused no unrest. In the mirror she could see, rather than hear, her husband saying 'Let's face it', and watch her eldest son, Jeremy, blond and beloved, behaving beautifully. She saw the rings on her fingers, and a bracelet that was insured. Look as she might, she could not see Angus Dance in that mirror (he had been taken to the dining-room for a slice of the ham), and knew she never would.

The head of Christian's department had a Common Market face. He put his drink down on the Chopin and said, 'I don't really know you well enough to tell you this story.' Grace watched the room rippling in mirrored waters: such slow movement, such pastels; and, again, herself – upholstered, decorated, insured, and, for the first time, utterly alone. A big woman in violet leaned against the mantel, purpling the view. Christian's chief said, 'Now comes the bawdy part.' Grace listened abstractedly to the end of the joke. When she did not smile, Sir Manfred was displeased; and looked at her white flesh as if to say, You started it. He took up his drink and moved off toward the bookcase: 'I'm a voracious reader.' He had left a circular stain on a nocturne.

She saw, or knew, that Angus Dance had come back into the room. Making sure about some cheese puffs, she found him close to her, talking to a black-haired, blue-eyed girl who had come with the Dalrymples.

And why on earth not? A man like that could not possibly be leading a celibate life, abstinent in tribute to her own romantic fancies.

'Grace, I've got the info for you on the *Tirpitz*.'

It was their oldest friend, whom she at once wished dead.

'Don't say I ever let you down. A promise is a promise. Twelfth of November forty-four.'

Grace folded her hands before her. Sunk.

'Capsized at her moorings. We'd disabled her with midget subs the year before, but the RAF gave her the coo de grass in forty-four. Somewhere in the Arctic Circle, up in the Norwegian fjords. Don't ask me to pronounce the place; it's one of those names with dots over the top of it.'

Angus Dance was back to back with them, well within earshot.

'Damn fool Germans brought her well within our range, you see. Always be relied on for the stupid thing. Utterly gormless. Well, does that take care of everything?'

'I'm grateful, Ernie.'

Ernie spoke no German but could do a good accent at parties. 'Effer at your serffice.' He clicked his heels.

Angus Dance was fetching an ashtray for the Dalrymple girl. He had said, 'They sank.' For Grace and Ernie, it was 'We sank' – even the schoolgirl Grace had attacked the great battleship *Tirpitz* with all her nine-year-old might. Angus Dance was out of it, free from guilt or glory. For him, Ernie and Grace might as well have rioted on Mafeking night.

Grace revolved a cold glass between her palms. Ernie ran a proprietary finger along the black waist of the piano, in the same way Christian had done with the rim of her dress. 'She took a thousand men to the bottom with her.'

People were kissing her, one after the other: 'Dored it, dored it. Simply dored it.' Angus Dance left on a wave of departures, shaking hands.

When it was over, they brought the Spode out from a safe place. Someone had broken a goblet of cut crystal.

Jeremy remarked, 'You did say smash.'

Two calico cats were let out mewing from the upstairs bathroom, but would not touch leftovers. Jeremy and Hugh put the chest back between the windows. Rupert, who was not allowed to lift, helped Christian count empty bottles: 'I liked Doctor Dance the best.'

I, too.

Christian half-turned his head to where Grace stood, and lightly winked. 'So we have a crush on Doctor Dance, do we?' He had assembled the bottles in a box. 'I liked him myself.'

Later still, winding his bedside clock, Christian asked, 'Why on earth was Ernie babbling on like that about the *Tirpitz*? Or was it the *Scharnhorst*?'

Grace was drawing the black dress over her head. 'I think it was the *Scharnhorst*.'

He could have called next day to thank for the party but did not, although the phone rang all morning and Christian's chief sent flowers.

'It was a success, then,' announced Jeremy, who was becoming worldly.

Grace was turning over the mail.

Christian said, 'I don't know when I've seen a finer bunch of marguerites.'

Mrs Thrale was now embarked on the well-known stages of love: the primary stage being simple, if infinite, longing. She might, in a single morning, see a dozen Dances in the streets. Then, high-strung to an impossible phone-bell whose electric drill reverberated in her soul, she constructed myths and legends from a doorway kiss; that was the secondary phase. Tertiary was the belief that all significance was of her own deranged contriving, and any reciprocity on the part of Angus Dance a fantasy. She had no revelation to make to him: he had even seen her best dress.

The trouble was the very abundance of her feelings sufficed for mutuality. So much loving-kindness also made it appear moral.

The phases mixed and alternated. If he came on Sunday, to the art show, she would know.

Grace lay awake, then slept uneasily.

Christian said, 'You're up so early these days.'

'It's that dog next door, barking at daybreak.'

Rupert cackled. 'Like a rooster.'

By now, Mrs Thrale had committed adultery in her heart many times.

On the Sunday, Christian took the boys to a horse show. Christian knew quite a bit about horses – their dimensions and markings and matings, their agilities. The boys, too, could adroitly use words like 'roan', 'Skewbald', and 'Gelding'.

'We should be back by six.'

Grace said, 'I might look in at the art show.'

When they had gone out she made up her face with care. She put on a heavy blue coat that was old but became her. It was a raw day, almost lightless; heavy clouds suggested snow. In a shop window she saw herself clasping her scarf together – hurrying, aglow.

A woman at the door charged her 10p. The floor of dirty wooden boards was uneven, and scrunched as she walked in. She was almost alone in the hall but could not bring herself to look about for Angus Dance. A fat man in a mackintosh stepped back to get perspective and collided: 'Sorry.' There were two or three elderly couples who had nothing else to do, and a dejected girl who was perhaps one of the exhibitors. The paint was in many cases green and red, in whorls; or had been applied thinly in angular greys. She knew he would not come.

When she left the place it was getting dark and there was sleet. She did not want to go home; it was as if her humiliation must be disclosed there. She shrank from home as from extra punishment – as a child, mauled by playmates, might fear parental scolding for torn clothes. But stumbled along with no other possibility. Pain rose up from her thorax, and descended like sleet behind her eyes. It was scarcely credible there should be no one to comfort her.

She thought: My mortification. And for the first time realised that the word meant death.

Alone at home, she went into the bathroom and leaned both hands on the sink, pondering. This anguish must be centred on some object other than Angus Dance. Such passion could scarcely have to do with him – the red-haired Doctor Dance of flesh and blood and three months' acquaintance – but must be fixed on a vision. This mirror, in its turn, showed her intent, exposed, breathing heavily. She had never seen herself so real, so rare.

She had just taken off her coat when they came in from the horse show, speaking in a practised manner of chestnuts and bays. Christian had been jostled in the Underground: 'Perhaps I'm not suited to the mass society.'

Grace said, 'Perhaps we are the mass society.'

Monday was Mrs Thrale's day for the hairdresser. She said, 'Mario, I have some grey hairs,' and put her hand to her brow. 'Here.' He took her head between his hands, under a light, as if it were a skull held *norma frontalis*. Alas, poor Grace. After a while he said, 'It is not a case for dyeing.'

He released her. 'You are not ready to dye.'

'No.'

'Being fair, you can wait a bit.' Grace sat in a plastic chair and he said, 'It is worse for the dark ladies.'

When she was settled under the dryer with *Vogue* and *The Gulag Archipelago*, the immemorial pathos of the place struck at her. There was hardly a young woman present, except the shampoo girl whose hipless jeans and prominent pectoral arch made Grace Thrale's soft flesh appear historic. Grace looked down at her own round little arms, stared at them as into a portrait by an Old Master. She thought of her body, which had never been truly slim, and showed a white mesh from bearing children, and now must passively await decay and mutilation. Her hands, clasped over a magazine picture of a bronze man on a beach, instinctively assumed an attitude of resignation. She read, 'The Aga Khan in a rare moment of relaxation.' But perceived herself in that instant entering into a huge suspense, lonely and universal.

That night Grace dreamed her own death.

The following morning she made an excuse to telephone the hospital.

'Doctor Dance has been off with a heavy cold.'

She said it was not important, and hung up. The bad cold arousing scorn, she said aloud, 'I would have got there,' meaning to the art show; which was perfectly true. She went upstairs and made the beds, and thought in derision: Scotsmen are scarcely Latin lovers.

Equilibrium did not last. On her way downstairs there was the same thoracic pain, a colossal suffering, grandiose, of a scale and distinction to which she, Grace Thrale of London W8 7EF, hardly seemed entitled. She sat in the kitchen and thought: I am overwrought; and perhaps am mad. Oh God, I must break myself of this.

Break, break, break. You said smash. A crush.

It occurred to her, in her isolation, that books might have helped. It was the first time she had reckoned with the fact she did not read, that neither she nor Christian read – and here was the true discovery, for she had relied on him to maintain a literary household. They had dozens of books, on shelves that took up half a wall; not to speak of the Penguins. And would send to the library regularly for the latest: she had the Iris Murdoch in the house, as well as the Solzhenitsyn. Voracious readers. But a state of receptiveness in which another's torment might reach into her own soul, through which her infatuation might be defined and celebrated – there was none of that. Christian confidently presented himself as a man of letters: 'I'm rereading Conrad this winter.' But *Within the Tides* had lain on his night table since December.

Christian came home and kissed her. 'I have spoken to those people about that yipping dog.'

'You haven't.'

'Certainly. You can't go sleepless for ever. They have agreed to keep the animal indoors.'

She wished he had not said 'the animal'.

He thumped his briefcase on to the hall table. 'And I actually used the word "yip".'

In her dream, Christian had been weeping.

Grace got up in the night and went downstairs. She took *Wuthering Heights* from a shelf and stood by the windows in the moonlight, keeping the ceaseless watch of her passion. She had no right to utter the name of Angus Dance, or to give him an endearment even in thought – never having done these things in life. She might as well have called on Heathcliff, or Aeneas. The book, an old edition, weighed in her hand. She knew she would not read it; but wondered if you might open at any page and find truth, like the Bible. She passed her other hand down her body, and thought her small feet irresistibly beautiful as they showed beneath her nightgown.

In the morning Christian said, 'Perhaps we need a new mattress.'

When the marguerites began to fester, Grace put them in the garbage. The card, still attached, said 'With Homage', and had an ink line through the surname. She swirled water in the vase and remembered: 'I didn't laugh at his off-colour joke.'

Christian was worried, but said, 'You certainly don't have to take insults to further my career': to forestall her thoughts. After a moment he asked, 'What was the joke anyway?'

'I couldn't for the life of me work it out.' They both burst out laughing. No reply could have pleased him more. Perfect, sheltered Grace. Once, during a holiday on Corsica, he had turned her face away from the spectacle, as he called it, of a fistfight.

Late that day she met Angus Dance in the street. She had bought narcissus to replace the daisies, and stood holding them downward in her hand. She could think of nothing to say that would equal the magical silent discourse of her reverie.

He said, 'Are you all right?'

'I haven't been sleeping properly.' She might as well have said, I love you. 'Except with pills.'

'What are you taking?' For a moment authority passed back to him.

They then spoke of his heavy cold. And she would bring Rupert in for a check-up at the end of the month. Despite sleeplessness, her skin glowed like his own.

He said, 'Do you have time for a coffee?'

So Grace Thrale sat at a Formica table and Angus Dance hung his flannel jacket on a peg. He wore a pale woollen waistcoat knitted by his mother. His hair in itself was enough to attract attention: his northern light, his blaze of midnight sun. They scarcely spoke, though leaning forward from a delicate readiness, until the girl came to take their order. Both his accent and an oddly aspirated *r* were more pronounced. Grace thought her own speech indistinct, and made an effort to talk out.

'I have been wondering how you were.' All things considered, the boldest remark she had ever made. She was surprised by her definite voice, her firm hand efficiently taking sugar, when the whole of Creation, the very texture of the firmament, was wrought, receptive, cream-coloured, like his sweater.

He said he ought to go to Burnham-on-Crouch to see about his boat, which was up on the slips for scraping and red lead. Some recaulking was also needed. 'I don't feel up to it, somehow.' The commonplaces, the withholdings, were a realisation in themselves. Her scented flowers stood between them in a tumbler of water, pent within a green string. 'I'm not much of a sailor – the genuine ones are fanatical. I took it up after a bad experience. I suppose it was a means of motion when everything was standing still.'

'Was it when your marriage broke up?'

'No. This was a later repudiation.' He smiled. 'I don't know that any of this can be very interesting. Such usual griefs.'

'To me they are not usual.' She could not imagine Christian, for whom acceptance was imperative, recounting his rebuffs, or acknowledging 'my griefs'. Even in the entrancement of the coffee-shop the threat came over her that Christian was in this the more infirm, the more defenceless; and that Angus Dance was fortified by reversals, and by his refusal to dissimulate. She recalled his simple commitment to Rupert, how he had said, 'I promise.' Such fearlessness could not be required of Christian.

When she made contrasts to Christian it was not just the disloyalty but that Christian always seemed to gain.

Doctor Dance offered buns. 'I had a grand time at your party. I should have called to say so.'

Grace thought of the scuttling of the *Tirpitz*, and the chief's commemorative flowers, a soaked wreath on swirling waters. Lest we forget. 'It seems so long ago.'

'I've not seen you since.'

It was the mingling of great and trivial that could not be misunderstood.

He went on, 'Yet we are so close.'

She fell silent, leaning back into colours and shadows of the room: not in fulfilment, which could hardly be, but in voluptuous calm, at peace. Her hand was outstretched on the table, the sleeve pushed up. It was the first time he had seen her inner arm. She knew it might be the only such passage between them, ever. If the usual griefs were coming to her at last, so was this unprecedented perfection.

Grace was seated at the piano. She turned a sheet of music, but did not play. Rupert came and stood beside her. 'What is it?'

'It's Scarlatti.'

He had meant, What's wrong?

Like a lover, he stood near enough to suggest she should embrace him. With her right arm she drew him against her side. Her left hand rested on the keys. She leaned her head to his upper arm. It was like an Edwardian photograph. She said, 'I do love you, Rupey.' This was the last child with whom she could get away with such a thing – and only then because his illness had given them an extension during which a lot might be overlooked. They both knew it. Emulating her mood, the boy became pensive, languid; and at the same time remained omnipotent.

She said again, 'I do.' To get him to say it back. She thought: So now it has come round: *I* am trying to draw strength from *them*. She thought the word 'adulteress', and it was archaic as being stoned to death – a bigoted word like 'Negress' or 'Jewess' or 'seamstress' or 'poetess'; but precise.

Her left hand sounded notes in the bass: sombre, separate, instructed. The room received them dispassionately. There was a click of her ring on ivory. She rocked the boy a little with her arm, and could feel the plaster armouring his X-rayed ribs. She took her hand from the piano and put both arms about him, her fingers locked over his side, her breast and brow turned to his body. This was less like a photograph.

He said, 'What's up, Mum?' Moving his imprisoned arm, he put his own hand to the treble and struck a discordant series of keys, stressing and repeating vehement high notes. She released him, but he jarred a few last preplexed excited sounds; and stood, still touching her, swayed between childhood and sensuality.

Christian came in with papers in his hands. 'What's this, a duet?'

The boy sauntered off and switched on the telly. The News flickered over jagged devastations – Beirut or Belfast, the Bronx or Bombay.

Christian said, 'Grace, I must speak to you.'

Rupert yelled, 'It is a programme on Pompeii.'

Grace sat with Christian on a sofa that was rarely used because of the velvet. He told her, 'Something momentous has occurred.'

In her mind, Grace Thrale swooned.

'I have been given Africa.'

He might have been Alexander, or Antony. The younger Scipio, Grace stared whitely, and he added, 'South of the Sahara.'

She was looking through such tears as would never rise for Angus Dance, who could not need, or evoke, pity for impercipience of self-exposure. She wept for Christian, insulated in the non-conducting vainglory of his days, and might then have told him all, out of sheer fidelity to the meaning of things. She said, 'My darling.'

'There's nothing in the world to cry about.' Christian touched her face, pleased. 'I can assure you.' Perfect Grace. He unrolled the departmental chart in his hand. A small box at the top of the page littered into larger boxes underneath, fathering endless enclosures of self-esteem. He pointed – here, and here. 'Talbot-Sims will only be Acting. But for me it's the real thing.' As he leaned to show the pedigree, there was a sparse, greying place on top of his sandy head. He said, 'My youth was against me,' brushing a speck from the flawless page. 'But in the end they waived seniority.' The chart started to curl at the edges, struggling to rescroll. 'It will make a whopping difference in the pension.'

Grace wondered if their severance from each other's thoughts and purposes had at any time appeared so conclusive to him; if ever she herself had so grossly disregarded. She wondered whether, during summer separations, or the time she went to Guernsey, he had perhaps loved, or slept with – the one need not preclude the other – someone else. It was hard to imagine him sufficiently headstrong for it, now he did not have the self-reliance to read a book. If he had loved another woman, Grace of all people would understand it. Magnanimity shaped a sad and vast perspective. Or it was merely a plea for leniency in her own case.

Christian put his arm around her, stooping from heights where officials waved seniority. 'I'm afraid we'll have to call off the Costa Brava. But when I've got things in hand I'll take you somewhere quiet.' His mind ranged, like the News, over ravaged nations, seeking a possibility. All was pandemonium – Portugal, Palestine, Tibet: called off, one after one. Elation weirdly faltered in his throat, as on a sob; but recklessly resumed: 'So you brought me luck, telling the old bastard off about his joke.'

Angus Dance came into the brick passage as the rain began. He started to run; at the same moment that Grace Thrale, entering from the opposite end, ran, too, under the rain.

Had it been possible to observe their meeting from above or alongside, like a sequence on film they would have been seen at first precipitate, heads lowered against weather; then slowed in realisation; and finally arrested. The arrestation being itself some peak of impetus, a consummation. They were then facing, about a yard apart, and rain was falling on Dance's hair and, like gauze, on Grace's coat of calamine blue. Ignored, the heavy rain was a cosmic attestation, more conclusive than an embrace.

Anyone seeing them would have said lovers.

Rain was silvering Dance's eyelids. He had taken hold of himself by the coat lapel. His expression was disarmed, pure with crisis. 'This is what I meant about being close.'

'Yes.'

'Shall we get to shelter?' As if they had not already got to shelter.

Sloshing along the narrow tunnel, he took her arm at last. By not embracing they had earned some such indulgence. They then stood under an awning at the exit of a supermarket; and he said, proving her more right than she had ever been about anything, 'You know that I love you.' It was the response she had not been able to compel from her own child.

She would not even brush the water from her hair or coat; and perhaps need never consider her appearance again. After moments during which the rain continued and they were nudged by shopping-bags, she said, 'It makes me happy.' She thought she would tell the simple truth, now that she was indomitable.

Opposite, there was the new hotel that took groups. Dance said, 'It would be a place to talk.'

'We can cross when it lets up.' Her self-possession surprised, as in the tea-shop.

He hesitated; and decided. 'Yes. I'll have to telephone about the appointments.'

She did not urge him to keep them. Nor did he ask if she was due in the Crescent. When the sky lightened, they crossed.

As they came into the hotel, the man at the desk put down the phone, saying 'Christ.' A heap of baggage – suitcases, golf-bags, holdalls in nylon plaid – was piled by the foot of the stairs. In the lounge, which was one floor up, they might already have been at an airport, waiting to depart. Pylons of the building were thinly encased in plastic wood, with little counters around them for ash trays or drinks. The sofas were hard and bright, yet far from cheerful. Slack curtains were tawdry with metallic threads, and on one wall there was a tessellated decoration of a cornucopia greenly disgorging.

As they entered, a group of women in trouser-suits got up to leave. An old man with an airline bag said, near tears, 'But they only had it in beige.'

Grace Thrale sat near a window, and Angus Dance went to telephone. Had it not been for him, how easily she might have fitted in here. The enclosure, nearly empty, enjoined subservience – was blank with the wrath, bewilderment, and touching faith of its usual aggregations. It was no use now trying this on Grace, who scarcely saw and was past condescending. With detachment that was another face of passion, she wondered in what circumstances she would leave this place and if she would ever go home. Abandoned by her, the house in the Crescent was worse than derelict, the life in it extinct; the roast attaining room temperature on the kitchen counter, an unfinished note to Grace's sister announcing Christian's promotion, a rock album that was a surprise for Hugh; and *Within the Tides*, unopened on the bedside table. All suspended, silent, enigmatical – slight things that might have dressed the cabins of the *Mary Celeste* or embellished a programme on Pompeii; trifles made portentous by rejection.

She got up and spread the two damp coats on a nearby seat, to deter. She stood at a concrete embrasure looking at the rain, and knew he had come back.

He sat beside her on hard red plastic and said, 'There's nothing to be afraid of.' He touched his fingers to hers, as once at the hospital. 'I am going away.' You could see the colour ebbing down through clear lit levels of his skin. 'I have been offered a position in Leeds.'

She sat with the air of supremacy, the triumphant bearing summoned for a different outcome. When she did not speak, he went on, 'You must not think I would ever try to damage your life.' Her life, which she stood ready to relinquish:

whose emblems she had been coolly dispersing, as she might have picked off the dead heads of flowers.

He said, 'As if I would seek to injure you.'

As if she would not have gone up with him to a room in this place and made love, if he had wished it.

He was making an honest woman of her. She deserved no credit from the beneficiaries, having already thrown them over: love would be concealed, like unworthiness, from them, from him. When she had coveted his standards, she had naïvely imagined them compatible with her passion. It was another self-revelation – that she should have assumed virtue could be had so quickly, and by such an easy access as love. It was hard to tell, in all this, where her innocence left off and guilt began.

Scrutinising Angus Dance's drained face and darkened eyes, his mouth not quite controlled, Grace Thrale was a navigator who seeks land in a horizon deceitful with vapours. Eventually she asked, repeating her long lesson, 'Is this a promotion?'

'An advancement, yes.'

Such conquerors, with their spoils, their cities and continents – Leeds, Africa. Advancing, progressing, all on the move: a means of motion. Only Grace was stationary, becalmed.

'In that way, also, it's necessary. I can't go on doing the present job for ever.'

Only Grace might go on doing for ever. Might look up Leeds in the phone book, like Dorset. Realisation was a low protracted keening in her soul. Here at last was her own shipwreck – a foundering beyond her parents' capsized ferry. She might have howled, but said instead what she had heard in plays: 'Of course there would have been no future to this.'

Colour came back on his cheeks like blood into contusions. He got up quickly and, as if they were in a private room, stood by the concrete window; then leaned against a column, facing her, his arms spread along the ridge meant for ash-trays, his durable body making a better architecture, a telamon. 'A man should have past and present as well as future.' He moved his hand emphatically, and a dish of peanuts spilled in silence: it was a gesture that laid waste, as if a fragment of the column disintegrated, 'Do you not think I see it constantly, the dying who've not lived? It is what we are being, not what we are to be. Rather, they are the same thing.'

'I know that.' Even her children were already staked on the future – their aptitudes for science or languages, what did they want to be, to be; they had never been sincerely asked what they would be now. She said, 'Even those who have truly lived will die. It is hard to say which is the greater irony.' Such discoveries were owed to him. She rose to his occasion, and no doubt would soon sink back, incurious; would go, literally, into a decline.

He said, 'I am near thirty-three years of age, and live with too much vacancy.'

She saw his rectitude existing in a cleared space like his parents' uncluttered house. He told her, 'You cannot imagine – well, I do not mean that unkindly. But you with your completeness – love, children, beauty, troops of friends – how would you understand such formlessness as mine? How would you know solitude, or despair?'

They were matters she had glimpsed in a mirror. She felt his view of her existence settling on her like an ornate, enfeebling garment; closing on her like a trap. She leaned back on the unyielding sofa, and he stood confronting. It was an allegorical contrast – sacred and profane love: her rapture offered like profanity. To assert, or retrieve, she said, 'Yet there has been nothing lovelier in my life than the times we sat together at the hospital and looked at the photographs.'

He came back to the sofa and replaced his hand on hers – a contact both essential and external, like the print of fingers on X-rays. 'It was like Paolo and Francesca.'

She would have to look it up when she got home. But stared at his hand on hers and thought, without mockery: Scarcely Latin lovers.

He said, 'It's true we could not have stood the lies.'

The first lie was Grace drawing off her dress, her head shrouded in black, her muffled voice saying, '*Scharnhorst.*' She said, 'In my married life I never so much as exchanged an unchaste kiss, until with you on my birthday.'

He smiled. Perfect sheltered Grace. 'There is so little laughter in illicit love. Whatever the theme, there must always be the sensation of laughing at someone else's expense.'

Grace had last laughed with Christian, over Sir Manfred's joke. She said, 'I am serious.' The kiss, the lie, the laughter – nothing would be serious again by that measurement. 'I am serious,' she said, as he smiled from his greater experience and lesser insight; as he looked with the wrong solicitude. Grace would not be called upon to testify. She remembered how, on tumultuous Corsica, her head had been turned away.

'In a new place', she supposed, 'you will get over this.'

'I still dream about a girl I knew when I was eighteen.' He would not conform with her platitudes; he would not perceive her truth. He would dream of Grace, in Leeds. He said, 'Memories cool to different temperatures at different speeds.' He glanced about, at the figured rug and tinselled curtains, the column splintered into peanuts, the drab cornucopia: 'What an awful place.' And his condemnation was the prelude to farewell.

Grace Thrale said, 'It is the world.'

'I've said many things to you in thought, but they were never hopeless like this. Nor did they take place in any material world.' He then corrected himself. 'Of course there has been desire,' dismissing this extravagance. His accent intruded, and he allowed time for speech to recover itself, mastering language like tears. 'What I mean is, in thoughts one keeps a reserve of hope, in spite of everything. You cannot say goodbye in imagination. That is something you can only do in actuality, in the flesh. Even desire has less to do with the flesh than goodbye.'

His face had never appeared less contemporary. Was one of those early photographs, individual with suffering and conscience.

'So I am to lose you.' She might have been farewelling a guest: Dored it, dored it. Dored you.

He said, 'I cannot do any more,' and withdrew his refractive touch and passed his hand through his bright hair as in some ordinary bafflement. He got up again and took his coat from the chair, and stood over her. All these actions, being performed very rapidly, reminded that he was expert in contending with pain. 'I'll drop you. I'm taking a taxi.' His reversion to daily phrases was deathly. It was ultimate proof that men were strong, or weak.

They stood up facing, as if opposed; and onlookers were relieved to see them normal.

'I'll stay on here a few minutes.' She could not contemplate the taxi in which he resolutely would not embrace her. She clasped her hands before her in the composed gesture with which she sometimes enfolded desperation; raising her head to his departure, she was a wayside child who salutes a speeding car on a country road.

When Grace came down into the street, the rain had stopped and the darkness arrived. Men and women were coming from their work, exhausted or exhilarated, all pale. And the wet road shone with headlamps, brighter than the clear black sky with stars. Engines, voices, footsteps, and a transistor or two created their geophysical tremor of a world in motion. This show of resumption urged her, gratuitously, toward the victors – to Jeremy whose eye needed bathing with boric acid, and Hugh's bent for mathematics, and Rupert's unexpected interest in Yeats, and Christian saying 'This is the best lamb in years.' All of that must riot in triumph over her, as she would find out soon enough. They would laugh last, with the innocent appalling laughter of their rightful claim and licit love.

With these prospects and impressions, Grace Marian Thrale, forty-one years old, stood silent in a hotel doorway in her worn blue coat and looked at the cars and the stars, with the roar of existence in her ears. And, like any great poet or tragic sovereign of antiquity, cried on her Creator and wondered how long she must remain on such an earth.